PENGUIN BOOKS

## The Prisoner and The Fugitive

Marcel Proust was born in Auteuil in 1871. In his twenties he became a conspicious society figure, frequenting the most fashionable Paris salons of the day. After 1899, however, his chronic asthma, the death of his parents and his growing disillusionment with humanity caused him to lead an increasingly retired life. From 1907 he rarely emerged from a cork-lined room on the Boulevard Haussmann. Here he insulated himself against the distractions of city life, as well as the effect of the trees and flowers – though he loved them they brought on his attacks of asthma. He slept by day and worked by night, writing letters and devoting himself to the completion of *In Search of Lost Time*. He died in 1922.

Christopher Prendergast is Professor of French at the University of Cambridge and a Fellow of King's College.

Carol Clark is a Fellow and Tutor in French at Balliol College, Oxford. She has previously published selections from Baudelaire in Penguin Classics.

Peter Collier is Senior Lecturer in French at Cambridge University and a Fellow of Sidney Sussex College. He has previously translated Pierre Bourdieu's *Homo Academicus* and Emile Zola's *Germinal*, and has written a book on *Proust and Venice*.

# MARCEL PROUST

## The Prisoner

*Translated and with an Introduction
and Notes by Carol Clark*

## The Fugitive

*Translated and with an Introduction
and Notes by Peter Collier*

*General Editor: Christopher Prendergast*

PENGUIN BOOKS

PENGUIN BOOKS

Published by the Penguin Group
Penguin Books Ltd, 80 Strand, London WC2R ORL, England
Penguin Putnam Inc., 375 Hudson Street, New York, New York 10014, USA
Penguin Books Australia Ltd, 250 Camberwell Road, Camberwell, Victoria 3124, Australia
Penguin Books Canada Ltd, 10 Alcorn Avenue, Toronto, Ontario, Canada M4V 3B2
Penguin Books India (P) Ltd, 11 Community Centre, Panchsheel Park, New Delhi – 110 017, India
Penguin Books (NZ) Ltd, Cnr Rosedale and Airborne Roads, Albany, Auckland, New Zealand
Penguin Books (South Africa) (Pty) Ltd, 24 Sturdee Avenue, Rosebank 2196, South Africa

Penguin Books Ltd, Registered Offices: 80 Strand, London WC2R ORL, England

www.penguin.com

*La Prisonnière* first published 1923
*Albertine disparue* first published 1925
This translation first published by Allen Lane The Penguin Press 2002
Published in Penguin Classics 2003

3

Translations and editorial matter copyright © Carol Clark, Peter Collier, 2002
All rights reserved

The moral rights of the translators and editors have been asserted

Set by Rowland Phototypesetting Ltd, Bury St Edmunds, Suffolk
Printed in England by Clays Ltd, St Ives plc

ISBN-13: 978-0-141-18035-9
ISBN-10: 0-141-18035-8

# Contents

# *Translator's Introduction:* The Prisoner

*The Prisoner* is the first part of what is often called the *roman d'Albertine*, the Albertine novel, an intense, two-handed story of love and jealousy set within the larger social fresco of *In Search of Lost Time*. This novel-within-a-novel did not form part of Proust's original plan for the work, but the idea for it seems to have come to him in 1913, and to have occupied more and more of his writing time between then and his death in 1922. The 'prisoner' is Albertine Simonet, a young woman whom the narrator first sees at the seaside at Balbec in the second part of *In the Shadow of Young Girls in Flower*. Then in her late teens, she is the lively, indeed almost rowdy, ringleader of a group of young girls referred to as '*la petite bande*', the little gang, who fly around the resort on their bicycles and dominate the beach and promenade with their racy style. The narrator also meets her at the studio of the painter Elstir. She does not appear in the next volume, *The Guermantes Way*, Part I, and only briefly in *The Guermantes Way*, Part II, when she visits the narrator in Paris, at a time when he is wholly preoccupied with another young woman, Mme de Stermaria. In the second part of *Sodom and Gomorrah*, however, the narrator returns to Balbec, meets Albertine again and begins to think that he is in love with her. He goes into society with her, notably into the Verdurin circle at its summer quarters at La Raspelière, introducing her as his cousin. His is a complicated and reluctant love, however: he is fascinated by the whole 'little gang', and wonders intermittently whether he would not do better to love a different member of it, Andrée; also he suspects the girls, and particularly Albertine and Andrée, of being attracted to each other, and even of having lesbian relations. His love really takes hold only when he has a conversation with Albertine in the little stopping train (the 'slowcoach' or 'tram') which winds its way along the coast, and learns from her that when even younger she was a close associate of Mlle Vinteuil and her friend, whom he knows to be lesbians. He feels a desperate need to keep Albertine away from these dangerous contacts, and, convincing her of his deep unhappiness (for which he supplies a false motive), he persuades her to come and live for the time being in his family's flat in Paris where he can keep a constant watch on her. He also holds out the prospect of marriage to her, and briefly believes in it himself: indeed, the final words of *Sodom and Gomorrah*, addressed by the narrator to his mother, are '*il faut absolument que j'épouse Albertine*' (I absolutely must marry Albertine). Thus from the beginning his love is grounded in jealousy and a project of control.

The opening of *The Prisoner* finds Albertine and the narrator living in the family flat, watched over only by the old family servant Françoise, since the narrator's mother is detained in their home village of Combray by the illness of an aunt. The story is told exclusively from the narrator's point of view and we are never allowed to learn of Albertine's reactions to his behaviour towards her: like him, we can only guess at them. Indeed, nowhere in the whole work are we given any fully reliable information about Albertine, apart from her name, family situation (she is an orphan, brought up by an aunt, Mme Bontemps), build and colouring (tall, plumpish, dark). Most strikingly, we do not learn, any more than the narrator does, whether she is exclusively lesbian in her tastes, or indeed actively lesbian at all. Indeed, what does 'being lesbian' mean to the narrator? He sees lesbians everywhere, and attributes to them a kind of promiscuous, predatory sexual behaviour (see, for example, p. 324) which, nowadays at least, we are told is not at all characteristic of female homosexuals.

But against the narrator's image of a vicious Albertine, Proust allows the reader to set his or her own image, formed from Albertine's kindly actions (beginning with her agreement, at the end of *Sodom and Gomorrah*, to leave Balbec and come to Paris to comfort the narrator), and above all her speech. Her rather slangy language with its simple sentence constructions (all the more striking by contrast with the narrator's highly complex written style) establishes her as a modern girl, emancipated for the period, not very reflective, affectionate, fond of the narrator but (it seems) genuinely unable to follow the tortuous pathways of his jealous thinking. A healthy, outdoor girl – golfer, cyclist – who says what she thinks: on the face of it the most unsuitable of matches for an aesthete – indoor, sedentary, physically frail – like the narrator. Can a girl like this really be the sexually rapacious incorrigible liar that the narrator imagines?

It is true that at the time of the action (not precisely specified but before 1914) middle- and upper-class young girls were strictly chaperoned and never allowed to be alone with young men: in such circumstances sexual contacts between girls might have been commoner than they would be today. Very late in the story (p. 368) the narrator admits the possibility that the young Albertine might have had sexual contact with other girls while seeing in this only *'des jeux avec une amie'*, games with a friend, and believing that the moral crime of 'being a lesbian' was something different. As well as a tragedy of possessive love, *The Prisoner* is also a dreadful comedy of misunderstanding.

Yet it is not the straightforward kind of ironic fiction (like, say, the first part of John Fowles's *The Collector*) in which the reader's sympathy goes to the narrator's victim rather than to the narrator himself. For a start the narrator – what Proust called *'le monsieur qui dit je'* – is at least double: he is the (presumably) middle-aged, older-and-wiser character who is telling the story in the past tense and who shares reflections with the reader about love, jealousy, the characteristic behaviour of men and women and so forth, and also the very young man living through the episode with Albertine: his speech is presumably meant to reproduce that of the young man. The way the story is told suggests that a reader's sympathies are expected to lie largely with the male character, even though, in his youthful incarnation, he is sometimes presented in a mildly comic light. In the many generalizations about how 'we' feel in our dealings with 'them', 'we' are always men and 'they' women. Yet Proust had close women friends, and must have hoped for many female readers for his book: how are women to take these generalizations, and the narrator's behaviour?

Albertine cannot be seen as a character of equal weight with the narrator, even in *The Prisoner*, since for about half of its duration she is offstage, and, for the greater part of that time, forgotten. The narrator returns into Paris artistic society for a long musical evening at the Verdurins' (pp. 174–301) and the dramatic focus of this part of the book is the relationship between the Baron de Charlus, an elderly homosexual who has played an increasingly important role in previous volumes, and his protégé Morel, the violinist, who is finally persuaded to reject him publicly. If the book's subject were simply the narrator's 'imprisonment' of Albertine then all this part would be irrelevant. But it is not: the *roman d'Albertine* is inextricably involved with the larger novel's themes of time, memory, art, social and class relationships, fashion, snobbery, and human irrationality generally. More specifically, it is located almost from the beginning within the world of 'unnatural' sexuality: the hero's love develops in *Sodom and Gomorrah*, and it is in the company of M. de Charlus that he spends the evening preceding the climactic quarrel that opens the last part of the book. Indeed, his return home is delayed by a lengthy discussion with the Baron and Brichot, the elderly don, about homosexuality from ancient Greece to the present day.

There is a temptingly easy explanation for the preponderance of this theme: Proust himself was a homosexual. Though he never admitted his orientation in his writings, it was an open secret among his Parisian friends, and the topic has been extensively explored by biographers since his death. From this it was a short step to interpreting the relationships in his novels as disguised versions of homosexual relationships in his life. As the joke went, 'In Proust, you have to understand that all the girls are boys.' In particular, *The Prisoner* was seen as a rewriting of Proust's relationship with his chauffeur Alfred Agostinelli, to whom he undoubtedly had a strong, possessive attachment and with whom – though this is not certain – he may have had sexual relations. A certain amount of trivial gender reassignment does seem to be going on in *The Prisoner*: it is very curious that in the narrator's Paris all the young people who bring goods to the house and whom he watches from the window, and all messengers except telegram boys, are girls: were there no delivery-boys in Paris in 1900? But one really cannot accept Albertine as a chauffeur in a wig. The narrator is too obviously fascinated by her very femininity: her shape and colouring, her clothes, hair, speech, pursuits, her relationship to other women (and also, alas, other more stereotyped traits like her impulsiveness, fickleness and economy with the truth). Proust had several close emotional friendships with women, and seems to have been particularly fascinated by young girls. It is almost as if in this book he is conducting a thought-experiment, trying to imagine what it would be like to have such a being sharing one's living-space.

The narrator's physical relations with Albertine are shrouded in a mystery only partly explained by the conventions of what was and was not publishable in 1923. They have separate rooms, but clearly spend part of many nights in each other's beds. They appear not to have penetrative sex (Albertine says that they are not 'really' lovers, p. 84), but see each other naked and caress each other in a clearly sexual way, using sexual language to excite each other (p. 312). There is a thinly veiled description of the narrator reaching orgasm next to Albertine (but without her help) (p. 62) and it is suggested that she sometimes does so with his help (p. 74). At the end of the book, when they are increasingly at odds, Albertine withdraws sexual favours ('[I was] no longer receiving from her even the physical pleasures that I valued', p. 373). All this can be explained in commonsense terms by the fact that Albertine is an unmarried girl and the narrator wishes to keep open the possibility of her marrying someone else: he would not therefore wish to take her virginity. But it is an additional irony that the 'shameful' practices the narrator imputes to Albertine and her friends and the ones in which he himself engages with her should be so similar. Strange, too, is the way that throughout a relationship of considerable intimacy, the young people go on calling each other *vous* (the formal, polite mode of address) and not the *tu* which would be expected between lovers. This strangeness, and perhaps Albertine's wish for a closer relationship, are pointed up when she signs a note to the narrator '*Toute à vous, ton Albertine*'.

*The Prisoner* is a strange mixture of the improbable and the painfully realistic. A man's story of his carnal passion for a woman, written by a man who had probably never experienced such a passion, its plot rests on two large implausibilities: first, Albertine's presence in the narrator's house, and second, the narrator's almost limitless financial resources. At the time of the action no family with any pretensions to respectability would have allowed its unmarried daughter or ward to live unchaperoned under a man's roof as Albertine does here. We see Proust acknowledging this difficulty on p. 39:

'A young dressmaker go into society?' you will say, 'how improbable.' If you stop to think, it was no more unlikely than that Albertine should formerly have come to see me at midnight, and should now be living with me. And that would perhaps have been improbable in anyone else, but not at all in Albertine . . .

His solution is to present Mme Bontemps as an almost unbelievably neglectful guardian, who tolerates Albertine's irregular behaviour in the hope that she will marry a rich man, some of whose money will then find its way to the aunt. But this is not convincing: a family like the narrator's would be less, not more, likely to agree to their son's marrying a girl if her family had been so lax as to allow her to live with him beforehand. And once devalued by her association with the narrator, Albertine would find it more difficult to catch another husband.

In any case, how rich is the narrator? He thinks he can hold on to Albertine until he is ready to leave her by showering gifts upon her: couture dresses, furs, jewellery. He keeps a car and chauffeur (in some passages, a carriage and coachman) so as to send her on daily supervised outings, and even talks of buying a yacht for her: not a small sailing-boat but presumably a steam yacht, as it is to have living quarters equipped with English furniture and French eighteenth-century silver! It is difficult to imagine such riches in the hands of the young son of an upper-middle-class professional family such as the narrator's seems to be, and Proust's own family was. The origin of his fortune is left unclear. Mention is made of a legacy from an aunt, but we have already met the narrator's aunts in *The Way by Swann's* and seen the modest way in which they live. Also, we have already been told in *In the Shadow of Young Girls in Flower* that the narrator, when hardly more than a schoolboy, was already squandering his aunt's legacy, selling a Chinese vase to buy flowers for the girl with whom he was then in love, and parting with his aunt's silver so as to send daily baskets of orchids to the girl's mother. The mother's response is to say that if she were the narrator's father, she would assign him a *conseil judiciaire*, a legal trustee with complete control over his fortune. (Baudelaire's family, among others, had already taken this step.) But, though we are never told that the narrator's father has died, he plays no role whatever in *The Prisoner*. The narrator's mother from time to time expresses anxiety about his extravagance, but to no effect.

Even quite a modest legacy will buy a good many orchids; a yacht suggests a completely different level of affluence. But practical considerations of money, which would be at the centre of a novel by Balzac or Zola, seem to be of little importance here. Again, one feels that Proust is carrying out a thought experiment: let there be a young man M and a girl A, living in flat F. Let the money available to M be infinite . . .

If we accept the terms of the experiment, however, we shall find that the relationship and its developments are worked out in the most careful and convincing psychological detail. Obsession, dependence, revolt, wishful thinking, despair: the whole spectrum of human irrationality is explored by a supremely rational and analytical narrator, none of whose reason or power of analysis offers him the least protection against his propensity to 'make a hell in heaven's despite'. The question of sexual orientation becomes irrelevant: anyone can read the account of the narrator's 'love' for Albertine with a shudder of recognition.

Reading the book is not a penance, however; indeed it is often extremely funny. The closet drama between the narrator and Albertine (almost all of the scenes between them take place in enclosed spaces, his or her bedroom, the back of the car or carriage) alternates with large scenes for many characters, notably the Verdurins' music party, around which the narration travels as a film camera would do, stopping for a moment to eavesdrop on one small group or other, or simply focussing on a visual 'shot' – Mme Verdurin sleeping through the music, for example, with her little dog under her chair, or M. de Charlus silencing the fashionable audience with an imperious glare. The sequences at Mme de Guermantes's and Mme Verdurin's offer a wider comic panorama of human folly, but all of it, from the Duc de Guermantes's offended pride to Mme Verdurin's pretension and the hubris of M. de Charlus, is still grounded in what Charlus's famous ancestor, the Duc de la Rochefoucauld, would have called *amour-propre*, self-regard. Yet it is in the Vanity Fair of Mme Verdurin's party, surrounded by this supporting cast of more or less likeable grotesques, that the narrator has an intimation, through the music of Vinteuil's septet, of the possibility of escaping human pettiness and finding a kind of salvation through art. This new faith in art will be the concluding theme of his final volume, *Finding Time Again*.

On a less elevated plane, what seems above all to make the narrator's life worth while is the simple sensory experience of living: variations in the weather, the sound of street cries, the sight of landscapes, architecture or human features, even – perhaps especially – those of people he does not know. He can appreciate all these better, it seems, in the absence of the person with whom he is in love, or indeed of any person he knows well, or who knows him. The excitement of freedom and the joy of one's own company are among the strongest themes of *The Prisoner*.

When Proust died in November 1922 only *The Way by Swann's*, *In the Shadow of Young Girls in Flower*, *The Guermantes Way* and *Sodom and Gomorrah* had been published; *The Prisoner*, *The Fugitive* and *Finding Time Again* were still in manuscript. But the phrase 'in manuscript' gives a wholly inadequate idea of the task facing his original editors. Proust composed by an immensely complex process of writing and rewriting, weaving together passages sometimes composed years apart, filling his margins with additions and, when the margins ran out, continuing on strips of paper glued to the pages. (Some of the most memorable passages in *The Prisoner*, the death of Bergotte for example, appear for the first time only in these last-minute '*paperoles*'.) After a time he would have a clean copy typed, but this by no means marked the end of the rewriting process, which might continue to the proof stage and beyond. As he never saw proofs of *The Prisoner*, the only thing of which we can be certain is that, had he lived to sign the *bon à tirer* (ready to print), the book would have been considerably different from the one we have now. All editions of it are based on three typescripts held in the Bibliothèque Nationale (now Bibliothèque de France) in Paris: the first quarter of the first typescript had been corrected by Proust before his death and further clean copies made, but it had not yet been given the *bon à tirer*. Consequently his first editors, the novelist and essayist Jacques Rivière and the author's brother Robert Proust, had to correct the rest and establish a text as best they could. Later editors, Pierre Clarac and Andre Ferré for the editions de la Pléiade in 1954 and Jean-Yves Tadié (general editor) and Pierre-Edmond Robert (for *The Prisoner*) for the same house in 1988, have relied on the same typescripts, supplemented by an increasing quantity of manuscript material which has become available as collectors have died and left it, or their heirs have sold it, to the Bibliothèque Nationale. The distinguishing characteristic of the 1988 edition, from which this translation is made, is the inclusion of a large number of *esquisses*, preliminary sketches for passages which the assiduous reader can compare with the versions adopted for the main text. The Pléiade editions are scholarly in a way the original edition was not. Rivière and Robert Proust were more concerned to produce a readable text which would please critics and buyers, and so they ironed out a considerable number of inconsistencies and, as they thought, faults of style which the later editors have reinstated.

In the case of Proust, such editorial decisions are much more difficult to make than one might suppose. His composition is very rarely linear or chronological: most of the events described take place in a timeless or repetitive past indicated by the use of the imperfect tense: only from time to time is an episode narrated in the past historic, indicating that it happened only once. (These alternative past tenses present a real problem to the translator.) In one paragraph the narrator can be years older than in the preceding one or, for that matter, younger. (Evelyn Waugh noticed this and facetiously complained to John Betjeman: 'Well, the chap was plain barmy. He never tells you the age of the hero and on one page he is being taken to the W.C. in the Champs-Elysées by his nurse & the next page he is going to a brothel. Such a lot of nonsense' (letter, ?February 1948).) Characters can be both masculine and effeminate (M. de Charlus), odious and kind (the Verdurins), corrupt and conscientious. For most of the time this is deliberate. Proust may be showing the passage of time (M. de Charlus is originally very masculine in his bearing, then becomes increasingly effeminate), or the complexity of human character (M. Verdurin bullies Saniette abominably and then supports him when he loses all his money, and it is Mlle Vinteuil's friend, the very personification of depravity throughout the preceding volumes, who proves to have saved the composer's music for posterity by her patient deciphering of his manuscripts). At other times the same characters can be seen differently by different people, either because some are more observant than others, or because they have had some particular revelatory experience. By the time of the Verdurins' music party, the narrator sees M. de Charlus as the caricature 'old queen', no doubt partly because he has overheard his sexual encounter with Jupien at the beginning of *Sodom and Gomorrah*. But the more knowing members of the Verdurin circle share this view of him. On the other hand, the more conventional members of the audience have failed to notice his transformation, and the innocent young girl in Brichot's lecture audience sees only 'a stout, white-haired man with a black moustache, wearing the Military Medal', and is disappointed that a baron looks just like anybody else. If Albertine says on p. 92 that the Verdurins have always been kind to her and tried to help her, on p. 313 that Mme. Verdurin has always been vile to her and then again on p. 379 that she has been kind, this tells us something about Albertine, and perhaps about human judgements in general. To eliminate inconsistencies like these would be completely to denature Proust's work. On the other hand when Brichot arrives, on p. 180, in a tram which by p. 183 is a bus, when Mme Verdurin's husband is called first Auguste and then, a few pages later, Gustave, or when the vehicle in which the narrator and Albertine are riding through the Bois (pp. 149–158) is alternately a carriage and a motor-car, one wonders if Proust, had he lived, would not have eliminated such variations. Certainly, they are not found in the part of the manuscript that he did correct. The most unnerving concerns Dr Cottard. Mme Verdurin is 'deep in discussion' with him and Ski on p. 209, but at the same party she receives, without apparent surprise, condolences on his death (p. 221). By p. 257 he is alive again, and

General Deltour is consulting him about his health. In the same way, two completely different accounts are given of the death of Saniette, its causes, the duration of his last illness and Cottard's involvement in it, though pp. 221 and 244 would suggest that the doctor had died before the patient. These inconsistencies no doubt result from Proust's practice of writing and rewriting sequences individually (again, rather in the way a film is shot), sometimes at considerable intervals of time and not in the order in which they would appear in the finished novel. It is difficult to see that such continuity errors serve any literary purpose, and his first editors eliminated them. Later, more reverential editors, however, have restored them all, including the death and resurrection of Cottard.

One might make the same observation about verbal repetitions, which are frequent in *La Prisonnière*, particularly in the part which Proust did not live to correct. Some of these are plainly deliberate, and represent tics of speech, like the Duc de Guermantes's 'bel et bien' (here translated 'thoroughgoing') or M. de Charlus's 'enchaînement de circonstances'. But others, including some whole sentences repeated with minimal changes, or sequences of two or more sentences all beginning with the same word or words (e.g. 'D'autre part', 'on the other hand'), are probably accidental. Such repetitions were regarded as very bad style at the time of the first edition, were often corrected by the first editors and have been reinstated by their modern successors. This translation has attenuated them to some degree.

Carol Clark

# *Translator's Introduction:* The Fugitive

*The Fugitive* (together with *The Prisoner*) appears to form an integral element of *In Search of Lost Time*. The disappearance of Albertine, Marcel's anguish, and his first intuitions of the recovery of past selves while in Venice, seem to lead inevitably into the revelations of *Finding Time Again*. However, Proust's original plan included only an imprecise role for Albertine. As we know from his notebooks, the original cautionary tale of Swann's frustrated love for Odette was a model which was intended to run smoothly into the narrator's similar disappointments in love, art and society, with Marcel's amorous interests and experience dispersed between his childhood relationship with Gilberte and a variety of young women met later at Balbec and elsewhere, and his ultimate meeting with Gilberte on his return to society after his illness. It was only in 1914, after the publication of *The Way by Swann's* and while he was already working on *In the Shadow of Young Girls in Flower*, that Proust started to feel the need to develop a new, major section concentrating the narrator's own experience of sexuality, jealousy, anxiety and loss into his relationship with Albertine, and linking it to other virtuoso but unplaced passages – Marcel's reading of his article in the *Figaro* and his visit to Venice – creating a new dialectic of desire and creativity.

Between *The Way by Swann's* and *Finding Time Again* lay the open wastes of superficial encounters with artists and high society, attractive enough to Marcel, but destined ultimately to disappoint him. As Proust continued to write, this central part was steadily expanded from being contained within the *Guermantes* volumes to occupy the further volumes of *Sodom and Gomorrah*. Between 1914 and his death in 1922, Proust moved much material concerning Albertine back and forth between the various volumes of *Sodom and Gomorrah* (where *The Prisoner*, *The Fugitive* and *Finding Time Again* took on their separate identities only towards the end of Proust's life). *The Fugitive* finally assumed a dual function: on the one hand as the apotheosis of sexual passion and the jealous quest to know the elusive object of desire, on the other, as the premise of Marcel's rediscovery of self and its inner sources of creativity, which the protagonist had seemed for so long to have lost, and which would structure *Finding Time Again*. *The Fugitive* was first published in 1925 from the 1917 dictated manuscript corrected by Jacques Rivière, Jean Paulhan and Proust's brother Robert; a fuller version, with variants, was used for the 1954 Pléiade edition. Editors differ in their opinions as to what was actually written, finally revised and ultimately intended by Proust. Matters were complicated by the existence of Proust's separate review publication of a different version of 'Staying in Venice' in 1919, and the acquisition by the Bibliothèque Nationale in 1962 and the publication by Nathalie Mauriac in 1986 of another *Fugitive* (edited by Proust, and probably intended to be published separately). The Pléiade edition here translated is the best assessment of what Proust would have published if he had lived (although he notoriously rewrote whenever faced with queries by typists or editors).

*The Fugitive* is in many ways a novel, or even a drama, of identity. One function is to develop Marcel's realization that gender and desire are often misleading and usually ambiguous. The homosexuality of Charlus and the bisexuality of Saint-Loup are gradually affirmed against the background of Albertine's lesbian relationships. These orientations turn out to be systematic for Proust. Like Freud, he sees a fundamental bisexuality in the human animal. The discovery by Marcel of Albertine's likely sexual relations with Andrée or Léa, or her casual encounters in the showers at Balbec, leads him to realize that he did not know her thoughts or desires. And as happened for Swann with Odette, it is this failure to know the beloved, this failure to grasp the core of another person's being, which leads Marcel into an anguished search for the inner truth of Albertine even after her death, since as long as he fails to find the object of his desire, he cannot, by definition, know the nature of his own passion. Desire, love and jealousy in Proust are all part of a search for truth and knowledge. Albertine, like Gilberte, indeed like Charlus and Saint-Loup, constantly reveals hidden selves, while suggesting yet others, unknown or unknowable. Marcel's whole project as mature narrator is an investigation into the self, as he struggles to reconstruct his past, while simultaneously displaying and analysing his own tendency towards self-deception. Proust shows a quasi-Freudian insight into the processes of negation, repression and displacement, as Marcel's feelings for the allegedly forgotten Albertine erupt here and there in devious guises – through the taste of cherries, a shade of twilight or a half-remembered phrase. The focus is also on the dynamic search for his own elusive selves, a search which drives the older Marcel's narrative and the younger protagonist's obsessive desire for knowledge of Albertine and exploration of his own suffering and jealousy, leading to a continual process of interpretation by Marcel of all the surface signs of meaning inscribed by individuals in their relations with him and society. These hypotheses, these fictions, these scenarios are also symptomatically woven around past experience, as whole areas of Albertine's missing life are rewritten by Marcel in order to make sense of the psychodrama that the two lovers had been enacting. Marcel's attempts to interpret Albertine are constantly deflected – by Aimé's unreliable letters, by Albertine's misinterpreted telegrams, by Marcel's failure to recognize Gilberte at the Guermantes.

All of these misreadings could be seen as part of a general comedy or tragedy of social misunderstanding and psychological failure to grasp the nature of other people, as well as one's own self. These fluctuations and deliberate ambiguities include the resonant interchange of names and situations between Gilberte and Albertine. Gilberte, the daughter of Swann, was as elusive and unfaithful to the young Marcel in *The Way by Swann's* as her mother had been to Swann himself. Now in *The Fugitive* it is Albertine who repeats the role of the evasive and fleeting fugitive. Their similar-sounding names lead to moments of high drama as Gilberte's telegram announcing her return and marriage are misread by Marcel as announcing the return from the dead of Albertine and even a marriage proposal from her. Thus the relationship between Saint-Loup and Gilberte in marriage will ironically re-echo those of Marcel and Albertine, and of Swann and Odette. The ironies of fate and reversals of fortune which punctuate *In Search of Lost Time*, and which culminate in the revelation of the work of time, ageing and death in *Finding Time Again*, are already accelerating in *The Fugitive*, which presents the outcome of tendencies, actions and facts half-hidden in previous volumes. This process of coming out, revelation and discovery of latent truths prefigures the crucial insight provided at the end of *The Fugitive* by the realization that the apparently separate Guermantes and Méséglise ways not only lie side by side, but actually meet outside Marcel's garden gate. And a key factor in this gradual revelation of what people are and how we construct their topology includes the position of the narrator himself as the protagonist who has in fact been guiding us forward and showing us significant moments of his past, without fully revealing or even grasping their significance.

It is in *The Fugitive* that Marcel at last gains more insight into the key moments of temporal and spatial overlap initiated by the mysterious 'epiphany' of the founding madeleine incident in the 'Combray' section of *The Way by Swann's*. As the sights and sensations of Venice trigger a revival within him of the dead Albertine, he starts to understand the mechanisms of involuntary memory, stored in the senses. The Baptistery of St Mark's and the canals of Venice reactivate the experience of the church and the streets of Combray. As daytime Combray lay embedded in the lime-flower tea, so artistic and spiritual Combray lies embedded in the stones and canals of Venice. But Marcel's retrieval of lost memories is offset by his terror during the moments when he has premonitions of the possibility of forgetting, the possibility of learning to let go of the all-pervasive and all-important emotion of love which previously structured his whole existence. Marcel retrospectively remembers moments of anxious anticipation just as he imagines in advance moments when he will have forgotten what he is now feeling. For in fact we negotiate with the memory of our emotions, as much as, if not more than, with our raw emotions themselves.

From the start of *The Fugitive*, the narrator notes a split between his intellect and his intuition. He understands rationally that Albertine has left, but all his emotional and bodily responses continue to behave as if she were still there. The problem is that the rational mind is situated at one present moment in time, and does not take into account the whole series of successive selves that we have been over a period of time. We have constructed ourselves largely from a series of habitual actions and visions. The interplay of conscious and unconscious memory structures the dreams and fantasies which occupy most of Marcel's time in *The Fugitive*. The force at work behind the dialectic of remembering and forgetting is largely that of the unconscious – and Proust is one of the earliest modern novelists to use 'the unconscious' as a noun. His retrospective narrative is interrupted, for instance by a dream of his dead grandmother turned to marble but walking around the room. Likewise, his waking thoughts, too, often assume a dream-like quality as every seasonal sound and every change of weather bring back visions of past days spent with Albertine, or imagined scenarios of future days spent either together or alone. It is above all this dynamics of remembering, forgetting, dreaming, hypothesizing and imagining which drives the narrative, sometimes forwards, sometimes backwards and sometimes in spirals.

This may explain why Proust's style is often wrongly assumed to be composed solely of long and tortuous sentences. In fact Proust does not have, or use, one single style in *In Search of Lost Time* as a whole, nor in this volume. He uses many voices, ranging from Norpois's diplomatic pedantry and Aimé's semi-educated letters, through Françoise's rustic wisdom, to the conscious exchange of witticisms at the Guermantes salon. Proust is of course noted for his use of metaphor, which has a structural and functional role to play in his whole aesthetic, with its implied rejection of appearances and reality. But although the proliferation of metaphors used by Marcel is a sign of his rich and potentially creative imagination, at the same time Proust's references and metaphors are usually highly precise, scientific even, drawing on his interest in biology, medicine and chemistry. Proust, like Freud, uses metaphors taken from archaeology, hydraulics and thermodynamics to show how throughout our lives our identity is constantly fractured and shifting; our different selves rise to the surface and fall away, surge forward only to be repressed, or come into conflict with each other in the ebb and flow of psychological and emotional experience.

At other moments, however, Proust's style may be concise and aphoristic. Marcel's long and intricate analyses may be punctuated or summarized by brief maxims worthy of La Rochefoucauld, or interrupted by sudden attempts of the will to seize control of his obsessional fantasies, procrastination and doubt. Proust's use of tenses reinforces the dynamics of memory, imagination and waiting, as elaborate interference between the past historic and the imperfect disrupts the usual relations between singular events, repeated acts and habitual states. Past information may be translated into the future or the conditional tenses, engendering new hypotheses, or the imperfect subjunctive may reveal Marcel's refusal of visual or verbal reality. It is true that in *The Fugitive* Proust's style is unusually tortuous, repetitive, hesitant and self-questioning, as it reflects the obsessions and ramblings of the anxious, obsessively suspicious and jealous mind, but this is a performative use of language, enacting the temporal turmoil and fluctuating will of the anguished Marcel.

In *The Fugitive* we also recognize aspects of Marcel's artistic creativity in the context of a more profound experience of reading and writing in general. By the time Marcel is living with Albertine, he has discovered and traversed the desert of Guermantes high society, and has failed to build on the creative intuitions which he had felt when faced with the three steeples of Martinville. His disappointments seem confirmed by the failure of Swann to write, as well as by the shallowness of the novelist Bergotte and the neglect and the suffering of the composer Vinteuil. Marcel's only creative feat has been an article written for the *Figaro* which has not even been published. When this article suddenly appears it surprises Marcel, who at first reacts as reader rather than author. He struggles to recognize phrases which he had produced but forgotten. But then the process of reading recreates in his mind a performance which repeats, in another key, the performance of writing. For a moment, perhaps, Marcel becomes the author of the book that we are reading, as the narrative starts freewheeling in an extraordinary shift into the present tense, uniting the timescales of thinking, writing and reading.

Themes of writing and creativity flicker through *The Fugitive*, sometimes ironically, sometimes mysteriously, but always in counterpoint to

Marcel's overt concern with desire and with the knowledge of the object of that desire. His visual imagination is often privileged as Marcel learns of Albertine's seaside and riverside adventures. He constantly visualizes her erotic experience in terms of painting. He remembers Elstir's paintings of nude bathers (and we suspect that Proust himself is remembering similar paintings by Courbet and Cézanne), then he projects such images retrospectively on to the figure of Albertine. In its turn this artistically derived image is developed, creating a new configuration of naked statues cavorting at Versailles. Marcel proceeds to feed these images back into the reality of Albertine's desire. But then his mind leaps out again into myth and the imagination, with memories and fantasies based on Leda and the swan. In all this, Marcel is to some extent repeating the experience of Swann, who mapped on to the figure of Odette the visual experience of a Botticelli painting and the musical experience of listening to Vinteuil, before reading back from Odette these reflections of artistic form which he himself had placed in her. For much of the novel before *The Fugitive* Marcel seemed likely to follow the model of Swann, who subordinated his creative energies to conversation, seduction and dilettantism. Now in *The Fugitive*, however, we see that even in his jealous fantasies, Marcel is starting to weave more complex mental paintings around the figure of Albertine, rather in the manner of Elstir, whose painting has already been interpreted by Marcel in *In the Shadow of Young Girls in Flower* as a process of creative interchange of substances and qualities whereby, for instance, the sea is expressed in terms of land, and vice versa – the epitome of metaphor. This tendency is no doubt confirmed in the section 'Staying in Venice', where the absence of Albertine, gradually accepted by the mind and learned by the body and the emotions, leaves Marcel free to accomplish his long-deferred trip to Venice, quintessential city of art.

Marcel's desire-driven fantasies and fictional scenarios continue as he risks his mother's wrath by wandering the back-streets of Venice in search of sex, rather than return to Paris. Once he has left for Venice with his mother, the signs of artistic and spiritual renaissance multiply. The motif of the eagle inscribed in Albertine's rings which signalled sexual betrayal and emotional anguish by encoding Albertine's lover's initials is transformed in Venice from a venal sign to a spiritual icon as the eagle of St John the Evangelist appears in statues and mosaics all around. Albertine's Fortuny gowns, coloured flesh pink as if revealing the inside of the labile body, rejoin the marine blue and solar gold of Venice, in their artistic retranslation back into the original motifs of Carpaccio's paintings. The previously censorious presence of Marcel's mother, which had interrupted his emotional fulfilment with Albertine, now overlaps the sanctified figure of the Virgin Mary, nurturing her son in St Mark's Baptistery. At the same time she becomes an artistic figure stimulating him to translate his intellectual comments and emotional intuitions, inspired by Ruskin. This reminds us that Proust, like Ruskin and Wilde, tends to see art as a substitute for religion, although we should also note that Proust here pays ironic homage to his own translations of *The Bible of Amiens* and *Sesame and Lilies*, and his own visit to Venice, nearly two decades earlier, during the phase when he was overawed by Ruskin and felt unable to compose his own work. But Proust himself had laid the foundations of his creative fiction in his preface to *Sesame and Lilies*, entitled *Days of Reading*. The great creative power of reading, exercised by Marcel when faced with his *Figaro* article, Albertine's rings, Aimé's letters, Gilberte's and Saint-Loup's telegrams, or Ruskin's art criticism, is a creative power shared by Proust's reader, stitching away at these fragments of interpretation and already anticipating the patchwork aesthetic to be revealed in *Finding Time Again*. Readers of *The Fugitive* may feel that their experience resembles that of the translator, constantly anticipating, constantly supplying provisional meanings: '*On devine en lisant, on crée; tout part d'une erreur initiale.*'

Peter Collier

*The Prisoner*

From early morning, with my face still turned to the wall and before I had seen, above the tall window curtains, the colour of the line of morning light, I already knew what kind of day it was. I could tell from the first street noises, whether they reached me muffled and distorted by dampness or twanging like arrows in the empty, resonant space of a wide-open morning, icy and pure. The rumbling of the first tram told me whether it was huddled against the rain or forging gaily towards a blue horizon. And maybe even those sounds had been preceded by some swifter, more penetrating emanation which had slid into my sleep and suffused it with a sadness foretelling snow, or had found there a certain little intermittent figure which it set to singing so many rousing hymns in praise of the sun that, though still asleep, I would begin to smile, my closed eyes preparing to be dazzled, until a crash of music finally brought me awake. It was, in fact, mainly from my bedroom that I perceived the world around me at this period. I know Bloch spread the story that when he came to see me in the evening, he would hear the sound of conversation; since my mother was at Combray and he never found anyone in my room, he concluded that I was talking to myself. When, much later, he found out that Albertine had been living with me then and realized that I had been hiding her from everyone, he declared that he understood at last why, at that time in my life, I never wanted to go out. He was wrong. Very understandably so, since reality, even if it is inevitable, is not completely predictable; those who learn some correct detail about the life of another promptly jump from it to quite incorrect conclusions and see in the newly discovered fact the explanation for things which in truth are completely unrelated to it.

3

When I think now of how my friend had left Balbec with me and come back to Paris to live under the same roof, giving up her idea of going on a cruise; of how she slept twenty paces from my bedroom, at the end of the corridor, in my father's little room with the tapestries, and how every evening, very late, before leaving me to sleep, she would slip her tongue into my mouth like my daily bread, like a nourishing food having the almost sacred character of all flesh on which suffering – the suffering that we have endured for its sake – has conferred a kind of spiritual sweetness, then the analogy which springs to my mind is not the night which Captain de Borodino allowed me to spend at the barracks – a favour which, after all, cured a mere passing malaise – but that other night when my father sent Mama to sleep in the little bed next to mine. So true is it that life, if it decides once more to spare us a trial which seems inevitable, does so in a different manner – such a contradictory manner, sometimes, that it appears almost sacrilegious to recognize that the grace granted to us is the same!

Once Albertine had learned from Françoise that, in the darkness of my room with its still-closed curtains, I was not sleeping, she did not bother to avoid making a small amount of noise as she washed in her bathroom. So then I would often go into another bathroom adjoining hers, which was a pleasant place. In former times a theatrical producer would spend hundreds of thousands of francs to stud with real emeralds the throne from which the diva would play the part of an empress. The Russian Ballet has taught us that simple, well-directed lighting effects can flood the stage with jewels just as sumptuous and more varied. This new décor, already more immaterial, is still not so charming as the one which the eight o'clock sun produces in place of what we were accustomed to see when we did not rise until midday. The windows of our two bathrooms were not clear but, so that we could not be seen from outside, were all puckered into an old-fashioned, artificial frost effect. The sun suddenly turned this net of glass to yellow, gilded it and, gently uncovering in me a young man of former times who had been long hidden by habit, intoxicated me with memories, as if I had been in the open air looking at gilded foliage in which not even the presence of a bird was wanting. For I could hear Albertine endlessly whistling:

>Sorrows are crazy
>And listening to them is crazier still.

I was too fond of her not to smile happily at her bad musical taste. Mme Bontemps, I may say, had had a passion for that song the previous summer, until she heard that it was a silly thing, whereupon, instead of asking Albertine to sing it when people called, she began to ask for:

>A farewell song rises from troubled springs

which in turn became 'that old thing of Massenet's that the child is always trotting out'. A cloud would pass, hiding the sun, and I would see the modest foliage of the glass curtain turn dull and lapse into a grisaille.

Albertine's bathroom was just like mine but, since there was another at the other end of the flat, Mama had never used this one for fear of disturbing me with noise. The walls separating the two were so thin that we could chat to each other as we washed, carrying on a conversation interrupted only by the sound of the water, in the kind of intimacy which is often produced in hotels by the cramped space and nearness of the rooms, but which in Paris is so rare. At other times, I stayed in bed, dreaming for as long as I liked, for the orders were never to come into my room until I had rung. Because of the inconvenient way in which the bell-push had been hung over my bed, reaching it took so long that sometimes, tiring of the effort to grasp it and enjoying being alone, I almost went back to sleep. Not that I was completely indifferent to Albertine's presence in the family flat. By separating her from her friends I had succeeded in sparing my heart further suffering. I had placed it in a position of rest, of near immobility which would help it to heal. But the state of calm which my friend's presence produced in me was an alleviation of suffering rather than actual joy. Not that it did not allow me to enjoy many pleasures from which my previous, acute pain had closed me off, but far from owing these pleasures to Albertine, whom I hardly even found pretty any more, in whose company I was bored and whom I had a clear sense of no longer loving, I experienced them, on the contrary, when she was not with me. So I would begin the morning by not having her called at once, especially if the weather were fine. For a few moments, knowing that his company made me happier than hers, I remained in private colloquy with the little inner figure, singer of salutations to the sun, whom I mentioned a moment ago. Of all the persons who make up our individual selves, the most apparent are not the most essential. When illness has eliminated them one by one, there will survive in me a final two or three, the hardest to kill off, and notably one, a philosopher who is happy only when he has discovered, between two works of art or between two sensations, a common factor. But I have sometimes wondered if the last of all will not be the little man very like another little man that the Combray optician kept in his shop window, who took his hood off whenever the sun shone and put it back on again if it was going to rain. I know that little man, with all his egoism; I can be suffering an asthma attack which only the coming of rain would relieve, he does not care and, at the first drops that I have been so longing for, he scowls and crossly pulls up his hood. On the other hand, I feel sure that on my deathbed, when all my other 'I's' are already gone, if there is a blink of sun, while I am drawing my last breaths, the little barometer man will be delighted and will take his hood off and sing, 'Ah! The sun at last!'

I rang for Françoise. I opened the *Figaro*. I looked for, and once more did not find, an article or something calling itself an article which I had sent to that newspaper and which was nothing but a slightly rearranged version of the recently rediscovered page which I had written in Dr Percepied's carriage while looking at the steeples of Martinville. Then I read Mama's latest letter. She found it strange, shocking, that an unmarried girl should be living alone with me. It may be that on the first day, when we were leaving Balbec, when she saw me looking so unhappy and was worried about leaving me alone, she had been pleased to hear that Albertine was coming with us and to see loaded on to the train, next to our luggage (the luggage I had spent the night weeping over in the hotel in Balbec), Albertine's narrow black boxes, which had seemed to me to have the shape of coffins, so that I did not know whether they would bring life into our house, or death. But I did not even think about Mama's feelings, being entirely caught up in the joy of that radiant morning and the thought that, after all my fear of staying in Balbec, I was taking Albertine home with me. Mama may not have been hostile to the scheme at first (she spoke kindly to my friend, as a mother does whose son has been seriously wounded and who is grateful to the young mistress who is devotedly nursing him), but she became so as it was too thoroughly carried out, and as the young woman's stay in our house – in our house in the absence of my parents – became prolonged. I cannot say, however, that she ever made her hostility plain to me. Just as before, when she felt she could no longer reproach me with my nervous disposition, my laziness, now she was afraid – something I perhaps did not entirely understand at the time or did not wish to understand – that by expressing any reservations about the girl to whom I said I was going to become engaged, she might cast a shadow over my future life, make me less committed to my wife, perhaps lead me to reproach myself, once she was gone, for having hurt her by marrying Albertine. Mama preferred to seem to endorse a choice that she felt she would not be able to make me reconsider. But everyone who saw her at that time told me that her sorrow at having lost her own mother was aggravated by a look of perpetual worry. This mental strain, this constant argument with herself, made Mama's temples over-heat, and she was constantly opening windows to try to cool down. But she could not take a decision for fear of 'influencing' me in the wrong direction and spoiling what she thought was my happiness. She could not even make up her mind to stop me having Albertine in the flat in the meantime. She did not want to appear more strict than Mme Bontemps, whose place it was, if anyone's, to act, and who did not find the arrangement unsuitable, much to my mother's surprise. In any case she was sorry to have been obliged to leave the two of us together by having to set off just then for Combray, where she saw she might have to stay (and did indeed stay) for many months, during which time my great-aunt needed her by her day and night. Everything there was made easy for her by the kindness, the devotion of Legrandin, for whom nothing was too much trouble, who put off from week to week his return to Paris, simply because my aunt, whom he did not know particularly well, had been a friend of his mother's, and because he realized that the dying woman valued his attentions and could not do without him. Snobbery is a serious malady of the soul, but a localized one which does not affect it overall. I, on the other hand, was delighted by Mama's absence in Combray, for it meant that Albertine (whom I could not ask to conceal it) would not be able to mention to her her friendship with Mlle Vinteuil. This relationship would, in my mother's eyes, have utterly precluded not only a marriage, which she had in any case asked me not to discuss in too definite terms with my friend and which furthermore was coming to seem intolerable to me, but even a stay in our house by Albertine as a guest. Failing such a serious reason, of which she was not aware, Mama, under the double effect of her mother's edifying and liberating example on the one hand (Grandmother, that admirer of George Sand, who defined virtue as nobility of heart) and on the other my own corrupting influence, now showed tolerance for women of whose conduct she would once have been severely critical and whom she would have condemned even now if they had been middle-class friends of hers from Paris or Combray, but whose great souls I praised to her and whom she forgave much because they were fond of me. In spite of everything, and even setting aside the question of propriety, I think Albertine would have exhausted Mama's patience, for Mama had learned at Combray, from Aunt Léonie and from all her female relations, habits of order of which my friend had not the slightest inkling. She would no more have closed a door nor, on the other hand, hesitated to enter a room where the door was open than would a dog or a cat. Her somewhat inconvenient charm consisted in being in the house not in the manner of a young girl but of a domestic animal which comes into a room, goes out, turns up in the place you least expect it, jumps on to the bed – I found this deeply restful – lies down beside one, makes a place for itself and lies there without moving, without annoying one as a person would. However, she finally adapted herself to my sleeping hours and learned, not just not to try to come into my room, but even not to make any noise until I rang. It was Françoise who set these rules for her. Françoise was one of those Combray servants who know their master's importance, and that the least they can do is to make everyone show him the respect they think is his due. When a visitor from outside gave Françoise a tip to be shared with the kitchen-maid, the donor hardly had time to hand over his coin before Françoise, with equal speed, discretion and energy, had primed the girl to appear and thank him, not under her breath but loudly and clearly, as Françoise had told her was the right way to do. The curé of Combray was not a genius, but he too knew how things should be done. Under his instruction, the daughter of some Protestant cousins of Mme Sazerat's had been converted to Catholicism, and the family had shown him all due appreciation. There was a question of her marrying a nobleman from Méséglise. The young man's parents wrote asking for information about her, a rather disdainful letter in which they showed contempt for her Protestant birth. The priest replied in such terms that the nobleman had to swallow his pride and write a very different letter, begging as the most precious favour to be allowed to form an alliance with the young lady.

There was no personal merit in the way Françoise taught Albertine to respect my sleep. She was steeped in the old tradition. Her silence, or her brusque reply to Albertine's no doubt innocent suggestion that she might enter my room or that Françoise might ask me for something, made my friend realize with astonishment that she had entered a new world of unknown customs, ruled by laws of behaviour that no one could think of breaking. Albertine had had a foretaste of this in Balbec, but in Paris she did not even try to resist, and waited patiently each morning for the sound of my bell before daring to make any noise.

Her education by Françoise was in any case good for our old servant herself, for it gradually moderated the level of the complaints that she had been uttering ever since our return from Balbec. For, just as we were getting into the tram, she had realized that she had forgotten to say goodbye to the 'housekeeper' of the hotel, a moustachioed person who watched over the landings and corridors, who barely knew Françoise but had been reasonably polite to her. Françoise was determined to turn back, to get off the tram, go back to the hotel, say a proper goodbye to the housekeeper and not leave until the next day. Good sense and above all my sudden horror of Balbec prevented me from allowing this, but ever since then she had been suffering from a feverish ill-humour, which the change of air did not relieve and which was persisting in Paris. For according to Françoise's code, as it is set forth in the bas-reliefs of Saint-André-des-Champs, to desire the death of an enemy, even to inflict it on him, is not forbidden, but it is dreadful not to do the right thing, not to return a favour, to be ignorant and not say goodbye to the lady on the landing. Throughout the journey, the constantly recurring memory of not having said goodbye to this woman would bring an alarming scarlet flush to Françoise's cheeks. And if she refused to eat or drink until we got to Paris, it was perhaps because this memory really 'weighed on her stomach' (every social class has its own pathology), and not just that she wanted to punish us.

One of the reasons why Mama wrote me a letter every day, every letter including a quotation from Mme de Sévigné,[1] was the memory of her mother. Mama would write to me, 'Mme Sazerat gave us one of her special little luncheons, the kind which, as your poor grandmother would have said, quoting Mme de Sévigné, take us from solitude without offering us company.' In an early answer, I was foolish enough to write to her, 'Your mother would recognize you at once from your choice of quotations,' only to receive the reply: 'Silly boy, imagine quoting Mme de Sévigné to talk to me about *my mother*. She would have answered you as she did Mme de Grignan: "Was she nothing to you? I thought you were related".'

At this point, I would hear my friend's footsteps coming or going from her bedroom. I would ring the bell, because this was the time when Andrée came with the chauffeur (a friend of Morel's, lent by the Verdurins) to collect Albertine. I had mentioned to Albertine the distant possibility of our marrying, but I had never made a formal proposal; she, for her part, out of modesty, when I had said, 'I don't know, but perhaps we could,' had shaken her head with a sad smile, saying, 'No, of course we couldn't,' meaning, 'I am too poor.' And so, while dismissing any long-term project with the words 'it's all very uncertain', I did everything possible to amuse her, to make her life pleasant, perhaps also, unconsciously, trying to make her want to marry me. Albertine herself laughed at all this luxury. 'Wouldn't Andrée's mother pull a face if she saw I'd become a rich lady like her, what she calls a lady with "horses, carriages, pictures". What? Didn't I ever tell you about her saying that? Oh, she's a real character. What surprises me is that she puts the pictures on the same level as the horses and carriages.'

For, as we shall see later, in spite of some silly habits of speech that she had retained, Albertine had developed astonishingly, something which was a matter of complete indifference to me, superior intelligence in a woman having always interested me so little that if I remarked on it to one or other of them, it has always been from mere politeness.

Only the curious genius of Céleste might have appealed to me. I could not keep from smiling for a few moments when, for example, knowing that Albertine was not there and seizing the opportunity, she approached me with the words, 'O heavenly being set down on a bed.' I said, 'Really, Céleste, what do you mean, "heavenly being"? – Well, if you think you're anything like the creatures who walk on our humble earth, you're much mistaken – But why "set down" on a bed? You can see that I'm lying down. – You never lie down. No one lies down like that. You floated down there. Those white pyjamas you're wearing today and the way you move your neck make you look like a dove.'

Albertine, even when she was talking about trivial things, now spoke in quite a different manner from that of the little girl she had been just a few years before, at Balbec. She would go so far as to say, about a political event of which she disapproved, 'I think that's beyond everything,' and I am not sure if it was not around that time that she learned to say, meaning that she found a book badly written, 'It's interesting, but really, he's *made a pig's ear* of the writing.' The taboo on entering my room before I had rung amused her greatly. As she had caught our family habit of quotation, and chose hers from the plays in which she had acted at the convent and which I had said I liked, she always compared me to Ahasuerus:

> *Et la mort est le prix de tout audacieux*
> *Qui sans être appelé se présente a ses yeux.*
>
> .    .    .    .    .    .    .    .    .
>
> *Rien ne met a l'abri de cet ordre fatal,*
> *Ni le rang, ni le sexe, et le crime est égal.*
>
> .    .    .    .    .    .    .    .    .
>
> *Moi-même . . .*
> *Je suis à cette loi comme une autre soumise,*
> *Et sans le prévenir il faut pour lui parler*
> *Qu'il me cherche ou du moins qu'il me fasse appeler.*[2]

Physically, too, she had changed. Her long blue eyes – longer now – had taken on a new shape; they were still the same colour, but seemed to have changed to the liquid state, so that, when she closed them, it was like drawing curtains to shut out a view of the sea. It was no doubt this part of her that I chiefly remembered when I left her each night. For, on the contrary, the tight waviness of her hair, for example, came to me for a long time as a daily surprise, like something new, as if I had never seen it before. And yet, springing above the smiling gaze of a young girl, what is more beautiful than this curly crown of black violets? There is more promise of friendship in the smile; but the little shiny tendrils of flowering hair, nearer relatives of the flesh which they seem to transpose into tiny, moving waves, take a stronger hold upon our desire. She would come into my bedroom, jump straight on to the bed and sometimes begin to define the character of my intelligence, or swear in a genuine rush of feeling that she would rather die than leave me: those were the days when I had shaved before calling her in. She was one of those women who cannot disentangle the reasons for their feelings. Seeing a fresh complexion gives them pleasure; they attribute it to the personal qualities of the man who seems to promise them a future of happiness: happiness which seems to shrink and to become less necessary to them as one's beard grows back again.

I would ask where she planned to go that day. 'I think Andrée wants to take me to the Buttes-Chaumont;[3] I've never been there.' It was certainly beyond me to guess whether these words, among so many others, concealed a lie. In any case I trusted Andrée to tell me all the places she went to with Albertine. In Balbec, when I felt I had really had enough of Albertine, I had planned to say, untruthfully, to Andrée: 'Dear Andrée, if only I had met you again sooner! You're the one I should have fallen in love with. But now I'm in love with someone else. All the same, we can see a lot of each other, for my love for this other person is making me so unhappy and you will help me to get over it.' But these same lying words had become the truth only three weeks later. Maybe, once in Paris, Andrée did come to believe that it was a lie and that I did love her, as she would surely have come to think in Balbec. For the truth changes so much for us that other people can hardly keep track of it. And as I knew that she would tell

me everything she and Albertine did together, I had asked her, and
she had agreed, to come and take Albertine out practically every day.
In this way I could safely stay at home. And Andrée's privileged
position as one of the girls of the little gang gave me confidence that
she would be able to influence Albertine to do anything I wanted.
Truly, I could now have told her in all honesty that she would be able
to give me peace of mind.

It is also true that my choice of Andrée (who happened to be in
Paris at this time, having given up her plan to go back to Balbec) as
my friend's companion had been influenced by what Albertine had
told me about her friend's attachment to me when we were in Balbec,
at a time when I feared I bored her; had I known of this at the time I
might indeed have fallen in love with Andrée after all. 'What, you
mean you didn't know?' said Albertine. 'We used to joke about it
among ourselves. Anyway, didn't you notice how she'd started to talk
like you, to use your arguments? Especially when she'd just been with
you, it stood out a mile. She didn't have to tell us that she'd seen you.
As soon as she arrived, if she'd been with you, we could tell at once.
We'd look at each other and laugh. She was like a coalman trying to
pretend he isn't a coalman, but he's all black. A miller doesn't have to
tell you he's a miller, you can see the flour all over him and the place
where the sack was on his back. Andrée was just the same, she moved
her eyebrows like you, and then that long neck of hers, I can't explain.
When I pick up a book that's been in your bedroom, I can take it out
of doors, but anyone can still tell it's yours because there's always a
trace of your horrible disinfectants. It's a tiny thing, I can't tell you,
but there's just a hint which is actually quite nice. Every time somebody
said anything nice about you, or seemed to think a lot of you, Andrée
was in the seventh heaven.'

Even so, just to be sure that nothing had been planned without my
knowledge, I would advise them not to go to the Buttes-Chaumont
that day, but to go instead to Saint-Cloud, or somewhere else.

It was certainly not that I loved Albertine in the slightest: I knew
that. Perhaps love is nothing but the ripple effect of those disturbances
which, in the wake of an emotion, stir up the soul. My whole soul had
been profoundly agitated when Albertine had told me, at Balbec, about

Mlle Vinteuil, but these disturbances were over now. I no longer loved Albertine, for nothing remained of the pain, now cured, which I had suffered in the tram at Balbec when I learned what Albertine's adolescence had been, including, perhaps, visits to Montjouvain. I had turned it all over in my mind for too long, the pain was gone. But occasionally certain ways of speaking of Albertine's led me to think – I do not know why – that she must have received in her time, short as it still was, a great many compliments, declarations of love, propositions, and received them with pleasure: that is, sensual pleasure. For example, she said apropos of anything and everything, 'Really? Is that really true?' Certainly, if she had said like Odette and others of her kind, 'Really? Are all those lies really true?' I would have taken no notice, for the absurdity of the saying would simply have been typical of the stupid banality of women's humour. But her questioning look as she said 'Is it really?' gave, on the one hand, the strange impression of a creature which cannot take in things for itself, which appeals to your judgment, as if it did not have the same faculties as you (if you said, 'We left an hour ago' or 'It's raining', she would reply 'Did we really?' or 'Is it really?'). On the other hand, unfortunately, this apparent difficulty in registering outward phenomena for herself was probably not in fact the origin of her 'Really? Is it really?' It seemed more likely that these words had developed, at the time of her precocious sexual maturity, as a response to 'You know, I've never known anyone as pretty as you,' 'You know I'm really in love with you, I'm dreadfully excited,' sayings which were received with the yielding, coquettishly modest 'Really?', 'Are you really?' which, with me, Albertine now only used in response to such observations as, 'You've been dozing for an hour' – 'Really?'

Without feeling at all in love with Albertine, without numbering among my pleasures the moments we spent together, I still worried about how she spent her time; certainly, I had fled Balbec so as to be sure that she would no longer be able to see certain women or girls with whom I was afraid that she might transgress, laughing the while – perhaps laughing at me – so afraid that I had craftily tried, by my departure, to break off in one go all her dangerous friendships. And Albertine's passivity was so intense, her ability to forget and to submit so extreme, that these friendships had in fact been broken off and the phobia which obsessed me, cured. But this phobia can take on as many forms as the uncertain evil which is its object. For so long as my jealousy was not reincarnated in new persons, I had enjoyed, after my earlier sufferings, an interval of calm. But a chronic illness needs only the smallest pretext to recur, just as the perverse impulses of the being which is the cause of the jealousy need only the slightest opportunity to reassert themselves (after an interval of chastity) with new partners. I had managed to separate Albertine from her accomplices and thereby to exorcize my hallucinations; but even though it was possible to make her forget particular people, to shorten her attachments, still her love of pleasure, like my jealousy, was chronic and perhaps was only waiting for an opportunity to resurface. Now, Paris offers as many such opportunities as Balbec. Whatever city she found herself in, she had no need to look for temptation, for the evil was not in Albertine alone, but in other women, for whom every chance of pleasure was worth taking. A look from one of them, immediately understood by the other, brings the sex-starved pair together. And a clever woman can easily appear not to have seen anything, and then five minutes later follow the other person, who did understand and is waiting for her in a side-street, and in a few words arrange a meeting. Who is to know? And to keep the relationship going, it was so easy for Albertine to tell me that she wanted to go back to some part of Paris that had appealed to her. It follows that she only had to come home late, her outing only had to have lasted an inexplicably long time (though no doubt it could easily have been explained without introducing any sexual motive) and my sufferings would begin again, attached this time to mental images that did not date from Balbec, and which I would try to erase, as I had erased their predecessors, as if the destruction of a temporary cause could bring about the cure of a congenital disease. I did not realize that by these eradications, in which I was assisted by Albertine's own changeability, her readiness to forget, even to hate the recent object of her love, I sometimes caused deep suffering to one or another of these unknown beings with whom she had, in turn, taken pleasure, and I caused them to suffer in vain, for they would be cast off, but replaced; parallel to the path marked out by so many light-hearted desertions, there would be a pitiless one for me, broken only by the shortest of respites, so that my sufferings, as I should have realized, could end only with Albertine's life or with my own. Even in our early days back in Paris, when I was dissatisfied with the information that Andrée and the chauffeur had given me about their outings with my friend, I had felt the surroundings of Paris to be as cruel as those of Balbec and I had gone off on a few days' journey with Albertine. But everywhere my uncertainty about what she was doing was the same, the possibilities for wrongdoing were just as numerous, keeping a watch on her was even more difficult, so that I had brought her back to Paris. The truth was that in leaving Balbec I had thought that I was leaving Gomorrah behind, that I was tearing Albertine away from it; alas! Gomorrah was dispersed to the four corners of the Earth. And, partly because of my jealousy, and partly out of ignorance about these pleasures (a most unusual ignorance), I had unwittingly set up this game of hide-and-seek in which Albertine would forever escape me. I would fire questions directly at her: 'Ah, that reminds me, Albertine, am I imagining it, or didn't you tell me you used to know Gilberte Swann?' – 'Yes, that's to say, she talked to me once at school, because she had the French history notes, she was really nice, she let them me borrow them and I gave them back to her the next time I saw her.' – 'Is she one of those women, you know, the kind I don't like?' – 'Oh no, not at all, quite the opposite.'

But, rather than engaging in these investigative conversations, I often expended on imagining Albertine's outing the energy I was saving by not taking part in it, and when I spoke to my friend about a project, it was with all the enthusiasm that is not dissipated by actually carrying it out. I would express so strong a desire to go and look again at such-and-such a stained-glass window in the Sainte Chapelle, such regret that we could not go there alone, that she would tenderly reply, 'But darling, if you want to go there so much, you can do it, come with us. We'll wait for you as long as you like, until you're ready to go. And then, if you'd rather go with just me, I can easily send Andrée home, she can come another time.' But by begging me to go out like this, she calmed me down to the point where I was able to stay at home.

I did not stop to think that by relying on Andrée or the chauffeur to keep me calm, by using them to keep watch on Albertine, I was becoming apathetic, allowing all the imaginative powers of the intelligence, the inspirations of the will which allow one to foresee and prevent the actions of another, to stiffen and become inert. This was all the more dangerous in that my nature has always made me more open to the world of the possible than to that of real-life contingencies. This approach helps one to understand the human soul, but one runs the risk of being deceived by individuals. My jealousy sprang from images, its purpose was suffering; it did not derive from any probability. Now, in the life of men and of nations there may come (and did come, one day, in my own life) a moment when one needs to find within oneself a prefect of police, a clear-sighted diplomat, a head of criminal investigation who, instead of letting his mind wander among all the possibilities between here and the four corners of the universe, reasons logically and says to himself, 'If Germany announces this, it's because she wants to do something else, not any odd thing at random, but precisely this or that, which she has perhaps already begun to do' – 'If such-and-such a person has escaped, he will not be heading for *a*, *b*, or *d*, but for *c*, and the place to begin our search is, *etc.*' Alas, this faculty was not very highly developed in me, and I was letting it grow sluggish, fade, disappear as I formed the habit of calm, relying on others to do my surveillance for me. As for my desire to stay at home, I had no wish to explain it to Albertine. I told her that the doctor said I had to stay in bed. That was not true. And even if it had been, his directions would not have had the power to stop me going out with my friend.

I asked her to excuse me from coming with her and Andrée. I shall give only one of my reasons, which was a reason of self-preservation. As soon as I was in public with Albertine, if she was out of my sight for a moment I was anxious, I began imagining that she had been speaking to someone or even looking at someone. If she was not in the very best of moods, I would think that I was making her miss or have to postpone some planned meeting. Reality is always a mere starting-point towards the unknown, on a path down which we can never travel very far. It is better not to know, to think as little as possible, not to feed jealousy on the smallest concrete detail.

Unfortunately, failing contact with the outside world, the inner world can also provide incidents; even when I did not go out with Albertine, chance meetings in my own solitary thoughts sometimes provided those little fragments of reality that magnetically draw to themselves scraps of the unknown which immediately begin to hurt. One may choose to live under the equivalent of a bell jar; associations of ideas and memories continue their play. But these internal shocks did not appear immediately; as soon as Albertine had left for her drive I was filled with life, if only for a few moments, by the elating powers of solitude. I shared in the pleasures of the day to come; the arbitrary desire – the capricious, purely personal wish – to enjoy them would not have been enough to put them within my reach, had not the day's special weather not only called up the images of such pleasures in the past, but affirmed their real existence in the here and now, immediately accessible to all men not obliged by an accidental (and therefore negligible) circumstance to stay at home. On certain fine days it was so cold, one was in such extensive communication with the street outside, that it was as if the walls of the house had been wrenched apart, and each time the tram passed, its note sounded out as if a silver knife were striking a house made of glass. But it was above all inside myself that I heard with delight a new sound struck from the inner violin. Its strings are tightened or slackened by simple variations in temperature, in exterior light. Within our being, that instrument which the uniformity of habit has reduced to silence, melody springs from these changes, these variations, which are the source of all music: the weather on particular days makes us move immediately from one note to another. We hear once more the forgotten tune whose mathematical necessity we could have worked out and which, for the first few moments, we sing without recognizing it. Only these inner changes (though they came from outside) brought the outer world alive again for me. Connecting doors, long walled up, were opening again in my brain. The life of certain towns, the gaiety of certain promenades took their place within me again. With my whole being trembling around the vibrating string, I would have given my dreary past life and all my life to come, both rubbed flat by the eraser of habit, to prolong this peculiar state.

I had not gone with Albertine on her long drive, but my mind would only travel the further and, having refused to experience with my senses that particular morning, I could enjoy in imagination every morning of the same kind, past and future, or, more exactly, a certain type of morning of which all mornings of the same kind were a fleeting apparition and which I had quickly recognized; for the sharp air itself turned up the right pages and set before me, so that I could follow it from my bed, the Gospel for the day. This ideal morning filled my mind with permanent reality, identical with all similar mornings, and with a gaiety unimpaired by my weak physical state; for, since our well-being results much less from our good health than from the surplus of our unexpended energy, we can attain it not only by increasing our strength, but by reducing our activity. I was overflowing with energy, held in reserve in my bed; it made me start, inwardly leap, like a machine with the brake on running in neutral.

Françoise came in to light the fire, and to get it going threw on a few twigs whose smell, forgotten all through the summer, traced a magic circle around the fireplace in which, seeing myself reading now at Combray, now at Doncières, I was as happy, staying in my room in Paris, as if I had been on the point of leaving for a walk towards Méséglise or meeting Saint-Loup and his friends on field exercises. It often happens that the pleasure that everyone takes in recalling his store of remembered scenes is more intense, for example, in those who on the one hand are prevented by the tyranny of physical illness and the hope of a cure from seeking in nature pictures which resemble their memories, but on the other can still hope that they will soon be able to do so, so that their attitude towards these scenes remains one of desire, of appetite, and they do not consider them simply as scenes, as pictures. But even if they could have remained mere pictures for me; if, recalling them, I could simply have gazed upon them, they still immediately recreated in me, in my whole being, by the power of an identical sensation, the child, the adolescent who had first seen them. It was not just the weather outside that had changed, or the smells in my room, but inside me there was a change of age, the replacement of one person by another. The smell of the twigs in the icy air was like a piece of the past, an invisible ice-floe broken off from a distant winter and floating into my room, striated here and there with a perfume or a light as if by different years into which I found myself plunged once again, swept away even before I had recognized them by the light-heartedness of hopes long since abandoned. The sun reached my bed and shone through the transparent barrier of my thin body, warmed me, made me as fiery as crystal. Then, like a starving convalescent feeding already on all the dishes he is not yet allowed to have, I would ask myself whether marrying Albertine would not ruin my life, both by making me take on the impossible task (impossible for me) of dedicating myself to another human being and by separating me from myself by her continual presence, depriving me for ever of the joys of solitude. And not only of those. Even if we ask of the day only desires, there are some – those provoked not by things, but by human beings – which by nature cannot be shared. Thus, if I got out of bed and went to open my curtains for a moment, it was not only in the way a musician opens his piano for a moment, and to see whether on the balcony and in the street the light had exactly the same quality as in my memory, it was also to see some laundry-woman carrying her linen-basket, a baker's wife in her blue apron, a dairy-woman in white linen bib and sleeves holding the hook for the milk-jugs, some proud, fair-haired young girl following her governess, an image which tiny differences in outline (perhaps so small as to be insignificant) made as different from any other as a musical phrase differs from another by a note or two. Without this vision I should have deprived my day of the objects it could offer to my desires for happiness. But if the increase in joy, brought to me by the sight of women I could not have imagined *a priori*, made the street, the town, the world seem more desirable, more worthy of being explored, it made me, for that very reason, more anxious to get well, to go out, and, without Albertine, to be free. How many times, at the moment when the unknown woman of whom I would soon be dreaming was passing in front of the house, sometimes on foot, sometimes with all the speed of her motor-car, I suffered because my body could not follow my gaze in its pursuit of her and, falling upon her as if shot from my window by a stone-bow, arrest the flight of that face in which there awaited me the promise of a happiness that, shut away as I was, I should never enjoy.

Albertine, on the other hand, held nothing new for me. Every day I found her less pretty. Only the desire which she excited in others, when I learned of it and began to suffer again, in my desire to keep her from them, could put her back on her pedestal. Suffering alone gave life to my tedious attachment to her. When she disappeared, taking with her the need to alleviate my pain, which demanded all my attention like some dreadful hobby, I realized how little she meant to me – as little, no doubt, as I meant to her. It made me unhappy that things should go on this way, and sometimes I longed to hear of some really unforgivable thing that she had done, something that, until I was cured, would come between us, so that we could then make it up, remake, in a different and more flexible form, the tie that held us together. In the meantime, I relied on a thousand circumstances, a thousand pleasures, to give her, while she stayed with me, the illusion of that happiness which I felt incapable of giving her myself. I wanted to go to Venice as soon as I was better, but how could I do that, married to Albertine, when I was so jealous of her that, even in Paris, when I did decide to move, it was to go out with her? Even when I stayed at home all afternoon, my thoughts followed her wherever she went, tracing out a distant, blue horizon, creating, around the centre where I lay, a moving zone of uncertainty and vagueness. 'Albertine could spare me so much of the anguish of separation,' I said to myself, 'if only, on one of these outings, seeing that I no longer speak to her of marriage, she would decide not to come back, and go off to her aunt's without my having to say goodbye!' My heart, now that its wound was forming scar tissue, was beginning to detach itself from that of my friend. I could imagine her removed, at a distance from me, without suffering. Failing myself, some other man would no doubt be her husband, and, once free, she would perhaps have some of those adventures that filled me with horror. But it was such a fine day, I was so sure that she would be back in the evening, that even if this idea of possible transgressions came into my mind, I could by an act of free-will shut it off in one part of my brain, where it impinged on me no more than the vices of an imaginary person would on my real life. Turning my thought on its newly oiled hinges, using a new energy which I could feel, in my head, as both a physical and a mental force, like a muscular movement and a spiritual departure, I had left behind the customary state of preoccupation in which I had hitherto been confined and was beginning to move in the free air, so that the idea of sacrificing everything to stop Albertine marrying someone else and to frustrate her taste for women seemed as unreasonable in my eyes as it would have to someone who had never known her. Besides, jealousy is one of those intermittent diseases whose causes are arbitrary, inescapable, always the same in a given patient but sometimes entirely different in another. Some asthmatics can moderate their attacks only by opening the windows, breathing a strong breeze or the pure air of the mountains; others take refuge in the centre of town, in a smoky room. There is hardly a victim of jealousy whose illness does not admit of some palliations. One accepts being deceived provided he is told of it, another provided it is hidden from him, and in this one is hardly more absurd than the other, for if the second is more truly deceived, since the truth is hidden from him, the first needs the truth to feed his sufferings, to extend and renew them. What is more, these two inverse obsessions of jealousy often go beyond words, whether they beg for confidences or refuse them. We see some victims who are jealous only of men with whom their mistress has relations far away from them, but who allow her to give herself to another man if it is with their permission, near them, and if not actually in front of their eyes, at any rate under their roof. This behaviour is quite often found in old men in love with a young woman. They know how difficult it is to please her, sometimes feel themselves incapable of satisfying her, and, rather than be deceived, prefer to allow someone to come into their house, to a neighbouring room, someone who they think will not be able to give her bad advice, even if he is able to give immediate pleasure. Others are quite the opposite: not allowing their mistress to go out alone for a moment in a city they know, keeping her in veritable slavery, they let her go away for a month to a country they do not know, where they cannot imagine what she is doing. In relation to Albertine I longed to achieve peace by either of these means. I would not have been jealous if she had taken pleasures close to me, encouraged and entirely overseen by me, sparing me in that way my fears of her lying; perhaps the same would have been true if she had gone somewhere far away and so unfamiliar to me that I could not imagine how she was living, nor have any hope of finding out, nor be tempted to try. In either case, doubt would have been suppressed, whether by complete knowledge or complete ignorance.

The waning of the day plunged me back, through memory, into a cool atmosphere of former times; I breathed it in with the same delight as Orpheus did the rarefied air, unknown to this earth, of the Elysian Fields. But already the day was ending and I was engulfed in my evening sadness. Looking mechanically at the clock to see how many hours had still to pass before Albertine came home, I saw that I still had time to dress and go downstairs to ask my landlady, Mme de Guermantes,[4] for some ideas about certain pretty items of dress that I wanted to give to my friend. Sometimes I used to meet Her Grace in the courtyard, going out to do her shopping on foot, even in bad weather, wearing a small, neat hat and a fur coat. I knew very well that for many intelligent people she was no different from any other lady, the name of Duchesse de Guermantes having no meaning now that there are no more dukedoms or principalities, but I had adopted another point of view as part of my way of deriving enjoyment from people and places. All the manors of the lands of which she was duchess, princess or viscountess seemed to accompany this fur-coated lady striding out in the rain; she bore them with her, as the characters carved on the lintel of a church door carry in their hand the cathedral they built or the city they defended. But those châteaux, those forests could be seen only by my inward eye in the gloved hand of the fur-clad lady, cousin to the King. My bodily eye could see only, on days when the weather was threatening, an umbrella,[5] with which the Duchesse did not disdain to equip herself. 'You never know, it makes sense, suppose I'm very far from home and a cab is much too *dear*.' The words 'too dear', 'beyond my means' recurred constantly in the Duchesse's conversation, along with 'I'm too poor'; it was impossible to tell whether she spoke this way because she found it amusing to call herself poor when she was so rich, or whether it seemed to her elegant, as a great aristocrat, to speak like a country-woman and show that she did not attach any importance to wealth, unlike people who have nothing but riches and who despise the poor. Maybe it was, rather, a habit which she had contracted at a time in her life when she was already rich, but not rich enough to cover the upkeep of so many properties, and felt a certain lack of money which she did not wish to seem to be concealing. The things people joke about most are usually those which irritate them, but which they do not want to seem to be irritated by; there is perhaps, too, an unspoken hope of further advantage: that the person we are speaking to, hearing us admit something jokingly, will believe that it is not true.

But most often, at that time, I knew I would find the Duchesse at home, and I was glad of that, for it made it easier to question her at length about the subjects which interested Albertine. And I went downstairs, hardly stopping to think how extraordinary it was that I should be going to see the mysterious Mme de Guermantes of my childhood, simply to use her as a source of practical information, as one uses the telephone, that supernatural instrument before whose wonders we were once all in awe, and which we now use unthinkingly, to call our tailor or order an iced dessert.

The 'little touches' of dress gave Albertine enormous pleasure, and I could not resist making her a small present of this kind every day. And every time she spoke to me about a scarf, a stole, a parasol which, looking out of the window or passing in the courtyard, with her sharp eyes that picked out so quickly anything relating to elegance, she had seen around the neck, on the shoulders or in the hand of Mme de Guermantes, I knew that her naturally demanding taste (which had been further refined by those lessons in elegance which Elstir's conversations had been to her) would not be content with some approximation, even a pretty thing which, to the vulgar eye, would be a perfect substitute but in no way resembles the original, and I would go in secret to have the Duchesse explain to me how, where, on what pattern, the thing Albertine admired had been made, how I should go about procuring exactly the same object, what was the maker's secret, the charm (what Albertine called 'the knack') of his manner, the precise name – for the beauty of the material was important too – and the quality of the fabrics which I should ask to be used.

I had told Albertine, when we arrived home from Balbec, that the

Duchesse de Guermantes lived opposite us, in the same building; when she heard the grand title and the great name, her face had taken on that indifferent look – no, more than indifferent, hostile, contemptuous – which is the sign of frustrated desire in proud and passionate natures. Albertine's nature was splendid, but its hidden qualities had been able to develop only under the restrictions constituted by our tastes, or our mourning for the tastes which we have had to renounce – in Albertine's case, the taste for social superiority: the result is what people call hatreds. Albertine's hatred for upper-class people was, however, a very small element in her character and I liked its hint of the revolutionary spirit – that is to say, unrequited love for the nobility – which forms the opposite face of the French character from the aristocratic style of Mme de Guermantes. Being unable to achieve it herself, Albertine would perhaps have thought nothing of this aristocratic style, but when she remembered that Elstir had spoken of the Duchesse as the best-dressed woman in Paris, my friend's republican disdain for a Duchess was replaced by an intense interest in a woman of fashion. She often asked me about Mme de Guermantes and liked me to go and visit the Duchesse to collect fashion hints for her. No doubt I could have asked Mme Swann for the same advice, and I even wrote to her once for this purpose. But Mme de Guermantes seemed to me to carry the art of dress to even greater heights. If I went down to see her for a moment (having first made sure that she had not gone out, and arranged to be told as soon as Albertine came home) and found her enclouded in the mists of a dress of grey crêpe de Chine, I accepted this appearance, which I felt to be due to complex causes and unchangeable, I let myself be swept into the atmosphere it created, like that of certain late afternoons muffled in a pearl-grey floating mist. If, on the other hand, the chosen gown were Chinese with a pattern of red and yellow flames, I saw it as a brilliant sunset; these costumes were not a trivial decoration which could have been replaced by any other, but an inescapable reality, poetic in the same way as the weather, or the light peculiar to a certain time of day.

Of all the gowns or tea-gowns that Mme de Guermantes wore, the ones which seemed most expressive of a particular intention, most endowed with a special meaning, were those gowns which Fortuny based on ancient Venetian designs. Is it their historic appearance, is it rather the fact that each one is unique, which gives them such an individual character that the pose of the woman who is wearing one to wait for you, to talk with you, takes on an exceptional importance, as if this costume had been chosen after long deliberation, and makes the conversation stand out from everyday life like a scene from a novel? In Balzac's novels we see the heroines choose particular costumes to wear on the days when they are to receive a particular visitor. The costumes of today have no such clearly defined character, with the exception of Fortuny dresses. There can be no vagueness in the novelist's description since this dress really exists, the smallest elements of its design as unalterable as those of a work of art. Before putting on this or that dress, the woman has had to make a choice, not between two that are more or less similar, but between two wholly individual ones, each of which could have its own name.

But the dress did not keep me from noticing the woman. Mme de Guermantes herself seemed to me more likeable then than at the time when I was still in love with her. I expected less of her now that I was not going to see her for her own sake, and as I listened to her talk I felt almost the same peaceful informality that one enjoys when home alone, with one's feet on the fender. It was like reading a book written in the language of another time. I had enough detachment to enjoy, in what she said, that pure, particularly French grace that one no longer finds either in the speech or the writing of the present day. I listened to her conversation as if to a deliciously French popular song, and I understood how I could once have heard her laugh at Maeterlinck (whom she now admired with all the weakness of a woman's judgment, swayed by late-flowering literary fashion), just as I understood how Mérimée could have laughed at Baudelaire, Stendhal at Balzac, Paul-Louis Courier at Victor Hugo, Meilhac at Mallarmé. I knew that the laugher's mind was narrow compared to the mind he laughed at, but his vocabulary was purer. Mme de Guermantes's vocabulary, almost as much as Saint-Loup's mother's, was so to an enchanting degree. The old language and the true pronunciation of words are not to be found in the pedantic pastiches of today's writers who say *in truth* (for *in fact*), *peculiar* (for *particular*), *dumbfounded* (for *astonished*), and so forth, but in the conversation of a Mme de Guermantes or a Françoise. I had learned from the second of these, by the age of five, that you do not say 'le Tarn' but 'le Tar', not 'le Béarn' but 'le Béar'. So that when at twenty I went into society, I did not have to learn not to say, as Mme Bontemps did: Madame de Béarn.

I would be lying if I said that this 'country', this almost peasant side of her was something the Duchesse was unconscious of, or that there was not a shade of affectation in the way she displayed it. But in her, it was not so much the fake simplicity of a great lady playing the country-woman, or the pride of a duchess cocking a snook at rich ladies and their contempt for the peasantry, but rather a sign of the almost artistic taste of a woman who understands the charm of what she possesses and does not mean to spoil it with a coat of modern distemper. In just the same way, everyone remembers a Norman restaurant-keeper, the owner of the *William the Conqueror* at Dives, who had been at pains – a very rare thing – not to give his inn the modern luxury of a hotel and who (though a millionaire himself) retained the speech and the smock of a Norman peasant and let the customers come into the kitchen, as in the country, to see him making the dinner himself – a dinner which was none the less far better and even more expensive than in the grandest four-star hotels.

All the local sap in the veins of old aristocratic families is not enough; they also have to give birth to a being intelligent enough not to despise it, not to hide it under a fashionable varnish. Mme de Guermantes, unfortunately a witty Parisian who when I first knew her had nothing left about her of her native region but the accent, had at least, when she wanted to describe her girlhood, found a language half-way between the involuntarily provincial and what might have seemed too consciously literary: one of those compromises which make George Sand's *La Petite Fadette* so delightful, or some of the legends repeated by Chateaubriand in the *Mémoires d'outre-tombe*. I especially loved to hear her tell some story in which peasants appeared alongside her. The ancient names, the old customs gave a pleasing quaintness to these meetings between the manor and the village. Having remained in contact with the lands where they once ruled, a certain part of the aristocracy remains regional, so that their simplest remark unrolls before our eyes a whole historical and geographical map of the history of France.

If there was no affectation in Mme de Guermantes's speech, no wish to create a personal language, then her pronunciation was a real oral museum of French history. 'My great-uncle Fitt-jam' did not come as a surprise, for everyone knows that the Fitz-James always insist that they are French nobles and do not wish their name to be pronounced in the English fashion. One is, however, forced to admire the touching docility of those people who had hitherto felt they must make the effort to pronounce certain names according to the rule-book, and who, once they had heard the Duchesse de Guermantes say them differently, applied themselves to learning the new, unsuspected pronunciation. Thus the Duchesse, one of whose great-grandfathers had been in the circle of the Comte de Chambord, liked to tease her husband, who had become an Orléanist, by saying, 'We, the old guard of Frochedorf'. The visitor, who up to that moment had always said 'Frohsdorf', would turn his coat then and there and take every opportunity of saying 'Frochedorf'.

Once when I asked Mme de Guermantes who a delightful young man was whom she had introduced to me as her nephew and whose name I had not caught, I had no more success when, in her throaty voice, the Duchesse said very loudly but indistinctly: 'It's . . . le Éon, Robert's brother. He says he has the head-shape of the ancient Gauls.' Then I realized that she had said, 'It's little Léon' (the Prince de Léon, in fact Robert de Saint-Loup's brother-in-law). 'I don't know if he has an ancient Gaul's skull,' she went on, 'but his way of dressing, which in fact is very smart, certainly doesn't come from that quarter. One day when I was staying at Josselin with the Rohans, and we went to a religious fête, country people had come to it from all over Brittany and a great villager from Léon was looking in astonishment at Robert's brother-in-law's fawn breeches. "Why are you staring at me?" said Léon. "I bet you don't know who I am." And when the man said no, "Well, I am your prince." "Well I never!" said the man, doffing his cap and apologizing, "and I thought you was an Englishman."' And if I picked up on the name of Rohan and encouraged Mme de Guermantes to say more about that family (with which her own had repeatedly intermarried), her conversation took on some of the melancholy charm of Breton religious gatherings and, as that real poet Pampille[6] would say, 'the bitter taste of buckwheat pancakes cooked over a furze fire'.

Speaking of the Marquis du Lau (whose sad end is well known, when he was deaf and used to have himself taken to the house of Mme H***, who was blind), she told of the happier years when after hunting, at Guermantes, he would put on his slippers to have tea with the King of England, whom he did not regard as his superior and in whose company he clearly did not stand on ceremony. She described all this in such a lively fashion that she added to his portrait the musketeer's plume of the somewhat boastful noblemen of the Périgord.

Anyway, even when she was giving the simplest descriptions of people, her careful way of assigning them to their home provinces gave to Mme de Guermantes, faithful in this to her origins, a charm that no native Parisian could ever have had, and the very names of Anjou, Poitou or Périgord recreated whole landscapes in her conversation.

To return to Mme de Guermantes's pronunciations and vocabulary, it is in things like these that the aristocracy shows itself truly conservative, in the full sense of that word: at the same time slightly childish and slightly dangerous, resistant to evolution but amusing for the artist. I wanted to know how the word Jean used to be written. I found out when I received a letter from Mme de Villeparisis's nephew, who signs his name – as he received it in baptism, as it appears in the Almanac de Gotha – Jehan de Villeparisis, with the same beautiful, useless, heraldic *h* that one loves to see, illuminated in vermilion or ultramarine, in a book of hours or a stained-glass window.

Unfortunately I could not prolong these visits indefinitely since I wished, if possible, not to arrive home after my friend. Now, it was always a slow and painful business extracting information from Mme de Guermantes about her clothes so as to have them copied (in so far as a young girl could wear them) for Albertine.

'For example, Ma'am, the day you were going to dinner with Mme de Saint-Euverte before going on to the Princesse de Guermantes's, you were wearing an all-red dress with red shoes, you were beyond belief, you looked like some kind of great flower of blood, a burning ruby, now what was that called? Could a young girl wear something like that?'

The Duchesse's tired face took on the radiant expression that the Princesse des Laumes would wear when Swann paid her compliments in the old days; she laughed gaily and directed a mocking look, questioning and delighted, towards M. de Bréauté, who was always there at that time of day, and behind whose monocle a lukewarm smile of indulgence stood ready for the intellectual's overblown compliment, which he imagined hid a young man's physical desire. The Duchesse seemed to be saying, 'What's the matter with him? He's mad.' Then, turning to me with a gently teasing look, 'I didn't know that I looked like a burning ruby or a flower of blood, but I do remember wearing a red dress; it was red satin, the way they were making them just then. I suppose a young girl *could* wear it, but you said that your friend never goes out in the evening. That was definitely an evening dress, you couldn't wear it to pay calls.'

What is remarkable is that in recalling that evening, not after all so long past, Mme de Guermantes should remember only the dress she was wearing and forget one thing which, as we shall see, should have been close to her heart. It is as if the minds of people of action, and smart people are people of action (on a minuscule, microscopic scale, but still action), are so consumed by attention to what will be happening in an hour's time that they commit very little to memory. Very often, for example, it was not a wish to deceive or to seem not to have been mistaken that made M. de Norpois, when the conversation turned to prognostications he had made about a German alliance that never, in fact, came off, say, 'You must be mistaken, I can't remember saying that, and it doesn't sound like me, for in that kind of conversation I usually say the minimum, and I would never have predicted success for one of those unplanned initiatives that begin as a show of strength and usually have to end with a show of force. There is no doubt that, in the very distant future, we could see a Franco-German rapprochement which would greatly benefit both countries, and would not, I believe, be a bad bargain for France, but I have never spoken of it, because the time is not yet ripe and, if you ask my opinion, I believe that if we tried to push our old enemies into a shotgun wedding we should be heading for a great fall and have to pick up the pieces.' When he said these things, M. de Norpois was not lying, he had simply forgotten. One quickly forgets thoughts which had no depth, ideas dictated by imitation or the passions of the moment. They change and our memories change with them. Even more than diplomats, politicians forget the positions they took at a given point in time, and some of their volte-faces owe less to ambition than to a failure of memory. As for grand people, they remember very little at all.

Mme de Guermantes maintained to me that at the party when she wore the red dress, she couldn't remember seeing Mme de Chausse-pierre, that I must be wrong to think she was there. Now heaven knows the Chaussepierres had figured largely enough since in the thoughts of the Duc, and even of the Duchesse! Here is why. M. de Guermantes was the senior vice-president of the Jockey Club when the president died. Some members of the club who have no connections in society and find their only pleasure in blackballing people who do not ask them to their parties, got up a campaign against the Duc de Guermantes, who, in the certainty of being elected, and caring little for this presidency, which was of small importance to a man in his social position, did nothing to secure it. It was argued that the Duchesse had been a Dreyfus supporter (the Dreyfus Affair was long over, but twenty years later people would still be talking about it, and at this time only two years had passed), that she received the Rothschilds, that too much favour had been shown recently to powerful cosmopolitan figures like the Duc de Guermantes, who was half a German. The campaign quickly took root: clubmen always envy the famous and hate great fortunes. Chaussepierre was not poor, but no one could be offended by his wealth as he never spent a penny of it; he lived with his wife in a modest flat, she appeared dressed in black woollen. A passionate music-lover, she did give little parties where many more singers were seen than at the Guermantes'. But nobody talked about them, no food was served, the husband did not even come, and all this happened in the obscurity of the rue de la Chaise. At the Opéra, no one noticed Mme de Chaussepierre; she was always with people whose names recalled the most reactionary circles of former times, the intimates of Charles X, but obscure people, not smart at all. On the day of the election, to everyone's surprise, Chaussepierre, the junior vice-president, was elected president of the Jockey Club and the Duc de Guermantes was left standing, that is, had to continue as senior vice-president. Certainly, being president of the Jockey Club is a trifle to a family of princely rank like the Guermantes. But not being elected when your turn comes, seeing the post going to a Chaussepierre, when Oriane had not only failed to acknowledge his wife's bow two years before, but had even showed her displeasure at being greeted by this unknown, dowdy figure, all this was hard for the Duc to bear. He claimed to be above noticing his failure, maintaining at the same time that it was his long-standing friendship with Swann that had caused it. In fact, he was furious. It was characteristic that the Duc had never been heard to use the banal expression 'thoroughgoing', but after the Jockey Club election, whenever the Dreyfus case was mentioned, 'thoroughgoing' would pop up: 'The Dreyfus case, the Dreyfus case, it's all very well to call it that, but it's a misnomer; it wasn't a matter of religion but a thoroughgoing political quarrel.' Five years could pass without 'thoroughgoing' being heard again, provided that during that time no one mentioned the Dreyfus case, but if at the end of the five years the name of Dreyfus was heard again, 'thoroughgoing' would follow immediately upon it. In any case, the Duc could not bear anyone to mention the case, 'which caused so much unhappiness', he would say, though in reality he was conscious of only one instance of unhappiness, his own failure to win the presidency of the Jockey Club.

So, on the afternoon I am speaking of, when I reminded Mme de Guermantes of the red dress she was wearing at her cousin's party, M. de Bréauté struck a wrong note when he broke into the conversation and, by an obscure association of ideas he did nothing to elucidate, manoeuvring his tongue to the point of his pursed lips, began by saying, 'Speaking of the Dreyfus case . . .' (why the Dreyfus case? we were only talking about a red dress, and certainly poor Bréauté, who only ever wanted to please, did not mean anything unkind). But the mere name of Dreyfus wrinkled the Jove-like brow of the Duc de Guermantes. 'Someone told me a very clever saying, really sharp, of our friend Cartier's (I should make it clear that this Cartier, Mme de Villefranche's brother, had nothing whatever to do with the jeweller of the same name!), and of course I wasn't surprised, for he always has wit and to spare. – Well, Oriane interrupted, I can certainly spare his wit. I can't tell you how much your friend Cartier has always *paralysed* me, and I've never been able to understand how Charles de la Trémoïlle and his wife can be so in thrall to such a crashing bore: I find him there every time I go to their house. – My d-dear d-Duchesse, replied Bréauté, who had a slight stammer, you are very hard on Cartier. Perhaps he has rather moved in on the La Trémoïlles, but he's a sort of, what shall I say, b-bosom friend to Charles, and that is a *rara avis* these days. Anyhow, here is the saying I was told about. It seems Cartier said that if M. Zola had gone out of his way to be charged and convicted, it was so as to experience a completely new sensation: going to p-prison. – And that's why he fled the country before he could be arrested, said Oriane. It doesn't make sense. And anyway, even if it were true, I think the remark was simply idiotic. If that's what you call wit . . . – Oh, Oriane d-dear, replied Bréauté, beginning to retreat in the face of opposition, *I* didn't say it, I'm just repeating what was said to me, take it for what it's worth. Anyway, it earned M. Cartier a severe telling-off from La Trémoïlle – excellent chap – who won't have anybody talking in his house – and he's quite right – about – what shall I say – the politics of the day, and who was all the more angry because Mme Alphonse Rothschild was there. Cartier had to take a real dressing-down from La Trémoïlle. – Of course, said the Duc very crossly, we all know that the Alphonse Rothschilds, though they are tactful enough never to speak of the wretched affair, are Dreyfusards at heart, like all Jews. In fact, that's an argument *ad hominem* (the Duc used the expression *ad hominem* in rather a slapdash way) that could be used more often to show how dishonest the Jews are. If a Frenchman commits theft or murder, I don't feel I have to say he's innocent, just because he's a Frenchman like me. But the Jews will never admit that one of them could be a traitor, even though they know it's true, and they don't care in the least about the terrible repercussions (the Duc was naturally thinking about the unspeakable election of Chaussepierre) that can result from

33

their friend's crime . . . Really, Oriane, you must admit it's disgraceful, the way all the Jews defend a traitor. You won't tell me that it's not because they're Jews themselves. – Yes I will, said Oriane (by now somewhat annoyed and feeling a certain desire to resist the Jove-like thunderings, and also to show 'intelligent' people's detachment from the Dreyfus case). But perhaps it's just because, being Jewish and knowing themselves, they know that a man can be a Jew without having to be treacherous and anti-French, as M. Drumont apparently would have us believe. Certainly if Dreyfus had been a Christian the Jews wouldn't have taken such an interest in his case, but they did, because they realize that if he hadn't been a Jew, people wouldn't have been so ready to believe him a traitor *a priori*, as my nephew Robert would say. – Women don't understand anything about politics, cried the Duc, glaring at the Duchesse. That appalling crime wasn't only a Jewish affair, but a *thoroughgoing* national scandal which may have the most dreadful consequences for France. And France should expel all the Jews, even though I recognize that the only measures so far have been taken (in the most disgraceful fashion, which should be reversed at once) not against them but against their most distinguished opponents, men of the first rank, excluded from public life to our country's great cost.'

I saw danger ahead and hurriedly began to talk frocks again.

'Do you remember, Ma'am, I said, the first time you were kind to me? – The first time I was kind to him,' she repeated with a laughing look towards M. de Bréauté, the end of whose nose got even thinner, while his smile became more tenderly polite towards Mme de Guermantes and his voice, like a knife being sharpened, let out a few vague, rusty sounds. 'You were wearing a yellow dress with big black flowers. – But dear boy, it's the same thing, those are evening dresses. – And your hat with the cornflowers that I liked so much! But anyway, that's all in the past. What I'd really like to have made for the girl I mentioned is a fur coat like the one you were wearing yesterday morning. Could I see it? Would that be out of the question? – No, Hannibal has to go in a moment. You can come into my dressing-room and my maid will show it to you. The only thing is, I can lend you anything you like, but if you have Callot's, or Doucet's, or Paquin's designs made up by a little dressmaker, they won't ever look the same. – But I've no intention of going to a little dressmaker, I know that wouldn't be the same, but I'd love to be able to understand why it wouldn't. – But you know I can't explain anything, I'm a *h*idiot, I talk like a peasant woman. It's a question of skill, of handling; for the furs I can at least introduce you to my furrier, which will mean he doesn't rob you. But you know it will cost you another eight or nine thousand francs. – And that loose gown you were wearing the other evening, the one that smells so strange, it's dark, velvety, with spots and gold streaks like a butterfly's wing? – Oh, that's a Fortuny dress. Your young friend can certainly wear that kind of thing at home. I have lots of them, I'll show you some, I can even give you some if you like. But I'd really like you to see the one my cousin Talleyrand has. I must write and ask her to lend it to me. – But you had such pretty shoes too, are they Fortuny as well? – No, I know the ones you mean, they're gold kid that we found in London, when I was shopping with Consuelo Manchester. They're extraordinary. I could never understand how they gilded the leather, it looks like a golden skin. Just that, with a little diamond in the middle. The Duchess of Manchester is dead, sadly, but if you like I'll write to Lady Warwick or the Duchess of Marlborough to see if I can find some more like it. In fact, I think I might have some of the skin left. Perhaps we could have some made up here. I'll have a look this evening and let you know.'

Since I tried as far as possible to have left the Duchesse before Albertine got home, I was often leaving Mme de Guermantes's at an hour that meant I would meet M. de Charlus and Morel, crossing the courtyard on their way to have tea with . . . Jupien, high favour for the Baron! I did not meet them every day, but they went there every day. We should note that the regularity of a habit is usually a function of its absurdity. Striking actions are usually carried out on irregular impulse. But insensate lives, where the madman deprives himself of all pleasures, and seeks out the most terrible sufferings, are usually the lives that change the least. At ten-year intervals, if one cared enough to check, one would find the sufferer still sleeping away the hours when he could be living, going out at hours when the best that could happen to him is to be murdered in the streets, drinking iced drinks when he is hot, always nursing a cold. A tiny burst of energy, on a single day, could change everything for him. But these lives are usually led by beings devoid of energy. Perversity is another aspect of these monotonous existences, which the smallest exercise of will would make less dreadful. Both aspects came into play when M. de Charlus paid his daily tea-time visit to Jupien. Only one cloud had ever shadowed the daily ritual. One day the waistcoat-maker's niece had said to Morel: 'That's right, come tomorrow, I'll treat you to tea.' The Baron had, rightly, thought the expression a vulgar one, particularly in the mouth of someone he was planning to make his almost-daughter-in-law. But, with his love of wounding and carried away by his own anger, instead of simply asking Morel to teach her the right thing to say, he had made a violent scene that lasted all the way home. In the most haughty, insolent tone he began: 'Your "touch", which I see has nothing to do with "tact", must have prevented the normal development of your sense of smell, since you allowed that fetid expression "treat you to tea" (twopenny tea no doubt) to lift up its cesspit odour to my royal nostrils. When you finish a violin solo at my house, have you ever been rewarded with a fart, instead of delirious applause or the silence which is even more eloquent as it comes from the fear of being unable to hold back – not what your fiancée gives us in such quantity, but tears, tears that you have brought to the edge of our lips?'

When a junior civil servant has received such a dressing-down from his superior, he is inevitably sacked the next day. But nothing would have been more painful to M. de Charlus than to have to send Morel away and, even fearing that he might have gone too far, he began to praise the young girl: detailed praises, showing fine taste, with every now and then unintended notes of impertinence. 'She is delightful. As you are a musician, I suppose you were charmed by her voice; it's beautiful in the high notes, where she seems to be waiting for your accompanying B sharp. I like her lower register less; I'm sure that must have something to do with the slimness of her neck and the strange way it seems to stop and start three times, always stretching a little higher; rather than commonplace details, it's her shape that is so pleasing. And as she's a dressmaker and clever with her scissors, she must make me a pretty silhouette of herself out of paper.'

Charlie had not been listening to these praises, all the less since the beauties they celebrated in his fiancée had always passed him by. But he answered M. de Charlus, 'That's all right, dear boy, I'll tell her what's what, I'll make sure she doesn't talk like that again.' If Morel called M. de Charlus 'dear boy', it was not that the handsome violinist did not know he was barely a third of the Baron's age. He did not say it, either, with Jupien's insinuating manner, but in the simple way that shows how, in certain relationships, a forgetting of the age difference has tacitly preceded the development of affection. Feigned affection in Morel's case, sincere affection in others. For example, about this time, M. de Charlus received a letter written in these terms: 'Dear Palamède, when am I going to see you? I'm missing you ever so much and thinking about you all the time (etc.) Your loving PIERRE.' M. de Charlus racked his brains to discover which of his relatives had dared to write to him in so familiar a style; it must be someone he knew very well, and yet he did not recognize the writing. For several days all the princes mentioned, however briefly, in the Almanac de Gotha trooped through M. de Charlus's brain. At last, suddenly, an address written on the back of the letter gave him the answer: it was the work of the pageboy at a gaming club where M. de Charlus occasionally called. The pageboy had not thought he was being rude in writing in this style to M. de Charlus, whom in fact he greatly admired. No, he thought it would not be nice not to call someone '*tu*' who had kissed you several times, and thereby – as he naïvely imagined – given you a sign of his affection. M. de Charlus was in fact delighted by his familiarity. He even walked back from an afternoon party with M. de Vaugoubert so as to show him the letter. And yet heaven knows M. de Charlus did not like to be seen with M. de Vaugoubert. For the diplomat, with his monocle stuck in his eye, stared in all directions at the lads passing by. What was more, when he was with M. de Charlus, he grew more daring, and began to use a language which the Baron hated. He put all men's names in the feminine and, as he was very stupid, thought this was the height of wit and was constantly bursting out laughing. As he was also hugely attached to his diplomatic post, his deplorable giggliness in the street was constantly interrupted by waves of terror when he saw his social equals, or worse, civil servants approaching. 'There goes little Miss Telegram,' he would say, nudging the scowling Baron, 'I used to know her, but she's settled down now, horrid thing! Ooh, isn't that Galeries Lafayette messenger delicious! Oh Lord, there's the chief secretary for Commercial Affairs. I hope he didn't see me nudging you! He's the sort who might talk to the minister about it and he might suspend me from duties, especially as he's one of the girls himself, so they say.' M. de Charlus was trembling with rage. Finally, to bring the infuriating walk to an end, he decided to take out his letter and give it to the ambassador to read, requesting his discretion, however; he pretended that Charlie was jealous in order to suggest that he loved him. 'Now, he added, with an inimitable air of benevolence, we should always try to cause as little unhappiness as we can.'

Before returning to Jupien's shop, the author wishes to make clear how unhappy he would be if the reader were offended by these strange scenes. On the one hand (and this is the less important aspect) it may be thought that the aristocracy, in this book, is disproportionately taxed with degeneracy as compared to the other social classes. If that were so, it would not be surprising. As time passes, old families develop peculiarities – a red, hooked nose, a deformed chin – which are admired as specific signs of 'blood'. But among these persisting and ever intensifying traits, there are some which are not visible: tendencies and tastes.

It would be a more serious objection, if true, to say that all these feelings are remote from us, and that poetry should be drawn from what is true and near at hand. Art derived from the most familiar reality does exist, and its range is perhaps the greatest. But it is none the less true that great interest, sometimes even beauty, can spring from actions which derive from a mode of thinking and feeling so remote from anything we feel, anything we believe, that we cannot even begin to understand them, that they unfold before us like an unexplained spectacle. What is more poetic than Xerxes, son of Darius, having the sea whipped with rods, the sea that had swallowed up his fleet?[7]

Morel, using the power that his good looks gave him over the young girl, must certainly have passed on the Baron's comment, disguised as his own, for the expression 'treating to tea' disappeared as completely from the waistcoat-maker's shop as a former close friend disappears from a salon where he used to be welcomed every day, when the hosts have quarrelled with him for some reason or other, or wish to hide their friendship with him and see him only in other people's houses. M. de Charlus was pleased at the disappearance of 'treating'; he saw in it the sign of his power over Morel and the removal of the only little flaw in the perfection of the young person. Then, like all men of his kind, while being genuinely a friend to Morel and his near-fiancée, and looking forward eagerly to their marriage, he took a certain pleasure in his power to stir up at will more or less trivial quarrels between them, above which he could float with the Olympian detachment that his brother would have shown in the same circumstances. Morel had said to M. de Charlus that he loved Jupien's niece and wanted to marry her, and the Baron was delighted to accompany his young friend on visits where he played the part of the future father-in-law, indulgent and discreet.

My own opinion is that 'treat you to tea' was a saying of Morel's own, and that, blinded by love, the young dressmaker had adopted an expression of her adored one's which, in its ugliness, stood out painfully against her pretty, young girl's speech. Thanks to this speech, the charming manners that matched it, and the protection of M. de Charlus, many of her customers treated her as a friend, asked her to dinner, accepted her into their social circle, though she only accepted with the Baron's permission and on the evenings when it suited him. 'A young dressmaker go into society?' you will say, 'how improbable.' If you stop to think, it was no more unlikely than that Albertine should formerly have come to see me at midnight and should now be living with me. And that would perhaps have been improbable in anyone else, but not at all in Albertine, an orphan, living such a free life that in Balbec, at first, I had taken her for the mistress of a cycle-racer, and having as her nearest relative Mme Bontemps, who in the old days, at Mme Swann's, saved all her admiration for her niece's worst behaviour, and now turned a blind eye to everything in the hope that she would take herself off and marry money, some of which might find its way to her aunt (in the highest society mothers who are very well born and very poor, once they have found a rich wife for their son, are happy to live at the young couple's expense, accepting furs, a motor-car, money from a daughter-in-law they do not like but whom they launch in society).

Perhaps the day will come when dressmakers – and I wouldn't find that at all shocking – will go into society. Jupien's niece, being an exception, cannot yet allow us to foresee that day, one swallow does not make a summer. In any case, if the modest social success of Jupien's niece scandalized anyone, it was not Morel, for on some points his stupidity was such that not only did he find the girl, who was a hundred times more intelligent than he was, 'not very bright' – perhaps only because she loved him – but he saw adventuresses, dressmakers in disguise pretending to be ladies, in persons of very good social position who welcomed her to their houses and of whom she never boasted. Naturally these were not Guermantes, nor even people who knew them, but rich, elegant bourgeoises, emancipated enough to think there was no disgrace in having a dressmaker as a guest and conventional enough to derive some pleasure from taking under their wing a young girl whom His Highness the Baron de Charlus visited – on terms of complete propriety – every day.

Nothing gave the Baron more pleasure than the idea of this wedding, which would ensure – so he thought – that Morel could not be taken away from him. Apparently Jupien's niece had once, when she was still hardly more than a child, made a 'slip'. And M. de Charlus, in the course of singing her praises to Morel, would not have been averse to mentioning this fact to his friend, who would have been furious, thus creating bad blood between them. For M. de Charlus, though thoroughly malevolent, was like a large number of good people who praise this man or that woman to show how good they are themselves, but would sooner die than say the kind words, so rarely spoken, that would end a quarrel. Nevertheless, the Baron did not allow himself any insinuation, for two reasons. 'If I tell him', he said to himself, 'that his fiancée is not spotless, his self-conceit will be wounded and he will be angry with me. And then how do I know that he is not in love with her? If I don't say anything, this little passion will soon be over, and I shall be able to control their relationship to suit myself; he will only love her as much as I want him to. Whereas, if I tell him about about the girl's fall from grace, how do I know that Charlie isn't still enough in love to be jealous? I would be turning an insignificant little affair, that I can direct as I please, into a grand passion, which is something difficult to control.' For these two reasons, M. de Charlus kept a silence which bore only a superficial resemblance to discretion, but which was still meritorious, given that not speaking is almost impossible for people of his sort.

Besides, the girl was enchanting, and M. de Charlus, in whom she satisfied all the aesthetic taste for women that he could possibly have, would have liked to have hundreds of photographs of her. Not so stupid as Morel, he learned with pleasure of the smart ladies who invited her to their houses and whom, with his experience, he was able to place socially. But he was careful (wishing to maintain the upper hand) not to enlighten Charlie, who, utterly ignorant of social matters, continued to think that outside the 'violin class' and the Verdurin circle, there existed only the Guermantes, the few almost royal families enumerated by the Baron, the rest of society being only the 'dregs', the 'plebs'. Charlie took these expressions of M. de Charlus's literally.

What, you will say, M. de Charlus, awaited in vain every day of the year by so many ambassadors and Duchesses, declining to dine with the Prince de Croy because he would have to give precedence to him, the same M. de Charlus spent all the time that he refused to these great lords and ladies with the niece of a waistcoat-maker? First and most important reason, Morel was there. But even if he had not been, I do not think the thing is so improbable; if you do, you are thinking like one of Aimé's boys. Only restaurant waiters think that an extremely rich man always wears eye-catching new clothes, and that a real swell gives dinners for sixty people and goes everywhere by motor. They are wrong. Very often an extremely rich man always wears the same shabby coat. A swell is the sort of man who, in a restaurant, talks only to the waiters and, when he gets home, plays cards with his footmen. That does not mean that he will not refuse to go through a door after Prince Murat.

Among the reasons for M. Charlus's happiness at the thought of the young people's wedding was his feeling that Jupien's niece would be a kind of extension of Morel's personality and hence of the Baron's knowledge of and power over him. The idea of 'deceiving', in the conjugal sense, the violinist's wife-to-be would not have given the Baron one moment's scruple. But having a 'young couple' to guide, feeling himself the mighty, all-powerful protector of Morel's wife (who, by considering the Baron as a god, would prove that the beloved Morel had inspired her with this notion and so would contain within her something of Morel), these things varied the form of M. de Charlus's dominance and brought to birth in his 'creature' Morel another being, the husband, that is, gave him something more, something new and curious to love in him. Perhaps this domination would now be even greater than before. For while Morel on his own, naked as it were, often resisted the Baron, whom he could be sure of winning over again, once he was married his fears for his household, for his flat, for his future would give M. de Charlus's wishes a stronger purchase upon him. All these prospects, and even, if necessary, on evenings when he was bored, the thought of setting the two at loggerheads (the Baron had always rather liked battle-scenes), gave pleasure to M. de Charlus. Less, however, than the thought of the young couple's future dependence on him. M. de Charlus's love for Morel took on a charming novelty when he thought to himself: 'His wife will belong to me as well, he belongs to me so completely; they will behave only in ways that cannot annoy me, they will obey my every whim and in that way she will be a sign (of a kind I have never had before) of the thing I had almost forgotten and which is so close to my heart: everyone will see, as they see me protecting them, putting a roof over their heads, I shall see myself that Morel is mine.' This unmistakeableness in the eyes of everyone, in his own eyes, made M. de Charlus happiest of all. For the possession of what one loves is a joy greater than love itself. Often those who hide their possession from everyone do so only for fear that the loved object will be taken away from them. And their happiness, by this prudent choice of silence, is diminished.

The reader will perhaps remember that Morel had once said to the Baron that his dream was to seduce a young girl, in particular this girl;

to do so he would promise to marry her, but, once the rape was accomplished, he would 'clear off out of it'. But all that was forgotten after the confession of love for Jupien's niece that Morel had made to M. de Charlus. Indeed, it may be that Morel had forgotten it himself. There was perhaps a genuine gap between Morel's nature, as he had cynically described it – or perhaps even cleverly exaggerated it – and the moment when it would assert itself once more. As he got to know the young girl better, he was attracted to her, he fell in love with her. He knew himself so little that no doubt he thought he loved her, perhaps even that he would love her for ever. Certainly his initial desire, his wicked scheme were still there, but overlaid with so many different feelings that we cannot be certain that the violinist would have been insincere in saying that this perverse desire was not the true motive of his present actions. There was, furthermore, a brief period when, without his entirely admitting it to himself, he saw marriage as necessary. At that moment Morel had quite severe cramps in his hand and was having to consider the possibility of giving up the violin. Since, in everything outside his art, he was unbelievably lazy, he would need to find someone to keep him, and he felt he would rather it were Jupien's niece than M. de Charlus. This arrangement would offer him more freedom and also a great choice of different women, from the ever-changing apprentices that Jupien's niece would hire and provide for him to the rich and beautiful ladies to whom he would prostitute her. The thought that his future wife might be so unreasonable as to refuse to take part in these schemes did not cross Morel's mind for a moment. In any case, they soon sank into the background, replaced by pure love, once the cramps got better. The violin would provide for them, with his allowance from M. de Charlus, who was sure to become less demanding once he, Morel, was married to the young woman. Marriage was the urgent thing now, because of his love and for the sake of his freedom. He asked for Jupien's niece's hand in the proper way; her uncle asked her what she felt. There was no need. The young girl's passion for the violinist streamed around her like her hair when it was down, like the joy that overflowed in her eyes. In Morel everything that was pleasant or profitable for himself produced moral sentiments and words of the same order, sometimes even tears.

It was therefore with sincerity – if such a word can be applied to him – that he made to the young girl speeches as sentimental (young noblemen who want to live in idleness can be sentimental too, when they are talking to the delightful daughter of some middle-class moneybags) as the theories he had set forth to M. de Charlus about seduction and deflowering had been unrelievedly base. The only thing was, that the virtuous enthusiasm he felt for a person who gave him pleasure, and the solemn commitments he made to her, had, in Morel's case, a debit side. As soon as the person no longer gave him pleasure, and even, for example, if the need to face up to the promises he had made to her caused him any displeasure, then she at once became, in Morel's mind, the object of a violent antipathy which he justified to himself and which, after some neurasthenic disturbances, allowed him to prove to his own satisfaction, once he had re-established the euphoria of his nervous system, that, even looking at things from the point of view of strict virtue, he was now freed from all obligation.

In the same way, at the end of his stay in Balbec, he had somehow or other lost all his money and, not daring to confess to M. de Charlus, was looking for someone who might give him some more. He had learned from his father (who nevertheless had forbidden him ever to 'touch' people) that in this situation it is permissible to write to the person one wants to approach, saying that one 'needs to talk to him about a business matter', and asking for a 'business meeting'. This magic formula so delighted Morel that I almost think he would have chosen to lose money so as to have the pleasure of asking for a 'meeting to talk about business'. In the years that followed, he had seen that the spell was not always so powerful as he had thought. He had noted that some people, to whom he himself would never have written except in such circumstances, did not reply to him within five minutes of receiving the 'business' letter. If the afternoon passed without Morel's receiving a reply, he did not imagine that, perhaps, the gentleman he approached was not at home, or had had other letters to write, if indeed he wasn't on holiday or ill, etc. If, by extraordinary luck, Morel were given an appointment for the following morning, he would open the conversation with these words, 'There you are! I was so surprised when you didn't answer, I wondered if you were all right, but you are, aren't you, quite well, etc.' So, at Balbec, and without telling me he wanted to speak to him about 'business', he had asked me to introduce him to Bloch, the same Bloch to whom he had been so unpleasant in the tram the week before. Bloch had immediately agreed to lend him – or rather, to get M. Nissim Bernard to lend him – five thousand francs. From that day forward, Morel had adored Bloch. He asked with tears in his eyes how he could ever repay someone who had saved his life. Finally, I approached M. de Charlus and asked him to give Morel a thousand francs a month, which Morel would immediately give to Bloch, paying off the debt reasonably quickly. The first month Morel, still impressed by Bloch's goodness, sent him the thousand francs straight away, but after that he reflected, no doubt, that a more agreeable use could be made of the remaining four thousand francs, for he began to speak ill of Bloch. The very sight of him put him in a black mood, and when Bloch, having forgotten exactly how much he had lent to Morel, asked him for three thousand five hundred francs instead of four thousand, which would have saved the violinist five hundred francs, Morel reacted by saying that in the face of such an irregularity, not only would he not pay a centime, but Bloch should think himself lucky he did not sue him. All this was said with flashing eyes. Not only did he say that Bloch and M. Nissim Bernard had no reason to be angry with him, but soon that they should be glad he was not angry with them. Finally, when he heard that M. Nissim Bernard had been saying that Thibaud played as well as he did, Morel threatened to drag him before the courts for doing him professional damage; then, as there was no justice in France any more, especially when one was up against the chosen race (for anti-Semitism was, in Morel, the natural result of having been lent five thousand francs by a Jew), he refused to leave the house without a loaded revolver. Such a nervous state, following upon an intense affection, was bound to occur soon in Morel, in relation to the waistcoat-maker's niece. It is true that M. de Charlus perhaps unintentionally played a part in the change, for he often said, without meaning it for a moment and simply to tease them, that once they were married he would not see them any more and would leave them to stand on their own feet. This idea on its own would certainly not have been enough to detach Morel from the girl, but, lodging in

Morel's mind, it would, when the time came, join up with other related ideas to form a powerful force for break-up.

I did not meet M. de Charlus and Morel all that regularly. They were often already inside Jupien's shop when I took leave of the Duchesse, for I enjoyed her company so much that it made me forget not only the period of anxious waiting which would precede Albertine's return, but even the time when I expected her. Among the days when I stayed late at Mme de Guermantes's, I shall single out one which was marked by a little incident whose cruel significance escaped me entirely and which I only came to understand much later. That late afternoon, Mme de Guermantes had given me, because she knew I liked them, some syringas that had come from the South of France. When I left the Duchesse and went upstairs, Albertine was already back, and on the stairs I met Andrée, who seemed distressed by the overpowering smell of the flowers I was carrying.

'Goodness, are you back already? I said. – Just this minute, but Albertine had a letter to write and she sent me away. – You don't think she was planning something unsuitable? – Of course not, she's writing to her aunt, I think. But she hates strong scents, remember: she won't be pleased with your syringas. – Oh dear, how silly of me. I'll tell Françoise to put them on the backstairs landing. – Don't you think Albertine will pick up the smell of them about you? After tuberoses, it's the most persistent scent there is. Anyway, I think Françoise has gone to the shops. – But I haven't got my key today, however shall I get in? – Ring the bell, Albertine will let you in. Or perhaps Françoise will be back by now.'

I said goodbye to Andrée. As soon as I knocked on the door, Albertine came to let me in, but it was quite a complicated business, for with Françoise being out Andrée did not know where to switch on the light. Finally she let me in, but fled at the smell of the syringas. I put them down in the kitchen, and while I was doing so my friend, abandoning her letter (I had no idea why), had time to go into my bedroom, lie down on the bed and call to me from there. I repeat that at the time everything seemed quite normal to me, perhaps a little confused, but quite insignificant. I had almost surprised her with Andrée, and she had given herself a breathing-space by switching off all the lights, had gone into my bedroom so that I should not go into hers and see her unmade bed, and pretended she had been writing. But all this will be explained later, all these things which might have been true or not, I have never been able to say.

Apart from this one incident, everything followed a predictable pattern when I came back up from the Duchesse's. Albertine, not knowing whether I would want to go out with her before dinner, usually left her hat, coat and parasol untidily in the hallway. When I saw them as I came in, the atmosphere of the house became breathable. I felt that, in place of a thin, depleted air, happiness filled it up. I was released from my sadness, the sight of these trivial things made Albertine mine, I ran to find her.

The days I did not go down to Mme de Guermantes's, to make the time pass more quickly during the hour before my friend's return, I would leaf through an album of Elstir's or one of Bergotte's books.

Then – as even those works which seem to be addressed solely to our sight or hearing require, if we are to appreciate them fully, a close collaboration between our awakened intelligence and these two senses – I unconsciously brought out of myself the dreams which Albertine had sown there in former times when I did not know her and which had shrivelled away in the familiarity of daily life. I threw them into the musician's phrase or the painter's image as if into a crucible, I used them to nourish the book that I was reading. And no doubt they made it more vivid for me. But Albertine gained just as much by being thus transported from one to the other of the two worlds we live in and in which we can alternately place the same object, by escaping the crushing pressure of matter and floating free in the weightless spaces of thought. I found myself able, suddenly and for a moment, to have ardent feelings for the fastidious young girl. At that moment she seemed like a work of Elstir or of Bergotte, I felt a moment of lofty enthusiasm for her, seeing her distanced by imagination and art.

Soon I was told that she had come home; but I had given orders that her name was not to be mentioned unless I were alone. If, for example, Bloch was visiting me, I would make him stay a few minutes longer, so as to be sure that he would not cross paths with my friend. For I was concealing the fact that she lived with me and even that I ever saw her at home, such was my fear that one of my friends might take a fancy to her, might wait for her outside the flat, or that in the split second of an encounter in the corridor or the hall, she might make a sign to him and arrange a meeting. Then I heard the rustle of Albertine's skirt moving towards her bedroom, for, out of discretion and, no doubt, also the consideration that she had shown in the old days when we dined at La Raspelière and she did her best to prevent me from being jealous, she would not come near my room, knowing I was not alone. But that was not the only reason, I suddenly realized. I remembered now, I had known an initial Albertine, then all of a sudden she had turned into another, the present one. And no one could be blamed for this change but myself. All the confessions she would have made to me readily, even gladly, when we were just friends, had dried up once she believed that I loved her, or perhaps, without mentioning the word Love to herself, recognized an inquisitorial feeling which desires knowledge, even when knowledge means pain, and constantly seeks to find out more. From that day onwards she had hidden everything from me. She turned away from my room if she thought, not even that I was with a woman friend, but with any friend, she whose eyes used to light up at the mention of any girl: 'You must have her round, I'd like to meet her. – But she has what you call a reputation. – Exactly, it'll be all the more fun.' At that moment, I could have perhaps heard the whole story. And even in the little casino, when she moved her breasts away from Andrée's, I do not think it was because I was there, but because of Cottard, who she no doubt thought might gossip about her. And yet even then she had begun to freeze, the confident words no longer sprang from her lips, her gestures were more reserved. Then she distanced herself from everything that might bring an emotional reaction from me. When she spoke of the parts of her life that I did not know, she colluded with my ignorance to give them the most reassuringly harmless character. And now the transformation was complete, she went straight to her room if I was not alone, not only so as not to disturb me, but to show that she cared nothing for anyone but me. There was only one thing she would not do for me, a thing she would have done only at the time when I would have cared nothing for it, and which she would have happily done then for that very reason: that is, tell me the truth. I would therefore always be reduced, like an examining magistrate, to drawing uncertain conclusions from slips of language which could perhaps be explained without invoking the hypothesis of guilt. And she would always see me as jealous and judging of her.

Our engagement was turning into a trial and giving her the timid manner of a guilty prisoner. Now she changed the subject when we spoke of anyone, man or woman, who was not old. If only I had seized the time before she knew I was jealous of her to ask her the things I wanted to know. One should make the best use of that time. That is when the woman we love will tell us what she enjoys, and even the means she uses to keep her tastes from other people. Albertine would never have confessed to me now, as she had at Balbec, partly because it was true and partly to excuse herself for not showing her feelings for me more clearly in public (for I had already begun to bore her and she had seen from my kindness to her that she did not have to show me as much affection as to other people in order to receive more in return), she would not have said to me now as she did then: 'I think it's stupid to let people see who you love; with me it's the opposite, as soon as I'm attracted to somebody, I seem to take no notice of them. That way nobody knows what's going on.' What! Was it the Albertine of today, with her pretensions to honesty and to treating everyone the same, who told me that? She would never have spelled out that rule for me today! She simply applied it when talking to me about anyone who might worry me: 'Oh, I don't know, I've never taken any notice of her, she's too uninteresting.' And from time to time, to forestall me in areas that I might find out about, she would own up to things in that tone of voice which, even before one learns of the reality the confession is designed to disguise or whitewash, marks it out as a lie.

As I listened to Albertine's footsteps, reflecting comfortably that she would not be going out again that evening, I thought again with surprise and delight that for this young girl, whom I had once despaired of getting to know, coming home every day now meant coming to my home. The mysterious, sensual, fleeting, fragmentary pleasure that I had experienced in Balbec the night that she came to sleep at the hotel had become whole, stable, and now filled the emptiness of my dwelling with an enduring provision of domestic, almost familial sweetness, which shone into the very corridors, and on which all my senses, sometimes directly and at other times, when I was alone, by imagination and in the promise of her return, could peacefully feed. Once I had heard Albertine's door close, if I had a friend with me I would hurry him out, not leaving him until I was quite sure that he was on his way downstairs, even if I had to go down a few steps myself. In the corridor Albertine would come towards me: 'Listen, while I take my things off, here's Andrée, she came up for a moment to say hallo.' And, still wrapped in the long grey veil which fell from the chinchilla toque I had given her at Balbec, she would disappear into her room, as if she guessed that Andrée, whom I had set to watch over her, would, by giving me copious details, describing how the two of them had met someone they knew, introduce some clarity into the vague regions where their whole day had been spent, and which I had not been able to imagine. Andrée's faults had become more marked, she was not such pleasant company as when I had first met her. A sort of sharp uneasiness hovered about her, ready, like a mist over the sea, to gather into storm-clouds if I were to mention any pleasure that Albertine and I shared. This did not stop Andrée being kinder to me, fonder of me than – and I have had many proofs of this – many more obviously pleasant people. But the smallest sign of happiness, if not caused by her, made an impression on her nerves as unpleasant as the sound of a slamming door. She could accept suffering in which she was not involved, but not pleasure; if she found me ill, she took it to heart, felt sorry for me, would have looked after me. But if I seemed pleased at anything, however small, if I stretched out blissfully as I closed a book and said, 'There! I've spent a delightful two hours reading such-and-such an amusing book,' these words, which would have given pleasure to my mother, to Albertine or Saint-Loup, produced in Andrée a kind of reproach, perhaps simply a nervous reaction. My pleasure irritated her in a way she could not conceal. Alongside these weaknesses were other, more serious faults; one day, when I was speaking of the young man, such an expert on racing, sport, golf and so ignorant about everything else, whom I had met with the little gang at Balbec, Andrée began to sneer: 'You know his father was a thief, he only just escaped the courts. They try to brazen it out, but I make sure I tell everyone. I'd like to see them charge me with slander. I could make quite a statement!' Her eyes were glittering. Now, I learned later that the father had done nothing wrong; Andrée knew that as well as anyone. But, imagining that the son looked down on her and wanting to find something that would embarrass and shame him, she had invented this whole fanciful story of statements to be made and had repeated it so many times to herself that perhaps by now she half believed it was true.

So, given the way Andrée had changed (and even ignoring her short, passionate bursts of hatred) I would not have chosen to spend time with her, if only because of the ill-natured edginess that set a sharp, chilly barrier around her warmer, kinder real nature. But the information that only she could give me about my friend was too important for me to neglect such a rare opportunity of acquiring it. Andrée came in, closed the door behind her; they had met a friend, one that Albertine had never mentioned to me. 'What did they say to each other? – I don't know; seeing that Albertine was with a friend, I went to buy some wool. – Buy some wool? – Yes, Albertine asked me to get it. – That's the very reason why you shouldn't have gone, she was probably trying to get you out of the way. – But she asked me before we met her friend. – Ah!' I said, breathing freely once more. But immediately my suspicion returned: 'But supposing she had arranged beforehand to meet her friend and thought of this as a way to be alone with her when the time came.' Anyway, could I be certain that my first idea (that Andrée was not telling me the whole truth) was not the right one? The person we love, I used to say to myself at Balbec, is a person whose actions seem particularly to attract our jealousy; we feel that if she told us of all her doings, we could perhaps easily stop loving her. No matter how cleverly the jealous lover hides his feelings, they are easily discovered by the woman who inspires them and who begins to use strategies of her own. She tries to deceive us about the things that might make us unhappy, and she succeeds, for how could a harmless phrase betray to the unwary hearer the lies that it conceals? We do not distinguish this phrase from others; spoken in fear and trembling, it is heard without particular attention. Later, when we are alone, we will come back to this phrase, and find that it does not seem to correspond exactly to reality. But are we remembering the phrase itself perfectly? It is as if there arises in us, in relation to the phrase and to the exactness of our memory, a doubt of the same kind as is found in certain neurotic states, when we can never remember whether we bolted the door; the fiftieth attempt is as uncertain as the first, as if we could carry out the action any number of times without its ever giving us the clear, liberating memory of having performed it. But at least we can shut the door for the fifty-first time, whereas the phrase exists in the past, in an uncertain body of sound which we have not the power to recreate. So we begin to dwell on other phrases which hide nothing, and the only, unacceptable cure would be not to know anything, so as not to want to know more. As soon as jealousy is discovered, it is considered by its object as a lack of trust which gives her a right to deceive us. Furthermore, in order to try to find out something, we ourselves have taken the initiative in lying, in deceiving. Andrée, Aimé promised not to say anything, but will they keep their word? Bloch could not promise as he knew nothing, and Albertine will only have to talk to the three of them separately and do some of what Saint-Loup would have called 'triangulation', to find out that we are lying when we pretend to be indifferent to what she does, and far too honourable to have her followed. Thus, coming to replace – in relation to Albertine's actions – my usual infinite doubt, which was too indistinct not to be painless, and was to jealousy what those beginnings of forgetfulness, where peace comes from sheer vagueness, are to grief, the little fragment of an answer which Andrée had just brought me immediately raised further questions; by exploring a small part of the great empty zone that spread around me, I had succeeded only in pushing further back into it that unknowable thing – when we actually try to picture it for ourselves – the real life of another human being. I went on questioning Andrée while Albertine, to be discreet and to give me time (did she do that on purpose?) to interrogate her as much as I wanted, spun out her undressing in her bedroom.

'I think Albertine's uncle and aunt like me,' I was sometimes foolish enough to say to Andrée, forgetting her character. Immediately I would see her sugary face turn sour, like a fruit syrup going off; she looked as if she would never smile again. Her mouth was bitter. Andrée had lost all the youthful gaiety which, like the rest of the little gang and in spite of her sickly disposition, she had shown at Balbec and which now (it is true that Andrée was now some years older) had deserted her so quickly. But I could make it reappear before Andrée left to go home for dinner. 'I met someone today who was full of praise for you,' I would say to her. Immediately a ray of joy lit up her face, it was as if she really loved me. She would not look straight at me, but laughed aimlessly, her eyes suddenly quite round. 'Who was it?' she would ask with naïve, greedy interest. I would tell her and, whoever it was, she would be happy.

Then the time came for her to leave. Albertine reappeared at my side; she had taken off her outdoor clothes and was wearing one of the crêpe de Chine dressing-gowns or Japanese kimonos made to the designs I had got from Mme de Guermantes; for the final details of several of them I had written to Mme Swann, who had replied in a letter beginning with the words, 'After your long eclipse, when I read your letter asking about my *robes de chambre*, I thought I was hearing from a ghost.' Albertine was wearing black slippers with rhinestone ornaments (which Françoise angrily called house-shoes) like the ones she had seen Mme de Guermantes wearing at home in the evening when she looked through the salon window, just as a little later she was to wear mules, some of gilt kid and others of chinchilla, which I loved to see because they were both signs (as other shoes would not have been) that she really lived with me. She had other things too, that I had not bought her, like a handsome gold ring. I admired the open eagle's wings that adorned it. 'My aunt gave me that,' she said. 'I must admit she sometimes is kind to me. It makes me feel old, because she gave it to me for my twentieth birthday.'

Albertine's taste for these pretty things was much sharper than the Duchesse's, because, like any obstacle placed in the way of possession (like my illness, which made travel so difficult and so desirable for me), poverty, more generous in this than riches, gives women something more than the clothes they cannot buy: the desire for these clothes, which is the true way, detailed, thorough, of getting to know them. She, because she could not afford to buy these things herself, and I, because by having them made for her I was trying to please her, were like students who know every detail of the pictures they long to go and see in Dresden or Vienna. Meanwhile rich women, surrounded by their countless hats and dresses, are like people who, having had no desire to visit a museum, find there only sensations of dizziness, fatigue and boredom. A particular hat, a sable coat, a Doucet indoor gown with pink-lined sleeves, took on for Albertine, who had spotted them, coveted them and, with the exclusive and detailed attention that are the mark of desire, isolated them in a vacuum in which the lining or the scarf stood out perfectly, and come to know them in every particular – and for me, who had gone to Mme de Guermantes's to try to have her explain to me what constituted the uniqueness, the superior character, the smartness of each thing, and the inimitable manner of the great craftsman – an importance, a fascination which they certainly did not have for the Duchesse, who was sated before she could even have an appetite, and which they would not have had even for me if I had seen them a few years earlier when I was accompanying some fashionable woman or other on her tiresome trail round the couturiers. Certainly, Albertine herself was developing into a woman of fashion. For if each thing I had made for her was the prettiest of its kind, with all the fine points that Mme de Guermantes or Mme Swann would have brought to it, she was coming to own quite a few such things. But that did not matter, given that she had begun by loving each of them for itself. When one has fallen in love first with one painter, then with another, one can finally admire the whole museum in a way that is not chilly, for the admiration is made of successive loves, each of which in its time was exclusive, but which have finally coalesced. I should add that she was not empty-headed; she did a great deal of reading when she was alone, and read aloud to me when I was at home. She had become extremely intelligent. She used to say (wrongly, in fact): 'It frightens me to think that if I hadn't met you I'd have gone on being stupid. Don't deny it, you opened up a world of ideas for me that I didn't know existed, and if I've made anything of myself, it's because of you.'

I have already mentioned that she spoke in similar terms of my influence over Andrée. Did either of them care at all about me? And, in themselves, what were Albertine and Andrée? To know the answer, we should have to be able to arrest your movement, stop our lives being one long wait for you, who when you arrive are always different; to fix your image we should have to stop loving you, no longer experience your endlessly postponed and always disconcerting arrival, O young girls, O successive flashes in the whirlwind where we tremble to see you reappear, barely recognizing you in the dizzying velocity of light. We should perhaps remain unaware of this rapid movement, and everything might seem to be standing still, if sexual attraction did not make us rush towards you, O drops of gold, each different from the next and always defying our expectation. Each time, a girl is so unlike what she was the time before (shattering as soon as we see her the memory we had kept of her and the desire we had planned to experience) that the stable identity we ascribe to her is purely fictitious, a convenience of language. We have been told that a certain beautiful girl is kind-hearted, loving, full of the most delicate feelings. Our imagination takes all this as gospel, and when we behold for the first time, under the curling halo of her blond hair, the disc of her rosy face, we almost fear that this too-virtuous sister will chill our passion by her very virtue, and will never be the mistress we have dreamed of. And yet, how many things we confide in her from the first moments, trusting in that nobility of heart, how many plans are made together! But a few days later, we regret having been so trusting, for the rosy young girl, when we meet her again, speaks to us in the words of a lubricious Fury. In the successive faces presented to us by the interception, after a lapse of several days, of the rosy light, it is not certain that a *movimentum* independent of the young girls has not played a part. That could have happened in the case of my young friends at Balbec. People praise to us the sweetness, the purity of a virgin. But quite soon one feels that something spicier would be more appealing and one advises her to be bolder in her manners. In herself, was she rather one than the other? Perhaps not, but capable of taking on so many different forms in the rushing current of life. There were others whose whole attraction lay in a certain implacable quality (which we planned to bend in our favour), for example the terrifying jumping girl of Balbec,[8] whose leaps just cleared the heads of frightened old gentlemen; what a disappointment when this figure showed us a different face, on our beginning to utter compliments inspired by the memory of her cruelty to others, and told us that she was shy, that she could never think of anything sensible to say to anyone the first time they met, she was so scared, and we'd have to wait a fortnight to have a proper conversation. The steel had turned to cotton wool, there would be no question of trying to break her resistance as she had already completely changed consistency. Of her own accord, it seemed, but perhaps the fault was ours, for the soft words we had addressed to Hardness had perhaps suggested to her, without there having been any conscious calculation, that she ought to become soft. (A depressing outcome for us, but perhaps only half a miscalculation on her part, since our gratitude for her yieldingness would perhaps produce a stronger commitment than our imagined delight in overcoming ferocity.) I do not suggest that one day we shall not assign quite clear-cut characters even to these radiant young girls, but that will be when they no longer appeal to us, when their entrance is no longer the apparition that our heart was awaiting in a different form, and which stuns it each time with new incarnations. Their fixity will be the product of our indifference, which delivers them up to our considered judgment. Even this, however, will not be much more conclusive, for having established that a certain fault, conspicuous in one girl, is happily absent from another, we shall notice that this fault was accompanied by a precious compensating virtue. So the false judgment of the intelligence, which comes into play only when they no longer interest us, will establish stable characters of young girls, which will tell us no more than the surprising faces, new every day, of our friends when, caught up in the dizzying whirl of our expectation, they appeared each day, each week so different that we could not arrest them in their passage, classify or rank them. As for our feelings, we need hardly repeat that love is often only the association between the image of a girl (of whom otherwise we would very quickly have tired) and the increased heart rate inseparable from a long, futile wait when the young lady in question has 'stood us up'. All this is true not only of imaginative young men and fickle young girls. At the time when our story is set, I have since learned, it seems that Jupien's niece had already changed her view of Morel and M. de Charlus. My chauffeur, trying to strengthen the love she already felt for Morel, had praised to her the violinist's supposed infinite delicacy of feeling, in which she was only too ready to believe. And on the other hand, Morel never tired of telling her what a slave-driver M. de Charlus was to him; she put this down to an evil nature, not guessing at the Baron's love. She could not, in any case, fail to notice M. de Charlus's tyrannical determination to attend all their meetings. And in corroboration of this impression, she heard her ladies speaking about the Baron's great cruelty.

Now, shortly before this, her judgment had been completely reversed. She had discovered in Morel (though it did not make her stop loving him) depths of wickedness and treachery, balanced however by frequent gentleness and real sensitivity, and in M. de Charlus an astonishing and limitless kindness, mixed with an occasional hard-heartedness that she had not yet experienced for herself. So she had been no more able to form a more definite judgment on what, each in himself, the violinist and his protector were, than I about Andrée, whom I saw every day, and Albertine, who lived in my house.

The evenings Albertine did not read aloud to me, she played the piano for me or we embarked on games of draughts or conversations, both of which I would interrupt to kiss her. Our relationship was restfully simple. The very emptiness of her life seemed to make Albertine all the more obedient, all the readier to do the few things I asked of her. Behind her young girl's shape, as once behind the crimson light that glowed beneath my curtains at Balbec, while the band's concert blared out, one could sense the bluish, mother-of-pearl undulations of the sea. Was she not, after all (she in the depths of whose being there lived an idea of me, so much at home there that, after her aunt, I was perhaps the person whom she distinguished least from herself), was she not the young girl that I had seen for the first time at Balbec, with her bold, laughing eyes under her jockey-cap, still unknown to me, thin as a cut-out figure silhouetted on the waves? These effigies, stored intact in the memory, when we return to them, astonish us by their lack of resemblance to the being we know now; we understand then how they are daily, painstakingly remodelled by habit. In Albertine's charm, as she sat by my fireside in Paris, there still lived the desire I had felt for the whole insolent, flower-decked procession as it wound along the beach, and just as Rachel retained for Saint-Loup, even after he had made her give it up, the glamour of the stage, so in the new Albertine, shut up in my house, far from Balbec, from where I had snatched her away, there survived the excitement, the social unease, the anxious vanity, the roving desires of seaside life. Her cage was so secure that some evenings I did not even call for her to come from her room to mine, she, the former leader of every party, whom I could never catch as she flew past on her bicycle and whom even the liftboy could not bring back to me, leaving me with no hope that she would come, yet still ready to wait for her all night. Albertine in front of the hotel – was she not the leading actress of the fiery beach, stirring up jealousies as she advanced on that natural stage, speaking to no one, disdaining the regular audience, dominating her friends; and this actress, so lusted-after, was she not now (removed from the stage by me, enclosed in my quarters) safe from all those whose desires would seek her in vain, as she sat, sometimes in my bedroom and sometimes in her own, drawing or doing some small piece of carving.

Certainly, in the first days at Balbec, Albertine seemed to be living in a parallel plane, separate from mine. But the two had come closer (after my visit to Elstir) and had finally touched, as I came to know her better, at Balbec, in Paris and then at Balbec again. Besides, if I compare my two pictures of Balbec, on the first visit and the second, though they are made up of the same villas from which the same girls appear in front of the same sea, what a difference there is! In Albertine's friends of the second stay, whom I knew well, whose good and bad qualities were so clearly written on their faces, how could I find again the freshness of those mysterious strangers who, the year before, could not make their chalet doors squeak on the sand or brush the trembling tamarisks as they passed, without making my heart beat faster? Their wide eyes had shrunk since, no doubt because they were no longer children, but also because these enchanting strangers, dramatis personae of the romantic first year, about whom I was constantly seeking details, held no more mystery for me. They had become, now that they accepted my demands, simply girls in the bloom of youth, among whom I felt no little pride in having plucked, carried off, the fairest rose.

Between the two, so different pictures of Balbec, there was an interval of several years in Paris, its length punctuated by repeated visits from Albertine. I saw her, in different years of my life, occupying different positions in relation to myself, which made me conscious of the beauty of the intervening spaces, the long periods when I had not been seeing her; against this diaphanous background the rosy person before my eyes took shape, a strongly modelled figure with mysterious shadows. Its three-dimensional character was due to the superposition, not only of the successive images that Albertine had been for me, but also of admirable traits of intelligence and feeling, and grave faults of character, all unsuspected by me, which Albertine, in a kind of germination, a multiplication of herself, a sombre-hued flowering of flesh, had added to a nature once almost characterless, but now difficult to know in depth. For human beings, even those of whom we once dreamed so much that they seemed to us mere images, Benozzo Gozzoli figures standing out against a greenish ground, the only variation in which depended (so we thought) on our distance from them, our angle of vision, the prevailing light, these same beings, while they change in relation to us, are also changing within themselves; and there had been enrichment, solidification and growth in volume in the two-dimensional figure once silhouetted against the sea. Nor was it only the sea at twilight that lived for me in Albertine, but sometimes the calm of the sea on the shore on moonlit nights. Sometimes, when I left my room to fetch a book from my father's study, my friend would ask if she could lie there till I got back. She would be so tired from her long excursion, all morning and all afternoon in the open air, that, even if I had only been gone for a moment, I would come back to find Albertine sound asleep. I did not wake her. Lying at full length on my bed, in a pose so natural that it could never have been adopted deliberately, she seemed to me like a long, flowering stem that had been laid there; and that was what she was: normally I could dream only when she was not there, but at these times the power of dreaming returned as I lay next to her, as if in her sleep she had turned into a plant. In that way her sleep realized, to a certain degree, the promise of love; when I was alone, I could think about her, but she was not there, she was not mine. When she was there, I could speak to her, but was too removed from myself to be able to think. When she was asleep, I did not have to speak any more, I knew that she could not see me, I did not have to live on the surface of myself. By closing her eyes, by losing consciousness, Albertine had put off, one by one, the various marks of humanity which had so disappointed me in her, from the day that we first met. She was animated only by the unconscious life of plants, of trees, a life more different from my own, stranger, and yet which I possessed more securely. Her individuality did not break through at every moment, as it did when we talked, through unconfessed thoughts and unguarded looks. She had drawn back into her self all the parts of her that were normally on the outside, she had taken refuge, enclosed and summed up in her body. Watching her, holding her in my hands, I felt that I possessed her completely, in a way I never did when she was awake. Her life was subject to me, was breathing out its light breath in my direction. I listened to that mysterious, murmuring emanation, gentle as a soft breeze over the sea, fairylike as the moonlight: the sound of her sleep. So long as it continued I could dream of her and look at her at the same time, and when her sleep became deeper, touch her and kiss her. What I experienced then was a love for something as pure, as immaterial, as mysterious as if I had been before those inanimate creatures that we call the beauties of nature. And indeed, once she had fallen into a deeper sleep, she was no longer just a plant; her slumber, on the edge of which I dreamed, experiencing a new, limpid pleasure of which I would never have tired and which I could have gone on enjoying indefinitely, had become for me a whole landscape. Having her asleep at my side offered something as sensually delicious as my moonlit nights on the bay at Balbec, when the water was calm as a lake amid scarcely moving branches, and one could lie on the beach forever, listening to the sound of the sea.

On entering the room I had stood still on the threshold, not daring to make any noise, and I heard no other sound than her breath, rising and dying away on her lips, like the sound of waves, but softer and more subdued. And at the moment when my ear picked up that heavenly sound, it was as if it held, condensed in itself, the whole person, the whole life of the charming captive who lay there before my eyes. Traffic was passing noisily in the street, her forehead remained as motionless, as pure as before, her breath as light, reduced to the simple expiration of the necessary air. Then, seeing that her sleep would not be disturbed, I advanced carefully, sat down on the chair beside the bed, then on the bed itself. I have spent delightful evenings talking or playing games with Albertine, but I was never so happy as when watching her sleep. When chatting or playing cards, she had a naturalness that no actress could have imitated, but it was a far deeper naturalness, a naturalness in the second degree, that her sleep offered to me. Her hair, falling the length of her rosy face, lay beside her on the bed, and sometimes a stray lock, standing on end, gave the same perspective effect as those frail, pale lunar trees that stick up in the background of Elstir's Raphaelesque paintings. If Albertine's lips were closed, on the other hand, from where I was sitting her eyelids seemed partly open, so that I could almost have wondered whether she was actually sleeping. Still, her lowered lids gave her face that perfect unity that open eyes would have disrupted. There are some faces which take on an unaccustomed beauty and majesty the moment they no longer have a gaze. My eyes measured Albertine as she lay at my feet. Every now and then a slight, inexplicable tremor ran through her, like an unexpected breeze momentarily convulsing the leaves. She touched her hair, then, not having had the effect she wanted, put her hand to it again, in such a coherent, apparently intentional set of movements that I was sure she was going to wake up. But no, she settled into her sleep again without stirring, and from then on stayed quite still. Letting her arm fall, she had dropped her hand on her breast in such a naïvely childish pose that, as I looked at her, it was hard not to smile as we do at babies in their innocent gravity and grace. I already knew several Albertines in one; now I felt I was seeing many more at rest beside me. Her eyebrows, arched as I had never known them, surrounded the globes of her lids like a halcyon's downy nest. Whole races, atavisms, vices slept in her face. Every time she moved her head she created a new woman, often undreamed of by me. I felt that I possessed not one, but innumerable young girls. Her breathing, growing deeper, raised and lowered her breast, and on it, her folded hands and her pearls, which moved differently under the same impulse, like boats and their mooring-chains oscillating in the ebb and flow of the waves. Then, realizing she was in a deep sleep, and that I would not go aground on reefs of consciousness now covered by the waters of oblivion, I carefully, noiselessly moved up on to the bed; I lay down alongside her, put one of my arms around her waist, touched my lips to her cheek and her heart, and then rested my free hand on every part of her body in turn. My hand, too, was raised and lowered, like the pearls, by Albertine's breathing: my whole body was gently rocked by its regular movement. I had set sail on Albertine's sleep.

Sometimes, it brought me a less pure pleasure. I did not have to move at all, I let my leg loll against hers, like a trailing oar to which one gives every now and then a tiny impulsion like the occasional wing-beat of a bird asleep in mid-air. I looked at her, choosing the profile that she never showed, and which was so beautiful. It is just possible to understand how the letters someone writes to us could be so similar to each other, could create an image so distinct from the person we know, that they constitute a second personality. But how much stranger it is that a woman should be attached, like Rosita and Doodica,[9] to another woman whose different beauty makes us deduce the existence of another personality, and that to see the one we should have to look at her in profile, the other full face. The sound of Albertine's breathing, growing louder, could almost have been mistaken for the breathlessness of pleasure, and as my own pleasure reached completion, I could kiss her without breaking into her sleep. It seemed to me at those moments that I had possessed her more completely, like an unconscious and unresisting part of dumb nature. I paid no attention to the words she sometimes uttered in her sleep, their meaning escaped me, and in any case, whatever unknown person they might refer to, it was on my hand, my cheek, that her hand closed, when a slight shudder occasionally passed through it. I experienced her sleep with a disinterested, calming love, as I might spend hours listening to the unrolling of the waves. Perhaps it is only people who can make us suffer a great deal who can offer us, in our hours of remission, that same, pacifying calm that nature can give. I did not have to answer her, as I did when we talked, and even had I been able to keep silent, as I did when she was speaking, listening to her did not allow me to enter so deeply into her as I did now. As I went on listening, collecting up from moment to moment the murmur, calming as an imperceptible breeze, of her sweet breath, a whole physiological existence was laid before me, was mine; the hours that I had once spent lying on the beach in the moonlight, I would now gladly have spent looking at her, listening to her. Sometimes it seemed that the sea was beginning to swell, that the coming storm could be sensed even in the bay, and I listened to the gentle rumble of her breathing as it turned into a snore.

Sometimes when she was too warm, already almost asleep she would slip out of her kimono and throw it over a chair As she slept, I said to myself that all her letters were in the inside pocket of her kimono, where she always kept them. A signature, an appointment would have been enough to convict her of a lie or disprove a suspicion. When I knew that Albertine was sound asleep, leaving the foot of her bed from which I had been studying her for a long time without moving, I took one bold step, gripped by a burning curiosity and conscious that the whole secret of her life lay there for the taking, limp and defenceless in that armchair. And so, one step at a time, constantly turning round to check that Albertine was not waking up, I moved towards the chair. When I got there I stopped, for a long time I stood looking at the kimono as I had stood looking at Albertine. But (perhaps mistakenly) I never touched the kimono, never put my hand in the pocket or looked at the letters. Finally, realizing that I would not take the step, I crept back to Albertine's bed and went on looking at her as she slept, she who told me nothing, while I could see on the arm of the chair the kimono which could have told me so much. And just as people pay a hundred francs a day for a hotel room at Balbec just to breathe the sea air, I thought it quite natural to spend more than that on her, since I had her breath near to my cheek or in her mouth, which I slowly opened upon mine, feeling her very life pass over my tongue. But this pleasure of watching her sleep, which was as sweet as that of feeling her live, was soon replaced by another: that of seeing her wake up.

This was the same, though in an intenser and more mysterious form, as the pleasure of having her living with me. Certainly I loved to think that when she got out of the car in the afternoons, it was to my flat that she was coming home. But it was even more delightful to think of her rising from the depths of sleep, climbing the last steps of the ladder of dreams and awakening to consciousness and life in my bedroom; asking herself for a moment 'where am I?' and seeing the objects that surrounded her, the lamp whose light hardly even made her blink, and being able to say 'at home', as she realized she was waking up under my roof. In this first delicious moment of uncertainty I felt that I was taking a new, more complete possession of her, for when she came back from outside, she would go first into her room, but now it was my room, as Albertine recognized it, that would enfold her, contain her, without my friend's eyes giving any sign of anxiety, for they remained as untroubled as if she had never been asleep. The hesitancy of waking, revealed in her silence, made no mark on her gaze.

Now she began to speak; her first words were 'darling' or 'my darling', followed by my Christian name, which, if we give the narrator the same name as the author of this book, would produce 'darling Marcel' or 'my darling Marcel'. From that moment I stopped allowing my relations, at home, to call me 'darling', so as not to destroy the unique charm of the words Albertine used in speaking to me. As she said them, she formed her lips into the shape of a kiss, which she soon turned into a real one. She had fallen asleep in an instant; now she woke up just as quickly. But it was not my movement through time, any more than the fact of looking at a girl sitting close to me under the lamp which cast a different light on her from the light of the sun as she strode along the sea-shore; not the real enrichment or independent progress of Albertine's character that were the true cause of the difference between the way I looked at her now and the way I had looked at her in the early days at Balbec. Many more years could have separated the two images without bringing about such a complete change; it had happened, radical and sudden, when I learned that my friend had been almost brought up by the associate of Mlle Vinteuil. Once I had been excited by the mystery I thought I saw in Albertine's eyes, but now I could be happy only when I briefly managed to eliminate from those eyes, or from her cheeks, which were almost as expressive as her eyes, sometimes so kindly but so quickly turning to brusqueness, any suggestion of the mysterious. The image I sought, the image in which I found repose, lying next to which I would have longed to die, was no longer the Albertine with a secret life; it was an Albertine I knew, as thoroughly as a person can be known (and that was why my love for her could last only so long as it remained unhappy, for by definition it could not satisfy the need for mystery), it was an Albertine who did not reflect a distant world, but instead desired nothing – and there were indeed moments when that seemed to be true – nothing but to be with me, to be exactly like me, an Albertine who was precisely the image of what was mine and not of the unknown. When, as here, love is born in a particular, anguished moment of our relation to a person, born of our uncertain hold on that person and the fear that he or she may escape, then that love always bears the sign of the upheaval of its creation; there is little left of the vision we previously had when we thought of the one we now love. My first impressions of Albertine at the edge of the waves perhaps survived in some small measure in my love for her: but really such previous impressions play only a very small part in a love of this kind, in its strength, its pain, its need for gentleness and its harking-back to a peaceful, pacifying world of memory, where one would wish to live forever, learning no more about the loved one, even if some vile revelation were there for the asking, but rather relying only upon such earlier impressions: a love of this kind is made of very different stuff! Sometimes I put out the light before she came in. It was in darkness, guided only by the light of an ember, that she came to my side. Only my hands, my cheeks recognized her, without my eyes seeing her, my eyes which so often feared to find her changed. So that, thanks to this blind love, she perhaps felt herself bathed in more tenderness than she was used to.

I would undress and get into bed, and with Albertine sitting at one corner of the bed, would take up again the game of cards or the conversation that our kisses had interrupted; and our desire (the only thing that makes us take any interest in the existence or character of a person) is such a constant reflection of our underlying nature, even if we abandon in turn the various beings we have loved, that once, catching sight of myself in the glass as I kissed Albertine, calling her 'little girl', and seeing the sad, passionate expression of my face, just as it would have been years ago when I was with Gilberte, whom I had now forgotten, and would be again, perhaps, with someone else if I were ever to forget Albertine, I thought that beyond any consideration of persons (for instinct demands that we always consider the present partner as the only true one) I was carrying out a duty of ardent and painful devotion, offered like a tribute to feminine youth and beauty. And still this desire which I placed like an *ex voto* in honour of youth, those memories of Balbec too, only partly explained the need I had to keep Albertine beside me every evening; there was another thing which so far had been alien to me, to me as a lover at any rate, even if it was not wholly new to my life. It was a calming effect so powerful that I had experienced nothing like it since the far-off evenings in Combray when my mother came and, leaning over my bed, brought me rest in a kiss. Certainly I would have been astonished in those days if someone had told me that I was not a wholly kind person, and still more that I would ever try to deprive someone of a pleasure. Clearly I had little self-knowledge at that time, for my pleasure in having Albertine living with me now was much less a positive pleasure than satisfaction at having removed from the world, where everyone could enjoy her in turn, the blossoming young girl who, even if she caused no great joy to me, at least could not offer it to anyone else. Ambition, glory could never have meant anything to me. Still less was I capable of experiencing hatred. All the same, carnal love for me was above all the joy of triumphing over so many competitors. I cannot repeat it too often, more than anything else it was relief from pain.

Before Albertine came home I might have suspected her, imagined her in the room at Montjouvain, but once she was in her dressing-gown, sitting facing my armchair or my bed, if, as usual, I was lying at the foot of it, I brought all my doubts to her, placed them before her so as to be freed from them, laying down my burden as a believer does when he prays.

She might have spent the whole evening mischievously curled up on my bed, playing with me like an oversized cat; her little pink nose, whose tip seemed all the smaller for her flirtatious way of glancing, giving her the special daintiness that some quite plump people have, might have given her a fiery, rebellious look; she might have let a lock of her long black hair fall across her pink wax doll's cheek and, half closing her eyes and uncrossing her arms, have seemed to be saying, 'Do what you like with me.' Still, when it was time for her to leave and she came close to me to say good-night, what I kissed was the now almost familial sweetness of the two sides of her strong young neck, which never seemed to me sufficiently tanned or coarse-grained, as if these robust qualities had been the sign of some reliable goodness in Albertine.

'Are you coming out with us tomorrow, bad boy?' she would ask me before she left. – 'Where are you going?' – 'That depends on the weather, and on you. *Did* you write anything this afternoon, dearest? No? Well then, you might just as well have come out. By the way, when I came in just now, you recognized my footsteps, didn't you, you guessed it was me?' – 'Of course. How could I mistake them? I'd know my little goosey's footsteps anywhere. Little goosey sit down and let me take off her shoes before she goes to bed. I'd like that. You're so sweet and pink among all that snowy lace.'

That was how I answered her; among the expressions of carnality, the reader will recognize others belonging to my mother and my grandmother. For I was slowly coming to resemble all my relatives: my father who – in a completely different manner from myself, of course, for if things repeat themselves it is always with wide variations – took such a strong interest in the weather; and not only my father, but more and more my aunt Léonie. Without her influence, Albertine would have been an obvious reason for me to go out, so as not to leave her alone, outside my control. Yes, Aunt Léonie, steeped in piety and with whom I would have sworn I did not have a single thing in common, I who was so mad for pleasures, quite unlike that obsessive who did not know what pleasure was and spent the whole day saying her rosary, I who was desperate to establish a life in literature, when she was the only person in the family who had never managed to understand that reading was not simply a pastime, something one did 'for fun', so that even in the Easter season reading was allowed on Sundays, when all serious work is forbidden, so that the whole day can be sanctified by prayer. Now, even though I found the explanation in some different ailment each day, what made me so often spend the whole day in bed was another being, not Albertine, not a being I loved but one with more power over me than any I did love; it was a soul transmigrated into me, despotic enough to reduce my jealous suspicions to silence, or at any rate to stop me going to find out whether they were true or not: it was Aunt Léonie. Was it not enough that I should bear an exaggerated resemblance to my father, not just consulting the barometer as he did but becoming a kind of human barometer myself, was it not enough that I should be driven by my aunt Léonie to spend the day observing the weather, but from my room and even from my bed? Here I was now talking to Albertine, sometimes like the child I had been at Combray talking to my mother, and sometimes like my grandmother talking to me. Once we pass a certain age, the soul of the child we used to be and the souls of the dead from whom we spring come and scatter over us handfuls of their riches and their misfortunes, asking to bear a part in the new feelings we are experiencing: feelings which allow us, rubbing out their old effigies, to recast them in an original creation. Thus, all my past since my earliest years, and beyond those, my relatives' past, mixed into my carnal love for Albertine the sweetness of a love both filial and maternal. Once a certain hour has come we have to welcome them, all those relatives who have come so far to assemble around us.

Before Albertine, obeying my wishes, had taken off her shoes, I would open her nightdress. The two high little breasts were so round that they seemed not so much integral parts of her body as two fruits that had ripened there; and her belly (hiding the place which, in men, is made ugly by something like the metal pin left sticking out of a statue when it is removed from its mould) was closed, at the meeting of the thighs, by two curves as gentle, as restful, as cloistered as the horizon when the sun has disappeared. She took off her shoes and lay down beside me.

O noble attitudes of Man and Woman in which, with all the

innocence of the first days and the humility of clay, what Creation put asunder tries to join together once more, in which Eve is astonished and compliant before the Man by whose side she awakes, as he is, still alone, before the God who made him! Albertine twisted her arms behind her black hair, her hip swelling, her leg falling away in a swan's-neck curve, lengthening and turning back on itself. Only when she was lying quite on her side did her features (so kind and beautiful when seen full face) appear intolerably ugly, hooked like certain Leonardo caricatures, seeming to reveal wickedness, greed, the deviousness of a spy whose presence in my house would have appalled me, and who seemed to be unmasked by those particular profiles. I would immediately take Albertine's face in my hands and reposition it to face me.

'There's a good boy, promise me that if you don't come out tomorrow you'll do some work,' said my friend, putting her night-dress back on. 'All right, but don't put your dressing-gown on yet.' Sometimes I fell asleep next to her. The bedroom had got cold, we needed more wood. I would try to find the bell-rope behind me, but I could not; I would feel all the brass posts but the two between which it hung, and say to Albertine, who had jumped out of bed so that Françoise would not see us together, 'No, get back in for a minute, I can't find the bell.'

These were happy, cheerful moments, innocent in appearance but hiding the growing possibility of disaster: this is what makes the life of lovers the most unpredictable of all, a life in which it can rain sulphur and pitch a moment after the sunniest spell and where, without having the courage to learn from our misfortunes, we immediately start building again on the slopes of the crater which can only spew out catastrophe. I was carefree in the way of those who think their happiness can last. It is just because this sweetness was necessary to give rise to suffering – and will also return intermittently to relieve it – that men can be being sincere with their friends, and even with themselves, when they speak warmly of a woman's kindness to them, even though, to tell the truth, their relationship is undermined secretly, in a way they do not confess to others or which is revealed involuntarily in response to questions, to inquiries, by a painful anxiety. But this anxiety could not have arisen if not for the previous happiness: and later, the intermittent happiness is necessary to make the suffering bearable and to avoid a complete break; and the way the lover hides the secret hell which living with this woman has become, even going so far as to boast of their intimacy and its pretended happiness, has an element of truth in it, expresses a general connection between cause and effect, one of the means by which the production of suffering is made possible.

It no longer surprised me that Albertine should be there and should only be able to go out the following day with me or under the protection of Andrée. These shared habits, these boundaries which marked off my existence and which no one could cross but Albertine, and also (in the plan, as yet unknown to me, of my future life, drawn as if by an architect designing monuments which will be built only much later) the distant lines, parallel to these but on a grander scale, which sketched out in me, like a lonely hermitage, the somewhat rigid, monotonous pattern of my future loves, had in fact been drawn that night in Balbec when, after Albertine had told me, in the little tram, who it was who had brought her up, I had decided at all costs to remove her from certain influences and prevent her from being out of my sight for several days. Days had followed upon days, my habits had become mechanical, but as with those rites for which History tries to discern a meaning, I could have said (and would not have wished to say) to anyone who asked me what was the meaning of this sequestered life, where I shut myself away to the point of no longer going to the theatre, that it had its origin in the anxiety of a single evening, and the need to prove to myself in the days that followed that the girl whose unfortunate childhood had just been revealed to me would no longer have the chance, even if she wished to do so, of exposing herself to similar temptations. I rarely thought about these temptations any more, but they must still have been present at the back of my mind. The fact of destroying them day by day – or of trying to do so – was no doubt what made me so happy as I kissed those cheeks, in themselves no more beautiful than many other cheeks; under every physical pleasure of any intensity there lies an abiding sense of danger.

I had promised Albertine that if I did not go out with her I would start work. But the next day, as if, while we were asleep, the house had miraculously travelled, I found myself waking up to different weather, a different climate. No one works immediately on landing in a strange country; there are the new conditions to get used to. Now, for me, each new day was a new country. Even my laziness constantly took on new forms: how could I have recognized it? Sometimes, on days when the weather was pronounced hopelessly bad, just living in a house placed at the centre of steadily falling rain had the gentle smoothness, the calming silence, the absorbing interest of a sea-voyage; then, on a bright day, simply lying still in bed would allow the shadows to pivot around me as if around a tree-trunk. Or else, from the first sound of the bells of a nearby convent, few and hesitant as their early morning worshippers, barely lightening the dark sky with their tentative showers of sound which were fused or broken up by the warm wind, I had already recognized one of those stormy days, mild and unpredictable, when the roofs, briefly dampened by rain, then dried by a breath of wind or a ray of sunshine, poutingly display a few drops and, as they wait for the wind to turn again, preen in the passing sunshine the rainbow glints of their shot-silk slates; one of those days which is filled with so many changes in the weather, so many atmospheric incidents, so much turbulence, that the lazy man feels he has not wasted it, since he has taken an interest in all the activity that the atmosphere, failing any action on his part, has undertaken in his place; days like those times of rioting or war that do not seem empty to the schoolboy missing his classes, since, hanging around outside the Palais de Justice or reading the newspapers, he has the illusion that the unfolding events replace the work he is not doing, developing his intelligence and excusing his idleness; days, in a word, to which we can compare those which bring our lives to some exceptional crisis and which make the man who has never done anything believe that he will, if all turns out happily, adopt new habits of diligence: for example, it is on the morning when he is going out to fight a duel in particularly dangerous circumstances that, when he is perhaps on the point of losing it, he suddenly becomes aware of the value of a life which he might have used to establish a body of work, or simply to enjoy himself, and of which he has made no use at all. 'Only let me not be killed,' he says to himself, 'and see how I shall work, starting this minute, and how I shall enjoy life!' Life suddenly seems more valuable to him, because he has included in it everything it might be able to give, and not the small amount that he usually makes it give to him. He sees it through the eyes of desire and not as what experience has shown him he can make of it, that is, something so very common-place. It has, in an instant, been filled with work, travel, mountain-climbing, all the fine things that he thinks the dreadful outcome of this duel may make impossible for him, without realizing that they were already impossible long before the duel was thought of, because of his bad habits which, even without the duel, would have continued. He comes home without a scratch. But he goes on finding the same objections to pleasures, to outings, to journeys, to everything of which he feared for a moment being deprived by death; life is enough to cut him off from them. As far as work is concerned – since extreme cir-cumstances exaggerate what was already present in a man, diligence in the hard worker and laziness in the idler – he awards himself a holiday.

I followed his example, and did as I had always done since the original decision to start writing which I had made long ago, but which always seemed to date from the day before, since I treated each day, one after another, as if they did not count. Today was just the same; I was letting its showers and spells of sunshine pass without doing anything and still promising myself that I would start working tomorrow. But I was not the same person under a cloudless sky; the golden sound of the bells contained not only, as honey does, light, but the sensation of light (and also the sweetish scent of preserved fruit, since at Combray it had often hung around our table, like a wasp, after the dishes had been cleared). On a day of such brilliant sunshine, keeping one's eyes closed all day was something permissible, usual, healthy, pleasant, seasonable, like closing one's shutters against the heat. The weather had been like this at the beginning of my second stay in Balbec, when I would hear the violins of the band between the bluish flows of the rising tide.

How much more Albertine belonged to me now! There were some days when the sound of a bell striking the hour bore on the sphere of its sound a patch of dampness or of brightness that was so fresh, so powerfully applied that it was like a translation for the blind, or, if you like, a musical transposition of the charm of the rain or the sunshine. So that at that moment, lying in bed with my eyes shut, I would say to myself that everything can be transposed, and that a universe made up only of sound could be as varied as any. Travelling lazily upstream from day to day as if on a boat, and seeing appear before me ever-new, magical memories which I had not chosen, which, the moment before they appeared, were invisible, and which memory presented to me one after the other without my being able to choose, I lazily pursued, over these smooth spaces, my outing in the sun.

The morning concerts at Balbec did not belong to the distant past. And yet, even after such a relatively short lapse of time, I was not thinking of Albertine. In fact, in the days just after my arrival, I had not known that she was in Balbec. Who was it who had told me she was there? Ah yes, Aimé. It was a lovely day, like today. Dear Aimé! He was glad to see me again. But he doesn't like Albertine. Not everyone can like her. Yes, he was the one who told me she was in Balbec. How did he know? He had met her, he thought she looked 'not quite the thing'. At this moment, approaching Aimé's account from a different angle from the one it had presented when I first heard it, my thoughts, which had so far been sailing smilingly over the happy waters I have just described, exploded, as if they had hit an invisible, dangerous mine, treacherously placed at this point in my memory. He said he had met her and she was looking 'not quite the thing'. What did he mean by that? I had thought he meant vulgar: indeed, I had immediately contradicted him by saying she looked distinguished. But no, perhaps he meant a lesbian look. She was with a friend, perhaps they had their arms round each other's waists, perhaps they were eyeing other women, maybe they had that 'look' that I had never seen on Albertine when I was around. Who was the friend? Where had Aimé met this hateful Albertine? I tried to remember exactly what Aimé had said, to see if it fitted with what I was now imagining, or if he was simply suggesting that her manners were common. But I asked these questions in vain, the person asking and the person who could supply the memory were, alas, one and the same person, myself, who could split himself in two for a moment, but could not add anything to himself. All my questioning was useless. I myself was giving the answers and I learned nothing new. I had stopped thinking about Mlle Vinteuil. Born of a new suspicion, the fit of jealousy I was suffering was also new, or rather it was simply an extension, a prolonging of this new suspicion; it had the same setting, no longer Montjouvain but the stretch of road where Aimé had met Albertine, and for characters the small group of friends, one or other of whom could have been the person with Albertine on that day. Perhaps it was a certain Élisabeth, or perhaps the two girls Albertine had watched in the mirror at the casino, when she didn't seem to be watching them. No doubt she had sexual relations with them, and with Esther besides, Bloch's cousin. Such relations, if they had been revealed to me by a third person, would have been almost enough to kill me, but as it was I who was imagining them myself, I was always careful to include enough uncertainty to make the pain bearable. One can absorb, in the form of suspicions, an enormous daily dose of the idea that one is deceived: when the same idea would be fatal in a much smaller quantity, if administered in the single injection of a destructive word. And that is no doubt the reason, allied to a form of the self-preservation instinct, why the jealous man is ready to form the most dreadful suspicions on the basis of innocent events, provided that, when the first piece of real evidence is brought to him, he can refuse to recognize the obvious. In any case, love is an incurable ailment, like those groups of related diseases in which respite from, say, rheumatism can be had only when it is replaced by epileptiform migraines. My jealous suspicions once pacified, I would begin to blame Albertine for not being loving, for having perhaps laughed about me with Andrée. I was afraid to think what idea she might have formed of me if Andrée had repeated all our conversations, the future seemed appalling. This sadness left me only if a new jealous suspicion plunged me into further inquiries or if, on the other hand, Albertine's affectionate behaviour robbed my happiness of meaning. Who could the girl have been? I must write to Aimé, try to see him, and then I could check on what he said by talking to Albertine, by drawing her out. In the meantime, convinced that it must be Bloch's cousin, I asked him, without giving him the least idea why, to show me a picture of her or, better still, to introduce me to her.

How many people, towns, pathways jealousy makes us desperate to know! It is a thirst for knowledge thanks to which we come to have, on a series of isolated points, all possible information except the information we really want. We never know when a suspicion will arise, for suddenly we remember a phrase that was unclear, an alibi which must have been given for a purpose. It is not that we have seen the person again, but there is a jealousy after the event, which arises only after we have left the person in question, a 'staircase jealousy' like staircase wit. Perhaps the habit I had developed of keeping certain desires secret within myself, the desire for a young girl of good society like the ones I saw passing under my window followed by their governesses, and particularly the one Saint-Loup, who frequented brothels, had told me about, the desire for pretty lady's-maids, and particularly Mme Putbus's, the desire to go to the country in spring and see the hawthorns again, the desire for storms, for Venice, to set to work, to live like other people, perhaps the habit of keeping all these desires alive in me without satisfying them, simply promising myself that I would not forget to realize them one day, perhaps this habit, formed over so many years, of perpetual postponement, of what M. de Charlus damned under the name of procrastination, had become so general in me that it had invaded even my jealous suspicions and led me, while making a mental note that one day I would certainly demand an explanation from Albertine about the young girl (or young girls, for this part of the story was confused, half erased, in other words unreadable in my memory) in whose company Aimé had met her, to delay this demand. In any case, I would not raise the subject with my friend this evening, for fear of seeming jealous and annoying her. Nevertheless, the following day when I received the photograph of Bloch's cousin Esther, I immediately sent it on to Aimé. And at the same moment I remembered that in the morning Albertine had refused me a pleasure which could, indeed, have tired her. Was she keeping it for someone else, that afternoon perhaps? For whom? It is in this way that jealousy knows no bounds, for even if the loved one, perhaps because of her death, can no longer provoke it by her actions, it can happen that memories, occurring long after any events, can behave in our minds like events in their own right: memories that we had not explored until then, which we had thought unimportant but which our own reflection on them, without bringing any further facts to bear, can endow with a new, dreadful meaning. There is no need for two players, one need only be alone in one's room, thinking, for new betrayals by one's mistress to occur, even after she is dead. It is not enough in love, as in everyday life, to fear only the future: one must fear the past, which often becomes real to us only after the future, and I am not simply speaking of the past about which we learn only after the event, but of the one we have carried within us for many years, and which we only now learn to read.

No matter, I was very happy, as the afternoon ended, that the hour was approaching when I would be able to seek in Albertine's presence the source of calm that I needed. Unfortunately, the evening was one of those which did not bring me that calm, one when the kiss Albertine gave me as she left, unlike her usual kiss, would not settle me, any more than my mother's kiss did on those evenings when she was cross with me, when I dared not call her back even though I knew I would not be able to go to sleep. Those evenings were now the ones when Albertine had made some plan for the following day that she did not want me to know about. If she had confided in me, I would have applied myself to realizing her plans with an energy that no one but Albertine could have inspired in me to the same degree. But she said nothing, and indeed had no need to say anything: as soon as she came in, as she stood at her bedroom door with her hat still on, I had already seen in her face the unknown, fractious, determined, irrepressible desire. Now these were often the evenings when I had looked forward to her return with the tenderest thoughts, imagining throwing my arms round her with the greatest affection. Alas, misunderstandings like the ones I had often had with my parents, whom I found distant or cross at the moment I ran towards them overflowing with affection, are nothing compared with those that come between lovers. Suffering here is much less superficial, much harder to bear; they affect a deeper layer of the heart. On this evening, Albertine could not avoid telling me a little about the plan she had made: I understood immediately that she wanted to go to Mme Verdurin's the next day, to make a visit to which normally I would not have objected at all. But certainly she meant to meet someone there, to prepare the ground for some pleasure. Otherwise she would not have been so determined to go. That is, she would not have kept repeating that she did not care whether she went or not. As I got older, I had developed in the opposite direction from those peoples who adopt a phonetic script only after having used characters as symbols; for so many years I had looked for people's real lives and thoughts only in the direct expressions of them that they deliberately provided, but now, thanks to them, I had come to do the opposite, to attach importance only to those statements that are not a rational, analytical expression of the truth; I relied on words only when I could read them like the rush of blood to the face of a person who is unsettled, or like a sudden silence. A certain phrase (like the one M. de Cambremer used when he thought I was 'a writer' and when, not having yet spoken to me, he was describing a visit he had made to the Verdurins, and said, turning to me, 'De Borrelli was there – *you* know') flaring up, sparked by the unintended, sometimes dangerous proximity of two ideas unexpressed by the speaker, from whose discourse I could, by appropriate methods of analysis or electrolysis, extract them, told me more than a whole speech. Albertine sometimes left such loose ends trailing in her speech, precious compounds which I hastened to 'process' so as to turn them into clear ideas.

It is one of the most dreadful things for the lover that, while particular facts – which only the test of experience, or even spying, can verify from among so many possibilities – are so difficult to unearth, the truth, on the other hand, is so easy to discover or simply to intuit. I had often seen her at Balbec give passing girls an offhand, lingering look, like a touch, and then, if I knew them, say, 'Shall we have them round? I'd like to be rude to them.' And for some time now, since she had learned to understand me, no doubt, there had been no requests to invite anyone, not a word, and even a turning-away of her gaze, which was now unfocussed and silent, and accompanied by a faraway, absent-minded look that was just as revealing as their former intensity. Now I could not reproach or question her about things which she would have said were so tiny, so insignificant that I must just be noticing them for the fun of 'nitpicking'. It is not easy to say, 'Why did you look at that girl we passed?' but even harder to say, 'Why didn't you look at her?' And yet I knew, or at least I would have known, if I had not chosen to believe what Albertine said rather than all the tiny signs included in a glance, proved by a glance, and certain inconsistencies in her words that I often did not notice until after I had left her, and which then made me suffer all night; I did not dare mention them to her afterwards, but they would nonetheless favour my memory with periodic return visits. Often these furtive or averted looks on the beach at Balbec or in the streets of Paris left me wondering if the person who provoked them was simply the subject of a passing desire, or whether she were not an old acquaintance, or else a girl to whom Albertine had simply spoken and to whom, when I learned of it, I was astonished that she should have spoken, so far removed was she, apparently, from the range of girls it was possible for Albertine to know. But modern Gomorrah is a jigsaw puzzle made up of pieces from the most unlikely places. I once observed a grand dinner at Rivebelle all of whose ten female guests I happened to know, if only by name; they were as disparate as possible socially and yet had a perfect understanding, so that I never saw a dinner where the guests, seemingly so ill-matched, mixed so well.

To return to the young passers-by, Albertine would never have looked at an old lady or an elderly man with that degree of fixity or, on the other hand, of discretion, seeming not to see them. Deceived husbands who 'do not know', in fact know everything. But one needs a stronger basis of factual evidence before making a jealous scene. Then, while jealousy teaches us to recognize a propensity to lying in the woman we love, it also multiplies that propensity a hundredfold once she has learned that we are jealous. She lies (on a scale on which she has never lied to us before), whether from pity, or fear, or an instinctive desire to hide, to flee which is proportionate to the energy of our investigations. Certainly there are affairs in which from the beginning a woman with a past has tried to pose as irreproachable in the eyes of the man who loves her. But in how many more do we see two completely contrasting phases! In the first, the woman speaks almost carelessly, simply softening the truth a little, about her taste for pleasure and the irregular life it has led her into, admissions which she will later deny with the utmost force to the same man, once she has sensed that he is jealous of her and is spying on her. He will come to look back fondly on the days of those early confidences, the memory of which none the less tortures him. If the woman would still confess to him in the same way, she would almost herself be giving up to him the secret of those offences which he vainly pursues every day. And then what a proof of confidence it would be, of trust, of friendship! If she cannot live without deceiving him, at least she would be deceiving him like a friend, telling him of her pleasures, sharing them with him. And he mourns the loss of such a life, which the beginning of their affair had seemed to hint at, but its development had made impossible, turning their love into something atrociously painful, and making a separation either inevitable or, as it might be, wholly impossible.

Sometimes the script in which I deciphered Albertine's lies was not ideographic, but simply had to be read backwards; thus, on this particular evening she had thrown out in my direction the message, designed to pass almost unnoticed: 'I might perhaps go to the Verdurins' tomorrow, I don't really know, I don't much feel like going.' A childish anagram of the admission, 'I'm going to the Verdurins' tomorrow, I simply must go, it's really important.' This apparent hesitation was the sign of a firm resolve and was designed to reduce the importance of the visit in the very moment of telling me about it. Albertine always used a tentative tone for irrevocable decisions. I was no less resolved: I would see to it that the visit to Mme Verdurin did not take place. Jealousy is often nothing but an uneasy desire for domination, applied in the context of love. I had no doubt inherited from my father this sudden, arbitrary need to threaten the beings I loved the most in their most comfortable hopes, so as to show that their security was illusory. When I saw that Albertine had planned, without consulting me, while hiding her scheme from me, an outing which I would have been the first to try to make easier and more pleasant for her if only she had told me about it, I would carelessly suggest, so as to alarm her, that I intended to go out that day myself.

I began to suggest to Albertine other places to visit which would have made calling on the Verdurins impossible, colouring my words with a feigned indifference under which I tried to disguise my annoyance. But she had spotted it. In her it encountered the electric force of a contrary will which repelled it strongly, throwing off sparks which I could see in Albertine's eyes. Anyway, why should I have paid attention to what her eyes were saying at that moment? How could I not have noticed long ago that Albertine's eyes belonged to the family of those (found even in unremarkable beings) which seem made up of different elements for all the different places where their owner would like to be – and will not admit that she would like to be – on a given day? Eyes always lyingly motionless and passive, but dynamic, measurable by the metres or kilometres to be covered in order to arrive at the desired – implacably desired – meeting-place, eyes given not so much to smiling at the temptations of pleasure, as to clouding over with sadness and discouragement at the thought of possible difficulties separating them from the goal. Even held in one's hands, these beings are creatures of flight. To understand the feelings they inspire and which other beings, even more beautiful ones, cannot, we must consider them not as immobile but in movement, and add to their description a sign corresponding to the sign for speed in physics.

If you upset their day's programme, they admit to the pleasure they were hiding from you: 'I was so looking forward to having tea with So-and-so, I do love her.' Well, if six months later you finally meet So-and-so, you discover that the girl whose plans you upset, who in order to escape your trap admitted to you that on the afternoons when you did not see her she always had tea with this friend, had in fact never been to her house; you learn that they never had tea together, for your friend was always too busy: that she was, in fact, seeing you.

So, the person she had confessed she was going to have tea with, that she had begged you to let her have tea with, this person, whose name she had produced under the pressure of necessity, was not the person at all, it was someone else, something quite different. What? Who was the other person? Alas, those fragmented eyes, sadly reaching into the distance, might perhaps allow you to judge distances, but not directions. The field of possibilities extends to infinity, and if by chance the truth appeared before us, it would be so utterly improbable that, suddenly stunned, we should charge into this wall that had appeared from nowhere and knock ourselves out. Actual movement, observed flight are not even necessary, it is enough that we should intuit their possibility. She had promised us a letter, we were calm, no longer in love. The letter does not come, successive posts do not bring one, 'what is happening?', anxiety is reborn and with it, love. These are the creatures we usually fall in love with, only to suffer the more. For each new anxiety they cause us blots out from our eyes a part of their personality. We were resigned to suffering, thinking we loved something outside ourselves, and we come to realize that our love is a function of our sadness, that perhaps it is our sadness, and that its object is only to a small extent the young girl with raven hair. But there it is, these are the creatures that above all inspire love. Most often love has for its object a body only if an emotion, the fear of losing the loved object, the uncertainty of finding it again, are fused with that body. Now this kind of anxiety has a great affinity for bodies. It gives them a quality which surpasses even beauty: that is one of the reasons why we see men, indifferent to the most beautiful women, fall in love with certain others who seem to us ugly. To those creatures, creatures of flight, their nature, our anxiety attaches wings. And even when they are with us, their eyes seem to say that they are about to fly away. The proof of this beauty beyond beauty which is lent to them by their wings, is that often the same being is first wingless for us, and then winged. As soon as we fear losing it, we forget all others. If we are sure of keeping it, we can compare it to others and quickly prefer them. And as these emotions and certainties can vary from one week to the next, a person can one week see everything that previously pleased us sacrificed to her, and the next week be sacrificed herself, and this can go on for a long time. All this would be incomprehensible if we did not know, from the experience every man has of having, at least once in his life, stopped loving a woman, of having forgotten her, how insignificant in itself a human being is when it has ceased to be, or has not yet become, permeable to our emotions. And certainly if we use the phrase 'creatures of flight', it is equally true of imprisoned creatures, the captive women whom we feel we shall never possess. Men hate procuresses, because they encourage flight, hold out temptations, but if they are in love with a woman who is shut away, they will seek out a procuress to help her escape and bring her to us. If relationships with women who have been 'carried off' end more quickly than others, it is because the fear of not being able to win them or the apprehension of their escape was all our love, and once stolen from their husbands or torn from their theatres, cured of the temptation to leave us, in a word dissociated from our emotion, whatever it is, they are only themselves, that is, next to nothing, and, having been so long desired, they are soon left by the very man who was so afraid of being left by them.

I said: 'Why hadn't I guessed?' But had I not guessed from the first day in Balbec? Had not I recognized in Albertine one of those girls under whose fleshly covering there palpitate more hidden beings, not just than in a deck of cards still in its box, in a locked cathedral or a theatre before the doors open, but in the whole vast, ever-changing crowd? Not simply so many beings, but the desire for, the voluptuous memory of, the anxious search for so many more. At Balbec I had not been worried by this, because I had never imagined that I should one day be following trails, even false ones. But still this multiplicity had given Albertine the plenitude of a being filled to overflowing with so many other, superimposed beings, so many desires for and pleasure-laden memories of other beings. And now that she had once said to me 'Mlle Vinteuil' I longed, not to tear off her dress and see her body, but to see through her body to the whole note-book of her memories and plans for further, ardent lovers' meetings.

What an extraordinary value the most insignificant things take on as soon as the person we love (or whom it will take only this piece of duplicity to make us love) hides them from us! Pain in itself does not necessarily produce love or hatred in us for the person who causes it: we remain indifferent to a surgeon who hurts us. But a woman who has been telling us for some time that we are everything to her, without her being quite everything to us, a woman whom we delight in seeing, kissing, taking on our knees, surprises us if we sense, from a sudden resistance, that she is not completely at our disposal. Disappointment can then awaken in us the forgotten memory of an old sorrow, which we know was not caused by this woman, but by others whose treacheries punctuate our past. How, then, can one dare hope to go on living, how can one take the least step to preserve oneself from death, in a world where love is provoked only by lies and consists only of our need to have our sufferings calmed by the person who makes us suffer? To escape from the dejection we experience when we discover this lie, this moment of resistance, there is the sad expedient of trying, without her knowledge, using people who we feel are closer to her everyday life than we are, to act upon the woman who is lying to us and resisting us, to become devious ourselves, to make her hate us. But the pain of such a love is of the kind that makes the patient seek in changes of position an illusory relief. Such means of action are not hard to find, alas! And the horror of these loves born only of anxiety comes from the way we sit in our cages, turning over and over insignificant remarks; to say nothing of the fact that the creatures we love in this way rarely appeal completely to us physically, since it is not our conscious taste, but a chance moment of suffering, a moment endlessly multiplied by our weakness of character, which returns each evening to its experiments and descends to the use of sedatives, that made the original choice for us. No doubt my love for Albertine was not the most impoverished of those to which the want of will-power can reduce us, since it was not entirely platonic; she did give me physical pleasures, and she was also intelligent. But all that was secondary. What stayed in my mind was not something intelligent she might have said, but some remark that aroused my suspicion about her actions. I tried to remember whether she had said this or that, with what expression, at what moment, in response to what words of mine, to reconstitute the whole dialogue of her scene with me, at what point she had said she wanted to go to the Verdurins', what it was I had said that had given her face its angry expression. I could not have been more concerned to establish the truth, to reconstitute the atmosphere and exact colour of the most important event. No doubt these anxieties, even when they have reached an intolerable intensity, can sometimes be wholly pacified for a single evening. Our friend is to attend a party, and for days we have been worrying about what kind of party it will be. Suddenly we are asked too, our friend has eyes only for us, talks only to us, we take her home and, with all our worries set aside, enjoy a repose as complete, as restorative as the deep sleep which follows upon long marches. But usually we are only changing one anxiety for another. One of the phrases which was supposed to set our mind at rest sets off our suspicions on a new track. Certainly, such relief is worth a high price. But would it not have been simpler not to buy, of our own free will, new worries, and more dearly than before? In any case, we know very well that however deep these moments of respite may be, anxiety will soon have the upper hand again. Often it is renewed by the phrase that was supposed to bring us relief. The demands of our jealousy and the extent of our blind credulity are both greater than the woman we love could have imagined. When she swears, unasked, that such-and-such a man is just a good friend, we are horrified to learn – what we had never suspected – that he is a friend at all. While she displays her sincerity by telling us how they had tea together, this very afternoon, with every word that she says the invisible, the unsuspected take shape before our eyes. She admits that he asked her to be his mistress, and we are tortured by the idea of her listening to his advances. She said no, she says. But soon, going through her account again, we shall wonder if she really refused, for between the various things she said there is a lack of that logical, necessary connection which, rather than the facts one recounts, is the sign of truth. And then she used that dreadful tone of contempt: 'I said no, absolutely not' which one hears at every level of society when a woman is lying. And yet we must thank her for having refused, encourage her by our kindness to make more such agonizing confessions in the future. At the most we remark, 'But if he had already propositioned you, why did you agree to have tea with him? – So that he wouldn't be angry with me and say I had been unkind.' And we do not dare point out that to have refused would perhaps have been kinder to us.

Albertine always alarmed me when she said that I was quite right to protect her reputation by saying that I was not her lover, since, as she said, 'you aren't, are you, not really'. Perhaps I was not, in the complete sense, but was I then to think that she did with other men all the things that we did together, only to say that she had not been their mistress? Knowing at all costs what Albertine was thinking, whom she was seeing, whom she loved – how strange it was that I should sacrifice everything to this need, given that I had felt the same need, in relation to Gilberte, for knowledge of proper names, facts which were now so indifferent to me! I knew quite well that in themselves Albertine's actions held no greater interest. It is strange how a first love, by the lesions it leaves on our heart, may open the way for later loves, but yet fail to offer us, in the identical character of our symptoms and sufferings, the means of curing them. In any case, do we need to know any single fact? Do we not have an initial, general understanding of the habits of lying and even of discretion of these women who have something to hide? Can we possibly be mistaken? They pride themselves on their silence when we long to make them speak. And we can hear them saying to their accomplice, 'I never say anything. He won't learn anything from *me*, I never say a word.'

We give up our fortunes, our very lives for someone, even while knowing that at ten years' distance, earlier or later, we would hold back the fortune, hold on to the life. For then this being would be detached from us, on its own and therefore a blank. What attaches us to other human beings is the thousand tiny roots, the innumerable threads formed by memories of the previous evening, hopes for the following morning; it is this continuous web of habit from which we cannot extricate ourselves. Just as there are misers who pile up wealth from generous motives, we are prodigals who spend from avarice, and we sacrifice our lives not so much to a particular human being, but to all the sum of our hours, our days that he has managed to accrete around himself, everything in comparison with which the life we have still to live, the relatively future life, seems to us a life more distant, more detached, less close to us, less ours. What we would need to do would be to break these bonds which are so much more important to us than he is, but they have the effect of creating in us a transient sense of obligation to him; we feel obliged not to leave him for fear of incurring his displeasure, whereas later we would do so, since then, detached from us, he would no longer be us; in reality, we are only creating obligations (even if, paradoxically, they drive us to suicide) towards ourselves.

If I did not love Albertine (and I was not sure whether I did or not), her place in my household was not extraordinary: we choose to live only with the thing we do not love, which we have brought to live with us precisely in order to kill off intolerable love, whether the thing in question is a woman, a country or a woman embodying a country. We would even be afraid of beginning to love once more, were the thing once more absent from us. I had not reached this point with Albertine. Her lies, her confessions left me with the unfinished task of uncovering the truth. Her lies were so numerous, because she did not simply lie in the way all human beings do when they believe themselves to be loved, but because she was by nature, quite independently, mendacious and, what is more, so changeable that even if she had told me the truth every time I asked, for example, what she thought of a person, the answer would have been different each time. Her confessions were so few and stopped so short that they left between them, in so far as they concerned the past, great blanks which it was my duty to fill in with the story of her life, which I therefore had to learn. As for the present, in so far as I could interpret Françoise's deliberately cryptic utterances, it was not just on particular points but on a whole range of things that Albertine was lying to me, as I should 'find out one fine day'; Françoise pretended to know the answer already, but would not tell me, and I dared not ask. No doubt it was the same jealousy she had once felt towards Eulalie that made Françoise drop the most improbable hints, so vague that they seemed to add up to no more than the unlikely suggestion that the poor captive (who preferred women) was angling for a marriage to someone who did not quite seem to be me. If that had been true, how could Françoise, for all her telepathic powers, have known about it? Certainly Albertine's accounts of her doings could offer me no certainty on the subject, for they were as different every day as the colours of a top which is slowing to a halt. In any case, it did seem as if Françoise's stories were inspired by hatred. No day passed without her saying to me, and my submitting to hear, in my mother's absence, things like: 'Of course, *you* are kind and I shall never forget everything I owe you (this probably so that I should create new claims on her gratitude). But the air in this house has been poisoned, ever since someone who is kindness itself has brought trickery into it, since the picture of intelligence has started protecting the stupidest creature ever seen. To see a gentleman with brains, manners, taste, dignity in everything, a real prince and not just in his ways, letting a vulgar, vicious creature, the lowest of the low, lay down the law to him, hatch her plots, and humiliate a person who has served this family for forty years.'

Françoise particularly held against Albertine the fact of having to take orders from someone outside the family, and the extra housework tired our old servant to the point of impairing her health (not that she became any readier to accept help with her work: *she* wasn't one of those 'useless females'). All this would have explained her irritation, her malevolent rages. Certainly she would have liked to see Albertine–Esther banished. That was Françoise's wish. And by relieving her feelings, it would already have given a respite to our old servant. But, in my opinion, that was not the whole story. Such hatred could have been born only in an exhausted body. And more even than regard for her feelings, Françoise needed sleep.

While Albertine was taking off her things, and to make my plans as quickly as possible, I picked up the telephone receiver and invoked the implacable Divinities, but succeeded only in arousing their ire, which expressed itself in the words 'The number is engaged.' Andrée was busy talking to someone else. While I waited for her to finish her call, I let myself wonder why, when so many of our painters are trying to revive the traditions of female portraiture of the eighteenth century, with its ingenious settings forming a pretext for expressions of anticipation, pique, interest or reverie, none of our modern Bouchers or Fragonards has painted, instead of *The Letter*, *The Harpsichord*, etc., the scene which could be called *On the Telephone*, with, playing on the lips of the lady listener, a smile all the more genuine because she knows it is unseen. Finally Andrée heard me say, 'Are you calling for Albertine tomorrow?' and as I pronounced Albertine's name, I thought of how I had envied Swann when he had said, on the day of the Princesse de Guermantes's party, 'You must come and see Odette,' and I had thought what strength there was in a name which in the eyes of the whole world and in Odette's own eyes had only in the mouth of Swann this sense of absolute possession. Such control – summed up in a single word – over the whole of a human existence must be so delightful, I had thought every time I was in love. But in reality, once one can speak that word, either one's power has become indifferent, or else habit has not blunted one's love, but has changed all its pleasures into pains. Lying is a trivial thing, we live in the midst of it and simply smile at it, we practise it without imagining we are hurting anyone, but jealousy suffers from it and sees in it more than is really behind it (often our friend refuses to spend the evening with us and goes to the theatre simply so that we shall not see her looking off-colour), just as it often is blind to what is hidden by truth. But jealousy cannot be satisfied, for women who swear that they are not lying would not admit to their true character even under the knife. I knew that only I could say 'Albertine' to Andrée in that particular way. And yet I knew that I was nothing to Albertine, to Andrée, to myself. And I understood the impossible obstacle facing love. We imagine that love has for its object a being which can lie down before us, enclosed in a body. Alas! It is the extension of that body to every point in space and time which that being has occupied or will occupy. If we do not grasp its point of contact with a given place, a given time, then we do not possess it. But we cannot touch all these points. If at least they were indicated to us, perhaps we could stretch out to reach them. But we can only feel for them blindly. Hence our mistrust, our jealousy, our persecutions. We waste irreplaceable time on an absurd trail and pass by the truth without knowing it.

But already one of the irascible Divinities, she of the dizzyingly fleet-fingered handmaidens, was becoming angry, not at my speaking but at my failing to speak. 'Speak up, sir, the line is clear! You've been connected for such a long time, I'm going to cut you off.' But she did not, and instead produced Andrée for me, wrapped, thanks to the poetic magic shared by all young ladies of the telephone, in the unique atmosphere of the home, the neighbourhood, the very life of Albertine's friend. 'Is that you?' said Andrée, her voice conveyed to me with instant speed by the goddess who has the power to make sounds move faster than light. 'Listen, I answered, go wherever you like, anywhere, except Mme Verdurin's. You simply must keep Albertine away from there tomorrow. – But that's exactly where she's planning to go tomorrow. – Oh.' But at that point I had to stop speaking and make threatening gestures, for while Françoise still refused – as if it were something as unpleasant as vaccination or as dangerous as flying – to learn to use the telephone, which would have allowed her to make our calls for us, at least those that she could safely know about, on the other hand she invariably came into my room as soon as I was making any call that I was determined to keep secret from her. When she finally left the room, having painstakingly removed various objects which had been there since the day before and could perfectly well have waited for another hour or two, and put back on the fire a log whose heat was made quite superfluous by the burning sensation caused in me by her intrusion and the fear of being 'cut off' by the young lady, 'Sorry, I said to Andrée, I was interrupted. You're absolutely sure that she means to go to the Verdurins' tomorrow? – Absolutely, but I can tell her you'd rather she didn't. – No, don't do that, what I thought is that I might come with you. – Oh,' said Andrée, sounding rather put out, almost as if she were alarmed by my daring, which only increased as a result. 'So I'll ring off now; I'm sorry to have troubled you for nothing. – Not at all, said Andrée, adding (for now that the telephone was in common use, a decorative language of special phrases had grown up around it, as formerly around 'tea-parties'), it's a pleasure to hear your voice.'

I could have said the same, and more truthfully than Andrée, for I had just been particularly struck by her voice, never having noticed before how different it was from others I had heard. And so I began to recall other voices, women's voices especially, some slowed down by the precision of a question and attention to the reply, others out of breath and even brought to a brief halt by the lyric enthusiasm of the story they were telling; I remembered one by one all the voices of the young girls I had known at Balbec, then Gilberte's, then my grandmother's, then Mme de Guermantes's, I found them all different, each moulded to a language peculiar to its owner, each played on a different instrument, and I thought to myself what a poor concert must be given in Heaven by the three or four angel-musicians of the old painters, when I saw rising up towards God the dozens, hundreds, thousands, the many-sounding, harmonious salutation of all the Voices. I did not hang up the telephone without a few, propitiatory words of thanks to Her who reigns over the speed of sounds, for having deigned to endow my humble words with a power which made them a hundred times faster than thunder. But my prayer of thanksgiving met with no other reply than being 'cut off'.

When Albertine came back into my room, she was wearing a black satin dress which made her skin paler, gave her the look of the pallid Parisienne, intense, her colour destroyed by the want of fresh air, the atmosphere of crowds and perhaps habits of vice, whose eyes seemed more anxious because not brightened by any pinkness in the cheeks. 'Guess who I've just been talking to on the telephone, I said, Andrée. – Andrée?' she cried, with a note of astonishment and emotion not demanded by such a simple piece of news. 'I hope she remembered to tell you that we met Mme Verdurin the other day. – Mme Verdurin? I don't remember,' I answered, as if thinking of something else, both in order to seem indifferent to this meeting and so as not to betray Andrée, who had told me where Albertine was going the following afternoon. But who knows if she, Andrée, were not betraying me, if she would not tell Albertine that I had begged her at all costs to stop her going to the Verdurins', if she had not already given away to her that I had often made such requests in the past. She swore to me that she had never repeated them, but the force of this promise was counterbalanced in my mind by my impression that for some time now Albertine's face no longer showed the confidence in me that she had had for so long.

The pain of love sometimes stops for a moment, but only to return in a different form. We weep to see the one we love no longer drawn to us by rushes of spontaneous feeling, no longer taking the initiative in loving as she did in the early days; we suffer even more to think that, having lost them for us, she perhaps now has these feelings for others; then we are distracted from that pain by a new, more desperate one, the suspicion that she lied to us about where she was the previous evening, when no doubt she was deceiving us; that suspicion also fades, our friend's sweetness to us pacifies us; but then a forgotten remark comes back into our mind, someone once told us that she was passionate in her love-making, whereas we have only ever seen her calm; we try to imagine what her frenzy with others could have been like, we realize how little we mean to her, we find a hint of boredom, of nostalgia, of sadness in her manner when we are speaking to her, we notice with foreboding the simple dresses she wears when with us, keeping for others the splendid ones with which, at the beginning, she tried to dazzle us. If for once she is affectionate, what a moment of joy! But seeing that little tongue poking out, like a signal to attract someone's eyes, we think of all the girls at whom it was directed, so often that even when Albertine was with me, and not thinking of them, it had become, from long habit, an automatic sign. Then the feeling returns that we are boring her. But suddenly that pain shrinks to something insignificant at the thought of the dastardly presence in her life, the unknowable places she has been, perhaps still is during the hours when we are not with her, assuming she is not intending to go and live there permanently: those places where she is far from us, does not belong to us, is happier than when with us. Such is the revolving fire of jealousy.

Jealousy is also a demon that cannot be exorcized and always reappears, clad in a new form. Even if we managed to exterminate them all, to hold on to the one we loved for ever, the Evil One would take on a new, still more pathetic form: despair at having been able to win her fidelity only by force, despair at not being loved.

Between Albertine and myself there was often the barrier of a silence made up no doubt of grievances which she kept to herself, believing them beyond repair. However sweet Albertine could be on some evenings, there were no more of those spontaneous reachings-out that I had seen in her at Balbec, when she would say, 'You really *are* nice, you know!' and the depths of her heart seemed to move towards me, uninhibited by any of her present grievances, which remained unspoken, no doubt because she judged them irreparable, unforgettable though unadmitted, but which still placed between her and myself the telling caution of her words or the gap of an uncrossable silence.

'And why did you telephone Andrée, or is it a secret? – To ask if she wouldn't mind my joining you tomorrow and paying the Verdurins the visit I've been promising them since La Raspelière. – As you please, but I should warn you that there's a terrible fog this evening and I'm sure it will be the same tomorrow. I'm telling you because I don't want you to make yourself ill. If it was up to me, you know I'd much rather you came with us. Anyway, she added with a preoccupied look, I'm not at all sure I shall go to the Verdurins. I really should, they've been so kind to me. Apart from you, they're the people who've done the most for me, but there are some things about their house I don't like. I must go to the *Bon Marché* or the *Trois Quartiers* and buy a white trimming for this dress, it's too black.'

The idea of Albertine's going alone to a department store, rubbing shoulders with so many people, in a place with so many exits that one can say afterwards that on leaving one could not find one's carriage which was waiting down the street, was quite unacceptable to me, but more than anything I felt sad. And still I had not admitted to myself that I should have stopped seeing Albertine long before, for she had entered, in relation to me, that wretched period when a being, dispersed in space and time, is no longer a woman in our eyes, but a series of events on which we cannot shed light, a series of insoluble problems, a sea which, like Xerxes, we absurdly try to beat, to punish it for all that it has swallowed up. Once this period has begun, one is inevitably defeated. Happy are those who see it in time not to be drawn into a useless, exhausting battle, surrounded on all sides by the limits of our imagination, where jealousy struggles so humiliatingly that the same man who once, if the eyes of his constant companion fell for a moment on another man, imagined a conspiracy, suffered who knows what torments, may later allow her to go out alone, sometimes with the man he knows is her lover, choosing this torture which is at least familiar in preference to the terrible unknown. It is a question of finding a rhythm which one afterwards follows from habit. Some sufferers from nervous ailments will not miss a dinner-party, after which they follow rest-cures which never seem long enough; women lately loose now live a life of penance. Jealous men who sacrificed their sleep, lived without rest in order to spy on the woman they loved, feeling now that her desires, the world with all its secrets, time itself are too strong for them, first let her go out without them, then travel, and finally separate from her. Jealousy finally peters out for want of fuel and lasted as long as it did only because it endlessly sought new supplies. I was far from having reached this state.

Certainly I controlled much more of Albertine's time than I had at

Balbec. I could now go out with her as often as I wanted to. As aircraft hangars had quickly grown up around Paris – they are to aeroplanes what harbours are to boats – and ever since the day at La Raspelière when my almost mythical meeting with an aviator, whose flight overhead had made my horse rear, had become for me a kind of image of freedom, I liked – and Albertine, with her passion for all sports, agreed – to conclude our days out with a visit to one of these aerodromes. We went there, she and I, drawn by the incessant bustle of arrivals and departures which enlivens walks on piers and even by the shore for those who like the sea, and attracts to airfields those who like the sky. At every moment, among the resting and, as it were, anchored craft, we would see one being dragged along by several mechanics, as a boat is dragged along the sand for a tourist who wants to go for a sail. The engine was started, the plane was running, it gathered speed, finally, suddenly, at right angles, it rose,[10] slowly, in rigid ecstasy, as if motionless, its horizontal speed transformed into majestic, vertical climbing. Albertine could not contain her joy and would ask for explanations from the mechanics who, now that the craft was safely launched, were coming back. The passenger meanwhile was quickly covering the miles, the great ship on which our eyes were still fixed was no more than an indistinct point in the sky, though it would slowly recover its materiality, its size, its volume when it was time to return to the harbour. And we gazed enviously, Albertine and I, on the passenger who had been out at sea, in those solitary horizons, enjoying the limpid calm of the evening. Then from the aerodrome, or from some church or museum that we had been visiting, we would come home in time for dinner. And yet I was not pacified, as I had been at Balbec by our less frequent outings, which made me so proud if they lasted a whole afternoon, and on which my mind dwelt afterwards, seeing them standing out like imposing floral borders from the rest of Albertine's life, as if against an empty sky where one's eyes can rest thoughtlessly, in a dream. Albertine's time did not belong to me then in the measure it did today. And yet it seemed much more mine, because I counted only – as a great favour to my love – the hours that she spent with me; and now – my anxious jealousy seeking in them opportunities for betrayal – only the hours we spent apart.

Now, tomorrow, she was sure to want some of these. I would have to choose to stop suffering, or to stop loving. For, just as it is first created by desire, love is later kept alive only by painful anxiety. I could feel that part of Albertine's life escaped me. Love, in painful anxiety as in happy desire, is the need for complete possession. It is born, it lives only for so long as there is something left to conquer. We love only that which we do not wholly possess. Albertine was lying when she said that she would probably not go to the Verdurins', just as I was lying when I said I did want to go there. She was simply trying to stop me going out with her, and I, by the sudden mention of this plan which I had no intention of carrying out, to touch her at the point where I felt she was most vulnerable, to hunt down the desire she was hiding and make her admit that my presence at her side tomorrow would prevent her from satisfying it. She had already done that, in fact, when she suddenly lost interest in going to the Verdurins'.

'If you don't want to come to the Verdurins',' I said, 'there's a marvellous charity performance at the Trocadéro.' She listened to this piece of advice with an expression of deep gloom. I was starting to be unkind to her again, as I had been at Balbec, in the days of my first jealousy. Her face showed her disappointment and I used against my friend the same arguments that had so often been used against me by my parents when I was small and which had seemed so stupid and cruel to my misunderstood childhood. 'No, I don't care how long a face you pull,' I would say to Albertine, 'I'm not sorry for you, I'd be sorry for you if you were sick, if something bad had happened to you, if you'd lost one of your relations, though that might not upset you at all, given the way you throw away your feelings on things that don't matter. Anyway, I don't think much of the feelings of people who say how much they love someone and then can't do the least thing to help them, and who are so busy thinking of the person that they can't remember to post a letter for them, even when their whole future depends on it.'

All of these words — for a large part of what we say is merely recitation — I had already heard from my mother, who (concerned as she was that I should not confuse real sensibility, which the Germans, whose language she greatly admired despite my father's loathing for that nation, called *Empfindung*, and mere tearfulness, *Empfindelei*) once went so far, when I was crying, as to say to me that Nero might have been highly strung, but that did not make him any more admirable. In truth, as in those plants which develop double forms as they grow, over against the nervous child which I had once alone been, there now stood a man who was the opposite: full of good sense, stern with the over-sensitivity of others, a man who was to others what my parents had been to me. No doubt, since everyone must carry on in himself the life of his progenitors, the steady, humorous man who had not existed in me at the beginning had come to join the sensitive one, and it was natural that I should become in turn what my parents had been. Furthermore, as this new me took shape, he found his words ready and waiting for him in the memory of the ironic, reproving language that had been used to me, and which I was now to use to others, and which came to my lips quite naturally, whether I was reviving it by imitation and association of memories, or whether the delicate and mysterious incrustations of genetic power had also drawn in me, without my knowing, patterns like those on the leaves of a plant: the same intonations, the same gestures, the same postures as had belonged to those from whom I sprang. For sometimes, as I played the wise man to Albertine, I seemed to hear my grandmother speaking. Had my mother not had the experience (such were the obscure, unconscious influences moulding even the way I flexed my fingers, to make them conform to the same patterns as my parents') of thinking that it was my father who was coming in, so similar was my way of knocking to his? After all, the coupling of opposites is the law of life, the principle of fertilization and, as we shall see, the cause of much misery. Normally, we detest what is like us, and our own failings, seen in others, exasperate us. How much more a person who has passed the age when weaknesses are voiced naïvely, and who has learned to keep an icy countenance at the most burning moments, will execrate these same failings, if it is another person, younger, more naïve or more foolish, who gives them expression. There are some sensitive people for whom the sight, in the eyes of another, of the tears that they themselves are holding back, is insufferable. It is over-strong resemblance that divides families despite the affection between their members, and sometimes all the more the fonder they are of each other. Perhaps in me, and in many people, the second man I had become was only another face of the first, idealistic and sensitive in his dealings with himself, a sage Mentor to others. Maybe the same was true of my parents according as one considered them in relation to me or in themselves. It was only too easy to see that my grandmother and my mother forced themselves to be strict with me, and perhaps even suffered as they did so, but perhaps even my father's coldness was an outward manifestation of his sensibility? For it was perhaps the human truth of this double aspect, one side facing the inner life, the other social relationships, that people meant to express in those words which seemed to me in those days as false in their content as they were banal in their expression: 'Behind his chilly exterior, he's extraordinarily sensitive; he's ashamed to show his feelings, that's what it is.' Had it not perhaps been a cover for constant, secret storms within, that calm marked where necessary by sententious observations, by ironic responses to clumsy manifest-ations of sensibility, which was so characteristic of him, but which I myself now affected in all my dealings with others, and in particular never set aside when discussing certain topics with Albertine?

I believe that that day I was really about to decide to break with her and leave for Venice. What chained me again to the relationship had to do with Normandy, not that Albertine showed any intention of going to that part of the country where I had first been jealous of her (for her plans fortunately never took her near the real danger points in my memory), but because, when I happened to say to her 'That would be like talking about your aunt's friend who lived in Infreville,' she angrily replied, with the joy of a person who wants to have all the arguments on her side, to show me that I was wrong and she always in the right: 'But my aunt doesn't know anyone at Infreville, I've never even been there.' She had forgotten the lie she had told me one evening about the easily offended lady at whose house she absolutely had to go and have tea, even if seeing the lady were to cost her my friendship, even if she died in the attempt. I didn't remind her of her lie. But it dealt me a terrible blow. And again I put off the separation to another day. To be loved, one need not be sincere, nor even good at lying. By love, I mean here a kind of mutual torture. I saw nothing wrong, this evening, in speaking to her as my grandmother, that excellent woman, had spoken to me, nor in using, to tell her I would be going to the Verdurins' with her, the same brusque manner as my father, who never told us of a decision except in the way that would cause us the maximum, and in this case wholly disproportionate, anxiety. In this way it was easy for him to find us absurd for showing such dismay at something so unimportant, when in fact the reason was the upset he had caused us. And if – like my grandmother's inflexible wisdom – these arbitrary impulses of my father's had come to complete in me the sensitive nature to which they had so long been alien, and to which, throughout my childhood, they had caused so much suffering, the same sensitive nature kept them very precisely informed of the most effective points at which to aim: there is no better police informer than a retired thief, or spy than a subject of the nation we wish to conquer. In certain families given to lying, a brother who visits his brother for no obvious reason and asks him, apropos of nothing, in the doorway, as he is leaving, a question the answer to which he hardly seems to take in, conveys to his brother by his very off-handedness that this question was the purpose of his visit, for the brother recognizes the faraway look, the words spoken as if between brackets, at the last moment, from having often used them himself. Now there are also pathological families, related sensibilities, sibling temperaments, initiated into that silent language which allows families to understand each other without speaking. After all, who can 'string us up' more than the highly strung? And then, there was perhaps a more general, deeper cause for my behaviour on these occasions. It is that, during those brief but inevitable moments when one hates someone one loves – moments that can last a lifetime with people one does not – one does not wish to appear good, and be pitied, but evil – as evil as possible and as happy as possible, so that one's happiness should be really detestable and eat into the soul of the temporary or permanent enemy. I have told dreadful, invented stories about myself to so many people, simply so that my 'conquests' should seem immoral to them, and make them all the more furious. One ought, of course, to do the opposite: show, without ostentation, that one has good feelings, rather than hiding them so carefully. And it would be easy if one knew how never to hate, always to love. Then, one would be so happy only ever to say the things that make other people happy, make them warm to one, love one!

Certainly, I felt some remorse about being so irritating to Albertine, and I said to myself, 'If I didn't love her, she'd be more grateful to me, for then I wouldn't be nasty to her; no, that's not right, it would balance out, for I wouldn't be so nice to her either.' And I could have justified myself by telling her that I loved her. But admitting my love in this way, besides the fact that it would not have told Albertine anything she did not already know, would perhaps have made her cool towards me even more than the very unkindnesses and the tricks for which love was the only excuse. Unkindness and deviousness in love are so natural! If the interest we take in other people does not prevent us from being gentle with them and helpful to them in their wishes, then that interest is feigned. Other people are a matter of indifference to us, and indifference does not prompt us to cruelty.

The evening was passing away; there was not much time to spare before Albertine went to bed, if we wanted to make it up and start kissing again. Neither of us had yet made the first move. Sensing that she was angry in any case, I took the opportunity of speaking to her about Esther Levy. 'Bloch told me', I lied, 'that you used to be a good friend of his cousin Esther's.' 'I wouldn't know her if I saw her,' said Albertine with a vague look. 'I've seen her picture,' I added angrily. I did not look at Albertine as I said this, so that I did not see her expression, which would have been her only reply, since she did not speak.

What I experienced with Albertine on these evenings was not the calming effect of my mother's kiss at Combray, but on the contrary, the anguish of the evenings when my mother said good-night to me only hurriedly, or worse, did not come up to my room at all, whether she was cross with me or kept downstairs by guests. That anguish, not its transposition into love, but the anguish itself, which had once been hived off to love, assigned to that single passion when the division, the specialization of the passions had taken place, now seemed to spread again over them all, to have returned to its undifferentiated state, as if all my feelings, which trembled at being unable to keep

Albertine next to my bed as a mistress, a sister, a daughter all at once, and as a mother whose good-night kiss I was beginning, in childish fashion, to need once more, had begun to coalesce again, to become one in the premature evening of my life, which promised to be no longer than a winter's day. But though I suffered the anguish of my childhood, the changed being who now inspired it, my different feelings about her, the very changes in my own character made it impossible for me to seek peace from Albertine as I had from my mother. I no longer knew how to say 'I am sad.' I restricted myself, with death in my heart, to talking about trivial things which did not help me at all in moving towards a happy solution. I marked time, repeating painful banalities. And with the intellectual egotism that leads us, the moment some insignificant truth seems to have a bearing on our love, to think the world of the person who voiced it, perhaps by sheer chance, like the fortune-teller who makes some commonplace prediction which then comes true, I came near to thinking Françoise more intelligent than Bergotte or Elstir because she had said to me, at Balbec, 'That girl will bring you nothing but grief.'

Every moment brought me closer to Albertine's 'Good-night', which she would eventually say to me. But on these evenings her absent-minded kiss, which did not really touch me, left me so anxious that, with my heart pounding, I would watch her walk to the door, thinking, 'If I want an excuse to call her back, to keep her here, to make up with her, I must hurry, a few more steps and she'll be out of the room, just two more, one, she's turning the handle, she's opening the door, too late, she's closed it.' But perhaps it was not too late. Just as at Combray in the old days, when my mother had left me without her calming kiss, I longed to run after Albertine, I felt that there could be no more peace for me until I had seen her again, that this seeing her again would be something immense that it had never been hitherto, but also, that if I did not manage to overcome this sadness by myself I would perhaps fall into the shameful habit of begging Albertine for comfort; so I would jump out of bed when she was already in her room and walk up and down the corridor, hoping that she would come out of her room and call to me; I would stand stock-still outside her door so as to be sure of hearing even the faintest call, then go back

99

into my own room for a moment to see if my friend had not, by great good luck, left behind a handkerchief, a bag, something that I could seem to think she might need and which would give me a pretext to go into her room. But no. I took up my station outside her door again. But there was now no light under the door. Albertine had put out her light, she was in bed, I stood there motionless, hoping in vain for I am not sure what; and much later, chilled to the bone, I would go back, get under my blankets and cry all the rest of the night.

So sometimes, on those evenings, I used a trick to get Albertine's kiss for myself. Knowing how quickly, once she had lain down, she fell asleep (she knew it too, for instinctively, as soon as she stretched out, she took off the mules I had given her and her ring, which she put down beside her as she did in her own room before going to bed), knowing how soundly she slept and how affectionate she was on waking, I would make the excuse of going to fetch something and persuade her to lie down on my bed. When I came back she would be asleep, and I saw before me the other woman she became when seen full face. But her personality soon changed again, for I would lie down beside her and look at her in profile once more. I could put my hand in hers, touch her shoulder, her cheek, Albertine went on sleeping. I could take her head, tip it back, place it against my lips, put my arms round her neck, she went on sleeping like a watch that never stops, like an animal that goes on living whatever position you put it in, like a climbing plant, a convolvulus that goes on throwing out branches whatever kind of support you give it. Only her breathing was affected by each of my touches, as if she had been an instrument I was playing and from which I drew new chords by producing from one and then another of its strings a variety of notes. My jealousy was being calmed, for I felt that Albertine had become a creature of respiration and nothing more, as was shown by her regular breathing, the expression of this purely physiological function, which in its fluidity lacks the consistency of either speech or silence; lacking all knowledge of evil, this sound, which seemed to be drawn from a hollow reed rather than a human being, was truly heavenly for me who at those moments felt Albertine removed from everything, not just materially but morally; it was the pure song of the Angels. And still in this breathing, I would suddenly say to myself, human names, the residue of memory, must be suspended.

Sometimes, indeed, the music of breathing was supplemented by the human voice. Albertine spoke some words. If only I could have understood them! The name of a person we had been talking about, someone I was jealous of, might rise to her lips, but without making me unhappy, since it seemed that the memory that accompanied the name was simply that of the conversations she had had with me about its owner. All the same, one evening, just as she was waking, with her eyes still shut, she spoke lovingly to me, calling me 'Andrée'. I hid my alarm. 'You're dreaming, I'm not Andrée,' I said laughingly. She smiled too: 'Don't be silly, I wanted to ask you what Andrée had been talking to you about this afternoon. – I'd be more inclined to think you had once lain like that next to her. – Of course not, never.' Only, just before making me that answer, she had hidden her face in her hands for a moment. Her silences, it seemed, were only veils, her surface affection kept out of sight a thousand memories which would have torn me apart – her life, then, was full of those events the mocking account of which, recounted with laughter, fills up our everyday chatter about others, those we do not care about; but when a creature is lodged in our heart every such detail seems to cast such precious light on its life that to know this hidden world we would gladly sacrifice our own. Her slumber seemed to me then like a wonderful, magic world where there can rise up, through the barely translucent element, the revelation of a secret which we shall not understand. But normally, when Albertine was sleeping, she seemed to have recovered her innocence. In the position where I had placed her, but which in sleep she quickly made her own, she seemed to be trusting herself to me. Her face had lost any expression of deviousness or vulgarity, and when she raised her arm towards me or laid her hand upon me, each of us seemed entirely given up to the other, indissolubly joined. Besides, her sleep did not take her away from me; the notion of our affection survived somewhere in her; it was all the rest that was wiped out; I could kiss her and say I was going out for a little walk, she would half-open her eyes and say in astonishment – it was already night-time – 'But where are you going, darling?' calling me by my name, and then go straight back to sleep. Her slumber was a kind of blotting-out of the rest of life, a level silence from which familiar words of affection would sometimes take flight. By piecing these words together one could have composed the perfect conversation, the secret intimacy of pure, unalloyed love. The calm of her sleep delighted me as a child's sound sleep delights its mother, who elevates it into a moral virtue. And hers was a child's sleep. Her awakening too: it was so natural, so tender, even before she knew where she was, that I sometimes asked myself trembling whether she had lost the habit, before she came to me, of sleeping alone, and was used to waking to find someone else beside her. But her childish grace overpowered me. Like a mother again, I marvelled at the way she always woke in such a good temper. After a few moments she came to herself, and said such charming, disconnected things, like a bird chirping. By a kind of interchange, her neck, which I normally hardly noticed, but which now seemed almost too beautiful, took the place of her eyes, once so important but now veiled in sleep – her eyes, with which I usually communicated but which I could not address now that her lids had closed over them. Just as closed eyes lend an innocent, solemn beauty to the face by eliminating everything that is only too clearly expressed when they are open, the not wholly meaningless but fragmentary words that Albertine spoke as she awoke had the pure beauty that is not constantly sullied, as conversation is, by verbal habits, repetition, traces of incorrect speech. Furthermore, when I decided to wake Albertine, I knew I could safely do so, for her awakening would bear no resemblance to the evening we had just spent together, but would emerge from her sleep as morning does from night. She would smile as she opened her eyes, hold up her mouth to me, and before she had said anything I would have tasted its freshness, calming as that of a garden still silent before the break of day.

The morning after the evening when Albertine had told me that she was, then was not going to the Verdurins', I woke early, and before I was properly awake my joy told me that, interpolated into the midst of winter, this was a day of spring. Outside, a series of popular melodies, elegantly arranged for various instruments, from the china-mender's horn to the chair-caner's trumpet, and including the flute of the goat's-milk seller who, on this fine day, seemed like a Sicilian shepherd, were lightly orchestrating the morning air into a Festival Overture. Hearing, that delightful sense, brings indoors all the company of the street, tracing out its lines, sketching all the forms which pass through it and showing us their colours. The metal grilles of the butcher's or the dairy, which had come down last night, closing off every possibility of feminine attraction, were now going up like the light pulleys of a ship making ready to sail away across the transparent sea on a dream of pretty shop-girls. This sound of grilles going up might have been my only pleasure, had I lived in a different neighbourhood. In this one there were a hundred others for my delight, and I would not have wanted to miss one of them by sleeping too late. The enchantment of old aristocratic quarters is that they are working-class as well. Just as cathedrals had a variety of trades being carried on not far from their doors (and sometimes preserved their names, as at Rouen with its 'Booksellers' Door', from the tradesmen who displayed their goods in the open air directly opposite it), various street-traders would pass in front of the noble Guermantes town house and recall for a moment the France of former times and the power of its Church. For the call that they addressed to the neighbouring small houses did not, except in a very few cases, at all resemble a song. It was as different from it as the declamation – coloured by barely perceptible variations – of *Boris Godunov* or *Pelléas*;[11] on the other hand, it recalled a priest intoning offices of which these street scenes are the good-natured, raffish counterpart, but still half liturgical in their character. I had never enjoyed them so much as I did now that Albertine was living with me. They seemed to me the joyous signal of her awakening and, by involving me in the life outside, made me more conscious of the calming power of a dear presence, now as constant as I could wish. Some of the foodstuffs being sold in the street, which I myself hated, were among Albertine's favourites, so that Françoise sent her kitchen-boy out to buy them, even if he perhaps felt it beneath his dignity to have to mingle in this way with the common herd. The cries sounded clearly in this quiet neighbourhood, where noise was no longer a grievance for Françoise, and had become a source of pleasure to me. Each had its different modulation: they were recitatives

declaimed by these common people, as they would be in the music
of *Boris*, with all its folk influences, where an initial intonation is
barely varied by the inflection of one note leaning on another: music
of the crowd which is more language than music. 'Winkles, winkles,
two sous your winkles' had us rushing to buy the paper cones in
which they sold those ghastly little molluscs which, had it not been
for Albertine, I should have refused in disgust, just like the snails
which I could hear being sold at the same time. Here again the
seller's voice recalled the barely musical declamation of Mussorgsky, but that was not all. For after having delivered 'Snails, snails,
lovely fresh snails' almost *parlando*, it was with the vague sadness of
Maeterlinck, transposed into music by Debussy, that the snail man, in
one of those sorrowful final phrases which the author of *Pelléas* seems
to have learned from Rameau[12] ('If I am to be conquered, must you
be my conqueror?'), added, with melancholy plangency, 'Six sous a
do-zen . . .'

I have never been able to understand why these perfectly clear
words were sighed out in such an inappropriate manner: mysteriously,
like the secret of why everyone is so sad in the old palace where
Mélisande has not been able to bring joy, and profoundly, like a saying
of old Arkel, who tries to utter in very simple words the whole of
wisdom and destiny. The very notes on which the voice of Golaud or
of the old king of Allemonde[13] rises, ever more sweetly, to say 'No
one knows what they will find here. It may seem strange. Perhaps
everything that happens has a meaning,' or 'You must not be frightened
. . . He was a poor, mysterious little thing, like all of us,' were the
ones the snail-seller used to repeat, in an unending cantilena, 'Six sous
the do-zen . . .' But his metaphysical lament did not have time to fade
away to infinity, it was interrupted by a lively trumpet. This time it
was not food, the words of the libretto were, 'We clip dogs, we clip
cats, we cut tails and ears.'

Certainly imagination, the wit of each seller, often introduced
variations into the words of these melodies I heard from my bed. Still
a ritual pause, placing a moment of silence in the middle of a word,
constantly revived the memory of old churches. In the little donkey-
cart which he stopped in front of each house so as to go into the

courtyards, the old-clothes man, whip in hand, would intone, 'Old clothes! Have you any old clo-othes?' with the same gap in the last syllable as if he had been chanting '*Per omnia saecula saeculo-rum*' or '*Requiescat in pa-ce*',[14] even though he could hardly have believed in the eternity of his wares, and was not offering them as shrouds for perpetual rest. And in the same way, as the tunes began to interweave in the morning air, a coster-woman, pushing her cart, used a Gregorian mode for her litany:

> Tender, sweet, fresh to eat,
> Here they are, ar-ti-chokes!

even though she probably knew nothing of the antiphonal and the seven tones, four of them symbolizing the quadrivium and three the trivium.

Drawing from a penny whistle or bagpipes melodies from his southern homeland, whose light the fine morning recalled, a man in a smock with a bludgeon in his hand and wearing a beret, stopped in front of the houses. This was the goat's-milk man with his two dogs and his herd of she-goats in front of him. As he had come a long way he arrived late in our neighbourhood; and the women came running with bowls for the milk which was to build up their children. But the Pyrenean melodies of this beneficent shepherd were already being interrupted by the knife-grinder's bell as he cried 'Knives, scissors, razors.' The saw-doctor, who had no instrument, could not compete with him and was reduced to calling out, 'Sharpen your saws? Sharpen your saws?' while the tinker more cheerily sang a list of all the things he could mend, soup-pots, saucepans and so forth, with the recurring refrain,

> Tinker, tinker, tin, tin, tin
> Any old hole, I'll fill it in

and little Italians carrying large metal boxes painted red and marked with winning and losing numbers, swung their rattles and called out, 'Come on, girls, give it a whirl.'

Françoise brought me the *Figaro*. A glance was enough to show me that my article had still not appeared. She said that Albertine was asking to come in and see me and had asked her to tell me in any case that she had given up her idea of going to the Verdurins' and would be going instead, as I had suggested, to the 'special' matinée at the Trocadéro (this was what would now be called a 'gala' matinée, but on a much less grand scale), after a short ride with Andrée. Now that I knew she had gone back on her perhaps dangerous wish to visit Mme Verdurin, it was with a smile that I said, 'Let her come in!' and I said to myself that she could go wherever she pleased for all I cared. I knew that by the end of the afternoon, when twilight came, I would no doubt be a different man, a sadder one, attaching to Albertine's smallest comings and goings an importance which they did not have now, on this beautiful morning. For my insouciance was accompanied by a clear understanding of its cause, which however did not diminish it. 'Françoise said you were awake and I wouldn't be disturbing you,' Albertine said as she came in. And since, after the danger of giving me a chill by opening her window at the wrong time, Albertine most feared coming into my room when I was still dozing, 'I hope it's all right,' she added. 'I was afraid you'd say

Quel mortel insolent vient chercher le trépas?

And she laughed, with the laugh that always moved me so strongly. I answered in the same joking tone

Est-ce pour vous qu'est fait cet ordre si sévère?

And so that she should never infringe it, I added, 'Though I would be furious if you woke me up.' – 'I know, I know, don't worry,' said Albertine. And to soften my harshness I went on playing the scene from *Esther* with her, while the street cries continued as a wholly confused background to our conversation, saying,

Je ne trouve qu'en vous je ne sais quelle grâce
Qui me charme toujours et jamais ne me lasse[15]

(while thinking to myself, 'She does, though, often'). And remembering what she had said the day before, while I thanked her fulsomely for having given up the Verdurins, so that she would be equally ready to obey me on another occasion, I added: 'Albertine, I love you but you don't trust me: you trust other people who don't love you' (as if it were not natural to mistrust those who love us, the only people who have an interest in lying to us, whether to find things out or to stop us doing what we want), and I added these lying words: 'You don't really believe I love you, it's strange. Of course, I don't *worship* you.' She went on to lie to me, saying that I was the only one she trusted, and then told the truth, assuring me that she knew I loved her. But this statement did not seem to imply that she did not think me a liar or suspect me of spying on her. And she seemed to forgive me, as if she had seen in my jealousy the intolerable consequences of a great love, or as if she had come to see herself as less good.

'Now darling, please, no gymnastics this time, not like the other day. Just think, Albertine, if you were to have an accident!' Naturally I did not wish her any harm. But how wonderful if, once on horseback, she had ridden off into the blue yonder, liked it there, and never come home! How much simpler it would have been if she could have gone and been happy somewhere else, I didn't even want to know where! 'Oh, I know you couldn't live without me, you'd kill yourself within two days.'

This was how we lied to each other. But a deeper truth than the one we would be speaking if we were sincere can sometimes be expressed and foretold by another means than that of sincerity. 'Don't you mind all those noises from outside? she asked. I love them. But you sleep so lightly . . .' On the contrary, I often slept very soundly (as I have said before, but as the event I am soon to speak of forces me to repeat), and especially when I did not get to sleep until early morning. Since that kind of sleep has usually been four times more restorative, it seems to the sleeper to have been four times as long, when in fact it was four times shorter. Splendid, sixteenfold error which lends such beauty to our awakening and introduces a real transformation into life, like one of those great changes of rhythm which in music mean that a quaver in an *andante* lasts as long as a minim in a *prestissimo*, and which never occur in the waking state. There life is almost always the same – hence the disappointments of travel. Dreams do seem sometimes to be made from the coarsest material of life, but this material is processed, kneaded, with an elasticity deriving from the fact that there are none of the time limits of the waking state to prevent its being spun so fine, raised to such heights, as to be unrecognizable. On the mornings when I had had this good fortune, when sleep had wiped from my brain the signs of my daily preoccupations which are written there as if on a blackboard, I had to set my memory going again; by the exercise of will one can relearn what the amnesia of sleep or of a stroke has blanked out: it returns very slowly, as the eyes open or paralysis recedes. I had lived so many hours in a few minutes that when I called Françoise and wanted to speak to her in a language connected to reality and appropriate to the hour, I had to use all my inner powers of control not to say, 'Well, Françoise, here we are, it's five o'clock and I haven't seen you since yesterday afternoon,' and to suppress my dreams. Ignoring them and lying to myself, using all my strength to keep the truth unspoken, I would shamelessly say, 'Françoise, is it ten o'clock yet?' I did not even say 'ten in the morning', so as to be able to speak the unbelievable words in a more convincing manner. Still, to say these words instead of the ones which still seemed true to the half-awakened sleeper cost me the same effort as someone who jumps from a moving train and runs along the track beside it has to make to keep his balance. He runs for a moment because the world he is leaving is a world in rapid movement, very unlike the motionless earth on which his feet do not at first feel at home. Because the world of dreams is not the waking world, it does not follow that the waking world is less real, quite the opposite. In the world of sleep our perceptions are so densely layered, each overlaid by another, superimposed one which duplicates it, obscures it needlessly, that we can hardly work out what is happening in the disorientation of waking; had Françoise come in, or had I tired of calling and gone to look for her? At that moment, silence was the only means of giving nothing away, as when one has been arrested by a judge who is informed about all sorts of things concerning one, but which have not been divulged to oneself. Was it Françoise who had come, was it I who had called out? Wasn't it perhaps Françoise who had been sleeping, and I who had wakened her? Or rather, wasn't Françoise somehow enclosed within me, for distinctions between people and their interactions hardly exist in that sepia darkness where reality is no more translucent than in the body of a porcupine, and where our minimal perceptions can perhaps give an idea of those of certain animals? Furthermore, even in the lucid madness which precedes these periods of heavy sleep, if fragments of wisdom float luminously, if the names of Taine or George Eliot are not unknown, the waking world still enjoys the superiority of being able to be continued every morning, unlike dreams which are different every night. But perhaps there are other worlds more real than the waking world. For have we not seen how the 'real world' is transformed by every revolution in the arts, and without waiting for that, by the degree of aptitude or cultivation which distinguishes an artist from an ignorant fool?

And sometimes an hour of sleep is a paralytic stroke after which we must regain the use of our limbs, learn to speak again. Will is not enough. We have slept too long, we have ceased to exist. Waking is barely experienced, without consciousness, as a pipe might experience the turning-off of a tap. This is followed by a life more inanimate than that of a jelly-fish; one might think one had been dredged up from the depths of the sea, or released from prison, if one could think anything at all. But then the goddess Mnemotechne[16] leans out from heaven and offers us, in the form of 'habit of calling for coffee', the hope of resurrection. But the sudden gift of memory is not always so simple. One often has at hand, in those first minutes when one is letting oneself slip towards awakening, a range of different realities from which one thinks one can choose, like taking a card from a pack. It is Friday morning and one is coming back from a walk, or else it is tea-time at the seaside. The idea of sleep and that one is in bed in one's nightshirt is often the last to occur. Resurrection does not come immediately, you think you have rung, you haven't, you turn over insane ideas in your mind. Movement alone restores thought, and when you have actually pressed the electric bell-push, you can say, slowly but clearly, 'It must be ten o'clock. Bring me my coffee please, Françoise.'

Wonders! Françoise could not have guessed at the sea of unreality in which I was still submerged, and through which I had managed to utter my strange question. For she answered, 'It's ten past,' which made me sound reasonable, and allowed me to keep hidden the strange conversations in which I had been so long caught up (on the days when it was not a mountain of nothingness that had swept my life away). By force of will, I had rejoined the world of reality. I was still enjoying the last remains of sleep, that is to say the only originality, the only novelty which exists in the telling of stories, since all waking narratives, even those embellished by literature, lack the mysterious incongruities which are the true source of beauty. It is easy to speak of the beauty created by opium. But for a man accustomed to depend on sleeping drugs, one unexpected hour of natural sleep will uncover the morning immensity of a landscape just as mysterious and far fresher. Varying the time and place where one goes to sleep, inducing sleep by artificial means or, on the other hand, returning to natural sleep – the strangest of all for those accustomed to rely on sleeping draughts – will produce varieties of sleep a thousand times more numerous than any gardener's varieties of roses or carnations. Gardeners manage to grow some flowers which are like delicious dreams, and others like nightmares. When I fell asleep in a certain manner, I would wake up shivering, thinking I had measles or, much more distressing, that my grandmother (whom I never thought of now) was suffering because I had laughed at her that day in Balbec when she had thought she was dying and wanted me to have a photograph of her. Immediately, even though I was awake, I wanted to go to her and tell her she had misunderstood me. But I was already warming up. The fear of measles was gone and my grandmother so far away from me that she could no longer pain my heart.

Sometimes these various forms of sleep were overshadowed by a sudden darkness. I felt fear as I walked further than usual, into a dark avenue where I could hear prowlers moving about. Suddenly I would hear a argument between a policeman and one of those women who often worked as drivers and whom, from a distance, one could mistake for young coachmen. On her box, surrounded by darkness, I could not see her, but she was speaking, and in her voice I could read the perfections of her face and the youth of her body. I walked towards her, meaning to get into her carriage before she set off again. It was a long way. Fortunately, she was still arguing with the policeman. I got to the carriage while it was still stationary. This part of the avenue was lit by street-lamps. The driver could now be seen. It was a woman, but an old woman, big and strong, with white hair escaping from her peaked cap and a large, red mark disfiguring her face. I would walk away, thinking, 'Is this what happens to the youth of women? We meet them, and then, if suddenly we want to see them again, will they always have grown old? Is the young, desirable woman like one of those stage roles which are created by particular actresses and then, as they decay, inevitably passed on to other stars? But then it is no longer the same role.' Then I was overcome by sadness. We experience in our sleep many instances of Pity, like the different *pietàs* of the Renaissance, but unlike them ours are not carved in marble but evanescent. They have their value, however, which is to keep us in touch with a certain kinder, more humane view of things that is only too easily submerged in the chilly, even hostile good sense of the waking state. Thus I was reminded of the promise I had made to myself at Balbec, always to feel pity for Françoise. And for the rest of that morning at least I would manage not to be irritated by Françoise's quarrels with the butler, and to be gentle with her, in whom others saw so little good. For that morning only, however; and I should have tried to provide myself with a somewhat more stable code of conduct, for, just as a people cannot long be governed by policies based on pure sentiment, men cannot be in thrall to the memory of their dreams. Already this dream was beginning to fade. By trying to hold on to it in order to describe it, I sent it fleeing all the faster. My eyelids were no longer so firmly sealed over my eyes. If I tried to reconstruct my dream, they would open altogether. We constantly have to choose between health and wisdom on the one hand, and spiritual pleasures on the other. I have always been too much of a coward to choose the second. What is more, the dangerous power I was renouncing was even more dangerous than we realize. By deliberately varying the conditions in which we fall asleep, we can forfeit the power, not only of dreaming but of falling asleep: it is not only our dreams that vanish but, sometimes for days or years together, sleep itself, which is divine but unstable: the smallest shock can render it volatile. It is to be found in the company of habit, which anchors it every evening to its accustomed place, preserving it from any disturbance. But if habits are altered, if it is no longer tied to them, it dissolves like a vapour. Like youth and love, once lost it cannot be found again.

In these various kinds of sleep, as in music, it was the augmentation or diminution of the interval that created beauty. I delighted in this beauty, but it was true that my morning sleep, however brief, had cost me a good part of the street-cries that brought home to me the circulating life of the trades and foodstuffs of Paris. So I usually tried to wake early so as not to miss them (without, alas, foreseeing the drama which was soon to be brought into my life by my late waking and the draconian, Persian laws acted out in my Racinian Ahasuerus scenes). As well as the pleasure of knowing how much Albertine liked these cries, and of getting outdoors without leaving my bed, I heard in them a symbol of the atmosphere outside, the dangerous, bustling world in which I would not let her move around except under my guardianship, in a kind of outdoor extension of her confinement, from which I could recall her whenever I wished and make her come home to me.

So it was with complete sincerity that I was able to reply to Albertine, 'Not at all, I like them because I know that you do. – Fresh from the sea, oysters, fresh from the sea – Oh, oysters, I must have some!' Fortunately Albertine's combination of fickleness and docility meant that she quickly forgot her wants, and before I could even say that she would get better ones at Prunier's, she had wanted in turn everything that she heard the fishwife crying: 'Shrimps, lovely shrimps, skate all alive, all alive-oh. – Whiting to fry, whiting! – Here's mackerel, fresh mackerel, new mackerel. Mackerel, ladies, lovely mackerel! – Mussels, all fresh, mussels!' At the words, 'Here's mackerel' I could not suppress a shudder.[17] But as this announcement could hardly apply to my chauffeur, I thought only of the fish I hated and my anxiety was short-lived. 'Ooh, mussels,' said Albertine. 'I'd *love* some mussels.' – 'Darling, mussels at Balbec was one thing, but here they'll be no good; anyway, remember what Cottard said about mussels.' But my remark

was ill-timed, for the next thing we heard was a coster-woman selling
something Cottard disapproved of even more:

> Lettuces-oh, lettuces-oh
> They're not for sale, they're just for show.

Still Albertine agreed to do without the lettuce provided I promised
her that in a few days I would make Françoise buy from the woman
who calls out, 'Lovely Argenteuil asparagus, get your fine asparagus.'
A mysterious voice, which one would have expected to hear making
odder offers, insinuated, 'Barrels, barrels!' One had to swallow one's
disappointment that he was offering only barrels, since the word was
almost completely drowned out by the cry of 'Glazier, mend your
panes, gla-zier', on a Gregorian division; still more reminiscent of
the liturgy, however, was the cry of the rag-and-bone man which
unwittingly reproduced one of those sudden changes of sonority in
the middle of a prayer which are quite frequent in the ritual of
the Church: '*Praeceptis salutaribus moniti et divina institutione formati
audemus dicere*,'[18] says the priest, finishing hurriedly on '*dicere*'. Without irreverence, just as the pious townsfolk of the Middle Ages acted
farces and fools'-plays in front of the cathedrals, the ragman recalled
that '*dicere*' as, having dragged out the words of his call, he spoke the
last syllable with an abruptness worthy of the rules of accentuation of
the great seventh-century pontiff: 'Rags, old iron to sell'[19] (all slowly
intoned, as were the two syllables that followed, while the last one was
dispatched even more rapidly than '*dicere*') 'raa-bbit *skins*'. 'Valencia,
Valencia, oranges straight from Spain', even humble leeks ('Lovely
lovely leeks!'), onions ('Eight sous your onions'), the cries rolled on
for me like an echo of the waves where Albertine, left to herself, could
have been lost, and took on the sweetness of a *Suave mari magno*.[20]

'Carrots, carrots, tuppence a bunch.' 'Oh,' cried Albertine, 'cab-
bages, carrots, oranges. I feel like eating them all. Do have Françoise
buy some. She can cook the carrots in cream. And then we'll eat
everything together, it'll be wonderful. All these sounds that we're
listening to, turned into a lovely meal. No, ask Françoise to make
skate with black butter, won't you, it's so good!' – 'Of course I will,

dearest. But you mustn't stay, otherwise you'll want to buy everything on all the barrows.' 'Right, I'm going, but for our dinners I want us only ever to have the things we've heard being sold in the street. It'll be such fun. To think we'll have to wait another two months before we hear "Fresh beans, tender beans, fresh green beans". Doesn't that sound delicious: tender beans! You know I want the thin, thin ones, dripping in vinegar, you hardly know you're eating them, it's like dew. And those little heart-shaped cream cheeses, they don't come for ages yet: "Cream cheese, lovely cream cheese", and chasselas grapes from Fontainebleau, "Buy my chasselas!"' And my heart sank to think how long I would have to stay with her, right up to the chasselas season. 'Listen, I know I said only wanted to eat things that I'd heard them selling in the street, but of course I'll make a few exceptions. I might very well call at Rebattet's and order an ice dessert for the two of us. You'll say it's not the season for ices, but I do so want one!' The mention of going to Rebattet's alarmed me, the phrase 'I might very well' particularly arousing my suspicions. Today was the Verdurins' at-home day, and since Swann had told them that Rebattet's was the best place, that was where they ordered their ices and *petits fours*. 'I've no objection to an ice, Albertine dearest, but let me order it; I'll get it from Poiré-Blanche's, or Rebattet's or the Ritz, I'm not sure, I'll see. – Are you going out, then?' she asked suspiciously. She always said that she would be delighted if I went out more, but if I ever said anything that implied I might not be staying at home, her anxious reaction suggested that her joy at seeing me constantly going out would not be wholly sincere. 'I may go out, I may not, you know I never make plans. Anyway, they don't sell ices in the street,[21] why do you want one?' The answer brought home to me how much intelligence and latent good taste had suddenly developed in her since Balbec; her words were of a kind that she maintained were owed solely to my influence, to her living permanently with me, but they were words that I myself would never have used, constrained as I felt by some unknown influence never to use literary forms in conversation. Perhaps Albertine's future and mine were not going to be the same. I almost felt it must be so when I saw her at pains to use such 'written' images, which I felt should be put to another, more sacred use with

which I was not yet familiar. She said to me (and I was deeply moved
in spite of everything, for I thought, 'I should never speak like that,
of course, but still, without me she would never have spoken that way,
she has really come under my influence, so she can't not love me, she
is my creation'): 'What I love about the food they sell in the street, is
to see a sound I have heard, like a rhapsody, change its nature on the
table and address itself to my palate. As for ices (and I hope you will
order me only the old-fashioned sort, moulded into every kind of
improbable architecture), every time I eat one, the temples, churches,
obelisks and rocks are like a picturesque geographical tableau that I
study first, before changing its raspberry or vanilla monuments into a
cool sensation in my throat.' I thought that was a little too elegantly
phrased, but she sensed that I did find it well phrased, and went on,
stopping for a moment to laugh when she felt she had drawn an
effective comparison; her laugh, though beautiful, hurt me because it
so clearly expressed her love of pleasure: 'Oh dear, I'm afraid that at
the Ritz hotel you will find Vendôme columns of ice, chocolate or
raspberry ice, and then you will have to buy several so that they can
look like votive columns or an avenue of pylons raised to the glory of
Cold. They make raspberry obelisks too, which can stand here and
there in the burning desert of my thirst until I melt their pink granite
in the back of my throat and they cool it better than an oasis (and
here she laughed deep in her throat, whether impressed by her own
eloquence, or amused by her ability to sustain such a lengthy metaphor, or, alas, from the physical sensation of imagining something
so delicious, so cool in her mouth, which gave her an almost sexual
pleasure). Those ice mountains you get at the Ritz sometimes look
like the Monte Rosa, but when the ice is lemon-flavoured I don't mind
if it doesn't have a monumental shape; it can be a bit irregular, with
cliffs, like one of Elstir's mountains. In that case it shouldn't be too
white, more yellowish, with that look of dirty, bleak snow that he
gives to his mountains. It needn't be a big one, a half-ice if you like,
but those lemon ices are always like miniature mountains, tiny ones,
but your imagination puts everything in scale, like those little dwarf
trees from Japan that you can see are really oak trees or cedars or upas
trees, so that if I put some next to a little trickle of water, in my room,

I could have a huge forest sloping down to a river, where little children could get lost. So, at the foot of my yellowy lemon half-ice, I can see postilions, travellers, post-chaises on whom my tongue brings down icy avalanches to swallow them up' (the cruel pleasure with which she said this aroused my jealousy); 'then', she added, 'I use my lips to demolish, pillar by pillar, those Venetian porphyry churches that are made of strawberry ice-cream, and bring down what I don't swallow on the heads of the faithful. Yes, all those monuments will leave their stony sites and travel into my chest: I can feel their melting coolness there already. But leaving ices aside, nothing is more exciting and thirst-inducing than advertisements for thermal springs. When I was at Mlle Vinteuil's, at Montjouvain, there was no good place to buy ices nearby, but we used to sit in the garden and travel all round France by drinking a different sparkling mineral water every day: there's Vichy water, for example; when you pour it it sends up a white cloud from the bottom of the glass that settles down again if you don't drink it fast enough.' But the mention of Montjouvain was too much for me to bear, and I would interrupt her. 'I'm boring you, darling, good-bye.' What a change from Balbec, where I would defy even Elstir himself to have spotted in Albertine such rich potential for poetry. Not such strange or such personal poetry as Céleste Albaret's was, when she had come to see me the day before and, finding me in bed, had said, 'O heavenly majesty set down on a bed – Why heavenly, Céleste? – Oh, because you're like nobody else, you're quite wrong if you think you have anything in common with those who tread the humble earth. – Well, why "set down", then? – Because you don't look like a man lying down, you're not *in* bed, it looks as if angels flew down and put you there.' Albertine would never have thought of anything like that, but love, even in its last stages, is biased. I preferred the 'picturesque geography' of sorbets, whose rather facile fantasy seemed to me a reason for loving Albertine more, and a sign of my power over her, a proof that she loved me.

Once Albertine had gone out, I felt how fatiguing her perpetual presence was for me, endlessly hungry for movement and life, disturbing my sleep with her comings and goings, making me live in a perpetual draught by leaving the doors open, obliging me – in order to find daily pretexts for not going out with her, without ever seeming too ill, and while making sure that someone else did go – to deploy an ingenuity worthy of Scheherazade.[22] Unfortunately, while the Persian storyteller's ingenuity delayed her death, I was bringing mine closer. Such situations do occur in life, not always caused, as here, by sexual jealousy and frail health which does not allow one to share the life of someone young and active, but where the problem of whether to go on living together or revert to separate lives poses itself in almost medical terms: which sort of peace should one put first (either by continuing one's daily, exhausting activity, or by resuming the pain of separation) – peace of mind, or the peace of the heart?

In any case, I was pleased that Andrée was going to the Trocadéro with Albertine, for certain recent incidents – tiny ones, it is true – without, of course, shaking my confidence in my chauffeur's honesty, had suggested a certain falling-off in his vigilance or at any rate his powers of observation. Thus, one day quite recently when I had sent Albertine to Versailles alone with him, she said she had lunched at the Reservoirs. As the chauffeur had mentioned Vatel's, noting the discrepancy I made an excuse to go down and talk to him (it was still the same chauffeur we had had at Balbec), while Albertine was dressing. 'You said you had lunch at Vatel's, but Miss Albertine mentioned the Reservoirs: how do you explain that? The chauffeur replied, 'Ah, I said I ate at Vatel's; I've no way of knowing where Miss Albertine ate. She left me when we got to Versailles and took a horse-cab; she prefers them when she hasn't any distance to go.' I was already furious to think that Albertine had been on her own; still, it was only for the time it took to eat lunch. 'Couldn't you, I said pleasantly, (for I did not want him to think that I was actually having Albertine watched, which would have been humiliating for me, and doubly so as it would have meant she was keeping me in the dark about her actions) have eaten your lunch, not actually with her of course, but in the same restaurant? – But she told me to be in the Place d'Armes at six o'clock, not before. I wasn't to pick her up after lunch. – Ah!' I said, trying to conceal the depths of my dismay. And I went back upstairs. So Albertine had been alone, left to her own devices, for more than seven hours together. It was true that taking the cab was not simply a trick to get rid of the chauffeur. In town Albertine liked riding slowly in a cab better than in the car; she said you could see better, that the air was sweeter. But still, she had had seven hours to herself, about which I would never know anything. And I dared not think about how she must have spent them. I thought the chauffeur had been thoroughly inept, but my confidence in him now became complete. For if he had been at all in league with Albertine, he would never have admitted to me that he had left her alone from eleven o'clock in the morning till six in the evening. Only one other explanation of the chauffeur's admission was possible, and that was absurd. If he had quarrelled with Albertine, he might have decided to give me an inkling of what was going on, and thus to show my friend that he could talk if he chose; if, after this harmless revelation, she did not do things his way, he really would spill the beans. The idea was ridiculous: one had to imagine a non-existent quarrel between him and Albertine, and credit the chauffeur, that handsome young man, with a blackmailer's outlook, when he had always shown himself so good-natured and obliging. In any case, a mere two days later, he showed that, more than I had ever dreamed in my jealous madness, he could keep a discreet but effective watch over Albertine. I had taken him on one side and, coming back to what he had told me about Versailles, I smiled and said off-handedly, 'That visit to Versailles that you were telling me about the other day, you were right to do as you did, of course, you always do the right thing. But if I can make just a small point, it's not important at all, I do feel such a responsibility since Mme Bontemps left her niece with me, I'm so afraid of accidents, I feel so bad about not going everywhere with her, that I'd rather you always drove Miss Albertine yourself, you are such a good driver, so clever with the car, you'd never have an accident. That way I needn't worry at all.' The charming, apostolic chauffeur laid his hand on his wheel as a saint might on his crucifix[23] and said these words which, dispelling all anxiety from my heart and immediately replacing it with joy, made me feel like throwing my arms around him: 'Don't worry, he said, she won't come to any harm, for even when I'm not driving her around I keep my eye on her. At Versailles, without anybody noticing, I went all round the town with her, you might say. From the Reservoirs she went to the Château, from there to the Trianons, and I followed her all the time without seeming to look at her, and the best of it is she never saw me. Well, and if she had, there'd have been no harm done, after all, with the whole day in front of me why shouldn't I have decided to see the Château as well? Especially as Miss Albertine must have noticed that I'm a reader myself and I love to see all the old things.' (It was true, and if I had known then that he was a friend of Morel's, I should have been surprised, he was so superior to the violinist in intelligence and taste.) 'But she never did see me. – She must have met some friends, she knows several ladies in Versailles. – No, she was on her own the whole time. – People must have been looking at her, then, such a striking young lady and all alone. – They looked at her all right, but she didn't take any notice of them, all the time with her head in her book, when she wasn't looking at the pictures.' The chauffeur's account seemed all the more convincing as the cards Albertine had sent me that day were one of the Château and the other of the Trianons. The care with which the kind chauffeur had followed in her footsteps touched my heart. How could I have imagined that his lengthy, reassuring expansion of his previous story could have been caused by a meeting with Albertine in the intervening two days, when, alarmed at the chauffeur's having spoken to me, she had submitted her will to his and made it up with him? I did not dream of such a thing.

The chauffeur's story, by removing any fear that Albertine had been deceiving me, naturally reduced my interest in my friend and the day she had spent at Versailles. I do believe, however, that his explanations, which by exonerating Albertine made her even more tedious to me, might perhaps not have been enough in themselves to pacify me so quickly. Two little pimples which appeared on my friend's forehead were perhaps more effective in changing the feelings of my heart. These feelings were finally turned away from her, to the point that I forgot her very existence except when I was in her presence, by the extraordinary confidence made to me by Gilberte's maid, whom I met by chance at this time. I learned from her that at the time I was calling on Gilberte every day, she was in love with another young man of whom she saw much more than she saw of me. I had briefly suspected this at the time, and remembered questioning this same maid. But as she knew I loved Gilberte, she had denied everything, sworn that Mlle Swann never set eyes on the young man. But now, knowing that my love was so long dead, that for years I had left all Gilberte's letters unanswered – and perhaps also because she was no longer in Gilberte's service – she told me of her own accord the whole story of the amorous episode I had known nothing about. It seemed to her quite natural to do so. Remembering her protestations then, I supposed that she had not known about the affair at the time. But she had: it was she who, on Mme Swann's orders, had gone to let the young man know whenever the girl I loved was alone. The girl I loved then . . . But I wondered for a moment whether my old love was as dead as I had thought, for the maid's story caused me pain. As I do not think that jealousy can revive a dead love, I imagined that my pained reaction was due, at least in part, to wounded self-esteem, for several people whom I disliked, and who at this time and for some while after – things were to change later – affected a contemptuous attitude towards me, must have known quite well, while I was so in love with Gilberte, that I was being fooled. And that made me look back and wonder whether my love for Gilberte had not had an admixture of vanity, since it was now so painful for me to realize that all the hours of friendly intimacy which had made me so happy were seen as nothing but a trick of my friend's at my expense, by people whom I did not like. Whether it was love or vanity, Gilberte was almost dead within me, but not entirely, and this new displeasure quite made me forget to worry over-much about Albertine, who occupied only such a narrow part of my heart. Nevertheless, to return to her (after such a long parenthesis) and her visit to Versailles, the postcards she sent me from there (can one's heart really be simultaneously assailed from different angles by two jealousies, each relating to a different person?) gave me rather a disagreeable feeling whenever I turned them up among the papers on my desk. And I thought that if the chauffeur hadn't been such a good sort, the way his second story matched Albertine's choice of cards would not have proved very much, for what would anybody send one from Versailles but 'views' of the Château and the Trianons, unless the choice were being made by a connoisseur in love with a particular statue, or by some idiot whose idea of a view was the horse-tram depot or the goods station?

I should not say an idiot, for that kind of postcard is not always sent by them, chosen simply because it came from Versailles. There were two years during which intelligent men, artists, decided that Siena, Venice and Granada had been done to death, and greeted the first omnibus or wagon with cries of 'Now that's beautiful'. Then that fad passed like the others. I am not even sure that we have not returned to the 'sacrilegious destruction of relics of the past'. In any case, a first-class railway coach is no longer considered *a priori* more beautiful than St Mark's in Venice. They used to say, 'Those are the *real* things, looking backwards is so artificial,' but without drawing any clear conclusions. In any case, and though I still trusted the chauffeur completely, I made sure that Albertine would not be able to park him and go off without his daring to refuse for fear of being thought a spy: I would only let her go out escorted by Andrée, whereas before I had thought the chauffeur was protection enough. I had even once let her (a thing I would never have done later) be away for three days, just her and the chauffeur, and go almost as far as Balbec, she was so keen to make the journey in a stripped-down vehicle, at great speed. During these three days I had been quite relaxed, even though the deluge of postcards she sent me did not arrive, so dreadful is the post from Brittany (good in summer, but no doubt disorganized in winter), until a week after Albertine and the chauffeur had returned. They came back so full of energy that on the very morning of their return they went out, quite undaunted, on their usual daily excursion. But since the Versailles incident I had changed. I was delighted that Albertine should be going to the 'special' matinée at the Trocadéro, but above all reassured that she was going there in company, the company of Andrée.

Setting these thoughts aside, now that Albertine was gone, I went to the window for a moment. First there was a silence, against which the tripe-seller's whistle and the tramway horn resonated in the air octaves apart, like a blind piano-tuner at work. Then I was able to distinguish the interwoven melodies, to which new ones were constantly added. There was also a different whistle, blown by a seller of

I never discovered what, which sounded exactly like a tram-whistle, and as it was not borne away at speed like the others, one imagined a single tram, lacking the power of movement or broken down, stuck in one position and piping feebly like a dying animal. And it seemed to me that if ever I had to leave that neighbourhood – unless for a completely working-class one – the streets and boulevards of the city centre (where the fruit, fish and other trades had been brought together in large food shops, rendering obsolete the cries of the street sellers which would in any case have been inaudible in the traffic) would strike me as very dull, unliveable in, stripped, emptied of all the litanies of the petty trades and perambulating delicacies, deprived of the orchestra which came to charm me at break of day. On the pavement, a woman, ill-dressed or following an ugly fashion, was passing, a too-light shape in a mohair sacque; no, it wasn't a woman, it was a chauffeur in his goatskin driving-coat, going on foot to his garage. Set loose from the grand hotels, the winged tribe of messengers in their rainbow colours sped towards the stations, bent over their bicycles, to meet the travellers from the morning trains. The throbbing of strings meant sometimes the passing of a car, and sometimes that I had not put enough water in my electric bed-warmer. In the middle of this modern symphony a false note was struck by an old-fashioned 'tune': replacing the sweet-seller who usually accompanied her song with a rattle, the toy-man, on whose military cap was mounted a puppet which he moved in all directions, was showing off other puppets and, with no regard for the ritual declamation of Gregory the Great, the reforms of Palestrina[24] or modern, operatic recitative, was bellowing out, like an old-fashioned partisan of pure melody,

> Come on Dad, come on Mum,
> Look, the kiddies' best friend has come.
> You've got the pennies, I've got the toys,
> All home-made for your girls and boys.
> Tra la la, tra la la la lero
> Tra la la la la la la la.
> Come on boys and girls!

Little Italians in berets did not try to compete with this *aria vivace*, but stood silently holding out their statuettes. Meanwhile a little fife-player was driving the toy-man to beat a retreat, still singing *presto* but more confusedly, 'Come on Dad, come on Mum'. Was the fife-player one of the dragoons I used to hear in the mornings at Doncières? No, for his notes were followed by the words, 'China to mend, china or earthenware? I mend everything, glass, marble, crystal, bone, ivory and antiques. Here's the men-der!' In a butcher's shop with on the left a sunburst and on the right a whole ox hanging up, a butcher's boy, very tall and thin, with blond hair, his neck emerging from a sky-blue collar, was, scrupulously and with dizzying speed, placing on one side exquisite fillet steaks and on the other low-grade rump, weighing them in gleaming scales with a cross on top, from which dangled fine chains, and though he was only setting out the displays of kidneys, tournedos or entrecôtes, he looked in fact much more like an angel on Judgment Day, separating out for God, according to their qualities, the Good and the Wicked, and weighing their souls. And now the thin, sharp note of the fife rose into the air again, announcing not the destruction that Françoise so feared every time she saw a cavalry column pass by, but 'restorations' to be done by an 'antique specialist', innocent or just cheeky, and in any case very eclectic, since far from specializing he exercised his skill on the most diverse materials. The little bakers' girls were hurriedly piling up in their baskets the long, thin loaves for 'midday dinner', and the dairy-girls speedily hanging from their carrying-poles the bottles of milk. Could the romantic view I had of these little girls have been accurate? Would it not have been different if I had been able to stop one of them for a moment and keep her beside me, instead of seeing them from my window, always in the shop or flying down the street? To understand what I was losing by always being shut indoors, and to measure the riches the day was offering, I would have had to stop the unrolling of the living frieze and catch one girl carrying her laundry or her milk, frame her, like a silhouette in a moving decoration, between the uprights of my door and focus on her, making sure to obtain enough information about her to be able to find her again another day, like the tags that ornithologists and ichthyologists attach to birds' legs or fishes' fins before freeing them to study their migrations.

I therefore told Françoise that I had an errand I wanted done, and that she should send up, as soon as one arrived, one or other of the little girls who were always coming to collect or deliver laundry or bread or milk, and whom she often sent with messages of her own. In this I was like Elstir, who, unable to leave his studio on certain spring days when the knowledge that the woods were full of violets made him desperate to see some, would send his portress to buy a bunch of them; then, his heart melting, almost hallucinating, he would see not the table on which he had placed the small botanical specimen, but all the carpet of the undergrowth where formerly, in their thousands, he had seen the twisting stems bending under their blue, beak-like blossoms; his eyes created an imaginary zone, marked off in his studio by the pure scent of the evocative flower.

There was no chance of a laundry-girl today, a Sunday. As for the baker's girl, ill luck would have it that she had rung while Françoise was out, left her loaves in the basket on the landing and made her escape. The greengrocer's girl would not come till much later. Once I had been in the dairy ordering a cheese, and among the shop-girls I had noticed one, extravagantly blond in colouring, very tall though still childish-looking, and who, among the other errand-girls, seemed to be far away, with a proud, dreamy look. I had seen her only from a distance, and so quickly that I could not really have described her, except to say that she must have shot up all at once, and that she had a head of hair that looked much less like individual locks than like a stylized sculpture of the meandering curves of parallel banks of snow. That was all I had noticed, apart from a strongly modelled nose (very unusual in young girls), recalling the beak of a baby vulture. It was not only her position, surrounded by the other shop-girls, that made it difficult for me to see her clearly, but also my uncertainty about the feelings that I, at that moment and later, might inspire in her: fierce pride, mockery, disdain which she would afterwards express to her friends? These various speculations which, in the first second, I made about her, had made even more impenetrable the troubled atmosphere in which she hid, like a goddess in a cloud shaken by thunder. For mental uncertainty is even more of an obstacle to clear visual perception than a physical defect of the eye would be. In this over-thin, over-eye-catching young person, the excess of what another man might have called attractions was exactly what I liked least, but all the same it had had the result of preventing me from noticing, still less remembering, anything about the other girls in the dairy, whom the first girl's hooked nose and her unpleasantly independent, thoughtful look, as if she were judging them, had relegated to obscurity, like a bolt of blond lightning throwing the countryside into darkness. And so from my visit to the dairy to order the cheese, I had remembered only (if one can speak of remembering a face so poorly recalled that one adapts ten different noses to the mist of the features) the little girl whom I had thought disagreeable. That can be a sufficient starting-point for love. Still, I would have forgotten the improbable blonde and would never have thought of seeing her again, if Françoise had not told me that, young as she was, she was very knowing and was going to leave her job because she spent too much on dress and owed money in the neighbourhood. It has been said that beauty is the promise of happiness. Reversing the idea, the prospect of pleasure can also be the beginning of beauty.

I began to read Mama's letter. Behind her quotations from Mme de Sévigné ('If my thoughts at Combray are not completely black, they are at least a dark grey-brown; I long for you and think of you every moment, your health, your business affairs, how far away you are, how do you think that feels on dark evenings?') I could feel that my mother did not like to see Albertine's stay in our house becoming so prolonged, and my ideas of marriage, though not yet declared to my intended, taking deeper root. She no longer said these things, because she was afraid that I would leave her letters lying around. Indeed, though they were written in such veiled terms, she complained if I did not let her know when I received each one. 'You remember what Mme de Sévigné said: "When one is far away one no longer laughs at letters that begin 'Thank you for your letter'".' She did not speak of what worried her most, but complained about my extravagance: 'What can you be spending all your money on? It's bad enough for me that you are like Charles de Sévigné, not knowing what you want and being "two or three different men at once", but try at least not to be as extravagant as he was, so that I do not have to say of you, "He has found the secret of spending money without making an impression, of losing without gambling and of paying his debts without removing the obligation".' I had just finished Mama's note when Françoise came back to tell me that the little dairy-girl whose forwardness she had told me about was in the kitchen at that moment. 'She can easily take your letter, sir, and do your errands if it's not too far. You'll see, sir, she's just like a Little Red Riding-Hood.' Françoise went to get her and I heard her showing her the way, saying, 'Look at you, you're scared because there's a corridor. Whatever next, I thought you had more sense, do I have to take you by the hand?' And Françoise, like a good and faithful servant who wants to make others respect her master as she respects him herself, had cloaked herself in the majesty which ennobles the bawd in those old master paintings where the lover and the mistress fade almost into insignificance next to her grandeur.

When Elstir gazed at his violets, he did not have to worry about what they were doing. The entrance of the little dairy-girl immediately dispelled my contemplative calm; now I had to concentrate on making the story of the letter to be delivered plausible, and I began to write rapidly, hardly daring to look at her, so as not to seem to have summoned her for that reason. She had for me all the charm of the unknown, which I would not have found in a pretty girl discovered in one of those houses where they are always waiting for you. She was not naked, nor in fancy dress, but a real dairy-maid, one of those girls one always thinks so pretty when one has not the time to get to know them, she had something of what makes for eternal desire, eternal regret in this life, whose double current has now at last been diverted, brought close to us. Double, because it is a question of the unknown, of a being we guess to be divine, given its stature, its proportions, its indifferent gaze, its haughty calm; on the other hand, we want the woman in question to belong to a clearly specialized trade, so that we can escape into the world which a particular costume convinces us must be romantically different. If one wanted to reduce to a formula the laws of amorous curiosity, one would have to seek it in the maximum divergence between a woman seen and a woman won, caressed. If the women in what used to be called houses of ill-fame, if even kept women (provided we know that is what they are) attract us so little, it is not that they are less beautiful than others, it is that they are ready and waiting for us: what we are trying to attain is already on offer, they are not conquests. Divergence here is at a minimum. A tart smiles at us in the street in the same way she will smile when she is alone with us. We are sculptors. We want to find in a woman a statue quite different from the one she first showed to us. We see an indifferent, insolent young girl at the seaside, a respectable shop-assistant busy at her counter who replies to our question abruptly, if only so as not to be teased by her workmates, a fruit-woman who barely answers us. Well, we cannot rest until we have tried to see whether the haughty seaside girl, the shop-girl with her worries about what people will think, the preoccupied fruit-seller cannot be persuaded, by crafty manœuvres on our part, to soften their unbending attitude, to wind round our neck the arms that carried the fruit, to turn upon our mouth, with a smile of consent, those hitherto chilly or faraway eyes – oh, the beauty of those eyes, so stern in working hours, when their owner feared the gossip of her companions, eyes which avoided our insistent looks and which, now that we are alone with her, drop their lids under the sunny weight of laughter when we speak of making love! Between the shop-assistant, the laundry-woman intent on her ironing, the fruit-seller, the dairy-woman, and the girl who is about to become our mistress, the maximum divergence is attained, stretched to its extreme limits, and varied by the habitual gestures of her trade, which make of her arms, during her hours of work, a pattern of curves as different as can be from the supple bonds which already, each evening, are winding round our neck, while her mouth prepares for our kiss. That is why we spend our lives in anxious, endlessly repeated approaches to respectable girls whose work seems to make them remote from us. Once in our arms, they are no longer what they were, the gap that we hoped to cross has disappeared. But we start again with other women, we give our whole time, all our money, all our strength to these pursuits, we roundly curse the coachman for driving too slowly and perhaps making us miss the first meeting, we are feverish with passion. The first meeting – and yet we know that it will mean the dispelling of an illusion. No matter: so long as the illusion lasts, we want to know if we can turn it into reality, and then we think of the laundry-woman whose coolness has struck us. The curiosity of love is like our curiosity about place-names: always disappointed, it is always reborn and remains insatiable.

Alas, once in my room, the blonde dairy-girl with the platinum streaks was stripped of all the imagination and desires I had invested in her and reduced to her unvarnished self. The trembling cloud of my curiosity no longer enveloped her in excitement. She looked shamefaced now at having only one nose (instead of the ten or twenty that I had been recalling in turn without being able to call up a precise memory), and that rounder than I had thought, giving a suggestion of stupidity to her face, which had in any case lost the power of self-multiplication. This captured flight, dead, pinned-down, incapable of adding anything to its pitiful obviousness, was no longer supplemented by my imagination. Falling into static reality, I tried to bounce back; the cheeks, which I had not observed in the shop, looked so pretty that I felt intimidated and, to give myself a countenance, I said to the girl, 'Would you be kind enough to pass me the *Figaro*, it's on the table there, I must look up the address of the place I want to send you.' As she picked up the paper she uncovered the red sleeve of her jacket up to the elbow, and held out the conservative sheet to me with a neat, helpful gesture which pleased me by its homely speed, its yielding appearance and its scarlet colour. As I opened the *Figaro*, so as to have something to say and without raising my eyes, I asked the child, 'What is that red, knitted thing you are wearing? It's very pretty.' She answered, 'That's my cardigan.' For, by a process of degeneration common to all fashions, the garments and words which, a few years earlier, had seemed to belong to the relatively elegant world of Albertine and her friends, had now passed down to working-girls. 'You really wouldn't mind', I went on, pretending to look in the *Figaro*, 'if I sent you quite a long way?' As soon as I appeared to think that sending her on an errand would be asking a great deal, she began to suggest that it would be difficult for her. 'The thing is, I'm supposed to be going for a bicycle ride later. We only get Sunday afternoons off, you know.' – 'But won't you be cold, bare-headed like that?' –

'Oh, I won't be bare-headed, I'll wear my jockey-cap, and anyhow, with all my hair . . .' I raised my eyes to the mass of curly yellow locks and felt their whirlwind carry me away, my heart beating faster in the light and gusts of wind of a hurricane of beauty. I kept on looking at the newspaper, but even though it was only to give myself a countenance and gain time, I did take in the sense of the words before my eyes and was struck by these: 'To the advertised programme of the matinée taking place this afternoon in the main hall of the Trocadéro, we must add the name of Mlle Léa, who has agreed to appear in *Naughty Nérine*. She will, naturally, play the part of Nérine, in which she displays dazzling verve and an enchanting gaiety.' It was as if some brutal hand had torn from my heart the dressing under which, since my return from Balbec, it had begun to heal. The flux of my anguish poured out in torrents. Léa was the actress who was friendly with the two young girls whom Albertine had looked at in the glass that afternoon in the casino, without seeming to see them. It is true that at Balbec Albertine, on hearing the name of Léa, had been at particular pains to assure me, as if she were shocked that such a virtuous person could possibly be suspected: 'Oh no, she's not that sort of woman at all, she's completely above board.' Sadly for me, when Albertine gave an assurance of this kind, it was only ever the prelude to further, contradictory affirmations. Soon after the first would come the second: 'I don't know her.' The third stage was when, Albertine having mentioned someone 'above suspicion', whom in any case (stage two) 'she did not know', she would first of all gradually forget that she was supposed not to know the person, and unwittingly 'trip herself up' by using some phrase which showed that she did know her.

After this first piece of forgetfulness and with the new story now established, she would then forget something else: that the person was above reproach. 'Isn't such-and-such a person one of them? – Of course she is, she's famous for it!' The original note of compunction returned, to support an assurance that was a distant, faint echo of the first one: 'I must say that she's always been perfectly all right with me. Of course she knew that I'd have put her in her place, no mistake about that. But that's not the point. I have to admit that she's always shown me complete respect. Obviously she knew who she was dealing with.' We can remember the truth because it bears a name, has roots in the past, but an improvised lie is quickly forgotten. Albertine would forget this last lie, her fourth, and one day when she was trying to gain my confidence by confiding in me, she would go so far as to say this same person, originally so respectable and whom she did not know: 'She fancied me at one time. She asked me back to her place three or four times. I didn't mind walking home with her, out in the open air in front of everybody, but when I got to the house I always found an excuse not to go upstairs.' Some time later Albertine would refer to the beautiful things the same lady had in her house. By piecing together the various partial accounts, it would no doubt have been possible to get the truth out of her, a truth perhaps less serious than I was inclined to believe, for perhaps, though she had once been free with women, she preferred a man, and now that I was her lover she might have taken no notice of Léa. It would already have been enough, at least where a large number of women were concerned, for me to bring together in front of my friend her various contradictory statements about them, in order to convict her of her transgressions (transgressions which, like the laws of astronomy, are easier to establish by reasoning than to observe, to uncover in reality). But she would still have chosen to say that one of her statements was a lie and withdraw it, thus throwing my whole system out of kilter, rather than admit that the whole story from the beginning was a tissue of lying tales. There are such tales in the *Arabian Nights*, and there they delight us. In someone we love, they make us suffer, and for that reason allow us to go deeper in our knowledge of human nature, rather than happily playing on its surface. Sorrow enters into us, and painful curiosity forces us to dig deeper. There we learn truths which we feel we have not the right to hide, so much so that a dying atheist who has learned these truths, though he knows he is going into nothingness and is indifferent to glory, will still use up his last hours in trying to make them known.

No doubt I was still at the first stage of affirmation in relation to Léa. I did not even know if Albertine knew her or not. But it did not matter: the problem was the same. I simply had to stop her going to the Trocadéro and renewing this acquaintance, or getting to know this stranger. I say that I did not know if she knew Léa or not; but I must have known when I was at Balbec: Albertine herself must have told me. For a large part of what she told me there had vanished from my memory, just as from her own. For memory is not a copy, always present to our eyes, of the various events of our life, but rather a void from which, every now and then, a present resemblance allows us to recover, to resurrect, dead recollections; but there are also thousands of tiny facts which never fell into this well of potential memories and which we shall never be able to check. Everything which we think irrelevant to the day-to-day life of the person we love is dismissed without consideration; we immediately forget what she tells us about this or that fact or person unknown to us, and the expression on her face when she was saying it. So, when later our jealousy is aroused by these same persons and we need to know that we are not mistaken, that it is they who are the cause of our mistress's haste to go out, her annoyance with us for depriving her of their company by coming home too early, our jealousy, digging in the past for clues, finds nothing; always turned towards the past, it is like a historian trying to write a history for which there are no documents; always late, it rushes like a mad bull into the place just vacated by the haughty, shining being who irritates it with his darts, and whom the crowd admires for his splendour and guile. Jealousy thrashes about in the void, uncertain, as we are in those dreams in which we are distressed not to find in his empty house someone whom we knew in life, but who here is perhaps someone else, simply wearing the features of another character; uncertain as we are, to an even greater degree, on waking, when we try to identify this or that detail of our dream. How did our friend look as she said those words? Did not she look happy, was she not even whistling, something she does only when she is thinking of love and our unwelcome presence annoys her? Did she not say something then which contradicted what she is saying now, that she knew or did not know such and such a person? We do not know, we shall never know, we struggle to put together the debris of a dream, and in the meantime our life with our mistress goes on, our life of inattention to what we do not know is important to us, attention to what we think important but perhaps is not, a life made nightmarish by beings who have no real connection with us, filled with forgetfulness, gaps, vain anxieties: a life most like a dream. I realized that the dairy-girl was still there. I said that it was really a very long way, and that I would not send her on my errand. She agreed at once that it would be too much trouble: 'There's a big match later on, I don't want to miss it.' I guessed that she would already call herself 'a sports fan', and that soon she would talk about 'leading her own life'. I said that I would not be needing her, and gave her five francs. This unexpected tip made her think that, if she could get five francs for nothing, she would certainly be well paid for running my errand, and she began to suggest that her match was not so important after all. 'I could have gone for you. I can always make time.' But I pushed her towards the door: I needed to be alone. I absolutely had to stop Albertine going to the Trocadéro and meeting those friends of Léa's. I had to, I simply had to manage it; I didn't as yet see how, and I spent the first moments opening and closing my hands, staring at them, cracking my knuckles, whether it is that our mind, when it cannot see a solution, is overcome by laziness and decides to suspend its activity for a moment, during which it registers with great clarity the most irrelevant things, like the blades of grass on the embankment which we see trembling in the wind while our train is stopped in the middle of nowhere – this immobility, however, is not always any more productive than that of a captured animal which, paralysed with fear or spellbound, stares without moving – or whether I was holding my whole body in reserve, with my intelligence inside it and along with that the possibility of acting on a given person, as if it were simply a weapon which I should presently wield to separate Albertine from Léa and her two friends. Certainly, in the morning when Françoise had come to tell me that Albertine was going to the Trocadéro, I had thought, 'Albertine can do as she pleases,' and I had said to myself that until the evening of that glorious day her actions would have no perceptible importance for me. But it was not simply the morning sun, as I had thought, that had made me so confident; it was because, having forced Albertine to give up the plans that she could have embarked on or even carried out at the Verdurins', and having reduced her to going to a matinée that I had picked out for her myself, where she could not possibly have plotted anything, I knew that what she did all day could only be innocent. In the same way, when Albertine said a few moments later, 'I don't care if I get killed,' it was because she felt sure that she would not be. In front of my eyes, in front of Albertine's, there had been not just the morning sunshine but that invisible, translucent yet changeable medium through which we looked, I at her actions, she at the importance of her own life: that is to say, those beliefs which we do not perceive but which are no more a pure vacuum than the air we breathe; they compose around us a changing atmosphere, sometimes excellent, often unbreathable, which we could usefully measure and note as carefully as the temperature, pressure and season, for each of our days has its individual character, physical and psychological. The belief, unnoticed by me that morning, and which nonetheless had enveloped me in happiness until the moment I reopened the *Figaro*, that Albertine would spend the whole day in harmless pursuits, had now abandoned me. I was no longer living in that beautiful day, but in another day created within the first one by my anxious fear that Albertine would renew her friendship with Léa and – what would be even easier – with the two girls, if they went, as seemed likely, to see the actress at the Trocadéro, where it would not be difficult for them, during one of the intervals, to meet up with Albertine. Mlle Vinteuil had gone out of my mind: the name of Léa had brought back to me, reviving my jealousy, the image of Léa at the casino with the two girls. For I held in my memory only isolated, incomplete sequences of Albertines, silhouettes, snapshots; my jealousy was therefore focussed on a particular, intermittent expression, both elusive and fixed, and on the people who had caused it to appear on Albertine's face. I remembered how she had been at Balbec, when the two girls, or other women of their kind, looked too long and hard at her; I remembered how I had suffered to see her face raked by their eyes, as intent as a painter's when he wants to make a sketch; it was wholly covered by them, but, because of my presence no doubt, it underwent this contact without seeming to notice, with a passivity which perhaps concealed a secret pleasure. And before she recovered her wits and spoke to me, just for a second Albertine did not move, stood smiling at nothing in particular, with the same look of feigned naturalness and hidden pleasure as if she had been being photographed, or even were trying to adopt a more appealing pose for the camera – as she had done when we were walking with Saint-Loup at Doncières, laughing and licking her lips, as if she were teasing a dog. Certainly at these moments she was not at all the same as when it was she who was interested in some passing girl. In that case, her narrow, velvety gaze fastened on the passer-by, stuck to her, so gluey and corrosive that you felt it would not be able to detach itself without removing a patch of skin. But at this moment that particular look, which at least gave her expression a seriousness which made her seem almost ill, would have been welcome to me, compared to the blank, happy expression which her face took on when the two girls were there, and I would have preferred the sombre expression of desire which she perhaps sometimes felt herself, to the smiling look caused by the desire she inspired in others. It was in vain that she tried to veil her consciousness of it: the knowledge bathed her, enveloped her in a mist of pleasure, made her face rosy with delight. But all the feelings that Albertine held in suspension within herself at these moments, though they radiated around her and made me suffer so terribly, who could tell whether, in my absence, she would continue to suppress them: whether, once I was gone, she would not respond boldly to the two girls' advances? Certainly, these memories caused me much suffering. They were like a complete admission of Albertine's tastes, a general confession of her unfaithfulness, against which nothing could carry any weight: Albertine's individual promises, much as I wanted to believe them, the negative results of my incomplete enquiries and the assurances, perhaps concocted in collaboration with Albertine, of Andrée. Albertine could deny particular betrayals, but by words that she let slip, which contradicted these declarations, by these very looks, she had revealed what she would have most wanted to hide, much more than any individual fact: what she would have let herself be killed rather than admit: her sexual tastes. For no being wants to give up its soul. In spite of the pain that these memories caused me, could I have denied that it was the afternoon's programme at the Trocadéro that had revived my need for Albertine? She was one of those women in whom ordinary attractions can be replaced by their offences and, almost as much, by the kindness which, following on these offences, restores to us the happiness which when we are with them, like an invalid who is never well two days running, we must constantly try to recover. Besides, even more powerful than the offences they commit while we love them, there are the offences they committed before we knew them, and the earliest of all: their nature. What makes this kind of love so painful is that it is preceded by what we might call an original sin by the woman, a sin which makes us love her, so that when we forget it, we need her less, and to begin loving her again we have to begin to suffer once more. At this moment, what mattered to me was ensuring that she should not see the two girls again, and finding out whether she knew Léa or not, although one should not concern oneself with particular facts except in so far as they have a general meaning, and it is childish, just as childish as the desire for travel or to know many women, to dissipate one's curiosity on whatever fragment of the invisible torrent of cruel realities which one will never know has chanced to crystallize in one's mind. Besides, even if one could destroy this fragment, it would promptly be replaced by another. Yesterday my fear was that Albertine should go to Mme Verdurin's. Now I was concerned only by Léa. Jealousy, whose eyes are bandaged, is not only powerless to see anything in the surrounding darkness; it is one of those tortures where a task has constantly to be begun again, like that of the Danaids or of Ixion.[25] Even if the two girls were not at the theatre, would not Albertine be impressed by Léa, more beautiful in costume, at the height of her success: would she not carry away dreams of her, desires which, even if they had to be suppressed in my house, would lead her to hate a life where she could not satisfy them? Then, perhaps she already knew Léa and would go to see her in her dressing-room, and even if Léa did not know her, how could I be sure that, having at least seen her at Balbec, she would not recognize her and make some sign to her from the stage that would allow Albertine to be admitted backstage? A danger seems avoidable once it has been averted. This one was not so yet, I was afraid that it could not be, and it seemed to me all the more terrible for that reason. And still my love for Albertine, which seemed almost to vanish when I tried to act upon it, seemed in a way proved by the intensity of my suffering at this moment. Nothing else mattered to me, I could think only of how to stop her staying at the Trocadéro, I would have given any money to Léa not to go there. If therefore one can judge one's true feelings by the action one takes rather than the idea one forms of them, I must have loved Albertine. But this renewal of my anguish did not give any greater consistency to my inner image of Albertine. She caused my sufferings like a goddess who remains invisible. Turning over countless possibilities in my mind, I tried to deaden my pain without thereby giving any more reality to my love.

First, I had to be certain that Léa really was appearing at the Trocadéro. Having sent the dairy-girl home with two francs, I rang Bloch, who was also a friend of Léa's, to ask him. He knew nothing about it and seemed surprised that I should want to know. I thought that I would have to act quickly, that Françoise was already dressed and I was not, I asked my mother to let me keep Françoise all day, and while I was getting up myself, I made her take a taxi; she was to go to the Trocadéro, buy a ticket, look for Albertine everywhere in the auditorium and give her a note from me. In the note, I said that I had been badly upset by a letter from the same lady who she knew had made me so unhappy one night at Balbec. I reminded her that the following day she had scolded me for not having had her called. So I felt, I said, that I could ask her to give up her afternoon at the theatre and come to collect me, so that we could go out together in the fresh air which I hoped would make me feel better. But as it would take me quite a long time to get dressed and be ready, I would like her to make use of her time with Françoise to go to the *Trois Quartiers* (this was a smaller shop which worried me less than the *Bon Marché*) and buy the white tulle collar that she needed.

My note probably served a purpose. To tell the truth, I knew nothing of what Albertine had been doing since I had known her, or even before. But in her day-to-day speech (Albertine could, if I had raised the matter with her, have said that I had misheard her), there were certain contradictions, certain alterations which seemed to me as conclusive as if I had caught her in the act, but they were less easy to use against Albertine, who, caught out like a child, would each time, by these quick strategic rephrasings, deflect my cruel attacks and regain control of the situation. The cruelty was turned on me. Not as a refinement of style, but to cover her careless mistakes, she used sudden leaps of syntax resembling what grammarians call anacoluthon or something like that. Talking about women, she would let slip the words, 'I remember not long ago I . . .'; then suddenly, after a 'quaver rest', 'I' would become 'she', and the action would be something she had seen while out for an innocent walk, and not something she had done herself. I wished I could remember the beginning of the sentence so as to decide myself, when she shifted her ground, what the ending would have been. But as I had been listening for the end, I could hardly remember the beginning, though it was perhaps the look of interest it had produced on my face that had made her change her tune, and I was left to my anxiety about her real thoughts, her authentic memory. The origins of one of our mistress's lies are unfortunately like the origins of our love, or of a vocation. They begin to form, take shape, pass, unnoticed by our attention. By the time one wants to remember how one began to love a woman, one is already in love; during earlier reveries, one did not say to oneself, 'this is the beginning of love, I must pay attention', and the feelings crept up on us almost unnoticed. In the same way, except in relatively rare cases, it is only to ease the telling of my story that I have often set one of Albertine's untruthful statements against her first assertions on the same subject. This first statement, given that I could not see into the future or guess what contradictory assertion would come to balance it, often slipped past me unnoticed; my ears certainly heard it, but without isolating it from the flow of Albertine's speech. Later, faced with a blatant lie or seized by anxious doubts, I longed to be able to remember it, but in vain; my memory, not forewarned, had not seen the need to take a copy.

I told Françoise, once she had got Albertine out of the theatre, to ring me and bring her home, whether she wanted to come or not. 'Not want to come home to you, sir, said Françoise, the very idea! – But I don't know if she likes seeing me all that much. – There's gratitude for you,' replied Françoise, in whom Albertine revived after so many years the torments of envy she had suffered when Eulalie was in favour with my aunt. Not knowing that Albertine's relationship to me was not of her seeking but mine (a fact that I preferred to hide from

Françoise out of self-regard, and also to irritate her all the more), she admired and cursed her cleverness, and when speaking of her to the other servants called her a 'play-actress', a 'hussy' who could wind me round her little finger. She did not dare carry the fight to her openly, spoke pleasantly to her, and made sure I knew how she helped me in my relations with her enemy; thinking it would be useless and would achieve nothing to say anything to me against Albertine, she was still always looking for an opening, and if ever she spotted a crack in Albertine's position, she would work to widen it and to separate us completely. 'Gratitude? But Françoise, I feel I'm the ungrateful one, you don't know how kind she is to me. (I loved to seem to be loved!) Go quickly. – I'll toddle off then, pronto.'

Her daughter's influence was beginning slowly to debase Françoise's vocabulary. That is how all languages lose their purity, by the accretion of new terms. This decadence of Françoise's speech, which I had known in its golden age, was furthermore in part my responsibility. Françoise's daughter would never have made her mother's classical parlance degenerate into the lowest slang if she had been content to go on speaking patois to her. She had always done so, and if they were both with me and wanted to tell each other secrets, they did not go into the kitchen but built around themselves in the middle of my bedroom a protective wall more impassable than the most carefully closed door, by speaking patois. I could only guess that the mother and daughter did not always get on very well, by noting the frequent recurrence of the only word I could understand: *m'esasperate* (unless the source of their exasperation was myself). Unfortunately one learns to understand the most impenetrable language if one hears it constantly spoken. I was sorry it was patois I learned in this way, for I could have equally well learnt Persian if Françoise had been accustomed to speak in that tongue. Françoise, when she noticed my progress, began to speak faster and her daughter too, but all in vain. The mother was upset that I should understand patois, then pleased to hear me speaking it. To tell the truth, this pleasure was a kind of mockery, for though I was finally able to pronounce it much as she did, she could hear a gulf between our two pronunciations which delighted her, and she began to be sorry that she no longer saw certain people from her village that she had not thought about for years and who, according to her, would have split their sides laughing – she would have loved to hear them – when they heard me speaking patois. The very idea filled her with gaiety and regret, and she would list one peasant after another who would have laughed till he cried. In any case, no joy could relieve her unhappiness at the fact that, even if I pronounced patois badly, I understood it well. Keys are useless when the person we are trying to keep out can use a skeleton key or a jemmy. Patois having become a worthless defence, she began to speak French to her daughter – a French which soon became that of the most decadent period.

I was ready. Françoise had not telephoned yet: should I leave without waiting? But how did I know if she would find Albertine? If she were not already backstage? And even if Françoise found her, would she let herself be taken home? Half an hour later, the telephone rang and hope and fear beat wildly in my heart. A flying column of sounds, commanded by an employee of the telephone company, brought to me with instant speed the words of the operator, not of Françoise, whose ancestral shyness and melancholy, applied to an object unknown to her forefathers, forbade her to approach a telephone receiver, even if the alternative were to visit a contagious invalid in person. She had found Albertine alone in the promenade gallery and she, taking only a moment to tell Andrée that she was going, had promptly left with Françoise. 'She wasn't angry? Oh, sorry! Would you please ask the lady if the young lady wasn't angry? – The lady asked me to tell you that she wasn't angry at all, quite the opposite; anyway, if she wasn't pleased, you couldn't tell. They're going to the *Trois Quartiers* now and they'll be back at two o'clock.' I knew that two o'clock must mean three o'clock, since it was after two already. But it was one of Françoise's particular weaknesses, a permanent, incurable weakness of the kind we call congenital, never to be able to tell the time correctly. I have never been able to understand what went on in her head when she looked at her watch and, if it were two o'clock, said that it was one o'clock, or three; I have never been able to tell whether the phenomenon which occurred then had as its locus Françoise's eyesight, or her thought, or her language; what is certain is that it always occurred. Humanity is very old. Heredity and breeding have given an irresistible strength to bad habits and vicious reflexes. One person sneezes and his chest rattles when he passes a rose-bush, another comes out in a rash at the smell of fresh paint; many people have stomach-aches when they have to travel, and grandsons of thieves who are millionaires and generous cannot resist robbing us of fifty francs. As far as explaining Françoise's inability to tell the time is concerned, she herself certainly never gave me any clues. For in spite of the anger usually produced in me by her wrong answers, Françoise would neither apologize for her mistake nor try to explain it. She stayed mute, looking as if she could not hear me, which completed my exasperation. I would have liked to hear one word of excuse, if only to throw it back at her, but there was nothing, only indifferent silence. In any case, as far as today was concerned, it was clear, Albertine was going to come back with Françoise at three o'clock, Albertine would not see Léa or her friends. So the danger that she would resume her relations with them having been averted, it promptly lost its importance in my eyes, and I was surprised, seeing how easily the thing had been done, that I should have doubted that it could be. I felt a lively sense of gratitude towards Albertine, who, I could now see, had not gone to the Trocadéro to meet Léa's friends, and who had shown me, by leaving the theatre and coming home at a word from me, that she belonged to me, even for the future, much more completely than I had realized. My gratitude was even more intense when a cycle messenger brought me a note from her to read while I waited, which was full of the charming expressions she so often used: 'Dear darling Marcel, I'll take longer than this cyclist, though I wish I could borrow his bike and get to you quicker. How could you think I would be angry, or that I could like anything as much as being with you? It will be fun to go out together, it would be even more fun to go out together always. Whatever is going through your head? Oh Marcel, Marcel! Your very own Albertine.' The very dresses I bought her, the yacht I had talked about, the Fortuny dresses, all the things which were, not repaid, but mirrored in this biddableness of Albertine's, seemed to me like privileges which I exercised; for the duties and expenses of a master form part of his dominion, define it and prove its existence just as much as his rights. And her recognition of my rights over her made clear the true character of my spending; I now had a woman of my own who, at one, unexpected word from me, would send a submissive telephone message to say that she was coming straight back, was letting herself be brought back, immediately. I was more of a master than I had thought. More of a master, that is to say, more of a slave. I was now in no hurry at all to see Albertine. The certain knowledge that she was shopping with Françoise, that they would arrive home together very shortly, was like a radiant, peaceful star lighting up a time which, now, I would have much preferred to spend on my own. My love for Albertine had made me get up and dress to go out, but it would now prevent me from enjoying my outing. I thought of how, on that Sunday afternoon, little working-girls, dressmakers, tarts would be walking in the Bois. And on the basis of these words, 'dressmakers', 'working-girls' (as had often happened with a proper name, the name of a young lady in the newspaper account of a ball) and of the image of a white bodice, a short skirt, because I placed behind them an unknown person who might love me, I created for myself desirable women, and said to myself, 'How attractive they must be!' But what use was their attractiveness to me, as I would not be going out alone?

Making the most of the fact that I was still alone, and half closing the curtains so that the sun would not stop me reading the notes, I sat down at the piano, opened Vinteuil's sonata which happened to be lying there, and began to play, since, Albertine's return being some time in the future but still absolutely certain, I had both some time at my disposal and a certain peace of mind. Secure in the expectation of her return with Françoise, my confidence in her docility bathed me in a blessed, inner light as warming as the sunlight outside; I could choose the direction of my thoughts, turn them for a moment away from Albertine and apply them to the sonata. Even in the piece of music, I did not trouble to notice how much more closely now the alternation of the sexual pleasure motif and the anxiety motif corresponded to my love for Albertine – a love from which jealousy had so long been absent that I had once been able to admit to Swann my ignorance of that feeling. No, approaching the sonata from another point of view, looking at it in itself as the work of a great artist, I was carried back on the wave of sound towards the old days at Combray – I do not mean Montjouvain and the Méséglise way, but our walks towards Guermantes — when I myself had wanted to be an artist. Having in practice abandoned this ambition, had I given up something real? Could life make up to me for the loss of art, or was there in art a deeper reality where our true personality finds an expression that the actions of life cannot give it? Each great artist seems so different from all the others, and gives us such a strong sense of individuality, which we seek in vain in everyday life! At the moment of having that thought, I was struck by a bar of the sonata, a bar which I knew very well, but sometimes a shift of attention casts a new light on things we have known for a long time, and shows us aspects of them that we had never noticed before. As I played the bar, and despite the fact that Vinteuil was at that point expressing a dream that would have remained quite alien to Wagner, I could not help murmuring, '*Tristan!*' with the smile of a family friend recognizing something of the grandfather in an intonation, a gesture of the grandson who never knew him. And just as people then turn to a photograph to confirm the resemblance, I set on the music-stand the score of *Tristan*, fragments of which were being performed that very afternoon in the Lamoureux concert series. I could admire the master of Bayreuth without any of the scruples of those who, like Nietzsche, feel that duty requires them to flee, both in art and life, from any beauty which appeals to them, who tear themselves away from *Tristan* as they renounce *Parsifal*, and by a spiritual ascesis, piling mortification upon mortification, follow the bloodiest path of suffering until they raise themselves to the pure knowledge and perfect adoration of *The Longjumeau Postilion*.[26] I realised how intensely realistic Wagner's work is, as I recalled those insistent, fleeting themes which appear in one act, fade away only to return and, sometimes distant, muted, almost detached, are at other times, while still vague, so immediate, so pressing, so internal, organic, visceral that their return seems not so much that of a motif as of a nerve pain.

Music, unlike Albertine's company, helped me to go deeper into myself, to find new things there: the variety which I had vainly sought in life and in travel, yet the longing for which was stirred in me by that surge of sound whose sunlit wavelets came to break at my feet. It was a double diversity. Just as the spectrum makes the composition of light visible to us, the harmonies of a Wagner, the colour of an Elstir let us know the qualitative essence of another's sensations in a way that love for another being can never do. Then there is the variety within the work itself, achieved by the only means there is of being genuinely diverse: bringing together different individualities. Where a lesser musician would claim he is depicting a squire or a knight, while having them sing the same music, Wagner, on the other hand, places under each name a different reality, and each time his squire appears, a particular figure, at once complex and simplistic, bursts, with a joyous, feudal clashing of lines, into the immensity of sound and leaves its mark there. Hence the fullness of a music which, in fact, is filled with countless different musics each of which is a being in its own right. A being, or the impression given by a fleeting aspect of nature. Even the thing which is most independent of the feeling it arouses in us, the song of a bird, the note of a huntsman's horn, the tune a shepherd plays on his pipe, all these leave on the horizon the silhouette of their sound. Certainly, Wagner was to bring it closer to us, appropriate it, work it in to an orchestral score, subordinate it to the loftiest musical ideas, but while still respecting its original character, as a woodcarver does the grain, the individual essence of the wood he sculpts.

But despite the richness of these works, in which the contemplation of nature is found next to action, next to individuals who are not only the names of characters, I found myself thinking how strongly these works partake of the character of being – wonderfully, it is true – incomplete: that incompleteness which characterizes all the great works of the nineteenth century; the nineteenth century, whose greatest writers failed in their books, but, watching themselves at work as if they were both worker and judge, drew from this self-contemplation a new beauty, separate from and superior to their work, conferring on it retrospectively a unity, a grandeur which it does not have in reality. Setting aside the man who saw after the event, in his novels, a *Human Comedy*, and those who named disparate collections of poems or essays *The Legend of the Centuries* or *The Bible of Humanity*,[27] cannot we say of this last that it represents the nineteenth century so perfectly, that we must look for the greatest beauties in Michelet not in his writings but in the attitude he takes to his writings, not in his *History of France* or his *History of the Revolution*, but in his prefaces to these two books? Prefaces, that is to say, pages written afterwards, in which he considers them, and to which we must add a few phrases here and there, generally beginning with a 'Dare I say?' which is not a scholar's precaution, but a musician's cadence. The other musician, who was causing me such delight at this moment, Wagner, as he took from his desk a delicious fragment to introduce, as a retrospectively necessary theme, into a work of which he had not yet dreamed when he was composing it, and when, having written one mythological opera, then a second, then more, he realized he had composed a Ring Cycle, must have known something of the same intoxication Balzac felt when, casting over his novels the eye of both a stranger and a father, and seeing in one the purity of a Raphael and in another the simplicity of the Gospel, he suddenly saw, with the light of hindsight, that they would be even more beautiful if brought together in a cycle in which the same characters would recur, and added to his work the final brushstroke, the most sublime of all. This unity was an afterthought, but not artificial. Otherwise it would have crumbled into dust, like so many systematic constructions by mediocre writers who, by lavish use of titles and subtitles, try to make it look as if they have followed a single, transcendent design. Not artificial, perhaps all the more real for being an afterthought, born in a moment of enthusiasm when it is discovered between parts which only need to come together, a unity which was unaware of itself, and which therefore is vital and not born of logic, which has not ruled out variety or put a damper on execution. This new-found unity (but this time on the scale of the whole work) is like certain pieces composed independently, born of inspiration, not demanded by the artificial working-out of a plan, which appear and take their place in the larger work. Before the large-scale orchestral movement which precedes the return of Isolde, it was the work itself which called into being the half-forgotten shepherd's pipe tune. And just as the swelling sound of the orchestra, as the ship approaches, takes hold of those pipe notes, changes them, associates them with its elation, breaks their rhythm, lightens their tone quality, speeds up their movement, varies their instrumentation, just so Wagner, no doubt, felt his joy increase when he discovered in his memory the shepherd's tune, built it into his work, gave it all its meaning. This joy, indeed, never leaves him. In his music, however sad the poet is, his sadness is consoled, transcended – and therefore, unfortunately, in some measure destroyed – by the enthusiasm of the maker. But then, as much as by the similarity I had just noticed between Vinteuil's phrase and Wagner's, I was disturbed by this Vulcan-like skill. Could it be this power which creates in the work of great artists the illusion of an essential, irreducible originality, apparently the reflection of a superhuman reality, when it is in fact the product of unremitting industry? If art is nothing but that, it is no more real than life, and I needed to have no regrets. I went on playing *Tristan*. Separated from Wagner by the intervening sound, I could hear him exulting, inviting me to share his joy, I could hear over and over again the eternally youthful laughter and the hammer-blows of Siegfried, in which further-more, the more perfectly struck out the phrases were, the more the workman's technique served to make them soar more freely above the earth, like birds resembling not Lohengrin's swan, but the aeroplane I had seen at Balbec turning its energy into elevation, gliding above the waves and disappearing into the sky. Perhaps, just as the birds who soar highest, who fly fastest, have the most powerful wings, we need those thoroughly material devices to explore the infinite, those hundred-and-twenty-horsepower Mysteries[28] in which, it must be said, however high one soars, one's appreciation of the silence of space is somewhat impeded by the powerful rumble of the engine!

I do not know why my wandering thoughts, which so far had been following memories of music, now turned to some of the best musical performers of our age, among whom, exaggerating his talent some-what, I placed Morel. Immediately my thoughts took a sudden new direction and focussed on the character of Morel, and some of the strangenesses of that character. In fact – and that fact might be related to, but not confused with, the neurasthenia from which he suffered – Morel often spoke of his own life, but gave an image of it so shrouded in darkness that it was difficult to make anything out. For example, he was M. de Charlus's to command, provided he could keep his evenings free, for he wanted to go to an algebra class after dinner. M. de Charlus gave his permission, but wanted to see him afterwards. 'Impossible, it's an old Italian painting' (transcribed in this way, the joke is meaningless; but since M. de Charlus had given Morel *L'Éducation sentimentale*[29] to read, in the penultimate chapter of which Frédéric Moreau makes this statement, Morel now never spoke the word 'impossible' without adding, 'it's an old Italian painting'). 'The course often goes on very late; and the teacher's already doing us a big favour, and of course he'd be offended . . . – But you don't need to go to lessons, algebra isn't swimming, or even English, you could just as well learn it out of a book,' M. de Charlus would reply, having immediately recognized in the algebra lessons one of those images behind which one could see nothing. Perhaps Morel was sleeping with a woman, or, trying to raise money by dubious means, was having secret dealings with the police and now had to go on an expedition with them: or worse, perhaps he was on call as a gigolo in a house of prostitution. 'Even better from a book, Morel would reply to M. de Charlus, for you can't understand a word of algebra lessons. – Then why don't you study it at my house instead, where you'd be so much more comfortable?' M. de Charlus could have replied, but he was careful not to, knowing as he did that, keeping only the necessary characteristic of occupying all the evening hours, the imaginary algebra course would immediately have changed into indispensable drawing or dancing lessons. Actually, M. de Charlus could have observed that he was mistaken, at least in part: Morel often spent time at the Baron's house in solving equations. M. de Charlus did object that algebra was of little use to a violinist. Morel replied that he enjoyed it, that it passed the time and relieved his neurasthenia. No doubt M. de Charlus could have tried to learn the truth, to find out the real nature of these mysterious, indispensable algebra lessons that were given only at night. But M. de Charlus had not time to unravel the twisted skein of Morel's occupations: he was too taken up himself with those of society. Calls received or paid, hours spent at his club, fashionable dinner-parties, evenings at the theatre took his mind off Morel's doings and let him ignore the aggression, both violent and underhand, which Morel had, it was said, both displayed and concealed in the various social milieux, the successive towns through which he had passed, and where his name was now only mentioned with a shudder, in an undertone and without giving any details. It was one of these outbursts of nervous aggression that I had the misfortune to overhear that day when, having left the piano, I went down into the courtyard to meet Albertine, who had still not arrived. As I passed in front of Jupien's shop, where Morel was alone with the girl I imagined he was soon to marry, Morel was shouting at the top of his voice, which brought out an accent in him that I had not heard before, a peasant accent he normally suppressed, which sounded very strange. His words were no less strange, the French was bad, but then he knew nothing properly. 'Get out, slut, great slut, you great slut,'[30] he was repeating to the poor girl, who certainly at first had not understood what he was saying, but now, proud and trembling, stood stock-still in front of him. 'I said get out, great slut, you great slut, go and get your uncle till I tell him what you are, you whore.' Just at that moment I heard Jupien's voice coming into the courtyard, talking to one of his friends, and as I knew that Morel was extremely cowardly, I did not think it necessary to offer my help to Jupien and his friend, who would be entering the shop at any moment, and I went back upstairs so as to avoid Morel, who, although he had been loudly demanding (no doubt in order to frighten and dominate the girl by some kind of probably groundless blackmail) that Jupien should be fetched, made himself scarce as soon as he heard him in the courtyard. The words in themselves are nothing, they cannot explain the beating of my heart as I went back up the stairs. These scenes which we witness in real life gain an incalculable power from what soldiers call, when describing an attack, surprise effect, and despite the blessed calm which I felt at the thought that Albertine, instead of staying at the Trocadéro, was coming home to me, my ears were still full of the sound of those constantly repeated words, 'great slut, great slut', which had so upset me.

Slowly my agitation receded. Albertine would be home soon. I would hear her ring the door-bell in a moment. I could feel that my life was no longer what it once might have been; and that to have, in this way, a woman with whom, quite naturally, when she came home, I would be expected to go out, to whose embellishment the strength and activity of my being would be increasingly devoted, made me into something like a twig which has grown in length, but is weighed down by the plump fruit in which all its reserves of strength have been concentrated. In contrast with the anxiety I had been suffering a mere hour before, the calm produced in me by Albertine's return was more complete than the one I had experienced in the morning, before she left. Confident in the future, of which I saw myself as master, thanks to my friend's docility, it was a stronger, fuller sense of calm, made stable by her imminent, inevitable, irritating, sweet presence: the calm (lulled by which we need not seek happiness within ourselves) of family feeling, of domestic happiness. Family, domestic bliss: that was the feeling which not only had brought me such peace while I was waiting for Albertine, but which I experienced again when I went out with her later. She took off her glove for a moment, either to touch my hand, or to dazzle me by letting me see, on her little finger, next to the ring Mme Bontemps had given her, another on which there gleamed the large, liquid expanse of a bright sliver of ruby. 'Another ring, Albertine! Your aunt is certainly generous! – No, this one isn't from my aunt, she laughed. I bought it myself: you're so good to me, I can save lots of money. I'm not even sure who it did belong to. A customer who had run out of money left it with the owner of a hotel I stayed in at Le Mans. He didn't know what to do with it and would have let me have it for much less than it was worth. But it was still much too dear for me. But now, thanks to you, I'm a smart lady, and I sent to ask him if he still had it. And here it is. – That's a lot of rings, Albertine. Where will you put the one I'm going to give you? Anyhow, this one is very pretty; I can't make out the carving around the ruby, it looks like the head of a man making a face. But I can't see well enough. – Even if your eyesight was better, you wouldn't be any further on. I can't make it out either.' In the past it had often happened to me while reading a novel, or memoirs, in which a man is always going out with a woman, having tea with her, to wish that I could do the same. I sometimes thought I had managed it, when I took out Saint-Loup's mistress, for example, and had dinner with her. But however hard I tried to believe that I was successfully playing the part of the character in the novel, this idea convinced me that I ought to be enjoying my time with Rachel, rather than allowing me actually to do so. The truth is that every time we try to imitate a truly real experience, we forget that that experience was produced, not by a wish to imitate anything, but by an unconscious force, itself also real. But this particular impression, which all my desire to experience a rare pleasure in going out with Rachel had not been enough to procure for me, now appeared spontaneously, without my having sought it at all, for quite different reasons, and sincere, profound ones: to name just one, for the reason that my jealousy did not allow me ever to be far from Albertine or, on the days when I could go out, to allow her to go out without me. It was only now that I felt this pleasure, because our knowledge is not of those things outside ourselves that we wish to observe, but of our involuntary sensations; because then, even though a woman was in the same carriage with me, she was not *really* beside me, so long as she was not recreated for me there from moment to moment by a need of her such as I had for Albertine, so long as the constant caress of my gaze did not renew in her complexion those colours that constantly need to be retouched, and my senses, ever-wakeful even when satisfied, lend taste and consistency to those colours; and so long as jealousy, joined with the senses and the imagination which exalts them, did not keep this woman suspended next to us by a balanced attraction as powerful as the law of gravity.

Our car was going quickly down the boulevards and avenues, whose rows of large houses, frozen pink cliffs of sun and cold, recalled to me my visits to Mme Swann, those afternoons gently illuminated by chrysanthemums as we waited for the lamps to be lit. I had hardly time to notice, being just as cut off from them by the car windows as I would have been behind the window of my bedroom, a young fruit-seller, a dairy-girl standing in front of her shop door, lit up by the winter sun, like a heroine whom my desire could involve in the most delicious complications, on the threshold of a novel which I should never read. For I could hardly ask Albertine to stop, and I had already lost sight of the young women, almost before my eyes had had time to distinguish their features and caress their youthful freshness in the blond vapour in which they were enveloped. The intensity of feeling which seized me at the sight of a wine-merchant's cashier at her desk or a laundry-girl chatting in the street was the feeling we have when we recognize goddesses. Now that there is no more Olympus, its inhabitants live on earth. And when, working on a mythological subject, painters have got working-class girls from the most humble occupations to pose as Venus or Ceres, far from committing a sacrilege, they have only restored to them the divine attributes of which they had been unjustly stripped. 'What did you think of the Trocadéro, sweetheart? – I'm jolly glad I left it to come and meet you. It's Davioud, isn't it? – Well, well, little Albertine is certainly learning a lot! It *is* Davioud, I'd forgotten that. – While you're asleep I read your books, lazybones. As a monument it's not much to look at, is it? – Dear child, you're changing so fast and getting so clever (it was true, but I was also quite pleased that she should have the satisfaction, in the absence of others, of being able to tell herself that the time she spent at my house was not completely wasted) that if I needed to I could tell you things that most people would think were nonsense but which have a kind of truth that I'm looking for. Do you know what Impressionism is? – Yes, of course. – Then think about this: do you remember the church at Marcouville-l'Orgueilleuse that he[31] didn't like because it was new? Well, isn't he going against the ideas of his own Impressionism when he isolates these important buildings from the general impression surrounding them, takes them out of the light they're dissolved in and examines their intrinsic value like an archaeologist? When he is painting, don't a hospital or a school or a poster on a wall have the same value as a priceless cathedral standing next to them, in one indivisible image? Remember how the façade was baked in the sun, how the relief of those Marcouville saints floated in the light. What does it matter if a building is new, if it looks old; or even if it doesn't! The poetic quality of old neighbourhoods has been squeezed out to the last drop, but there are some houses newly built for the shopkeeper class, in new neighbourhoods, where the newly cut stone is still too white, that scream in the burning midday air of July, when the shopkeepers are coming home to lunch in the suburbs, with a note as acid as the smell of cherries waiting for the meal to be served in the shuttered dining-room, where the glass prism knife-rests glint with multicoloured lights as beautiful as the stained-glass windows of Chartres? – What a lovely idea! If I ever develop any intelligence, it will be thanks to you. – Why, on a beautiful day, should one take one's eyes off the Trocadéro, whose giraffe-neck towers[32] remind one of the Charterhouse at Pavia? – It made me think of something else, sitting on its little hill like that: a Mantegna reproduction of yours, *Saint Sebastian* I think, where there's a town in the background arranged in the shape of an amphitheatre and you'd swear one of the buildings is the Trocadéro. – You see! But how did you come to see the Mantegna? You're amazing.'

We had arrived in a more working-class neighbourhood, and the setting-up of an ancillary Venus behind every counter turned it into a kind of suburban altar before which I would gladly have spent my life in adoration. As one does on the eve of an untimely death, I was drawing up a list of the pleasures of which I was being deprived by Albertine's having set a final period to my freedom. In Passy the pavements were so crowded that young girls walking in the roadway itself, with their arms round each other's waists, showed me the wonder of their smiles. I had not time to make them out very clearly, but I do not think I exaggerated their beauty; for in any crowd, any youthful crowd, it is common to find the effigy of a noble profile. So that unruly holiday mobs are as fruitful terrain for the voluptuary as for the archaeologist the disorderly aftermath of an excavation which may turn up ancient medals. We arrived at the Bois.

I was thinking that if Albertine had not come out with me, I could, at that moment, have been in the Champs-Elysées Circus,[33] listening as the Wagnerian tempest set all the rigging of the orchestra groaning and drew towards itself like an airy foam the shepherd's pipe tune that I had just been playing, setting it flying through the air, kneading it, pulling it out of shape, splitting it, catching it up in an ever-growing whirlwind. At the very least, I wanted our outing to be a short one, and for us to go home early, since, unknown to Albertine, I had decided to spend the evening at the Verdurins'. They had recently sent me an invitation which I had thrown in the wastepaper basket like all the others. But I had changed my mind about this evening, for I wanted to try to find out who the people were that Albertine had been hoping to meet at their house that afternoon. To tell the truth, I had reached the point with Albertine where (if everything continues in the same way, if things follow the normal course) a woman has no more interest for us except as the means of transition to another woman. She still has a place in our heart, but only a very small place; we cannot wait to go out each evening and meet women we do not know, and particularly women unknown to us but known to her, who will be able to tell us how she has lived. Her we have already taken possession of, exhausted everything she has been willing to tell us about herself. Her life is her, of course, but precisely the part of her that we do not know, the things we vainly questioned her about and which we shall be able to collect from new lips.

If my life with Albertine was to keep me from going to Venice, from travelling, then today I could at least, if I had been alone, have got to know the young working-girls who were dotted about in the brilliant sunshine of that fine Sunday, and in whose beauty I mentally located a large part of the unknown life which animated them. When one sees a person's eyes, are they not suffused with a look which bears within it, inseparable from it, its own images, memories, expectations, disdains? Will not this existence, which is that of the passing being, give, according to its own nature, a different meaning to the frown that we observe, to the dilation of the nostrils? Albertine's presence deprived me of the chance of approaching these girls and thereby, perhaps, of ceasing to desire them. The man who wants to keep alive in himself the wish to go on living and belief in something more delicious than the things of every day, must go out walking; for the streets, the avenues are filled with Goddesses. But Goddesses do not let us approach them. Here and there, among the trees, a servant kept watch like a nymph at the entrance to a sacred grove, while in the distance three young girls sat by the immense arc of their bicycles, which lay on the ground next to them, like three immortals leaning on the cloud or the magic steed which would bear them on their mythological journeys. I noticed that Albertine would look for a moment, with deep attention, at these girls and then turn immediately back towards me. But I was not unduly tormented by the intensity of this contemplation, nor by its brevity, for which the intensity compensated; as far as the latter was concerned, it often happened that Albertine, whether from tiredness or a characteristically attentive habit of looking, would let her eyes rest as if in a kind of meditation upon, perhaps, my father, or Françoise; and as for her way of rapidly turning back towards me, it could have been explained by the fact that Albertine, knowing my suspicions, might wish, even if they were unjustified, not to give them any grounds. The attention paid to these young girls would have seemed criminal to me in Albertine (and just as much so if she had been looking at young men); yet I directed the same attention, without a moment's guilt – and almost feeling that Albertine was guilty for keeping me, by her presence, from stopping the car and getting out – upon every shop-girl we passed. We find desiring innocent, and hideous that the other should desire. And this contrast between what applies to us and to the woman we love, is not only a matter of desire, but also of lying. What is more usual than to lie, whether we wish to conceal, say, the daily fluctuations of our health when we want to represent it as strong, or to hide a vice, or to go, without hurting another, towards the thing which we prefer? Lying is the most necessary means of self-preservation, and the most used. And yet it is the thing we are determined to expunge from the life of the woman we love, lying is what we spy upon, sniff out, hate above all. It turns our feelings upside down, it is enough to make us break off a relationship, it seems to us to hide the greatest faults, unless of course it hides them so well that we do not suspect their existence. What a strange state it is in which we are so sensitive to a pathogen whose ubiquitous pullulation makes it harmless to the world at large, and yet so dangerous to the unfortunate subject who happens to have lost his immunity to it! The life of those pretty girls, since – spending so much time as I did shut away indoors – I so rarely met any of them, seemed to me, as it does to all those in whom the ease of achievement has not impaired the power of ambition, something as different from anything I knew, something as desirable as the most wonderful cities to which one might dream of travelling.

The disappointment I had experienced with women whom I had known, or in cities to which I had travelled, did not prevent me from giving myself up to the attraction of new ones and believing in their reality, just as seeing Venice – Venice, which this springlike weather made me long for all the more, and which marriage to Albertine would prevent me from ever getting to know – seeing Venice in a panorama which Ski might have said was more prettily coloured than the city itself, would have in no way replaced for me the actual journey to Venice, a journey which, despite its length, arrived at without any reference to me, it seemed to me absolutely necessary to complete. In the same way, a young dressmaker artificially procured for me by a bawd would have been no possible substitute for the tall yet almost childish figure I saw passing under the trees at this moment, laughing with a friend. The one I found in a house of assignation might have been prettier, still it would not have been the same, because when we look at the eyes of a girl we do not know, it is not like looking at a little opal or agate plaque. No, we know that the little ray of light which strikes prismatic glints from them, the diamond dust which seems to glitter there, are all that we can see of a mind, a will, a memory in which dwell the family house we do not know, the dear friends whom we so envy. The hope of taking possession of all that – such a difficult, such a thankless task – is what gives her eyes their value, much more than any mere material beauty (and this explains how the same young man can set in train a whole romance in the imagination of a woman who has heard that he was the Prince of Wales, and be of no further interest to her as soon as she learns she was mistaken); to find the little dressmaker in the house of ill-fame is to find her emptied of that unknown life which we hope to possess in the act of possessing her, it is to look into eyes which have now indeed become nothing but precious stones; when she wrinkles her nose, the folds have no more meaning than those of a flower. No, in relation to the unknown working-girl who was passing just then, it seemed to me just as vital, if I wished to go on believing in her reality, as it would be to make a long railway journey if I wished to believe in the Pisa I would see at the end of it, which would then be something more than a pavilion at a universal exhibition, to put up with her refusals and wear down her resistance by changing my approach, risking an insult and returning to the attack, winning her agreement to a meeting, waiting for her when she came out of work, learning incident by incident what made up the girl's life, getting through the layers that, in her mind, surrounded the pleasure I was seeking, and covering the distance that her different habits and particular life placed between me and the attention, the favour that I wanted to win and make my own. But these very similarities between desire and travel made me promise myself that one day I would grasp more effectively the nature of this force, invisible but as strong as religious belief, or in the world of physics as atmospheric pressure, which so raised in my estimation cities, or women, for so long as I did not know them, but fell away beneath them as soon as I approached them, depositing them on the flat earth of vulgar reality. Further off another girl was kneeling by her bicycle, mending it. As soon as the repair was done, the young rider jumped on her machine, but without throwing her leg over it as a man would do. For a moment the bicycle swerved from side to side, and the young body seemed to have acquired a sail, a huge wing, and presently we saw the youthful being, half-human and half-winged, an angel or a peri, continuing her journey.

There exactly was what Albertine's presence, what my life with Albertine, was depriving me of. Depriving? Should I not have said, on the contrary, the gift it brought to me? If Albertine had not been living with me, if she had been free, I should have been imagining all these women, and quite rightly, as possible, as probable objects of her desire, of her pleasure. They would have appeared to me like dancers in some diabolical ballet, representing Temptations for one character, firing their arrows into the heart of another. Working-girls, young ladies, actresses, how I should have hated them all! Objects of horror to me, they would have been set apart from the beauty of the universe. The subjection of Albertine, by sparing me the suffering they could have caused me, replaced them in the world's beauty. Harmless as they now were, deprived of the dart which plants jealousy in our heart, I could freely admire them, caress them with my eyes and perhaps one day even more intimately. By shutting away Albertine, I had restored to the world all those glittering wings which rustle in public promenades, at balls, at the theatre, and which were coming to tempt me once more now that she could no longer succumb to their temptation. These wings made up the beauty of the world. They had once made the beauty of Albertine. It was because I had seen her as a mysterious bird, then as a great actress of the beach scene, desired and, who knows, enjoyed, that she had seemed wonderful to me. Once a captive in my house, the marvellous bird I had once seen walking with measured pace on the promenade, surrounded by the gathering of other girls like gulls alighting from nowhere in particular, had lost all its colours: they had vanished along with other people's chances of making Albertine their own. Little by little she had lost her beauty. It was only on outings like today's, when I could imagine her, if she were out without me, being accosted by some young woman or young man, that I could see her once more amid the splendour of the beach, even though my jealousy was on another plane from the declining pleasures of my imagination. But in spite of these sudden, recurring moments when, desired by others, she was beautiful once more in my eyes, I could easily divide the time she had spent with me into two periods: the first, when she was still, though less each day, the glittering actress of the beach, and the second when, having become the grey prisoner, reduced to her dull self, she needed those flashes in which I remembered the past to restore something of her brilliance.

Sometimes, during those hours when I felt the greatest indifference to her, a memory would return to me of a moment on the beach, when I did not know her yet; she was not far from a certain lady with whom I was now almost sure that she had had relations, and she was laughing loudly while giving me an insolent look. The polished, blue sea murmured all around. In the sunlight of the beach, Albertine, surrounded by her friends, was the most beautiful of all. She was a splendid-looking girl who, in this her usual setting of a vast seascape, had, under the eyes of this lady who so admired her, inflicted this slight upon me. It was ineradicable, for the lady might return to Balbec, might notice on the beach, full of light and the sound of the sea, the absence of Albertine. But she could not know that the girl now lived with me, belonged only to me. The vast, blue waters, her forgetfulness of the passing fancy she had had for Albertine, which had now turned towards others, had washed over Albertine's insult, enclosing it in a glittering and unbreakable casket. Then hatred for this woman would bite into my heart; for Albertine too, but that was a hatred mixed with admiration for the beautiful, worshipped young girl with her marvellous hair, whose sudden laugh on the beach was an affront.

Shame, jealousy, the memory of initial desire and its dazzling setting had given Albertine back her former beauty, her value to me. And thus there alternated, with the slight weight of boredom I felt when I was with her, a trembling desire, full of splendid images and regret for the past, according to whether she was sitting next to me in my room, or I gave her back her freedom in my memory, setting her walking on the promenade, in her gay beach-dresses, against the background music of the sea, Albertine, now removed from that setting, possessed and retaining little value, and now placed in it once more, escaping from me into a past I could not know, insulting me in front of the lady, her friend, as real as the splashing of the waves and the dazzling of the sun, Albertine, put back on the beach or withdrawn from it into my bedroom, in a kind of amphibious love.

Elsewhere in the Bois a large group of girls was playing ball. All these little girls had wanted to make the best of the sunshine, for February days, even when they are as bright as these, do not last long, and the brilliance of their light cannot postpone its fading. Even before darkness fell we had a considerable time of half-light, because, after we had driven as far as the Seine, where Albertine admired, and by her presence prevented me from admiring, the reflections of red sails in the blue, wintry water, and a tile-roofed house huddled in the distance like a single poppy on the bright horizon which seemed, further to the west, at Saint-Cloud, to have become petrified and fragmented, crumbly and ribbed, we got out of the car and walked for a long time. For a few moments I even took her arm, and it seemed that the ring that her arm made as it passed under mine joined our two selves as a single being and linked our futures one to the other. At our feet our shadows, first parallel, then close and finally merged, drew an enchanting pattern. Of course it still seemed wonderful to me at home that Albertine should be living with me, that it should be she who lay down on my bed. But it was like a transference of that wonder out of doors, into nature itself, when in front of the lake in the Bois that I loved so much, at the foot of its trees, it should be her very shadow, the pure, simplified outline of her leg, her torso, that the sun was called upon to paint in ink-and-wash on the fine gravel of the path. And I found a charm, more immaterial no doubt but no less intimate than that of the nearness, the joining of our bodies, in the fusion of our shadows. Then we got back into the car. And it started back, down little, twisting paths where the winter trees, hung in ivy and brambles, looked as if they should lead to a magician's lair. As we emerged from their gloom and headed out of the Bois, we found ourselves in broad daylight once more, so bright that I thought I would have time to do everything I wanted before dinner; however, it was only a few moments later, as our car approached the Arc de Triomphe, that I was surprised and alarmed to see, hanging over Paris, the full moon, premature as the dial of a stopped clock which makes one think one is already late. We had told the driver to take us home. For her, that meant coming home with me. The presence of women, however much we love them, who have to leave us to go home, does not give us that sense of peace which I now enjoyed with Albertine sitting in the back of the car beside me, a presence which was taking us, not towards the emptiness of the hours when we are apart, but to an even more stable unity, better enclosed in my home, which was also her home, the material symbol of my possession of her. Certainly, to possess something one must have desired it. We can possess a line, a surface, a volume only if our love occupies it. But Albertine, as we rode in the car, had not been for me, as Rachel had been all those years before, an empty dust-cloud of flesh and fabric. The imagination of my eyes, my lips, my hands at Balbec had so solidly built up her body, polished it so lovingly, that now, in this car, to touch her body, to contain it, I did not have to press mine against her, nor even to see her, it was enough to hear her voice and, if she fell silent, to know that she was there, near me; my senses woven together wrapped around her completely, and when we arrived home and she quite naturally got out of the carriage, I stayed behind for a moment to ask the chauffeur to come back for me, but my gaze still enfolded her as she disappeared from my sight into the entrance, and I still experienced the same pleasantly inert, domestic calm as I saw her, heavy, her cheeks flushed, opulent and a prisoner, coming home with me as if it were the most natural thing in the world, like a woman who belonged to me, and, protected by the walls, vanishing into our house.

Unfortunately she seemed to feel imprisoned there, and to agree with that Mme de la Rochefoucauld, who, asked whether she were not pleased to be in so fine a house as Liancourt, replied that 'there is no such thing as a fine prison', if I could judge by the sad, tired look that she wore that evening as we dined alone in her bedroom. I did not notice it at first, and indeed it was I who was disconsolate at the thought that if I had not had Albertine (for, with her, I would have suffered too much from jealousy in a hotel where she would have been in contact all day with so many other human beings), I could at that moment have been dining in Venice in one of those semi-subterranean little dining-rooms, like the hold of a ship, from where you can see the Grand Canal through little arched windows surrounded with Moorish moulding.

I should add that Albertine much admired a large Barbedienne bronze[34] in my parents' flat, which Bloch rightly considered hideous. He was perhaps less justified in being astonished at my keeping it. Unlike him, I had never tried to create artistic surroundings, to compose room settings, I was too lazy for that, too indifferent to the things I had before my eyes every day. Since my taste was not involved, I had the right not to take notice of décor. All the same, I could have got rid of the bronze. But ugly, expensive things can be useful: they can impress people who do not understand us, do not share our taste, but with whom we might be in love, more than a difficult object which does not yield up its beauty at once. Now it is precisely and only those people who do not understand us whom it may be useful to impress with possessions, since our intelligence will be enough to win the regard of superior beings. Albertine was beginning to have taste, but she still went in awe of the bronze to some extent, and this awe was transferred to me in the form of an admiration which, since it came from Albertine, was important to me (infinitely more important than the embarrassment of keeping a rather shaming bronze), since I loved Albertine.

But the thought of my slavery suddenly ceased to weigh upon me, and I even wished to prolong it when I seemed to see that Albertine was sorely oppressed by hers. Certainly, every time I had asked her if she found it tiresome living with me, she had always replied that she could not think of anywhere she would be happier. But these words were often belied by a look of longing or of irritation. Certainly, if her tastes were what I had imagined them to be, this situation of being unable ever to satisfy them must have been as irritating to her as it was pacifying to me; pacifying to the point that the hypothesis that I had accused her unjustly would have seemed to me the most probable, except that I would then have had great difficulty in explaining Albertine's extraordinary determination never to be alone, never to be free, not to stop for a moment outside the door as she came in, to have herself conspicuously accompanied to the telephone whenever she had a call to make, by someone who could repeat to me what she had said, Françoise or Andrée; always to leave me alone, as if by accident, with Andrée when they had been out together, so that I could get a detailed report of what they had done. In contrast with this wonderful docility, certain hints of impatience, quickly suppressed, made me wonder if Albertine had not formed the plan of shaking off her chains.

Other events underpinned this suspicion. For example, one day when I had gone out on my own, I met Gisèle near Passy and we talked about one thing and another. Presently, quite pleased to be able to give her this news, I told her that I was seeing quite a lot of Albertine these days. Gisèle asked me where she could find her as there was something she *really must* tell her. 'Oh, what? – Something about some little friends of hers. – What friends are those? I could pass on your message, not of course that that will stop you seeing her yourself. – Oh, just friends from the old days, I can't remember their names,' Gisèle answered with a vague look, beating a hasty retreat. She left me, imagining that she had spoken so cautiously that nothing could have aroused my suspicions. But untruth demands so little, needs only such tiny signs to make its presence obvious. If these had been friends of long ago, whose names she could not even remember, why would she have *really* needed to talk to Albertine about them just then? This adverb, closely related as it was to one of Mme Cottard's favourite expressions, 'it couldn't have come at a better time', could apply only to a particular piece of news, timely, perhaps urgent, concerning particular people. Besides, even her way of opening her mouth, as if in a stifled yawn, before saying vaguely (while almost pulling her body away from me, just as she began, from that moment, to backtrack in our conversation), 'Oh, I don't know, I can't remember their names,' turned her whole figure, and her voice along with it, into an embodiment of untruthfulness, just as her previous, quite different posture, intent, lively, forward-leaning, as she said 'I really must . . .', had been an indicator of truth. I did not question Gisèle. What would have been the use? Certainly, her way of lying was different from Albertine's. And certainly Albertine's lies hurt me more. But in the first instance there was a point of similarity between them, the mere fact of their being lies, which in some cases is thoroughly obvious. Not that the reality behind the lies is obvious. Everyone knows that although each single murderer thinks he has planned his crime so carefully that he will never be caught, in fact almost all murderers are caught. Liars, on the other hand, are rarely caught out, and among liars, particularly the women one loves. We do not know where she has been or what she has been doing there, but as soon as we hear her talking, talking about something different which conceals the thing she will not speak of, it is immediately obvious that she is lying. And jealousy is redoubled because we can hear the lie and cannot know the truth. With Albertine, the sensation of untruth was given by many details already mentioned in this story, but above all by the fact that, when she was lying, her account was either inadequate, whether from omissions or improbabilities, or else too complete, too full of little details intended to make it more plausible. Verisimilitude, whatever the liar may think, is not at all the same thing as truth. When, as we listen to a true account, we hear something which is merely plausible, which is perhaps more plausible than the truth, perhaps too plausible, the even slightly trained ear notices that something is wrong, as with a line of verse that does not scan, or a wrong word read aloud. The ear hears it and, if we are in love, the heart takes fright.

Why do we not stop to think, before changing our whole lives because we cannot know whether a woman went down the rue de Berri or the rue Washington, why do we not tell ourselves that those few metres of difference, and the woman herself, will shrink to a hundred millionth of their size (that is, to a size we can no longer perceive), if only we are wise enough not to see the woman for several years, and that she who was Gulliver-sized and much more will shrink to a Lilliputian whom no microscope – of the heart, that is, for the objective instrument of memory is more powerful and less fragile – will be any longer able to perceive! In any case, even if there was something in common between Albertine's and Gisèle's lies – the fact of being lies – still Gisèle did not lie in quite the same way as Albertine, or as Andrée, but their respective lies fitted so well one into the other, while still presenting a great variety, that the little gang had the impenetrable solidity of certain commercial, publishing or bookselling houses, in dealings with which the poor author, for example, can never succeed in finding out, despite the variety of different personalities making them up, whether or not he is being swindled. The newspaper or magazine editor lies with an air of sincerity all the more impressive for his need to conceal the fact that very often he is behaving in exactly the same way, resorting to the same commercial tricks, as the other editors, theatre directors or publishers he has condemned so roundly since raising and carrying into battle against them the standard of Sincerity. To have once proclaimed (as the leader of a political party, or in any capacity) that it is appalling to lie, usually obliges one to lie more than other people, without however putting aside the solemn mask, the august tiara of trustworthiness. The associate of the 'sincere man' lies in a different way and more naïvely. He deceives his author as he might deceive his wife, with tricks from stage farce. The managing editor, an honest, clumsy soul, lies quite straightforwardly, like an architect who assures you your house will be ready on a date when it will not have been started. The editor-in-chief floats in his unworldliness among the previous three and, not knowing what is going on, gives them, out of a sense of fraternal duty and loving solidarity, the valuable support of his unimpeachable word. These four people are constantly quarrelling, except when the arrival of the author reconciles them. Forgetting their particular disputes, they recall the great military duty to come to the aid of the threatened 'corps'. Without realizing it, I had long been playing the role of that author in relation to the 'little gang'. If Gisèle had been thinking, when she used the word 'really', about some friend of Albertine's who would have been happy to go travelling with her as soon as my friend found some pretext or other for leaving me, and had wanted to let Albertine know that the time had come or was at hand, Gisèle would have let herself be cut in pieces rather than give away the secret to me. There was therefore no point in asking her any questions.

Meetings like the ones with Gisèle were not the only thing which increased my suspicions. For example, I was looking at Albertine's paintings. And these paintings, touching pursuits of the prisoner, so moved me that I praised them to her. 'No, they're hopeless, but then I've never had a single drawing lesson. – But one evening at Balbec you sent me a message to say you were kept late at a drawing lesson.' I reminded her of the day and said that of course I had understood at once that people don't have drawing lessons at that time of night. Albertine blushed. 'You're right, she said, I wasn't taking drawing lessons, I told you a lot of lies at the beginning, I admit. But I never lie to you now.' How I should have loved to know what all those early lies were! But I knew already that her confessions would have been further lies. So I simply kissed her. I asked her to tell me just one of the lies. She answered, 'Well, for example, I said that the sea air was bad for me.' In the face of such an attitude, I asked no more.

Every being we love, up to a point every being, is a Janus, showing us its pleasant face as it moves away from us, and its gloomy face if we know it is permanently available to us. In the case of Albertine, living permanently with her was a source of pain in another way which I cannot describe in this story. It is dreadful to have another person's life attached to one's own, like carrying a bomb which one cannot let go of without committing a crime. But let us take as a comparison the elation and despair, the dangers, the worry, the fear of seeing people in later years believe things which are untrue but plausible, and which one will not then be able to explain, all the things one experiences if living in private contact with a madman. For example, I pitied M. de Charlus for living with Morel (and immediately the memory of that afternoon's scene made the left side of my chest feel much larger than the other); setting aside whatever their sexual relations might be, M. de Charlus could not have known at the beginning that Morel was mad. Morel's beauty, his commonplace mind, his pride must have ensured that M. de Charlus did not entertain such far-fetched ideas, until the appearance of the attacks of melancholy in which Morel blamed M. de Charlus for his unhappiness, without being able to offer any explanations, accused him of not trusting him, with a mixture of insults and devious but extremely subtle reasoning, and threatened him with desperate solutions, in the midst of which threats could still be discerned the most twisted manoeuvres of immediate cupidity. All this is just for comparison. Albertine was not mad.

To make her chains seem lighter, I thought the best idea was to convince her that I meant to break them. But I could not begin to feed her this lie now, when she had just been so good in coming back from the Trocadéro; what I could do, rather than upsetting her with threats of a separation, was to keep silent about the dreams of a permanent life together which were even then forming in my grateful heart. As I looked at her, I could hardly keep myself from pouring them out to her, and perhaps she realized it. Unfortunately the expression of such dreams is not contagious. The case of an affected old woman like M. de Charlus who, daily seeing in his own imagination only a proud young man, comes to believe in himself as a proud young man, the more so as he becomes more affected and more laughable, this case applies more generally, and the passionate lover is so unfortunate as not to recognize that, while he sees a beautiful face before him, his mistress sees his face which is not made more beautiful, quite the opposite, when deformed by the pleasure he feels at the sight of beauty. And love does not exhaust the applicability of this model; we do not see our own bodies, which others see, and pursue our own thought, the object invisible to others, wherever it leads. An artist is sometimes able to show this object in his work. That is why the admirers of the work are disappointed in the author, in whose face this inner beauty is but imperfectly reflected.

Retaining from my dream of Venice only what could relate to Albertine and make the time she spent with me more tolerable, I mentioned to her a Fortuny dress that we must go and order in the next few days. I was trying to discover new pleasures with which to divert her. I would have liked to be able to surprise her by giving her, if I could find any, some pieces of old French silver. In fact, when we had discussed the idea of having a yacht, a plan which Albertine dismissed as impossible – as I did whenever I thought her virtuous, and life with her therefore as ruinous as marriage with her would be impossible – we had, still without her thinking that I would buy one, taken advice from Elstir.

I learned that that day there had been a death which caused me great sadness, that of Bergotte. His illness had, of course, been a long one. Not his first, which had been of natural length. Nature seems unable to give any but short illnesses. But medicine has taken over the art of prolonging them. Medicines, the remission they secure, the symptoms which return when they are stopped, make up an artificial disease to which the patient's habituation gives a stable, stylized form, just as children regularly have coughing fits long after they have got over whooping-cough. Then the medicines become less effective, the dose is increased, they no longer do any good, but the patient has been keeping his bed so long that they begin to do harm. Nature would never have given them such a long reign. It is a marvellous thing that medicine should be almost as powerful as nature, should force the patient to stay in bed and, under pain of death, to continue a treatment. By this time, the artificially introduced disease has taken root, has become a secondary but true illness, the only difference being that natural diseases can get better, but never medical ones, for medicine knows nothing of the secrets of cure.

Bergotte had not been out of the house for years. He had never liked society, or rather he had once liked it for a single day, only to despise it afterwards as he despised everything, after his own fashion, which was not to despise what one cannot obtain, but what one has obtained, as soon as one has obtained it. He lived so simply that no one suspected how rich he was, and had people known it they would still have misunderstood him, imagining him to be a miser when in fact no one was more generous. He was particularly so to women, girls rather, who were ashamed to take so much from him in return for so little. He excused his behaviour to himself because he knew he could never produce so well as in an atmosphere where he felt he was in love. Love, no, pleasure well rooted in the flesh helps literary work because it cancels out other pleasures, the pleasures of social life, for example, which are the same for everyone. And even if this love brings disillusion, at least that too keeps the surface of the soul in motion, where otherwise it might become stagnant. Desire, therefore, can be useful to the man of letters, first by keeping him at a distance from other men and from resembling them, then by restoring some movement to a spiritual machine which otherwise, beyond a certain age, tends to seize up. None of this makes us happy, but we can examine the reasons that keep us from being so, reasons which would have remained hidden from us if not for these sudden irruptions of disappointment. And dreams cannot be made real, we know that; still, perhaps we would not form any without desire, and it is useful to have dreams so that we can see their collapse and learn from it. So it was that Bergotte said to himself, 'I spend more on girls than a multi-millionaire, but the pleasures or disappointments they bring me allow me to write a book and make money.' On economic grounds this reasoning was absurd, but no doubt he took some pleasure in transmuting gold into caresses in this way, and caresses back into gold. And then, as we saw when my grandmother died, his tired old age loved repose. Now in society, there is nothing but conversation. Stupid conversation, but it serves to eliminate women, who become nothing but questions and answers. Outside fashionable society, women become once more what is so restful for a tired old man – something to look at.

Anyway, none of that any longer arose. I said that Bergotte never went out, and when he got up for an hour in his room, he was covered in shawls and rugs, everything one wraps around oneself to face the bitter cold of a railway journey. He would apologize to the few friends whom he admitted to visit him, pointing to his plaids, his blankets and saying gaily, 'It can't be helped, dear boy, after all, as Anaxagoras said, life is a journey.' Thus he grew colder and colder, a little planet offering a foretaste of what the last days of the big one will be, when first warmth and then life recede from the Earth. Then there will be an end to resurrection, for however far into the world of future generations the works of men may cast their light, still they will need human beings to see them. Even if certain animal species stand up better than men to the encroaching cold, and even supposing Bergotte's glory to have survived for so long, at this moment it will suddenly be extinguished for ever. The last surviving animals will not read him, for it is hardly likely that, like the apostles at Pentecost, they will be able to understand the languages of the various human peoples without having learned them.

In the months preceding his death, Bergotte suffered from insomnia, and what is worse, as soon as he fell asleep, from nightmares, so that when he awoke he did his best not to go to sleep again. He had long been a lover of dreams, even bad dreams, because it is they, in the way they contradict reality, which give us, when we wake up if not before, the profound sensation that we have been asleep. But Bergotte's nightmares were not of that kind. When he spoke of nightmares, formerly he had meant unpleasant things happening in his brain. But now he experienced, as things coming from outside himself, a hand holding a wet cloth, the hand of an angry woman who was rubbing it over his face, trying to wake him up, intolerable itching of his sides, the fury – because Bergotte had muttered in his sleep that he was driving badly – of a raging mad coachman who threw himself on the writer, biting his fingers, trying to saw them off. Finally, as soon as darkness had gathered thickly enough over his sleep, nature would stage a kind of undress rehearsal of the apoplectic attack that was to carry him off: Bergotte would be passing through the carriage entrance of the Swanns' new house and wanting to alight. An overpowering dizziness would pin him to his seat, the concierge would try to help him down, but he would remain seated, unable to stand, to straighten his legs. He would try to hold on to the stone pillar in front of him, but would not find the support he needed to stay upright. He consulted the doctors who, flattered at having been called in by him, saw in his great commitment to work (he had done nothing for twenty years), in the way he had been over-working, the reason for his feeling so ill. They advised him not to read frightening stories (he never read anything), to get out more into the 'vital' light of the sun (if he had had a few years of somewhat better health, it was only because of never leaving the house), to eat more (which made him lose weight and above all intensified his nightmares). One of his doctors was endowed with the spirit of contradiction and teasing, and when Bergotte saw him in the absence of the others and, in order not to offend him, put forward as his own ideas what the other doctors had advised him, the disobliging doctor, thinking that Bergotte was trying to get him to prescribe something that he liked, forbade him it immediately, and often for reasons so quickly invented for the purpose that, faced with Bergotte's convincing, material objections, the contrary doctor had in the same breath to contradict himself, but still, for different reasons, maintained his prohibition. Bergotte went back to one of the original doctors, a man who prided himself on his intelligence, especially when faced with a master of the pen, and who, if Bergotte insinuated, 'I did think, though, that Dr X had said – long ago, of course – that that might produce congestion of the kidneys or the brain . . .', would smile knowingly, wag his finger and pronounce, 'I said use, not over-use. Of course any treatment, if one over-does it, becomes a two-edged sword.' There is in our body a certain instinctive sense of what is good for us, as in our heart of what is right, which no doctor or medicine or theology can replace. We know that cold baths are bad for us, but we like them, so we can always find a doctor to prescribe them for us, if not to stop them harming us. From each of his doctors Bergotte accepted the things that, out of natural wisdom, he had forbidden himself for years. After a few weeks, his old problems had returned, the new ones had worsened. Made desperate by constant pain, to which was added insomnia punctuated by brief nightmares, Bergotte gave up seeing doctors and tried, with success but to excess, various sleeping-draughts, confidently reading the leaflet which accompanied each one, each of which proclaimed the necessity of sleep but insinuated that all the products that can induce it (except the one in the bottle around which the leaflet was wrapped, which never produced harmful side-effects) were little better than poison, cures that were worse than the disease. Bergotte tried them all. Some are of a different family from the ones we are used to, being derived, for example, from amyl and ethyl. One swallows the new product, with its different chemical composition, in delicious anticipation of the unknown. Where will the newcomer take us, towards what unknown kinds of sleep, of dreams? Now it is inside us, controlling the direction of our thoughts. How shall we fall asleep? And once we are asleep, down what strange paths, to what peaks or unexplored abysses will the all-powerful master lead us? What new system of sensations shall we meet on this journey? Will it lead us to sickness? To blessedness?

To death? Bergotte's death had happened the previous day, a day when he had put his trust in one of these too-powerful friends (or enemies).

This is how he died: after a mild uremic attack he had been ordered to rest. But a critic having written that in Vermeer's *View of Delft* (lent by the museum at The Hague for an exhibition of Dutch painting), a painting he adored and thought he knew perfectly, a little patch of yellow wall (which he could not remember) was so well painted that it was, if one looked at it in isolation, like a precious work of Chinese art, of an entirely self-sufficient beauty, Bergotte ate a few potatoes and went out to the exhibition. As he climbed the first set of steps, his head began to spin. He passed several paintings and had an impression of the sterility and uselessness of such an artificial form, and how inferior it was to the outdoor breezes and sunlight of a palazzo in Venice, or even an ordinary house at the seaside. Finally he stood in front of the Vermeer, which he remembered as having been more brilliant, more different from everything else he knew, but in which, thanks to the critic's article, he now noticed for the first time little figures in blue, the pinkness of the sand, and finally the precious substance of the tiny area of wall. His head spun faster; he fixed his gaze, as a child does on a yellow butterfly he wants to catch, on the precious little patch of wall. 'That is how I should have written, he said to himself. My last books are too dry, I should have applied several layers of colour, made my sentences precious in themselves, like that little patch of yellow wall.' He knew how serious his dizziness was. In a heavenly scales he could see, weighing down one of the pans, his own life, while the other contained the little patch of wall so beautifully painted in yellow. He could feel that he had rashly given the first for the second. 'I would really rather not, he thought, be the human interest item in this exhibition for the evening papers.' He was repeating to himself, 'Little patch of yellow wall with a canopy, little patch of yellow wall.' While saying this he collapsed on to a circular sofa; then suddenly, he stopped thinking that his life was in danger and said to himself, 'It's just indigestion; those potatoes were undercooked.' He had a further stroke, rolled off the sofa on to the ground as all the visitors and guards came running up. He was dead. Dead for ever? Who can say? Certainly spiritualist experiments provide no more proof than religious dogma of the soul's survival. What we can say is that everything in our life happens as if we entered it bearing a burden of obligations contracted in an earlier life; there is nothing in the conditions of our life on this earth to make us feel any obligation to do good, to be scrupulous, even to be polite, nor to make the unbelieving artist feel compelled to paint a single passage twenty times over, when the admiration it will excite will be of little importance to his body when it is eaten by the worms, like the little piece of yellow wall painted with such knowledge and such refinement by the never-to-be-known artist whom we have barely identified by the name of Vermeer. All these obligations which do not derive their force from the here-and-now seem to belong to a different world founded on goodness, conscientiousness, sacrifice, a world quite different from this one, which we leave to be born on to this earth, and to which we shall perhaps return, to live under those unknown laws which we have obeyed because we carried their teaching within us without knowing who had written it there, these laws to which we are brought closer by any profound work of the intellect, and which are invisible – if ever wholly invisible – only to fools. So that the idea that Bergotte was not dead for ever is not at all implausible.

They buried him, but all the night before his funeral, in the lighted bookshop windows, his books, set out in threes, kept watch like angels with outspread wings and seemed, for him who was no more, the symbol of his resurrection.

I learned, as I said, that Bergotte had died that day. And I marvelled at the inaccuracy of the newspapers who, all copying the same piece of information, said that he had died the day before. For Albertine had met him the day before, she told me about it that evening, and he had even kept her a little late, for he had talked to her for quite a long time. Probably she had been the last person he spoke to. She had met him through me; I had not seen him for a long time, but since she had wanted to be introduced to him, a year or so earlier I had written to the aged master to ask permission to bring her to see him. He had agreed to my request, while being a little hurt, I think, that I should come to see him only in order to please someone else, thereby showing how indifferent I was to him myself. Such cases are common; sometimes, the man or woman one begs for a meeting, not for the pleasure of talking to him or her again, but for the sake of a third person, refuses so stubbornly that our protégée believes we have been claiming a power we do not have; more often, the genius or celebrated beauty agrees to our request, but, feeling their fame impugned, or offended in their affection for us, retains for us only a diminished feeling, slightly painful, with a touch of contempt. I guessed long afterwards that I had been wrong in accusing the newspapers of inaccuracy, for Albertine had not met Bergotte on that day at all. But I had not suspected it for a moment, she had told me the story so naturally, and it was only much later that I recognized her charming gift for lying with simplicity. What she said, what she confessed had so much the same character as the forms of the obviously true – those things we see or learn quite undeniably – that she scattered into the empty spaces of life the episodes of another life whose falsehood I did not then suspect. This word falsehood would repay further examination. The universe is true for all of us and different for each one. The evidence of my senses, if I had been outside at that moment, might have told me that the lady had not walked a little way with Albertine. But if I had learned the opposite, it was by a chain of reasoning (one of those chains in which the words of those we trust form strong links), and not by the evidence of the senses. To be able to call on the evidence of the senses, I would precisely have had to be out of doors, which had not been the case. It is easy to see, however, that the hypothesis is not implausible. And then I would have known that Albertine had been lying. But could I have been sure even then? The evidence of the senses is itself a mental event in which conviction creates belief. We have often seen the sense of hearing bring to Françoise not the word actually spoken, but the one she believed to be right, and that this was sufficient for her to ignore the correction implicit in a better pronunciation. Our butler was no different. M. de Charlus was at that time in the habit of wearing very light-coloured trousers which would have been recognizable anywhere. Now the butler, who thought that the word *pissotière* (meaning what M. de Rambuteau had been so distressed to hear the Duc de Guermantes call a 'Rambuteau shelter'[35]) was *pistière*, never in his whole life actually heard anyone say *pissotière*, even though the word was often pronounced that way in his hearing. But error is more stubborn than faith and does not examine its beliefs. I constantly heard the butler say, 'M. le Baron de Charlus must have caught a disease, he spends so much time in the same *pistière*. That's what he gets for all those years running after women. You can tell from those trousers he wears. This morning, Madam sent me on an errand to Neuilly. As I went past the *pistière* in the rue de Bourgogne I saw M. le Baron de Charlus going in. On the way back from Neuilly, a good hour later, I saw his cream-coloured trousers in the same *pistière*, in the same place, in the middle, where he always stands so that nobody can see him.' I knew no one more beautiful, more aristocratic nor younger than a certain niece of Mme de Guermantes. But I heard the doorkeeper of a restaurant where I sometimes went say as she passed, 'Look at that old trout, what a sight! Eighty if she's a day.' As far as the age was concerned, I could not see how he could believe it. But the pageboys standing around him, who laughed every time she passed the hotel on her way to visit her two delightful great-aunts, Mmes de Fezensac and de Balleroy, who lived nearby, saw on the face of the young beauty the eighty years which, jokingly or not, the doorkeeper had ascribed to the 'old trout'. They would have split their sides if one had suggested to them that she was more elegant than one of the two lady cashiers of the hotel, who, disfigured by eczema and absurdly fat, seemed to them a handsome woman. Perhaps only sexual desire could have kept their mistake from taking shape, if it had intervened during the passing of the so-called old trout, and if the boys had found themselves suddenly coveting the youthful goddess. But for unknown reasons, probably of social class origin, this desire had not come into play.

But after all I could have gone out that evening and could have been passing at the time when Albertine would have told me (not having seen me) that she had walked a little way with the lady. A sacred darkness would have taken possession of my mind, I would have begun to doubt that I had seen her alone, I would hardly have even tried to understand what optical illusion could have prevented my seeing the lady, for the world of the stars is no more difficult to know than the real actions of human beings, especially the beings we love, protected as they are against our doubts by stories invented to protect them. For how many years will these stories allow our apathetic love to believe that the beloved has a sister living abroad, or a brother, or a sister-in-law who have never existed! Indeed, if the order of our story did not oblige me here to restrict myself to trivial reasons, how many more serious ones might be revealed behind the fallacious slightness of the beginning of this volume in which, from my bed, I hear the world waking up, sometimes to one kind of weather, sometimes to another! Yes, I have been forced to cut down the facts and to belie the truth, for it is not one universe but millions, almost as many as the number of human eyes and human intelligences, that wake up every morning.

To return to Albertine, I have never known any woman more gifted than she with a happy aptitude for animated lying, lying with the very colouring of life, unless it were a friend of hers, another of my blossoming girls, pink as Albertine, but whose irregular profile, first hollow, then projecting, then hollow again, was just like certain pink flower-heads whose name I have forgotten, but which have the same sinuous outline. This girl, in the realm of invention, was even better than Albertine, for her stories did not include any of those painful moments, any of those hints of underlying rage, which were frequent in my friend's. I have said, though, how charming she was when she was inventing a story which left no room for doubt, for as she spoke one could see before one's eyes the – wholly imaginary – thing she was describing, her speech substituting itself for the power of one's eyes. That was my real perception.

I have added, 'when she was admitting something', and for this reason. Sometimes surprising coincidences gave me jealous suspicions about her, in which there figured beside her another person from the past or, alas, the future. In order to seem sure of what I was saying I would mention the name, and Albertine would reply, 'That's right, I met her a week ago, not far from home. She said hallo and I felt I should reply. I walked a little way with her. But there was never anything between us and there never will be.' Now Albertine had never even met this person, for the very good reason that she had not been in Paris for ten months. But my friend thought that to deny everything would not be convincing. Hence this short, fictitious meeting, so simply described that I could see the lady stopping, saying hallo, walking a little way with her. Plausibility alone had inspired Albertine, not at all the wish to make me jealous. For Albertine, though perhaps not self-interested, liked people to be nice to her. Now although in the course of this work I have had and will have occasion to describe how jealousy intensifies love, it has always been from the lover's point of view. But if the lover has any pride, and even if a separation would kill him, he will not respond to an imagined act of treachery by a kindness, he will withdraw or, without staying away from his mistress, will force himself to feign coldness. So his mistress gains nothing by making him suffer so. On the other hand, if she uses a clever word, or loving caresses, to dissipate the suspicions that were torturing him even if he pretended to be indifferent to them, the lover will not, indeed, experience that desperate heightening of love which jealousy induces, but, suddenly relieved from his suffering, happy, tender, relaxed as one is after a storm when all the rain has fallen and, under the great chestnut trees, one can barely still hear the drip of the hanging drops, already gleaming in the returning sun, he cannot think how to express his gratitude to the one who has cured him. Albertine knew that I loved to reward her for her kindnesses to me, and perhaps that explained why she would invent natural-sounding confessions to justify herself, like her stories which I never doubted, one of which was her meeting with Bergotte at a time when he was already dead. The only ones of Albertine's lies I knew about at this time were the ones Françoise had told me about at Balbec, for example, and which I have not mentioned, much as they hurt me at the time: 'She didn't want to come so she said to me, "Couldn't you tell your master you couldn't find me, I'd gone out?"' But our 'inferiors', when they love us, as Françoise did, always like to wound us in our self-regard.

After dinner, I said to Albertine that I wanted to take advantage of being out of bed to go and see some friends, Mme de Villeparisis, Mme de Guermantes, the Cambremers, I hardly knew, any of them that I found at home. The only name I did not mention was that of the people to whose house I was intending to go, the Verdurins. I asked Albertine if she wanted to come with me. She replied that she had nothing to wear. 'And besides, my hair's a mess. Do you really want me to go on wearing it in this style?' And to say goodbye to me she held out her hand in the abrupt fashion, arm extended, shoulders back, that she had used on the beach at Balbec, and never since. This forgotten movement, animating her body, turned it back into the body of the Albertine of those days, who hardly knew me yet. It restored to Albertine, formal under an air of abruptness, her original novelty, her unknownness, and even her setting. I saw the sea behind this girl, whom I had never seen take leave of me in this way since I had left the seaside. 'My aunt thinks it makes me look older,' she added crossly. 'If only her aunt were right! I thought. All she wants is for Albertine to look like a child, so that she, Mme Bontemps, will seem younger; that, and for Albertine not to cost her anything, while she waits for the day when, by marrying me, Albertine will start to bring in money.' But if Albertine could have looked less young, not so pretty, less able to turn heads in the street, that is what would have pleased me. For the aged looks of a duenna are less reassuring to a lover than the ageing of the face of the one he loves. My only worry was that the hair-style I had asked her to wear might seem to Albertine yet another form of imprisonment. And it was this same, new feeling of domesticity that continued to draw me towards Albertine, even when I was away from her.

Having told Albertine, who was not in the mood, so she said, to go with me to the Guermantes' or the Cambremers', that I was not sure where I would go, I headed straight for the Verdurins'. As I left for the Verdurins', and as the thought of the recital I would hear there reminded me of that afternoon's scene: 'great slut, great slut', a scene of disappointed love, jealous love perhaps, but in that case as bestial, with only the addition of words, as the scene an orang-utan might make to a woman for whom it has, so to speak, fallen, just as I was about to call a cab in the street I heard sobs, which a man, seated on a bollard, was trying to suppress. I walked up to the man, who had his head in his hands; he looked young, was elegantly dressed, and I was surprised to note, from the whiteness showing under his cloak, that he was in full evening clothes with white tie. Hearing me approach he uncovered his face, which was awash with tears, but immediately, recognizing me, he turned it away. It was Morel. He saw that I had recognized him and, trying to stem his tears, he said that he had stopped for a moment, he was so unhappy. 'I was appallingly rude, he said, just this afternoon, to someone I used to care a great deal about. It was a vile thing to do, for she still loves me. – Maybe in time she will forget,' I said, without thinking that by speaking in this way I might give the impression of having heard the afternoon's scene. But he was so wrapped up in his grief he did not even imagine that I could know anything about it. 'Perhaps she will forget, he said. But I can never forget. I feel so ashamed, I'm disgusted with myself! But there, I said those things, they can't be unsaid. When someone puts me in a rage, I don't know what I'm doing. And it's so bad for me, my nerves are all tied in knots now,' for like all neurasthenics he was very concerned for his own health. If in the afternoon I had seen the amorous rage of a furious animal, by this evening, a few hours later, centuries had passed, and the appearance of a new feeling, a feeling of shame, regret, grief, showed that a great step had been taken in the evolution of the animal towards human status. But I still heard 'great slut, great slut' and feared a sudden reversion to the savage state. In any case I had very little understanding of what had happened, and that was all the more natural given that M. de Charlus himself was wholly ignorant of the fact that in the preceding few days, and particularly on this day, even before the shameful episode which was not directly connected to the violinist's physical state, Morel had had a recurrence of neurasthenia. The month before he had pressed on as fast as he could, if much more slowly than he would have liked, with the seduction of Jupien's niece, whom, as her fiancé, he could now take out as much as he liked. But once his advances had come rather too close to rape, and, particularly when he had suggested that his fiancée should become friendly with other young girls and then procure them for him, he had encountered resistance which exasperated him. Suddenly (either because she had been too chaste, or, on the contrary, had given in to him), he lost his desire for her. He had made up his mind to break with her, but judging the Baron, with all his vices, to be more moral than himself, he was afraid that as soon as he broke the engagement M. de Charlus would throw him out. So he had decided, about a fortnight earlier, to stop seeing the girl, to let M. de Charlus and Jupien sort things out between them (he used a more Cambronnesque word[36]), and, before announcing the breaking-off, to 'piss off out of it' to an unknown destination. This ending to his love left him a little sad; so that, even though his behaviour to Jupien's niece corresponded exactly to the plan he had set out before the Baron when they were dining at Saint-Mars-le-Vêtu, it was probably quite different in fact, and less brutal feelings, unforeseen in his theoretical conduct, had lent beauty, given a sentimental colouring to his behaviour in reality. The only point at which, on the other hand, reality was worse than the plan, is that in the plan he did not think it would be possible to stay in Paris after such an act of treachery. But now, 'buggering off' seemed to him an unduly high price to pay for something so simple. It meant leaving the Baron, who no doubt would be furious, and losing the position he had made for himself. He would lose all the money the Baron gave him. The thought that this was inevitable gave him hysterical fits. He wept for hours together, and to stop thinking about it took morphine, in safe doses. Then suddenly an idea came into his mind (it had no doubt been taking shape and life there for some time), and this idea was that the dilemma, the choice between breaking his engagement and completely falling out with M. de Charlus,[37] was not inescapable. Losing all the Baron's money was serious. Unable to decide, Morel spent several days in a black mood, like the one into which he was plunged by the sight of Bloch. Then he decided that Jupien and his niece had tried to trap him, that they should be thankful for having got away with it so cheaply. In his view, the girl was in the wrong, having so clumsily failed to keep his attraction to her alive. Not only did it seem absurd to him to give up his position with M. de Charlus, but he now grudged even the money he had spent on dinners with the girl since their engagement; he could have told you the cost of each one, like the valet's son he was: his father came every month to go through his 'book' with my uncle. For 'book' in the singular may mean 'printed work' to the general run of mortals: it changes its meaning for Highnesses and valets. For the latter it means 'account-book', for the former the bound volume where one writes one's name.

(At Balbec, one day when the Princess of Luxembourg said she had not brought her book with her, I was about to lend her *A Fisherman of Iceland* and *Tartarin of Tarascon*, when I realized what she meant: not that she would be spending the time less pleasantly, but that I would not easily be able to write my name among those of her friends.) In spite of Morel's change of mind about the consequences of his conduct, even though such conduct would have seemed to him abominable two months previously, when he was madly in love with Jupien's niece, and despite the fact that for the last fortnight he had been constantly repeating to himself that this same conduct was natural, even praiseworthy, it still aggravated in him the nervous state in which he had, that afternoon, announced his decision to break with the girl. And he was ready at any moment to 'take out' his feelings, if not (except for one brief surge of rage) on the girl herself, for whom he still felt that residual fear which is the last trace of love, then certainly on the Baron. He was careful, however, not to say anything to him before dinner, for, placing above everything his own professional virtuosity, when he had difficult pieces to play (as he would have that evening at the Verdurins'), he avoided (as far as possible, and the afternoon's scene had already gone far too far) anything that could possibly make his movements jerky. In the same way, a surgeon who loves motoring will leave off driving when he has to operate. I realized that this was why, as he talked to me, he kept gently moving his fingers one after the other, to see if they had regained their suppleness. The hint of a frown seemed to suggest that there was still some nervous stiffness there. But so as not to increase it, he unwrinkled his face, as one tries not to let oneself be irritated by not being able to get to sleep or to possess a woman, for fear that the phobia itself should delay further the moment of sleep or of pleasure. So, wishing to regain his serenity so as to be able to give himself completely, as he always did, to the music he would be playing at the Verdurins', and wishing also, for so long as I was watching him, to be able to convey his suffering to me, the simplest solution seemed to him to ask me to leave immediately. There was no need to ask, and I was delighted to escape. I had been afraid that, as we were going to the same house at almost the same time, he would ask me to drive him there, and I remembered the afternoon's scene too well not to feel a certain disgust at the thought of having Morel next to me during the journey. It is quite possible that the love and then the indifference or hatred Morel felt towards Jupien's niece were both sincere. Unfortunately it was not the first time (and it would not be the last) that he had behaved in this way, suddenly 'throwing over' a young girl after swearing to her that he would love her for ever, even showing her a loaded revolver and saying that he would blow his brains out if he sank so low as to leave her. He left her just the same and felt, instead of remorse, a kind of resentment. It was not the first time he had acted like this, nor would it be the last, so that many young girls' heads – young girls less forgetful of him than he was of them – throbbed with pain – pain that Jupien's niece was to suffer for a long time yet, as she went on loving Morel and at the same time despising him – ready to split with the force of anguish surging up from inside – because each of them had, like a fragment of Greek sculpture, a glimpse of Morel's face, hard as marble and of an antique beauty, lodged in her brain, with his blossoming hair, his finely drawn eyes, his straight nose, a protuberance the skull was not designed to receive, and which could not be removed by surgery. But in the long run these rock-hard fragments slip into a place where they do not cause too much damage, settle there, and one no longer feels their presence; that is forgetfulness, or indifferent memory.

I had within myself two products of the day's experiences. One was the result of the calm produced by Albertine's docility: I saw that I could break with her and therefore resolved to do so. The other was the idea, formed from my reflections as I sat waiting for her at the piano, that Art, to which I planned to devote my new-found freedom, was not something for which I need make sacrifices, something apart from life, untouched by its vanity and emptiness, since the appearance of real individuality found in works of art was achieved only by the illusions of technical skill. If my afternoon had left other deposits in my mind, perhaps at a deeper level, they were not to rise to consciousness until much later. As for the two which I was consciously weighing, neither was to last; for that very evening, my ideas on art were to begin to recover from the downgrading they had experienced in the afternoon, while on the other hand the freedom which was to allow me to dedicate myself to art was to be once more taken from me.

As my carriage went along the embankment towards the Verdurins', I told the driver to stop, for I had just seen Brichot get off the tram at the corner of the rue Bonaparte, wipe his shoes with an old newspaper and pull on pearl-grey gloves. I went up to him. For some time now, since his sight had become much worse, he had been equipped – as elaborately as a laboratory – with new spectacles which, powerful and complicated as astronomical instruments, looked as if they were screwed into his eyes. He bent their exaggerated vision on me and recognized me. The glasses were marvellous. But behind them I saw the tiny, pale, convulsive, expiring gaze placed under this powerful apparatus, as in over-subsidized laboratories some insignificant little creature is left to die under a battery of the most up-to-date instruments. I offered my arm to the half-blind scholar to help him along. 'We meet this time not near the real Cherbourg, but the figurative Dunkerque,' a remark which seemed quite unamusing to me as I did not understand what it meant; however, I dared not ask Brichot, not so much for fear of his contempt as of his explanations. I replied that I was looking forward to seeing the salon where Swann used once to meet Odette every evening. 'What, do you know those old stories?' he said.

Swann's death had been a great shock to me at the time. Swann's death! The word Swann's, in this phrase, is not a simple genitive. I mean by it the particular death, the death sent by fate to release Swann. For we say 'death' for the sake of simplicity, but there are almost as many deaths as there are people. We lack the sense which would allow us to see them passing with great speed, flying in all directions, the various deaths, the active deaths sent by destiny after this man or that. Sometimes they are deaths which will not have fully accomplished their task until two or three years later. They fly to implant a cancer in the side of someone like Swann, then go off to do other work, and only return when, after the surgeons have operated, the cancer needs to be put back in position. Then the time comes when one reads in the *Gaulois* that Swann's health has been giving rise to concern, but that he is now on the way to making a full recovery. Then, a few minutes before one breathes one's last, death, like a nun who had been nursing rather than destroying one, comes to witness one's last moments and to set a final, crowning halo upon the being, now frozen for ever, whose heart has stopped beating. And it is this multitude of different deaths, the mystery of their functioning, the colour of their fatal draperies, that give a certain impressive ring to the lines in the newspapers: 'We regret to inform our readers that M. Charles Swann passed away yesterday at his home in Paris, after a long and painful illness. A Parisian whose wit was universally admired, as was his gift for select but faithful friendship, he will be much missed both in artistic and literary circles, to which he was drawn by his finely educated taste and where his opinions were eagerly sought after, and in the Jockey Club, of which he was one of the oldest and most respected members. He was also a member of the Union Club and the Society for the Promotion of Agriculture. He had recently resigned from the Rue Royale Club.

'His intelligent features and widespread reputation could not fail to arouse the curiosity of the public at the most important musical and artistic events, and particularly at the exhibition openings which he attended faithfully until recent years, when he only rarely went out. The funeral will be, etc.'

From this point of view, unless one is 'someone', the lack of a recognized title accelerates the decomposition of death. Certainly it is only in an anonymous fashion, without any marks of individuality, that one continues to be the Duc d'Uzès. But the ducal coronet keeps the elements of one's individuality together for a while, like the carefully sculpted ice-creams that Albertine liked so much. Meanwhile the names even of ultra-fashionable bourgeois, as soon as they are dead, are 'turned out', melt and disintegrate. We have heard Mme de Guermantes speaking of Cartier as the best friend of the Duc de la Trémoïlle, someone much in demand in aristocratic circles. For the following generation, Cartier has become something so formless that one would almost be raising him in the world by making him a relative of the jeweller Cartier, with whom he would have smiled to hear the ignorant confuse him! Swann, on the other hand, was an outstanding personality in the artistic and intellectual world, and so, even though he had not 'produced' anything, his name was able to survive a little longer. And yet, dear Charles Swann, whom I knew so little when I was still so young and you so near the grave, it is already because someone whom you must have considered a little idiot has made you the hero of one of his novels that people are beginning to talk about you again, and perhaps you will live on. If people talk so much about the Tissot painting[38] set on the balcony of the Rue Royale Club, where you are standing with Galliffet, Edmond de Polignac and Saint-Maurice, it is because they can see there is something of you in the character of Swann.

To come back to more general truths, it was of this expected and yet sudden death of Swann that I had heard himself speak at the Duchesse de Guermantes's house, on the evening of her cousin's party. This was the death whose particular strangeness had struck me one evening as I was scanning the newspaper and the announcement of it had brought me to a halt, as if it were written in mysterious lines inappropriately interpolated there. These lines had been enough to turn a living man into one who can no longer reply to what is said to him, a name, a written name, which has suddenly passed from the real world into the realm of silence. It was these same lines which now made me want to see the house where the Verdurins had once lived and where Swann, who was not then simply a set of letters printed in a newspaper, had so often dined with Odette. I must add (and this is something which long made Swann's death more painful to me than another's, even though these facts had nothing to do with the particular strangeness of *his* death) that I had not gone to see Gilberte as I had promised him at the Princesse de Guermantes's that I would; that he had never told me the 'other reason' that he referred to on that evening, which had made him choose me as confidant of his meeting with the prince; and that a thousand questions kept coming back to me (like bubbles rising through water), which I had wanted to ask him on the most varied subjects: about Vermeer, about M. de Mouchy, about himself, about a certain Boucher tapestry, about Combray, not urgent questions, clearly, as I had been putting them off from day to day, but which seemed to me of the utmost importance now that his lips were sealed and the answers would never come. Someone else's death is like being on a journey and remembering, a hundred kilometres from

Paris, that one has left behind two dozen handkerchiefs, forgotten to give a key to the cook, to say goodbye to one's uncle, or to ask the name of the town where the ancient fountain is that one so wants to see. But all these forgotten things the memory of which assails one and which one mentions aloud, for form's sake, to one's travelling companion, come up against the stern reality of the carriage seat and the station name called out by the guard which only marks the increasing impossibility of doing these things, so that, turning our thoughts away from these irremediable acts of omission, we undo our parcel of food and begin to exchange newspapers and magazines.

'No, no, added Brichot, it wasn't here that Swann used to meet his wife-to-be, or at least not until the very end of that period, after the accident which destroyed Mme Verdurin's old house.' Unfortunately, not wishing to display before Brichot a luxury which seemed to me out of place, since the academic could not share in it, I had got out of the carriage too hurriedly and the driver had not understood the words I had thrown in his direction in my haste to distance myself from him before Brichot should see me. As a result, the coachman drove up behind us and asked if he was to come back to collect me. I hastily said yes and redoubled my attentions to the old don, who had arrived by bus. 'Ah, you were driven here, he said solemnly. – By pure chance, I swear; it almost never happens. I always take the bus or walk. But perhaps I shall have the great pleasure of taking you home this evening, if you are prepared to ride in this old rattle-trap. It will be rather a tight fit. But you are always so kind to me.' Alas, making this offer will cost me nothing, I thought, since I shall have to leave early in any case, because of Albertine. Knowing that she was in the flat, at a time when no one could call on her, left me as much the master of my time as in the afternoon when I knew she was on her way back from the Trocadéro and was in no hurry to see her again. But there again, as in the afternoon, I had the sense of having a wife, and knew that when I returned home it would not be to the excitement, the bracing sense of solitude. 'I should be delighted, Brichot replied. At the time to which you refer, our friends lived in the rue Montalivet, in a splendid ground-floor flat with a mezzanine, giving on to a garden; it was less sumptuous, naturally, than the Hôtel des Ambassadeurs de Venise, yet

I preferred it.' Brichot informed me that that evening at 'Quai Conti' (that was how the faithful referred to Mme Verdurin's salon since it had migrated there), there was to be a great musical 'bunfight', organized by M. de Charlus. He added that in the old days I had been speaking of, the inner circle had been different and the tone quite other, and not only because the faithful were younger. He told me about tricks Elstir had played (what he called 'veritable harlequinades'); how one day, having pretended to cry off at the last minute, he came disguised as an extra butler and, as he handed the dishes, whispered improprieties in the ear of the highly prudish Baronne Putbus, whose face flushed red with alarm and annoyance; then, disappearing before the end of the dinner, he had had a bath full of water carried into the salon and, when the guests came through, jumped out of it stark naked, swearing at the top of his voice; also about the suppers to which everyone came in fancy dresses made of paper, designed, cut out and painted by Elstir, which were masterpieces. Brichot had come once as a nobleman of the court of Charles VII, with shoes with extravagantly turned-up toes, and another time as Napoleon I, when Elstir had made him a grand cordon of the Légion d'honneur out of sealing-wax. In a word, Brichot, seeing in his mind's eye the salon of those days, with its tall windows, its low sofas which, rotted by the midday sun, had had to be replaced, said that he still preferred it to today's. Of course I understood that by 'salon' Brichot meant – just as the word 'church' means not only the religious building but the community of believers – not only the mezzanine, but the people who frequented it and the particular pleasures they came to seek there, which in his mind had taken their form from the sofas on which, when one came to see Mme Verdurin in the afternoon, one sat to wait for her to be ready, while the pink flowers of the chestnut trees outside, and on the chimney-piece carnations in vases, seemed, in a gracious movement of sympathy for the visitor echoed in the smiling welcome of their rosy colours, to be fixedly watching for the belated arrival of the mistress of the house. But if that 'salon' seemed to him superior to the present one, it was perhaps because our spirit, like old Proteus, cannot remain the slave of any form and, even in the realm of fashion, suddenly detaches itself from a salon which has slowly and with difficulty been brought to its point of perfection, preferring some less brilliant gathering; just as the retouched photographs which Odette had had taken by Otto, showing her in a splendid princess-line gown and with her hair waved by Lenthéric,[39] did not appeal to Swann so much as a little carte-de-visite photograph taken in Nice where, wearing a cloth shoulder-cape and with her badly arranged hair protruding from a straw hat adorned with pansies and a black velvet bow (women usually do look older the older the photographs are in which they appear), despite being a woman of fashion twenty years younger, she looked like a little maidservant, but twenty years older. Perhaps it also gave him pleasure to cry up to me things that I should never know, to show me that he had tasted pleasures that I could not share. If that was his aim he succeeded, for simply by mentioning the names of three or four people who no longer existed and to whose charm he gave a mysterious quality by his way of speaking of it and of those moments of delicious intimacy, he made me wonder what it had been like, and feel that everything people had told me about the Verdurins was too coarsely drawn; even thinking of Swann, whom I had known, I reproached myself with not having paid enough attention to him, not having listened to him disinterestedly enough when I was at his house and he showed me beautiful things while we waited for his wife to come home to luncheon, now that I knew he could stand comparison with one of the finest talkers of former times.

As we arrived at Mme Verdurin's, I saw M. de Charlus steering his whole enormous body in our direction, unconsciously drawing along in his wake one of the street-arabs or young gangsters who now invariably sprang from the earth as he passed, even in the most apparently deserted spots, to escort the powerful monster, albeit at a certain distance, as a shark is accompanied by its pilot-fish, and presenting such a contrast with the haughty stranger of my first year at Balbec, with his stern aspect and affectation of manliness, that I felt I was seeing, accompanied by its satellite, a heavenly body at quite a different moment of its orbit and now appearing in its full phase, or a patient now invaded by the illness which a few years ago was a mere pimple, easily concealed and whose gravity no one suspected. Even though Brichot had undergone an operation which had restored to

him some of the sight he thought he had lost forever, I do not know
if he had spotted the street-boy following in the Baron's footsteps. It
hardly mattered in any case, for ever since La Raspelière, and despite
Brichot's liking for him, M. de Charlus's presence made him feel a
certain unease. No doubt for each man the life of every other man
extends unsuspected winding paths into the darkness. Lies, so often
misleading and which form the substance of all conversations, are less
effective in covering up a feeling of dislike or of self-interest, or a visit
one would rather people did not know about, or a one-day fling one
wants to conceal from one's wife – than a good reputation is in utterly
overshadowing disreputable habits. These habits can have remained
unknown for a lifetime, a chance meeting on a jetty one evening will
reveal them; even then the revelation is often misunderstood until a
third person, better informed, supplies the elusive solution known to
him alone. But once the truth is known, it is frightening, because it
seems to threaten our sanity rather than our morals. Mme de Surgis le
Duc's moral ideas were not at all highly developed, and she would
have accepted in her sons any behaviour which could have been
explained, and cheapened, by mercenary motives. But she forbade
them to have anything further to do with M. de Charlus when she
learned that, with a kind of clockwork regularity, whenever he came
to visit her, he was drawn to pinch them under the chin and get them
to do the same to him. She had the same disquieting sense of a physical
mystery in the offing that one has when one begins to wonder whether
the neighbour with whom one always got on so well is not affected by
cannibalistic urges, and to the Baron's repeated questions, 'When shall
I see the boys?' she replied, knowing the trouble she was storing up
for herself, that they were very busy with their lessons, were preparing
for a journey, etc. Diminished responsibility aggravates faults and
even crimes, whatever the law may say. Landru[40] (assuming that he
really killed women), if he did it for money, could be pardoned, but
not if he acted out of irresistible sadism. Brichot's heavy jokes, in the
early days of his friendship with the Baron, had been replaced, once it
was a question not of repeating clichés but of understanding, with a
painful feeling masked by gaiety. He reassured himself by repeating
pages of Plato, lines of Virgil, because, intellectually as well as physi-

cally blind, he could not understand that in those days loving a boy (Socrates' jokes make it clearer than Plato's theories) was like keeping a dancer today, before one becomes engaged and settles down. M. de Charlus himself would not have understood this, confusing as he did his mania with friendship, which it does not at all resemble, and the athletes of Praxiteles with accommodating boxers. He refused to see that nineteen hundred years later ('a courtier who is pious under a pious ruler would have been an unbeliever under an unbelieving ruler,' said La Bruyère[41]), all everyday homosexuality – that of Plato's young men or Virgil's shepherds – has disappeared, and all that survives and multiplies is the involuntary kind, the nervous disease, the kind that one hides from others and disguises from oneself. And M. de Charlus would have been wrong not to reject openly the pagan genealogy of his condition. By giving up a little physical beauty, what a gain in moral standing! The Theocritean shepherd who sighs for a boy will have no claim in later life to be less insensitive or more intelligent than the other shepherd whose flute sounds for Amaryllis. For the first one is not suffering from an illness, he is simply following prevailing fashion. It is the homosexuality that survives in spite of obstacles, condemned, covered in shame, that is the real homosexuality; only that kind can be accompanied in the same being by a refinement of the inner life. One trembles to think of the connection there can be between physical and moral qualities when one thinks of the small variation in purely physical taste, the slight defect in one sense, which bring it about that the world of poets and musicians, so closed to the Duc de Guermantes, should be partly open to M. de Charlus. That the latter should take an interest in the decoration of his rooms – which are as full of objects as a knick-knack-loving housewife's – is hardly surprising; but that the same little chink should open on to Beethoven and Veronese! But none of this means that healthy people should not be alarmed when a madman who has written a sublime poem, having explained to them in the most rational way possible that he has been locked away by mistake or through his wicked wife's scheming, begging them to speak to the superintendent on his behalf and weeping as he describes the dreadful company he is forced to keep, concludes by saying, 'Do you see that man who is waiting to speak to me in the yard, whom I shan't be able to avoid? He thinks he is Jesus Christ. That is enough to show me the kind of madmen I am shut up with; he can't be Jesus Christ, I am.' A moment earlier one was on the point of going to tell the alienist of the mistake. Having heard these last words, and despite the thought of the wonderful poem on which the same man works every day, one moves away, just as Mme de Surgis's sons moved away from M. de Charlus, not because he had hurt them in any way, but because of his persistent invitations which always ended in his tickling them under the chin. Unfortunate poet, unguided by any Virgil, who must go down through the circles of a hell of sulphur and pitch and plunge into the fire that falls from heaven in order to bring back some inhabitants of Sodom! His work can have no charm; his life must be as austere as that of unfrocked priests who still observe the strictest celibacy, so that no one can say they left off the soutane for any other reason than the loss of their faith. Not that the writers are always able to keep this rule. Where is the mad-doctor in whom daily contact with his patients will not produce his own moment of madness? He will be lucky if he can say with confidence that it was not a pre-existing, latent condition that drove him into his speciality. His subject of study often has an effect on a psychiatrist. But why this subject in the first place? What obscure attraction, what fascinating apprehension, had made him choose it?

Pretending not to see the dubious individual who was following in his footsteps (when the Baron ventured out on the boulevards or crossed the waiting-room of the gare Saint-Lazare, these followers could be counted in dozens, never, in the hope of a coin, letting him out of their sight), and for fear that the boy should be bold enough to speak to him, the Baron piously lowered his mascaraed lashes which, in their contrast with his papier-poudré cheeks, made him look like a Grand Inquisitor painted by El Greco. But this was a frightening priest and looked like one denied the sacraments, for the various compromises to which he had been forced by the need to indulge his tastes while keeping them secret had had the effect of bringing to the surface of the Baron's face exactly what he most wanted to hide, a squalid life reflected in moral decay. Such decay, whatever its cause, is easy to read in a face, for it takes material shape and spreads there, particularly in the cheeks and around the eyes, as unmistakably as the ochre tints of liver disease or the repulsive red patches of a skin complaint. In any case, it was not only in the cheeks, or rather jowls, of the painted face, in the plump breasts and bouncing buttocks of the self-indulgent body invaded by fat, that there now floated on the surface, visible as oil, the vice once so carefully hidden away by M. de Charlus in the furthest depths of his being. It now overflowed in his speech.

'I say, Brichot, out at night with a handsome young man! he said as he came up to us, while the disappointed street-boy faded into the background. Charming! We'll have to tell your little pupils at the Sorbonne that you're no better than you should be. Anyway, young company does you good, professor, you've got colour in your cheeks. And you, dear boy, how are you? he said, leaving off his bantering tone. We don't often see your youthful features at the Quai Conti. And your cousin, is she well? You haven't brought her with you. A pity, she's delightful. Shall we see the young lady this evening? How pretty she is! And she'd be even more so if she developed the art, such a rare art, for which she already has a natural gift, of dressing well.' I must point out here that M. de Charlus 'possessed' – in this the exact opposite of myself – the gift of carefully observing, of being able to describe in the finest detail, either an outfit or a 'canvas'. As far as the dresses and hats were concerned, certain unkind people or over-generalizing theoreticians will say that in a man the penchant for male charms is compensated by an inborn taste, a passion for the study, the science of female dress. And that does happen sometimes, as if, men having claimed all the physical desire, all the deep affection of someone like Charlus, the other sex found bestowed on it everything that could be called (very improperly) 'platonic' taste, or, more simply, taste itself, with all its most knowing and effective refinements. In this respect M. de Charlus would have deserved the nickname that was given him later, 'the Dressmaker'. But his taste, his powers of observation extended much further. I mentioned how, on the evening I went to visit him after a dinner at the Duchesse de Guermantes's, I had not noticed the masterpieces he had in his rooms until he showed them to me, one by one. He immediately recognized things that no one else would ever have noticed, and that was as true in works of art as in the dishes at a dinner (and everything else between painting and cookery). I have always been sorry that M. de Charlus, instead of restricting his artistic gifts to the painting of a fan as a present for his sister-in-law (we saw the Duchesse de Guermantes with it in her hand, opening it, not so much to fan herself with it as to boast of it, showing off her friendship with Palamède), or to the perfecting of his piano technique so as to be able to accompany Morel's violin bowings without making mistakes, I repeat I have always regretted and still regret that M. de Charlus never wrote anything. Of course I cannot assume from the eloquence of his conversation and even letter-writing that he would have been a talented writer. The two are not on the same level. We have all seen tiresome sayers of the obvious write masterpieces, and lords of the spoken word fall below mediocrity as soon as they put pen to paper. All the same I believe that if M. de Charlus had tried his hand at prose, beginning with the artistic subjects on which he was so knowledgeable, he would have struck a spark, the lightning would have flashed out, and the man of fashion would have become a master of the pen. I often said this to him, but he would never try, perhaps simply from laziness, or being constantly busy with brilliant parties and sordid amusements, or the Guermantes family need for endless chat. I am all the more sorry as in his most sparkling conversation, his wit could never be separated from his character, the ingenuity of the one from the insolence of the other. If he had written books, then instead of detesting him even while admiring him as one did in salons where, in his moments of most striking intelligence, he would at the same time be trampling on the weak, taking vengeance on those who had not insulted him, or trying contemptibly to set friends at odds — if he had written books, one would have been able to isolate his intelligent side, decant it from his nastiness, nothing would have interfered with one's admiration of him and many of his traits would have inspired friendship.

In any case, even if I am mistaken about what he could have put down on the page, he would have done us all a great service in writing, for not only could he make the finest distinctions, but when he distinguished a thing he always knew its name. It is true that in talking

with him, if I did not learn to see (my mind and my feelings were bent
on other things), at least I saw things that without him I should never
have noticed, but their names, which would have helped me to find
their shapes and colours again, those names were always quickly
forgotten. If he had written books, even bad ones, though I do not
think they would have been bad, what an enchanting dictionary, what
an inexhaustible work of reference they would have been! But then,
who knows? Instead of unlocking his knowledge and his taste, he
might have written undistinguished serial stories, or useless tales of
travel or adventure.

'Yes, she knows how to dress or more precisely how to present
herself, said M. de Charlus, returning to Albertine. My only doubt is
whether she dresses in accordance with her own particular beauty, and
perhaps I am slightly to blame for that, having given her advice
without taking enough thought beforehand. The things I often used
to say to her as we were going to La Raspelière – and now I see, and
I am sorry for it, that what I said was prompted more by the character
of the countryside, the nearness of the sea, than by the individual
character of your cousin's type – made her incline too much towards
light fabrics. I admit I've seen her in lovely tarlatans, charming gauze
scarves, a certain small rose-coloured toque set off perfectly by a
little pink feather. But I think her real, almost massive beauty needs
something more than just pretty things about her. Is a toque right for
that huge head of hair? A Russian tiara would hardly be excessive.
Very few women can wear those antique dresses that have a look of
stage costume about them. But this young girl, with her already
womanly beauty, is the exception, and ought to have a dress in old
Genoese velvet (I immediately thought of Elstir and the Fortuny
dresses), which I should not hesitate to weigh down further with
jewelled embroidery or pendants of those wonderful, old-fashioned
stones (that's the biggest compliment you can pay them) like peridot,
marcasite or the incomparable labradorite. In fact, she herself seems
to have the sense of counterweight that a rather heavy beauty needs.
Do you remember, when she went to dine at La Raspelière, all the
things she carried with her, pretty boxes, heavy bags . . . when she is
married, she will be able to put in them the carmine and white not just

of rouge and powder, but – in a not-too-indigo lapis lazuli jewel-case – of pearls and rubies, and not cultured ones, I feel sure, for she should be able to marry very well.'

'Goodness, Baron,' Brichot interrupted, fearing that these last words would upset me, since he had some doubts about the purity of my relations and the authenticity of my cousinly connection with Albertine, 'you do take an interest in the young ladies!'

'Not in front of the children, scandal-monger,' M. de Charlus sniggered, lowering one hand in the gesture of imposing silence on Brichot, but making sure that it landed on my shoulder. 'I interrupted you, I'm sorry, you looked as if you were having such fun, like two naughty girls, without any help from a boring old granny like me. Still, I shan't feel too guilty, as you'd nearly arrived.' The Baron was all the more cheerful as he knew nothing at all about the scene of that afternoon, Jupien having decided that it was more important to protect his niece against a possible further attack than to go and warn M. de Charlus. So the Baron still believed in the forthcoming marriage and was pleased about it. It is as if it were a kind of consolation to these lonely figures to soften their tragic bachelorhood with a fictitious paternity. 'But really, Brichot, he added, laughing as he turned towards us, I feel decidedly *de trop* when I see you in such attractive company. You looked like two lovers. Arm in arm, Brichot, I must say, you are going a bit far!' Could such words have been the sign of an ageing mind, less in control than formerly of its reflexes and, in a moment's automatic response, betraying a secret so carefully buried for forty years? Or was it the disdain for middle-class opinion that all the Guermantes had underneath, and which M. de Charlus's brother, the Duc, displayed in a different way when, not caring in the least whether my mother could see him, he would stand at his window shaving, with his nightshirt undone? Had M. de Charlus, during his over-heated journeys from Doncières to Douville, acquired the habit of relaxation, and just as he pushed his straw hat back on his head to let his enormous forehead breathe, had he begun to loosen, at first just for a few moments, the mask too tightly covering his real face? His matrimonial manners with Morel would have rightly astonished anyone who knew that he no longer loved him. But in M. de Charlus's case, the narrow range of pleasures offered by his vice had come to bore him. He had instinctively sought to break new physical limits and then, tiring of the strangers he met, had gone to the opposite extreme and chosen what he had thought he would always loathe, the simulacrum of a 'marriage' or of 'fatherhood'. Sometimes even that did not satisfy him, he had to do something new, and he would go and spend the night with a woman, in the way a normal man might, once in his life, want to sleep with a boy, out of the same kind of curiosity, each the mirror-image of the other, and each equally unhealthy. The Baron's life as 'one of the crowd', living as he did, because of Charlie, entirely within the Verdurin clan, had had the same effect, in undoing the efforts he had made for so long to keep up a false appearance, as a voyage of exploration or a stay in the colonies can have on certain Europeans, who lose while abroad the guiding principles that ruled their lives in France. And yet the inward revolution of a mind, unconscious at first of the abnormality within itself, then frightened by it when it had recognized it, and finally becoming so familiar with it that it no longer recognized the danger of admitting it to other people, having learned to admit it without shame to itself, had been even more effective in freeing M. de Charlus from the last ties of social constraint than the time spent at the Verdurins'. For no exile at the South Pole or at the top of Mont Blanc can detach us more from other people than a lengthy stay inside an inner vice, that is to say, a way of thinking different from theirs. A vice (for such the Baron used to call it), to which he now gave the amiable character of a mere fault, very common, quite likeable and almost amusing, like laziness, forgetfulness or too great a liking for food. Recognizing the curiosity that his odd personality aroused, M. de Charlus took a certain pleasure in satisfying it, stimulating and encouraging it. Just as a certain Jewish journalist daily defends Catholicism, probably not expecting to be taken seriously, but in order not to disappoint the readers who appreciate his humour, M. de Charlus jokingly attacked immorality, in the little set, as he might have affected an English accent or imitated Mounet-Sully,[42] without waiting to be asked, a talented amateur singing for his supper with a good grace; so that M. de Charlus now threatened to report Brichot to the Sorbonne for walking out with young men, as the circumcised columnist punctuates his prose with 'France, the eldest daughter of the Church' and the 'Sacred Heart of Jesus', without the least hypocrisy, but with a certain theatrical affectation. And it is not only his new vocabulary, so different from the words he formerly allowed himself to use, that would be a rewarding study, but also the change in his intonations and gestures, which both now bore a surprising resemblance to everything he had once most scathingly condemned; he now emitted, quite without thinking, something like the little squeals – involuntary in his case, and therefore all the more revealing – that homosexuals produce – in their case deliberately – when they call out to each other – 'darling!'; as if this purposely 'camp' manner, which M. de Charlus had so long avoided like the plague, were nothing but a brilliant, faithful imitation of the intonations that the Charluses of this world inevitably develop when they reach a certain phase of their disease, just as a tertiary syphilitic or a sufferer from ataxia cannot fail in the end to present certain symptoms. In reality – as this deep-rooted affectation revealed – the only difference between the stern Charlus I had once known, dressed all in black, with his hair cut short, and made-up young men dripping with jewels, was the purely superficial one that we see between an agitated person, talking all the time and constantly fidgeting, and a mental sufferer who speaks slowly, is impossible to rouse, but in the eyes of a clinician is plainly affected by the same neurasthenia, eaten up by the same anxieties and suffering from the same physical defects. There were other, physical signs that also showed M. de Charlus was getting old, like the surprisingly frequent repetition in his conversation of certain expressions which had multiplied there and now appeared at every other moment (for example 'the chain of circumstances'); the Baron's speech now advanced from sentence to sentence leaning on these phrases as if on a necessary support. 'Is Charlie here already?' Brichot asked M. de Charlus as we were about to ring the doorbell. 'I don't know, I'm afraid,' said the Baron, raising his hands in the air and half-closing his eyes like someone who does not want to be accused of indiscretion, the more so, no doubt, because he had been scolded by Morel for mentioning things which Morel (as cowardly as he was vain, and as ready to deny his friendship with the Baron as to boast of it) had thought revealing, though they were quite insignificant. 'You know I don't know anything about his plans. I don't know who else he is seeing, but I hardly see him at all.' If conversations between two people who are having an affair are full of lies, lies occur no less naturally in the conversations an outsider has with someone who is in love about the person he or she loves, regardless of that person's sex.

'Is it a long time since you saw him last?' I asked, not wishing to appear reluctant to speak to him of Morel, nor yet to seem to know that they lived together all the time. 'He called in for five minutes this morning, as it happens, while I was still half asleep, and came and sat on the end of my bed, as if he were going to rape me!' I immediately concluded that M. de Charlus had seen Charlie within the hour, for when one asks a man's mistress when she last saw the man one knows – and whom she perhaps thinks one believes – to be her lover, if she has just had tea with him, she will reply, 'I saw him just before lunch.' Between these two statements the only difference is that one is false and the other true, but each is as innocent or, if you like, as guilty as the other. So it would be difficult to understand why the mistress (or here, M. de Charlus) invariably chooses the falsehood, if one did not know that their replies are determined, in a way unknown to the speaker, by a number of factors which seems so disproportionate to the triviality of the issue that it seems absurd to dwell on them. But for a physicist the position of the tiniest ball of pith is explained by the action, the clash or the equilibrium of the same forces of attraction or repulsion whose laws govern much greater worlds. Let us simply recall the wish to appear natural and forthcoming, the instinctive movement to conceal a secret lovers' meeting, a mixture of modesty and ostentation, the need to speak of what is so pleasant to ourselves and to show that we are loved, a partial understanding of what the other person already knows, or guesses, which, outrunning or falling short of his understanding, constantly over- or under-estimates it, the involuntary drive to take risks or to cut one's losses. All these different laws, acting in conflicting directions, determine even the most general replies concerning the innocence, the 'platonic' character, or on the other hand the carnal reality of one's relations with the person one says one saw in the morning when in fact one saw him in the evening. Still, in general terms, we must say that M. de Charlus, despite the progress of his illness, which now constantly drove him to reveal, to hint at or simply to invent compromising details, was still at this period of his life trying to establish that Charlie was not the same kind of man as himself, and that there was nothing between them but friendship. Perhaps it was true, but that did not stop him sometimes contradicting himself on the subject (as he had just done about the time when he had last seen him), whether he was absent-mindedly telling the truth, or boastfully or sentimentally lying, or finding it amusing to mislead the listener. 'You know what he is to me, the Baron continued, a dear young friend, whom I'm so very fond of, as I'm sure (if he was so sure, why did he have to say it?) he is of me, but there's nothing else between us, none of that sort of thing, you know, none of that, said the Baron, as naturally as if he had been speaking of a lady. Yes, he came to shake me awake this morning, even though he knows how much I hate to be seen in bed. Don't you? Oh, it's dreadful, really upsetting, one looks so hideous, I know I'll never see twenty-five again, I'm not setting up to be Queen of the May, but one does have one's standards!'

Perhaps the Baron was being sincere when he spoke of Morel as a good friend, and unwittingly telling the truth when he said 'I don't know what he does, his life is a mystery to me.' Let us say (if we may now travel forward several weeks in the story, which we shall pick up again after this parenthesis which has opened up while M. de Charlus, Brichot and I are walking towards Mme Verdurin's), let us say that, shortly after this evening party, the Baron was plunged into suffering and amazement when he mistakenly opened a letter addressed to Morel. This letter, which was also, in a roundabout fashion, to cause me intense pain, was from Léa, the actress known for her exclusive attraction to women. Yet her letter to Morel (whom M. de Charlus had never even suspected of knowing her) was written in the most passionate terms. It was too indecent to be reproduced here, but one may note that Léa addressed him in the feminine throughout, calling him 'Dirty girl!' and saying 'Well, sweetheart, you *are* one and no mistake!' And the letter mentioned several other women with whom Morel seemed to be no less friendly than with Léa. Furthermore, the way she teased Morel about M. de Charlus, in the same way as she joked about an officer who was keeping her and about whom she said, 'He writes letters begging me to be a good girl! Me! What do you think, kitten?' had brought home to M. de Charlus a state of things of which he had had no more inkling than of Morel's unusual friendship with Léa.

The Baron was particularly worried by the expression 'you *are* one'. Having long been in ignorance of it, he had for a long time now accepted the fact that he 'was one'. Now this accepted idea was once more put in question. When he had discovered he 'was one', he had imagined it meant that his taste, as Saint-Simon puts it, was not for women. Now it appeared that for Morel the phrase had a range of meaning unfamiliar to M. de Charlus, to the point that the letter suggested Morel proved he 'was one' by having the same taste for women as certain women themselves. From then on M. de Charlus's jealousy had no reason to restrict itself to the men Morel knew, but would extend even to women. So it seemed that the beings who 'were one' were not only those he had thought, but covered a whole immense part of the planet, made up of women as well as men, and the Baron, encountering a new meaning for such a familiar expression, felt tortured by an uneasiness as much intellectual as emotional when faced with this double mystery involving both the expansion of his jealousy and the sudden inadequacy of a definition.

M. de Charlus had never in his life been anything but an amateur. It followed that incidents of this kind could never be of any use to him. He let the painful impression they produced on him spill over into violent scenes, in which he could sometimes be eloquent, or into underhand scheming. But for a person as gifted as Bergotte, for example, they could have had great value. It is perhaps this that partly explains (since we are always groping in the dark, but, like animals, head for the plant that does us most good) why beings like Bergotte generally live in the company of run-of-the-mill people, deceitful and unkind. The beauty of these people is all the writer needs; it elevates his goodness to a higher plane, but does nothing to transform the nature of the woman he lives with, whose life thousands of feet below him, whose improbable connections and lies carried to a degree and, above all, in a direction beyond all imagining, come to light in periodic flashes. A lie, a perfect lie about people we know, our past relations with them, our motives in acting which we presented to ourselves in quite a different light, a lie about who we are, about what we love, about what we feel for the person who loves us and thinks he has moulded us in his likeness because he holds us in a constant embrace, a lie of that kind is one of the few things in the world that can open up wholly new perspectives for us, can awaken our torpid senses to contemplate universes which otherwise we should never have known. We must say, in relation to M. de Charlus, that if he was astonished to learn a certain number of things about Morel that had been carefully hidden from him, he was wrong to conclude that it was a mistake to form close friendships with working-class people, and that such painful revelations (the most painful for him had been that of a journey which Morel had made with Léa at a time when he had assured M. de Charlus that he was studying music in Germany. To buttress the lie he had used well-disposed persons in Germany to whom he had sent the letters for posting on to M. de Charlus, who, in fact, was so convinced that that was where Morel was that he never even looked at the postmarks).[43] We shall see, in fact, in the last volume of this work, M. de Charlus doing things that would have been even more astonishing to his family and friends than the life revealed by Léa was to him.

But now we must return to the Baron, who, with Brichot and myself, was approaching the Verdurins' door. 'And what has happened, he added, turning towards me, to your young Jewish friend that we used to see at Douville? I thought that if you liked we might invite him one evening.' For M. de Charlus, while not hesitating to have Morel's comings and goings spied on by a detective agency, exactly like a husband or a lover, did not himself stop taking an interest in other young men. He had had an old servant organize, through an agency, surveillance of Morel which was so indiscreet that the very footmen thought they were being followed, and one chambermaid was living in terror and did not dare go out in the street, believing that a policeman was always on her trail. 'Let her do as she pleases, the old servant would exclaim ironically. I'd like to see us waste our time and money having her tailed! As if we cared what she gets up to!' for he was so passionately attached to his master that, even though he did not share the Baron's tastes at all, he served them with such heartfelt devotion that in the end he came to speak of them as if they were his own. 'He's the salt of the earth,' M. de Charlus would say of this old servant, for the people we value most are always those who have great virtues, and apply them unstintingly to the furtherance of our vices. It was, by the way, only of men that M. de Charlus could feel jealous in relation to Morel. Women had no such effect. This is, in fact, nearly always the rule with Charluses. The love that the man they love has for a woman is something else, happening within a different species (lions don't go after tigers), and does not worry them: indeed, it may reassure them. Sometimes, it is true, among those who regard inversion as a priesthood, such love is seen as disgusting. Then they are angry with their friend for having given way to it, seeing his action not as a betrayal, but a degradation. A different kind of Charlus from the Baron would have been as outraged to see Morel having relations with a woman, as he would have been to read on a poster that the distinguished interpreter of Bach and Handel was now going to start playing Puccini. That is why young men who, for money, accept the love of Charluses, tell them that they find sex with women disgusting, as they might say to the doctor that they never drink spirits and only like spring water. But on this point M. de Charlus diverged somewhat from the general rule. Admiring everything about Morel as he did, his successes with women, since they did not offend him, gave him the same pleasure as did his successes on the concert platform or at cards. 'He has women, you know,' he would say to a friend, with an air of amazement, of scandal, perhaps of envy, certainly of admiration. 'He's astonishing. The most famous whores can't keep their eyes off him. He stands out everywhere, not just at the theatre, even in the metro. It becomes a bore! I can't go to a restaurant with him without the waiter bringing him notes from at least three women. And always pretty ones. But it's not surprising. I was looking at him yesterday and I understand them, he's grown so beautiful, he looks like a kind of Bronzino, it is marvellous.' But M. de Charlus liked to show that he loved Morel and to persuade others, perhaps to persuade himself, that Morel loved him. He must always have him near him, in spite of the damage the boy might do to his reputation in society: it seemed to be a matter of pride. For (and we often see men who have achieved a good social position throw it away out of vanity in order to be seen everywhere with a mistress, a semi-whore or lady of tarnished reputation, who is not received anywhere, but with whom it seems to them flattering to be connected) he had reached the point where self-regard applies all its energy to destroying the ends it had previously attained, whether because, under the influence of love, one finds a new prestige, which one is alone in perceiving, in an ostentatious relationship with the object of one's affection, or whether the ebbing of worldly ambitions, now satisfied, and the rising tide of curiosity about other forms of life, all the more absorbing the more academic it is, now make it seem that one's social ascent has not only reached but passed the level where other people have difficulty in clinging on.

As far as his taste for other young men was concerned, M. de Charlus found that Morel's existence offered no obstacle, and even that his glittering reputation as a violinist and his growing fame as composer and journalist in some cases acted as an attraction. When a young composer of attractive appearance was introduced to the Baron, he would turn to the talents of Morel to find something pleasant to say to the new arrival. 'You should bring me some of your compositions, he would say, so that Morel can play them in a concert or on tour. There is so little attractive music written for the violin! It's a pleasure to find something new. And foreigners are very appreciative too. Even in the provinces there are little musical circles where they love music with extraordinary passion and intelligence.' With no greater sincerity (for all this was just a way of leading the young men on, and Morel rarely if ever performed any of the pieces), since Bloch had said that he was 'by way of being' a poet, with the sarcastic laugh with which he accompanied a cliché when he could not think of anything original to say, M. de Charlus said to me, 'Do tell the young Hebrew, since he writes verses, to bring me some for Morel. It's always a problem for a composer to find something pretty to set to music. We might even think about a libretto. That's not an uninteresting idea, and it could attract notice because of the poet's talent, my patronage, a whole chain of helpful circumstances, among which Morel's talent must come first.

For he does a lot of composing now and writes too, very prettily, I must tell you about it. As for his talent as a performer (you know he's quite a master now), you'll see this evening how well the boy can play Vinteuil's music. It takes my breath away to see how well he understands it at his age, when he seems such a child, just a schoolboy. Oh, this evening is just a rehearsal. The big performance is in a few days' time. But it will be much smarter today. We were so delighted you could come, he said, using the royal "we". Because it's such a splendid programme, I told Mme Verdurin she should have two parties. One in a few days' time, when she'll have all her duty guests, and the other this evening, when the Patronne will be, as they say in the law-courts, off the case. I sent out the invitations for this one and I asked some pleasant people from a different social world, who may be useful to Charlie and whom the Verdurins will like to meet. I'm sure you agree, it is wonderful to have the best music played by the finest artists, but what impact will the occasion have if the audience comes from the corner shop and the draper's across the way? You know what I think of the cultural standards of society people, but they can have an important part to play, for example the part the press plays on public occasions, of being an organ of publicity. You know what I mean: I've invited my sister-in-law Oriane, for example. She may or may not come, but if she does she certainly won't understand a thing. But the idea is not for her to understand, which would be beyond her, but to talk, which she is perfectly able to do and certainly will. Result: tomorrow, instead of the glum silence of the grocer and the draper's wife, there will be animated discussion at the Mortemarts', with Oriane telling how she heard the most wonderful things, how a certain Morel, etc., and indescribable fury on the part of the uninvited, who will say, "No doubt Palamède thought we were too uncultured; anyway, who on earth are these people at whose house it all happened": something just as useful in its own way as Oriane's praise, since the name Morel will keep coming back and will lodge in the memory like a lesson repeated a dozen times over. All this forms a chain of circumstances which can be valuable to the artist and to the hostess; it can act as a kind of megaphone to broadcast the event to a distant audience. It really is worth doing. You'll hear how he has come on. And then we've discovered a new talent in him, my dear, he writes like an angel. *Like an angel.*

'You know Bergotte, don't you? I thought you might perhaps have been able to refresh his memory about the writings of our young friend; you would be working along with me, helping me to create the right chain of circumstances to promote a double talent, for both music and writing, that might one day take its place alongside Berlioz's. You can see what you would have to say to Bergotte. You know what famous people are, they have their own preoccupations, everyone looks up to them, they often take no interest in anyone but themselves. But Bergotte, who is really unaffected and kind, should be able to make the *Gaulois*, or some other paper, take some of his little articles; they're half humorous, half musical, really charming, and I'd be so pleased to see Charlie adding to his violin a little bit of an Ingres pen.[44] I know I get too excited when I'm making plans for him, I'm like all the old sugar-mummies at the Conservatoire. What, dear boy, you didn't realize? But then you don't know how easily impressed I am. I stand about for hours outside the doors when the competitions are going on. I adore it, it's such fun. And Bergotte himself told me that Charlie's writing is really very good indeed.'

M. de Charlus, who had been introduced to him long before by Swann, really had been to see him to ask him to arrange for Morel to write a half-humorous column about music in a paper. On the way there M. de Charlus had felt a certain sense of guilt, for despite being a great admirer of Bergotte, he realized that he never went to see him for himself, but only to use his own half-intellectual, half-social standing in Bergotte's eyes to do a favour for Morel, for Mme Molé or certain other ladies. The fact of using his connections only for such purposes did not shock M. de Charlus, but it seemed to him worse to treat Bergotte in this way, since he felt that Bergotte was not simply someone useful like his society friends but deserved better of him. It was just that his life was extremely busy and he could find time in it only for something that he wanted very badly, for example anything involving Morel. Furthermore, though he was very intelligent himself, he cared little for conversation with another intelligent man, and particularly with Bergotte, who was too much the man of letters for his taste and belonged to another set which took a different view of things. Bergotte, for his part, was well aware of the utilitarian character of M. de Charlus's visits, but did not resent it; for he was incapable of sustained kindness but fond of giving pleasure when he could; he was understanding and incapable of taking pleasure in delivering a snub. As for M. de Charlus's vice, he did not share it in any degree but saw in it rather an element of colour in the character, *fas et nefas* consisting for an artist not in moral examples, but in memories of Plato or Il Sodoma.[45]

M. de Charlus had omitted to say that for some time now, like those great noblemen of the seventeenth century who disdained to sign or even to write their lampoons, he had been having Morel write little paragraphs loaded with low calumnies and directed against the Comtesse Molé. Insolent enough in the eyes of those who read them, how much more cruelly did they strike the young woman herself, who found in them, slipped in so cleverly that no one else could have noticed them, passages of her own letters, quoted verbatim but slanted in such a way as to make her feel on the edge of madness: cruellest of revenges. It killed the young woman. But every day in Paris brings forth, as Balzac would say, a kind of spoken newspaper, more to be feared than any of the others. We shall see later how that verbal press could annihilate the power of a Charlus once he had ceased to be fashionable, and elevate above him a Morel who was not worth a millionth part of his former protector. At least this intellectual fashion is naïve, and really believes in the insignificance of a brilliant Charlus, and the unquestionable authority of a stupid Morel. The Baron's implacable revenges were less innocent. Hence no doubt the bitter venom in his mouth, the invasion of which seemed to give to his cheeks the yellow tint of jaundice when he was in a rage.

'I should have liked him to be here this evening, to hear Charlie in the things he really plays best. But he's stopped going out, I hear, he doesn't want to be bored by people, he's quite right. But what about you, fair youth, we never see you on the Quai Conti. You're not exactly exhausting your welcome!' I said that I mostly went out with my cousin. 'Do you hear that! The boy goes out with his cousin, how sweet!' said M. de Charlus to Brichot. 'But we don't want to know how you spend your time, dear *che-ild*. You can do whatever you fancy. We are just sorry not to have any part in it. Anyway, you have excellent taste, your cousin is charming, ask Brichot, who could speak of nothing else when we were in Douville. We shall miss her this evening. But perhaps you were right not to bring her. Vinteuil's music is admirable, but I learned this morning through Charlie that the composer's daughter and her friend were to be there, and they are two young women of dreadful reputation. These things are always difficult for an unmarried girl. I'm even a little worried about my guests. But as they have almost all reached years of discretion it's less important for them. So they will be there, unless the two young ladies haven't been able to come, for they had promised faithfully to spend the whole of this afternoon at a study rehearsal that Mme Verdurin had arranged just for her bores, her family, the people who couldn't be asked for this evening. But just a moment ago, before dinner, Charlie told me that after all their promises the Misses Vinteuil, as we call them, hadn't turned up.' In spite of the dreadful pain that I felt on juxtaposing (as one does an effect, originally unexplained, and its finally discovered cause) Albertine's recent desire to come to the Verdurins' and the expected presence (unknown to me) of Mlle Vinteuil and her friend, I had enough presence of mind left to notice M. de Charlus's slip when, having told us a moment ago that he had not seen Charlie since the morning, he now admitted to having seen him before dinner. But my suffering was becoming apparent. 'What is the matter? said the Baron. You're turning green; come along, let's go inside, you really don't look well.' It was not that M. de Charlus's words had reawakened my original doubts about Albertine's virtue. So many further doubts had found their way into my mind; one thinks each one must be the last, that one can bear no more, and still one finds room for the newcomer, and once it has established itself in our inner life it finds itself competing with so many desires to believe, so many pretexts to forget, that quite soon they settle down together and in the end we hardly pay attention to it any more. It survives only as a half-deadened pain, a mere threat of future suffering, and being the other face of desire, a thing of the same order, it lodges at the centre of our thoughts and irradiates them, as if from an immense distance, with subtle hints of sadness, just as desire does with pleasures of unrecognizable origin, wherever anything can be associated with the idea of the woman we love. But pain springs back to life when a new, complete doubt, enters us; our first response may be to say 'I can cope, there will be a method of avoiding pain, the story can't be true,' all the same there was an initial moment when we suffered as much as if we believed it. If we had only limbs, only legs and arms, life would be tolerable. Unfortunately we have that little organ called the heart, which is subject to certain periods of weakness during which it is infinitely sensitive to everything that concerns the life of a certain person; at these times a lie – that harmless thing, alongside which we can live so happily whether it is told by ourselves or others – when it comes from this particular person, causes the little heart, which we ought to be able to have surgically removed, unbearable attacks of pain. Useless to mention the brain, for our thoughts can reason as much as they like during these attacks, they have no more impact on them than on a severe toothache. It is true that the person is wrong to lie to us, since she had sworn always to tell us the truth. But we know from experience, our own and others', what such promises are worth. And we chose to put our faith in them, when they were made by the person with the most obvious interest in lying to us, a woman whom we had not, in any case, chosen for her virtue. It is true that later she will hardly need to lie to us any more – precisely because our heart has become indifferent to her lying – because we shall then no longer have any interest in her life. We know that, and still we willingly sacrifice ours, either by killing ourselves for her, or having ourselves condemned to death for murdering her, or simply by spending our entire fortune on her in a few years, so that we then have to kill ourselves because we have nothing left. Anyway, no matter how calm one thinks one is when in love, the love in one's heart is always in unstable equilibrium. The smallest thing can move it into the positive position: one radiates happiness, one is overcome with tenderness, not for the beloved but for those who have set her in a good light, who have kept her away from wicked temptations; one believes oneself safe, and a single word: 'Gilberte isn't coming', 'Mlle Vinteuil has been invited', is enough to make the planned happiness towards which one was surging crumble away, to make the sun go in, the wind change and the inner storm break against which one day one will no longer be able to stand. On that day, the day when our heart is near breaking, friends who admire our work are distressed to see how such nobodies, such insignificant beings, can hurt us so badly, bring us to the point of death. But what can they do? If a poet is dying of infectious pneumonia, can one imagine his friends explaining to the pneumococcus that the poet is talented and that it should let him get better? The doubt related to Mlle de Vinteuil was not completely new. But such as it was, that afternoon's jealousy, prompted by Léa and her friends, had cancelled it out. Once I had removed the danger of the Trocadéro, I had experienced, I had thought I had regained for ever, complete peace. But what was really something new for me, was a certain outing about which Andrée had said to me, 'We walked a bit, here and there, we didn't meet anyone,' and during which in fact Mlle Vinteuil had obviously arranged to meet Albertine at Mme Verdurin's. Now I would have been happy to let Albertine go out by herself, go anywhere she liked, provided I could have locked away Mlle Vinteuil and her friend somewhere and be certain that Albertine would never see them. For jealousy is usually a partial thing, its location varies, either because it is the painful extension of an anxiety provoked sometimes by one person whom our friend might love and sometimes by another, or because of the narrow scope of our thought, which can make real only the area which it pictures to itself, and leaves the rest in a blur which cannot cause real suffering.

As we were about to enter the courtyard of the Verdurins' house, Saniette caught up with us, not having recognized us at first. 'I had been studying you for a while, however, he said in a breathless voice. Strange, was it not, that I should hesitate?' 'Wasn't it strange' would have seemed to him incorrect, and he was becoming infuriatingly familiar with historic forms of the language. 'And yet a man could own you for his friends.' His greyish skin seemed to reflect the leaden sky of a storm. His breathlessness which, the summer before, had still occurred only when M. Verdurin 'tore a strip off' him, was now constant. 'I know that a work of Vinteuil's is to be performed for the first time by excellent artists, and peculiarly by Morel. – What do you mean "peculiarly"?', asked the Baron, who took the adverb as a criticism. 'Our dear Saniette, Brichot hastily explained, playing the role of interpreter, often uses, as the cultured man he is, the language of a time when "peculiarly" corresponded to our "in particular".'

As we entered the ante-room, M. de Charlus asked me if I were working, and as I answered no, but that I was becoming very interested in old silver and porcelain services, he said that I could not see finer ones anywhere than at the Verdurins', as I must have seen at La Raspelière since, arguing that objects can also be also friends, they had the extravagant custom of taking all their possessions with them; it would be inconvenient, he said, to get everything out for me on a party day, but still he would ask them to let me see anything I wanted. I begged him not to. M. de Charlus unbuttoned his overcoat and took off his hat; I saw that the top of his head was turning silver in places. But, like a precious shrub which not only is coloured by autumn, but has had some of its leaves wrapped in cotton-wool for protection and others coated in plaster, M. de Charlus only appeared more colourful for these few white hairs at his top, when they were added to the patchwork of his face. And nevertheless, even under the layers of different expressions, of the make-up and hypocrisy which formed such an unconvincing mask, M. de Charlus's face still kept hidden from the world the secret which it seemed to me to be crying aloud. I was almost embarrassed by his eyes, in which I feared he would see me reading as if in an open book, and by his voice, which seemed to me to be repeating it in every possible tone, with an unflagging indecency. But human beings keep their secrets safe, for everyone who comes near them is deaf and blind. People who learned the truth from one source or another, for example from the Verdurins, believed it, but only until they met M. de Charlus. His face, so far from spreading dangerous rumours, quelled them. For we form such an exaggerated idea of certain entities that we could never identify them with the familiar features of someone we actually know. And it is hard for us to believe in the vices, just as it is impossible to believe in the genius, of a person we were at the Opéra with only yesterday.

M. de Charlus was handing over his overcoat with the familiarity of a frequent guest. But the footman to whom he was offering it was a new one, just a boy. Now M. de Charlus often lost the place, as they say, nowadays and no longer had a sense of what was and was not done. He had had a praiseworthy desire, at Balbec, to show that he was not alarmed by certain subjects, not afraid to declare of someone, 'He's good-looking,' to say, in a word, the same things as anyone might have said who was not like him; now he sometimes gave expression to this desire by saying things that no one who was not like him would ever have dreamed of saying, things on which his mind was so constantly fixed that he forgot they were not part of everyone's daily preoccupations. In this way, looking at the new footman, the Baron raised his index finger in the air in a threatening fashion, and, thinking he was making an excellent joke, said, 'You! How dare you make eyes at me like that!' and turning to Brichot, 'He has a funny little face, hasn't he? Cute little nose'; then, to complete his teasing, or giving way to an urge, he lowered his finger to the horizontal, pointed it straight at the boy, hesitated a moment, then, unable to contain himself any longer, poked the end of his nose saying 'Beep, beep!' and, followed by Brichot, myself and Saniette, who told us that Princess Sherbatoff had died at six o'clock, walked into the drawing-room. 'What sort of a house is this?' the footman thought to himself, and asked his friends if the Baron was a wise guy or a nut. 'That's just the way he is, replied the butler (who thought he was a bit 'touched', a bit 'crackers'), but he's one of Madame's friends I've always had the most time for, his heart's in the right place.'

At this moment M. Verdurin came towards us; only Saniette, already fearful of catching cold, for the outside door kept opening and closing, was still resignedly waiting for someone to take his things. 'What are you doing there, standing there like the faithful hound, M. Verdurin asked. – I am waiting for one of the people charged with the coats to take mine and give me a number. – What's that you say? said M. Verdurin sternly. "Charged with the coats"! are you going gaga? It's "in charge of the coats". Do we have to teach you the language again, like someone who's had a stroke? – "Charged with" is right, muttered Saniette in a halting voice; the abbé Le Batteux[46] – I've had enough of you, cried M. Verdurin in a terrifying voice. Listen to your wheezing! Have you just run up six flights of stairs?' M. Verdurin's overbearing rudeness had the effect of making the cloakroom attendants put other people before Saniette and when he tried to hand in his things they said, 'In a moment, sir, don't be in such a hurry.' 'Well done, chaps, order and system, that's the way,' said M. Verdurin with an encouraging smile, fortifying them in their inclination to make Saniette wait till last. 'Come on, he said to us, that damn fool's trying to make us catch our deaths in his beloved draught. Let's go and warm up in the drawing-room. Charged with the coats, what an idiot! – He is a little precious, but he isn't a bad sort, said Brichot. – I didn't say he was a bad sort, I said he was an idiot,' was M. Verdurin's sharp retort. 'Will you come to Incarville again this year, Brichot asked me. I think our Patronne has taken La Raspelière again, even though she had a disagreement with the owners. But none of that matters, the clouds will roll by,' he added in the same optimistic tone as newspapers use when they say, 'Mistakes have been made, but who does not make mistakes?' But I remembered in what a miserable state I had left Balbec and I had no wish to return there. I kept putting off from day to day my arrangements with Albertine. 'But of course he will come, he must, we insist upon it,' declared M. de Charlus with the high-handed and uncomprehending egoism of kindness. M. Verdurin, to whom we offered our condolences on the death of Princess Sherbatoff, said, 'Yes, I know she's very ill – No, no, she died at six o'clock, cried Saniette. – You're always exaggerating, said M. Verdurin brutally, for, the party not having been put off, he preferred to stick to the story of illness. Meanwhile Mme Verdurin was deep in discussion with Cottard and Ski. Morel had just refused, because M. de Charlus could not go there, an invitation to the house of some friends to whom she had promised the violinist's services. Morel's reason for refusing to play at the Verdurins' friends' party, a reason soon to be supplemented, as we shall see, by other, more serious ones, had acquired its force from a habit general in the circles of the idle, but particularly strong in Mme Verdurin's inner group. Certainly, if Mme Verdurin spotted a newcomer and one of the faithful exchanging a quiet word that led her to think they might already be acquainted, or wish to know each other better ('Till Friday then, at the So-and-sos'', or 'Come to the studio any day you like, I'm always there until five, I'd be delighted to see you') the Patronne, on edge, imagining that the newcomer had a 'position' which would make him a brilliant recruit to the little set, would pretend not to have heard anything and let her fine eyes drift (her Debussy habit had drawn darker rings under them than cocaine could ever have done, and their air of exhaustion was due only to the intoxication of music). Nevertheless, behind that domed forehead, swollen by so many quartets and their ensuing migraines, she would be turning over thoughts which were not exclusively polyphonic; till she could bear it no more, unable to wait a moment longer for her fix, and threw herself upon the two talkers, drew them to one side, and said to the newcomer, indicating the old hand, 'Wouldn't you like to come to dinner with *him*, let's say on Saturday, or whenever you like, with some nice people? Don't mention it too loudly because I won't ask all this mob' (a term describing, for five minutes, the inner circle, momentarily disdained in favour of the newcomer in whom such hopes were being invested). But this passion for new people, for bringing them together, had its counterpart. Faithful attendance at their Wednesdays produced in the Verdurins the opposite disposition. This was a desire to create quarrels, to push people apart. It had been intensified, brought to an almost insane pitch by the months they had spent at La Raspelière, where people were in each other's company from morning till night. M. Verdurin delighted in catching people out, in spinning webs to catch some innocent fly to feed to his spider bride. Where there had been no offence they invented contemptible traits. As soon as an old hand had been gone for half an hour, they made fun of him in front of the others, affected surprise that no one had noticed how he always had dirty teeth, or else brushed them obsessively twenty times a day. If someone presumed to open a window, such a want of manners made the Patron and the Patronne exchange looks of outrage. A moment later Mme Verdurin would ask for her shawl and give M. Verdurin the chance to say in furious tones, 'No, I'll close the window, I wonder who can possibly have opened it,' in the hearing of the guilty party, who would blush into his hair. They would reproach you with the amount of wine you had drunk. 'Doesn't it make you feel ill? It's one thing for a working man, but . . .' Walks taken together by two of the faithful without prior permission from the Patronne gave rise to endless comment, however innocent they might be. M. de Charlus's walks with Morel were not innocent at all. Only the fact that M. de Charlus was not living at La Raspelière (because Morel was in barracks) postponed the moment when they would have had enough of him, would turn against him, vomit him up. However, that moment was near at hand. She was furious and had made up her mind to 'open Morel's eyes' to the ridiculous and distasteful part which M. de Charlus was making him play. 'And besides, continued Mme Verdurin (who in any situation when she so much as felt herself under too heavy an obligation to someone she could not kill, would find some serious fault in him that would justify her in not showing him any gratitude), besides, I don't like the way he behaves in my house.' For Mme Verdurin in fact had an even more serious reason than Morel's letting down of her friends to feel angry with M. de Charlus. That gentleman, convinced of the honour he was doing the Patronne by bringing to the Quai Conti people who, indeed, would never have gone there on her account, had, at the first mention of names that Mme Verdurin put forward as possible guests, pronounced the most categorical sentence of exclusion, in a peremptory tone in which the vindictive pride of the testy great noble mingled with the dogmatism of the expert party organizer who would take off his play and refuse his collaboration sooner than descend to concessions which, according to him, would spoil the overall effect. M. de Charlus had only given his permission, hedged about with reservations, for Saintine, in relation to whom, so as not to be encumbered with his wife, Mme Guermantes had passed from daily intimacy to a complete break in relations, but whom M. de Charlus, finding him intelligent, continued to see. Certainly it was only in a bourgeois milieu with certain connections to the minor nobility, a world where everyone is very rich and related to an aristocracy of which the great aristocracy knows nothing, that Saintine, once the flower of the Guermantes set, had gone to seek his fortune and, as he thought, find support. But Mme Verdurin, knowing the pretensions to nobility of the wife's family, and not realizing the husband's position, for our impressions of elevation are formed from what is immediately above our heads and not from what is so high in the sky that we can barely see it, thought to justify an invitation to Saintine by boasting of his valuable connections 'since he married

Mlle \*\*\*'. The degree of Mme Verdurin's ignorance that this assertion revealed made a smile of indulgent contempt and generous understanding spread over the painted lips of the Baron. He did not deign to reply directly but, as he liked to build structures of theory about fashionable life which bore witness to the fertility of his intelligence and the massiveness of his pride, together with the hereditary frivolity of his interests, 'Saintine should have come to me for advice before he married, he said, there is a social as well as a physiological eugenics, and I am perhaps the only expert in it. Saintine's was an open and shut case, it was obvious that in making the marriage he did he was tying a millstone round his neck and hiding his light permanently under a bushel. His social life was over. I could have explained that to him and he would have understood, for he is clever. On the other hand, there was a different person who had everything needed to create a high, dominant, universally recognized position; but was being kept down by a dreadful attachment. I helped that person, half by pressure and half by force, to break his ties, and the resulting freedom, power and triumphant joy are owed to me. It took will-power, but what a reward! That is how it is, when people listen to me they can be the midwives of their own destiny.' It was only too evident that M. de Charlus had not been able to act on his destiny: action is not the same as words, even eloquent words, or thought, however ingenious. 'But as for myself, I am a philosopher; I observe with detachment the social reactions I have predicted, but do not influence them. I have continued to see Saintine, who has always shown me the affectionate deference that he owed me. I have even dined with him in his new establishment, where one is as bored amid all the luxury as one was formerly entertained when, living from hand to mouth, he brought together the choicest company in a little attic. You may invite him, I permit it. But I impose my veto on all the other names you mention. And you will thank me later, for I am not only an expert on marriages, but no less so on parties. I know the leading personalities who can lift an occasion, make it take off, give it height; and I can also spot the name that will puncture the balloon, make the whole thing fall flat.' These vetoes of M. de Charlus's were not always founded on crazy resentments or artistic hair-splitting; an actor's sharpness also came into play. When

he had a really successful ready-made speech to deliver about someone
or something, he liked to perform it to the largest possible number of
people, but without accepting in the second batch of guests any of the
first who might notice that the piece had not changed. He put together
a new audience, just because he was not changing the programme, and
when he had a real success in conversation would almost have been
willing to organize a tour and make appearances in the provinces.
Whatever the varied motives for these exclusions, M. de Charlus's
dicta not only offended Mme Verdurin, who felt her authority as
Patronne being undermined, they caused her real social damage, for
two reasons. The first was that M. de Charlus, even more over-sensitive
than Jupien, was constantly quarrelling for no perceptible reason with
the people one would have thought most fitted to be his friends.
Naturally, one of the first ways he thought of punishing them was not
to have them invited to parties he gave at the Verdurins'. Now these
outcasts were often people at the top of the tree, as they say, but who
in M. de Charlus's eyes had fallen from that position as soon as they
fell out with him. For he was equally imaginative in imputing faults
to people he wanted to quarrel with, and in denying all importance to
them once they were no longer his friends. If, for example, the guilty
party were a man of extremely ancient family, but whose duchy dates
only from the nineteenth century, the Montesquious for example, from
one day to the next M. de Charlus recognized only the antiquity of the
duchy, the family counted for nothing. 'They're not even dukes, he
would say. The title belonged to the Abbé de Montesquiou and passed
improperly to a relative, not eighty years ago. The present duke, if he
is a duke, is the third. Compare that to people like Uzès, La Trémoïlle,
Luynes who are the tenth or fourteenth dukes, or like my brother who
is the twelfth Duc de Guermantes and seventeenth Prince de Condom.
The Montesquious descend from an ancient family, what does that
prove, even if you could prove it? They've descended so far they're
at the bottom of the heap.' But if he was on bad terms with a gentleman,
heir to an ancient duchy, with the most magnificent connections,
related to ruling houses, but whose family had risen to this position
quickly without being able to trace its history very far back, a Luynes
for example, everything changed and only family now mattered. 'I ask

you, M. Alberti, who only rose out of the dirt under Louis XIII! What is it to us if they pulled strings at court to get their hands on duchies they had no right to?' Furthermore, with M. de Charlus, disgrace followed closely upon favour because of his characteristic Guermantes predisposition to demand from the conversation of friends things it cannot give, together with a symptomatic fear of being the object of ill-intentioned gossip. And the greater the favour, the harder the fall. Now no one had enjoyed such favour with the Baron as the Comtesse Molé. By what sign of indifference had she shown herself unworthy of it? The Comtesse herself always maintained that she had never been able to find out. It is true none the less that the very mention of her name would launch the Baron into the most violent rages, the most eloquent but most dreadful invectives. Mme Verdurin, to whom Mme Molé had been very kind and who was looking forward eagerly to the Comtesse's seeing at her house the most noble names 'in all France and lands adjoining', as the Patronne put it, immediately proposed inviting 'Mme de Molé'. 'Well, well, there's no accounting for tastes,' M. de Charlus had replied, and if yours, dear lady, is to spend your time with Mrs Todgers, Sarah Gamp and Mrs Harris[47] I have nothing to say, but please let it be on an evening when I am not here. I can see from your first words that we are not speaking the same language, since I was speaking of the aristocracy and you are quoting me the obscurest names from the legal world, crafty little commoners, poisonous gossips, little ladies who think themselves patrons of the arts because they copy a cut-down version of my sister-in-law's manners, like the jay imitating the peacock. Let me add that it would be almost indecent to introduce into a party that I have agreed to give at Mme Verdurin's house a person whom I have deliberately excluded from the circle of my friends, a female without birth, honour or wit, who is deluded enough to think that she can play the Duchesse de Guermantes or the Princesse de Guermantes, a combination which is itself ridiculous, since the Duchesse de Guermantes and the Princesse de Guermantes are exactly the opposite of each other. It's as if someone set up to be both Reichenberg and Sarah Bernhardt.[48] In any case, even if it were not contradictory, it would be deeply absurd. I may sometimes smile at the exaggerations of the one and be saddened by the limitations of the other, that is my right. But to see that little bourgeois frog trying to puff herself out to be the equal of those two great ladies who, at the very least, always show the incomparable distinction of their blood, it's enough, as they say, to make a cat laugh. *La* Molé! That is one name I never want to hear again, or I must wash my hands of the case,' he added, smiling, like a doctor who, desiring the good of his patient in spite of the patient himself, intends not to have forced on him the collaboration of a homeopath. However, certain persons judged insignificant by M. de Charlus might have been so for him, but not for Mme Verdurin. M. de Charlus, from the pinnacle of his birth, could disdain some of the smartest people whose presence would have made Mme Verdurin's salon one of the foremost in Paris. Now that lady was beginning to think that she had perhaps missed the bus once too often, to say nothing of the years she had lost by choosing the wrong side, in worldly terms, in the Dreyfus Affair. Her choice had done her some good, however. 'I don't know if I told you how displeased the Duchesse de Guermantes had been to see people from her social world subordinating everything to the Affair, shutting out elegant women and admitting others who were not, for reasons of revisionism or anti-revisionism, and how she had been criticized in her turn by the same ladies as lukewarm, unreliable and ready to place worldly etiquette before the interests of the country,' I might say to the reader as if to a friend with whom one has spent so much time that one no longer remembers whether one had thought or found the moment to tell him about a particular thing. Whether I did or not, the Duchesse's attitude at that time can be easily imagined and even, if we look back on it from a later period, can seem, from a social point of view, perfectly justified. It was a time when M. de Cambremer thought of the Dreyfus Affair as a foreign plot designed to destroy the Intelligence Service, to break down discipline, to destroy the army, divide the French and open the way for invasion. All literature, apart from a few fables of La Fontaine, being a closed book to the Marquis, he left it to his wife to establish that a cruelly observant literature, by creating disrespect, had brought about a comparable upheaval. 'M. Reinach and M. Hervieu[49] are in this together,' she used to say. No one will accuse the Dreyfus Affair of having had the same desperate designs on social life. But there too it broke down distinctions. Society people who do not want to let politics interfere with social life are just as wise as those soldiers who do not want to allow politics into the army. Society is like sexual tastes, about which one can never know what point of perversion they may reach once one lets aesthetic reasons determine the choice of them. Because they were nationalists, the ladies of the Faubourg Saint-Germain fell into the habit of receiving ladies of another social milieu; when nationalism disappeared, the habit persisted. Mme Verdurin, thanks to Dreyfusism, had attracted to her salon some good writers who at that time were of no value to her social schemes because they were Dreyfusards. But political passions, like all other passions, wane. New generations spring up who no longer understand them, even the generation which first felt them changes, experiences new political passions which, as they do not correspond exactly to the earlier ones, rehabilitate a certain proportion of the excluded, the reasons for their exclusion having altered. The monarchists no longer cared, during the Dreyfus case, whether someone had been a Republican, even a Radical, even an anti-clerical, provided he was now an anti-Semite and a nationalist. If ever there were to be a war, patriotism would take a different form, and if a writer were chauvinistic enough, no one would care whether or not he had been a Dreyfusard. That explains how, with each new political crisis, each artistic renewal, Mme Verdurin had collected the little drops of water, little grains of sand, presently useless, which would one day make up her salon. The Dreyfus Affair had passed, she still had Anatole France.[50] Mme Verdurin's real strength was her sincere love of art, the trouble she took for the faithful, the wonderful dinners she gave just for them, with no grand guests invited. Each of them was treated in her house as Bergotte had been in Mme Swann's. When, one fine day, a friend of this kind becomes a great man, a visit by him to someone like Mme Verdurin has nothing of the artificial, over-elaborate character of an official banquet or St Charlemagne's Day dinner with the dishes sent in from Potel and Chabot's, but is a deliciously homely occasion, with food that would have been just as perfect if no one had been invited. At Mme Verdurin's the company was perfectly trained, the repertory of the first order: she lacked only an audience. And since audiences' taste had begun to turn away from the rational, French art of a Bergotte and towards exotic music above all, Mme Verdurin, like a recognized Paris agent for all foreign artists, would soon, alongside the ravishing Princess Yourbeletieff, be playing the part of an elderly but all-powerful Fairy Carabosse in favour of the Russian dancers. This delightful invasion, against whose charms only those critics protested who were devoid of taste, brought to Paris, as is well known, a fever of curiosity less violent, more purely aesthetic, but perhaps just as intense as the Dreyfus Affair. In this battle too, Mme Verdurin was to be in the vanguard, but with a very different social dividend. As she had been seen shoulder to shoulder with Mme Zola, facing the might of the Cour d'Assises, so when the new humanity, rushing to acclaim the Russian Ballet, flocked to the Opéra crowned with the feathers of unknown birds, there again, in a grand circle box, was Mme Verdurin, flanking the Princess Yourbeletieff. And, just as after the day's excitement at the Palais de Justice we had gone in the evening to Mme Verdurin's to see Picquart or Labori at close quarters, and especially to hear the latest news, to find out what could be expected of Zurlinden, Loubet, Colonel Jouaust[51] or the Regulations, in the same way, not wanting to go to bed after the enthusiasm unleashed by *Shéhérazade* or the *Prince Igor* dances, we went to Mme Verdurin's, where every evening delicious suppers, jointly presided over by Princess Yourbeletieff and the Patronne, brought together the dancers who had not yet eaten, so as to be able to jump even higher, their director, the scene-painters, the great composers Igor Stravinsky and Richard Strauss, an unchanging inner circle around which, as at M. and Mme Helvetius's suppers, the greatest ladies in Paris and foreign Highnesses did not disdain to come and go. Even those society people who laid claim to taste and drew otiose distinctions between the various Russian ballets, finding the production of *Les Sylphides* 'subtler' than that of *Shéhérazade*, in which they saw an almost African influence, were delighted to observe close at hand these great men who were revolutionizing taste in the theatre and who, in an art perhaps somewhat more artificial than painting, had produced a renewal as radical as Impressionism.

To return to M. de Charlus, Mme Verdurin could have borne it if he had proscribed only Mme Bontemps, whom Mme Verdurin had singled out at Odette's for her love of the arts and who, during the Dreyfus Affair, had sometimes come to dinner with her husband, whom Mme Verdurin had called lukewarm since he did not support the call for a judicial review, but who, being highly intelligent and happy to create understandings with people from all the parties, was delighted to show his independence by dining with Labori, while carefully slipping in at the right moment a tribute to the honourable conduct, recognized by all parties, of Jaurès.[52] But the Baron had also proscribed certain ladies of the aristocracy with whom Mme Verdurin, in the context of musical celebrations, collections and charity events, had begun to establish contact, and who, whatever M. de Charlus thought of them, would have formed a good basis, much better than the Baron himself, on which to build a new Verdurin inner circle, an aristocratic one this time. She had in fact been counting on this party, to which M. de Charlus was bringing ladies of the same class, as an occasion to mix her new friends with his, and had been looking forward happily to their surprise on meeting at her house their own friends or relations, invited by the Baron. She was disappointed and furious at his prohibitions. It remained to be seen whether the evening, in these circumstances, would add up to a profit or a loss for her. The loss would not be too severe if at least M. de Charlus's lady guests, when they came, were so well disposed towards Mme Verdurin that they would become friends of hers in the future. In that case there would be something to be gained, and one day soon the two halves of society that M. de Charlus wanted to keep apart would be brought together, at the cost, of course, of not inviting him that evening. Mme Verdurin was therefore awaiting the arrival of the Baron's guests with a certain apprehension. She was soon to learn the frame of mind in which they were coming, and what kind of relations the Patronne could hope to enjoy with them. As she waited, Mme Verdurin consulted with the faithful, but seeing Charlus come in with Brichot and me, she immediately stopped speaking.

To our great astonishment, when Brichot said how sad he was to hear that her great friend was so ill, Mme Verdurin replied, 'Listen, I have to admit that I don't feel sad at all. There's no point in pretending that one feels something when one doesn't . . .' No doubt she spoke this way because she was tired and lacked the energy to put on a sad face for the whole length of her party; she was proud, too, and did not want to look as if she were hunting for excuses for not having put the whole thing off, but also concerned for her reputation and clever enough to see that the lack of sorrow she displayed would be more honourable if attributed to a particular antipathy, only now revealed, to the Princesse, than to a general want of feeling; then, no one could fail to be disarmed by such unquestionable sincerity: for if Mme Verdurin had not really been indifferent to the Princess's death, would she have chosen, in order to explain why she had not cancelled her party, to accuse herself of a much graver fault? This was to forget that in admitting her grief she would also have been confessing an inability to forgo any pleasure; now her hard-heartedness as a friend was something more shocking, more immoral, but less shaming, and consequently easier to admit to than the frivolous values of a hostess. In the case of a crime, when the culprit is in danger, any confession is dictated by self-interest. Where there is no punishment for the offence, the cause is self-esteem. Whether it was that, finding woefully hackneyed the excuse that people use to avoid having their life of pleasure interrupted by bereavements, when they say that they find it unnecessary to wear outward signs of mourning when their grief is in their heart, Mme Verdurin had chosen to imitate those intelligent criminals who reject the clichés of innocence and whose defence (half-way to an admission of guilt, if only they knew it) is to say that they would have seen no objection to the crime with which they are charged, but by chance, as it happens, they did not have the opportunity of committing it, or whether, having decided on indifference as the explanation of her conduct, and having once given way to her bad impulse, she had seen a certain originality in this feeling, unusual perspicacity in recognizing it, and unmistakable 'nerve' in proclaiming it so openly, Mme Verdurin continued to insist on her lack of sorrow, not without a certain pride such as might be felt by a paradoxical psychologist or a daring playwright. 'Yes, isn't it strange, she said, I felt almost nothing. Not that I wouldn't rather she had lived, heaven knows, I had nothing against her. – I had, interrupted M. Verdurin. – Oh, he doesn't like her, he thought it didn't look good for me to have her here, but he shouldn't have worried. – Now you must admit that I never approved of you seeing her. I always told you her reputation was bad. – But I have never heard that said, Saniette protested. – What!, cried Mme Verdurin, everyone knew. It wasn't just bad, it was shocking, dreadful. But no, it's not because of that. I just can't explain my reaction; I didn't dislike her, but I cared so little about her that, when we heard she was very ill, even my husband was surprised and said, "You don't seem affected at all." Listen, this evening he offered to call off the rehearsal, but I said no, we must go on with it, because I thought it would be hypocritical to pretend to be sad when I wasn't.' She said this because it had a curiously modern, 'problem-play' sound to it, and also it was gloriously convenient; for want of feeling or immorality, once confessed, simplify life as effectively as loose morals: they remove the need to find excuses for blameworthy actions, and transform them into obligations of sincerity. And the faithful listened to Mme Verdurin's words with the mixture of admiration and unease that certain cruelly realistic, painfully observed plays used once to provoke; and while they marvelled at this new display of their beloved Patronne's honesty and independent spirit, more than one, while saying to himself that of course it would be different for him, thought of his own death and wondered whether the sad day would be marked by tears or a party at the Quai Conti. 'I'm glad the evening wasn't cancelled, because of my own guests,' said M. de Charlus, little thinking that by speaking in this way he was further offending Mme Verdurin.

Meanwhile I was struck, as everyone was who came near Mme Verdurin that evening, by a strong and rather disagreeable smell of nose-drops. This was the reason. The reader will remember that Mme Verdurin's artistic emotions were never expressed by psychological, but only by physical means, so that they should seem deeper and more ineluctable. Now if anyone spoke to her of Vinteuil's music, her favourite, she would remain indifferent, as if she did not expect it to cause her any emotion. Then after a few minutes of looking straight in front of her, almost absent-mindedly, she would answer in a precise, down-to-earth, barely polite tone, as if she had been saying, 'I don't mind your smoking, of course, if it weren't for the carpet, which is a very fine one. Not that that matters either, but it would catch fire very easily, I'm terribly afraid of fire and I wouldn't want you all to be roasted alive just because somebody dropped a cigarette end.' With Vinteuil it was the same. If someone spoke of him, she did not express any admiration, but a moment later said how sorry she was that he was to be played that evening: 'I've nothing against Vinteuil, in fact I think he's the greatest composer of the century, it's just that I can't listen to one of those pieces without crying all the way through (she did not say "crying" in a pathetic tone of voice, but with the same, natural voice as she would have said "sleeping" and indeed some unkind people maintained that the second verb would have been more appropriate, for she always listened to Vinteuil's music with her head in her hands, and certain snoring noises could have been sobs). I can cry, I don't mind, but the trouble is, crying gives me the most dreadful cold. My nose gets all congested, and two days later I look like an old drunkard and to get my vocal cords working again I have to have days of inhalations. So one of Cottard's pupils . . . – Oh, but I didn't have a chance to say, poor Dr Cottard, you must have been so sorry to lose him, and so young . . . – Well, there you are, he's dead, we all die, he'd killed patients enough, it was time to take his own medicine. Anyhow, as I was saying, one of his pupils, a lovely man, has been treating me for my colds. He has quite an original saying, "Prevention is better than cure". So he puts stuff up my nose before the music starts. The effect is dramatic. I can cry like I don't know how many mothers who have lost all their children, not a hint of a cold. Sometimes a touch of conjunctivitis, but that's all. Total relief. If it wasn't for that I couldn't have gone on listening to Vinteuil. It was just one bronchitis attack after another.' I could not keep any longer from talking about Mlle Vinteuil. 'Isn't the composer's daughter here? I asked Mme Verdurin, with one of her friends? – No, I've just had a telegram, said Mme Verdurin evasively, they've had to stay in the country.' And for a moment I dared hope that perhaps they had never agreed to come, and that Mme Verdurin had promised the appearance of these representatives of the composer only in order to make a favourable impression on the musicians and the audience. 'What, weren't they even at the afternoon rehearsal?' asked M. de Charlus with feigned interest, wishing to seem not to have spoken to Charlie. Morel himself came to say hallo to me. I questioned him in a whisper about Mlle Vinteuil's non-appearance. He seemed to know very little about it. I motioned to him not to speak of it aloud and said that we would talk about it later. He bowed to me and assured me that my wish would be his command. I noticed that he was much more polite, more respectful than formerly. I praised him – the man who could perhaps help me to clarify my suspicions – to M. de Charlus, who replied, 'Of course he is, there would hardly be any point in his living with people who know how to behave if he went on being ill-mannered.' Good manners, in M. de Charlus's eyes, were old French manners, without a hint of British stiffness. So when Charlie, coming back from a tour in the provinces or abroad, arrived in his travelling clothes at the Baron's, the older man, if there were not too many people present, would unaffectedly kiss him on both cheeks, perhaps in part to show by such an open display of his affection that there was nothing improper in it, perhaps in order not to deny himself a pleasure, but probably more from a sense of history, to uphold and demonstrate the old manners of France and, just as he would have protested against Secession style or Art Nouveau by keeping his great-grandmother's old armchairs, to set against the British stiff upper lip the affectionate sensibility of an eighteenth-century father not hiding his joy at the return of his son. Was there an incestuous streak in this paternal affection? It is more likely that the way in which M. de Charlus habitually relieved his lusts, and about which we shall learn more at a later stage, did not satisfy his emotional side, which had lain fallow since the death of his wife; it is certainly true that after having thought several times about marrying again, he was now exercised by an obsessive desire to adopt a child, and that some people in his circle were afraid it would fix upon Charlie. And this is not surprising. The invert who has been able to nourish his passion only with a literature written for men who love women, who thought of men as he read Musset's *Nights*, feels a need to share, in the same way, all the social roles of the man who is not an invert, to keep someone as the admirer of chorus-girls does, or the old habitué of the Opéra, and also to settle down, to marry or live with a man, to be a father.

He walked away with Morel, ostensibly to have him explain the pieces they would be playing, but more because he took great pleasure, while Charlie showed him his music, in this public display of their secret intimacy. I too spent this time in pleasure. For, even though the Verdurin set did not include many unmarried girls, they made up for this by inviting plenty of them to their big evening parties. Some of these, and some very pretty ones, I already knew. They were catching each other's eyes across the room, signalling a welcome and filling the air with the repeated brightness of a lovely young girl's smile. Such is the multiple, scattered ornament of evening parties, as of days. One recalls an atmosphere because of the young girls who smiled there. People would have been very surprised if they had picked up any of the furtive messages that M. de Charlus had been exchanging with several other important male guests. These were two dukes, an eminent general, a famous writer, great doctor and distinguished lawyer. The remarks were these: 'By the way, did you ever find out if the footman, no, the little one who rides on the coach ... And at your cousin Guermantes's, is there anything? – Not at the moment, no. – I say, did you see, at the main door, looking after the carriages, there was a little blond thing in knee-breeches who looked very appealing. She called my carriage for me quite charmingly, I'd have liked to get talking. – Yes, but she's dead against, anyway she makes such difficulties, you know you like things to move quickly, you'd hate that. – Anyhow I know it's no go, one of my friends tried. – What a shame, the profile's wonderful and the hair! – Really, do you think so? I think if you'd seen more of her you'd soon have lost interest. No, you should have been at the buffet two months ago, you'd have seen something amazing, a great big lad over six feet tall, perfect skin, *and* he likes it. But he's in Poland now. – Oh! That's rather far. – You never know. He may come back. People do reappear.' There is no fashionable party, if one takes a cross-section of it at sufficient depth, that is not like those parties to which doctors invite their patients; the patients talk very sensibly, display excellent manners, and would give no sign of being mad if they did not whisper in your ear as an old gentleman passes, 'Do you see him? That's Joan of Arc.'

'I think we really have a duty to tell him, said Mme Verdurin to

Brichot. It's not that I mean any harm to Charlus, quite the opposite. He's good company and as for his reputation, it's not one that can do *me* any harm! All right, I know that for the sake of our little set, at our dinners when we get together to talk, I hate flirting, men saying silly things to women off in a corner instead of talking about something interesting, but with Charlus I didn't have to worry the way I did with Swann or Elstir or any of those others. With him I knew I was safe, there could have been all the women in the world there, you knew that the conversation wouldn't break up into tête-à-têtes, there'd be no whispering in corners. Charlus is in a class by himself, like a priest. But he mustn't start thinking he can lay down the law to the young men who come here and upset the balance in our little group, otherwise it will be worse than having a ladies' man.' And Mme Verdurin was sincere in thus pronouncing her tolerance of Charlisme. Like every ecclesiastical power, she regarded mere human weaknesses as less serious than anything that could weaken the authority principle, damage orthodoxy, alter the ancient creed, in her little church. 'Otherwise, I shall have something to say. There's a gentleman who stopped Charlie coming to a recital because he was not invited. So, we shall give him a severe warning, I hope that will be enough for him, for if not he will have to take himself off. I swear he wants to make a fool of him.' And, using exactly the same expressions that almost anyone else would have, for there are some quite uncommon ones that a given subject, particular circumstances almost inevitably bring back to the speaker, who imagines that he is freely expressing his own thoughts while he is simply mechanically repeating the universal lesson, she added, 'You never see him without that great bogyman hanging over him, like some kind of a bodyguard.' M. Verdurin suggested taking Charlie on one side for a moment, saying he needed to ask him about something. Mme Verdurin feared that he would be upset and play badly. 'No, you'd better not say your piece until after the performance. Perhaps better wait for another time.' For much as Mme Verdurin looked forward to the delicious feeling of knowing that her husband was enlightening Charlie in a room nearby, she was afraid, if things went wrong, that he might be angry and let her down on the sixteenth.

What doomed M. de Charlus on that evening was the bad manners

– so common among society people – of his guests, who were now
beginning to arrive. They had come out of friendship for M. de
Charlus, and curiosity about visiting such an unlikely spot; every
duchess headed straight for the Baron as if he were the host, saying, a
yard away from the Verdurins, who could hear everything, 'Show me,
where is old Mother Verdurin, do you think I really have to be
introduced to her? I do hope she doesn't put my name in the newspaper
tomorrow, or I shall be in disgrace with all my relations. What, that
woman with white hair? But she doesn't look too bad.' Hearing the
name of Mlle Vinteuil, who in any case was not there, more than one
lady said, 'What, the sonata girl? Do let me see her,' and meeting up
with their own friends, they huddled together and kept watch, bubbling
with ironic curiosity, for the arrival of the faithful, finding little to
single out but the rather unusual hair-style of a person who, some
years later, was to make the same style fashionable in the very smartest
circles; all in all, they were disappointed to find this salon less different
than they had hoped from those they were used to, just as smart people
would feel let down if, having gone to Bruant's night-club in the hope
of being picked on by the singer, they were welcomed on arrival with
a polite 'good evening' instead of the expected, 'Cor, what a mouth,
what a North and South! Blimey, what a mouth she's got!'

M. de Charlus, at Balbec, had made a penetrating criticism in my
hearing of Mme de Vaugoubert, who, despite her great intelligence,
had caused first the unexpected success and then the irremediable
disgrace of her husband. The sovereigns to whom M. de Vaugoubert
was accredited, King Theodosius and Queen Eudoxia, having returned
to Paris, this time for a stay of some length, there had been daily
celebrations in their honour, during which the Queen, a close friend
of Mme de Vaugoubert, whom she had known for ten years in her
own capital, and not knowing the wife of the President nor of any of
the ministers, had turned her back on them to spend her time with the
ambassador's wife. For that lady, who believed her position to be
unassailable, since M. de Vaugoubert had been the architect of the
alliance between King Theodosius and France, the marked favour
shown her by the Queen had been balm to her pride, but had not given
her any sense of the danger which threatened her and which was to

overwhelm her a few months later with the sudden, and to the over-confident couple unbelievable, announcement of M. de Vaugoubert's brutally sudden forced retirement. M. de Charlus, commenting in the 'slowcoach' on the fall of his childhood friend, expressed his surprise that such a clever woman should not, in these circumstances, have used all her influence with the sovereigns to make it appear that she had no such influence, and to have them direct all their amiability towards the President's and ministers' wives: an attention which would have flattered the wives all the more, and made them feel all the more grateful to the Vaugouberts, the more they thought that such amiability was unprompted, and not orchestrated by them. But the man who can see another's mistake need only be intoxicated, however gently, by circumstances and he will often fall into it himself. And M. de Charlus, as his guests pushed their way through the crowd to come and congratulate him, to thank him as if he had been the host, did not think to ask them to say a word to Mme Verdurin. Only the Queen of Naples, in whose veins ran the same noble blood as in her sisters, the Empress Elizabeth and the Duchesse d'Alençon, began to talk to Mme Verdurin as if she had come to the house for the pleasure of seeing Mme Verdurin, more than for the music or to see M. de Charlus. She said a hundred kind things to the Patronne, spoke at length of how long she had wanted to meet her, complimented her on her house and talked to her of the most varied things as if she were paying a call. She would have so liked to bring her niece Elizabeth, she said (the one who was soon afterwards to marry Prince Albert of Belgium); the girl would be so sorry not to have come! She fell silent as she saw the musicians appear on the platform, and asked for Morel to be pointed out to her. She could have been under no illusion about M. de Charlus's motives in wanting the young virtuoso to be bathed in such glory. But the wisdom of an old sovereign in whose veins ran some of the noblest blood in history, the richest in experience, scepticism and pride, only led her to consider the inevitable blemishes of some of the people she loved most, like her cousin Charlus (the child, like her, of a Duchess of Bavaria), as misfortunes which made them value all the more the support they found in her, and made her take even greater pleasure in offering it to them. She knew that M. de Charlus would be doubly pleased that she had taken the trouble to come in these circumstances. It was just that, being as kind as she had once shown herself brave, this heroic woman who, as a soldier-queen, had fired the cannon on the ramparts at Gaeta,[53] was always chivalrously ready to go to the help of the powerless and, seeing Mme Verdurin alone and neglected (and quite unaware of the fact that she should not have left the Queen's side), had tried to pretend that for her, the Queen of Naples, the focal point of the evening, the attraction which had drawn her there, was Mme Verdurin. She apologized repeatedly for not being able to stay to the end, since she had, most unusually, to go to another party, and particularly asked that when she left no one should be disturbed on her account, thus forgoing the honours which Mme Verdurin did not in any case know should be paid her on her departure.

We must, however, do M. de Charlus the justice of remarking that, even though he forgot Mme Verdurin entirely and allowed her to be neglected to a scandalous degree by the people 'of his own world' whom he had invited, he did understand that he must not allow them to show the same offhand disregard for the 'musical entertainment' as they had for the Patronne herself. Morel had already gone up on the platform, the artists were taking their places, and the conversations were continuing, with laughter and comments that 'apparently you have to be in the know to make much of this'. Suddenly M. de Charlus, drew himself up, as if he had entered a different body from the one I had seen dragging its bulk towards Mme Verdurin's, took on the expression of a prophet and turned upon the assembled audience a look of seriousness that told them the time for laughter was past; more than one lady suddenly blushed, like a schoolgirl caught in misbehaviour before the whole class. I found something comical in M. de Charlus's attitude, noble as it was; for at one moment he silenced his guests with fiery looks, and then, so as to indicate to them, as if by an order of service, the religious hush, the detachment from all earthly things, that they were to observe, he offered them, lifting his white-gloved hands to his fine forehead, a model, to be imitated by all, of gravity, almost of ecstasy, not acknowledging the greetings of late arrivals, who lacked the decency to understand that it was now time for great Art. Everyone was hypnotized, no one dared make a sound or move a chair; respect for music – thanks to the prestige of Palamède – had suddenly been instilled into a crowd as ill-mannered as it was smart.

Seeing the little platform occupied not just by Morel and a pianist but other instrumentalists, I thought that they were going to begin with works by composers other than Vinteuil. For I thought that only his piano and violin sonata had survived.

Mme Verdurin was sitting off to one side, the hemispheres of her white and pale-pink forehead swelling magnificently, her hair drawn back and upwards, partly in imitation of an eighteenth-century portrait and partly by the need for fresh air of a fever patient reluctant to speak of her suffering, isolated, a divinity presiding over the musical solemnities, a goddess of Wagnerism and migraine, a kind of almost tragic Norn, summoned up by genius in the midst of all these bores, in whose presence she was going to disdain even more than usual to show any sign of being affected by this music which she knew so much better than they did. The concert began, I did not know what they were playing; I was in unknown territory. Where could I place it? In which composer's work was I? I longed to know, and not being near anyone I could ask, wished I could have been a character in the *Arabian Nights*, which I constantly reread, and in which at moments of uncertainty there appears a genie or a maiden of ravishing beauty, invisible to all but the perplexed hero, to whom she reveals exactly what he wants to know. Now at this moment I was suddenly vouchsafed just such a magic apparition. Just as, when walking in a landscape one does not know and which one has indeed approached from a new direction, one turns a corner and finds oneself suddenly on a new path every twist and turn of which one knows perfectly, but which one has never joined from this direction before, one says to oneself 'But this is the little path that leads to the back gate into my friends the ***s' garden; I'm only two minutes from their house,' and there indeed is their daughter who has seen one approaching and come out to say hallo; just so I found my bearings in this music which was new to me, and recognized the landscape of the Vinteuil sonata; and, more wonderful than any girl, the little phrase, wrapped, caparisoned in silver, streaming with brilliant sonorities light and soft as scarves, came towards me, still recognizable under these new ornaments. My joy at meeting it again was increased by the familiar, friendly tone in which it spoke to me, so persuasive, so simple, yet allowing its rich, shimmering beauty to unfold in all its splendour. Its purpose this time, however, was simply to show me the way, a different path from that of the sonata, for this was a different, hitherto unperformed work by Vinteuil, where he had simply chosen to make an allusion (explained at this point by a note in the programme which we should have had before us) by introducing, just for a moment, the little phrase. Having been recalled for a moment in this way, it disappeared and I found myself in an unknown world once more, but I now knew, and everything I heard confirmed, that this was one of the worlds that I had not even imagined Vinteuil could have created; for when, tiring of the sonata, whose universe was exhausted for me, I tried to imagine others equally beautiful but different, I simply did as those poets do who fill their imagined Paradise with meadows, flowers and rivers duplicating those on Earth. What I now heard caused me as much joy as the sonata would have done if I had not known it; that is to say, it was just as beautiful, but different. Whereas the sonata opened on a lily-like dawn in the country, dividing its floating whiteness but only to attach it to the light but thick tangle of a rustic bower of honeysuckle and white geraniums, the new work took off on a stormy morning over flat, level surfaces like those of the sea, amid an acid silence, in an infinity of emptiness, and then it was in a rosy dawn that this unknown universe began to be built before me, drawn out of silence and night. This new, red light, so absent from the tender, rustic and candid sonata, tinged all the sky, as dawn does, with a mysterious hope. And a cry was already piercing the air, a cry of seven notes, but the most unheard-of, the most different from anything I could ever have imagined, something both unvoiceable and strident, no longer a murmuring of doves as in the sonata, but something that tore the air, as bright as the scarlet note that had suffused the opening bars, something like a mystic cock-crow, an inexpressible but shrill call of eternal morning. The cold, rain-washed, electric atmosphere – so different in quality, its pressures so other, belonging to a world so remote from the virginal, grass- and tree-inhabited world of the sonata – kept changing every moment, washing away the crimsoned promise of the Dawn. At midday, however, in a spell of burning sunshine, it seemed to reach a heavy, villagey and almost rustic happiness, in which the repetitive clanging of unleashed bells (like those which poured their burning heat down on the church square at Combray and which Vinteuil, who must often have heard them, had perhaps found at that moment in his memory, like a colour ready to hand upon a palette) seemed to give material form to the coarsest joy. To tell the truth, I did not find this joy motif aesthetically pleasing; it seemed to be almost ugly, its rhythm bumped so heavily along the ground that one could have copied it in almost all essentials just by a certain way of banging sticks on a table. I felt that in this passage Vinteuil had been lacking in inspiration, and as a result I allowed my own attention to drift slightly.

I looked at the Patronne, whose fierce stillness seemed a protest against the rhythmically nodding, ignorant heads of the ladies of the Faubourg. Mme Verdurin did not say, 'You know, I know this music really pretty well! If I had to express everything *I* feel, you'd be here all night!' She did not say it. But her straight-backed, unmoving posture, her expressionless eyes, her escaping locks of hair, said it for her. They also expressed her courage, said that the musicians could do their worst, trample her nerves, she would not flinch at the *andante* nor cry out at the *allegro*. I looked at the musicians. The cellist was dominating the instrument he held between his knees, his head to one side and his vulgar features giving his face, at particularly mannered moments, an involuntary expression of disgust; the double-bassist leaned over his instrument, plucking it with the same homely persistence with which he would have cleaned a cabbage, while next to him the harpist, still a child, in a short dress, with the horizontal rays of her golden quadrilateral extending beyond her in all directions, like those which stand for the ether in the magic chamber of a sibyl, according to conventional modes of representation, seemed to be trying to pluck from pre-arranged points in the network a delicious sound, in the same as way as, were she a little allegorical goddess standing before the golden trellis of the night sky, she would have picked stars one by one. As for Morel, a lock of hair hitherto invisible and lost among the others had come loose and now formed a curl on his forehead.

I turned my head a fraction towards the audience to see what M. de Charlus seemed to think of this curl. But my eyes only met the face, or rather the hands of Mme Verdurin, for the one was entirely hidden behind the others. Did the Patronne, by this meditative posture, mean to show that she considered herself to be somewhere like church, finding this music no different from the sublimest prayer; was she trying, as some people in church do, to hide from prying looks either, out of modesty, their imagined fervour or, for more worldly reasons, their guilty wandering thoughts or irresistible sleep? This last hypothesis I thought for a moment, hearing a regular, non-musical sound, must be the right one, but then I noticed that it came from the snoring, not of Mme Verdurin but of her little dog. But soon, the triumphant bell-motif having been dispelled, chased away by others, my attention was captured by the music again, and I realized that if the various voices in the septet came to the fore in turn only to combine at the end, in the same way his sonata and, I was later to learn, all his other works were mere sketches, charming but slight, compared to the complete, overwhelming masterwork that was now revealed to me. And I could not help making the comparison and remembering that I had thought of all the other worlds Vinteuil might possibly have created as closed universes, like each one of my loves; but in reality I had to admit to myself that, just as my latest love – the love for Albertine – contained within itself all my first impulses to love her (at Balbec at the very beginning, then after the ring game, then the night she had slept at the hotel, then on the foggy Sunday in Paris, then on the evening of the Guermantes party, then at Balbec again, and finally in Paris, where my life was now closely entwined with hers), in the same way, if I considered not just my love for Albertine but my whole life, then all my previous loves had been mere, slight essays preparing the way for, calling into existence this vaster love . . . love for Albertine. And I stopped listening to the music to wonder again whether Albertine had seen Mlle Vinteuil in the past few days or not, as one reinvestigates an inward pain from which one has been for a moment distracted. For it was inside me that all Albertine's actions took place. For every being that we know, we possess a double. But, normally located on the edge of our imagination, our memory, it remains relatively external to ourselves, and what it has or might have done has no more painful impact upon us than an object placed some distance away and able to cause only the painless sensations of sight. When something affects such beings as these, we perceive it in a detached manner, we can deplore it in the right terms which will convince others of our good-heartedness, we cannot really feel it. But since my injury at Balbec, it was in my heart, at a depth making removal impossible, that Albertine's double had lodged. What I saw of her hurt me as it might a patient whose senses were so unfortunately transposed that he experienced the sight of a colour as an incision deep into the flesh. Happily I had not yet given way to the temptation to break with Albertine; the irritation I felt, knowing that I would soon have to return to her as to a woman one loves, was insignificant compared to the anxiety I would have felt if the separation had been accomplished at a time when I still had doubts and before I had had time to become indifferent to her. And at the moment when I imagined her waiting for me at home, feeling the time passing slowly, perhaps having fallen asleep for a moment in her room, I felt the passing caress of a tender, homely phrase in the septet. Perhaps – everything is so closely intertwined and superimposed in our inner life – the phrase had been inspired by Vinteuil's daughter's sleep – that daughter who was now the cause of all my uneasiness, when its tranquillity surrounded the musician's work of an evening; the phrase calmed me by its soft background of silence which underlies certain reveries of Schumann's, during which, even when 'the poet is speaking', one senses that 'the child is asleep'.[54] Sleeping or waking, I would find her waiting for me this evening when I chose to go home, Albertine, my little girl. And yet, I said to myself, something more mysterious than Albertine's love seemed to be promised by the beginning of this work, by those first dawn cries. I tried to put aside the thought of my friend so as to concentrate on the musician. For he seemed to be there with us. It seemed as if the composer, reincarnated, was living for ever in his music; one could hear the joy with which he was choosing this or that tone-colour, matching it to the others. For, alongside deeper gifts, Vinteuil enjoyed one which few musicians and even few painters have possessed, that of choosing colours which are so durable but also so personal that not only can time not fade their freshness, but the pupils who imitate the original colourist, and even the masters who outperform him, cannot tarnish their originality. The revolution accomplished by their appearance will not be assimilated into anonymity with the passing of time; it is unleashed, it explodes anew and only when the works of the perpetual innovator are played again. Each timbre was underlined by a colour which all the rules in the world, learned by the best-educated musicians, could never imitate, so that Vinteuil, even though he had appeared at the appropriate moment to fill his assigned place in the evolution of music, would always break ranks and appear in the vanguard when one of his pieces was played, a piece which would give the impression of having been written after those of more recent musicians, because of its apparently contradictory and in fact deceptive character of enduring novelty. A passage of Vinteuil's symphonic work, first encountered in piano reduction and then heard in full score, was like a ray of sunshine broken up by a prism as it enters a dark dining-room; it unfolded an unsuspected, multicoloured treasure like all the jewels of the *Thousand and One Nights*. But how can one compare to such a static if glittering flood of light something that was life, blissful perpetual motion? M. Vinteuil, whom I remembered as so shy and so sad, had, when it was a matter of choosing a timbre, joining it to another, a boldness and in every sense of the word a happy touch of which there could be no doubt when one listened to his music. The joy that such sounds had caused him, the new strength they had given him to seek out more, still led the listener on from one discovery to the next, or rather it was the creator who led him on himself, drawing from the colours as he found them a wild joy which gave him the power to press on, to discover those which they seemed to summon up next, ecstatic, trembling as if at a spark when sublimity sprang spontaneously from the clash of brass, panting, intoxicated, dizzy, half-madly painting his great musical fresco, like Michelangelo tied to his ladder and, head down, flinging tumultuous brushstrokes at the ceiling of the Sistine Chapel. Vinteuil had been dead for many years now; but in the midst of these instruments he had loved, he had been allowed to pursue, without limit of time, at least one part of his life. Of his human life only? If art was indeed only an extension of life, was it worth sacrificing anything for, was it not as unreal as life itself? The more I listened to the septet, the less I could believe so. No doubt the flaming red septet was singularly different from the white sonata; the timid questioning answered by the little phrase from the breathless insistence on finding the fulfilment of the strange promise which had sounded forth so sharply, so briefly, vibrating so uncannily in the still, motionless red light of the morning sky over the sea. And yet these phrases, different as they were, were all made up of the same elements, for just as there was a parallel universe, perceptible to us in fragments dispersed here and there in museums and private collections, which was Elstir's universe, so Vinteuil's music spread out, note by note, touch by touch, the unknown, priceless colorations of an unsuspected universe, fragmented by the lacunae which separated successive hearings of his work; these two such different questionings which determined the different progress of the sonata and the septet, one breaking up into short appeals a line in itself continuous and pure, the other welding scattered fragments together to form an indivisible framework, one so quiet and timid, almost detached and as it were philosophical, the other so pressing, anxious, imploring, were in fact the same prayer, springing up before different inner sunrises, and simply refracted through different milieux of disparate thoughts, artistic experiments in progress during the years when he had been trying to create something new. A prayer, a hope which was always essentially the same, recognizable under its disguises in the various works of Vinteuil, yet found only in the works of Vinteuil. Musicologists could take those phrases and find their analogues, their antecedants, in the works of other great musicians, but only for secondary reasons, outward resemblances, analogies discovered through ingenious reasoning rather than felt through direct impression. The impression conveyed by these phrases of Vinteuil's was different from any other, as if, in spite of the conclusions which science seems to be reaching, individuals did exist. And it was just when he was doing his utmost to be novel, that one could recognize, beneath the apparent differences, the deep similarities and the planned resemblances that underlay a work, when Vinteuil would pick up a given phrase several times, diversify it, playfully change its rhythm, bring it back again in the original form; this kind of deliberate echo, the product of intelligence, inevitably superficial, could never be so striking as the hidden, involuntary resemblances which sprang to the surface, under different colours, between the two distinct masterpieces; for then Vinteuil, striving powerfully to produce something new, searched into himself, and with all the force of creative effort touched his own essence, at a depth where, whatever question one asks, the soul replies with the same accent – its own. A particular accent, this accent of Vinteuil's, separated from the accent of other musicians by a distinction much more marked than the one we perceive between the voices of different people, or even between the bellowing and the cry of two animal species; a real difference, the one that existed between the thought of some other musician and the eternal investigations of Vinteuil, the question that he put to himself in so many different forms, his speculation, endlessly painstaking but as free from the analytical forms of reasoning as if it had been conducted in the realm of the angels, so that we can measure its depth but no more translate it into human speech than disembodied spirits can when they are called up by a medium and interrogated about the secrets of death; his own accent, for in the end and even taking into account the acquired originality which had struck me in the afternoon, the family relationship which musicologists could trace between composers, it is to a single, personal voice that those great singers, the original musicians, always return in spite of themselves, a voice which is the living proof of the irreducible individuality of each soul. Vinteuil might try to make his music more solemn, grander, or to aim at liveliness and gaiety, to produce what he could see reflected as beauty in the mind of the public, the same Vinteuil, in spite of himself, saw everything else submerged in a groundswell which makes his song eternal and consequently recognized. This song, so different from everyone else's, so similar in all his own works, where had Vinteuil learnt it? Each great artist seems to be the citizen of an unknown homeland which even he has forgotten, different from the land from which another great artist will soon set sail for the earth. At most, Vinteuil seemed to have got nearer to this homeland in his last works. The atmosphere in them was not the same as in the sonata, the questioning phrases had become more pressing, more uneasy, the answers more mysterious; the damp breezes of its morning and evening seemed to exercise an influence even on the strings of the instruments. Morel was playing wonderfully, yet the sounds issuing from his violin seemed to me strangely piercing, even shrill. This sharpness was pleasing and one seemed to hear in it, as one does in certain voices, a kind of moral quality, as if of superior intelligence. But it could also be shocking. When an artist's vision of the universe changes, becomes purer, closer to the memory of the lost homeland, it is natural that that should be reflected in a general alteration of sound quality in the musician, as of colour in the painter. In any case, the most intelligent part of the audience understands, for it would later be said that Vinteuil's last works were his most profound. Now there was no programme here, no title to allow one to form an intellectual judgment. So one simply guessed that this was a transposition, into the realm of sound, of profundity.

It is not that musicians can remember this lost homeland, but each of them always remains unconsciously in tune with it; he is overcome with joy when he sings the songs of his country, he may sometimes betray it for the sake of glory, but when he seeks glory in this way he moves further away from it, and only finds it when he turns his back on it, and when, whatever his subject may be, he gives voice to that particular song whose repetitive character – for whatever the ostensible subject it remains identical – proves the continuity in the musician of the constituent elements of his soul. But is it not the case that these elements, this final residue which we are obliged to keep to ourselves, which speech cannot convey even from friend to friend, from master to pupil, from lover to mistress, that this inexpressible thing which reveals the qualitative difference between what each of us has felt and has had to leave on the threshold of the phrases which he uses to communicate with others, something which he can do only by dwelling on points of experience common to all and consequently of no interest to any, can be expressed through art, the art of a Vinteuil or an Elstir, which makes manifest in the colours of the spectrum the intimate make-up of those worlds we call individuals, and which without art we should never know? Wings, another respiratory system which allowed us to cross the immensity of space, would not help us. For if we went to Mars or Venus while keeping the same senses, everything we might see there would take on the same aspect as the things we know on Earth. The only real journey, the only Fountain of Youth, would be to travel not towards new landscapes, but with new eyes, to see the universe through the eyes of another, of a hundred others, to see the hundred universes that each of them can see, or can be; and we can do that with the help of an Elstir, a Vinteuil; with them and their like we can truly fly from star to star.

The *andante* had just finished on a phrase full of tenderness to which I had given myself up completely; then there was, before the next movement, a moment's break during which the musicians put down their instruments and the listeners began to exchange impressions. A duke, to show his knowledge of the subject, said, 'That piece is very difficult to play well.' Some more likeable people talked to me for a moment. But what was I to make of their words, which like all spoken human words seemed so meaningless in comparison with the heavenly musical phrase that had just been occupying me? I was really like an angel fallen from the delights of Paradise into the most insignificant reality. And just as certain creatures are the last examples of a form of life which nature has abandoned, I wondered whether music were not the sole example of the form which might have served – had language, the forms of words, the possibility of analysing ideas, never been invented – for the communication of souls. Music is like a possibility which has never been developed, humanity having taken different paths, those of language, spoken and written. But this return to the unanalysed was so intoxicating that on leaving its Paradise contact with other, more or less intelligent beings seemed to me extraordinarily insignificant. I might have remembered certain human beings during the music, have involved them with it; or rather, I had really connected the memory of only one person with the music, Albertine. And the final phrase of the *andante* seemed to me so sublime that I said to myself it was a pity that Albertine should not know – and if she had known, would not have understood – what an honour it was for her to be connected with something so splendid which brought us together, and with whose moving voice she had seemed to speak. But once the music ceased, the people who were there seemed too colourless for words. Refreshments were handed round. M. de Charlus spoke every now and then to a servant: 'How are you? Did you get my message? Will you come?' No doubt this hailing of them was in part a sign of the freedom and condescension of the great noble who is closer to working people than the bourgeois is, but it also showed the deviousness of the guilty individual who thinks that anything one does in the public eye will for that very reason be judged innocent. And he added, in Mme de Villeparisis's Guermantes voice, 'He's a fine lad, a good type, I often use him at home.' But his cleverness often misfired, for people were astonished by his intimately friendly manner and the *pneumatiques* he sent to footmen. The footmen themselves were not so much flattered as embarrassed by what their friends would say.

Meanwhile the septet, having begun again, was moving towards its end; several times a phrase from somewhere in the sonata reappeared, but each time changed, set to a different rhythm, with a different accompaniment, the same and yet another, as things are when they recur in life; and it was one of those phrases which, though one cannot tell which affinity has determined as their only possible dwelling-place the past of a given musician, can be found only in his works and constantly appear there, being the fairies, the dryads, the familiar divinities of the place. I had first noticed two or three such phrases in the septet which reminded me of the sonata. Soon – emerging from the violet mist which above all pervaded the last period of Vinteuil's work, so that even when he introduced a dance measure here or there, it remained trapped in an opal – I noticed another phrase of the sonata, still keeping so aloof that I barely recognized it; hesitantly it approached, disappeared as if startled, then returned and began to link arms with others arriving, as I was to learn later, from other works, called together still others which quickly became equally appealing and persuasive as they became more familiar, and entered into the dance, the heavenly dance which remained invisible to the majority of listeners who, seeing before them only a confused mist behind which they could discern nothing, punctuated with random, admiring exclamations a boredom of which they thought they would die. Then the phrases faded away, except one which I saw pass by again up to five or six times, not letting me see her face, but so tender, so different – as the little phrase from the sonata no doubt was for Swann – from anything that any woman had yet led me to desire, that that phrase, offering me in such a gentle voice a kind of happiness which would have truly been worth attaining – that invisible creature whose language I could not understand and yet whom I understood so well – was perhaps the only Unknown Woman it has ever been granted to me to meet. Then that phrase dissolved, changed its shape, like the little phrase in the sonata, and turned into the mysterious call of the beginning of the piece. A phrase of sorrowful character came to counter it, but it was so deep, so formless, so inward, so almost organic and visceral that each time it reappeared one was not sure if what was recurring was a theme or a nerve-pain. Soon the two motifs vied for supremacy in a struggle in which sometimes one disappeared entirely, and then one saw only a small part of the other. It was a wrestling-match of pure energies, however; for if these beings struggled against each other, it was without the encumbrance of their bodies, their outward appearances, their names, and they found in me an inward spectator – equally indifferent to names and individual character – ready to involve himself in their immaterial, dynamic combat and to follow with passion its vicissitudes of sound. Finally the joyous motif triumphed, it was no longer an almost anxious call from behind an empty sky, it was an inexpressible joy which seemed to come from heaven itself; a joy as different from that of the sonata as, compared to a sweetly grave Bellini angel playing the theorbo, would be an archangel of Mantegna robed in scarlet and blowing into a mighty trumpet. I knew that I should never forget this new kind of elation, this appeal to a joy not of this earth. But should I ever be able to attain it? The question seemed to me all the more important since this phrase was what could best have summed up – as something set apart from the rest of my life, from all the visible world – those impressions, separated by long intervals, which I recalled from my previous existence as landmarks, points of departure for the construction of a true life: the impression I had felt before the spires of Martinville, before a line of trees near Balbec. In any case, to return to the particular sound of this phrase, how strange it was that that this premonition, so completely at odds with anything day-to-day life can offer, this, the most daring approximation to the joys of the next world, should have come to me from the sad, respectable lower-middle-class figure that we used to meet at the Month of Mary services at Combray! But above all, how could I possibly owe this revelation, the strangest I had yet received, of an unknown type of joy, when, it was said, he had died leaving only his sonata, with the rest non-existent, buried in indecipherable notes? Indecipherable, perhaps, but in the end, by dint of endless patience, intelligence and respect, they had been deciphered by the one person who had lived alongside Vinteuil long enough to know his way of working, to understand his hints for orchestration: Mlle Vinteuil's friend. During the lifetime of the great composer she had already assimilated the daughter's veneration for her father. It was because of this veneration that the two girls had taken an insane pleasure in the desecrations described earlier. Adoration of her father was the very precondition of the daughter's sacrilege. And no doubt they should have denied themselves the pleasure of this sacrilege, but it did not completely define them. And besides, such pleasures had become less frequent and finally disappeared altogether as their morbid physical relations, that dark, choking fire, had given way to the clear flame of a lofty, pure friendship. Mlle Vinteuil's friend was sometimes troubled by the thought that she had perhaps caused the premature death of Vinteuil. If so, by spending years sorting out the impenetrable mass of notes he left behind, by establishing reliable readings of those unknown hieroglyphs, she had had the consolation of ensuring for the composer whose last years she had darkened, a compensating immortality. Relationships not sanctioned by the law can give rise to family connections no less varied and complex, and only more solid, than those created by marriage. Without dwelling on relationships as unusual as this one, do we not see every day that adultery, when it is based on true love, not only does not shake family attachments and duties, but gives them new life? A good daughter who will, out of a sense of propriety, wear mourning for her mother's second husband, will weep real tears for the man whom her mother had chosen from among all others to be her lover. Then, Mlle Vinteuil acted as she did simply out of sadism, which does not excuse her, but comforted me a little when I thought about it afterwards. She must have understood, I would say to myself, that all this was just an illness, a form of

madness, and not the true delight in wickedness that she wanted it to
be. But if she was able, later, to think of this for herself, it must have
eased her suffering as it had formerly spoiled her pleasure. 'That wasn't
me, she must have said, I was out of my mind. I can still pray for my
father, and not despair of his goodness.' However, it is possible that
this idea, which must have come to her during her pleasure, did not
occur to her during her suffering. I wished I could have put it into her
mind. I am sure it would have done her good, and that I could have
re-established between her and the memory of her father a reasonably
pleasant form of communication.

As if from the illegible note-books where a chemist of genius, not
knowing death is at hand, has written down discoveries which will
perhaps remain for ever unread, she had extracted from papers more
illegible than papyri marked with cuneiform script, the ever-true,
ever-fertile formula for that unknown joy, that mystic hope of the
scarlet angel of morning. And even I to whom, even if not in the same
degree as to Vinteuil, she had caused, and had that very evening, by
reviving my jealousy of Albertine, continued to cause, and would
cause even more in the future, such suffering, owed to her, in compen-
sation, the possibility of receiving the strange call which had come to
me and which I would never again cease to hear − as it were the
promise that something else existed, something perhaps reachable
through art, besides the nothingness that I had found in all pleasures,
and even in love, and that even if my life seemed so empty, at least it
was not over.

The part of Vinteuil that she had made accessible through her work
was indeed the entire work of Vinteuil. In comparison with this piece
for ten instruments, the few passages of the sonata that were all the
public had known before seemed so banal that one could not understand
how they had excited such admiration. In the same way we are
surprised that for years such insipid pieces as 'O Star of Eve' or
'Elisabeth's Prayer' could have brought audiences to their feet,
applauding wildly and crying 'encore' at the last notes of what seems
to us poor, colourless stuff now that we have heard *Tristan*, *The
Rhinegold* and *The Mastersingers*. We must suppose that these characterless melodies nevertheless contained in tiny and therefore perhaps

more easily assimilable quantities something of the originality of the masterworks which now are the only important ones for us, but which then would perhaps have been too perfect to be understood; the first ones may have prepared the way for them in the public's hearts. It is none the less true that, though they may have given a confused premonition of the beauties to come, they left them still completely undiscovered. The same is true of Vinteuil; if at his death he had left nothing – if we except certain parts of the sonata – but what he had been able to finish, what we could have known of him would have been as little, in comparison with his real greatness, as we should have known of Victor Hugo if he had died after 'The Combat of King John', 'The Silversmith's Daughter' or 'Sarah Bathing', without having written anything of *The Legend of the Centuries* or *The Contemplations*. What we think of as his real work would have remained in a virtual state, as unknown as those universes our perception cannot reach, and of which we shall never have an idea.

The same apparent contrast and profound unity between genius (talent too, and virtue) and the sheath of vices within which, as had happened for Vinteuil, it is so often contained and protected, could be read, as in a crude allegory, in the collection of guests among whom I found myself when the music was finished. This group, confined this time to Mme Verdurin's drawing-room, was like many others whose composition is unknown to the general public, and which journalists with intellectual pretensions – if they are a little better informed – call Parisian, or Panamist, or Dreyfusard, without realizing that they can be found just as well in St Petersburg, Berlin or Madrid, and at all historical periods; for if the Under-Secretary for Arts, a man of real taste and perfect manners, with a strong sense of his position, several Duchesses and three ambassadors with their wives were at Mme Verdurin's this evening, still the real, proximate reason for their presence lay in M. de Charlus's relations with Morel, relations which made the Baron wish to achieve the greatest possible publicity for his young idol's artistic success, and to get him the cross of the Légion d'honneur, another reason, at several removes, which had made the evening possible, was that a young woman enjoying the same sort of relations with Mlle Vinteuil as the Baron's with Charlie, had brought to light a whole series of works of genius that had come as such a revelation that a subscription was soon to be got up, under the patronage of the Ministry of Education, to put up a statue of Vinteuil. The cause of these works had, in fact, been served not only by Mlle Vinteuil's relations with her friend but by Charlie's with the Baron, and a sort of field path or short-cut would now allow the public to reach them without going the long way round via an incomprehension which might have lasted for years, if not complete ignorance lasting for ever. Every time something happens which can be grasped by the vulgar mind of the high-class journalist, that is to say usually something in the world of politics, the high-class journalists become convinced that nothing will be the same in France, there will be no more such evenings, people will stop admiring Ibsen, Renan, Dostoevsky, d'Annunzio, Tolstoy, Wagner or Strauss. For these journalists allow the dubious undercurrents of these official evenings to convince them that there is something decadent about the art celebrated there, which is often the most austere of all. For there is no name among those most revered by high-class journalists that did not in its time give rise to equally strange gatherings, though their strangeness was perhaps less flagrant, better concealed. At this party, the impure elements which came together there struck me from another point of view; certainly, I was as well placed as anyone to dissociate them, having met them separately; but the memories connected with Mlle Vinteuil and her friend, especially, spoke to me of Combray and also of Albertine, that is to say of Balbec, since it was because I had once seen Mlle Vinteuil at Montjouvain and then learned of her friend's association with Albertine, that I would be going home in a moment to find not solitude but Albertine awaiting me; and my memories of Morel and M. de Charlus's first meeting on the platform at Doncières, spoke to me of Combray and its two walks, for M. de Charlus was one of those Guermantes who lived in Combray without having a house there, half-way to heaven like Gilbert the Wicked in his stained-glass window, while Morel was the son of the old valet who had let me in to meet the lady in pink and had been the means of my recognizing her, so many years later, as Mme Swann.

'Well played, eh? said M. Verdurin to Saniette. – I only fear, he replied with a stutter, that Morel's very virtuosity may have obfuscated the general feeling of the work. – Obfuscated, what on earth do you mean?' yelled M. Verdurin, as the guests closed in, like lions ready to devour a man on the ground. 'Oh, I do not advert only to him. – He doesn't know what he's saying. Advert to what? – I should . . . have . . . to hear it again to form a considerate judgment. – Considerate! He's insane!' said M. Verdurin clutching his head in his hands. 'I mean, one that is well weighed. You speak of judging with d-d-due consideration. I say that I cannot form a considerate judgment – And I say to you, get out!' cried M. Verdurin, drunk on his own anger, pointing to the door. 'I won't have people talking like that in my house.' Saniette went out, weaving in circles like a drunk man. Some people thought that he had not been invited, and that was why he was being put out in such a way. And a lady who had been very friendly with him up to that point, to whom he had lent a valuable book the day before, sent it back to him the next day, loosely wrapped in a piece of paper on which she simply had her butler write Saniette's address; she did not want to be 'under any obligation' to a person who was obviously in such bad odour with the inner circle. Saniette never knew anything of this insult. For not five minutes had passed from M. Verdurin's outburst when a footman came to tell the Patron that M. Saniette had dropped unconscious in the courtyard of the house. But the evening was not over yet. 'Have him taken home, he'll be all right,' said the Patron, whose house ('private house', the Balbec hotel manager would have said) thus came to resemble those grand hotels where sudden deaths are swiftly concealed so as not to frighten the guests, and where the dead man may be hidden in a larder until, however grand, however generous he may have been in life, he can be smuggled out of the back door used by the sauce-cooks and the washers-up. Saniette was not quite dead, however. He lived for some weeks more, but without regaining consciousness for more than a few minutes at a time.

When the music was finished and his guests began to take their leave, M. de Charlus fell into the same error as on their arrival. He did not ask them to speak to the Patronne, to include her and her husband in the thanks they were expressing to him. A long line of people were waiting, but only to see the Baron, and he was not unconscious of them, for he said to me a few minutes later, 'The artistic evening took on a rather comical "after Mass" aspect afterwards.' People protracted their thanks in different ways, in the hope of spending a moment more with the Baron, while those who had not yet congratulated him on the success of *his* party stood waiting, marking time. (More than one husband wanted to leave; but his wife, socially ambitious even though a duchess, would protest: 'No, no, even if we have to wait an hour we can't leave without thanking Palamède, he's taken such trouble. He's the only person who gives parties like this any more.' No one would have thought of asking to be introduced to Mme Verdurin, any more than to an old usherette at a theatre where some great lady has invited the whole aristocracy for one evening.) 'Did you go to Eliane de Montmorency's yesterday evening, Palamède dear? asked Mme de Mortemart in the hope of prolonging the conversation. – Well no, I didn't; I do love Eliane, but I can never understand her invitations. No doubt I'm dreadfully stupid,' he added with a beaming smile, while Mme de Mortemart prepared herself to be the first recipient of a 'Palamedism', just as she often received 'Orianisms'. 'I did receive a card about a fortnight ago from dear Eliane. Above the slightly suspect name of Montmorency there was a delightful invitation: *Dear cousin, do think of me this Friday at 9.30.* Underneath were written two less charming words: *Czech Quartet.* I couldn't understand them at all, they seemed to have no more connection with what went before than those letters where one finds that on the back the writer has begun another with the words "Dear friend" and no more, without taking a clean sheet of paper, whether from absent-mindedness or the spirit of economy. I'm fond of Eliane, so I wasn't angry with her, I simply ignored the strange, irrelevant words *Czech Quartet*, and, orderly as always, I put the invitation on my chimney-piece with its instruction to think of Mme de Montmorency at half-past nine on Friday. In spite of my obedient nature, steady and gentle, as Buffon says of the camel[55] – and here a laugh spread among all M. de Charlus's hearers, for, as he knew, he was regarded as particularly difficult to get on with – I was a few minutes late (the time it took me to take off my day clothes), but did not feel too much remorse, thinking that nine-thirty might have meant ten o'clock. And on the stroke of ten o'clock, wearing a nice warm dressing-gown, with my feet in thick slippers, I sat down at my fireside to think about Eliane as she had asked me to do, and with a concentration that only began to flag at about half-past ten. You will tell her, won't you, that I complied strictly with her unusual request. I'm sure she will be pleased.'

Mme de Mortemart was helpless with laughter, in which M. de Charlus joined. 'And tomorrow, she added, not caring that she had over-run, and by a long way, the time allotted to her, will you go to our cousins the La Rochefoucaulds'? – Oh no, that is out of the question, they have invited me, as they have you, I see, to something quite impossible to imagine and to carry out, something called, if I can believe the invitation card, a *thé dansant*. Dancing tea! I was considered very agile as a young man, but even then I doubt if I could, without offending propriety, have drunk tea while dancing. I've always hated the idea of eating or drinking messily. Now you will say that a man of my age won't be called upon to dance. But even if I were sitting comfortably drinking tea – and what strange tea it must be, if it's described as dancing – I should be afraid that younger guests, perhaps not so agile as I was at their age, might spill their cup over me and spoil my pleasure in emptying mine.' And M. de Charlus was not content to leave Mme Verdurin out of the conversation as he spoke on every kind of subject (seeming to take delight in developing and varying them for the cruel pleasure, which he had always enjoyed, of keeping his friends standing in a 'queue' as they waited with long-suffering patience for their turn to speak to him). He went so far as to criticize all that part of the evening for which Mme Verdurin had been responsible: 'But, speaking of cups, what were those near-bowls like the ones the sorbets used to come in from Poiré-Blanche's when I was a boy? Someone told me a moment ago that they were for iced coffee. But I haven't seen any coffee or any ice. What strange objects, and what can be their function?' To say these words M. de Charlus had placed his white-gloved hands vertically over his mouth, and narrowed the focus of his gaze as if he were afraid to be heard or even seen by the owners of the house. But this was only a feint, for a moment later he was to voice the same criticisms to the Patronne herself, and later still to add, with further insolence, 'And please, no more iced coffee cups! Give them away to one of your friends, someone whose house you want to spoil. But don't let her put them in the drawing-room, people might think they've wandered into the wrong room, for they look exactly like chamber-pots.' 'But, dear, his cousin was saying, lowering her voice too and giving M. de Charlus a tentative look, not for fear of offending Mme Verdurin but of offending him, perhaps she doesn't know exactly what . . . – She'll learn. – Well, laughed the guest, she couldn't have a better teacher. How lucky she is! With you to guide her she'll never strike a wrong note. – Well, there weren't any in the music at least. – Oh, it was wonderful. Unforgettable. The violinist was a genius, and that reminds me, she continued, believing in her innocence that M. de Charlus was interested in the violin for its own sake, there's another one I heard the other day playing a Fauré sonata wonderfully, he's called Frank . . . – I know, he's dreadful, M. de Charlus replied, not caring how rudely he contradicted his guest and implied that she had no taste. If you want a violinist I advise you to stick to mine.' A new exchange of looks now began between M. de Charlus and his cousin: lowered, furtive looks because, blushing at her gaffe and determined to repair it by enthusiasm, Mme de Mortemart was about to suggest to M. de Charlus that she should give a party and ask Morel to play. She was not really concerned to launch a talent but more to display what she thought was her own, when it really belonged to M. de Charlus. She saw in this occasion only an opportunity to give a particularly smart party, and was already planning whom she would invite and whom leave out. This exercise of choice, the chief preoccupation of party-givers (those people whom the fashionable papers have the nerve or the stupidity to call the 'elite'), immediately changes the look of the eyes – and written style – more deeply than hypnotic suggestion can do. Even before thinking about what Morel might play (a consideration she judged secondary and with good reason, for even if everyone, thanks to M. de Charlus, had the good manners to be quiet during the music, certainly no one would dream of listening to it), Mme de Mortemart, having decided that Mme de Valcourt would not be among the chosen, had taken on, for that very reason, that conspiratorial, plotting look that so disfigures even those women in fashionable society who have the least need to care what others think of them. 'Couldn't I give a party to introduce your friend?' said Mme de Mortemart in a low voice; though her question was directed to M. de Charlus alone, she could not keep her eyes from drifting, as if mesmerized, towards Mme de Valcourt (the excluded one) so as to check that that lady was far enough away not to hear her. 'No, she can't make out what I am saying,' Mme de Mortemart privately concluded, reassured by her swift look, which had had quite the opposite effect on Mme de Valcourt from that intended. 'Well, well, thought Mme de Valcourt, intercepting the look, Marie-Thérèse is plotting something with Palamède that is not going to include me.' 'You mean my protégé,' corrected M. de Charlus, who had no higher opinion of his cousin's linguistic knowledge than of her musical gifts. Then, taking no notice of the her silent pleas and the smiles with which she attempted to excuse them, 'But of course . . . , he boomed, in a voice loud enough to be heard by the whole room, though there is always a danger in that kind of transplantation of a mesmeric personality into a context in which it cannot but suffer a depletion of its transcendental powers and the setting of which, in any case, is yet to be determined.' Mme de Mortemart felt that the *pianissimo*, the *mezza voce* of her question had been wasted, given the triple-*forte* delivery of the reply. But she was wrong. Mme de Valcourt heard nothing for the simple reason that she did not understand a single word. Her uneasiness lessened and would have quickly died away if Mme de Mortemart, fearing to be outmanoeuvred and to find herself having to invite Mme de Valcourt, who was too close a friend to be 'left out' if she found out about the party beforehand, had not raised her eyes in Edith's direction to forestall an impending danger, only to drop her lids hurriedly again so as not to establish real contact. She had planned to write to her the day after the party, one of those letters which is the unfailing accompaniment of the tell-tale look, letters which the writer thinks cleverly worded and which are like an open, signed confession. For example: *Dear Edith, I can't wait to see you, I didn't really think that you would come yesterday evening* (how could she imagine I would come, Edith would think, when she hadn't asked me?) *for I know you're*

*not over-fond of that sort of gathering, and find them rather boring. Still,
we should have been honoured to have you with us* (Mme de Mortemart
never used the term 'honoured' except in letters where she was trying
to give a lie the appearance of truth). *You know we're always delighted
to see you here. Anyway, you did the right thing, for the evening was a
complete frost, as things always are when they've been put together at the
last minute*, etc. But already the furtive look turned upon her for a
second time had made Edith aware of everything that lay behind M.
de Charlus's convoluted language. Indeed, the look was so powerful
that after striking Mme de Valcourt, the unmistakable mystery and
secretive intention that it conveyed bounced off and hit a young
Peruvian whom Mme de Mortemart was in fact intending to invite.
But he, filled with suspicion, seeing so plainly the smokescreen that
was being set up without realizing it was not meant for him, promptly
experienced a violent hatred for Mme de Mortemart and swore to play
countless cruel jokes on her: to have fifty iced coffees sent to her on a
day when she had no guests, for example, or, when she did have a
party, to put a note in the papers saying it was postponed, and to
write lying accounts of subsequent parties which would include the
well-known names of people whom, for various reasons, no one would
wish to invite, or even be willing to meet.

Mme de Mortemart was wrong to worry about Mme de Valcourt.
M. de Charlus was about to undertake a transformation of the planned
party much more radical than Edith's presence could ever have
achieved. 'But cousin,' said Mme de Mortemart, in response to the
phrase about the 'setting' whose meaning, in her momentary state of
hyperaesthesia, she had been able to guess at, 'you needn't trouble
yourself with that. I promise to ask Gilbert to make all the arrangements. – No, don't think of it, especially as he won't be invited. I will
do everything. The important thing is to keep out all of those who
have ears but hear not.' M. de Charlus's cousin, who had banked on
the attraction of Morel to give a party at which she would be able to
say, unlike so many of her female relations, that she had 'had Palamède',
began to reconsider her sense of M. de Charlus's prestige in the light
of all the enemies he would make for her if he took charge of the
inviting and excluding. The thought that the Prince de Guermantes

(to whom her decision to exclude Mme de Valcourt was partly due, since she was not accepted in his house) might not be invited, filled her with fear. 'Is the light a little too bright for you?' M. de Charlus asked with an apparent seriousness whose underlying irony passed unnoticed. 'No, not at all, I was thinking of the difficulties it might create, not for me of course, but with my relations, if Gilbert found out that I had had a party and not invited him, when he never has the smallest get-together without . . . That's it exactly, where two or three are gathered together we can expect nothing but pointless gossip; I think that with all this noisy conversation going on you have failed to understand that it's not a question of giving a party to flatter all your friends, but of carrying out the due rites of any true celebration.' Then, judging, not that the next person had been waiting too long, but that it was not appropriate to show further favour to the woman who was much less concerned with Morel than with her own invitation lists, M. de Charlus, like a doctor who brings the consultation to an end when he feels he has spent the due time on it, gave his cousin leave to withdraw, not by saying goodbye to her but by turning to the person immediately following her. 'Good evening, Madame de Montesquiou; wasn't that wonderful? I didn't see Hélène here, do tell her that any general policy of renunciation, even the noblest, that is to say, hers, must make exceptions where the occasion is a brilliant one, as it was this evening. To be seen rarely is good, but the rare, which is a negative value, must sometimes give way to the precious. No one values more than I do your sister's systematic *absence* from places where there is nothing worthy of her, but on a memorable occasion like this to be present would have been to take her due precedence, and would have added a further prestige to your sister's already prestigious reputation.' With that he passed on to a third lady.

I was very surprised to see there, now as pleasant and flattering to M. de Charlus as he had once been cutting to him, insisting on being introduced to Charlie and saying that he hoped he would come and visit him, M. d'Argencourt, once the scourge of men of Charlus's sort. Now he lived surrounded by them. It was not, certainly, that he had become one of the Charlus kind. But some time earlier he had practically abandoned his wife for a young society woman whom he adored. She was intelligent and had brought him to share her liking for intelligent people, and dearly wished to have M. de Charlus as a regular visitor. But above all M. d'Argencourt, who was extremely jealous and not very potent, felt that he was not satisfying his conquest and, wishing both to hold on to her and to amuse her, could safely do so only by surrounding her with unthreatening men, whom he thus cast in the role of guardians of the harem. They in turn found that he had become most agreeable and declared him much more intelligent than they had thought, thus pleasing both his mistress and himself.

M. de Charlus's lady guests melted away quite rapidly. Many of them said, 'I'd rather not go to the vestry (the small drawing-room where the Baron, with Charlie at his side, was receiving congratulations), but I must make sure Palamède sees me and knows I stayed right to the end.' None took the least notice of Mme Verdurin. Some pretended not to recognize her and to say a mistaken goodbye to Mme Cottard, saying to me of the doctor's wife, 'That's Mme Verdurin, isn't it?' Mme d'Arpajon asked me, within earshot of the real hostess, 'Was there ever really a M. Verdurin?' The Duchesses who were last to leave, not finding any of the expected strangenesses in this place which they had hoped would be different from everything they knew, consoled themselves by stifling wild giggles in front of Elstir's paintings; everything else, which they found much more similar than they had expected to what they were used to, they put to the credit of M. de Charlus, saying, 'Isn't Palamède clever! He could stage a fairy-play in a broom-closet, it would still be breathtaking.' The highest-ranking among them were those who congratulated M. de Charlus most fervently on the success of an evening whose secret motive was known at least to some of them and did not embarrass them at all, for this society – in memory, perhaps, of certain earlier historical periods when their family was already fully conscious of its destiny – carried its contempt for scruples almost as far as its reverence for etiquette. Several booked Charlie on the spot to come and play Vinteuil's septet for them, but none of them dreamed of inviting Mme Verdurin to hear him. She was consumed with rage, when M. de Charlus, floating on a cloud and unable to register her fury, magnanimously chose to invite the Patronne to share his joy. And this expert in artistic parties was perhaps rather giving way to his literary tastes than to an outrush of pride when he said to Mme Verdurin, 'Well, are you pleased? I think you have cause to be; you can see that when I take the trouble to organize a party, I do the thing properly. I do not know if your grasp of heraldry would allow you to measure exactly the importance of this occasion, to understand the impact I have made, the job I have done for you. The Queen of Naples came, the brother of the King of Bavaria, the holders of the three oldest peerages. If we think of Vinteuil as Mahomet, we can say that we moved the least movable of mountains on his account. Just think that for your party the Queen of Naples came from Neuilly, which she finds much more difficult than leaving the Two Sicilies,' he said with unkind humour, despite his admiration for the Queen. 'It's a historic occasion. Think of it, she had probably never been out since the fall of Gaeta. I expect that in the biographical dictionaries her key dates will be the fall of Gaeta and Mme Verdurin's party. The fan that she put down to applaud Vinteuil will take its place alongside the one that Mme de Metternich broke when she heard them hiss Wagner – Look, she left the fan behind,' said Mme Verdurin, momentarily pacified by the memory of the Queen's kind manner to her, and she showed M. de Charlus where it was lying on a chair. 'Oh, how moving! cried M. de Charlus, approaching the relic with veneration. All the more moving as it's so ugly; the little violet is beyond belief.' Emotion and irony ran through him in alternating spasms. 'I don't know if these things touch you as they do me. Swann would simply have died in convulsions if he had seen that. Now I know that, however high the price goes, I shall have to buy that fan when the Queen's things are sold up. And they will be, he added, for she's as poor as a church mouse,' cruel detraction being always mixed in the Baron's speech with the most genuine veneration, each springing from one of the two opposing natures that were brought together in him.

Each of them could indeed be brought to bear on the same occurrence. For the M. de Charlus who, from his comfortable position as a rich man, could mock the Queen's poverty, was the same one who often praised that poverty to the skies and who, if someone mentioned

Princess Murat, queen of the Two Sicilies, would reply: 'I don't know whom you mean. There is only one Queen of Naples, a sublime woman, who does not have her own carriage. But from her seat in the omnibus she annihilates all the smart carriages and a man would kneel in the dust to watch her go by.'

'I shall leave it to a museum. In the meantime we must send it back to her so that she does not have to send a cab to fetch it. The cleverest thing, given the historic value of such an object, would be to steal the fan. But that would be unkind to her – since she probably doesn't own another,' he added, laughing aloud. 'Anyway, you see that she came for my sake. And that's not the only miracle I worked. I don't think that anyone else at this moment can make as many people turn out for something as I can. But we must give credit where credit is due, Charlie and the other musicians played like angels. And you, dear Patronne, he added condescendingly, you too had your part to play in this festivity. Your name will not be absent from the record. History has preserved the name of the page who armed Joan of Arc for her first encounter: you have been, how shall I say, the vital link, you have brought together Vinteuil's music and its brilliant interpreter, you have been intelligent enough to see the capital importance of a chain of circumstances which would throw behind the performer all the weight of a personality of some standing, if I were not speaking of myself I should say of providential standing, and had the excellent idea of asking that person to ensure the success of the gathering, and to bring together before Morel's violin the ears directly attached to the most influential tongues; no, no, that is not unimportant. Nothing is unimportant in such a complete success. Every little helps. *La* Duras was marvellous. But then everything was; that is why, he concluded, for he loved to lecture, why I was so against your inviting those human divisors I mentioned, who would have acted upon the substantial figures I brought like decimal points in a sum, reducing the others to a tenth part of their value. I have a natural feeling for these things. You understand, we must avoid blunders when we are giving a party that must be worthy of Vinteuil, of his brilliant interpreter, of you and, dare I say it, of myself. Invite *la* Molé and everything would have been ruined. She is the little contrary, neutralizing drop that makes a potion powerless. The lights would have gone out, the *petits fours* would have been late, the orangeade would have given everybody a stomach-ache. At the mere sound of her name, as in a fairy-story, the brass would have fallen silent; the flute and the oboe would suddenly have lost their voices. Morel himself, even if he could have scraped out a few sounds, would not have been up to his task, and instead of Vinteuil's septet, you would have heard Beckmesser's parody[56] of it, finishing in a chorus of boos. I really believe in the influences of certain people, I could feel in one particular *allargando* as it opened right out like a flower, in the overwhelming satisfaction of the finale which was not just *allegro* but genuinely full of matchless *allegria*, that the absence of *la* Molé was inspiring the musicians and dilating the very instruments themselves with joy. Anyway, the day one plays host to one's sovereigns is not the day to invite the concierge.' In calling her *la* Molé (he also said *la* Duras though he was very fond of her) he was doing her justice. For all these women were actresses on the social stage, and it is true that even considered in that light Mme Molé was not equal to the extraordinary reputation for intelligence that she had acquired, and which reminded one of those mediocre actors or novelists who at a certain period come to be thought of as geniuses, either because of the mediocrity of their contemporaries, who do not include any outstanding artist who could show what real talent is, or the poor taste of the public, who, if a really individual genius did come to light, would be incapable of understanding him. The world being the kingdom of vanity, there is so little to choose among the various society hostesses that only the spite or wild imagination of M. de Charlus could make much of a distinction. And certainly, when he talked as he had just been doing, in this language which was a recherché amalgam of artistic and fashionable concerns, it was because his old woman's rages and his drawing-room culture provided his real eloquence with only cut-rate themes. The world of real differences does not exist on the surface of the earth, among all the countries levelled by our perception; how much less, therefore, does it exist among the 'worldly'. Does it in fact exist anywhere? The Vinteuil septet had seemed to tell me that it did. But where?

As M. de Charlus also loved tale-bearing and setting people at odds, following a policy of divide and rule, he added, 'And by not inviting her, you did not give Mme Molé the chance to say, "I can't think why that Mme Verdurin asked me. Who are those people, I don't know them." She was already saying last year that you were trying so hard to attract her it was becoming a bore. She's a fool, don't ask her again. What is she, anyway? Nothing out of the ordinary. She could perfectly well come to your house without making such a fuss; after all, I do. All in all, he concluded, I think you can be grateful to me, for, as it turned out, the evening was perfect. The Duchesse de Guermantes didn't come, but I don't know, perhaps that was for the best. We shan't be angry with her and we shall think of her again for another time, anyway, how could we not remember her, with those blue eyes of hers always saying "forget me not".' (And I thought to myself how powerful the Guermantes spirit – the decision to go here and not there – must be in the Duchesse to have overcome her fear of Palamède.) 'In the face of such a complete success, one is tempted to be like Bernardin de Saint-Pierre and see the hand of Providence everywhere. The Duchesse de Duras was delighted with everything. She even asked me to tell you so,' M. de Charlus added, emphasizing each word, as if Mme Verdurin should consider the message honour enough. So great an honour, indeed, as to be hardly believable, for he felt it necessary to convince her by adding, with the folly the gods send to those they wish to destroy, 'Truly.' 'She has engaged Morel to play at her house, the programme will be the same, and I think I can even get an invitation for M. Verdurin.' This courtesy extended to the husband alone was, though M. de Charlus did not realize it, the blackest insult to the wife, who, believing herself to enjoy, in relation to the performer and thanks to a kind of Moscow decree[57] operating within the little set, the right to forbid him to play anywhere else without her express permission, was already determined to cancel his appearance at Mme de Duras's party.

By this mere fluency of speech, M. de Charlus was already irritating Mme Verdurin, who did not appreciate private relationships within the little set. How often, and even at La Raspelière, when she heard the Baron talking uninterruptedly to Charlie rather than taking part in the *concertante* ensemble of the set, she had cried, pointing to the

Baron, 'What a gossip! What a gossip! Talk about a gossip, he's a gossip all right!' But this time it was much worse. Drunk on his own words, the Baron did not understand that by recognizing Mme Verdurin's role but fixing strict limits to it, he was unleashing that feeling of hatred which in her was a particular form, a social form, of jealousy. Mme Verdurin truly loved her regulars, the faithful members of the little set, she wanted them to belong wholly to their Patronne. She had to settle for less, like those jealous men who let themselves be deceived, but only under their own roof and even under their eyes, that is, where they are not deceived; she would allow the men to have a mistress, or a lover, provided the relationship had no social ramifications outside her house; it must have begun and had all its existence under the umbrella of her Wednesdays. Every suppressed laugh from Odette as she sat next to Swann had formerly gnawed at her heart, as had, recently, every private conversation between Morel and the Baron; she could find only one consolation for her pain, which was to destroy the happiness of others. She could never have tolerated the Baron's for much longer. But now his own rashness was bringing on the catastrophe by seeming to restrict the power of the Patronne within her own little clan. Already she could see Morel going into society without her, under the protection of the Baron. There was only one solution – to force Morel to choose between the Baron and herself and, using the ascendancy she had established over Morel by displaying, as he thought, an extraordinary insight which was due to reports she commissioned, lies that she invented and served up to him as corroboration of things he already wanted to believe, and, something he was about to experience for himself, traps that she set for the unwary to fall into: using this ascendancy, to make him choose herself in preference to the Baron. As for the society ladies who were there and who had not even asked to be introduced to her, as soon as she had understood their reluctance or simple indifferent rudeness, she had said, 'All right, I've got it, this is a bunch of old slappers that we can do without, they won't see the inside of this house again.' For she would sooner have died than admit they had been less friendly to her than she had hoped.

'Ah! My dear General,' M. de Charlus suddenly exclaimed, dropping

Mme Verdurin as he spotted General Deltour, the President's secretary, who might be very helpful in the matter of Charlie's decoration, and who, having consulted Cottard about his health, was quickly slipping away. 'Good-evening, dear and delightful friend. Sneaking off without saying good-bye to me, eh? said the Baron with a smile of happy confidence, for he knew that people were always delighted to spend a moment longer talking to him. And, as in his over-excited state he was both asking questions and supplying the answers, all in a high-pitched voice, 'Well, did you enjoy it? he asked. Wasn't it beautiful? The *andante* especially. It's the most moving thing ever written. I defy anyone to listen to it all through without tears in his eyes. How good of you to have come! I say, Froberville telegraphed me this morning, to say that as far as the Grand Chancellery is concerned there are no more problems, as they say.' M. de Charlus's voice continued to rise, sounding unusually shrill, as different from his normal voice as a barrister's is when he is making a highly rhetorical speech: a phenomenon of vocal amplification through over-excitement and nervous euphoria similar to that which, at her dinners, raised both Mme de Guermantes's voice and her look to such an unaccustomed pitch. 'I meant to send you a note tomorrow morning to say how glad I was, while I waited for an opportunity to tell you face to face, but you had so many people waiting to talk to you! Froberville's support is certainly worth having, but the minister has promised me his, said the General. – Oh, excellent. Well, you have seen how talented he is, how much he deserves it. Hoyos[58] was delighted, I didn't manage to speak to the ambassador's wife, was she pleased? Of course she was, who would not have been, except for those who have ears and hear not, and what does that matter provided they have tongues and speak?'

Seeing the Baron taken up with the General, Mme Verdurin called over Brichot. He, not knowing what Mme Verdurin was going to say, decided to make her laugh and, without realizing the suffering he was causing me, said to the Patronne, 'The Baron is delighted that Mlle Vinteuil and her friend aren't here. He is thoroughly scandalized by them. He said that their way of life was appalling. You can't imagine how prudish and stern the Baron is on the subject of morals.' Contrary to Brichot's expectation, Mme Verdurin was not amused. 'He is disgusting,' she replied. 'Take him out to smoke a cigarette with you, so that my husband can take his inamorata on one side without old Charlus seeing, and show him the danger he is falling into.' Brichot seemed to be hesitating. 'Let me tell you,' said Mme Verdurin, to remove his last scruples, 'I don't feel safe with that man in my house. I know he's been mixed up in some very dirty business, and the police are watching him.' And, since she had a certain gift of improvisation when inspired by malice, Mme Verdurin did not stop there: 'Apparently he's been in prison. Oh yes, I heard it from some people who ought to know. And someone I know who lives in his street says you can't imagine the characters that go up to his house.' And as Brichot, who often went to the Baron's himself, protested, Mme Verdurin replied even more emphatically, 'It's true, I tell you! You have my word for it,' an expression she generally used to support allegations made more or less at random. 'He'll be murdered one of these days, that's the way they all go. Perhaps he won't get that far because he's in the clutches of that Jupien. He had the nerve to send him here to me, a gaolbird, he is, you know, I know it for certain. He's got a hold on Charlus through some letters, the most dreadful things apparently. Someone I know has seen them, and he told me. "They'd make you sick if you read them," he said. That's how Jupien keeps him under his thumb and makes him cough up all the money he wants. I'd rather a thousand times be dead than living in terror as Charlus does. Anyway, if Morel's family decides to take him to law, I don't want to be charged as an accomplice. Let him go on, but at his own risk: I'll have done my duty. I'm sorry, but doing the right thing isn't always fun.' And already in a pleasant fever of anticipation at the thought of the conversation her husband was going to have with the violinist, Mme Verdurin said to me, 'Ask Brichot what kind of friend I am, and if I can do what it takes to save my friends.' (She was alluding to the way in which she had made him break just in time, first with his laundress and then with Mme de Cambremer; following upon these quarrels Brichot had become first almost completely blind and then, it was said, a morphine addict.) 'A pearl among friends, far-sighted and brave,' replied the old don with genuine if naïve feeling. 'Mme Verdurin kept me from doing something extremely foolish, Brichot continued, when she had moved away. She doesn't hesitate to cut deep, to do heroic surgery, as Cottard would say. I must admit, however, to great sadness at the thought that the poor Baron does not yet know of the blow that is going to fall upon him. He is quite mad about that boy. If Mme Verdurin succeeds, he is going to be a very unhappy man. But in any case it is by no means certain that she will not fail. I fear that she may be able to create certain misunderstandings between them which, in the end, will not separate them but only estrange them from her.' This had often happened between Mme Verdurin and her flock. But one could see that the need to keep their friendship was increasingly dominated in her by the need to ensure that that friendship was never imperilled by any feeling they might have for each other. Homosexuality did not offend her, so long as it did not threaten the faith, but, like the Church, she would have accepted any sacrifice rather than any compromise on orthodoxy. I began to fear that she might be annoyed with me because she had learned that I had prevented Albertine from being there that afternoon, and that she might begin, if she had not already done so, the process of separating her from me, the same work that her husband was about to undertake, in relation to Charlus, with the violinist. 'Come on, go and find Charlus, think of something, now's the time,' said Mme Verdurin, and above all, don't let him come back until I send someone to fetch you. What an evening! Mme Verdurin added, revealing the real cause of her rage. Playing those masterpieces in front of those dimwits! I don't mean the Queen of Naples, she is intelligent (meaning: she was friendly to me). But the others! It's enough to drive you mad. I'm sorry, but I'm not a girl any more. When I was young we were told you had to be able to stand boredom, and I tried, but now it's too much, I can't take any more, I'm old enough to do as I please, life is too short, and being bored, spending time with imbeciles and trying to look as if I find them intelligent, no, no, that's all over. Come on, Brichot, there's no time to lose – I'm going, Madame, I'm going,' said Brichot as General Deltour moved away. But first the professor took me on one side. 'Moral duty, he said, is not so categorically imperative as our ethics courses teach. Theosophical cafés and Kantian brasseries can say what they like, we are deplorably ignorant of the nature of the Good. I myself, in all modesty, have expounded for my pupils, to the best of my ability, the teachings of the aforesaid Immanuel Kant, yet I can find no precise guidance on the problem in social casuistry that faces me in that *Critique of Practical Reason* in which the great unfrocked pastor of Protestantism rewrote Plato in Teutonic style for a prehistorically sentimental Germany of princedoms, all for the greater good of a certain Pomeranian mysticism. It is the *Symposium* all over again, but this time in Königsberg, in the local style, healthy and indigestible, with sauerkraut and no rent-boys. It is evident, on the one hand, that I cannot refuse our excellent hostess a small favour that she asks of me, one which conforms fully with traditional Morality. We must above all avoid letting ourselves be deceived by words, for there are few things that lead to greater foolishness. But we must, in the end, admit that if mothers of families could vote, the Baron would run the risk of being deplorably blackballed for the post of professor of morals. Unfortunately it is with the constitution of a roué that he pursues his pedagogical vocation; note that I am not saying anything against the Baron; that charming man, who can carve a roast better than anyone, combines a genius for anathema with a heart of gold. He can be as amusing as the best of clowns, while with a certain colleague, a member of the Academy if you please, I yawn away sixteen drachmas to the dozen, as Xenophon might have said. But I fear he compromises his constitution with Morel a little more than sound morals would prescribe, and without knowing how docilely or otherwise the young penitent submits to the special exercises with which his catechist teaches him to mortify the flesh, one need not be an expert casuist to be certain that we should commit a sin of excessive indulgence, as you might say, towards that occult practitioner who seems to have come from the pages of Petronius via Saint-Simon, if we closed our eyes and gave him an open licence to flirt with Satan. Yet on the other hand, if I keep the man occupied while Mme Verdurin, for the sinner's own good and justly tempted by the thought of such a conversion, speaks plainly to the foolish young man and takes away from him all that he loves, perhaps strikes a fatal blow at him, I cannot say that the thing is indifferent to me, it seems to me that I am luring him into an ambush, as you might say, and I shrink from it as from an act of cowardice.'

Having said this, he did not hesitate to commit the act, and taking me by the arm, said, 'Come, Baron, let us go and smoke a cigarette, this young man has not yet seen all the treasures of the house.' I tried to excuse myself, saying that I had to go home. 'Wait a moment, said Brichot, you know you promised to take me home and I shall hold you to your promise. – Wouldn't you really like me to make them get out the silver for you? Nothing would be easier, said M. Charlus to me. Now remember your promise, not a word to Morel on the subject of the decoration. I want to surprise him with it in a moment, when we've left. I know he says it's not important for an artist, but his uncle would like it (I blushed, because the Verdurins knew, through my grandfather, who Morel's uncle was). Now, wouldn't you like me to have the best pieces brought out for you? But of course you know them, you've seen them time and again at La Raspelière.' I dared not tell him that what would have really interested me was not the run-of-the-mill table-silver of a bourgeois household, but some example, even in the form of a fine engraving, of Mme du Barry's. I was much too preoccupied and – even had I not been unsettled by the recent revelation of Mlle Vinteuil's expected presence at the party – too distracted and ill-at-ease whenever I went into society to be able to fix my attention on vaguely pretty objects. It could have been arrested only by the appeal of something which addressed my imagination, as, that evening, a view of Venice might have done, that city on which my thoughts had dwelt for so long in the afternoon, or some general element common to several appearances and more real than any of them, something which always spontaneously aroused in me an inner spirit, normally slumbering, but whose rise to the surface of my consciousness caused me the greatest joy. Now, as I came out of the room they called the theatre, and walked with Brichot and M. de Charlus through the other reception rooms, noticing, placed here and there among other furniture, certain pieces I had seen at La Raspelière without paying any attention to them, I grasped a certain family resemblance between the layout of the town house and the château, an underlying identity, and I understood Brichot when he said with a smile, 'Look, do you see the far end of this room, that might just give you an idea of what the rue Montalivet house was like twenty-five years ago, *grande mortalis aevi spatium*.'[59] His smile, at the thought of the departed salon which he could see once more, let me understand what it was that Brichot, perhaps unconsciously, preferred about the old room: not its big windows, not the youthful gaiety of the Patrons and their friends, but that unreal part (which I had reconstructed myself from a few similarities between La Raspelière and the Quai Conti) of which, in a drawing-room as in everything, the outer part, present and observable by everyone, is simply an extension: that part which had become purely spiritual, whose colour existed only in the mind of my old companion, who could not show it to me, that part which detaches itself from the outer world to find refuge in our souls, which it enhances, and with whose normal substance it merges, transforming itself there – vanished houses, people of former days, dishes of fruit from remembered suppers – into the translucent alabaster of our memories, whose colour we cannot show to others as only we can see it (so that we can truthfully say to them that they cannot imagine the past, that it was nothing like anything they have seen), and which we cannot contemplate inwardly without being moved, when we think that the existence of our thought is the condition of these things' continued survival, for a little while, the light of lamps that have gone out and the scent of arbours that will flower no more. And it was no doubt for this reason that the rue Montalivet drawing-room outshone, in Brichot's eyes, the Verdurins' present house. But, on the other hand, it added to the new house, for the professor, a beauty which it could never have for a newcomer. Those pieces of the old furniture which had been relocated here, the same groupings sometimes retained, and which I myself recognized from La Raspelière, integrated into the present salon parts of the old one which sometimes recalled it to the point of hallucination and then seemed almost unreal in the way they evoked, in the midst of ambient reality, fragments of a destroyed world which seemed to be existing elsewhere. A dream sofa rising up among new, all-too-real armchairs, the brocade cover of a gaming-table raised to the dignity of a person since, like a person, it had a past, a memory, still scorched by the sun shining through the windows of the rue Montalivet (the hour of whose arrival it knew as well as Mme Verdurin herself) and through the french windows at Douville, where it had been taken and from where it looked out all day over the carefully planted flower garden and across the deep valley of the \*\*\*, waiting for the time when Cottard and the violinist would have their game of cards, a bunch of violets and pansies drawn in pastel, the gift of a friend, a great artist now dead, sole surviving fragment of a life vanished without trace, the summing-up of a talent and a long friendship, recalling his gentle, intent gaze, his fine, plump hand with its sad look while he was painting; this charming clutter, this disorderly display of the gifts of the faithful which followed the mistress of the house everywhere she went and finally took on the structure, the fixity of a character trait; a profusion of bouquets, of chocolate boxes which developed systematic-ally, here as there, according to an identical pattern of flowering; a sprinkling of those strange, superfluous objects that look as if they had just emerged from their gift-wrappings and remain throughout their lives what they were to begin with, New Year's presents; all those objects that one could not consider in isolation, but which for Brichot, an old habitué of the Verdurins' parties, had the patina, the velvety touch of those things which acquire a kind of depth from being inhabited by their spiritual doubles; these things, strewn about, all set singing before his eyes as many musical notes which awakened beloved resemblances in his heart, confused reminiscences which marked off and cut out of the present-day salon, which they patterned here and there, as a frame of sunlight does on a fine day, pieces of furniture and carpets, pursuing from a cushion to a flower-stand, from a stool to a waft of perfume, from a lighting effect to a predominance of colours, moulding, calling up, making spiritual, bringing to life a form which, as it were, was the ideal figure, immanent in all their successive dwellings, of the Verdurins' drawing-room.

'Let us try, Brichot murmured in my ear, to get the Baron on to his favourite subject. He is prodigious on it.' On the one hand, I hoped to be able to obtain from M. de Charlus the information I wanted about the coming of Mlle Vinteuil and her friend, information in pursuit of which I had decided to leave Albertine. On the other, I did not wish to leave her alone for too long, not that (uncertain when I would return and at an hour, in any case, when anyone calling on her, or any attempt by her to leave the flat, would have been far too noticeable) she could have put my absence to any bad use, but because I did not wish her to find it too protracted. So I said to Brichot and M. de Charlus that I would not come with them for long. 'But do come,' the Baron said, whose social excitement was beginning to wane, but who felt that need to prolong, to draw out conversations that I had already noticed in the Duchesse de Guermantes as well as in him, and which, very strongly marked in that family, is found generally among all those who, giving no play to their intelligence except in conversation, that is, in an imperfect realization, remain unsatisfied even after hours spent together and hang on ever more desperately to their exhausted interlocutor, from whom they mistakenly demand a final satisfaction that social pleasures cannot give. 'Do come, won't you, he continued, this is the best moment of a party, when the guests have gone, Doña Sol's time,[60] though we hope that this party will not end so unhappily. But you are in a hurry, what a pity, probably in a hurry to go and do things you would do better not to do. Everyone is always in a hurry, and people leave when they should just be arriving. Here we are like Couture's philosophers,[61] now would be the time to go over the evening again, to do a post-mortem as we soldiers call it. We could ask Mme Verdurin to order a little supper for us, to which we would carefully not ask her, and have Charlie – *Hernani* again[62] – to play the sublime *adagio* again just for us. How wonderful that *adagio* is! But where is the young violinist? I want to congratulate him, it's hugs and kisses time. Admit it, Brichot, they did play like gods, especially Morel. Did you notice the moment when his forelock came adrift? No? Ah then, my dear chap, you didn't notice anything. We had an F sharp that Enesco, Capet or Thibaud[63] would have died for; I'm not normally emotional, but I admit that at that sound my heart was so full that I could hardly hold back my tears. The whole room was gasping; my dear Brichot, the Baron cried, violently shaking the professor by his arm, it was sublime. Only young Charlie stood as still as a statue, you couldn't even see him breathe, he was like those things in the inanimate world that Théodore Rousseau[64] talks about, which cannot think but inspire us to thought. And then all of a sudden,' cried M. de Charlus dramatically, gesturing as if for a *coup de théâtre*, 'then

. . . the Lock! And at that very moment, the graceful entry, like a little country-dance, of the *allegro vivace*. You know, that lock was the signal for revelation, even to the most slow-witted. The Princess of Taormina, who had been deaf up to that point, for there are none so deaf as those who have ears but hear not, realized that this was music and that there wouldn't be any poker later on. Oh, it was a solemn moment. – Pardon me for interrupting you, sir, I said to M. de Charlus to get him on to the subject that interested me, didn't you say that the composer's daughter was coming. I should have liked to meet her. Are you sure that she was really expected? – I have no idea.' In saying this, M. de Charlus was conforming, perhaps unintentionally, to the universal rule which says that we never give information to the jealous, whether out of an absurd wish to show that we are, out of decency and even if we detest her personally, 'on the side' of the suspected one; or from spite towards her, guessing that jealousy will only redouble his love for her; or out of that need to be unpleasant to others which takes the form of telling the truth to almost everyone but hiding it from the jealous, since not knowing will multiply their sufferings, or so they think; while, in order to hurt people, we head straight for what they themselves, perhaps wrongly, imagine to be the most painful subjects. 'You know the Verdurins, he went on, exaggeration is pretty much their stock-in-trade, they are delightful people, but they do love to promise celebrities of one kind or another. But you don't look well, you'll catch cold in this damp room, he said, pushing a chair towards me. You have been ill, haven't you, you must be careful, let me go and find your warm things. No, don't go yourself, you'll get lost and catch cold. That's how trouble starts, but you're not a baby, you should take more care, what you need is an old nanny like me to look after you. – Please, Baron, let *me* go, said Brichot who immediately disappeared: not quite realizing, perhaps, the real affection that M. de Charlus felt for me, and what charming remissions, full of simplicity and kindness, punctuated his wild delusions of grandeur and persecution, he had been afraid that M. de Charlus, whom Mme Verdurin had placed like a prisoner under his guard, might have simply been trying, with the excuse of finding my greatcoat, to rejoin Morel, and might thus have undone the Patronne's plan.

In the mean time Ski had sat down at the piano without waiting to be asked and, putting together a humorous frown, a far-off look and a slight twist of the mouth to form what he considered an artistic expression, was trying to talk Morel into playing something by Bizet. 'What, don't you like that childlike side of Bizet's music? But, my dear boy, he said, with his distinctive pronunciation, it's enchanting.' Morel, who did not like Bizet, said so in exaggerated terms, and (since, amazingly enough, the little set regarded Morel as a wit) Ski, pretending to take the violinist's diatribes as paradoxes, began to laugh. His laugh was not, like Mme Verdurin's, a sound like a smoker choking. Ski adopted an intelligent look, then there escaped from him, as if against his will, a single laugh, like the first note of a bell, followed by a silence during which the clever look seemed to be carefully examining the humorousness or otherwise of what was being said, then a second bell rang out, and soon the complete angelus of laughter.

I said to M. de Charlus how sorry I was that M. Brichot had been troubled. 'What? no, he's happy to do it, he's fond of you, we're all very fond of you. The other day someone was saying: where is he, we haven't seen him for ages, he's hiding away! He's a really good soul, is Brichot,' M. de Charlus continued, little suspecting, no doubt, given the frank, affectionate way in which the professor of ethics used to speak to him, that in his absence he did not hesitate to hold him up to ridicule. 'He's a very distinguished man, enormously learned, and his knowledge hasn't dried him up, hasn't turned him into a bookworm like so many of the others, who stink of ink. He has kept a breadth of mind, a tolerance, which is rare in his world. Sometimes when one sees how he understands life, how he gives everyone his due with such discernment, one wonders where a mere Sorbonne professor, an old school usher, can have learned about all that. I wonder at it myself.' I wondered even more to see the conversation of Brichot, which the least discerning of Mme de Guermantes's guests would surely have found laboured and dull, find favour with the most critical of them, M. de Charlus. But this result had been brought about by various influences, in particular two distinct ones, the first of which had led Swann to feel at home for so long in the little set, when he was in love with Odette, and the other, after his marriage, to feel warmly towards

Mme Bontemps, who pretended to adore the Swanns, constantly called on the wife, loved to listen to the husband's stories and, elsewhere, spoke of them with disdain. Like the writer who ascribed the highest intelligence, not to the man who was most intelligent, but to the dissipated one who could make daring yet tolerant comments about a man's passion for a woman, comments which made the writer's bluestocking mistress agree with him that of all the people who came to her house the least stupid was indeed this old ladies'-man who knew all about love, in the same way M. de Charlus found Brichot more intelligent than his other friends, for not only was he friendly to Morel, but he could collect from the Greek philosophers, the Latin poets and oriental storytellers texts which furnished the Baron's taste with strange and charming garlands. M. de Charlus had reached the age at which a Victor Hugo will choose to be surrounded by Vacqueries and Meurices.[65] He preferred above all others to be surrounded by people who accepted his point of view on life. 'I see a lot of him,' he added in a fluting, rhythmical voice; no movement but that of his lips disturbed the solemn, white-face mask upon which his clerical eyelids were half lowered. 'I go to his lectures, the Latin Quarter atmosphere is a change for me, the youth there is studious, thoughtful, made up of middle-class boys who are more intelligent and more knowledgeable than my contemporaries were in our very different sphere. It's another world, these are young *bourgeois*,' he said, spitting out the word as if it were preceded by several *b*s, and underlining it by a sort of habit of speech which corresponded to a taste for distinctions in thought that was peculiar to him, but perhaps also because he could not resist the pleasure of showing me a certain insolence. This last in no way reduced the great, affectionate pity that M. de Charlus inspired in me (ever since Mme Verdurin had unveiled her plan before me); it only amused me, and even if the circumstances had been different, if I had not felt so much on his side, it would not have offended me. I had inherited from my grandmother a lack of vanity so extreme that it could easily have made me wanting in self-respect. No doubt I was hardly conscious of this, and having seen at school and later the people I most admired refuse to accept a slight or forgive anyone who had behaved badly to them, I had learned to show in my words and actions a certain pride, as it were by second nature. I was even thought to be extremely proud since, not being at all fearful, I readily fought duels, the moral prestige of which I diminished by laughing at them myself, which soon led others to see them as ridiculous. But the nature we repress nonetheless survives in us. That is why, when we read the new master-work of a genius, we are sometimes delighted to find in it thoughts of our own which we had dismissed as valueless, moments of gaiety or sadness which we suppressed, a whole world of feeling we treated as beneath notice; the book in which we recognize them suddenly teaches us their value. I had learned from experience that it was wrong to smile affectionately when someone made fun of me and not to be angry with him. But this lack of self-esteem and resentment, even if I had stopped giving it expression, to the point that I hardly knew it existed in me, was nevertheless the original medium in which I had grown and still lived. Anger and malice arose in me in quite a different manner, by sudden acute fits. What is more, the sense of justice was absent in me, to the point of complete moral idiocy. In the depths of my heart I was immediately on the side of the underdog, of whoever was unhappy. I had no opinion about the extent to which right and wrong might be involved in the relations between Morel and M. de Charlus, but the idea of the suffering that was being prepared for M. de Charlus revolted me. I wanted to prevent it, but I did not know how. 'The sight of that little world of hard work is most agreeable to an old relic like me. I don't know those boys,' he added, raising his hand in a gesture of caution, so as not to seem to be boasting, to attest his own purity and ensure that the students' virtue was not in doubt, 'but they are very well-mannered; they are often kind enough to keep a place for me, as I am a very old gentleman. Yes, yes, dear boy, don't say no, I shan't see forty again, said the Baron, who was well into his sixties. It's rather hot in the lecture-room where Brichot speaks, but it's always interesting.' Though the Baron preferred standing, and even being jostled, in the crowd of students, sometimes, to save him a long wait, Brichot would take him in with him. Even though Brichot was on his own territory in the Sorbonne, as he walked in behind the bedel in all his chains,[66] the admired teacher among his pupils, he could not control a certain apprehension, and, while wishing to make the most of this

moment when he felt sufficiently important to behave graciously to
Charlus, he was still slightly at a loss; to get him past the bedel, he
would say, in an artificially bustling voice, 'Follow me, Baron, we
shall find you a seat,' then, paying no more attention to him and in
order to make his entrance, he would advance in sprightly fashion
alone down the corridor. On either side, a double row of young
teachers would greet him; not wishing to seem overbearing to these
young men, for whom he knew he was a great panjandrum, he gave
them endless winks and conspiratorial nods, but as he was careful to
remain martial and French in his manner, the result was a kind of
manly encouragement, the *sursum corda*[67] of an Old Contemptible
saying, 'By God, we'll show 'em.' Then the students' clapping would
break out. Brichot sometimes used M. de Charlus's attendance at his
lectures to please a visitor, even to return a favour. He would say to
some relative, or one of his middle-class friends, 'If you think your
wife or your daughter might be interested, may I say that the Baron
de Charlus, the Prince of Agrigentum, the descendant of the Condés,
will be at my lecture. It's something for a child to remember, that she
saw one of the last truly characteristic descendants of our aristocracy.
If they come, they'll be able to pick him out because he'll be sitting
next to me at the lectern. Anyway, he will be the only other person on
the platform, a stout, white-haired man with a black moustache,
wearing the Military Medal. – Oh, thank you,' the father would say.
And even though his wife had other things to do, so as not to offend
Brichot he would make her go to the lecture, while his daughter, in
spite of the heat and the crowd, would stare in curiosity at the
descendant of the great Condé, astonished that he was not wearing a
ruff and looked just like people today. He, however, did not spare her
a look, but more than one student, not knowing who he was, was
astonished by his friendly approaches, became busy and offhand, and
the Baron left the room full of dreams and melancholy. 'Excuse me
for bringing you back to my concerns,' I said hurriedly to M. de
Charlus as I heard Brichot coming back, but would it be possible for
you to send me a *pneumatique* if you heard that Mlle Vinteuil and her
friend were coming to Paris, and tell me exactly how long they would
be staying, without telling anyone that I had asked you?' I did not

really think that they would be coming now, but I wanted to take precautions for the future. 'Of course I will. First, because I owe you a great debt. By refusing the suggestion I once made to you, you did me a great favour at some cost to yourself, you left me my freedom. It's true that I've lost it now, in another way, he added in a melancholy tone suggesting a desire to confide in me; but what I always consider the most important aspect of your choice is there was a whole chain of circumstances that could have benefited you, and you ignored them, perhaps because Destiny warned you at that moment not to divert my course. It's the old saying again, "Man proposes and God disposes". Who can tell, perhaps if on that day when we came out of Mme de Villeparisis's together you had accepted my offer, many things that have happened since would never have come about.' Embarrassed, I changed the subject, seizing on the name of Mme de Villeparisis and saying how sad I had been to hear of her death. 'Ah, yes,' M. de Charlus murmured drily, in the most insolent tone, acknowledging my condolences while not seeming for a moment to believe them sincere. Seeing that in any case the subject of Mme de Villeparisis was not painful to him, I tried to find out from him, so well qualified in every way to give me the answer, why Mme de Villeparisis had been kept at such a distance by the aristocratic world. Not only did he not solve this little problem of social behaviour for me, he did not even seem to be aware of it. I understood then that Mme de Villeparisis's social situation, which was to seem impressive to posterity, and even in the Marquise's lifetime to ignorant commoners, had seemed hardly less so at the other end of social scale, in Mme de Villeparisis's own world, to the Guermantes. She was their aunt, they were chiefly aware of her birth, her connections by marriage, the importance she retained in their world through her influence over this or that sister-in-law. They saw her less from the society than the family point of view. Now Mme de Villeparisis's family position was much better than I had thought. I had been surprised to hear that the name Villeparisis was an assumed one. But there are other examples of great ladies marrying beneath them and managing to keep a strong social position. M. de Charlus began by telling me that Mme de Villeparisis was the niece of the famous Duchesse de ***, the most famous member of the high aristocracy during the July Monarchy, but someone who had refused to know the Citizen King[68] and his family. I had so wanted to hear stories about this Duchesse! And Mme de Villeparisis, good, kind Mme de Villeparisis whose cheeks seemed to me the pattern of *bourgeois* cheeks, Mme de Villeparisis who sent me so many presents and whom I could have seen every day if I liked, Mme de Villeparisis was the Duchesse's niece, brought up by her in her own house, the *hôtel de* ***. 'She asked the Duc de Doudeauville, said M. de Charlus, speaking of the three sisters, "Which of the sisters do you prefer?" Doudeauville said, "Mme de Villeparisis", and the Duchesse de *** answered, "Dirty beast!" For the Duchesse was so *witty*,' said M. de Charlus, giving the word the emphasis and the pronunciation usual among the Guermantes. I was not surprised that he should find the reply so 'witty', for I had often noticed the centrifugal, objective tendency which leads men to set aside, when judging the wit of others, the severe criticism they would apply to their own, and to set down and retain as something valuable sayings that they would disdain to originate themselves.

'But what's wrong with him? That's my overcoat he's got, he said, seeing that Brichot had been gone so long and brought back the wrong garment. I should have gone myself. Anyway, put it round you. You know that that's very compromising, dear boy? It's like drinking out of the same glass, I shall be able to read your thoughts. No, no, not like that, let me,' and as he put his coat round me he squeezed it against my shoulders, drew it up round my neck, turned the collar up and stroked my chin with his hand, apologizing the while. 'At his age he can't even dress himself properly, we'll have to make him cosy, I'm in the wrong job, Brichot, I should have been a children's nurse.' I wanted to leave but, M. de Charlus having expressed the intention of going to find Morel, Brichot held both of us back. Besides, the certain knowledge that when I got home I should find Albertine there, the same certainty that I had had in the afternoon that Albertine would come back from the Trocadéro, made me as little anxious to see her as I had been then, when I was sitting at the piano, after Françoise had telephoned. And it was this inner calm which allowed me to obey Brichot, who feared that if I left Charlus would not wait until the moment when Mme Verdurin came and called us. 'Don't go, he said to the Baron, stay with us for a little while, you can kiss him on both cheeks presently,' Brichot added, turning his almost dead eye on me; the many operations he had undergone had restored a little life to it, but nothing like the mobility required for the expression of mischief. 'Kiss him on both cheeks, really! cried the Baron with shrill delight. I tell you, dear boy, he thinks he's still at a school prize-giving, he's dreaming of his little pupils. I bet he sleeps with them. – You'd like to see Mlle Vinteuil, said Brichot to me, having heard the tail-end of our conversation. I promise to let you know if she comes, I'll hear about it from Mme Verdurin, he added, no doubt foreseeing that the Baron was in imminent danger of exclusion from the little set. 'Oh, do you think I am in less close touch with Mme Verdurin than you are, said M. de Charlus, less likely to hear of the coming of those two highly notorious young women? Everyone knows about them, you know. Mme Verdurin should not invite them, they belong in more dubious circles. They're part of a dreadful crew, they must all get together in the most frightful places.' With every word new suffering was piled upon my suffering, which changed its shape. For suddenly remembering certain movements of impatience in Albertine, which she had, however, immediately suppressed, I was struck by the alarming idea that she had begun to think of leaving me. This suspicion made it all the more vital for me to extend our life together until a time when I should have recovered my peace of mind. And to dispel from Albertine's mind, if it had taken root there, the idea of forestalling my plan of breaking with her, in order to make her chains seem lighter until the moment when I could break them without pain to myself, I thought the best plan (perhaps I had been cross-infected by M. de Charlus's presence and the unconscious memory of the games he loved to play), the best plan would be to make Albertine believe that I myself intended to leave her; as soon as I got home I would pretend to break with her, to be on the point of saying good-bye. 'Indeed not, I do not think I am closer to Mme Verdurin than you are,' Brichot declared, enunciating each word clearly, for he feared he had awakened the Baron's suspicions. And seeing that I wanted to leave and trying to keep me by the promise of amusement, he continued, 'It seems to me that the Baron fails to consider one thing when he speaks of those ladies' reputation, and that is that a reputation can be both dreadful and undeserved. Thus for example, in what I may call parallel history, it is certain that judicial errors have been frequent, and that history has recorded convictions for sodomy against famous men who were quite innocent of it. The recent discovery of Michelangelo's great love for a woman is a piece of new evidence which should give Leo X's friend the benefit of a posthumous judicial review. The Michelangelo Affair seems to me to have all the prerequisites to stir up high society and set the East End on the march, when that other Affair, which made anarchy the fashionable vice among our smartest dilettantes, but whose name one dare not mention for fear of quarrels, is finally forgotten.' From the moment Brichot had begun talking about men's reputations, M. de Charlus's whole face had betrayed the particular kind of impatience that we see in an expert on medical or military matters, when lay people who know nothing about them begin to say foolish things about therapeutics or strategy. 'You haven't the first idea what you're talking about, he finally said to Brichot. Just tell me one undeserved reputation. Give me the names. Yes, I know, he burst out when Brichot timidly attempted a reply, the people who tried it once out of curiosity, or a particular feeling for a dear friend who's dead now, and the one who's afraid he once gave himself away and now, when you say that a man is good-looking, replies that that's all Greek to him, that he can no more tell a handsome man from an ugly one than one motor engine from another, since he hasn't the bump for mechanical things. That's all hogwash. Good Lord, I don't mean to say that a bad reputation (or what people call a bad reputation) can never possibly be unjustified. But it's so rare, so out of the ordinary that for practical purposes it doesn't exist. I'm an expert on the subject, I hunt out examples, and I've found one or two that weren't mythical. Yes, in my whole life I've established the existence (I mean established scientifically, I don't go by what I hear) of two undeserved reputations. They usually occur because of the similarity of two names, or certain outward signs, like wearing too many rings, which people who know nothing about it think are absolutely unfailing signs of what you are talking about, just as they believe a peasant never opens his mouth without saying *Aar*, or an Irishman *Begorrah*. These are just clichés from the middlebrow theatre.'

I was very surprised to hear M. de Charlus mention as an invert the 'actress's friend' whom I had seen at Balbec and who was the leader of the Club of four friends. 'But what about the actress? – She's a blind, and anyway he sleeps with her, more perhaps than he does with men: he's not very active with them. – Does he sleep with the other three? – Never! Absolutely not. They're friends, that's all, they don't do anything like that. Two of them are women-only, the third is one, but isn't sure about his friend, and in any case they hide their affairs from each other. What is really surprising is the way undeserved reputations are the ones that people believe in most strongly. You, Brichot, for example, you'd go to the stake for the virtue of this or that man who comes here, and to those in the know he stands out like a sore thumb. At the same time, you're like everyone else, you believe the stories about such-and-such a famous man who, in the eyes of the public, is the personification of the vice we're speaking of, while he wouldn't practise it for worlds. I say for worlds because that's vague: if we tied it down to a few hundred in cash, then the number of the strictly pure would soon fall to zero. Without any inducement, the proportion of the virtuous, if you call that virtue, would fall somewhere between thirty and forty per cent.' Brichot had transferred our consideration of bad reputations on to the male sex: I, on the other hand, preoccupied with Albertine, had begun once more to apply M. de Charlus's words to women. I was appalled by his statistics, even though I realized that his figures must be inflated by wishful thinking and the reports of gossips, perhaps untruthful and in any case led astray by their own desires which, added to those of M. de Charlus himself, must have thrown out the Baron's calculations. 'Three out of ten virtuous! cried Brichot. Even if the proportions were reversed, I should still have had to multiply the numbers of the wicked by a hundred. If there are as many as you say, Baron, if you are not mistaken, then we must confess that you are one of the few clear-sighted observers of a truth that few can recognize around them. You are like Barrès,[69] who made discoveries about parliamentary corruption that were confirmed later, like the existence of Leverrier's planet.[70] Mme

Verdurin could probably mention some men whom I would rather not name, who suspected the existence in the Secret Service, in Army Headquarters, of behaviour prompted, no doubt, by patriotism but of which I could never have dreamed. Think of freemasonry, German spies, drug-addiction: Lucien Daudet[71] writes about them every day, stories that seem the height of fantasy and then turn out to be true. Three out of ten!' he repeated in astonishment. And it is true that M. de Charlus ascribed inversion to the great majority of his contemporaries, excepting only those with whom he had himself had relations; their case – provided the relations had been in the smallest degree romantic – he regarded as more complex. In the same way confirmed seducers, usually cynical about women's honour, will give a little credit only to the woman who has been their mistress, protesting, with apparent sincerity and an air of mystery, 'No, no, you're wrong, she's not like that.' This unlikely respect is dictated partly by their self-esteem, for it is naturally more flattering to suppose that such favours have been reserved for them alone, partly by their naïvety, which readily swallows everything their mistress tells them, and partly by the way in which, the closer one becomes to human beings and their existences, the more one is convinced that ready-made labels and classifications are too simple. 'Three out of ten! But be careful, Baron: unlike those historians whom the future will vindicate, if you were to present to posterity the picture you have just been describing, it might be rejected. Posterity demands evidence, and will want to see your documents. Now, as there will be no documentary evidence to support the existence of such collective phenomena, which the small number of those involved will be only too anxious to leave in obscurity, there would be outrage in the circles of the high-minded, and you would be regarded as a slanderer or, dare I say it, a madman. Having achieved full marks and first place as *arbiter elegantiarum*,[72] you would suffer the misfortune of a posthumous blackballing. That would be a slap in the face, as – God forgive me – our dear Bossuet says somewhere or other. – I am not working for posterity, M. de Charlus replied, I am content with life, it is quite interesting enough, as poor Swann used to say. – What! Did you know Swann, Baron, I didn't know that. Was he one of them? Brichot asked uneasily. – Really! Do you think I only know people like that? No, I don't think so,' said Charlus with lowered eyelids, weighing the pros and cons. And then, thinking that, given Swann's well-known reputation for quite the opposite propensity, a half-hint could not harm the man against which it was aimed, and might flatter the originator of the insinuation, 'Perhaps at school, I don't know, once or twice . . .' He let the words slip, as if thinking aloud, then took them back with a 'But that was two centuries ago! How do you expect me to remember? How tiresome you are,' he concluded with a laugh. 'He wasn't exactly pretty,' said Brichot who, though hideous, thought himself handsome and was quick to describe others as ugly. 'Don't say that, said the Baron, you don't know what you're talking about, his complexion in those days was peaches and cream and, he added in a measured, sing-song voice, he was a per-fect che-rub. And he stayed attractive all his life. Women were wild about him. – But did you know his wife? – I introduced them! She caught my eye in a semi-breeches part, when she was playing Miss Sacripant; I was with some chaps from the club, each of us took a woman home, and though I only felt like sleeping, some unkind people said – people are so unkind – that I had slept with Odette. But then she kept bothering me afterwards, and I thought I would get rid of her by introducing her to Swann. She wouldn't let go of me after that, she couldn't spell to save her life, I had to write all her letters. And then I had to take her everywhere. See, child, what happens when you have a good reputation. And yet it was only half deserved. She used to force me to organize the most dreadful sessions for her, four, five people at a time.' And Odette's successive lovers (she had been with Such-and-such, then So-and-so – all these men not one of whom poor Swann had known anything about, blinded as he was by jealousy and by love, now calculating probabilities and now accepting protestations of innocence more damning than any contradiction into which his mistress might have fallen, a contradiction harder to pin down and still more telling, on which the jealous lover might more logically rely, than on the information he pretends to have received so as to disturb his mistress), Charlus now began to enumerate them as matter-of-factly as he might have recited the list of the kings of France. And in fact the jealous lover is, like contemporaries, too close to the events, he can know nothing of them, and it is for the uninvolved that a series of adulteries takes on the precision of history, expanding into lists, quite dispassionate in themselves and saddening only for another jealous lover such as I was, who cannot avoid comparing his own case to the one he is hearing about, and wondering whether, for the woman he doubts, there does not exist another equally famous list. But he will never know, it is as if there is a general conspiracy, a joke of which he is the victim, in which everyone cruelly participates and which involves, while the woman he loves flits from one man to another, holding a blindfold over his eyes which he constantly tries to tear off, but without success, for everyone keeps him in the dark, poor soul, kind people out of kindness, unkind out of unkindness, vulgar people from a taste for low jokes, well-brought-up people from politeness and good manners, and everyone in observance of one of those conventions which the world calls principles. 'But did Swann ever know that you had been her lover? – Good heavens, of course not! Tell poor Charles about that! What a dreadful idea! My dear fellow, he would have killed me on the spot, he was as jealous as a tiger. I didn't tell Odette either, not that she would have cared, that I . . . but let's leave that. And to think it was she who fired a revolver at him, and nearly hit me! Oh, I could tell you a lot about that couple; and of course it was on me he called to be his second against d'Osmond, who has never forgiven me. D'Osmond had gone off with Odette, and to show he didn't care Swann had taken Odette's sister as his mistress, or pretended to. Anyhow, you mustn't ask me to tell you the whole story of Swann, or we'll still be here in ten years' time, but you can see I know more about it than anyone. I used to walk out with Odette when she didn't want to see Charles. It was all the more embarrassing as I have a close relative who has adopted the name of Crécy, though of course he has no right to it, and he didn't like the way Odette used it. For she called herself Odette de Crécy, and quite legitimately as she was only separated from a Crécy who had married her, a perfectly genuine one, a decent chap she had cleaned out, down to his last centime. But you're just keeping me talking, you know him, I saw you with him in the "slowcoach", you used to give him dinner at Balbec. He must need it, poor soul: he used to live on a tiny income that Swann gave him, and now that my friend is dead I should be surprised if any of it is still paid. What I can't understand, said M. de Charlus to me, is that you often visited Charles, and yet you didn't care to be presented to the Queen of Naples. It looks to me as if you have no curiosity about *people*, and that always surprises me in someone who knew Swann, for he was extremely curious in that way, to the point that I'm not sure whether I developed it in him, or he in me. I'm just as surprised as I would be to meet someone who knew Whistler and had no idea of taste. Anyway, the person who really needed to meet her was Morel. He desperately wanted to, for he is really extremely intelligent. It's a pity she's gone. But I shall bring them together one day soon. He must get to know her. The only thing that could stop it would be if she died tomorrow. So let's hope that she doesn't.' Suddenly, having been ruminating on the 'thirty per cent rule' revealed to him by M. de Charlus, Brichot, determined to pursue the subject, broke in with what seemed like the brusque manner of an examining magistrate trying to make a prisoner confess, but was in fact the result of the professor's desire to seem perspicacious and his uneasiness at uttering such a grave accusation. 'Isn't Ski one of them?' he asked M. de Charlus with a sombre look. To show off his imagined powers of intuition he had chosen Ski, saying to himself that since only three men out of ten were innocent, he would not run much risk by choosing someone who appeared to him somewhat bizarre, who slept badly, wore scent, and in a word was out of the ordinary. 'No, *not at all*, cried the Baron, giving his expert decision in a sarcastic, exasperated tone. You're absolutely wrong, quite on the wrong track, it's absurd! Ski is just people's idea of that sort of man, people who don't know anything about it. If he were, he wouldn't look it so much; I don't say that to criticize him, for he is an attractive man, there's something really likeable about him. – Tell us some of their names, then,' Brichot persisted. M. de Charlus drew himself up haughtily: 'My dear man, you know I live in a world of abstraction, these things only interest me from a transcendental point of view,' he replied with the touchiness of his kind and the assumed grandiloquence which marked his conversation. 'I am only interested in general principles, I'm talking to you of these things as I might discuss the law of gravity.' But these moments

of annoyed reaction in which the Baron tried to hide his real life were
few and fleeting as compared with the hours during which he constantly
let it show through, or displayed it with an irritating self-satisfaction,
the need to confide being much stronger in him than the fear of
self-revelation. 'What I meant to say, he went on, is that for every bad
reputation that is undeserved, there are hundreds of good ones that
are equally groundless. Obviously the number of those who do not
deserve their reputation for virtue varies according to whether you
listen to people like them or to the others. And while it is true that the
readiness of the latter to believe ill of the virtuous is limited by the
excessive difficulty they would have in ascribing a vice as horrible in
their eyes as theft or murder to people they know to be sensitive and
scrupulous, the first group is over-excited by the wish to believe that
people they find attractive are, how shall I put it, attainable, and by
information derived from others led astray by a similar desire, and
finally by the very distance at which they are generally held by the
rest of society. I have heard a man, generally avoided for this reason,
say that he thought a certain gentleman had the same tastes. And his
only reason for thinking so was that the man had spoken pleasantly to
him! These are some of the reasons for *optimism*, said the Baron
naïvely, in guessing the number. But the real reason for the enormous
gap between the number as calculated by outsiders and by the initiates,
is the mystery with which the insiders surround their doings in order
to hide them from the others, who, cut off from any source of
information, would be literally astounded if they learned even a quarter
of the truth. – So our times are just like those of the Greeks, said
Brichot. – What do you mean, like the Greeks? Do you think nothing
went on between the Greeks and us? Look at Louis XIV's time,
with Monsieur,[73] little Vermandois, Molière, Prince Louis of Baden,
Brunswick, Charolais, Boufflers, the great Condé, the Duc de Brissac.
– Stop there, I knew about Monsieur, Brissac is in Saint-Simon,
Vendôme naturally and lots of others too, but Saint-Simon, that old
slanderer, often talks about the great Condé and Prince Louis of Baden
and he never says anything about that. – Dear me, to think I have to
give history lessons to a teacher at the Sorbonne. But professor, you
don't know the first thing. – True, Baron, cruel but true. But wait a

moment, I have a story you will like. I've just remembered a song from the period, in macaronic Latin, about the great Condé being caught in a storm as he sailed down the Rhine with his friend the Marquis de la Moussaye. Condé says:

> Carus Amicus Mussaeus,
> Ah! Deus bonus! Quod tempus!
>   Landerirette,
>   Imbre sumus perituri.

And La Moussaye comforts him by saying:

> Securae sunt nostrae vitae
> Sumus enim Sodomitae
> Igne tantum perituri
>   Landeriri.

— I take it all back, said Charlus in a high, affected voice, you're a mine of information, you'll write that out for me, won't you, I must have it for my family archives, since my great-great-grandmother was the sister of M. le Prince. — Yes, Baron, but I've never read anything about Prince Louis of Baden. Besides, I think that in general the military vocation . . . — What nonsense! In those days, Vendôme, Villars, Prince Eugène, the Prince de Conti, and if I were to mention all our heroes in Indo-China, in Morocco, and I mean the very noblest ones, pious too, and "modern-minded", you would be astonished. Ah, I could tell some tales to those people who are examining how the new generation has rejected the needless complications of its elders, as M. Bourget says.[74] I have a young friend in the army who is making quite a name for himself, who has done great things; but let me not gossip, let's go back to the seventeenth century, you know what Saint-Simon says about the Maréchal d'Huxelles — among so many others: "pleasure-loving, given to Greek debauchery which he did not trouble to conceal, he drew in young officers and made them his companions, along with handsome young serving-men, all quite openly, when on service and at Strasbourg." You have probably read Madame's letters, the men never called him anything but "Putana." She speaks of it quite openly. – And she knew whereof she spoke, with that husband. – Such an interesting character, Madame, said M. de Charlus. She could serve as the complete model of the "Queen's Woman". Mannish, for a start; the Queen's wife is usually a man, that's why it's so easy for him to get children on her. Then Madame never speaks of her husband's vices, but talks endlessly of the same vice in other people, and obviously knew what she was talking about; it's the same quirk that makes us love to find in other people's families the same weaknesses that we suffer from in our own, so as to prove to ourselves that there is nothing exceptional or shameful about them. As I was saying, it's always been like that. However, our own age stands out particularly from this point of view. And in spite of the examples I took from the seventeenth century, if my great ancestor François de la Rochefoucauld were alive today, he could say with even more truth than when speaking of his own time, come along, Brichot, help me out: "Vices belong to every age; but if certain people whom everyone knows had appeared in the first centuries, should we still speak today of the excesses of Heliogabalus?"[75] *Whom everyone knows*, I like that. I can see that my wise relative could tell when his most famous contemporaries were "spinning a line", just as I can with mine. But it's not just that there are even more people like that today. There's also something particular about them.' I saw that M. de Charlus was going to tell us in what way that mode of life had changed. But not for a moment as he talked, as Brichot talked, was the more or less conscious image of my flat where Albertine was waiting for me, an image associated with the homely, caressing motif of Vinteuil's music, dispelled from my mind. I kept coming back to Albertine, just as I would soon have in reality to go back to her, as if to a kind of ball and chain which prevented me from leaving Paris and which at this moment, as from the Verdurin salon I thought of my own home, made me see it, not as an empty space, exciting to the personality and rather sad, but as filled – just as the hotel at Balbec had been filled on a certain evening – by that unmoving presence, which continued to inhabit it for my sake, and which I could be sure of finding there again whenever I wanted to. The insistence with which M. de Charlus kept returning to his theme – in relation to which his intelligence, always exercised in the same direction, did possess a certain penetration – was distressing in quite a complex way. He was as boring as a scholar who can see nothing beyond his own subject, irritating as an insider who prides himself on the secrets he knows and cannot wait to give away, disagreeable as those who, in the matter of their own faults, let themselves go without realizing what offence they are giving, obsessive as a maniac and fatally rash as one who knows himself guilty. These characteristics, which at some moments became as striking as those which distinguish a madman or a criminal, did however offer me some comfort. For, transposing them into a form which allowed me to draw conclusions from them about Albertine, and remembering her attitude to Saint-Loup and to me, I said to myself that, however painful one of those memories was for me, and however melancholy the other, they seemed to rule out the kind of severe mental warping, the intensely one-sided specialization, which was so strongly evident in the conversation and in the person of M. de Charlus. But the man himself, sadly, now began to destroy these reasons for hope in the same way in which he had provided me with them, that is, unintentionally. 'Yes, he said, I'm not a boy any more and I have already seen many things changing around me, I can no longer understand a society where all barriers are broken down, where a noisy crowd with no elegance or even decency dances the tango even in the houses of my family, nor fashion, nor politics, nor the arts, nor religion, nothing. But I will admit that the thing that has changed most of all is what the Germans call homosexuality. Good heavens, in my day, if one set aside the men who simply hated women, and those who, while actually preferring them, did other things for money or their careers, homosexuals were good family men and really only kept mistresses as a blind. If I had had a daughter to settle I should have gone to them to find her a husband, if I had wished to make sure she would not be unhappy. But now everything is changed, alas. Now they recruit even among men who are the maddest about women. I used to be able to spot them, and when I said to myself "no, not that one" I would never be wrong. But now I give up. One of my friends who is famous for it had a coachman that my sister-in-law Oriane had found for him, a boy from

Combray who had been a bit of a jack-of-all-trades but was chiefly known as a ladies' man: I would have sworn no one could have been more averse to that kind of thing. He had a regular girl-friend but tormented her by seeing two other women he was mad about, not to mention all the others – an actress and a barmaid. My cousin the Prince de Guermantes, who is intelligent in the irritating way of people who are too ready to believe everything, said to me one day, "Why doesn't X sleep with his coachman, do you suppose? Théodore (that's the coachman's name) might like it, you never know; perhaps he's even offended that his master hasn't made any advances to him." I couldn't stop myself telling Gilbert to be quiet; I was annoyed by two things: his pretence at understanding, which when it is too general shows a lack of understanding, and the transparent scheming of my cousin, who wanted to see our friend X test the water and then, if he was successful, follow in his footsteps. – Is the Prince de Guermantes that way inclined as well, then? Brichot asked with a mixture of astonishment and unease. – Goodness, replied M. de Charlus delightedly, it's so well known that I don't think I'm being indiscreet in saying yes. Anyway, the next year I went to Balbec and there I learned from a sailor who sometimes took me fishing that the same Théodore, whose sister, by the way, is maid to one of Mme Verdurin's friends, the Baronne Putbus, was now in the habit of coming down to the harbour as bold as brass to pick up one sailor or another and go out with them for a sail "and that's not all, and that's not all". It was now my turn to ask whether the proprietor, in whom I had recognized the gentleman who played cards all day with his mistress, was like the Prince de Guermantes. 'Of course he is, everyone knows that, he doesn't even trouble to hide it. – But his mistress was with him. – And so? How naïve these children are,' he said in a paternal tone, not guessing the suffering I extracted from his words when I applied them to Albertine. 'His mistress is delightful. – So his three friends are like him? – No, no, no, he cried, stopping his ears as if I had just played a wrong note on a musical instrument. Now he's gone off to the other extreme. Can't a man have friends any more? Youth, youth, they get everything wrong. We shall have to take your education in hand, young man. Now I admit, he continued, that this case, and I know of many others of the same kind, puts me in difficulty, however hard I try to keep an open mind. I may be old-fashioned, but I can't understand, he said, like an old Gallican speaking of certain forms of Ultramontane religion, a liberal Royalist of Action française or a disciple of Claude Monet of the cubists. If they like women so much, why, especially in the working-class world where it's so disapproved of, do they feel they must have what they call a gay boy as well? It must represent something different for them. But what?' 'What is the "something different" that a woman represents for Albertine?' I wondered, and that, indeed, was the painful question for me. 'Really, Baron, said Brichot, if the General Board of the University ever decides to set up a chair in homosexuality, I shall put your name forward at once. No, perhaps a special Institute of Psychopathology would suit you better. Best of all, I could see you with a chair at the Collège de France, able to pursue your own researches and report on them, as the professors of Tamil or Sanskrit do, to the very small number of people who take an interest. You would have an audience of two and the porter, if I may say so without casting aspersions on our caretaking staff, a splendid body of men. – You don't know what you're talking about, said the Baron harshly. Anyway, you are mistaken if you think the subject interests only so very few people. Quite the opposite, in fact,' and, seemingly unaware of the contradiction between the unfailing tendency of his own conversation and the reproaches he was about to address to other people: 'It's dreadful, he said to Brichot with a scandalized, shamefaced look, no one talks of anything else. Shameful, I know, but that's the way it is, my dear fellow. Imagine, if women start talking about it now, what a scandal! The worst of it is, he added with extraordinary force, they get their information from real horrors, shockers like little Châtellerault, against whom there'd be more to say than anyone else, and who tell them stories about other people. I hear he says the most dreadful things about me, but I don't care, I think that any mud thrown by someone who was nearly thrown out of the Jockey Club for cheating at cards can only fall back on himself. But I do know that if I were Jane d'Ayen I should have enough respect for my guests not to allow these subjects to be discussed in their hearing, nor to let my family be dragged through the mud in my own house. But there is no society any more, no rules, no propriety, whether in conversation or dress. Ah, my dear friend, it's the end of the world. Everyone has become so wicked. They compete to see who can say the worst things about each other. Horrible!'

Still cowardly as I had been as a child at Combray, when I fled so as not to see them offering my grandfather brandy and my grandmother vainly trying to persuade him not to drink it, I now had only one wish, to escape from the Verdurins' before the execution of Charlus was carried out. 'I really must go, I said to Brichot. – I'll come with you, he replied, but we can't just walk out like that. Let's go and say good-bye to Mme Verdurin, the professor concluded, walking towards the drawing-room with the look of someone playing a parlour game, going into the room to ask 'May we come in?'

While we were talking, M. Verdurin, at a signal from his wife, had taken Morel off to another room. Even if Mme Verdurin had decided, after reflection, that it would be wiser to postpone the revelations to be made to Morel, it was now too late to turn back. We can allow certain desires, sometimes purely oral in nature, to become so strong that they must be satisfied, whatever the consequences: we simply must plant a kiss on a bare shoulder that we have been looking at for too long, and our lips fall on it like a bird of prey on a snake; we cannot resist the impulse, stronger than hunger, to sink our teeth in a cake, or forgo the astonishment, the alarm, the sorrow or the gaiety which we can unleash in a human soul by saying something unexpected. In this frame of mind, drunk on melodrama, Mme Verdurin had impressed on her husband that he must take the violinist on one side and, at all costs, speak to him. The young man had begun by complaining that the Queen of Naples had left before he could be introduced to her. M. de Charlus had repeated to him so often that she was the sister of the Empress Elizabeth and the Duchesse d'Alençon that the royal lady had taken on extraordinary importance in Morel's eyes. But the Patron had explained to him that they were not there to discuss the Queen of Naples, and had gone straight to the heart of the matter. 'That's how it is, he had said after some time had passed, but look, if you like, we'll ask my wife's advice. I haven't said anything to her about this, I swear. Let's see what she thinks about it. Maybe my idea isn't the right one, but you know how clever she is, and then she's immensely fond of you: let's consult her.' And while Mme Verdurin waited impatiently for the delicious excitement she would feel in talking to the virtuoso, and then, after he was gone, in making her husband go over every word of the scene that had passed between them, and as she waited kept repeating, 'What on earth can they be doing? Auguste is taking so long, I hope at least he'll have got him properly sorted out,' M. Verdurin had come downstairs again with Morel, who seemed to be experiencing strong emotion. 'He would like to ask your advice,' said M. Verdurin to his wife, with the air of someone who does not know if his request will be granted. In the grip of passion, Mme Verdurin spoke not to her husband but directly to Morel: 'I think my husband's absolutely right, you can't put up with this any longer!' she cried violently, forgetting the futile fiction agreed with her husband beforehand, that she was not supposed to know anything of what he had said to the violinist. 'What? Put up with what?' M. Verdurin stammered, trying to feign astonishment and, with understandable clumsiness, to cover up his lie. 'I guessed it, I guessed what you told him,' Mme Verdurin replied, without the least concern for the probability or otherwise of the explanation, and regardless of what, when he thought over this scene again, the violinist might think of the veracity of his Patronne. 'No, Mme Verdurin repeated, I believe that you should no longer accept this shameful familiarity with a disgraced character who is not received anywhere, she added, quite unconcerned that this was a lie and forgetting that she herself received him in her house almost daily. Everyone at the Conservatoire is talking about you, she added, feeling that this would be the most telling argument; one more month of this life and your musical career is finished, whereas without Charlus you should be earning a hundred thousand a year. – But I've never heard a word of this, I'm dumbstruck, I can't thank you enough,' murmured Morel with tears in his eyes. But, obliged to feign astonishment and hide his shame at the same time, he was redder in the face and sweating more freely than if he had played all Beethoven's sonatas in quick succession, and his eyes were filling with tears that the master of Bonn could never have drawn from them. The sculptor, interested by the tears, smiled and pointed out Charlie to me with a sidelong glance. 'If you haven't heard about him you're the only one who hasn't. He's a gentleman with a very nasty reputation who's been mixed up in all sorts of scandals. I know the police are watching him and it's a good thing for him that they are, otherwise he would end up like all the rest of them, murdered by street riff-raff,' she added, for the thought of Charlus had brought back the memory of Mme de Duras and, intoxicated with rage, she was trying to wound the wretched Charlie ever more deeply, in revenge for the insults she had suffered in the course of the evening. 'Anyway, even in practical terms he can't be of any use to you, he is completely ruined since he fell into the clutches of blackmailers; he can't even pay them, so how could he help you, everything is mortgaged to the hilt, his town house, his country estate, etc.' Morel was all the more convinced by this lie as M. de Charlus liked to confide in him about his dealings with apaches, a race which a manservant's son, however squalid his own life, must regard with a horror equal to his attachment to Bonapartist ideas.

Already his crafty mind had formed the idea of a reversal analogous to what was called in the eighteenth century the Diplomatic Revolution. Determined never to speak to M. de Charlus again, he had decided to go back the next evening to see Jupien's niece and patch everything up again. Unfortunately for him, this plan was a failure, M. de Charlus having already made an appointment for the evening of the party with Jupien, an appointment which the former waistcoat-maker, despite the day's events, did not dare break. Other people, as we shall see, having made rash decisions in relation to Morel, when a tearful Jupien recounted his misfortunes to the Baron, that nobleman, no less unhappy, announced that he would adopt the unfortunate girl, that she could take one of the titles in his gift, probably that of Mlle d'Oloron; he would give her an appropriate education and find her a rich husband. These promises caused deep joy to Jupien and did not impress his niece at all, for she still loved Morel, who was foolish or shameless enough to come into the shop when Jupien was out. 'What's the matter, he asked, laughing, you've got rings under your eyes. Unhappy in love? Come along, tomorrow is another day. After all, surely a man has the right to try on a pair of shoes, or a woman, and if they don't fit . . .' He got angry only once, when she cried; he thought that cowardly, an unworthy manœuvre. It is not always easy to bear the tears that are shed for us.

But we are running on too fast, for all these things happened after the Verdurin soirée; we must pick up our account of it where we left off. 'I'd never have dreamed . . . , Morel sighed in response to Mme Verdurin. – Of course no one says it to your face, but still everyone in the Conservatoire is talking about you, she repeated spitefully, wishing to show Morel that not only the Baron but he himself was the subject of gossip. I believe you when you say you weren't aware of it, but people do say the most dreadful things. Ask Ski what they were saying the other day at Chevillard's just a few yards away from us, when you came into my box. Everyone's eyes were on you. I must say that for myself I don't care in the least, but I do think it makes a man a complete laughing-stock, and that's something that can last a lifetime. – I don't know how to thank you,' said Charlie in the tone one uses to a dentist who has just been causing one excruciating pain to which one does not want to admit, or to an over-bloodthirsty second who is dragging one into a duel over some harmless remark of which he says, 'You can't swallow that.' 'I think you've got backbone, that you're a man, Mme Verdurin replied, and you'll speak up for yourself even though he tells everyone that you daren't, that he has a hold on you.' Charlie, trying to find a borrowed dignity to cover the tatters of his own, found in his memory a phrase which he had read somewhere or heard someone say, and promptly proclaimed, 'I wasn't brought up to take that sort of thing. I'll break with M. de Charlus this very evening. The Queen of Naples has left, hasn't she? Otherwise, before breaking with him, I'd have asked him . . . – You don't have to break off with him completely, said Mme Verdurin, not wishing to disrupt the inner circle. You can safely meet him here, in our little group, where people appreciate you, where no one will say anything unkind. But insist on your independence, and don't let him drag you to all those two-faced old trouts' houses; I wish you could have heard what they said behind your back. Don't feel any regret about it, not only will you be getting rid of a cloud that would have hung over you all your life, but from the professional point of view, it's not just the shame of being introduced by Charlus, I should tell you that getting mixed up in that phoney society would make you look completely unserious, like an amateur, a little drawing-room musician, and that's terrible at your age. I can see that it's a great idea for all those fine ladies to return favours to their friends by getting you to play for them for nothing, but it's your future as a musician you should be thinking of. I don't say you can't go to one or two houses. I think I heard you mention the Queen of Naples, she *has* left by the way, now she was planning a party and she's a good sort, who doesn't think much of Charlus or so I hear. I really do think she came chiefly to see me. In fact I know it's true, she wanted to meet M. Verdurin and myself. Now there is somewhere you could play. And then let me say that if you were introduced by me, someone all the musicians know, you know, someone they're always really decent with, for they see me as one of themselves, their own Patronne, that would be quite different. But don't even think of going to Mme de Duras's. Don't make a blunder like that! Artistes I know have come to tell me about the problems they have had with her. You know, they know they can trust me, she said in the sweet, simple tone she knew how to assume at a moment's notice, giving her features an air of modesty and her eyes the appropriate charm. They come and tell me their little troubles; the ones who are supposed to have the least to say sometimes talk to me for hours, and I can't tell you how interesting they are. Poor Chabrier always said, "Mme Verdurin's the only one who can get them talking." Well, you know, I've seen all of them, every last one, in tears after they had been to play at Mme de Duras's. It's not just the way she encourages her servants to humiliate them, but they found no one else would hire them afterwards. The concert bookers said, "Oh yes, he's the one who plays at Mme de Duras's." And that was that. It's the kind of thing that will really cut short a career. You know, working for society people just doesn't look serious, you can have all the talent in the world, but sadly one Mme de Duras is enough to make you look like an amateur. And the artistes themselves, well, you know I've known them for forty years, taking an interest in them, getting them started, well, you know how it is, once they call somebody an amateur that's that. And they were just starting to say it about you. How many times I've had to stand up for you, to swear that you wouldn't play in this or that ridiculous salon! Do you know what they answered? "But he'll have to, Charlus will fix it without consulting him, he never asks him what he wants to do." Someone tried to please him by saying "We all so admire your friend Morel." Do you know what he answered, with that insolent look of his? "What do you mean, my friend? We come from different classes: he is my protégé, my creature if you will."' At this moment something was fermenting behind the domed forehead of the music-lover, the only thing that certain persons cannot keep to themselves, a remark to repeat which would be not only contemptible but dangerous. But the need to repeat it is stronger than honour or prudence. It was to this need that, after a few convulsive movements of the spherical, angry forehead, the Patronne gave way. 'Someone even told my husband that he said "my servant", but I can't be sure of that,' she added. It was a similar need that had driven M. de Charlus, shortly after swearing to Morel that he would never reveal his background to anyone, to tell Mme Verdurin, 'His father was a manservant.' It would again be this kind of need that, once the word was out, would make it pass from one person to another, each revealing it under the promise of a strict secrecy which would not be kept, any more than the first person had kept it. As in the ring game, these remarks eventually found their way back to Mme Verdurin, losing her the friendship of the subject, who had finally become aware of them. She knew this, but could not hold on to the word which was burning her tongue. 'Servant' was bound to hurt Morel. However she said it: 'servant', and if she added that she could not be sure of it, it was both in order to suggest that she *was* sure about the other insults, and to show her own impartiality. The thought of this impartiality gave her such a warm feeling that she began to speak to Charlie in tender tones: 'Of course I don't hold it against him that he tried to pull you into the mud beside him, since he is wallowing in it himself, wallowing in it, she repeated a little louder, pleased by the vividness of the image which had escaped her faster than her attention could follow it, and now struck her as deserving more prominence. 'No, what I blame him for, she continued tenderly, with a note of feminine triumph in her voice, is his lack of consideration for you. There are some things we don't repeat to everyone. Just a moment ago he was betting people that he would make you blush with pleasure by getting you (he must have been joking, for his recommendation would be enough to make sure you didn't get it) the cross of the Légion d'honneur. There was no harm in that, though I've never thought it was very nice, she added primly, to make a fool of one's friends, but you know, there are some things he says that do hurt. Like the way he laughed aloud when he said that you really wanted the decoration to please your uncle, and your uncle was a flunkey. – He said that!' cried Charlie, convinced by these carefully remembered last words that everything Mme Verdurin had said was true. Mme Verdurin felt flooding over her the joy of an old mistress who, about to be dropped by her young lover, has found a way to stop his marriage. And perhaps her lies were not deliberately planned, nor even conscious. It was perhaps a logic of feeling, or even something more elementary, a kind of nervous reflex that moved her, when it was a question of enlivening her existence or preserving her happiness, to 'make mischief' inside the little set, that brought to her lips these assertions, devilishly useful if not entirely exact. 'It wouldn't matter if he'd only said it to us, the Patronne continued, we know we have to take what he says with a pinch of salt, and then there is no shame in honest work, each man has his own worth; but to go and make Mme de Portefin giggle over it (Mme Verdurin mentioned Mme de Portefin on purpose, knowing that Charlie liked her), that's the kind of thing we hate. My husband said, when he heard him say it, "I'd rather have had a slap in the face."' For Gustave likes you just as much as I do (it was thus that we learned M. Verdurin's name was Gustave). He's quite tender-hearted really. – I never told you I liked him, muttered M. Verdurin in the role of kindly curmudgeon. It's Charlus who likes him. – Oh, no, now I can tell the difference; I was being used by someone despicable, but you are kind, Charlie cried with sincere feeling. – No, no, said Mme Verdurin, magnanimous in victory (for she now felt her Wednesdays safe), despicable is too strong: he does damage, lots of damage, without meaning to; you know, that Légion d'honneur business didn't go on for very long. And I'd rather not tell you all the other things he said about your family (she would have been hard put to it to think of any). – I don't care if it only lasted a second, that's enough to show he's a wretch,' cried Morel.

It was at this moment that we came back into the drawing-room. 'Ah!' M. de Charlus cried, seeing Morel there, and, walking towards the musician with the spring in his step of a man who has organized his whole evening perfectly to lead up to a rendezvous with a woman and who, intoxicated with his cleverness, does not realize that he has himself set the trap in which he will be caught and soundly thrashed in front of everyone by the husband's spies. 'Well, there you are at last. Are you happy, young maestro and soon to be young Chevalier de la Légion d'honneur? For soon you'll be able to show off your cross,' said M. de Charlus to Morel with a look of tender triumph, but this very mention of the decoration seemed to confirm Mme Verdurin's lies, which now seemed indisputably true to Morel. 'Leave me alone, don't you dare come near me, cried Morel to the Baron. I bet this isn't your first time, you must have tried to corrupt other people before me.' My only comfort was the belief that I would soon see Morel and the Verdurins pulverized by M. de Charlus. I had had to face his insane rages for a thousand times less than this, no one was safe from them, a king would not have intimidated him. Now the most extraordinary thing happened. We saw M. de Charlus dumbstruck, aghast, realizing the scale of his misfortune but not its cause, not finding a word to say, turning his eyes upon everyone present, one by one, puzzled, indignant, helpless, as if to ask them not so much what had happened as what he should now do. Perhaps what had struck him dumb was (seeing M. and Mme Verdurin turning away from him and no one else coming to his aid) his present suffering and above all the fear of further sufferings to come; or perhaps it was that, not having used the power of his imagination to work himself up and develop a rage in advance, and having no ready-made fury to draw on (for with his sensitive, nervous, hysterical temperament he was genuinely impulsive but not a natural fighter, nor for that matter, and this made me like him better, truly aggressive, and he lacked the normal reactions of the man wounded in his honour), he had been taken by surprise, attacked when he was unarmed; or perhaps it was that in a milieu not his own he felt less confident and consequently less brave than he would have been if at home in the Faubourg. For whatever reason, in this salon that he despised, this great noble (whose superiority over commoners was no more self-evident than had been that of certain of his tormented ancestors appearing before the Revolutionary courts) found his whole body and tongue seemingly paralysed, and could do nothing but cast frightened glances in all directions, expressing incomprehension, indignation at the attack on him and mute calls for help. And yet M. de Charlus could call on all the resources not only of eloquence but of boldness when, possessed by a rage which had been bubbling up inside him against someone, he would transfix him, reduce him to utter despair by the cruellest words in the hearing of polite people who stood aghast, never having imagined that anyone could go so far. In those situations M. de Charlus was on fire, in the grip of genuine nervous attacks which left everyone trembling. But in those cases he had the initiative, he could go on the attack, say whatever he pleased (just as Bloch could make jokes against Jews, but blushed if anyone mentioned their name to him). When he hated people, it was because he thought those people despised him. If they had been pleasant to him, then instead of becoming intoxicated with rage against them, he would have put his arms round them. In a situation so cruelly unforeseen as this one, the great talker could only stammer, 'What's the meaning of this? What's going on?' He could hardly even be heard. And the gestures expressive of panic terror have changed so little, that the old gentleman to whom something unpleasant was happening in a Paris drawing-room struck again, without knowing it, the small number of stylized attitudes which in archaic Greek sculpture indicated the alarm of nymphs being pursued by the god Pan.

The disgraced ambassador, the civil service chief forced into retirement, the man about town given a chilly reception, the lover shown the door sometimes spend months examining the event which destroyed their hopes; they turn it over and over like a bullet fired they do not know from where nor by whom, almost like a meteorite. They want to know what the strange device is made of that struck them down so suddenly, whose ill-will it embodies. At least chemists can turn to analysis; sufferers from an unknown disease can call in a doctor. And criminal cases are more or less clarified by the examining magistrate. But the disconcerting actions of our fellow-men rarely reveal their motives. Thus M. de Charlus, to move forward for a moment to the days which followed Mme Verdurin's party, to which we shall return, could see only one clear reason for Charlie's attitude. Charlie, who had often threatened to reveal the nature of the Baron's passion for him, must have decided to do it now that he felt 'established' enough to stand on his own feet. And out of sheer ingratitude he must have told Mme Verdurin everything. But how could she have allowed herself to be so deceived (for the Baron, having made up his mind to deny the charge, had already persuaded himself that the feelings he would be accused of were imaginary)? Friends of Mme Verdurin's, perhaps attracted to Charlie themselves, must have prepared the ground. So over the next few days M. de Charlus wrote dreadful letters to several entirely innocent members of the 'faithful', who simply thought he had gone mad; then he went to pour out to Mme Verdurin a long, pitiful tale which did not have at all the effect he intended. For on the one hand Mme Verdurin kept repeating to the Baron: 'Just ignore him, don't have anything more to do with him, he's a baby,' when the Baron desired nothing more than a reconciliation. On the other hand, trying to bring one about by denying Charlie everything he had thought he could rely on, he asked Mme Verdurin to stop inviting him to her house: her refusal earned her some furiously sarcastic letters from M. de Charlus. Alternating between one theory and another, M. de Charlus never hit on the right one, namely that the coup had not originated with Morel at all. It is true that he could have found that out by asking Morel to talk to him for a few minutes. But he thought that would be beneath his dignity and damaging to the interests of his love. He was the offended party, he was owed an explanation. In fact there is almost always, attached to the idea of a conversation which might clear up a misunderstanding, some other idea which for one reason or another makes us reluctant to have that conversation. The man who has backed down and shown weakness in twenty different circumstances, will stand on his pride the twenty-first time, the only time when it would have been useful not to dig his heels in and to dispel a misapprehension that can only grow stronger in his adversary for want of an explanation. As for the 'society' side of the incident, the word went around that M. de Charlus had been thrown out of the Verdurins' when he was discovered trying to rape a young musician. So no one was surprised when he did not reappear at the Verdurins', and when he bumped into one of the 'faithful' whom he had suspected and insulted, as the other man still felt resentment towards the Baron, who himself did not greet him, it was easy for others to assume that no one in the little set was now willing to speak to the Baron.

While M. de Charlus, felled on the spot by Morel's words and the Patronne's attitude, was adopting the pose of the nymph seized by panic terror, M. and Mme Verdurin had retired into the first drawing-room, as if to signal a break in diplomatic relations, leaving M. de Charlus alone, while Morel stood on the dais putting his violin back in its case. 'Tell us how it went, said Mme Verdurin greedily to her husband. – I don't know what you said to him, but he really looked upset, said Ski, he was crying.' Pretending not to understand, 'I don't think what I said made any impression on him,' said Mme Verdurin, making one of those feints which do not, in fact, deceive everyone, in order to make the sculptor repeat that Charlie had been in tears: tears which filled the Patronne with such swelling pride that she wanted to be sure no member of the faithful could possibly have failed to hear about them. 'No, it must have, I saw big tears glistening in his eyes,' said the sculptor in a low voice, smiling conspiratorially and looking out of the corner of his eye to make sure that Morel was still on the dais and could not hear what he was saying. But there was one person who did hear it and whose presence, as soon as it was noticed, restored to Morel one of his lost hopes. It was the Queen of Naples who, having left her fan behind, had thought it would be kinder, on her way back from another party, to call for it herself. She had slipped in as quietly as possible, as if coming to apologize and to make a short visit now that everyone had gone home. But her entrance had passed unnoticed in the excitement of the incident, which she had instantly understood and which filled her with burning indignation. 'Ski says that he was crying, did you see that? I didn't see any tears. Oh yes, I did, now I remember, she added for fear that her denial might be believed. As for old Charlus, he doesn't look so good, he ought to sit down, he's tottering on his feet, he'll fall over if he's not careful,' she said with a pitiless snigger. At that moment Morel ran towards her: 'Isn't that the Queen of Naples, he asked (though he knew it was she), pointing to the royal lady, who was now walking towards Charlus. After what's happened I can't very well ask the Baron to introduce me. – Wait a minute, I'll do it,' said Mme Verdurin, and followed by several faithful, but not by Brichot or myself, for we were hurrying to collect our coats and leave, she advanced towards the Queen, who was talking to M. de Charlus. He had thought that his great wish to see Morel presented to the Queen of Naples could be denied only by the improbable death of the sovereign. But we think of the future as a reflection of the present projected into an empty space, while it is often the immediate result of causes which for the most part escape us. Less than an hour had passed, and M. de Charlus would now have given anything to ensure that Morel was not presented to the Queen. Mme Verdurin curtsied to the Queen. Seeing that she did not seem to recognize her: 'I am Mme Verdurin, she said. Your Majesty does not recognize me. – Quite so,' said the Queen, continuing her conversation with M. de Charlus so naturally and with such an absent-minded manner that Mme Verdurin could not be sure whether the 'quite so', pronounced so distantly, and which drew from M. de Charlus, in the midst of his sufferings as a lover, the grateful, appreciative smile of a connoisseur of insolence, was really meant for her. Morel, seeing from a distance that the preliminaries to his presentation were under way, had come nearer. The Queen held out her arm to M. de Charlus. She was angry with him too, but only because he was not standing up more energetically to those who had dared to insult him. She blushed with shame on his behalf that the Verdurins should feel able to treat him in such a way. The unaffected friendliness she had shown them a few hours before and the insolent pride with which she now held herself erect before them had their source in the same place in her heart. The Queen was a woman of great goodness, but her idea of goodness was, first of all, an unshakeable attachment to people whom she loved, to her relations, to all the princes of her family, one of whom was M. de Charlus, then to all the middle-class or humbler people who showed respect to those she loved, who had the proper feelings towards them. It was as a woman endowed with these good instincts that she had shown friendliness to Mme Verdurin. And no doubt hers was a narrow, rather reactionary and increasingly outdated conception of goodness. But that does not mean that her goodness was any less sincere or less ardent. In ancient times men did not love the human group to which they devoted themselves with any less fervour because it was restricted to the city, nor do the men of today love their country less than those who will one day love the United States of the Earth. I have an example closer at hand in my mother, whom Mme de Cambremer and Mme de Guermantes were never able to interest in any philanthropic 'good works', in any patriotic sewing-circle or charity bazaar. I do not say that she was right in acting only when her own heart moved her, and in reserving to her own family, her servants, any unfortunates that chance put in her way, the treasures of her love and generosity, but I do know that those treasures, like my grandmother's, were inexhaustible and left far behind anything that Mmes de Cambremer and de Guermantes were ever able to achieve. The case of the Queen of Naples was quite different, but we must admit that she did not choose the objects of her sympathy, as Dostoevsky did in the novels Albertine borrowed from my bookshelves and made her own, among flattering parasites, thieves, drunkards, some of them dull and others insolent, debauchees and even murderers. But the two extremes are closer than we think, since the nobleman, the close friend, the offended relative that the Queen wished to defend was M. de Charlus, that is to say, despite his birth and his various family ties to the Queen, someone whose virtue was set off by numerous vices. 'You don't look well, my dear cousin, she said to M. de Charlus. Lean on my arm. It will always be there to support you. It is strong enough for that. You know how once, at Gaeta, it held the mob at bay. It will be a rampart to you.' Such was the departure, lending her arm to the Baron and without having let Morel be presented to her, of the glorious sister of the Empress Elizabeth.

One might imagine, given the appalling character of M. de Charlus, the way in which he persecuted and terrified even members of his own family, that in the aftermath of this evening he would have unleashed his rage and carried out violent reprisals against the Verdurins. But nothing of the kind took place, and the main reason was certainly that the Baron, having caught a chill a few days later and contracted one of those infectious pneumonias that were so common at the time, was judged by his doctors and judged himself to be at death's door, and then spent several months suspended between death and life. Was there simply a physical metastasis, and did another illness replace the neurosis which up to that point had made him forget himself and give way to veritable orgies of anger? For it would be too simple to think that, never having taken the Verdurins seriously from the social point of view, he could not feel resentment towards them as he would towards his equals; too simple, also, to recall that the highly strung, forever stirred up against imaginary and harmless enemies, become harmless themselves when anyone stands up to them, and that one can calm them down better by throwing cold water over them than by trying to show them the emptiness of their grievances. But the explanation of the Baron's lack of resentment is probably not to be found in a metastasis, but in the malady itself. It exhausted the Baron so completely that it left him little chance to think about the Verdurins. He was half-dead. We were speaking of counter-attacks; even those which can have only posthumous effects require, in order to be 'set up' effectively, the sacrifice of some part of one's forces. M. de Charlus had too little strength left to embark on such a preparation. We often hear about mortal enemies who open their eyes only to see each other on the point of death and die happy. That must be a rare occurrence, except where death has caught us in the midst of life. On the contrary, it is when we have nothing more to lose that we lose the will to face risks which we should have taken quite happily when in health. The desire for revenge is part of life; more often than not – in spite of exceptions which, within a single character, are mere human contradictions – it fades at the approach of death. When he had thought about the Verdurins for a moment. M. de Charlus felt too tired, turned towards the wall and stopped thinking altogether. It was not that he had lost his eloquence, but it now cost him less effort. It still flowed from him spontaneously, but had lost its previous character. Freed from its subjection to the violent feelings it had so often dignified, it was now an almost mystical eloquence adorned with words of gentleness, Gospel parables, seeming resignation to death. He spoke chiefly on the days when he felt he would survive. A relapse reduced him to silence. This Christian sweetness, into which his splendid violence had been transformed (as *Esther* represents a transformation of the very different genius of *Andromaque*), caused wonderment in all who saw it. Even the Verdurins would have been equally admiring; they could not have forborne to adore a man whose faults had made them hate him. Certainly some thoughts floated to the surface that were Christian only in appearance. He begged the Archangel Gabriel to come down and tell him, as he had told the Prophet, when the Messiah would come. And then, with a sweet, sorrowful smile, he would add, 'But the archangel had better not tell me to wait for "seven weeks and yet six times seven", for I shall be dead before then.' The coming he was waiting for was that of Morel. Indeed, he asked the Archangel Raphael to bring him to him, as he had the young Tobias. And, employing more human means (as sick popes go on having Masses said for them but are careful also to call in their doctors) he would hint to his visitors that if Brichot brought his young Tobias to him, then perhaps the Archangel Raphael would restore his sight, as he had done for Tobias's father, or as had happened at the pool of Bethsaida.[76] But despite these recurrences of human weakness, the new-found moral purity of M. de Charlus's conversation was still delightful. Vanity, slander, mad spite and pride had all disappeared. M. de Charlus had risen far above the moral level on which he had formerly lived. But this moral improvement, the reality of which was, it must be said, somewhat exaggerated by his oratorical powers in the minds of his sympathetic hearers, this improvement lasted only as long as the illness which had fostered it. M. de Charlus soon began to slide down the slippery slope again, and with ever-increasing speed, as we shall see. But the Verdurins' attitude to him was to remain a distant memory, which later, more immediate resentments pushed into the background.

To return to the Verdurins' party, that evening when the couple were left alone, M. Verdurin said to his wife: 'Do you know why Cottard didn't come? He's with Saniette, whose stock market gamble didn't come off. When he heard he was down to his last franc and owed more than a million, Saniette had some kind of stroke. – But what was he doing playing the market? How absurd, that isn't his kind of thing at all. Much cleverer people than he is lose their shirts, and he was just cut out to be swindled by everybody. – Of course he's an idiot, we've known that for years, said M. Verdurin. But the damage is done now. Here we have a man whose landlord is going to throw him out tomorrow, who won't have a penny to his name, his family don't like him, you don't imagine Forcheville will do anything for him. So I thought, I don't want to do anything you don't agree with, but perhaps we could arrange a little income for him so that he doesn't realize he's ruined, so that he can be looked after at home. – I quite agree, and you're a dear to have thought of it. But you say "at home"; the idiot has kept on a flat that's much too expensive, he can't go on like this, we must find him a couple of rooms somewhere. I think he's still renting a flat for six or seven thousand francs. – Six and a half. But he's very attached to his home. Well, this is his first attack, he can't live more than another two or three years. Even if we spend ten thousand a year on him for three years, I think we could manage that. Let's say that this year, instead of renting La Raspelière again, we take something more modest. With our income, it shouldn't be impossible to find another ten thousand francs for three years. – All right, but the only problem is that it'll get out, and we'll end up having to do the same for other people. – I thought of that, of course. I'll do it, but only on the strict condition that no one must know. I don't want us having to become the benefactors of the whole human race. No thank you very much! No philanthropy for me. What we could do would be to tell him that Princess Sherbatoff left him the money. – Will he believe it? She consulted Cottard when she was making her will. – We *could* tell Cottard, I suppose, if we really had to. It's his job to keep secrets, he makes a fortune in fees, he'll never be in line for a hand-out. Perhaps he'll even be willing to say that Princess Sherbatoff used him to set up the legacy. Then we wouldn't have to come into it at all. No tiresome scenes of thanks, no fuss, no prepared speeches.' M. Verdurin added here a word which evidently stood for the kind of emotional scene and embarrassing phrase which he wanted to avoid.

But my informant could not repeat it to me exactly, for it was not a normal French word, but one of those terms that are used within families to designate certain things, in particular annoying things, no doubt because the family wishes to be able to point them out without the offenders understanding. Such expressions are usually a throwback to an earlier state of the family in question. In a Jewish family, for example, the word will be a ritual term displaced from its original meaning, perhaps the only word of Hebrew that the family, now wholly French in its manners, has retained. In a very strongly provincial family, it will be a term of their provincial dialect, even though the family no longer speaks dialect and can barely understand it any longer. In a South American family which now speaks only French, it will be a word of Spanish. And in the next generation, the word will survive only as a childhood memory. The children will remember that their parents could speak about the servants waiting at table without being understood by them, using a particular word, but they cannot tell exactly what the word meant, whether it was Spanish, Hebrew, German or dialect, or even whether it had ever belonged to any real language and was not a proper name or simply something invented. The mystery can be solved only if there is a great-uncle, an elderly cousin still living who must have once used the word himself. As I never knew any of the Verdurins' relatives, I was never able to supply the exact word. However, it clearly made Mme Verdurin smile, for the use of this private, personal, secret language instead of the language of every day gives the users of it a self-centred feeling which is always accompanied by a certain satisfaction. When the moment of gaiety had passed, Mme Verdurin objected, 'But what if Cottard talks? – He won't talk.' But he did talk, at least to me, for it was from him that I learnt about the whole thing some years later, at Saniette's funeral in fact. I was sorry not to have known of it sooner. First of all, it would have allowed me to arrive more quickly at the idea that one should never bear grudges against people, never judge them by the memory of one unkind act, for we can never know all the good resolves and effective actions of which their souls may have been capable at other times. And so, even from the simple point of view of foresight, we make mistakes. For no doubt the bad pattern that we observed on that one occasion will recur. But the soul is richer than that, has many other patterns which will also recur in the same man, yet we refuse to take pleasure in them because of one piece of bad behaviour in the past. But from a more personal point of view, such a revelation would not have been without effect on me. For by changing my opinion of M. Verdurin, whom I was coming to think the very worst of men, Cottard's revelation, if he had made it earlier, would have dispelled the suspicions I had about the role the Verdurins might play in my relationship with Albertine. Wrongly dispelled them, perhaps, for if M. Verdurin had some good qualities, he was nevertheless given to teasing to the point of savage persecution, and so jealous of his dominant position in the little set that he did not shrink from the most shocking lies, from stirring up the most unjustified hatreds, so as to break any bonds between the faithful that were not solely directed to the strengthening of the little group. He was a man capable of disinterested kindness, of discreet generosity, but that does not necessarily mean a sensitive man, nor one who was likeable, nor scrupulous, nor truthful, nor even always good. A partial goodness – in which there perhaps survived something of the family who had been my great-aunt's friends – no doubt existed in him long before I came to know of it through this action, just as America and the North Pole existed before Columbus or Peary. Still, at the moment of my discovery, M. Verdurin's nature presented a new, unsuspected face to me; and I concluded from it how difficult it is to present a stable image, whether of a character or of societies and passions. For character changes just as much as these, and if we wish to fix it in its more immutable aspects, we find that it presents a series of different faces (suggesting that it cannot keep still, but is ever-moving) to the baffled camera.

Seeing how late it was and fearing that Albertine would be becoming discontented, I asked Brichot, as we left the Verdurins', whether he would be kind enough to drop me off first. My carriage would take him home afterwards. He congratulated me on going home so directly, not knowing that a girl was waiting for me there, and on finishing the evening so early and so soberly when, in fact, I had merely been delaying its real beginning. Then he began to talk about M. de Charlus, who would doubt have been astonished to hear the professor who was so pleasant to him, the professor who always said 'I never repeat anything', speak of him and his way of life without the slightest restraint. And Brichot's surprised indignation would, I am sure, have been no less sincere if M. de Charlus had said to him, 'I hear you have been talking scandal about me.' Brichot did, in fact, like M. de Charlus, and if he had been obliged to recall a conversation of which he was the subject, he would have found it easier to remember the warm feelings he had had about the Baron, as he said the same things about him that everyone said, than those things themselves. He would not have felt he was lying if he said, 'I always say such nice things about you', since he had experienced a friendly feeling while talking about M. de Charlus. The Baron could offer Brichot above all the charm which the professor chiefly sought in life outside the classroom, namely that it should offer him living specimens of what he had long thought an invention of the poets. Brichot, who had often lectured on Virgil's second eclogue without really knowing whether its fiction was in any way based on reality, now, late in life, found some of the same pleasure in talking to M. de Charlus which he knew his masters M. Mérimée and M. Renan or his colleague M. Maspéro had experienced when travelling in Spain, Palestine or Egypt, as they recognized in the present-day landscapes of Spain, Palestine or Egypt the settings and the unchanging characters of the ancient scenes which they had studied in books. 'I have no wish to disparage that noble scion of a mighty race, Brichot declared as we rode in the carriage, but he is simply miraculous when he expounds his devil's catechism with ever so slightly bedlamite zeal and the stubbornness, I was about to say the candour, of a Spanish reactionary or an aristocrat fleeing the Revolution. I can assure you, if I may borrow a phrase from Mgr d'Hulst,[77] that I have the time of my life when I am visited by that feudal figure who, wishing to defend Adonis in this age of unbelief, has simply followed the instincts of his race and, in all sodomitical innocence, has embarked on a crusade.' I was listening to Brichot and yet I was not alone with him. As indeed had been the case since I left the house, I felt, however obscurely, in contact with the young girl who even now was waiting in her room. Even while I was chatting to one person or another at the Verdurins', I could feel her somehow near me, I had that vague sense of her that one has of one's own limbs, and if I chanced to think of her, it was in the way one thinks, irritated by the sense of being wholly tied, enslaved to it, of one's own body. 'And what a mine of gossip, enough to fill all the appendices to the *Monday Conversations*,[78] in that missionary's conversation! Imagine, I learned from him that the treatise on morals which I have always revered as the most elaborate ethical construction of our times, was inspired in our venerable colleague X by a young telegraph messenger. Let us note that my eminent friend neglected to mention the name of this fair youth in the course of his expositions, thereby showing less moral courage than Phidias, who carved the name of the athlete he loved on the ring of his Olympian Zeus. The Baron did not know that last story, which needless to say charmed his orthodoxy. You can imagine that now when I am arguing with my colleague over a doctoral thesis, I find in his ever-subtle dialectic the same extra piquancy that certain spicy revelations added for Sainte-Beuve to the work of Chateaubriand, which he found insufficiently personal. From our colleague, whose wisdom is beyond price but who is somewhat short of money, the young telegraphist passed into the hands of the Baron ("all quite above board" – you should have heard him say it). And as that Satan is the most obliging of men, he found his protégé an opening in the colonies, from where the grateful youth sometimes sends him excellent fruit. The Baron passes it on to his important friends; some of the young man's pineapples recently appeared on the table at the Quai Conti, which made Mme Verdurin say quite innocently, "You must have an uncle in America, or a nephew, M. de Charlus, to get pineapples like these!" I admit I smiled as I ate them, reciting *in petto* the beginning of an ode of Horace which Diderot liked to recall. In a word, like my colleague Boissier strolling from the Palatine to Tibur, I derive from the Baron's conversation a singularly more vivid and colourful idea of the writers of the Golden Age. Let us not mention the Decadence, nor go back as far as the Greeks, though I once said to the excellent M. de Charlus that when I was with him I felt like Plato in the house of Aspasia.[79] I must say that I had greatly exaggerated the scale of the two characters, and that I should have taken my example from "much smaller creatures", as La Fontaine says. In any case, you must not imagine that the Baron was offended. I never saw him so straightfor-wardly delighted. A childish pleasure made him forsake his aristocrat's impassivity. "You dons are such flatterers! he cried with delight. To think I should have had to wait until this age to be compared to Aspasia! An old fright like me! O youth, youth!" I wish you could have seen him saying that, covered in powder as usual and, at his age, scented like a fop. But in fact, despite his obsession with genealogy, he's the best fellow alive. For all these reasons I should be sorry if this evening's quarrel were final. What surprised me was the way the young man reacted so violently. Latterly he had been behaving towards the Baron as a kind of henchman, he had a vassal's manner that hardly foreshadowed such a revolt. I hope that in any case, even if (*Dii omen avertant*[80]) the Baron were not to return to the Quai Conti, this aversion would not extend to myself. Each of us would have too much to lose from an interruption to our exchanges, my poor knowledge against his experience. (We shall in fact see that, while M. de Charlus did not express any violent resentment against Brichot, at least his liking for the scholar was reduced to such an extent that he felt able to express very harsh judgments of him.) And I swear that the exchange is such an unequal one that when the Baron lets me share what he has learned from his existence, I cannot agree with Sylvestre Bonnard's saying[81] that a library is still the best place to pursue the dream of life.'

We had arrived at my door. I got out of the carriage to give the coachman Brichot's address. From the pavement I could see the window of Albertine's bedroom, that window which had always been dark in the evening when she did not yet live in the house, and which the electric light from the inside, sectioned by the slats of the shutters, now striped with parallel golden bars. This magic spell-book was as clear to me, presenting to my untroubled mind precise images, close at hand, of whose reality I was shortly to resume possession, as it was obscure to the half-blind Brichot, still seated in the carriage; it would, in any case, have been incomprehensible to him, since the professor was no more aware than were those friends who came to see me before dinner, when Albertine had just got home from her outing, that I had a young girl waiting just for me in a bedroom close to mine. The carriage moved off. I stood for a moment alone on the pavement.

Certainly, the luminous stripes I could see from below, which would have seemed insignificant to anyone else, had for me a consistency, a plenitude, an extreme solidity which came from the meaning with which I endowed them, from the treasure, if you like, a treasure unsuspected by others, which I had hidden there and from which these horizontal rays emanated: a treasure, however, for which I had given my freedom, my solitude, my thoughts. If Albertine had not been up there, or even if I had been concerned only for pleasure, I could have gone and found it with unknown women, in Venice perhaps, or at least in some unknown corner of night-time Paris. But now what I had to do when the time for caresses was at hand, was not to embark on a journey, nor even to leave the house, but to go back there. And not to go home at least to find solitude, not, after leaving the others who provided from outside the matter for one's thoughts, to be forced to find it in oneself, but on the contrary, to be less alone than I had been at the Verdurins', since I was returning to the person to whom I surrendered my personality, handing it over completely to her, without having a moment to think of myself, nor any need to think of her, since she would always be beside me. So that lifting my eyes for the last time to the window of the room where I should shortly be, I seemed to see the cage of light that would presently close upon me, and of which I myself, for my eternal enslavement, had forged the golden bars.

Albertine had never told me that she suspected me of being jealous of her, of spying on everything she did. The only words we had exchanged about jealousy, a long time before, seemed to suggest the opposite. I remembered that, one fine moonlit evening, at the beginning of our time together, one evening when I had seen her home and would have preferred not to do so, wishing instead to leave her and run to other women, I had said to her, 'You know, it's not because I'm jealous that I'm offering to see you home, if you've got other things to do I can take myself off,' and she had answered, 'Oh, I know you're not jealous, you don't care what I do, but I don't want to do anything but be with you.' Another time at La Raspelière, M. de Charlus, while casting sidelong glances at Morel, had been ostenta-tiously attentive to Albertine, and I had said, 'He certainly kept a close eye on you.' And when I added half ironically, 'I suffered all the pangs of jealousy,' Albertine, using the language of the vulgar background from which she had emerged, or of the even more vulgar one which she now frequented, had replied, 'Stop pulling my leg! I know you're not jealous. For one thing you told me, and then I can see it anyway.' She had never said to me since that she had changed her mind, but she must have formed some new ideas on the subject, which she hid from me but which chance might reveal in spite of her, for that evening, once I had gone in, found her in her bedroom and taken her to mine, I had said (with a certain embarrassment that I could not understand myself, since I had already told Albertine that I was going to visit someone I knew, I did not know whom, perhaps Mme de Guermantes, perhaps Mme de Cambremer – it is true that I did not mention the Verdurins): 'Guess where I've been? To the Verdurins'.' I had no sooner said these words than Albertine, her face contorted with feeling, replied, her words seeming to explode with a force that could not be contained, 'I know it. – I didn't think you'd mind if I went to the Verdurins'.' (It is true she had not said that she did mind, but I could see it in her face. It is true too that I had not thought that she would mind. And still, faced with the explosion of her anger, as at those moments when a kind of retrospective double vision makes us feel we have experienced them before, it seemed to me that I could never have expected anything else.) 'Mind? Why on earth should I mind? I couldn't care less. Wasn't Mlle Vinteuil supposed to be there?' These words infuriated me, and 'You didn't tell me you'd met Mme Verdurin the other day,' I said, to show that I knew more about her doings than she realized. 'Did I meet her?' she asked with a faraway look, addressing both herself, as if she were trying to collect her memories, and me, as if I should be able to tell her; and no doubt too so that I should tell her what I knew, and to give her time to find an answer to a difficult question. But the thought of Mlle Vinteuil worried me much less than another fear which I had briefly felt, but which now took hold of me much more strongly. Even on the way home, I had been imagining that Mme Verdurin had quite simply invented out of vanity the story that Mlle Vinteuil and her friend were coming, so that I arrived home quite happy. Only Albertine's words, 'But wasn't Mlle Vinteuil supposed to be there?' had shown me that my first suspicions had been justified. However, I had nothing to fear for the future, as by not going to the Verdurins', Albertine had sacrificed Mlle Vinteuil to me. 'Anyway, I said to her angrily, there are lots of things you don't tell me, quite unimportant things for the most part. I could mention the three days you spent in Balbec, for example.' I had added the words 'I could mention' as a complement to 'quite unimportant things', so that if Albertine then said, 'Well, what was wrong with my trip to Balbec?' I could answer, 'Nothing, I can't remember, I get things mixed up in my head, it really doesn't matter at all.' And if I had mentioned the three-day trip to Balbec with the chauffeur, from which her postcards had reached me with such a long delay, it was really by chance, and I felt sorry to have chosen such a poor example, for indeed, given the time taken up by the journey there and back, it was certainly the one of their excursions on which she would have had the least chance of spending any length of time with anybody. But Albertine concluded from what I had said that this time I knew the real truth, and was only hiding from her the fact that I knew it. She therefore remained convinced of the idea she had recently formed that somehow or other, perhaps by having her followed or something of that kind, I now 'knew more about her', as she had said to Andrée the week before, 'than she knew about herself'. So she interrupted me to make the most unnecessary confession, for certainly I had suspected nothing of what she then told me, and the revelation hurt me terribly, so great can the gulf be between a lying woman's invention and the idea which her lover, relying on her lies, has formed of the truth. No sooner had I said the words, 'your three-day trip to Balbec', than Albertine broke in and said as if it were the most natural thing in the world, 'Are you going to tell me we never went to Balbec? Well of course we didn't! And I always wondered why you kept pretending you believed it! It wasn't a big thing, though. The driver had things to do on his own account for three days. He didn't dare tell you. So to do him a favour (just like me! and then I'm always the one who ends up in trouble), I invented a plan to go to Balbec. He simply dropped me off in Auteuil, at my friend's house in the rue de l'Assomption, where I spent the most boring three days of my life. You see, there was nothing to worry about, there's no harm done. I did begin to think that perhaps you knew all about it when I saw you laugh at the cards arriving a week later. I know that was ridiculous and it would have been better not to send any cards at all. But it wasn't my fault. I bought them in advance and gave them to the driver before he dropped me in Auteuil, and then the idiot left them in his pockets instead of sending them in an envelope to a friend of his who lives near Balbec, who was supposed to post them on to you. The driver didn't remember them until five days later, and instead of telling me the fool sent them straight off to Balbec. When he said he'd done that I really gave him hell, you can imagine! Worrying you for nothing, the great buffoon, that was my reward for shutting myself away for three days to let him go and sort out his bits of family business! I didn't even dare go out in Auteuil for fear someone would see me. I only went out once and then I was dressed as a man, just for a laugh. And with my luck, of course the first person I bumped into was your sheeny friend Bloch. But I don't think he can have been the one who told you that our trip to Balbec only ever existed in my imagination, for I don't think he recognized me.'

I did not know what to say, not wishing to seem surprised as I groaned under the weight of so many lies. A feeling of horror, which did not make me want to throw Albertine out of the house, quite the opposite, was accompanied by an extreme desire to weep. This was caused, not by the lies themselves or by the annihilation of everything which I had believed to be true – so that I felt as if I were in a razed town where not a house is left standing and the naked earth is covered only with rubble – but by the melancholy thought that during all the three days of boredom at her friend's house in Auteuil, Albertine should not have once felt the wish, or perhaps even had the idea, of coming to spend a day secretly with me, or sending me a *petit bleu* to ask me to go and see her there. But I had not the time to give myself up to these thoughts. Above all I did not wish to seem surprised. I smiled like someone who knows much more than he is willing to admit: 'But that's just one thing among so many. Why, this very evening at the Verdurins', someone told me that what you said about Mlle Vinteuil . . .' Albertine stared at me with a desperate look, trying to read in my eyes how much I knew. Now what I knew and was going to tell her, was the nature of Mlle Vinteuil. It is true that I had not learned this at the Verdurins', but at Montjouvain many years previously. But as I had, by design, never spoken of it to Albertine, I could seem to have learned it only that evening. And I was almost pleased – after having suffered so much in the little tram – to possess that memory of Montjouvain, which I would assign to a later period, but which nonetheless would be the conclusive proof, a dreadful blow to Albertine. This time at least, I did not have to pretend to know, or to 'draw out' Albertine: I knew, I had *seen* the truth through the lighted window at Montjouvain. Albertine might insist that her relations with Mlle Vinteuil and her friend had been entirely proper, how would she be able, once I swore to her (and I would be swearing the truth) that I knew how these two women lived, how could she maintain that having lived in daily intimacy with them, calling them 'my big sisters', she had never been subjected to advances which would have required her to break with them, unless of course they had been welcomed? But I did not have time to speak the truth. Albertine, believing that, as with the fictitious journey to Balbec, I had heard about it, either from Mlle Vinteuil if she had been at the Verdurins', or simply from Mme Verdurin herself, who could have discussed the matter with Mlle Vinteuil, Albertine did not let me speak, but plunged into a confession, the exact opposite of the one I had been expecting, but which, by making it clear that there had never been a time when she had not lied to me, perhaps caused me just as much pain (especially because, as I have just said, I had stopped being jealous of Mlle Vinteuil). So, forestalling me, Albertine spoke in these terms: 'You're going to say you found out this evening that I was lying when I said I was almost brought up by Mlle Vinteuil's friend. Perhaps I did lie a little. But I felt you looked down on me and I saw you getting so passionate about this fellow Vinteuil's music that, seeing one of my friends – this is really true, I swear – had been a friend of Mlle Vinteuil's friend, I had the silly idea of making myself more interesting to you by pretending that I'd known those two girls very well. I could feel that I was boring you, that you thought I was empty-headed; I thought that if I told you I had spent time with those people, that I could give you details about

Vinteuil's music, then I'd become a bit more interesting to you and that would bring us together. And it has taken this wretched evening at the Verdurins' for you to learn the truth, which has probably been twisted anyway. I bet Mlle Vinteuil's friend told you she didn't know me. Well, she's seen me at least twice at my friend's house. But of course I'm not smart enough for people who've become so famous. They'd rather say they've never met me.' Poor Albertine, when she thought that boasting to me of her friendship with Mlle Vinteuil's friend would put off the moment she was 'dumped', would bring her closer to me, as so often happens she had arrived at the truth by a different path from the one she meant to take. To have learned that she knew more about music than I had thought would not have deterred me in the least from breaking with her that evening in the little tram; and yet it was this very phrase, which she had pronounced with this aim in mind, which had immediately made it impossible for me to break things off, and much more than that. She had simply made a mistake, not about the likely effect of her statement, but about the cause of that effect: this cause was my learning, not about her knowledge of music, but about her dubious friendships. What had suddenly brought me closer to her, much more, had irrevocably tied me to her, was not a hope of pleasure – even the word pleasure is too strong, a passing fancy – it was the grip of pain.

This time too, I could not stay silent for more than a moment, for fear of letting her guess at my surprise. So, touched by her modesty and the way she had felt insignificant in the Verdurin circle, I said tenderly to her, 'But darling, now I think of it, I'd be happy to give you a few hundred francs to go anywhere you like and play the smart lady, you could give a grand dinner and ask M. and Mme Verdurin.' Alas, Albertine was several people in one. The most mysterious, the most basic, the most dreadful one now appeared as she answered with a look of disgust and, to tell the truth, using words which I did not perfectly understand (even her opening ones, as she did not complete her reply). I was only able to supply them all a little later, once I had guessed her meaning. One can hear retrospectively once one has understood. 'Thanks a lot! Spend money on those old gargoyles, I'd much rather you left me alone for once, let me go out and get . . .' The moment she had said this she blushed crimson, looked heartbroken, put her hand over her mouth as if she could have pushed back into it the words which I had wholly failed to understand. 'What was that, Albertine? – Nothing, sorry, I'm half asleep. – No you're not, you're wide awake. – I was thinking about the dinner for the Verdurins, it's very sweet of you to think of it. – No, I want to know what you said.' She gave me a whole series of different versions of it, but none of them corresponded, I will not say to her words, which, having been interrupted, remained vague in my mind, but to this very interruption and the furious blushing which had accompanied it. 'No, dearest, think, that can't have been what you wanted to say, otherwise why would you have broken off? – Because I felt I shouldn't be asking you for things. – For what? – To let me give a dinner. – No, it's not that, you don't have to feel ashamed with me. – Yes I should, you shouldn't exploit the people you love. I swear that was what it was.' One the one hand, I still could not doubt anything she actually swore to me; on the other, her explanations did not satisfy my reason. I kept insisting: 'At least be brave enough to finish your sentence, you just got as far as *casser* . . . – Oh no, please don't! – But why? – Because it's something horribly vulgar, I'd be too ashamed to say it in front of you. I can't think what I was doing using words I don't even know the meaning of, things I'd heard the most terrible people saying in the street, they just came back to me for no reason. They had nothing to do with me or with anyone, I was just rambling.' I could see that I would get nothing more out of Albertine. She had been lying to me a moment ago when she said that what had made her break off was a sense of discretion, and was so now when she blamed her reluctance to use over-vulgar language in my hearing. For when Albertine and I were together there were no ideas too perverse, no words too indecent for us to speak as we caressed each other. However, it was useless to insist at this moment. But the word '*casser*' continued to obsess my memory. Albertine often said '*casser du bois sur quelqu'un, casser du sucre*', meaning to run someone down when his back is turned, or even '*ah! ce que je lui en ai cassé*', 'I really let him have it'. But she regularly said these things in my hearing, and if that was what she had meant to say this time, why had she blushed so violently, put her hands over her mouth, turned her sentence another way, and when she saw that I had clearly heard '*casser*', given me a false explanation? But I was not going to keep on interrogating her, since she was clearly determined not to reply, so I thought it better to seem to have forgotten all about it, and returning in my mind to Albertine's objections to my having gone to the Patronne's, I said very clumsily, as a kind of attempted excuse: 'I really meant to ask you if you wanted to come to Mme Verdurin's party this evening' – a doubly ill-chosen remark, since if I had wanted to ask her, having had every opportunity to talk to her, why had I not done so? Enraged by my lie and emboldened by my half-heartedness: 'You could have asked me a thousand times over, she said, and I still wouldn't have gone. Those people have always been against me, they've done all they could to make things difficult for me. I was really nice to Mme Verdurin at Balbec and this is the thanks I get. She could ask for me on her deathbed and I wouldn't go. Some things you can't forgive. And as for you, this is the first really nasty thing you've done to me. When Françoise told me you'd gone out (and wasn't she pleased to be able to tell me!), I wished she'd split my head down the middle instead. I tried to stop her noticing anything, but I've never felt so insulted in my life.'

But as she talked, my mind was still pursuing, in the waking, creative sleep of the unconscious (a sleep in which things which first passed us by almost unnoticed now take full shape, in which our sleeping hands grasp the key to secrets hitherto sought in vain), the search for the meaning of the interrupted sentence whose intended conclusion I wished to discover. And suddenly two dreadful words, of which I had not even been thinking, burst upon my mind: '*le pot*'. I cannot say that they appeared as a single discovery, as when one has been in long subjection to an incomplete memory, gently, cautiously trying to extend it but always closely applied to it. No, this was unlike my usual way of trying to remember: there were, I think, two parallel lines of enquiry: one took note not only of the words Albertine had spoken, but of her angry look when I offered her a gift of money to give a grand dinner, a look which seemed to say, 'Thanks a lot for giving me money to do boring things, when without any money I could be doing things I like!' And it was perhaps the memory of that look on her face that made me approach the problem of finding the ending in a different way. Up to that point I had focussed obsessively on the last word, '*casser*'. Break what? Wood? No. Sugar? No. *Casser, casser, casser*. And suddenly, the sight of her shrugging her shoulders as I made my offer took me back into the earlier words of her sentence. And I realized that she had not said '*casser*' but '*me faire casser*'. Horrors! That is what she would have preferred.[82] Horror upon horror! For even the lowest prostitute, who lends herself to that activity, or even welcomes it, will not use in speaking to the man who performs it such a revolting expression. She would feel herself too humiliated. Only with another woman, if she prefers women, will she use it, as if to excuse herself for yielding to a man. Albertine had not been lying when she had said that she was dreaming. Absent-minded, impulsive, she had forgotten that she was with me, she had shrugged her shoulders and began to speak as she might have done to one of those women, perhaps to one of my blossoming girls. And then, suddenly brought back to reality, blushing for shame, pushing the words back into her mouth, desperate, she had refused to say anything more. I had not a moment to lose if I wanted to keep my despair from her. But already, after the first surge of fury, tears were coming to my eyes. As at Balbec the night after she had revealed her friendship with the Vinteuils, I had to find an instant explanation for my anguish that should be plausible and at the same time have such a profound effect on Albertine as to win me a few days' respite before I should have to make a decision. So, at the moment when she said that she had never been so insulted as when I went out without her, that she would rather have died than hear the news from Françoise, and just as, irritated by her absurd over-sensitivity, I was about to tell her that what I had done was quite unimportant, that my going out should not have offended her so – and while, at the same time, my unconscious search for what she had been going to say after the word '*casser*' had been reaching a conclusion, and the despair into which it had thrown me could not be completely hidden, instead of defending myself I began to blame myself: 'Albertine, dearest, I said to her in a gentle voice in which my first tears could be heard, I could say that you're making a mistake, that what I did was nothing, but that would be a lie; you *are* right, you've seen how things are, poor baby: six months ago, three months even, when I was so very fond of you, I'd never have done a thing like that. It's a tiny thing, but it's hugely important because it shows how much my feelings have changed. And since you have guessed what I've been trying to keep from you, I think it's time to say this: Darling Albertine, I said gently, with deep sadness, you must see that your life here is depressing for you, we should separate, and as the quickest separations are the best, I will ask you, to make my suffering a little less, to say good-bye this evening and leave tomorrow morning before I wake up, so that I do not have to see you again.' She seemed astonished, still unbelieving and already heartbroken: 'What? Tomorrow? Is that what you really want?' And despite the pain it caused me to speak of our separation as something already accomplished – perhaps, indeed, because of that suffering, I began to give Albertine the most precise instructions about things she would have to do after leaving the house. And as one recommendation followed another, I soon found myself going into the tiniest details. 'You will be kind, won't you, I said with infinite sadness, and send me the Bergotte book that's at your aunt's. There's no hurry, in a few days' time, a week will do, whenever you like, but do remember, so that I don't have to write to you about it, that would be too painful. We have been so happy, and now we can see that that would make us unhappy.' – 'Don't say it would make us unhappy, Albertine broke in, don't say *us* when it's just your idea! – Yes, well, you or me, it doesn't matter, but for whatever reason – look at the time, you must go to bed – we've decided to end it this evening. – I beg your pardon, *you* decided and I'm accepting it because I don't want to hurt you. – All right, I decided, but it hurts me a lot just the same. I don't say that it will hurt forever, I'm not good at holding on to memories for a long time, but at the beginning I shall miss you so much. So I don't think we should keep it going by writing to each other, let's make a clean break. – You're right, she said with a look of anguish which was intensified by the late-night droop of her features, rather than have my fingers cut off one by one I'd sooner put my head on the block right away. – I can't believe how late I'm keeping you up, this is crazy. But there, since it's our last evening! You'll have the rest of your life to sleep.' And so, by telling her it was time to say good-night, I was trying to put off the moment when she would actually say it. 'Would it help you to get through the first few days if I asked Bloch to send his cousin Esther to stay with you, wherever you are going? He'd do that for me, I'm sure. – I can't think why you're saying that (I was saying it to try to force a confession from Albertine). The only person I want to be with is you,' said Albertine, sending a warm feeling right through me. But this was immediately followed by a stab of pain when she said, 'I do remember giving my photo to that girl Esther because she kept on asking and I saw she would really like to have it, but as for being a friend of hers or wanting to see her now, it's absurd.' And still Albertine was so easy to influence that she added, 'If she wants to see me I don't mind, she's very nice, but really I don't care either way.' So, when I had spoken to her about Bloch sending me Esther's photograph (which I had not yet seen when I mentioned it to Albertine) she had thought I meant that Bloch had shown me a photograph of her, the one she had given to Esther. In my worst imagining I had never supposed that that degree of intimacy had existed between Albertine and Esther. Albertine had made no reply when I talked about the photograph before. Now thinking me, quite wrongly, well informed about it, she had thought it better to confess. I was cast into gloom. 'And then, Albertine, please do just one more thing for me, never try to see me again. If ever, a year from now, two, three years, we find ourselves in the same town, stay away from me.' And seeing that she did not assent, 'Dear Albertine, please don't do that, don't try to see me again in this life. It would hurt me too much. For I really cared for you, you know. I know when I told you the other day that I wanted to see the friend we had talked about at Balbec, you thought that I had it all planned. No, I assure you I didn't care about her at all. You think I had had my mind made up for a long time to leave you, and when I was nice to you it was all put on. – You're crazy, I didn't think that, she said sadly. – Well, you're right, you mustn't think so, I was really fond of you. Perhaps it wasn't love, but I was very, very fond of you, more than you would believe. – But I do believe you. And if you think I don't love you! – I hate leaving you. – And I hate it a hundred times more,' Albertine replied. For a moment now I had been feeling that I would not be able to hold back the tears which were welling up in my eyes. And these tears were not caused by at all the same kind of sadness as I had felt formerly when saying to Gilberte, 'We had better stop seeing each other, life is forcing us apart.' No doubt when I was writing those words to Gilberte, I was saying to myself that when I next loved, not her but some other person, the excess of my love would diminish the love that that person might otherwise feel for me, as if between two people there were inevitably a fixed amount of love, so that where one loved more the other must love less, and from that other, as from Gilberte, I should be forced one day to separate. But this situation was quite different for a variety of reasons, of which the first, which had gone on to produce all the others, was that the weak will that my mother and my grandmother had feared I was developing at Combray, only to capitulate in turn before it later, such is an invalid's power to impose his weakness on others, this already inadequate will-power had been ever more rapidly diminishing. When I had felt that I was becoming tiresome to Gilberte, I still had enough strength of character to give her up; by the time I observed the same feelings in Albertine, my strength had gone and all I could think of was how to keep her by any means necessary. So that while I had written to Gilberte that I was going to stop seeing her, intending to do just that, when I said it to Albertine it was a complete lie, intended to bring about a reconciliation. Thus each of us was presenting to the other an appearance very different from what lay behind. And no doubt that is how it always is when two people face each other, since each of them is unaware of a part of what is inside the other, even what he is aware of he only partly understands, and each of them shows the other only what is least personal in him, whether because they have not understood themselves and think that the rest is unimportant, or because certain attractions which are not truly part of them seem to them more important and more flattering, or because there are other qualities which they think they need in order not to be despised, but do not have, and so they pretend to care nothing for them, and these are the things which they seem to despise above all and even to abominate. But in love this misunderstanding is carried to the highest degree since, except perhaps when we are children, we try to ensure that the impression we give, rather than being an exact reflection of our thoughts, should be what these thoughts conclude will have the best chance of getting us what we want, which in my case, since arriving home that evening, was the assurance of being able to keep Albertine as submissive as she had been in the past, so that her irritation did not lead her to demand the greater freedom which I meant to give her one day, but which at this moment, when I found her desire for independence so threatening, would have made me too jealous. From a certain age onwards vanity and wisdom combine to ensure that the things we desire the most are those that seem not to matter to us. But in love, simple foresight – which is probably not real wisdom – forces us to develop this talent for duplicity early in life. As a child, when I dreamed of love what seemed most delightful in it, the very essence of it, was the idea of being able to give free rein, with the girl I loved, to all my affection, my gratitude for a favour, my desire to spend my whole life with her. But I had soon realized, through my own experience and that of my friends, that the expression of such feelings is anything but contagious. The case of an affected old woman like M. de Charlus who, seeing nothing in his imagination but a handsome young man, thinks he has become a handsome young man himself, and betrays more and more effeminacy in his laughable affectations of virility, this case is an example of a law which affects not only Charluses, a law so general that even the whole domain of love does not exhaust its application; we cannot see our bodies as others see them, and we 'focus on' our own thoughts, the thing which is in front of us but invisible to others (sometimes made visible by an artist in a painting, hence the frequent disappointment of his admirers when they are admitted to his presence and see this inner beauty so imperfectly reflected in his face). Once one has noticed this, one no longer 'lets oneself go'; I had been careful, that afternoon, not to tell Albertine how grateful I was to her for having left the Trocadéro. And now, in the evening, fearing that she might leave me, I had pretended to want to leave her, a pretence dictated, as we shall see presently, by the lessons I thought I had learned from my previous love affairs and which I was trying to put to use in this one. This fear I had that Albertine might be going to say to me, 'I want to be able to go out on my own at certain times, I want to be able to be away for twenty-four hours,' or some make some other demand for freedom which I did not define to myself, but which frightened me, the thought of it had occurred to me for a moment during the evening at the Verdurins'. But it had quickly faded, contradicted in fact by the memory of Albertine constantly telling me how happy she was in the flat. The intention to leave me, if Albertine were harbouring it, appeared only in a disguised fashion, in certain sad looks, certain moments of impatience, phrases which seemed to mean something else but if one thought them over (and there was really no need for thought since this language of passion is instantly comprehensible, even working-class people understand those phrases which can only be explained by vanity, resentment, jealousy, which they do not express directly but which are immediately decoded by an intuitive faculty in the partner which, like Descartes's 'common sense', is 'the most common gift in the world'), could only be explained by the presence in her of a feeling which she was hiding from me and which might lead her to begin planning another life without me. Just as this intention was not logically expressed in her words, in the same way the premonition of this intention which I had had since the beginning of the evening was still vague in my mind. I was still living on the principle of believing everything Albertine said. But it is possible that a quite different principle, which I did not want to think about, was already taking shape at the back of my mind; that seems all the more likely as otherwise I would have felt no embarrassment at telling Albertine that I had been to the Verdurins', and, otherwise, it would have been impossible to understand why I had been so little surprised by her anger. So that what had probably taken root in me was the idea of an Albertine quite the opposite of the one my reason had formed of her, and also of the one depicted by her own words, but still not a wholly invented Albertine, since it appeared to be the inner reflection of some of her emotional reactions, like her ill-temper at my having gone to the Verdurins'. Furthermore, my frequent moments of anguish, my fear of telling Albertine I loved her, had long corresponded to another hypothesis which explained many further things, and also had on its side the fact that, if one adopted the first, the second became more probable, for if I gave way to outpourings of affection with Albertine, she only responded with irritation (an irritation to which she, however, ascribed another cause).

I must say what had struck me as the most serious sign that she was anticipating my accusation was that she had said, 'I think Mlle Vinteuil will be there this evening,' and I had replied in the cruellest way possible, saying, 'You didn't tell me you'd seen Mme Verdurin.' When Albertine seemed to be unkind, instead of admitting my sadness to her, I became aggressive. Analysing my conduct on that principle, the famous rule that my answers had always to express the opposite of what I was feeling, I can be sure that if I told her that night I was going to leave her, it was because – even before I had quite realized it – I was afraid she was going to want more freedom (what this dangerous freedom would exactly be I could not have said, but the kind of freedom that would have allowed her to deceive me, or at least prevented me from being certain that she was not deceiving me) and I wanted to be clever and show her, out of pride, that I did not care, just as, at Balbec, I had wanted her to have a high opinion of me and, later, had wanted her to have so much to do that she could not be bored with me.

Finally, to deal with the possible counter-argument to my second hypothesis – the one not yet formulated – that everything Albertine was always saying to me about the life she preferred, a quiet life under my roof, with reading, time to herself, no contact with lesbians, etc., meant just that, it was not worth consideration. For if on her side Albertine had decided to judge my feelings by what I said to her, she would have learned the exact opposite of the truth, since I only ever showed the desire to leave her when I could not do without her, and at Balbec I had twice told her I loved another woman, once Andrée and once an unnamed person, each time when jealousy had revived my love for Albertine. My words therefore did not reflect my feelings in the least. If the reader has only a faint impression of this, that is because, as narrator, I describe my feelings to him at the same time as repeating my words. But if I were to hide the former from him so that he heard only the latter, my actions, which corresponded so little to my words, would so often give him the impression of strange changes in direction that he would think me almost mad. A method which would not be much more misleading than the one I have adopted, since the images which prompted my actions, so different from those that were depicted in my words, were still at this time very obscure: I had only an imperfect understanding of the nature to which I was bound, whereas today I know the truth about it, at least from a subjective point of view. As for its objective truth, that is, whether these semi-hidden intuitions were any better than my reasoning at capturing Albertine's real intentions, and whether I was right to trust to my nature or whether it did not in fact distort Albertine's intentions instead of clarifying them, is difficult for me now to say.

The vague fear I had felt at the Verdurins' that Albertine might leave me, had originally faded. Arriving home, I had had the feeling of being a prisoner, not at all of returning to a female captive. But the forgotten fear had gripped me much more strongly when, at the moment I told Albertine that I had been to the Verdurins', I saw on the surface of her face a look of mysterious irritation, which indeed was not appearing there for the first time. I knew that this look was the crystallization in the flesh of long-considered grievances, of ideas which were clear to the person forming them and keeping them secret, a synthesis become visible but no more rational, which the man who gathers the precious residue on the face of the woman he loves tries in his turn, in order to understand what is going on behind it, to analyse and break down into its intellectual components. The equation corresponding to that unknown thing which was Albertine's thought for me went something like this: 'I knew he was suspicious, I was sure that he would try to check up on me, and so that I wouldn't be able to interfere he went off and did all his snooping on the sly.' But if these ideas, which she had never voiced to me, were what Albertine lived with every day, would not she revolt against, feel unable to lead, would not she sooner or later decide to turn her back on a life where she was always, at least in her desires, guilty but felt that she had been seen through, was being watched and prevented from ever satisfying those desires unless she could circumvent my jealousy; but where, if she were innocent in intention and deed, she had every reason to feel discouraged, seeing that from the days at Balbec, where she had taken such trouble never to be alone with Andrée, until today, when she had given up her plans of going to the Verdurins' and of staying at the Trocadéro, she had never managed to regain my trust? All the more so since I could not say that her behaviour had been anything but perfect. At Balbec, when we talked about girls who were ill-behaved, she had often laughed aloud, twisted her body, imitated their walk in a way that tortured me with the fear of what all that might mean to her friends, but now that she knew my feelings about it, as soon as anyone alluded to that kind of thing she withdrew from the conversation, not only by her silence but by the expression of her face. Whether she wanted to avoid contributing to the unkind gossip about this or that girl, or for some other reason, the only noticeable thing about her highly mobile features was that, from the moment the subject was raised, they had demonstrated their inattention by holding exactly the same expression as the moment before. And this fixity of even an inconsequential expression weighed on the company like a silence. No one could have told whether she disapproved of such conduct, or approved of it, or knew anything about it at all. Each of her features now related only to another of her features. Her nose, her mouth, her eyes formed a perfect harmony, isolated from everything else, she looked like a pastel portrait, as if she had not heard what had just been said any more than if it had been said in front of a La Tour.[83]

My fetters, of which I was still conscious when I was giving the coachman Brichot's address and saw the lighted window, had ceased to weigh on me soon after when I saw how intolerant Albertine seemed to be becoming of hers. And to make hers feel lighter, so that she would not form the idea of breaking them herself, I had thought it best to give her the impression that her slavery would not last for ever, and that I myself wished to bring it to an end. Seeing that my trick had worked, I could have felt happy, first of all because the thing I had so dreaded, the plan to leave me with which I had credited Albertine, had been averted and then because, quite apart from the result I had brought about, the very success of my trick established me in Albertine's eyes as something more than an unwanted lover, jealous, frustrated, slow, all of whose devices are seen through in advance. This gave a kind of new virginity to our love, bringing back the Balbec days when she found it so easy to believe that I was in love with someone else. She probably would not have believed that any longer, but she did believe in my expressed intention to break off with her that same evening.

She seemed to suspect that the cause might lie with the Verdurins. I said that I had met a playwright there, Bloch, who was a close friend of Léa's and that he had heard some very strange things from her (my idea was to suggest to her that I knew more than I had admitted about Bloch's girl-cousins). But in order to calm the agitation into which I had been cast by my threat to break with her, I said, 'Albertine, can you swear that you have never lied to me?' She stared into space, then answered, 'Yes, that's to say no. I shouldn't have said that Andrée was smitten with Bloch, we hadn't met him yet. – But why did you say it then? – I was afraid you might think something else about her. – Is that all?' She looked at me again and said, 'I shouldn't have kept it from you that I'd been away for three weeks with Léa. But I didn't really know you then. – Was it before we were in Balbec? – Before the second time, yes.' And that very morning she had told me she did not know Léa at all! I watched as sudden flames tore through a novel I had spent ten million minutes composing. What was the use? What was the use! I saw quite clearly that Albertine was revealing these two facts to me because she thought I had already learned them indirectly from Léa, and that there was no reason to suppose that there were not a hundred facts in her past of a similar kind. I knew too that Albertine's words when questioned never contained an atom of truth, that she only ever let slip the truth involuntarily, as a sudden collision took place in her between the facts she had previously decided to keep hidden and the belief that they had already been discovered. 'Two things, that's nothing, I said to Albertine, why don't you go to four and leave me something to remember you by? What else can you tell me about?' She went on looking straight in front of her. To what beliefs in an after-life was she adapting her lies, with what gods, less indulgent than she had believed, was she trying to patch things up? The task cannot have been easy, for her silence and her fixed stare lasted for some while. 'Nothing else,' she finally said. And the more I insisted the more she stuck, without difficulty now, to her 'Nothing else'. And that was such an obvious lie, for from the moment she developed these tastes until the day I shut her away in my house, how many times, in how many houses, on how many excursions she must have satisfied them! Lesbians are rare enough but also common enough that wherever they go, in whatever crowd, they cannot fail to spot another of their kind. I remembered with horror an evening which at the time had seemed merely laughable. One of my friends had asked me to a restaurant with his mistress and a friend of his who had also brought his girl. The two girls were not slow to understand each other, but were so impatient to move to physical relations that by the soup course their feet were feeling for each other, often finding mine instead. Soon their legs were intertwining. My two friends had not noticed anything; I was dying of embarrassment. One of the two, who could not wait any longer, got under the table, saying that she had dropped something. Then one developed a migraine and had to go and lie down. The other discovered that it was time to go and meet a friend at the theatre. In the end I was left alone with my two friends, who still suspected nothing. The migraine sufferer came back downstairs and said she must leave; she would go to her lover's house, take some antipyrine and wait for him there. The two girls became great friends, were seen everywhere together, one dressed as a man and went around picking up little girls and taking them home to the other to initiate them. The other had a little boy and used to pretend to be angry with him so that the other could punish him, with a heavy hand by all accounts. You could safely say that there was no place, no matter how public, where they did not do the most secret things.

'But Léa was perfectly all right with me all through the trip, said Albertine. Actually she was more proper than a lot of respectable ladies. – Are there respectable ladies who have behaved improperly to you, Albertine? – Never. – So what do you mean? – Well, she was more careful in her language. – For example? – She'd never say "get on my nerves" like lots of ladies who go to the best houses, or, "I don't give a damn".' It seemed to me that the unburnt part of the novel was slowly crumbling into ashes. My discouragement might have been lasting. Indeed Albertine's words, when I thought about them, turned it into a wild rage. But that fell back in the face of a kind of hopeless tenderness. After all, since I had come in and begun to speak of wanting to break with her, I too had been lying. And this wish for separation that I persisted in feigning was producing in me something like the sadness I would have felt if I had really wanted to leave Albertine.

Furthermore, even as I returned intermittently, in twinges as we say for other kinds of physical pain, to the thought of the orgiastic life Albertine must have led before she knew me, I wondered all the more at the submissiveness of my captive and I stopped feeling angry with her. Obviously I had never, during our life together, allowed Albertine to think that that life would be anything but temporary, so that she should continue to find some attraction in it. But this evening I had gone further, fearing that vague threats of separation would no longer be effective, since they would no doubt be contradicted in Albertine's mind by her idea of a great, jealous love for her which had sent me, so she hinted, to make inquiries about her at the Verdurins'. That evening I realized that among the other causes which had made me take the sudden decision, without realizing it until the process was under way, to play out this comedy of separation, there was the fact that when, under one of those compulsions which also affected my father, I was threatening the security of another human being, then, lacking, like him, the courage to carry out my threats, and so as not to let the person think that they had just been empty words, I would go a long way towards doing what I threatened and not give way until my adversary, really convinced of my sincerity, had trembled in all seriousness.

Furthermore, we can feel that in these lies there is always a measure of truth, that if life does not bring changes to our love, soon we ourselves will want to do so, or to pretend that they have occurred, and to talk of separation, so evident is it that all loves and all things move rapidly towards farewells. We want to weep the tears that the ending will bring, long before it happens. No doubt this time, in the scene I had just been playing, there was a practical consideration. I suddenly felt I must keep Albertine because I felt her being was dissipated among various other people whom I could not prevent her from joining. But if she had given them all up for me, for ever, I should perhaps have decided even more firmly never to leave her, for while jealousy makes separation difficult, gratitude makes it impossible. In any case I felt that this was the final engagement in which I must be victorious or succumb. I would have offered Albertine in a single hour everything I possessed, for I was saying to myself, 'Everything depends on this battle.' But battles of this kind are not so much like those of former times, which lasted a few hours, as like present-day battles, which are not over in a day, or two days, or a week. Generals commit all their troops, because they always think these are the last they will need. And a year passes and the 'decisive' battle never comes.

Perhaps too an unconscious memory of the lying scenes made by M. de Charlus, with whom I had been when seized by the fear of Albertine's leaving me, had been an additional cause. But afterwards I once heard my mother telling this story, which I had not known at the time and which makes me think that I had found all the elements of this scene within myself, in one of those obscure, hereditary reserves which certain emotions, acting as coffee or alcohol do on our reserves of strength, can make available to us: when Aunt Octave learned from Eulalie that Françoise, convinced that her mistress would never leave the house again, had plotted some outing that my aunt was not to know about, the invalid, the day before, would pretend to have decided to try the fresh air the following day. She made the unbelieving Françoise not only get her things ready, airing those which had been shut away for too long, but even order the carriage, and arrange to the nearest quarter of an hour all the details of the day. It was only when Françoise, finally convinced or at least disconcerted, had been obliged to admit her own plans to my aunt that she would publicly renounce hers so as not, she said, to upset Françoise's. In the same way, so that Albertine would not think I was exaggerating and to keep her for as long as possible in the belief that we were going to separate, I had begun to plan the time which was to begin the following day and last for ever, the time when we should be apart, making all the same recommendations to Albertine as if we were not going to end our quarrel in a moment. Like generals who believe that in order for a feint to deceive the enemy it must be carried out in every detail, I had committed to this one almost as much of my reserves of feeling as if it had been happening in reality. This scene of fictitious separation in the end caused me almost as much unhappiness as if it had been true, perhaps because one of the actors, Albertine, believed that it was, and so added to the illusion for the other. We were living a day at a time, a life which though painful was bearable, kept in contact with everyday things by the ballast of habit and by the certain knowledge that the following day might be cruel, but would at least include the presence of the being we loved. And here I was suddenly, insanely destroying this solid existence. True, I was only pretending to destroy it, but that was enough to make me wretched; perhaps because sad words, when one speaks them, even untruthfully, contain their own sadness and inject it deep into one; perhaps because one knows that a feigned farewell is only anticipating an hour which must finally come; and then one is not quite sure that one has not triggered the mechanism which will make that hour strike. In every bluff there is an element, however small, of uncertainty about the reaction of the person one is deceiving. Suppose this game of separation led to a real separation! We cannot think of the possibility without a pang of anxiety. Indeed we are doubly anxious, for in that case the separation would come about at the very moment when it would be intolerable, for we would have been made to suffer by a woman who would be leaving us without having cured our pain, or at any rate soothed it. Lastly, we can no longer rely even on habit, which normally bears us up even in times of sorrow. We have thrown our habits away, we have made today uniquely important, detaching it from the surrounding days, it is mobile, rootless as a day of departure, our imagination, no longer paralysed by the predictable, has come alive, we have suddenly added to our everyday love sentimental dreams which enormously increase its power, making it impossible to do without someone on whose presence, unfortunately, we can no longer absolutely count. Of course it was precisely in order to retain this necessary presence for the future that we started pretending to be able to do without it. But we got caught up in the game ourselves, we began to suffer because we were doing something new, something unaccustomed, which turned out to be like those medicines that are to cure our sufferings in the long run, but whose first effect is to make them worse.

I had tears in my eyes like those people who, alone in their room, let their thoughts drift on to the death of a person they love, and imagine the sorrow it would cause them in such detail that they end up actually feeling it. In the same way, while making ever more detailed recommendations to Albertine on how she should behave to me once we were no longer together, I felt almost as sad as if we had not been going to make things up soon afterwards. And then, was I so sure that I could make it up, that I could bring Albertine back round to the idea of our living together, and if I managed it for this evening, could I be sure that the frame of mind which this scene had dispelled would not return? I felt, but did not believe, that I controlled the future, because I knew that my feeling came from the fact that the future did not yet exist and that I could not therefore be subject to its inevitability. And then, even as I lied perhaps I was putting more truth into my words than I thought. I had just had an example of this when I had said to Albertine that I should soon forget her. That was what had happened with Gilberte, whom I now avoided going to see, in order to spare myself not suffering but a tiresome chore. And certainly I had suffered when writing to Gilberte that I did not want to see her again. For I used only to go to Gilberte's house now and then. But every one of Albertine's hours belonged to me. And in love it is easier to uproot a feeling than to give up a habit. But if I was able to speak so many painful words concerning our separation, it was because I knew they were false; on the other hand they were sincere in the mouth of Albertine when I heard her cry out, 'Oh, I promise, I'll never see you again! I can't bear to see you cry like that, darling. I don't want to hurt you. If that's what you want, we won't see each other again.' They were sincere in a way they could not have been if I had spoken them, and this was because Albertine was fond of me, no more, and so on the one hand the promised renunciation was easier for her, and on the other hand my tears, which would have seemed insignificant in the context of a great love, seemed to her extraordinary and upsetting when transferred to that of affection, outside which she had never ventured, an affection greater than mine, if what she had said was true, and she had said it because in a separation it is always the one who is not really in love who says the affectionate things, love not expressing itself directly, and what she had said was perhaps not wholly false, for the thousand kindnesses of love may in the end call forth in the person who is loved without loving a fondness, a gratitude which are less selfish than the feeling which inspired them, and which may, after years of separation, when nothing survives of love in the former lover, live on in the beloved.

For just one moment I did feel a kind of hatred for her which only made me the more desperate to keep her with me. Preoccupied as I was that evening with Mlle Vinteuil alone, when my thoughts drifted to the Trocadéro I remained quite undisturbed, not only because I had sent Albertine there to keep her away from the Verdurins', but even when I pictured Léa there, Léa on account of whom I had summoned Albertine back home, so that she should not be introduced to her. I spoke Léa's name without thinking and Albertine, suspicious and fearing that I had perhaps learned more about the actress, forestalled me and said rapidly, with her face partly turned away, 'I know her very well, I went with some friends last year to see her on stage, after the play we went backstage to her dressing-room, we saw her dressing. It was very interesting.' Then my mind was forced to let go of Mlle Vinteuil and, in a desperate effort, in the impossible race to reconstitute the past, to focus itself on the actress and that evening when Albertine had gone to her dressing-room. On the one hand, after all the oaths she had sworn to me that had sounded so sincere, after the complete sacrifice of her liberty, how could I believe that there was any harm in it? And yet, were not my suspicions like antennae pointed towards the truth, since, while she had given up the Verdurins and gone to the Trocadéro to please me, all the same, Mlle Vinteuil was supposed to have been at the Verdurins', and at the Trocadéro, which she had also given up in order to come out with me, there had been, as a reason to bring her back from there, Léa, that same Léa about whom I seemed to be worrying needlessly but whom, in words that I had not forced out of her, Albertine said she knew, had met in a larger society than the one I particularly feared, but in very dubious circumstances, for who could have persuaded her to go backstage, to that dressing-room? If the thought of Mlle Vinteuil stopped hurting me when I thought of Léa – these two women who between them had destroyed my day –

it was either because my wounded spirit was unable to picture too many scenes at once, or because of the confusion of my nervous emotions, of which my jealousy was only the echo. I could conclude that Albertine had not belonged either to Léa or to Mlle Vinteuil, and that I was only imagining her with Léa because I still felt pain from that quarter. But because my jealousies were dying down – only to flare up again from time to time, one after the other – that did not mean that each of them did not correspond to some rightly suspected truth, and that I should say not 'none of these women', but 'all'. I say 'suspected', because I could not occupy all the necessary points of space and time, and then what instinct would have led me to combine the right ones, so as to surprise Albertine here at such-and-such a time with Léa, or with the young girls in Balbec, or with Mme Bontemps's friend who had brushed against her, or the young girl who had nudged her at the tennis match, or with Mlle Vinteuil?

'Dear Albertine, you are sweet to promise me that. Anyway, for the first few years at least I shall stay away from the places you want to go to. Do you know yet if you'll be in Balbec this summer? Because if you were, I'd arrange to be somewhere else.' If I went on in this vein, running ahead in my lying invention, it was not so much to frighten Albertine as to give myself pain. Like a man who at first had only trivial reasons for being annoyed, but, intoxicated by the sound of his own voice, lets himself be carried away by a fury engendered not by his grievances but by his burgeoning anger itself, I was rolling faster and faster down the slope of my sadness towards an ever deeper despair, with the inertia of a man who feels the cold gaining on him, but does not try to fight it and even finds a kind of pleasure in shivering. And if I presently found enough strength, as I was confident of doing, to reassert myself and go into reverse, it was not the unhappiness Albertine had caused me by giving me such an angry reception when I came home, but the pain I had felt while dreaming up, for the sake of pretending to settle them, all the formalities of an imaginary separation and foreseeing all its consequences, that would have to be made better this evening by Albertine's bedtime kiss. In any case, it was important that she did not say good-night of her own accord, for that would have made it difficult for me to change course and suggest we call off our separation. So I kept repeating that it was long past the time to say good-night, which left me the choice of when to say it, and allowed me to put it off a moment longer. And so I kept slipping allusions to the late hour, to our tiredness, into the questions I asked Albertine. 'I don't know where I'll go,' she replied to the last one, with a worried look. 'Perhaps to Touraine, to my aunt's.' This first suggestion made me shiver, as if it really marked the beginning of our final separation. She looked round the room, with its pianola and blue satin armchairs. 'I still can't take in the idea that I won't see all this tomorrow, nor the day after tomorrow, nor ever again. Poor little room! It seems impossible, I can't get it into my head. – We had to do it, you were so unhappy here. – No I wasn't, I wasn't unhappy, I'm going to be unhappy now. – No, believe me, it'll be better for you. – For you, you mean!' I began to look in front of me as if, deeply hesitant, I were wrestling with an idea which had just come into my head. Then suddenly: 'Listen, Albertine, you say you're happier here this elsewhere, that you're going to be unhappy if you leave. – Of course I am. – That makes me wonder; do you think you'd like us to try to go on for a few more weeks after all? You never know, a week at a time, we might manage to go on for a good long time, you know some temporary things can go on for ever. – Oh, that would be lovely! – But in that case it's crazy to have gone on hurting each other like this for hours over nothing, it's like getting ready for a journey and then not leaving. I'm worn out with it.' I sat her on my knees, took the Bergotte manuscript she so wanted to have and wrote on the cover, 'For little Albertine, a souvenir of a lease renewed.' 'Now, darling, I said, go to bed and sleep till tomorrow evening, you must be exhausted. – Happy is what I am. – Do you love me just a little? – A hundred times more now.'

I should have been wrong to feel pleased with this little comedy, were it not that I had managed to push it to the limit, so that it took on the form of a real theatrical performance. If we had simply talked about separating that would already have been serious. One imagines that one can have such conversations without meaning them, which is true, but also without paying a price. But they generally represent, unknown to us, murmured in spite of ourselves, the first rumblings of

an unsuspected storm. In fact, what we say at these times is the opposite
of what we want (which is to go on living with the woman we love),
but it is this very inability to live together which underlies our daily
suffering, a suffering which we prefer to the pain of separation, but
which will eventually, in spite of ourselves, drive us apart. Not usually
in one go, however. What most often happens – though not, as we
shall see, in the case of Albertine and myself – is that some time after
saying the words in which we did not believe, we set in action an
imprecise attempt at a voluntary, painless, temporary separation. We
ask the woman, in the hope that she will feel happier with us afterwards,
in the hope, also, of a brief escape from our continual sadness and
fatigue, to go away without us, or to let us go without her, for a few
days' travel, the first days for a very long time that we have spent – it
would once have seemed impossible – without her. Very soon she
returns home to us. But this separation, short but real, was not decided
on in so arbitrary a fashion as we think, nor was it the only one we
had in mind. The same sadness begins again, the difficulty of living
together becomes more marked, the only change is that separation
does not now seem so difficult; we began by talking about it, then we
carried it out in a harmless form. But these things are warning
symptoms which we have not yet recognized. Soon the smiling,
temporary separation is succeeded by the hideous, final parting for
which we unwittingly prepared the ground.

'Come to my room in five minutes and let me see you for a little
while, sweetheart. You'll be nice, won't you. But I'll go to sleep
straight after, for I'm half dead.' And it was a dead woman that I saw
when I went into her room a moment later. She had fallen asleep the
minute she lay down; her sheets, wrapped round her body like a
shroud, had fallen into fine folds with the apparent hardness of stone.
You would have said that, as in certain Last Judgments of the Middle
Ages, only her head was appearing out of her tomb, as she waited in
her sleep for the Last Trump. She had fallen asleep with her head
thrown back, her hair dishevelled. And seeing that meaningless body
lying there, I wondered what kind of logarithmic table it must constitute
for it to be possible that every action in which it had been involved,
from a nudge to the brushing of a dress, could, when projected to

infinity from all the points it had occupied in space and time or sometimes brought back to life again in my memory, cause me such terrible stabs of pain, which, however, I knew to be triggered by movements, desires of hers which in another woman, or in herself five years sooner or five years later, would have left me completely indifferent. It was a lie, but I dared not look for any solutions to it other than my death. So I stood there, still in the overcoat in which I had returned from the Verdurins', looking at that twisted body, that allegorical figure of what? Of my death? Of my love? Soon I began to hear her regular breathing. I went and sat on the edge of her bed to calm myself with her breath and the look of her. Then I slipped away so as not to wake her.

It was so late that the next morning I asked Françoise to walk as quietly as she could when passing Albertine's bedroom. And Françoise, convinced that we had spent the night in what she called orgies, duly warned the other servants, in an ironic tone, not to 'wake her Highness'. And this was one of my fears, that one day Françoise would lose her self-control and speak insolently to Albertine, thus facing me with complications in our life together. In former days she used to suffer pangs when she saw Eulalie in favour with my aunt; but now she was too old to bear her jealousy without showing its outward signs. It changed our servant's face, almost paralysing it, to the point where, sometimes, I wondered whether a surge of fury in her, unseen by me, had not caused a slight stroke. Having thus asked for Albertine's sleep to be protected, I could not sleep at all myself. I kept trying to guess at Albertine's true state of mind. Had the deplorable comedy I had just acted out served to defend me from a real danger, and despite her claims to be so happy in my house, had she really been hankering after her freedom, or ought I, on the contrary, to believe what she said? Which of the two hypotheses was the right one? Often at this time I took (and would do so even more often in the future) an occurrence in my past life and projected it on a historic scale so as to try to understand a political event; this morning I did the opposite, and kept identifying, despite the many differences between them, and in order to understand it better, the import of our scene of the night before with a diplomatic incident which had recently taken place.

Perhaps I was right to reason in that way. For it is very likely that I had, without knowing it, been guided by the example of M. de Charlus in that lying scene which I had seen him play so often and with such mastery; and on the other hand was it, in him, anything but an unconscious importing into the sphere of private life, of the profound tendency of his German race, challenging in its deviousness and, if necessary, warlike in its pride?

Various people, including the Prince of Monaco, having suggested to the French government that, if it did not dismiss M. Delcassé, German threats would be succeeded by real war, the Foreign Minister had been asked to resign. The French government had, therefore, accepted the hypothesis of an intention to declare war on us if we did not back down. But others thought that it had been simply a bluff, and that if France had stood its ground Germany would not have drawn the sword. Of course our scenario had been not just different but almost the reverse, since Albertine had never voiced any threat to break with me; but a system of impressions had led me to believe that she was thinking of doing so, just as the French government had believed of the Germans. On the other hand, if Germany wanted peace, leading the French government to think she was planning war was a doubtful and dangerous strategy. Certainly, my conduct had been rather clever, if it was the thought that I would never take the decision to break with her that had been leading Albertine to form sudden desires for independence. And was it not difficult to believe that she had no such desires, to refuse to see a whole secret life in her, directed towards the satisfaction of her vice? Everything showed it, even her anger on learning that I had been to the Verdurins', when she cried, 'I knew it,' and gave away her whole secret by saying, 'They were expecting Mlle Vinteuil.' All that was borne out by the meeting between Albertine and Mme Verdurin of which I had learned from Andrée. But on the other hand, perhaps those sudden desires for independence, so I said to myself when I tried to go against my instinct, were caused – supposing they existed at all – or would in the end be caused by the opposite idea, that is, that I had never intended to marry her, that it was when I alluded, as if involuntarily, to our impending separation that I was telling the truth, that I would in any case leave

her one day or another, a belief which my scene of the previous
evening could only have confirmed and which might in the end produce
in her the resolution: 'If it has to happen some time or other, it might
as well happen now.' Preparations for war, which the most false of all
proverbs recommends as a way of ensuring peace, in fact create the
belief in each of the adversaries that the other wants to break off
relations, a belief which brings about that very breakdown, and then,
once it has taken place, the further belief on each side that it was the
other side who wanted it. Even if the threat was not sincere, its success
encourages its repetition. But the exact limits of successful bluffing are
difficult to determine; if one party goes too far, the other, which up to
that point had been retreating, begins to advance; the first, unable
to change its methods, accustomed now to the idea that the best way
to avoid a breakdown is to seem not to fear it (as I had done this
evening with Albertine), and, in its pride, preferring defeat to surrender, continues its threats up to the point where neither party can any
longer retreat. Bluff can also be mixed with sincerity, can alternate
with it so that what was a game yesterday can become tomorrow's
reality. It can also sometimes be the case that one of the adversaries is
really committed to war: Albertine could have intended, sooner or
later, to stop living this life, or perhaps the idea of leaving it had never
entered her mind, and my imagination had invented the whole thing
from start to finish. These were the different hypotheses I turned over
in my mind as she slept, on that particular morning. However, as far
as the second is concerned, I can say that I never, in the time which
followed, threatened to leave Albertine except in response to a mistaken
desire for freedom on her part, an idea which she did not put into
words, but which seemed to me to be implied by certain mysterious
signs of dissatisfaction, by certain words, certain gestures which could
be explained only by some such underlying idea and for which she
refused to give me any other explanation. I still often noted these signs
without saying anything about a possible separation, hoping that they
were caused by a bad mood that would be gone by the next day. But
the mood sometimes went on for weeks together, it was as if Albertine
wanted to pick a quarrel with me, as if she knew of the existence, more
or less close at hand, of pleasures of which her enclosed life with me

was depriving her, and which exercised an influence upon her for as long as they lasted, like those atmospheric disturbances which reach us at our own firesides and act upon our nerves from as far away as the Balearic islands.

That morning, while Albertine was sleeping and I was trying to guess at her hidden feelings, I received a letter from my mother in which she expressed her uneasiness at knowing nothing of my intentions, using this remark of Mme de Sévigné's: 'I believe that he will not take a wife; but why then trouble this girl whom he will never marry? Why risk prompting her to refuse matches that she will come to look on with disdain? Why disturb the mind of a person whom he could so easily avoid?' My mother's letter brought me back to earth. Why am I searching out a mysterious soul, I thought, interpreting a face, feeling surrounded by forebodings which I dare not pursue? I have been dreaming, things are simple. I am an irresolute young man, this is one of those marriages that may or may not happen, it will take time to decide. Nothing here is peculiar to Albertine. This thought gave me profound relief, but it was short-lived. Soon I said to myself, 'The whole thing could be reduced, if one looks at it from the social point of view, to the most banal, everyday story: if it were happening to someone else, perhaps that is how I should see it. But I know that the truth, at least part of the truth, is everything I have been thinking, everything I have read in Albertine's eyes, the fears that have been torturing me, the questions I have been asking myself about my relation to Albertine.' The story of the hesitant fiancé and the broken engagement may correspond to all that, in the way a theatrical notice written by a commonsensical columnist may set out the subject of an Ibsen play. But there is more to it than the facts of the story. It is true that there may also be more, if one could see it, to the story of every hesitant fiancé and every engagement that drags on, because there is perhaps mystery in everyone's daily life. I could overlook it in the lives of others, but in Albertine's and my own life, I was living it from within.

Albertine did not say to me after that evening, any more than she had done before, 'I know you don't trust me, I'm going to try to dispel your suspicions.' But this idea, which she never expressed, could have explained every one of her actions. Not only did she take care never to be alone for a moment, so that I could not fail to know everything she had been doing, even if I did not believe her own account of it, but even when she had to speak on the telephone to Andrée, or the garage, or the riding-school, or anywhere else, she would say that it was too tiresome telephoning on one's own, the girls were so slow in putting one through, and she would see to it that I was there to hear her, or failing that Françoise, as if she feared that I might imagine reprehensible telephone calls in which she planned mysterious rendez-vous. Alas, this did nothing to calm my fears. Aimé had sent me back Esther's photograph, saying that that was not the girl. So there were others? Who? I sent the picture back to Bloch. The one I should have liked to see was the one Albertine had given to Esther. How was she dressed in it? Perhaps with a low neckline; who knows, perhaps they had been photographed together? But I did not dare speak to Albertine about it, for then she would know I had not seen the photograph, nor to Bloch, in whose eyes I did not want to seem to be interested in Albertine. And this life, so cruel for me and for Albertine, as anyone would have recognized who had known of my suspicions and her slavery, from the outside, in Françoise's eyes, appeared to be a life of undeserved treats cleverly wheedled out of me by the 'crafty one', as Françoise called her, or, using the feminine of the word much more often than the masculine, as she was more envious of women than of men, the '*charlatante*'.[84] She would even say, having expanded her vocabulary by contact with me but always using the new expressions in her own way, that she had never known anyone so 'perfidulous' as Albertine, that she knew how to get money out of me by play-acting (which Françoise, who was as likely to take the particular for the general as the general for the particular, and had only the vaguest idea of the various genres of drama, called 'pantomiming'). Perhaps this misunderstanding about our real life, Albertine's and mine, was partly my fault, since I confirmed it in some measure by the vague hints which I carefully let slip when talking to Françoise, either in order to tease her, or to seem, if not loved, at any rate happy. And yet my jealousy, my watchful surveillance of Albertine, which I was so anxious that Françoise should not suspect, were immediately guessed at by

her, as a medium, blindfolded, goes straight to an object, guided by
her unfailing sense of what could cause me pain, which could not be
diverted by any lies I told to put her off track, and also by the hatred
of Albertine which led Françoise – even more than to think her enemies
luckier, cleverer actresses than they really were – to hunt out what
could damage them and hasten their downfall. Françoise certainly
never had an open quarrel with Albertine. I wondered whether
Albertine, feeling herself watched, would not herself decide to bring
forward the separation with which I had threatened her, for life as it
changes turns our fantasies into reality. Every time I heard a door
open, I felt myself tremble as my grandmother had trembled in her
death-agony every time I rang the bell. I did not really think she had
gone out without telling me, but my unconscious mind thought so, as
it had been my grandmother's unconscious mind which jumped at the
sound of the bell even after she had lost consciousness. One morning, I
even had the sudden, anxious feeling that she had not only gone out, but
gone for good. I had heard the sound of a door which seemed to me to
be the door of her bedroom. I crept along to her room, opened the door
and stood on the threshold. In the half-darkness there was a semi-circular
mass under the sheets that must be Albertine sleeping with her body
in a curve, her head and feet pointing towards the wall. Only her head
could be seen above the sheets: its mass of black hair showed me that
this was she, that she had not opened her door, had not moved at all,
and I felt that this motionless, living semicircle, in which a whole
human life was suspended, was the only thing that held any value for
me, and that it was there, under my power, in my possession.

But I knew Françoise's powers of insinuation, her ability to set a
scene and exploit its significance, and I cannot believe she resisted the
temptation to remind Albertine daily of her humiliating position in my
household, to distress her by a carefully exaggerated depiction of the
confinement to which my friend was subject. I once found Françoise
with thick glasses on her nose, poking among my papers and putting
back one on which I had noted down a story about Swann and his
inability to do without Odette. Had she accidentally left it lying in
Albertine's room? In any case, above all Françoise's hints, which had
been only a whispered, insidious bass accompaniment to them, no

doubt there had sounded out, higher, clearer, more urgent, the voice of the Verdurins, with their accusations and calumnies, since they were angry to see how Albertine unwittingly kept me away, and I her quite deliberately, from the meetings of the little set.

As for the money I spent on Albertine, it was almost impossible for me to hide it from Françoise, since I could not hide any expenditure from her. Françoise had few vices, but these vices had developed in her some true gifts which were often evident only in the service of the said vices. Chief among them was the curiosity she brought to bear on any expenditure of money by us on anyone but herself. If I had a bill to pay, a tip to give, it was useless to go into another room, she would find a plate to put away, a napkin to collect, some pretext to get near me. And however little time I allowed her for observation, chasing her angrily away, this woman who could hardly see any longer, who could barely count, directed by the same instinct which makes a tailor look at you and assess the cloth of your suit and even reach out to finger it, or a painter respond to a colour effect, Françoise would steal a sidelong glance and calculate instantly what I was giving. If, to prevent her telling Albertine I was bribing her chauffeur, I forestalled her and made an excuse for the tip by saying, 'I wanted to be nice to the chauffeur, I gave him ten francs,' the pitiless Françoise, one glance from whose eagle eye – an old, near-blind eagle, but no matter – had been enough, would reply, 'No, sir, you gave him a forty-three franc tip. He said the bill was forty-five francs and you, sir, gave him a hundred and he only gave back twelve.' She had managed to see and count the total of the tip when I did not know it myself.

If Albertine's aim was to pacify me, she succeeded in part, since my reason, in any case, was only too anxious to convince me that I had been mistaken about Albertine's sinister plans, just as I had perhaps been wrong about her vicious instincts. No doubt in my ready acceptance of the arguments my reason put forward there was an element of wishful thinking. But in order to be fair and to have a chance of reaching the truth, unless we admit that it is only ever known by premonition, by some telepathic emanation, was it not necessary to say to myself that if my reason, working towards my cure, let itself be led by what I wished to believe, on the other hand, in the whole matter of Mlle Vinteuil, Albertine's vices, her intention to change her life and her plan to leave me, both of which were corollaries of her vices, my instinct, seeking to make me ill, could have let itself be led astray by my jealousy? In any case Albertine's removal from the world, which she herself took such ingenious pains to make complete, by ending my suffering, slowly reduced my suspicions until I was able, when evening brought back my anxieties, to find Albertine's presence as comforting as it had been at the beginning. Sitting by my bed, she would talk to me about one of the dresses or one of the objects which I was constantly giving her in the hope of making her life more pleasant and her prison more attractive, while sometimes fearing that she might agree with the Mme de la Rochefoucauld who, when she was asked if she were not glad to be living in such a fine house as Liancourt, replied that she knew of no fine prisons. Thus, if I had questioned M. de Charlus about old French silver, it was because, when we had formed the plan of buying a yacht, a plan which seemed impossible to Albertine – and to me whenever I began to believe once more in her virtue, and my jealousy, shrinking in volume, allowed the expansion of other desires, not involving her, which would also require money for their satisfaction – we had chanced, despite her belief that we would never have one, to ask the advice of Elstir. Now, just as in women's dress, the painter had a subtle, demanding taste in the decoration of yachts. On board, he would accept only English furniture and old French silver. Formerly all Albertine's thoughts had been for dress and furnishings. Now she was interested in silver as well, and this had led her, since our return from Balbec, to read books on the art of silverwork and on the marks of the old silversmiths. But since French silver was melted down twice, once at the time of the Treaty of Utrecht, when the king himself, followed by the great nobles, gave up his plate, and then in 1789, old pieces are extremely rare. True, modern silversmiths have reproduced all the lost pieces according to the Pont-aux-Choux drawings,[85] but in vain: Elstir pronounced these new-old designs unfit to enter the home of a woman of taste, even her floating home. I knew that Albertine had read a description of the wonders created by Roettiers for Mme du Barry.[86] She was dying to see some of these pieces, if any survived, and I longed to give them to her. She had even begun a collection of pretty pieces which she arranged charmingly in a glass case, and which I could not look at without feelings of pity and fear, for the art with which she arranged them showed that combination of patience, ingenuity, homesickness and the need to forget which we see in the art of prisoners.

As far as dress was concerned, her taste at that moment was particularly for everything that Fortuny was making. Those Fortuny dresses, one of which I had seen Mme de Guermantes wearing, were the ones whose appearance had been foretold by Elstir, when he spoke of the magnificent garments worn by the women of Carpaccio's and Titian's time; now they were being reborn from their sumptuous ashes, for everything must return, as it is written on the vaults of St Mark's, and as the birds proclaim that we see drinking from the marble and jasper urns of Byzantine capitals, signifying both death and resurrection. As soon as women started wearing them, Albertine had remembered Elstir's promises and had wanted one, and we were to go and choose one for her. Now these dresses, though they were not actually old, of the kind which on women of today always look a little too much like fancy dress and which it is nicer to keep as collector's pieces (I was also looking for some pieces of this kind for Albertine), did not have the cold, pastiche accuracy of reproductions. They were more like the stage designs of Sert, Bakst and Benois, who at this time, for the Ballets Russes, were bringing back to life the best-loved periods of art with the help of works steeped in period feeling, but still original; in the same way Fortuny's dresses, faithful to the antique spirit but powerfully original, called up as a backdrop, but with even more evocative power than a stage setting, since this backdrop had to take shape in our imagination, the Venice laden with Oriental riches in which they would have been worn; even better than a relic in the shrine of St Mark, they evoked the sun and crowding turbans of the east, its fragmented, mysterious and complementary colour. All of this time was lost, but everything was returning, called up, to be bound together in the splendour of the landscape and the swarming of life, by the surviving scraps, rising from oblivion, of the dresses of the Venetian noblewomen.

Once or twice I felt like asking Mme de Guermantes's advice on this subject. But the Duchesse did not like clothes with a fancy-dress look. She herself never looked so well as in black velvet and diamonds. And on dresses of the Fortuny kind her advice would not have been very useful. In any case I was afraid that if I asked her about them I would seem to be going to visit her only when I happened to need something from her, at a time when I was regularly refusing several of her invitations every week. She was not the only person to invite me so persistently. Certainly, she and other women had always been very welcoming to me. But my reclusive life had undoubtedly multiplied their interest tenfold. It seems as if in society life, a trivial reflection of the realm of love, the best way to make oneself sought after is to be hard to find. A man mentions all the points to his credit that he can think of in order to appeal to a woman; he keeps changing his clothes, tries to look his best, and she takes no notice of him, while another, whom he deceives, before whom he appears in disarray and whom he takes no trouble to please, is indissolubly attached to him. In the same way, if a man felt that society took too little notice of him, I should not advise him to pay still more calls, to have a still more splendid turn-out, I should tell him to refuse all invitations, to live shut away in his room, to admit no one, and that he would then see people queuing outside his door. Or rather, I should not give him this advice. For this method of achieving social success works only in the same way as the similar method of making oneself loved, that is if one does not adopt it deliberately, but, say, keeps to one's room because one is seriously ill, or believes oneself so, or has a mistress shut up with one whom one prefers to all the rest of the world (or all of these things); the world, knowing nothing of this woman, and simply because you withhold yourself from it, will see in that a perfect reason to prefer you to all the others who force themselves upon it, and to seek you out.

'Speaking of dresses,' I said to Albertine, 'it's time we thought about ordering your Fortuny dress.' And certainly, given how long she had wanted these dresses, the time she would spend choosing them with me, the space she had already made for them not only in her wardrobe but in her imagination, the way in which, before choosing them from among many others, she would dwell lovingly on every detail, they would mean more to her than to a rich woman who has more dresses than she wants and does not even look at them. Even so, despite the smile with which Albertine thanked me, saying, 'You are sweet,' I noticed how tired, even sad, she looked. Sometimes, as we waited for the dresses she had chosen to be ready, I borrowed some others, sometimes just the fabrics, and dressed Albertine in them, draped them over her, and watched her parade round my room with the majesty of a doge's consort or of a mannequin. The only difficulty was that my enslavement to Paris was made harder to bear by the sight of these robes that made me think of Venice. Certainly, Albertine was much more of a prisoner than I was. And it was strange to think how destiny, which transforms people, had been able to pass through the walls of her prison and change her very essence, turning the young girl of Balbec into a dutiful and tedious captive. No, the prison walls had not been able to stop this influence passing through; indeed, it was perhaps they who had produced it. She was no longer the same Albertine because she was no longer, as she had been in Balbec, constantly in flight on her bicycle, unfindable because of the number of tiny beaches where she might decide to stay with a friend, and where, furthermore, her lies made her even more impossible to reach; because, now imprisoned in my house, she was no longer what she had been at Balbec, on the beach, even when I was able to find her there, no longer the elusive, crafty, careful being whose presence was extended by all the lovers' meetings that she was so clever at concealing, the meetings that made me love her because they made me suffer, because behind her offhand manner to others and her meaningless replies, one could sense yesterday's meeting and the one planned for tomorrow, framed for me in distance and deception. Because the wind no longer billowed in her garments, because, above all, I had cut her wings, she had ceased to be a Victory, she was a heavy slave of whom I wished to be rid.

So, to change the direction of my thoughts, rather than beginning a game of cards or draughts with Albertine, I would ask her to play some music for me. I would stay in bed and she would go to the other end of the room and sit at the pianola, between the uprights of the book-case. She chose either pieces that were entirely new to me, or others that she had played only once or twice, for, as she came to know me better, she realized that I liked to give my attention only to things that were obscure to me and to be able, at successive hearings, to make connections, as they became clearer in the growing but, alas, foreign and denaturing light of my intelligence, between the fragmentary and broken lines of the overall construction, which at first had been almost entirely hidden in mist. She recognized and, I think, understood the mental pleasure which I took, at the first few hearings, in this work of modelling an initially formless nebula. As she played, the only part of the complex structure of Albertine's hair that I could see was a heart-shaped black twist of hair, applied along her ear like the knot of ribbons of a Velázquez infanta. Just as the third dimension of this angel-musician was supplied by the manifold distances between the various points in the past which her memory occupied in me and the various organs of memory, from sight to the most inward sensations of my being, which allowed me to enter into the hidden depths of hers, so the music she was playing also had its depth, produced by the unequal visibility of the different phrases, according to whether I had yet managed to throw light on them and connect up the various lines of a construction which at first had seemed to me almost entirely lost in the fog. Albertine knew that she could please me by presenting to my thought only things which were still obscure and giving me the task of modelling these nebulae. She guessed that on the third or fourth hearing my intelligence would have mastered all the parts of the piece, and consequently placed them at the same distance from me: there would be no more work to be done on them, they would all be laid out, motionless, on a single plane. She did not, however, move at once on to a new piece, for perhaps without quite understanding the work that was going on within me, she knew that at the moment when the action of my intelligence had managed to dispel the mystery of a work, it was very unusual for her not to have gathered, in return for her tedious labour, this or that useful observation. And by the time Albertine said, 'Let's give this roll to Françoise to take and change for another one,' there was often no doubt one less piece of music in the world for me, but one truth more.

I was now so convinced that it would be absurd to be jealous of Mlle Vinteuil and her friend, since Albertine was making no efforts to see them again, and among all the holiday plans we had discussed had, of her own accord, rejected Combray, which is so close to Montjouvain, that I often asked Albertine to play for me, without its making me suffer, some of Vinteuil's music. Only once had this music of Vinteuil been an indirect cause of jealousy in me. It was when Albertine, who knew that I had heard it played at Mme Verdurin's by Morel, spoke to me about him one evening, showing a strong desire to go and hear him play, and to be introduced to him. This was just two days after I had heard about the letter, which M. de Charlus had intercepted, from Léa to Morel. I wondered if perhaps Léa had spoken to Albertine about him. I recalled with horror the words 'dirty girl', 'kinky slut'. But, just because in this way Vinteuil's music was painfully linked to Léa – and not to Mlle Vinteuil and her friend – when the suffering caused by Léa was relieved, I was able to listen to the music without pain. In the music I had heard at Mme Verdurin's, certain phrases which I had not noticed at the time, mere formless larvae, now grew into dazzling, complex structures; and some which I had barely distinguished from the others, which at best had seemed to me ugly, became my friends, like those people to whom we do not 'take' at first, and of whom we could never believe that they will turn out as they do when we come to know them well. Between these two states there was a real transmutation. On the other hand, some phrases which had been distinct even the first time, but which I had not recognized in this position, I could now identify with phrases in other works, like the phrase from the *Religious Variations* for organ which at Mme Verdurin's had passed unnoticed in the septet, in which, however, like a saint who had come down the sanctuary steps, she found herself mingling with the fairies more familiar to the musician. On the other hand, the 'bells at midday' phrase which had seemed to me too unmelodic, too mechanically rhythmical in its heavy-footed joy, was now the one I loved most, whether it was that I had become used to its ugliness, or that I had discovered its beauty. This reaction to the initial disappointment caused by masterpieces can, indeed, be attributed either to a weakening of our original impression, or to the effort required to arrive at the truth. Two hypotheses that arise again in relation to all important questions, the questions of the reality of Art, of Reality itself, of the Eternity of the soul: we have to choose between them; and in the case of Vinteuil's music, one was faced with the choice at every moment, in a variety of forms. For example, this music seemed to me something more true than all known books. Sometimes I thought that the reason was that the things we feel in life are not experienced in the form of ideas, and so their translation into literature, an intellectual process, may give an account of them, explain them, analyse them, but cannot recreate them as music does, its sounds seeming to take on the inflections of our being, to reproduce that inner, extreme point of sensation which is the thing that causes us the specific ecstasy we feel from time to time and which, when we say 'What a beautiful day! What beautiful sunshine!', is not conveyed at all to our neighbour, in whom the same sun and the same weather set off quite different vibrations. In Vinteuil's music there were some of these visions which it is impossible to express and almost forbidden to dwell upon, since, when at the moment of falling asleep we feel the caress of their unreal spell, at that very moment, when reason has already left us, our eyes close and, before we have time to recognize not only the invisible but the ineffable, we fall asleep. It seemed to me, when I gave myself up to the hypothesis that art might be real, that music could convey not just the simple, nervous excitement of a fine day or a night of opium, but a more real, more productive ecstasy, or so I felt. But it is impossible that a sculpture, a piece of music which gives us an emotion that we feel to be higher, purer, truer, should not correspond to a certain spiritual reality, otherwise life would have no meaning. Thus, nothing came closer than a fine phrase of Vinteuil's to the particular pleasure which I had sometimes experienced in my life, before the spires of Martinville, for example, or certain trees on a road at Balbec, or more simply, as at the beginning of this work, when drinking a certain mouthful of tea. As the tea had done, the multiple sensations of light, the airy sounds, the noisy colours which Vinteuil sent us from the world in which he composed, presented to my imagination, forcefully but too rapidly for it to take it in, something which I could compare to the perfumed silk of a geranium. The only thing is, while in a memory the vagueness can be if not eliminated at least made more precise by pinpointing the circumstances which explain why a certain taste recalls sensations of light, since the vague sensations conveyed by Vinteuil came not from a memory but from an impression (like that of the steeples of Martinville), one would have had to explain the geranium fragrance of his music not by a material resemblance but by its profound equivalent, the unknown, multicoloured festival (of which his works seemed to be disparate fragments, dazzling shards with scarlet fracture lines), the mode according to which he 'heard' and projected the universe. This unknown quality of a unique world, which no other musician had ever shown us before, was perhaps, I said to Albertine, the most authentic proof of genius, much more than the content of the work itself. 'In literature too? Albertine asked. – In literature too.' And, thinking again about the repetitiveness of Vinteuil's work, I explained to Albertine that great writers have only ever written a single work, or rather, refracted through different media a single beauty which each of them has brought to the world. 'If it weren't so late, dear, I would say to her, I should point it out to you in all the writers you read when I am asleep, I could show you the same sameness as in Vinteuil. Those repeated phrases, you're beginning to recognize them, dearest, just as I do, the same ones in the sonata, the septet, in the other works too, well, in Barbey d'Aurevilly[87] it would be the revelation of a hidden reality in a physical trace, the red colouring of the Woman Bewitched, of Aimée de Spens, of La Clotte, the hand in "The Crimson Curtain", the old customs, old habits, old words, the strange, ancient trades that symbolize the Past, the oral history retailed by the shepherds in the mirror episode, the noble Norman cities with their aura of England, but pretty as a Scottish village, the curses put on people which they cannot throw off, La Vellini, the shepherd, a recurring sensation of anxiety in a landscape, whether it is the wife looking for her husband in *An Old Mistress*, or the husband of *The Woman Bewitched* searching the moor, and the Woman Bewitched herself coming out of Mass. And the pattern of the stone-cutters in Thomas Hardy's novels – that's Vinteuil's recurring phrases again.'

Vinteuil's phrases made me think of the little phrase and I told Albertine how it had been, as it were, the national anthem of Swann's and Odette's love, 'Gilberte's parents. You used to know her, didn't you? You said she had a reputation. Didn't she try to have an affair with you? She mentioned you to me. – Yes, her parents used to send the carriage to collect her from school when the weather was too bad, she gave me a lift once, I think, and she kissed me,' she said after a moment's thought, laughing as if the confidence were amusing. 'She suddenly asked me if I liked women.' (But if she only thought she remembered being taken home by Gilberte, how could she recall so precisely that Gilberte had asked her such a strange question?) 'I don't know why, I wanted to play a joke on her, I said yes.' (You would have thought Albertine was afraid I might have heard the story from Gilberte, and did not want me to catch her in a lie.) 'But we didn't do anything.' (Strange, if they had confided in each other in this way, that they should have done nothing, especially as before that, according to Albertine, they had kissed in the carriage.) 'She took me home like that four or five times, maybe a bit more, and that's all.' I had great difficulty in not asking her further questions, but, restraining myself so as not to seem to attach any importance to the matter, I came back to Hardy's stone-cutters. 'You remember them in *Jude the Obscure*, but do you remember how in *The Well-Beloved* the blocks of stone that the father quarries on the island are brought by water and piled up in the son's workshop where they become statues; how in *A Pair of Blue Eyes* there are the parallel graves, and the parallel lines of the ship, and the row of wagons where the lovers are next to the corpse, and the parallelism between *The Well-Beloved*, where the hero loves three women, and *A Pair of Blue Eyes*, where the woman loves three men, and so on, all those novels that could be superimposed on each other, like the houses piled vertically, one above the other, on the rocky soil of the island? I can't talk to you just now about the greatest writers, but you would find in Stendhal a certain feeling of height allied to spirituality, there is the high place where Julien Sorel is imprisoned, the top of the tower where Fabrice is held, the steeple where the Abbé Blanes studies astrology and from which Fabrice has such a wonderful view. You say you've been looking at some paintings by Vermeer, then you can see that they're all fragments of a single world, that it is always, whatever the genius recreating it, the same table, the same carpet, the same women, the same new and unique beauty, a complete enigma at this period when there is nothing else like it, nothing to explain it, unless one tries to relate him to other painters by his choice of subjects, while recognizing the particular, personal impression made by his colour. Well, we find just such a new beauty, the same in each one of his works, in Dostoevsky: isn't Dostoevsky's woman (just as peculiar to him as Rembrandt's was to him), with her mysterious face whose appealing beauty suddenly changes, as if she had only been playing at goodness, into a terrifying insolence (even though underneath it seems that she is good after all), isn't she always the same, whether it is Nastasya Philippovna writing love letters to Aglae and admitting that she hates her, or in a visit-scene exactly identical to that one – and also to the one where Nastasya Philippovna insults Gania's parents – Grushenka,[88] having been as gentle in Katerina Ivanovna's house as Katerina had expected her to be terrifying, suddenly revealing her aggression, insulting Katerina Ivanovna (even though Grushenka herself is essentially good)? Grushenka, Nastasya, figures as original, as mysterious, not just as Carpaccio's courtesans, but as Rembrandt's Bathsheba. Notice that he did not have a clear understanding of that striking, double face, those sudden explosions of pride which make a woman different from her normal self ("You are not like that," says Myshkin to Nastasya during the visit to Gania's parents, and Alyosha could have said the same to Grushenka during the visit to Katerina Ivanovna). And on the contrary when he tries to have an "idea for a scene", they are always stupid and would produce, at best, one of the pictures in which Munkácsy tries to represent a condemned prisoner at the moment of, etc., the Blessed Virgin at the moment of, etc. But to return to the new beauty which Dostoevsky brought into the world, as with Vermeer there is the creation of something like a soul, of a certain colour of draperies and settings, Dostoevsky does not create only people but their dwellings, and the house of the killing in *Crime and Punishment*, with its *dvornik*, is not so marvellous as that masterpiece of murder settings in Dostoevsky, the dark house, so long, so tall, so vast, where Rogosin kills Nastasya Philippovna. This new, terrible beauty a house can have, the new, hybrid beauty of a woman's face, that is the one great thing Dostoevsky brought into the world, and the comparisons literary critics may make between him and Gogol, or him and Paul de Kock[89] for that matter, are completely without interest, since they have nothing to do with this secret beauty. What is more, I have talked about the same scene recurring in different novels, but within the same novel scenes and characters can be repeated, if the novel is very long. I could easily give you an example from *War and Peace*, there's a particular scene in a carriage . . . – I don't want to interrupt you, but as I see you're moving on from Dostoevsky, I'm afraid I'll forget what you've been saying. Darling, what did you mean the other day when you said, "That's the Dostoevsky side of Mme de Sévigné"? I admit I didn't understand. The two seem so different. – Come here, little girl, and let me give you a kiss for being so good at remembering what I say. You can go back to the pianola afterwards. I admit that what I said then might have sounded stupid. But I said it for two reasons. One, a particular one. Mme de Sévigné sometimes, like Elstir or Dostoevsky, instead of presenting things in the logical order, that is to say starting with the cause, begins by showing us the effect, the illusion which strikes us. That is how Dostoevsky presents his characters. Their actions have as misleading an appearance as those Elstir paintings where the sea seems to be in the sky. We are astonished to learn afterwards that the man who seemed so sly is admirable underneath. Or the opposite. – Yes, but an example from Mme de Sévigné, please. – Well, this is a pretty far-fetched one, I replied, laughing, but here is a description.[90]

'But did he ever murder anyone, Dostoevsky? All of his novels that I've read could be called *The Story of a Crime*. He's obsessed with the subject, it's not natural always to be talking about it. – I don't think so, Albertine dear, I don't know much about his life. Certainly, like everyone else, he had experience of sin in one form or another, probably in a form punished by the law. In that sense he must have had a criminal side, like his heroes, and they of course are not wholly criminal, there are always extenuating circumstances. And perhaps he didn't need to be a criminal. I am not a novelist, but it is possible that writers of fiction are attracted by certain modes of life that they have not experienced themselves. If I come to Versailles with you as we planned, I will show you the portrait of the most honourable of men, an excellent husband, Choderlos de Laclos, who wrote the most appallingly perverse book, and facing it that of Mme de Genlis,[91] who wrote moral tales and, not content with deceiving the Duchesse d'Orléans, tortured her by turning her children against her. I do admit that Dostoevsky's preoccupation with murder has something extraordinary about it that makes me feel very remote from him. I'm already astonished to hear Baudelaire say,

> Si le viol, le poison, le poignard, l'incendie . . .
> C'est que notre âme, hélas! n'est pas assez hardie.[92]

But at least I can believe that Baudelaire is being insincere. But Dostoevsky . . . I feel as far away as possible from all that, unless there are parts of me that I don't know about, for one realizes oneself only one piece at a time. In Dostoevsky I find impossibly deep abysses, but only at some points of the human soul. But he is a great creator. First, the world that he describes seems genuinely to have been created for him. All those recurring buffoons, Lebedev, Karamazov, Ivolgin, Segrev, that incredible procession of fools, is a humanity more fantastic than the background figures in Rembrandt's *Night Watch*. But perhaps it is fantastic only in the same way, thanks to the costumes and lighting, and in fact is everyday and familiar. In any case it is full of truths, profound and unique, and belongs only to Dostoevsky. It almost seems, that series of buffoons, like a stock stage role which has ceased to exist, like certain characters in ancient comedy, and yet, how well they reveal certain unchanging aspects of the human soul! What I can't bear is the solemn way in which people talk and write about Dostoevsky. Have you noticed the part self-love and pride play in his characters? You would say that for him love and the wildest hatred, kindness and treachery, timidity and insolence, are only two states of the same nature, as self-love and pride prevent Aglae, Nastasya, the captain who has his beard pulled by Mitya, and Krassotkin, Alyosha's friend-cum-enemy, from showing themselves as they "truly are" in reality. But there are many other fine things. I know very little about his books. But can't we call it something simple and sculptural, worthy of the most ancient art, a frieze interrupted and resumed in which Vengeance and Expiation unfold their story, that tale of old Karamazov making the madwoman pregnant and the mysterious, unexplained, animal urge which drives the mother, the unwitting instrument of destiny's revenge, in obedience to her mama's instinct and perhaps also to a kind of resentment combined with physical gratitude to her violator, to go back and give birth at Karamazov's house? This is the first episode, mysterious, grandiose, majestic, like a Creation of Woman among the sculptures of Orvieto. And it is balanced by the second episode, more than twenty years later, the murder of old Karamazov by the madwoman's son, Smerdyakov, followed soon after by an action equally mysterious, sculptural and inexplicable, as obscurely beautiful and natural as the birth in old Karamazov's garden, Smerdyakov hanging himself, having carried out his crime. As for Dostoevsky, I was not leaving him behind as much as you thought when I spoke of Tolstoy, who imitated him a great deal. And in Dostoevsky there is, in a concentrated form, still turned in on itself and cramped, a lot of what will blossom in Tolstoy. Dostoevsky has that early, morose quality of primitives which their followers will open out. – Oh, darling, if only you weren't so lazy! Can't you see how you make literature so much more interesting than it was when we had to study it; oh, those answers we had to write on *Esther*. "My dear Sir", do you remember?' she said, laughing, not so much to make fun of her teachers and herself, as for the pleasure of finding in her memory, in our shared memory, something already quite old.

But as she talked, and as I thought about Vinteuil, the other hypothesis, the materialist one, that of nothingness, came to the fore in its turn. I began to doubt once more, I said to myself that after all it might be that, even though Vinteuil's phrases seemed to me to be the expression of certain states of the soul – analogous to the one I had experienced on tasting the madeleine soaked in tea – nothing proved that the vagueness of these states was a sign of their profundity, rather than of our inability, so far, to analyse them: there would therefore be nothing more real in them than in others. Still that happiness, that feeling of certainty in happiness, while I drank the cup of tea, or as I breathed in a certain scent of old wood in the Champs-Elysées gardens, was not an illusion. In any case, the spirit of doubt said to me, even if those states are more profound than others in our life, and are unanalysable for that very reason, because they bring into play too many forces of which we are not yet aware, the charm of certain of Vinteuil's phrases may make us think of them because it too is unanalysable, but that does not prove that it has the same depth. The beauty of a musical phrase can easily seem to be the image of or at least to be related to a non-intellectual impression we have had, but only because it too is unintellectual. But why, then, do we feel so strongly the particular profundity of those mysterious phrases which haunt certain quartets and the 'concert' of Vinteuil? In any case, it was not only his music that Albertine played for me; the pianola sometimes served us as a kind of educational (historical and geographical) magic lantern, and on the walls of that room in Paris, better equipped than the old one in Combray, I saw spread out, according as Albertine played some Rameau or some Borodin, now an eighteenth-century tapestry dotted with cherubs on a background of roses, and now the Eastern steppes where sounds are lost in the limitless distances and muffled by the snow. And these fleeting decorations were in fact the only ones in my room, for, even though when I came into my inheritance from Aunt Léonie I had promised myself I would be a collector like Swann, buying pictures and statues, in fact all my money went on horses, a motor-car, dresses for Albertine. But then, did not my room contain a work of art more precious than all those others? It was Albertine herself. I kept looking at her. It was strange for me to think that this was she, she whom I had so long thought it impossible even to meet, who now, a wild animal tamed, a rambling rose for which I had provided the support, the trellis, the framework of her life, sat each day, at home, near me, before the pianola, next to my book-case. Her shoulders, which I had seen low-slung and shifty as she brought home her golf-clubs, now leaned against my books. Her fine legs, which I had marked down on the first day, rightly, as having spent their whole adolescence turning the pedals of a bicycle, rose and fell on those of the pianola, where Albertine, who had acquired an elegance that made her seem all the more mine, as it was I who had provided it, now placed her cloth-of-gold slippers. The fingers which once knew the handlebars now rested on the stops like those of a St Cecilia; her neck, whose roundness, seen from my bed, was full and strong, at that distance and by lamplight seemed pinker, but not so pink as her face turned in profile, to which my gaze, coming from the depths of my being, laden with memories and burning with desire, added such brilliance, such intensity of life that its modelling seemed to detach itself and spin in the air with the same almost magic power as that day, in the hotel at Balbec, when my sight was blurred by my too-great desire to kiss her; I projected each surface of it beyond what I could see, and under the surfaces which hid it from me — eyelids half-closing the eyes, hair hiding the upper part of the cheeks — I felt only the more intensely the geometry of these superimposed planes; the eyes, like two polished opal plaques still trapped in their surrounding ore, had become more lucent than metal while remaining harder than light; they shone, amid the blind matter overhanging them, like the mauve silk wings of a butterfly in a case; and the hair, black and curly, showing different patterns of locks as she turned towards me to ask what she should play next, now a splendid wing, pointed at its tip and broad at its base, black, feathery and triangular, now a mass of three-dimensional curls like a mountain range, powerful and varied, full of ridges, watersheds, precipices, whipped up into a richness and multiplicity that seemed to exceed the normal variety of nature, as if a sculptor were accumulating difficulties so as to show off the suppleness, the dash, the freedom and lifelikeness of his execution, brought out more strongly, by covering and breaking it in places, the lively curve and, as it were, the rotation of the smooth, pink face, which had the shiny yet matt quality of painted wood. And by contrast with such varied relief, by the harmony too that brought them together with the girl, who had adapted her position to their shape and function, the pianola which half-hid her like an organ case, the bookshelves, all that end of the room seemed to be nothing but a candle-lit sanctuary, a crib for this angel-musician, this work of art which presently, by its own gentle magic, would step down from its niche and offer its pink, precious substance to my kisses. But no; Albertine was not at all a work of art for me. I knew what it was to admire a woman from an artistic point of view — I had known Swann. But for my own part I was incapable of seeing any woman, whoever she might be, in this way, having no spirit whatsoever of external observation, never knowing what it was I was looking at, and I was full of wonderment when Swann retrospectively bestowed artistic dignity – by comparing her for me, as he liked to do as a compliment to herself, to some portrait by Luini, or finding in her costume the dress or the jewels of a Giorgione – upon a woman who had seemed to me unremarkable. I had no such inclination. Indeed, to tell the truth, when I began to see Albertine as an angel-musician, a wonderfully patinated statue, a prized possession, I soon became indifferent to her, presently I was bored in her company, but these moments did not last for long. There must be something inaccessible in what we love, something to pursue; we love only what we do not possess, and soon I began once more to realize that I did not possess Albertine. I could see passing through her eyes first hope for, then the memory of, perhaps regret for joys that I could not guess at, joys which she preferred to renounce rather than tell me of them, and of which, seeing only their light reflected in her pupils, I could perceive no more than the late-comer who has not been allowed to enter the theatre and who, his eye glued to the glass panel in the door, can see nothing of what is happening on stage. (I do not know if it was true of her, but it is remarkable, something like a sign in the most irreligious of their continuing belief in good, how all those who deceive us persist in lying to us. We can tell them how their lies hurt us more than the truth would, they can believe us, it is no use: they will still lie to us again a moment later in order to stay consistent with what they originally told us they were, or what they told us we were to them. In the same way, an atheist who wants to go on living will let himself be killed rather than give the lie to his reputation for defiance.) During these hours, I would sometimes see floating around her, in her look, in a passing facial expression, in her smile, the reflection of these inner visions: dwelling on them made her different on those evenings, distant from me as she would not share them with me. 'What are you thinking of, darling? – Nothing.' Sometimes, in response to my complaints that she never told me anything, she would tell me either things that she knew quite well I knew already, things that everyone knew (like those politicians who would not part with the smallest piece of real news, but instead tell you at length about things you read in yesterday's newspaper), or stories lacking in all detail, seeming confidences that were nothing of the kind, about bicycle rides that she went on from Balbec the year before I met her. And it seemed that I had been right originally, when I thought of Albertine as a very loosely brought-up young girl, going on long outings away from home, when I saw, at the mention of these cycle rides, a mysterious smile slowly part Albertine's lips, the same smile that had attracted me to her on those first days, on the promenade at Balbec. She also told me about her cycle rides with girl-friends in the Dutch countryside, of coming back late in the evening to Amsterdam, when a dense crowd of people, all happy, most of whom she knew, filled the streets and the banks of the canals, whose countless, flickering lights I felt I could see reflected in Albertine's gleaming eyes, as if in the uncertain windows of a fast-moving carriage. People speak of aesthetic curiosity: how much more it would deserve the name of indifference, when compared to the painful, tireless curiosity I felt about the places where Albertine had lived, about what she might have been doing on this or that evening, how she had smiled, what she had looked at, the words she had spoken, the kisses she had received! No, the jealousy of Saint-Loup that I had felt one day, even if it had lasted, could never have given me this immense anxiety. This love between women was something too unknown: nothing could allow me to picture with confidence, with precision, its pleasures, its very nature. How many different people, how many places (even places not involving her directly, vague places of entertainment where she might have tasted some pleasure, places where crowds of people go, where they brush against one) Albertine – like someone who, ushering a whole group of people, all her friends, past the ticket-desk in front of her, gets them all into the theatre – had ushered in from the fringes of my imagination and my memory, where I was taking no notice of them, and installed in my heart! Now my knowledge of them was an internal thing, immediate, spasmodic, painful. Love is space and time made apprehensible to the heart.

And yet perhaps had I been entirely faithful, I should not have suffered so from infidelities which I should have been incapable of imagining. But what I could not bear to imagine in Albertine was my own unceasing desire to attract new women, to sketch out new novels in which they would figure; it was the thought of her casting her eye, as I had not been able to restrain myself from doing the other day, even when seated beside her, at the young girl cyclists sitting at the tables in the Bois de Boulogne. Just as one can know only oneself, one could almost say that one can be jealous only of oneself. Observation is of little use. Only from one's own pleasure can one derive both knowledge and pain.

At some moments, in Albertine's eyes, in the sudden flush that lit up her complexion, I felt something like a flash of warmth pass surreptitiously through regions more inaccessible to me than the heavens: the regions where her memories moved, memories unknown to me. Then the beauty which, when I thought of the successive years in which I had known Albertine, either on the beach at Balbec or here in Paris, I now found in her, and which was due to the fact that my friend now existed for me on so many different planes and contained in herself so many out-of-reach days, this beauty now seemed almost unbearably painful. Then behind her rosy, blushing face I felt a great gulf opening up, the inexhaustible space of the evenings when I had not known Albertine. I could take Albertine on my knees, hold her head in my hands, I could stroke her, run my hands all over her, but, just as if I had been handling a stone enclosing the salt of immemorial oceans or the light of a star, I felt that I was touching only the closed outer casing of a being which on the inside was in touch with the infinite. How I suffered from the position in which careless Nature placed us, when it instituted the separation of bodies from each other, and forgot to provide for the interpenetration of souls! And I realized that Albertine was not, even for me (for if her body was in the power of my body, her thought constantly escaped from my thought's grasp), the wonderful captive with whom I had thought to enrich my dwelling, while concealing her presence there, even from those who came to visit me and did not suspect her presence at the end of the corridor in a nearby room, as perfectly as did the character in the story, of whom no one suspected that he had the Princess of China shut up in a bottle;[93] no, by setting me to the pressing, cruel and endless task of unearthing the past she became something more like a great goddess of Time. And though I may have wasted years of my life and much of my fortune on her, provided I can say, though nothing is less certain, alas, that she herself lost nothing by it, then I need have no regrets. Certainly a solitary life would have been better for me, more productive and less painful. But the collector's life which Swann urged on me, which M. de Charlus reproached me with neglecting, when with a mixture of wit, insolence and taste he said, 'How ugly your house is!', what statues, what pictures long pursued and finally possessed, or even, at best, disinterestedly contemplated, could have given me, as did the little wound which was quite quick to heal, but which was soon opened again by the unthinking clumsiness of Albertine, of outsiders, or of my own thoughts, access to that way out of oneself, that private path which however links up with the high road where everything passes that we begin to know only from the day when we have first suffered by it: the life of others?

Sometimes the moonlight was so beautiful that barely an hour after Albertine had gone to bed I would go to her bedside to ask her to look out of the window. I am sure that was what made me go to her bedroom, not any wish to make sure that she was actually in it. How likely was it that she could have escaped, or would have wished to do so? It would have required a most unlikely collusion with Françoise. In the dark room I could see nothing but a frail diadem of black hair on the whiteness of the pillow. But I could hear Albertine's breathing. She was sleeping so deeply that I hesitated to go up to her bed; I sat on the edge of it; her sleep flowed on with the same gentle murmur. What is impossible to describe is the gaiety of her awakening. I would kiss her, shake her. Suddenly she would be awake, but without a moment's transition she would burst out laughing, wind her arms round my neck and say, 'I was just wondering if you would come,' and laugh affectionately all the more. You would have said that her lovely head, as she slept, was full of nothing but gaiety, tenderness and laughter. And waking her had been simply like opening a ripe fruit, sending the thirst-quenching juice spurting into one's mouth.

Meanwhile winter was coming to an end; the fine weather returned, and often, soon after Albertine had said good-night to me, when my room, my curtains, the wall above the curtains were still in pitch darkness, in the nearby convent garden I could hear, rich and precise in the silence as the sound of a church harmonium, the modulations of an unknown bird singing matins in the Lydian mode, and sounding in my darkness the rich, brilliant note of the sun he could already see. Soon the nights shortened, and before what used to be the hours of morning, I could already see encroaching upon my window-curtains the steadily growing whiteness of the day. If I resigned myself to letting Albertine go on living this life in which, despite her denials, I knew she felt herself to be a prisoner, it was only because every day I was sure that the next day I should be able to begin work and at the same time start getting up, going out, preparing for our departure to some country house which we should buy, where Albertine would be more free to live the country or seaside life, sailing or hunting, which she would enjoy.

However, the next day, that past time which I alternately loved and hated in Albertine (just as, when it is the present, each of us out of self-interest, or politeness, or pity, works at spinning a web of lies between it and ourselves, lies which we take for truth) came back: it would happen that, in retrospect, one of the hours which made it up, and even one of those that I had thought I knew all about, was suddenly presented to me in a new aspect which she did nothing to conceal, and which was quite different from the one under which it had originally appeared. Behind a certain look, instead of the kind thought which I had imagined I saw at the time, a hitherto unsuspected desire was revealed, alienating from me another part of Albertine's heart, which I had thought completely attuned to mine. For example, when Andrée had left Balbec in the month of July, Albertine had never told me that she expected to see her again soon; and I thought that they had met again even sooner than Albertine expected, since, because of my great sadness on the night of the fourteenth of September, she had left Balbec for my sake and come straight back to Paris. When she had arrived, on the fifteenth, I had suggested she go and see Andrée and had asked her, 'Was she pleased to see you again?' Now Mme Bontemps called to bring something or other for Albertine, I spoke to her for a moment and said that Albertine had gone out with Andrée. 'They've gone to the country. – Yes, Mme Bontemps replied, Albertine is easy to please where the country is concerned. Three years ago, nothing would do but she must go every day to the Buttes-Chaumont.' At this mention of the Buttes-Chaumont, where Albertine had told me she had never been, my breathing stopped for a moment. Reality is the cleverest of our enemies. It directs its attacks at those points in our heart where we were not expecting them, and where we had prepared no defence. Had Albertine been lying to her aunt then, when she said every day that she was going to the Buttes-Chaumont, or to me when she said that she had never been there? 'Fortunately, Mme Bontemps continued, poor Andrée will soon be leaving for a healthier part of the countryside, for real country, she needs it, she looks so poorly. It's true that last summer she didn't get all the fresh air she needs. Remember, she left Balbec at the end of July expecting to come back in September, then her brother put his knee out and she couldn't come back.' So Albertine had been expecting her back in Balbec and had not told me! It is true that that made her suggestion of coming back all the kinder. Unless ... 'Yes, I remember Albertine telling me about it ... (this was untrue). When was it the accident happened? I've got it all a bit mixed up. – Well, in one sense it happened just at the right moment, for one day later their lease on the villa would have started, and Andrée's grandmother would have had to pay a month's rent for nothing. He broke his leg on the fourteenth of September, she managed to wire Albertine on the morning of the fifteenth to say that she wasn't coming, and Albertine sent word to the agency. One more day, and they'd have had to pay up to the fifteenth of October.' In other words, when Albertine changed her mind and said, 'Let's leave this evening,' she had in her mind's eye a place which I had never seen, Andrée's grandmother's flat, where, as soon as we got back, she would be able to meet her friend again, the friend whom, unknown to me, she had been expecting to see again soon at Balbec. I had tried to explain the kind words with which she agreed to come back with me, which so contrasted with her stubborn refusal shortly before, by thinking that her kind heart was reasserting itself. They were simply the reflection of a change in a situation of which we are unaware, which is the whole secret of a change in the conduct of women who do not love us. They obstinately refuse to see us tomorrow, because they are tired, because their grandfather is insisting that they dine with him. 'But come round afterwards,' we insist. 'He always keeps me very late. Perhaps he'll take me home.' It is simple: they have arranged to meet someone they like better. Suddenly he is not available. And they come and tell us how sorry they are to have hurt our feelings, they have put off their grandfather and will spend the evening with us: there is nothing they want to do more. I should have recognized these phrases in Albertine's language to me the day I left Balbec. But perhaps they are not all I should have recognized: to interpret her language correctly, I should have remembered two particular traits of Albertine's character.

Two traits of Albertine's character came back to me at that moment, one to comfort and the other to appal me, for we can find everything in our memory: it is a kind of pharmacy or chemical laboratory, where one's hand may fall at any moment on a sedative drug or a dangerous poison. The first trait, the comforting one, was her habit of using a single action to give pleasure to more than one person: this use of her actions for multiple purposes was characteristic of Albertine. It was very like her to return to Paris (the fact that Andrée would not be coming back to Balbec could have made it inconvenient for her to stay there, without its being necessarily true that she could not live without Andrée), and then to see in this single journey the chance of touching the hearts of two people both of whom she sincerely loved: me, by making me think her purpose was not to leave me alone, to spare me suffering, out of devotion to me, and Andrée, by persuading her that since she would now not be returning to Balbec, Albertine did not want to stay there a moment longer, having stayed on only in the hope of seeing her, and was now rushing back to her side. Now, Albertine's departure with me in fact followed so closely both upon my unhappiness and wish to return to Paris, and on Andrée's telegram, that it was quite natural that both Andrée and I, knowing nothing, she of my sadness and I of her telegram, should have thought that Albertine's decision to leave was caused by the only factor that each of us was aware of, and upon which it followed so immediately and so unexpectedly. If this were true, I could still believe that Albertine's real object had been to come with me, but that she had not wished to lose the opportunity of making Andrée feel grateful to her. But unfortunately I also remembered at almost the same time another trait of Albertine's character, which was the alacrity with which she seized upon any opportunity of pleasure. Now I remembered, when she had made her decision to leave, how impatient she had been to reach the train, how she had hurried past the hotel manager, who by trying to speak to us might have made us miss the bus, the conspiratorial shrugs of her shoulders which had so touched me when, in the 'slowcoach', M. de Cambremer asked if we could not wait and leave a week later. Yes, what she saw in her mind's eye at that moment, what made her so desperate to leave, what she could not wait to see again, was an empty flat which I had once seen, belonging to Andrée's grandmother, a luxurious flat left in the keeping of one old valet, full of light, but so empty, so silent that the sun seemed to be putting dust-covers over the sofa, over the armchairs in the bedrooms where Andrée and Albertine would ask the respectful caretaker, naïve or perhaps knowing, to let them lie down. I could see it all the time now, empty, with a bed or a sofa, an easily deceived or complaisant guardian, the place where, every time Albertine looked busy and preoccupied, she was going to meet her friend, who would no doubt have arrived before her since she was less supervised. I had never thought before about this flat, which now took on a hideous beauty for me. The unknown element in the lives of human beings is like that of nature, which every new scientific discovery diminishes but does not eliminate. A jealous man exasperates the woman he loves by denying her countless unimportant pleasures. But the pleasures that mean the most to her she hides in places where, even at the moments when he thinks his intelligence is being the most perspicacious, and when other people are keeping him most effectively informed, he never thinks of looking.

But at least, in any case, Albertine was going to leave. But I did not wish her to be able to despise me for having been so easily deceived by herself and Andrée. One day soon I would tell her I knew. And thus perhaps I would force her to speak to me more frankly, by showing her that I knew even about things that she had kept hidden from me. But I did not want to talk to her about it yet, first of all because, so soon after her aunt's visit, she would have realized where my information came from, would have shut off that source and had no need to fear unknown ones. Then because I did not wish to take the risk, before I was perfectly certain of being able to keep Albertine as long as I wanted, of making her so angry that she would want to leave me. It is true that if I reasoned, sought the truth and foretold the future according to her own words, which always expressed agreement with everything I planned to do, told me how much she loved this life, how little hardship her confinement imposed on her, I could not doubt that she would stay with me for ever. I even found the idea highly tiresome, I felt life and the world which I had never explored slipping away from me, exchanged for a woman in whom I could no longer find anything new. I could not even go to Venice where, while I was in bed, I would be tortured by the thought of the advances the gondolier might be making to her, or the people in the hotel, or the Venetian women. But if I based my reasoning on the other hypothesis, the one which was supported not by Albertine's words, but by silences, looks, blushes, sulks and even fits of anger which I could easily have shown her were groundless but which I preferred to seem not to have noticed, then I said to myself that she found this life intolerable, that at every moment she found herself deprived of what she loved, and that inevitably she would leave me one day. All I wanted, if she was to do so, was to be able to choose the moment, one when it would not cause me too much pain, and at a time of year when she would not be able to go to any of the places where I imagined her misconduct occurring, not to Amsterdam, nor to Andrée's, nor to Mlle Vinteuil's, even though it is true she would be able to see them all again a few months later. But by then I should have regained my self-control and it would all have become a matter of indifference to me. In any case, before thinking of separation I should have to wait for the little relapse to pass which I had suffered on learning why Albertine, at a few hours' interval, had first not wanted to leave Balbec and then to leave it at once; I had to leave time for the disappearance of the symptoms which could only fade from now on, provided I did not learn anything else new, but which were still too acute not to add pain and difficulty to the operation I now saw was inevitable, but which was not yet urgent and would be much better carried out after a suitable interval. I should be able to choose the moment; for if she wanted to leave before I thought it right, when she told me she had had enough of this life, it would be time enough to think of countering her reasons, to give her more freedom, to promise her some treat in the near future which she herself would want to wait for, or even, if I had to have recourse to her feelings, to admit my own unhappiness. I had nothing to worry about from that point of view, though I was not being very logical in my thinking. For, following a chain of reasoning in which I chose not to pay any attention to the things she was saying and of which she was warning me, I assumed that, when she had decided to leave, she would tell me her reasons for doing so and would allow me to answer and overcome them.

I could feel that my life with Albertine was nothing but, on the one hand, when I was not jealous, boredom, and on the other, when I was, suffering. Even supposing it contained happiness, that could not last. In the same spirit of wisdom which inspired me at Balbec, the night we were so happy after Mme de Cambremer's visit, I wanted to leave her because I knew that in the long run things could never be better. However, even now, I imagined that the memory I should keep of her would be like a kind of vibrating echo, held by a pedal, of the last moment of our separation. So I wanted to choose a gentle moment, so that that would be the one to go on echoing in me. I must not be too difficult, not wait too long. I had to be wise. And yet, having waited so long, it would be crazy not to make myself wait a few days longer, until the acceptable moment came, rather than see her go with that angry feeling that I had had in the past when Mama left my bedside without saying a second good-night, or when she said good-bye to me at the station. I lavished more and more presents on her. Among the Fortuny dresses, we had finally decided on a blue and gold one lined with pink, which they had just finished making. And I had also ordered the other five which she had reluctantly rejected in favour of that one.

Still, at the beginning of spring, when two months had passed since her aunt's revelation, I let myself be carried away by anger one evening. It was the very evening when Albertine had put on the blue and gold Fortuny dress for the first time; calling up images of Venice, it made me even more conscious of everything I was giving up for Albertine, who was not in the least grateful for my sacrifice. I had never seen Venice, but I had been dreaming of it constantly, ever since the Easter holiday I had been supposed to spend there as a child, and even before that, since Swann had given me the engravings of Giorgione and photographs of Giotto at Combray. The Fortuny dress that Albertine was wearing that evening seemed to me like the tempting shadow of that invisible Venice. It was overrun with Arabic ornament like Venice, like the Venetian palazzi hiding like sultanesses behind a pierced veil of stone, like the bindings of the Ambrosiana library, like the columns whose oriental birds, signifying both life and death, were repeated in the shimmering of the fabric, of a dark blue which as I watched turned into malleable gold, by the same transmutations which, ahead of the advancing gondola, turn the azure of the Grand Canal into flaming metal. And the sleeves were lined with a cherry pink which is so characteristically Venetian that it is called Tiepolo pink.

Earlier in the day, Françoise had let slip in my hearing that Albertine was not happy with anything, that when I let her know that I would be going out with her, or that I would not, that the car would be coming to collect her, or that it would not, she almost shrugged her shoulders and her reply was barely polite. That evening, when I felt that she was in a bad mood and the first really hot day had made me edgy, I could not control my anger and reproached her with her ingratitude: 'Yes, you can ask anyone, I cried at the top of my voice, ask Françoise, they all say the same.' But I immediately remembered Albertine saying once how frightening she found me when I was angry, and how she had applied the lines of *Esther* to me:

> Jugez combien ce front irrité contre moi
> Dans mon âme troublée a dû jeter d'émoi . . .
> Hélas! sans frissonner quel cœur audacieux
> Soutiendrait les éclairs qui partent de vos yeux?[94]

I felt ashamed of my violence. And to reverse the effect of my action, without its seeming a defeat, so that my peace should be an armed peace leaving her something to fear, and because it seemed to me useful to show that I did not fear a separation, and thus to prevent her from thinking of one: 'I'm sorry, Albertine dear, I'm ashamed to be so violent, it really makes me despair. If we cannot get on together any more, if we have to leave each other, it mustn't be like this, this is unworthy of us. We shall separate if we must, but first of all I must humbly ask your forgiveness, with all my heart.' I thought that to put things right, and to make sure that she intended to stay for the next period, at least until Andrée had left, which would be in three weeks' time, it would be a good idea to begin the next day to plan some greater-than-usual treat for her, to happen quite some time in the future; so, since I was going to wipe out the offence I had just given her, maybe this would be the moment to show that I knew more of her life than she realized. Her displeasure would be wiped out the next day by my kindness, but the warning would remain in her mind. 'Yes, dear little Albertine, forgive me if I have been violent. But I am not quite so guilty as you think. There are unkind people who are trying to come between us, I've never wanted to talk to you about it so as not to hurt you, and I was finally too upset by some of their wicked stories.' And, intending to make the most of my ability to show that I knew the story behind her departure from Balbec: 'For example, you did know that Mlle Vinteuil was supposed to be coming to Mme Verdurin's the afternoon you went to the Trocadéro.' She blushed. 'Yes, I did. – But can you swear to me that you weren't meaning to start up your relationship with her again? – Of course I can. And anyway, what do you mean, "start again"? I never had any relationship with her, I swear it.' I hated to hear Albertine lying to me like this, denying the obvious truth which her blushing had only too clearly confirmed. Her deviousness appalled me. And yet, as her words contained a protestation of innocence which I was unconsciously ready to accept, they hurt me less than her sincerity when I asked her, 'Can you at least swear to me that the pleasure of seeing Mlle Vinteuil again had nothing to do with your wish to go to the Verdurins' party?', and she replied, 'No, I can't swear that. I was pleased at the thought of seeing Mlle Vinteuil again.' A second before, I had been angry with her for trying to hide her relationship with Mlle Vinteuil, and now her admission of pleasure at the thought of seeing her was like a hammer-blow. Certainly when Albertine had said to me, as I arrived back from the Verdurins', 'Wasn't Mlle Vinteuil supposed to be there?' she had brought back all my pain by proving to me that she had known of it. But no doubt I had explained the whole thing to myself afterwards, saying, 'She knew she was coming and didn't take any pleasure in the idea, but since she must have worked out afterwards that it was her telling me that she knew someone with such a bad reputation as Mlle Vinteuil that had so upset me at Balbec that I even thought of suicide, she preferred not to mention it to me.' But now I had forced her to admit that she had been pleased at the thought of seeing her. Anyhow, her mysterious determination to go to the Verdurins' should have been proof enough. But I had not given it enough thought at the time. So even though I was now saying to myself, 'Why does she tell me only half the truth? It's not just nasty and sad, it's stupid,' I was so crushed that I had not the strength to insist on this point, where I knew I could not give a good account of myself, having no incriminating document to produce, and to regain the upper hand I quickly moved on to the subject of Andrée, which I knew would allow me to rout Albertine, using the crushing revelation of Andrée's telegram. 'And another thing, I said, people keep on telling me about your affairs with other girls, I can't bear it: this time it's about Andrée. – Andrée? she cried, her face reddening with irritation. Her eyes were wide with astonishment, or the wish to seem astonished. *Charm*ing! And may one know who is telling you these delightful stories? Could I have a word with these kind people? And know where they get their filthy suggestions from? – Albertine, darling, I don't know, they're anonymous letters, but you might be able to guess who they are from (this to show that I did not care if she tried to find out) for they must know you quite well. I will admit that the last one annoyed me (and I'm mentioning that one because it's about something quite trivial and it's not too unpleasant to quote). It said that on the day we left Balbec, the reason why you first wanted to stay and then to leave was that in the intervening time you'd had a letter from Andrée to say that she wasn't coming back. – Of course Andrée wrote to say she wasn't coming back, she even sent me a telegram, I can't show it to you because I didn't keep it, but it wasn't that day, and even if it had been, why should I care whether Andrée was coming to Balbec or not?' 'Why should I care' was a sign of anger, and showed that she did care; but not necessarily a proof that Albertine had come back simply because she wanted to see Andrée. Every time that Albertine saw one of the real or alleged motives of her actions uncovered by a person to whom she had given a different reason, it made her angry, even if the person was the one for whose benefit she had really carried out the action. Did Albertine believe that this information about her doings was not sent to me by anonymous informants against my will, but eagerly sought out by me? One could not have guessed it from the words she now spoke to me, in which she appeared to accept my story about anonymous letters, but it was apparent from the angry looks she turned upon me, an anger which seemed to be merely the boiling-over of her previous ill-temper, just as the spying in which, if I was right, she thought I had engaged would have been only the logical consequence of a watch I kept over all her actions, of which she could not have failed to be aware for a long time now. Her anger extended even to Andrée, and no doubt realizing that I would no longer trust her to go out even with her friend, she cried, 'Anyhow, I'm fed up with Andrée. She's a complete bore. She's supposed to be coming back tomorrow, but I don't want to go out with her any more. So you can tell that to the people who said I'd come back to Paris just for her. Good Lord, after all the years I've known Andrée I couldn't even tell you what she looks like, I've never taken time to look at her!' Now the first year at Balbec, she had said to me, 'Andrée looks so lovely.' It is true that did not prove she had had sexual relations with her, and also true that I never heard her speak without indignation at the time of girls who did have such relations. But could she not have changed, even without realizing she had changed, not believing that her little games with a friend were the same thing as immoral relations, of which she had only a vague idea when she condemned them in others? Was that not possible, since the same change, and the same unconsciousness of change, had occurred in her relations with me, when at Balbec she had rejected my kisses with such indignation and later had offered me kisses herself every day, the same kisses which, I hoped, she would long continue to give me, which she would be giving me again in a moment? 'But darling, how can I tell them when I don't know who they are?' This answer was so convincing that it should have dissolved the objections and doubts that I saw suspended like crystals in

Albertine's eyes. But they did not touch them; I had fallen silent, and still she was looking at me with the continuing attention one gives to someone who has not finished speaking. I asked her forgiveness again, and she answered that she had nothing to forgive me for. She had become very gentle once more. But behind her sad, wan face it seemed to me that a secret had formed. I knew that she could not leave me without warning; she could not wish to (it was only a week till she was to try on the second set of Fortuny dresses), nor could she decently do so, since my mother and her aunt were coming back at the end of the week. Why, since it was impossible for her to leave, did I tell her repeatedly that we would go out together the next day to look at some Venetian glass that I wanted to give her, and why was I relieved to hear her say it was agreed? When she came to say good-night to me and I kissed her, she did not do as she usually did but turned her head away and – this was only moments after I had been thinking how sweet it was that she should give me every night what she had refused me at Balbec – did not return my kiss. It seemed as if, angry with me, she would not give me a sign of affection which I could have later have seen as dishonest, inconsistent with her anger. She seemed to be matching her actions to the quarrel between us, but gently, either so as not to spell it out, or because, despite breaking off carnal relations with me, she wished still to be my friend. So I kissed her again, clasping to my breast the glittering azure and gold of the Grand Canal and the paired birds, symbols of death and resurrection. But once again, instead of returning my kiss, she drew away with the kind of instinctive, sinister stubbornness of animals that feel death upon them. This premonition to which she seemed to be giving expression affected me as well and filled me with such fearful anxiety that when Albertine reached the door I did not dare let her leave and called her back to me. 'Albertine, I said, I'm not tired at all. If you don't feel like sleeping either, you might stay a little longer if you like, but there's no need and I really don't want to tire you.' I felt that if I could have got her to undress and seen her in her white night-gown in which she seemed so much pinker, warmer, more exciting to my senses, our reconciliation would have been more complete. But I hesitated for a moment, for the blue edge of the dress gave her face a beauty, a brightness, a heavenly quality without which she would have seemed to me harsher. She came back slowly and said very gently, still with the same sad, downcast face, 'I can stay as long as you like, I'm not sleepy.' Her answer comforted me for, so long as she was there, I felt that I could take thought for the future, and there was friendliness in it too, and obedience, but of a particular kind, which seemed to me to have limits set to it by the secret I could sense behind her sad look and her new manner, which she had changed half-reluctantly and half, no doubt, in order to bring it into line with something as yet unknown to me. I felt all the same that if only I could see her before me all in white, with her neck bare, as I had seen her in her bed in Balbec, it would give me the courage to make her yield to me. 'Since you're being so nice and staying to keep me company, you should take your dress off, it's too warm, too stiff, I don't dare go near you for fear of crushing that lovely velvet and there are those solemn birds in between us. Do take your clothes off, dear. – No. I can't undo this dress properly here. I'll get undressed in my room in a minute. – Then won't you even sit on my bed? – Yes, of course.' But she stayed at a distance, near my feet. We talked. Suddenly we heard the regular cadence of a plaintive call. It was the pigeons beginning to coo. 'You see, it's daylight already,' said Albertine; and almost frowning, as if living with me deprived her of the pleasures of the new season, 'Spring must be here, if the pigeons have come back.' The resemblance between their cooing and the cock's crow was as profound and as obscure as, in Vinteuil's septet, the likeness between the theme of the *adagio* and the first and last movements, which share the same key phrase, but so transformed by the differences in tone colour, rhythm and so on that the uninitiated reader, if he opens a book on Vinteuil, is astonished to learn that they are all three built on the same four notes, which he can indeed pick out with one finger on the piano without hearing anything resembling the three pieces. In the same way, the melancholy piece executed by the pigeons was a sort of cockcrow in the minor mode, which did not rise towards the heavens, did not soar vertically, but, regular as a donkey's braying, wrapped in gentleness, went from one pigeon to another along the same horizontal line, and never looked upwards, never changed its level complaint into the joyous call that had sounded out so often in the *allegro* of the introduction and the *finale*. I know it was then that I spoke the word 'death', as if Albertine were going to die. It seems that events extend further than the moments in which they happen, and cannot be completely contained within them. Certainly, they spill over into the future through the memories we retain of them, but they also demand space in the time that precedes them. Certainly you will say that at that time we do not see them as they will actually be, but are they not also changed in our memory of them?

When I saw that she made no move to kiss me, I realized that all this was a waste of time and that the true, soothing minutes would begin only when she had, so I said, 'Good-night, it's far too late,' because that would make her kiss me and we could begin from there. But, saying 'Good-night, try to sleep,' exactly as she had done the two previous times, she offered me only a kiss on the cheek. This time I did not dare call her back. But my heart was beating so fast that I could not go back to bed. Like a bird hopping from one end of its cage to the other, I kept coming and going between the fear that Albertine might leave me and a relative calm. This calm was produced by an argument that I ran through several times a minute: 'Anyway, she can't leave without telling me, and she hasn't said anything about leaving,' and I was almost reassured. But I immediately said to myself again, 'But suppose tomorrow I found her gone! If I am so anxious, it must be for a reason; why wouldn't she kiss me?' Then my heart pained me dreadfully. Then it was relieved to some extent by the argument which I began again, but I always ended up with a headache, because this toing and froing of my thoughts was so unending and so repetitive. There are certain psychological states, notably anxiety, which, presenting us in this way with only two alternatives, have something of the appallingly limited character of straightforward physical pain. I kept going over the arguments which justified my anxiety and those which countered it and reassured me, in as constricted a space as the one in which a sufferer continually touches, by an inner movement, the organ which is causing him pain, drawing away for a moment from the tender spot only to return to it a moment later. Suddenly, in the silence of the night, I was struck by an apparently insignificant noise, which none the less filled me with terror: the sound

371

of Albertine's window being violently thrown open. When no other sound followed, I asked myself why the noise had so alarmed me. By itself, there was nothing out of the ordinary in it by itself; but I was probably ascribing two meanings to it, each equally terrifying for me. First, it was one of the conventions of our life together that, as I dreaded draughts, no windows were ever opened at night. This had been explained to Albertine when she came to live in the house, and even though she was convinced that this was an irrational obsession on my part, and an unhealthy one, she had promised me never to infringe the prohibition. And she was so fearful of going against my wishes in anything, even if she did not agree with them, that I knew she would have slept in the fumes of a smoking fire rather than open her window, just as even the most important happening would not have led her to have me wakened in the morning. This was just one of our little agreements, but now that she had broken this one without asking me first, did it not mean that she had thrown caution to the winds, and would be equally ready to break them all? And then the noise had been violent, almost rude, as if she had been flushed with anger as she threw the window open, saying, 'I'm suffocating here, I don't care, I must have some air!' I did not spell all this out to myself, but I kept recalling, like an omen even more mysterious and sinister than an owl's cry, the sound of Albertine opening her window. More agitated than perhaps I had ever been since the night when Swann dined with us at Combray, I walked up and down the corridor all night hoping that the noise I made would attract Albertine's attention, that she would take pity on me and call out to me, but I heard no sound from her room. At Combray I had begged my mother to come to me. But with my mother I feared only her anger, I knew I could not reduce her affection for me by showing her mine. This thought made me reluctant to call Albertine. Gradually I realized that it really was too late. She must have been asleep for hours. I went back to bed. The next day, as soon as I woke, since no one ever came into my room unless I had called for them, I rang for Françoise. At the same time I thought, 'I'll speak to Albertine about a yacht I want to have built for her.' Taking my letters, I said to Françoise without looking at her, 'I want to talk to Miss Albertine about something presently; is she up? – Yes, she got up early.' I felt something like a wind rising within me, a thousand anxieties which I had not known I kept suspended within my bosom. Their tumult was so great it left me breathless, as if in a storm. 'Ah? But where is she now? – I expect she's in her room. – Ah! well then, I shall see her in a moment.' I breathed again, she was there, my agitation receded, Albertine was here, I hardly cared whether she were here or not. Anyhow, had it not been ridiculous to imagine that she might not be? I went back to sleep, but in spite of my conviction that she would not leave me my sleep was easily disturbed, though only by anything connected with her. As for sounds which might relate to building work going on in the courtyard, I might hear them vaguely as I slept, but I was not moved, while the slightest whisper from her room, or the sounds she made going out or coming back, pressing on the bell so gently, made me jump, ran right through me, left my heart pounding, even though I heard them in a deep slumber, just as my grandmother in the last days before her death, when she was sunk in an immobile state from which nothing could rouse her and which doctors call coma, still began to tremble like a leaf for a moment, so I have been told, when she heard the three rings of the bell with which I used to summon Françoise and which, even though I made them quieter that week so as not to disturb the death-chamber, no one, so Françoise assured me, could have confused, such was the personal way I had, unknown to myself, of touching the bell-push, with anyone else's way of ringing. Was I now too in my death agony? Was I going to die?

That day and the next we went out together, since Albertine did not want to go out with Andrée any more. I did not say anything more about the yacht, these outings were enough to restore me to complete calm. But she was still giving me my bedtime kiss in the new way, which enraged me. All I could see in it was a sign of stand-offishness, which seemed to me absurd given all the things I was doing to please her. So, no longer receiving from her even the physical pleasures that I valued, finding her ugly in her continuing ill-humour, I felt all the more strongly my deprivation of all the women and all the journeys the desire for which was revived in me by the first fine days. Thanks no doubt to scattered memories of meetings with women that I had

had while still at school, under the now thickening foliage, this region of spring where our journey through the seasons had now been halted for three days, under a clement sky, this region all of whose paths seemed to lead away towards lunches in the country, boating parties, pleasure excursions, seemed to me the land of women as much as of trees, and one where pleasure, everywhere on offer, could be permitted to my returning strength. Resignation to laziness, resignation to chastity, to knowing pleasure only with a woman I did not love, resignation to staying in my room, to not travelling, all these were possible in the old world where we had been only the day before, in the empty world of winter, but were no longer so in this new, leafy universe where I had awakened like a young Adam faced for the first time with the questions of existence, of happiness, and not weighed down by the accumulation of earlier, negative answers. I found Albertine's presence burdensome, I looked at her, gentle and depressed, and I felt it a mistake that we should not have separated. I wanted to go to Venice, and in the meantime I wanted to go to the Louvre to look at Venetian paintings, and to the Luxembourg to see the two Elstirs which I had just heard that the Princesse de Guermantes had sold to the museum, the ones that I had so admired at the Duchesse de Guermantes's house, the *Pleasures of the Dance* and the *Portrait of the X Family*. But I feared that in the first of these certain lascivious poses might remind Albertine of popular festivities, and set her to longing for them, making her say to herself that a certain life she had never led, a life of firework displays and open-air dance-halls, perhaps had something to recommend it. I was already fearful that on the fourteenth of July she would want to go to a street party and I dreamed of unlikely occurrences that might put paid to this festival. And then again in the Elstirs there were nude female figures in bosky Mediterranean landscapes that might make Albertine's thoughts turn to certain pleasures, even though Elstir – but would she not cheapen his work? – was thinking only of sculptural values when he painted them, the white, monumental beauty that women's bodies take on when seated amid greenery. So I resigned myself to giving up all that, and proposed a visit to Versailles. Albertine, who had refused to go out with Andrée, was sitting in her room reading, wrapped in a Fortuny dressing-gown. I asked her if she wanted to come to Versailles with me. She had the charming characteristic of always being ready to do anything, perhaps because of the way she had formerly spent half her time living in other people's houses, as was shown by the way she had decided in two minutes to come with us to Paris. She said, 'I can come like this provided we don't get out of the carriage.' She hesitated for a moment between two Fortuny cloaks to cover up her dressing-gown – as she might have done between two friends to take with her – took a dark blue one, quite beautiful, pinned on a hat. In a moment she was ready, before I could put my overcoat on, and we went to Versailles. This very speed, this utter docility reassured me, as if, without having any precise reason to be anxious, I had needed reassurance. 'You see, I've nothing to fear. She does everything I ask, despite the noise of the window the other night. As soon as I mentioned going out, she threw that blue cloak over her dressing-gown and she came, now that's not what somebody who was feeling rebellious would have done, somebody who didn't feel happy with me,' I said to myself as we travelled towards Versailles. We spent a long time there; the whole sky was filled with that radiant, palish blue that the walker lying in a field sometimes sees over his head, but so uniform, so deep that one feels that the blue of which it is made was used without any admixture and with such inexhaustible richness that one could delve deeper and deeper into its substance without finding an atom of anything but that same blue. I thought of my grandmother, who loved, both in human art and in nature, greatness, and who loved to see the steeple of Saint-Hilaire rise up against that same blue. Suddenly I felt once more a longing for my lost freedom when I heard a sound which I did not recognize at first and which my grandmother would also have loved. It was like the buzzing of a wasp. 'Look, said Albertine, there's an aeroplane, it's high, high up.' I looked all around me but, like the walker lying in a field, I could see nothing but the intact paleness of the unmixed blue, with not so much as a speck of black in it. I could still hear, however, the buzzing of the wings, which suddenly entered my field of vision. Up there, tiny, gleaming brown wings were puckering the blue expanse of the unchanging sky, I could finally attach the buzzing to its cause, the little insect throbbing up there, no doubt two thousand metres above us, I could see it making its noise. Perhaps, when distances on earth had not been shortened by speed as they have now been for a long time, the whistle of a train passing two kilometres away may have had the beauty which, for a few more years, will move us in the buzzing of an aeroplane at two thousand metres, at the thought that the distances covered in that vertical journey are the same as on the ground, that in this new direction where distances seem different to us because we thought we should never be able to go there, an aeroplane at two thousand metres is no further away than a train at two kilometres, indeed is nearer, since the same distance is to be covered in a more transparent medium, with no separation between the traveller and his point of departure, just as at sea or on an open plain, in calm weather, the wake of a faraway ship or the mere breath of a zephyr can draw lines across the ocean of waves or of corn.

I felt like having tea. We stopped at a large cake-shop almost on the edge of the town, which was quite fashionable at the time. A lady was coming out and asking the proprietress for her things. Albertine looked several times at the cake-shop owner as if to attract her attention as she cleared away plates, cups and little cakes, for it was already late. She would approach me only if I asked for something. And it happened then that, since the owner, who was very tall, was serving standing up and Albertine was sitting next to me, every time Albertine turned a blond gaze upon her to attract her attention she was obliged to turn her pupils upwards all the more sharply as, since the owner was directly opposite us, she could not have recourse to softening the angle of her gaze by its obliquity. She was obliged, without raising her head too much, to raise her eyes to the absurdly high plane on which the tea-shop lady's eyes could meet them. To spare my feelings, Albertine would quickly lower her eyes, and then, when the woman paid no attention to her, start the manoeuvre again. The result was a series of vain, imploring glances raised towards an inaccessible divinity. The woman had only one large table near us left to clear. There, Albertine could simply look sideways. But not once did the tea-shop owner's eyes alight on my friend. I was not surprised, for I knew that the woman, whom I knew very slightly, had lovers, though she was married, and managed to keep her affairs perfectly secret, which greatly surprised me as she was prodigiously stupid. I watched this woman as we finished our tea. Wholly taken up with her tidying, she was almost rude in the way she would not look at Albertine despite my friend's glances at her, which had nothing improper about them. The other woman kept on tidying, tidying, without raising her eyes for a moment. The putting away of the teaspoons and fruit-knives could have been entrusted, not to this tall, handsome woman but to some labour-saving machine, and one would have seen no greater imperviousness to Albertine's attention, and yet she did not lower her gaze, did not seem abstracted, let her eyes and her attractive physique shine out as usual, attentive only to her work. It is true that if this cake-shop owner had not been an unusually stupid woman (not only was that her reputation, I knew it to be true from my own experience), such detachment could have been a sign of the highest cleverness. And I know that the dullest being, if his desires or his interest are involved, can in this one case, amid the nullity of his stupid life, adapt immediately to the workings of the most complicated social mechanism; all the same, it would have been unduly subtle to imagine such behaviour in a woman as stupid as the cake-shop owner. Her stupidity was making her quite unbelievably rude! She did not once look at Albertine, though she could not have failed to see her. It was not polite to my friend, but in fact I was delighted that Albertine should be taught a lesson in this small way, and see that women would not always pay attention to her. We left the cake-shop, got back into the carriage and were already on the way home, when I suddenly regretted that I had not thought to take the owner on one side and ask her, if the lady who was leaving when we arrived should come back, not to give her my name and address, which the owner must have to hand as I had often ordered cakes from her. I had no wish for the lady to learn Albertine's address by this indirect means. But I thought that going back there would take too long for such a small thing, and would make the matter seem too important in the eyes of the foolish, lying owner. I simply thought that we should have to go for tea there again in a week or so's time to give the message to the owner, and how tiresome it was that one always forgets half of what one means to say, and has to come back several times to do the simplest things.

We came back very late, through the darkness in which, here and there, by the side of the road, the sight of uniform trouser-legs next to a petticoat indicated the presence of loving couples. Our carriage came back through the Porte Maillot. In place of the monuments of Paris we saw a pure, linear two-dimensional drawing of the monuments of Paris, such as might have been made to record the image of a destroyed city; but above them there rose up so sweetly the pale blue border against which they stood out that one's thirsty eyes turned in every direction to try to find out more of that delicious colour that was dispensed to them so grudgingly: the moon was shining. Albertine admired it. I dared not say to her that I would have enjoyed it more if I had been alone, or on my way to find some unknown partner. I repeated lines of poetry to her, or prose phrases about the moonlight, showing how, having once been silvery, it had become blue for Chateaubriand and the Victor Hugo of 'Eviradnus' and 'Theresa's Party', before becoming metallic yellow again for Baudelaire and Leconte de Lisle. Then, reminding her of the image of the crescent moon at the end of '*Booz endormi*',[95] I talked to her about the whole poem. I cannot express how much, when I think of it again now, her life was driven by alternating desires, fleeting and often contradictory. No doubt her habit of lying made it even more complicated, for, as she never remembered our conversations exactly, when she said to me, 'Now that was a pretty girl, and a good golfer too,' and I asked her the girl's name, she would reply with that detached, general, superior look which is no doubt always available, since every liar of this type adopts it for a moment every time he does not want to answer a question, and it never fails him: 'Oh, I don't know (seeming to regret not being able to inform me), I never did know it, I used to see her at the golf course but I didn't know what she was called'; if a month later I said to her, 'Albertine, you know that pretty girl you mentioned to me, the one who played golf so well. – Oh, yes, she would answer without thinking, Émilie Daltier, I don't know what became of her.' And the lie, like a mobile fortification, was transferred from defending the name, which had now fallen, to the possibility of tracing the girl. 'Oh, I don't know, I never knew her address. I can't think who might be able to tell you. Oh, no, Andrée didn't know her. She wasn't part of our little gang, and that's broken up now anyway.' At other times the lie was like an ugly admission: 'If only I had three hundred thousand a year . . .' She bit her lip. 'What, darling? – I'd ask if I could go on living with you, she would say, kissing me. Where else could I be happier?' But even taking her lies into account it was incredible how fragmented her life was, and how transient even her strongest desires. She was mad about someone, and three days later would not even have been at home to her. She could not wait an hour for me to buy her canvases and colours, for she wanted to begin painting again. She fretted for two days, almost weeping soon-to-be-dried tears, like a child who has lost its nurse. And this instability of her feelings in relation to people, to things, to her pursuits, the arts, whole countries, was in truth so universal that, if she did love money, she cannot have loved it more consistently than anything else. When she said 'If only I had three hundred thousand a year', even if she was expressing a mean but transient thought, she could not have held to it any longer than to her desire to go to Les Rochers, of which she had seen a picture in my grandmother's copy of Mme de Sévigné, or to meet an old friend from the golf-course, to go up in an aeroplane, to spend Christmas at her aunt's, or to start painting again.

'You know, neither of us is really hungry, we could have looked in on the Verdurins, she said, it's their at-home day and this is the time. – But I thought you were angry with them. – Oh, people gossip about them but underneath they're not so bad. Mme Verdurin has always been really nice to me. And then, we can't always be quarrelling with everybody. They have their faults, but who hasn't? – You're not dressed, you'd have to go home and dress, we'd be very late. – You're right, let's just go home,' said Albertine with the admirable docility that always astonished me.

The fine weather took another leap forward that night, as a thermometer rises with the heat. When I woke up on those early rising spring mornings, from my bed I could hear the trams moving through the scents in the air, with which the heat would coalesce more and more until it reached the almost solid density of midday. Fresher were the scents of my bedroom, once the smooth air had finished coating and separating the smells of the washbasin, of the wardrobe, of the sofa; the very clarity with which, standing upright, they formed distinct, juxtaposed layers, in a mother-of-pearl semi-darkness which gave a gentler sheen to the gleam of the curtains and the blue satin armchairs, allowed me to see myself, not by a simple quirk of my imagination but because it was really possible, walking through some newly developed part of the suburbs, like the one Bloch lived in at Balbec, following streets blinded with sunlight, and seeing not the dull butchers' shops and white freestone, but the dining-room of a country house where I might presently arrive, and the scents which I should find when I arrived there, the smell of the fruit-bowl of cherries and apricots, of cider, of Gruyère cheese, all suspended in the luminous congelation of shadow which they vein delicately like the depths of an agate, while the cut-glass knife-rests flash rainbows or deposit on the oilcloth table-cover peacock's-feather ocelli.

Like a steadily strengthening wind I heard with joy the sound of a motor-car under my window. I recognized its petrol smell. This smell may seem regrettable to the squeamish (who are always materialists and for whom it spoils the countryside) and to certain thinkers, also materialists in their way, who, believing in the importance of the fact, imagine that man would be happier, capable of a more elevated poetry, if his eyes could see more colours, his nostrils smell more perfumes: a philosophical version of the naïve belief of those who think that life was more beautiful when, instead of dark suits, people wore sumptuous costumes. But for me (just as an aroma, unpleasant in itself, of mothballs and vetiver would have delighted me by restoring to me the pure blue of the sea on the day I arrived at Balbec), this smell of petrol which, with the smoke that was escaping from the machine, had so many times risen into the pale azure sky, on those burning hot days when I went from Saint-Jean-de-la-Haise to Gourville, just as it had followed me on my outings on the afternoons when Albertine was painting, now set to flowering all around me, even though I was in my darkened room, cornflowers, poppies and red clover, it intoxicated me with a scent of the countryside, not circumscribed and precise, like the one which is affixed in front of hawthorns and, held there by its rich, heavy elements, floats without moving much in front of the hedge, but a scent at the appearance of which roads receded in front of me, the look of the ground changed, châteaux appeared from nowhere, the sky turned paler, my strength grew tenfold; this was a scent which seemed to symbolize leaping forward, power, and which renewed the desire I had felt at Balbec to get into the cage of glass and steel, not this time to go and pay visits in familiar houses with a woman I already knew too well, but to go and make love in new places with a woman I did not know at all. A scent which was always accompanied by the sound of passing motor horns, to which I added words as if to a bugle-call: 'Parisian, get up, get up,[96] come and have lunch in the country and go boating on the river, in the shade under the trees, with a pretty girl, get up, get up.' And I enjoyed all these daydreams so much that I congratulated myself on the 'stern decree' which meant that, until I called, no 'timid mortal', whether Françoise or Albertine, would dare to come and disturb me 'in the depths of my palace' where

> . . . une majesté terrible
> Affecte à mes sujets de me rendre invisible.[97]

But suddenly the scene changed; it was no longer the memory of old impressions, but of an old longing, recently reawakened in me by the blue and gold Fortuny dress, which spread out before me another spring, not a leafy spring but, on the contrary, one suddenly stripped of all its trees and flowers by the name I had just pronounced to myself: 'Venice', a spring decanted, reduced to its essence, where the lengthening, warming, gradual opening-up of the days is reflected in the progressive fermentation, not of impure earth, but of virgin, blue water, spring-like without blossom, which could respond to the month of May only by its reflections, animated by the month, giving itself perfectly to it in the glittering, fixed nudity of its dark sapphire gleam. And just as the seasons have been unable to change its unflowering channels, modern times have brought no change to the Gothic city; I knew this, I could not imagine it, or rather, when I imagined it that is what I longed for, with the same desire which once, when I was a child, in the very excitement of leaving, had taken from me the strength

I needed to make the journey: I wanted to come face to face with my Venetian imaginings, to see how this divided sea held within its coils, like the windings of the river Ocean,[98] an urban, refined civilization which, cut off by azure bands of water, had developed in isolation, had had its own schools of painting and architecture – a fabulous garden of fruits and birds carved in coloured stones, flowering in the middle of the sea which daily refreshed it, lapping with its tides the bases of the columns and casting on the deep-carved capitals watching in the darkness like a sombre blue gaze, patches of ever-moving light. Yes, I had to leave, the time had come. Since Albertine had stopped looking angry with me, possession of her no longer seemed to me one of those goods in exchange for which one is ready to give up all others. Perhaps because doing so would have freed us from a source of unhappiness, an anxiety which now no longer exists. We have managed to break the cloth of the hoop which we thought we should never jump through. We have made the storm clear, brought back smiling serenity. The painful mystery of an unexplained and perhaps unending hatred has been dispelled. Now we find ourselves face to face with the problem we had put on one side, the problem of a happiness we know to be impossible. Now that life with Albertine had become possible again, I could see that it would only ever make me unhappy since she did not love me; better to leave her in the happiness of her acquiescence, which I could prolong in memory. Yes, this was the moment; I should have to find out exactly the date on which Albertine meant to leave Paris, to take decisive steps, working through Mme Bontemps, to make sure that she could not then go to Holland, nor to Montjouvain. If we were better at analysing our love affairs, we might find that often we love the women we do only because of the counterweight of the men against whom we have to compete to win them; remove the counterweight, and the woman's charm will collapse. There is a painful and salutary example of this in some men's predilection for women who, before they knew them, had transgressed, for women whom they feel to be in danger and whom, for as long as their love lasts, they must always be trying to pull back from it; another example, not at all dramatic this time, comes later, when the man, feeling his attraction to the woman he loves waning, applies a new set of rules, and, in order to convince himself that he has not stopped loving her, sets her down in a dangerous milieu where he will have to protect her every day. (The opposite in this of the men who insist that their women give up the stage, when it was only because they were on the stage that they fell in love with them in the first place.)

And now that my departure no longer presented any problems, I must choose a fine spring day like this one – there would be many more – when I should be indifferent to Albertine, and tempted by a thousand other things; I must let her go out without seeing her, then get up, get ready quickly, leave her a note, making the most of the fact that, as she would not at that time be able to go anywhere that would make me uneasy, I might be able, on my journey, not to picture to myself how she might be misbehaving, something which I cared little about at that moment in any case, and, without seeing her again, leave for Venice. I rang for Françoise to ask her to buy me a guide-book and a train time-table, as I had done when I was a child, when I had once before wanted to plan a journey to Venice, in fulfilment of a desire as violent as the one I felt at that moment; I was forgetting that there was another such desire which I had fulfilled without any pleasure at all, the desire for Balbec, and that Venice, being another visible phenomenon, would probably be no more successful than Balbec in realizing an inexpressible dream, the dream of Gothic time made real above a springtime sea, which caressed my mind at every moment with a magical, ungraspable image, mysterious and confused. Françoise, having heard my bell, came in, obviously worried at how I would react to her words and what she had done. She said, 'I wish you hadn't rung so late today, sir. I didn't know what I should do. This morning at eight o'clock Miss Albertine asked me for her boxes, I didn't dare say no, I was afraid you would be angry if I came and woke you. I asked her what she was playing at, I told her to wait another hour because I was sure you would ring, sir, but she wouldn't hear a word, she left me this note for you, sir, and at nine o'clock she was off.' And then – so little does one know what one has inside one, since I was sure I cared nothing for Albertine – my breath stopped, I clutched my heart in both hands, which were wet with a sweat I had not felt since the moment in the little tram when Albertine told me about Mlle Vinteuil's friend, while I could say nothing but 'Very good, Françoise, thank you, you were quite right not to wake me, leave me for a moment, please, I shall ring for you presently.'

*The Fugitive*

CHAPTER I

*Grieving and Forgetting*

'Miss Albertine has left!' How much more sharply suffering probes the psyche than does psychology! A moment earlier, as I analysed my feelings, I had thought that leaving her, without ever seeing her again, was exactly what I wanted, and comparing the mediocrity of the pleasure which Albertine gave me with the richness of the desires which she prevented me from achieving, I had concluded my subtle heart-searching by finding that I no longer wanted to see her, that I no longer loved her. But these words: 'Mademoiselle Albertine has left' had just caused such pain in my heart that I felt that I could no longer hold out. Thus something which I had thought meant nothing to me, was quite simply my whole life. How little we know ourselves. I must immediately put an end to my suffering; feeling as gentle with myself as my mother had been with my grandmother on her deathbed, I told myself, with all the good will that we lavish on those we love in order to spare them from suffering, 'Be patient just one moment, we'll find a remedy, don't worry, we won't let you suffer like this.' It was in this realm of ideas that my instinct for self-preservation sought the first balm available in order to apply it to the open wound: 'None of this is of any importance, because I shall get her to return straight away. I'll have to think of a way, but in any case she will be here by this evening. Therefore there is no need to worry.' 'None of this is of any importance', I was not content merely to persuade myself of this, but I tried to give Françoise the same impression, by not revealing my torment in her presence, because, even at the moment when I suffered so violently, my love would not let me forget the importance of making it appear to be a mutually happy love affair, above all in the eyes of Françoise, who did not like Albertine and doubted her sincerity. It is true that a moment earlier, before Françoise had appeared, I had thought that I no longer loved Albertine, believing that I had taken everything into account, that I was completely lucid and that I had plumbed the depths of my heart. But however great our intelligence, it cannot conceive all the elements that constitute it and which remain undetected as long as no event capable of isolating them makes them start to solidify out of the volatile state in which they exist for most of the time. I was mistaken when I thought that I saw clearly into my heart. But this knowledge, which the finest insights of my intellect had not given me, had just been brought home to me, as hard, dazzling and strange as crystals of salt, through the sudden stimulus of pain. I had become so accustomed to having Albertine beside me, and now I suddenly saw Habit in a completely new perspective. Until now I had considered it above all as a negative force suppressing the originality and even our awareness of our perceptions; now I saw it as a fearsome goddess, so attached to us, with her inscrutable face so grafted on to our hearts that if she detaches herself and turns away from us, this deity, whose presence we were barely able to discern, inflicts upon us the most terrible suffering, and then she is as cruel as death.

The most urgent thing was to read Albertine's letter, since I needed to consider how to bring her back. I imagined that this was within my grasp, because, since the future exists only in our minds, we think that we are still able to control it by a last-minute act of will-power. But at the same time I remembered that I had seen the future inflected by powers other than mine, against which, even with more time available, I could have done nothing. What does it avail us that the hour has not yet struck, if we can do nothing to prevent what it will bring? As long as Albertine was still living with me, I was determined to maintain the impetus of our separation. But now she had left. I opened Albertine's letter. This is what it said:

*'My dear friend, do forgive me for not having dared to say to your face the few words that follow, but I am a coward, I have always been so afraid of facing you that, despite my efforts, I was unable to pluck up the courage to do so. This is what I would have liked to tell you: "Life together has become impossible, besides, you must have realized from your tirade the other evening that something in our*

*relationship had changed. What could have been remedied that evening was to become irreparable over the next few days. It seems better therefore, since we have been fortunate enough to settle our differences, to leave each other on friendly terms"; that is why, my dearest, I am sending you this note, and I beg that you will be kind enough to forgive me for causing you a little grief, when you think of the far greater pain that I shall suffer. My dear old friend, I do not want to become your enemy, I shall already find it difficult enough to see you gradually, but all too swiftly, becoming indifferent towards me; and so since my decision is irrevocable, before asking Françoise to hand you this letter I will already have asked her to bring me my trunk. Farewell, I leave you with the best of me. Albertine.'*

All of which means nothing, I told myself, it is even better than I had thought, for since she does not believe a word of all this, she has obviously written it only in order to make a scene, to frighten me, so that I will stop behaving unreasonably towards her. The most urgent thing to do is to make sure that Albertine returns home this evening. How sad to think that the Bontemps are corrupt people, using their niece to extract money from me. But no matter. Were I to offer half of my kingdom to Mme Bontemps in order to have Albertine back here this evening, enough would remain for Albertine and me to live in comfort. And at the same time I was calculating whether I would have time that morning to go out and buy the yacht and the Rolls-Royce that she desired, and, abandoning all hesitation, did not consider for a moment that I had thought it rather unwise to make her this gift. Even if Mme Bontemps's agreement is not sufficient, and Albertine refuses to obey her aunt and stipulates as the condition of her return that she shall henceforth enjoy complete independence, well then, however much sorrow it should cause me, let it be; she may go out unaccompanied, as often as she likes; we have to accept the need to make sacrifices, however painful, in the interest of what we hold most dear, which for me, despite what I believed this morning in the light of my precise and absurd calculations, is that Albertine should live here with me. Should I, however, add that granting her this freedom would have caused me great distress? I would be lying. I had often previously felt that the suffering caused by leaving her free to do wrong far away from me might well be less than the kind of sadness which I sometimes experienced when I sensed her boredom beside me at home. Of course if at any particular moment, when she asked me if she could pay some visit, I would have found the idea of letting her go appalling, imagining a whole programme of orgies. But I had often been tempted to say, 'Take our boat, take the train, go away for a month to some country that I don't know, where I've never been, where I won't know a thing about whatever you do,' because I thought that, once distant from me, she would prefer to be back with me instead, and would be happier when she had returned. Besides, this is surely what she wants: she does not actually demand such freedom, which, I might add, I would easily manage to restrict from day to day by offering her new pleasures every day. No, what Albertine wanted was for me to stop behaving intolerably towards her, and above all – like Odette with Swann in former times – for me to decide to marry her. Once married, she would not worry about her independence; we would be so happy living here together! Of course that would mean giving up any idea of Venice. But how those much-desired cities like Venice – not to mention hostesses like the Duchesse de Guermantes or entertainments like the theatre – tend to pale, fade and die, when we are chained to another heart by a bond so painful that it prevents us from parting! Besides, Albertine is absolutely right on the question of marriage. Even Mama finds all the delay ridiculous. Marrying her was what I should have done ages ago, it's what I must do now, that's what has made her write this letter, not one word of which she believes; it was in order to achieve this that she renounced for a few hours something that she must want as much as I want her to do it: to return home. Yes, that is what she wants, that is her main intention, my reason said compassionately; but I felt, as I argued, that my reason tended to pursue the hypothesis that it had adopted at the outset, while I felt quite clearly that it was the other hypothesis which had constantly been corroborated. Of course, this alternative version would never have made so bold as to overtly formulate the theory that Albertine might have had a relationship with Mlle Vinteuil and her female friend. And yet, when I was overwhelmed with this terrible news just as we were drawing into the station at Incarville, it was the second hypothesis that had been confirmed. This theory had never yet suggested that

Albertine might leave me of her own accord, in such a way, without warning and without giving me time to stop her. But even if, after the enormous mental leap that I had been obliged to take, the new reality which I had to face was as surprising as any revealed by a physicist's latest discovery, a prosecutor's fresh enquiry into a crime, or a historian's new insight into some revolution, this new reality went far beyond the half-hearted premonitions of my alternative hypothesis, and yet helped to prove them right. This alternative hypothesis was not one formulated by the intellect, and the panic which I had experienced on the evening when Albertine had not kissed me, or the night when I had heard her window opening, was not a rational fear. But – as many episodes may already have indicated and what follows will show all the more – the fact that the intellect is not the most subtle, powerful and appropriate instrument for grasping the truth is only one more reason in favour of starting with the intellect rather than with the intuitions of the unconscious or with unquestioning faith in our premonitions. It is life which little by little, case by case, allows us to realize that what is most important for our hearts or our minds is taught us not by reason but by other powers. And then it is the intellect itself, which, recognizing their superiority, uses its reasoning in order to abdicate in their favour and accepts the role of collaborator and servant. It has 'experimental faith'. The unexpected unhappiness which confronted me already felt familiar (as did Albertine's friendship with two lesbians) from having been indicated by so many signs in which (despite my rational arguments using Albertine's own pronouncements in order to prove the opposite) I had detected the tedium and repugnance that she felt at living in this slavish manner, in signs written as it were backwards and in invisible ink, in Albertine's sad and submissive eyes, on those cheeks suddenly inflamed by an unexplained blush, or in the sound of a suddenly opened window! Of course I had never dared analyse them fully enough to formulate the precise image of her sudden departure. My spirits lulled by Albertine's presence, I had envisaged only a departure arranged by me at an indeterminate date, that is, situated in a timeless zone; and consequently had only imagined that I thought of her departure, in the way that many people who think about death when they are in good health imagine that they do not fear it, and in fact do no more than introduce one purely negative notion into the heart of their good health, which would be precisely what the approach of death would alter. Moreover the idea of a parting planned by Albertine herself could have struck my mind a thousand times over, as clearly and unambiguously as you like, without my having any truer realization of what this departure would mean to me, that is, what it would mean in reality – something original, devastating, unknown, an entirely novel evil. Even if I had foreseen this departure, I might have thought of it ceaselessly year after year, without all such thoughts, even if joined together, having the slightest connection either in intensity or in quality with the unimaginable hell that Françoise had allowed me to glimpse when she said, 'Miss Albertine has left.' In order to represent an unknown situation, the imagination borrows elements already known, and for this reason fails to represent it. But our sensibility, even at its most physical, remains scored long afterwards by the original and long-indelible mark of the new event, as the furrow scored by a flash of lightning. And I hardly dared admit to myself that, if I had foreseen this departure, I would perhaps have been incapable of representing it to myself in its true horror, and even if Albertine had announced it to me, and I had threatened and implored her, might have been incapable of preventing her. How far my desire for Venice had now abated! Just as the desire to meet Mme de Guermantes in Combray in days gone by had abated, at those moments when I held but one thing dear, to have Mama in my bedroom. And it was in fact all the worries that I had felt since I was a child that had been solicited by this new source of anxiety and had rushed to reinforce it, amalgamating themselves with it into one homogeneous mass which suffocated me.

Certainly, the physical heartache which such a separation deals and which, through the body's terrible ability to keep records, renders any pain contemporary with all the periods in our lives when we have suffered, – certainly this heartache, perhaps somewhat calculated – so little do we care for the pain of others – by a woman desiring to make us miss her as acutely as possible, whether the woman only pretending to make her departure wishes merely to obtain more favourable conditions, or whether leaving for ever – for ever! – she wants to strike a blow, perhaps from vengeance, perhaps to continue to be loved, or perhaps to preserve the quality of the memory that she will leave, and violently break out of this network of tedium and indifference which she had felt being woven around her, – certainly we had promised each other that we would avoid such heartache, we had said that we would part on good terms. But it is in fact very rare to part on good terms, for if all were well we would not separate. And then again, the woman towards whom we affect the utmost indifference does none the less feel obscurely that, just as we have come to tire of her because of the force of habit, so we have become all the more attached to her, and she guesses that one of the essential requirements for parting on good terms is to warn her partner that she is going to leave. Yet she fears that warning him may prevent her. Every woman feels that, the greater is her power over a man, the more her only way of leaving him is just to take flight. She becomes a fugitive precisely because she was a queen, this is inevitable. Certainly, there is a yawning gap between the tedium which she inspired a moment ago and the furious need, once she has left, to have her back. But there are reasons for this, above and beyond those given in the course of this work and others which will be revealed later. First and foremost, the departure often occurs at a moment when our indifference – real or imagined – is at its greatest, at the farthest extent of the pendulum swing. The woman thinks: 'No, things cannot go on like this,' precisely because the man speaks only, or thinks only, of leaving her. So the pendulum, as it returns to its other extreme, opens the largest gap at this moment. A moment later it will return to its starting-point: once more, despite all the reasons proffered, everything seems so natural! Our heart starts to pound; and besides, the woman who has left is no longer the same as the woman who used to be there. Her life with us, which was too predictable, finds itself suddenly enriched by all those other lives with which she will inevitably become involved, and in order to become involved with which she may have left us. As a result, this new complexity in the life of the woman who has run away has a retrospective impact on the woman who previously lived at our side, and was perhaps premeditating her departure. To the set of psychological facts which we identify as part of our life together, and part of our jealousy too (which imply that men who have been left by several women have nearly all been left each time in the same manner because of their identical and entirely predictable characters and reactions: each has his own manner of being betrayed, as he does of catching cold), although we do not find this set of facts too mysterious, there doubtless corresponds a set of facts that we failed to notice. She must have been corresponding with or contacting some man, or woman, through a messenger, waiting for the signal which we may have given ourselves without realizing it, by saying, 'Monsieur X came to see me yesterday,' if she had agreed with Monsieur X that he would come to see me on the eve of the day when she was due to meet him. How many hypotheses were possible! But only possible. I constructed the truth so well, but only in terms of possibilities, that one day, having opened a letter addressed to one of my mistresses, a letter written in a coded format, 'Awaiting signal to visit Marquis de Saint-Loup, alert tomorrow by telephone,' I reconstituted some kind of planned escape; the name of the Marquis de Saint-Loup was there only to signify something else, for my mistress did not know Saint-Loup but had heard me speak of him, and moreover the signature was a kind of nickname, lacking any recognizable linguistic form. Yet the letter was not addressed to my mistress, but to another person in the building whose name was different but had been mistaken for hers. The letter was written not in a coded format but in poor French, because it had been written by an American lady, who was indeed one of Saint-Loup's friends, as he informed me himself. And the strange way in which this American lady formed some of her letters had given the appearance of a nickname to a perfectly authentic but foreign surname. I had therefore been entirely wrong in my suspicions that day. But the intellectual framework that had linked these facts together in my mind did provide a perfectly correct and unanswerable model for the truth when my mistress (who at the time had been thinking of spending her whole life with me) did leave me three months later, for it happened in a fashion absolutely identical to the way I had imagined on the previous occasion. A letter arrived, with the same characteristics which I had wrongly identified in the earlier letter, but this time having indeed the sense of a signal, and Albertine had thus premeditated her escape for some time. This was the greatest misfortune of my life. And in spite of everything, the suffering which it caused me was perhaps even exceeded by my curiosity to know the causes of this disaster: whom Albertine had desired, for whom she had left me. But the sources of these great events are like those of rivers, we may well travel the whole surface of the globe without being able to find them. Because at the time it seemed simply attention-seeking and bad temper, what in Françoise's case we called 'having the sulks', I did not note that, from the day when she had stopped kissing me, she took on a funereal air, looking stiff and unbending, adopting a sad voice for even the most simple things, moving slowly and never smiling. I cannot say that no evidence proved that she had no contact with the outside world. Françoise did in fact tell me that when she entered her room two days before her departure, she had found nobody there and the curtains drawn, but she had sensed from the atmosphere and the sounds in the room that the window was open. And in fact she had found Albertine on the balcony. But I cannot see with whom she could have communicated from there, and, besides, the open window behind drawn curtains was easy to explain by the fact that she knew how afraid I was of draughts, and that even if the curtains were not much protection for me, they would have prevented Françoise from seeing from the corridor that her shutters were open so early. No, I can think of only one small detail, which proves merely that she had decided the day before that she was going to leave. The day before she had in fact taken from my room without my noticing a considerable quantity of tissue paper and packing material, which I kept there, and which she used throughout the night to wrap her countless peignoirs and negligees in order to leave in the morning. That was the only detail, that was all. I cannot attribute any importance to the fact that during the evening she almost thrust upon me a thousand francs which she owed me, there was nothing special in that, for she was extremely scrupulous in matters of money.

Yes, she took the tissue paper the day before, but it was not just the day before that she knew that she was going to leave! For it was not sorrow that caused her to leave, but the decision that she had already taken to leave, to renounce the life of which she had dreamed, which gave her that sorrowful air. Sorrowful, almost solemnly cold with me, except the last evening, when, after staying with me longer than she wanted – which astonished me on her part since she usually wanted to stay as long as possible – she stopped at the door and said, 'Farewell, my dear, farewell, my dear.' But I paid no attention at the time. Françoise told me that the following morning, when Albertine told her that she was leaving, she was still so sad, and so much more stiff, so much more unbending than the previous days (but this is however also explicable through fatigue, for she had not undressed and had spent all night packing, except for those possessions that were not in her room or her dressing-room), that Françoise nearly fell over when she heard her say, 'Farewell, Françoise.' When we hear of such things, we understand that the woman who has come to please us so much less than all those who are so easy to meet on the most casual occasion, the woman we resent for making us sacrifice them for her, is on the contrary the one that we would now prefer a thousand times over. For we are no longer asked to choose between a certain pleasure – which custom and perhaps the mediocrity of its object have rendered almost null and void – and other more tempting and seductive pleasures, but between these pleasures and something even stronger, compassion for her suffering.

In promising myself that Albertine would return home by the evening, I had risen to the emergency and applied an emotional sticking plaster to the wound opened up by tearing away my old belief. But however swift my instinct for self-preservation had been, I had, when Françoise spoke, remained helpless for a moment, and even though I now knew that Albertine would be back that very evening, the pain I had felt during the instant when I had not yet convinced myself of this return (the instant that had followed the words, 'Miss Albertine asked for her trunk, Miss Albertine has left'), surged up again spontaneously within me exactly as before, that is, as if I were still unaware of the imminent return of Albertine. In any case, she must return, but of her own accord. Whichever hypothesis was right, if I seemed to plead with her or engineer her return, it would be counter-productive. There was no doubt that I did not have the strength to renounce her that I had had in the case of Gilberte. Even more than to see Albertine again, what I wanted was to put an end to the physical anguish that my heart, in a worse state than usual, could no longer bear. And then again, from the sheer habit of avoiding any effort of will-power, whether for work or for other things, I had become more of a coward. But above all my anguish was incomparably stronger this time, for many reasons, of which the most important was not perhaps that I had never tasted sensual pleasure with Mme de Guermantes or with Gilberte, but that since I did not see them every hour of every day and had no opportunity, and consequently experienced no need, to do so, my love for them lacked the all-powerful element of Habit. Perhaps, now that my heart, unable to exercise its will and unable to withstand suffering willingly, felt that there was only one possible solution, Albertine's return at all costs, or perhaps the contrary remedy (deliberate renunciation, gradual resignation), would have struck me as the ending of a novel, implausible in real life, if I had not already opted for this solution myself in the case of Gilberte. I knew therefore that this other solution could also be accepted, and by one and the same man, for I was still more or less the same person. Yet time had played its part, time which had aged me, time which had also placed Albertine perpetually by my side while we were sharing our lives together. But at least, while not renouncing Albertine, what remained for me of what I had felt for Gilberte was the pride of not wanting Albertine to see me as a pathetic puppet if I asked her to return. I did want her to return, but did not want to be seen to care. I got up, so as to waste no time, but suffering stopped me in my tracks: this was the first time that I had got up since Albertine's departure. And yet I must dress quickly in order to ask her concierge if there was any news.

Suffering, as the aftermath of an unwelcome moral shock, aspires to change form: we hope to dispel it by making plans, by seeking information; we want it to pass through its countless metamorphoses, for this requires less courage than keeping the suffering raw; we lie with our suffering as in a bed too narrow, too hard, and too cold. So I stood up again; I made my way around the room, but with infinite caution, I took up positions where I would not catch sight of Albertine's chair, the pianola whose pedals had felt the pressure of her golden slippers, or any of the objects which she had used, and which all, in the private language that my memory had taught them, seemed to offer me a new translation, another draft, announcing the news of her departure a second time. But even without looking I saw them; my strength drained away, I slumped down into one of those blue satin chairs whose sheen, in the chiaroscuro of the room anaesthetized by a single shaft of daylight, had an hour earlier invoked in me passionately nurtured dreams, which now seemed utterly remote. Alas! Before this moment I had never sat in one except in Albertine's presence. So I could not stay seated, I got back on to my feet; and thus at every moment, I had to meet one of those countless, humble selves that compose us who had not yet learnt of Albertine's departure and inform them of it – this task was all more cruel than if they had been strangers, and had not borrowed my sensitivity in order to suffer – to announce the impending misfortune to all of these people, all of these selves who did not yet know it; each one of them in turn needed to hear these words for the first time 'Albertine asked for her trunk' – that coffin-shaped trunk which I had seen loaded into the carriage at Balbec along with my mother's luggage – 'Albertine has left.' I had to inform every one of them of my sorrow, that sorrow which is not at all a pessimistic conclusion freely drawn from a collection of sinister circumstances, but the intermittent and involuntary revival of a specific impression, externally provoked rather than chosen by us. Some of these selves I had not seen for quite a while. For instance (I had not realized that it was the day for the barber to call) the self that I was when I had my hair cut. I had forgotten that self, his arrival made me burst out sobbing as would the arrival at a funeral of an old, retired servant who knew the lady who has just died. Then all of a sudden I remembered that over the last week I had been seized from time to time by panic attacks, which I had not admitted to myself. At those moments I had however argued with myself, saying, 'Surely there is no point in entertaining the hypothesis that she might suddenly leave. It is absurd. If I had submitted this hypothesis to a sensible and intelligent man (and I would have done, in order to gain peace of mind, if jealousy had not prevented me from taking anyone into my confidence), he would surely have replied: "But you are mad. It's impossible." And indeed during those last days we had not had a single quarrel. People leave for a reason. They tell you what it is. They offer the right of reply. They do not just leave. No, that is childish. That is the only absurd hypothesis.' And yet every day, when I found her still there when I rang for her in the morning, I had breathed an enormous sigh of relief. And when Françoise had handed me Albertine's letter, I had immediately felt sure that it was about the one unthinkable event, a departure somehow sensed several days in advance, despite my logical reasons for being reassured. I had told myself this in my despair with almost self-satisfied perspicacity, like a murderer who knows that he cannot be found out but who is afraid and suddenly sees the name of his victim written at the head of a file on the desk of the examining magistrate who has summoned him to appear. My only hope was that Albertine had gone to see her aunt in Touraine, where she would in fact be quite closely supervised, and could not get up to much harm before I collected her. My worst fear was that she might have stayed in Paris or left for Amsterdam or Montjouvain, that is, that she might have escaped to indulge in some intrigue whose preparations had escaped my attention. But in fact as I thought of Paris, Amsterdam, Montjouvain, that is, a variety of places, I was thinking of places which were no more than possible; so when Albertine's concierge replied that she had left for Touraine, the location which I had thought I preferred seemed to me the most awful of all, because it was real and because for the first time, tortured by the certainty of the present and the uncertainty of the future, I could visualize Albertine starting a life intentionally separate from me, perhaps for some time, perhaps for ever, and a life where she would attain that unknown which had formerly so often disturbed me, even though I was lucky enough to possess and to caress what lay outside, her sweet, captive, impenetrable face. It was this unknown which lay at the heart of my love.

Outside Albertine's door I found a little poor girl who looked at me wide-eyed and who appeared so kind that I asked her if she wouldn't like to come home with me, as I might have invited a dog with a faithful look. She seemed pleased. Once at home, I rocked her for a while on my knees, but soon her presence, which made me feel Albertine's absence too keenly, became intolerable. And I asked her to leave, after giving her a five-hundred-franc note. And yet, soon after, the thought of having some other little girl by my side, of never being alone without the succour of an innocent presence, was the only dream that made me able to bear the idea that Albertine might stay away for some time before she returned. As for Albertine herself, she hardly existed for me as more than a name which, apart from some rare moments of respite on waking, kept inscribing itself into my brain over and over again. If I had thought aloud, I would have repeated it endlessly, and my verbiage would have been as monotonous and limited as if I had been transformed into a bird, like the one in the legend whose call repeats endlessly the name of the woman that he loved when he was a man. You say it to yourself, but as you do not say it out loud, it seems as if you are writing it inside yourself, and it leaves its trace in the brain, which must finally, like a wall on which someone has enjoyed scribbling, be entirely covered by the name of the beloved, rewritten a thousand times. We write it over and over again in our minds as long as we are happy, even more when we are unhappy. And we feel the constantly renewed need to repeat this name which tells us no more than what we already knew, but, in the long run, we also feel fatigue. At this moment I did not even think of carnal pleasure; I did not even see in my mind's eye the image of that Albertine, although she had been the cause of such a revolution in my being, nor did I perceive her body, and if I had wanted to isolate the idea – for there always is one – that connected it with my suffering, it would have been in alternation, on the one hand, wondering about her state of mind on leaving, whether she hoped to return or not, on the other hand, wondering how to bring her back. Perhaps there is a symbolic truth in the infinitely small place taken up in our anxious feelings by the loved one to whom they relate. For her person itself has little to do with it; it is almost entirely concerned with the sequence of emotions and anxieties which chance made us feel for her at some time or other in the past, and which habit has attached to her. What proves this clearly (even more than the tedium that we find in the midst of happiness) is how indifferent we will feel at seeing or not seeing this same person, being esteemed by her or not, having her at our disposal or not, once we no longer need ask the question only in relation to this person alone (a question so superfluous that we will no longer bother to ask it), – once this sequence of emotions and anxieties is forgotten, at least in so far as they attach to her, for they may have reappeared, but attached to somebody else. Before that, when these emotions and anxieties were still attached to her, we believed that our happiness depended upon her person: but it depended only on ending our anxiety. At that time, therefore, our unconscious was more clear-sighted than we were, reducing the beloved figure to such a small size, a figure which we ourselves had perhaps forgotten, which we might have known imperfectly and believed mediocre, in the terrible drama we enacted where our very lives might have depended on tracking her down in order to cease waiting for her. This scaling-down of the figure of the woman is a logical and necessary effect of the way in which love develops, a clear allegory of the subjective nature of this love.

Albertine's state of mind when she left was no doubt similar in part to that of those peoples who use a display of armed force to prepare the ground for their diplomacy. She must have left me only to obtain from me better terms, greater freedom, more luxury. In that case, I would have emerged victorious, if I had had the strength to hold out, and wait for the moment when, seeing that she had won nothing, she would return of her own accord. But while in cards and in war, where winning alone matters, we can call someone's bluff, the situation created by love and jealousy, not to mention suffering, is not the same. If I were to let Albertine remain far away from me for several hours, perhaps for several weeks, in order to wait, to 'hold out', I would ruin what had been my goal for more than a year, which was never to leave her alone even for an hour. All my precautions became pointless if I gave her the time and the opportunity to deceive me at her leisure; and if in the end she did surrender, I would never be able to forget the time when she had been alone, and even if finally victorious, I would have suffered defeat in the past, that is to say irrevocably.

As for the means of bringing Albertine back, they were all the more likely to succeed if the hypothesis that she had left only in the hope of being recalled on more favourable terms appeared to be the most plausible. And doubtless for those who did not believe in Albertine's sincerity, certainly for Françoise for example, this was the case. But, as far as my reason was concerned, the only explanation for some of her bad moods and attitudes had seemed to be, even before I knew anything, that she was planning her final departure; it was difficult to believe, now that this departure had occurred, that it was only a pretence. I say for my reason, not for my self. I found the hypothesis of a pretence all the more necessary for being improbable and that it gained in strength what it lost in verisimilitude. When we see ourselves on the brink of the precipice and it seems that God has abandoned us, we no longer hesitate to ask him for a miracle. I acknowledge that in all that I was the most lax and yet the most vulnerable of policemen. But Albertine's flight had not restored to me the powers which the habit of having her watched by others had taken away from me. I could think of only one thing: entrusting someone else with the enquiry. This someone else was Saint-Loup, who agreed. Passing on the anxiety that had haunted me for so many days to someone else made me tremble with joy, as I felt certain of success, and my hands turned suddenly dry as they had been before becoming bathed in the sweat provoked by Françoise when she announced: 'Mademoiselle Albertine has left.' We should remember that when I resolved to live with Albertine and even marry her, I had done so in order to hold her, to know what she was doing, to prevent her from returning to her old habits with Mlle Vinteuil. Even while reeling from the savage blow caused by her revelation at Balbec, which she presented as if it were the most natural thing in the world, and even though my grief was greater than any I had ever experienced before, I did manage to find quite natural the one thing that in my worst imaginings I would never have dared suppose. (It is astonishing how jealousy, which spends its time inventing so many petty but false suppositions, lacks imagination when it comes to discovering the truth.) Yet my love, born above all of the need to prevent Albertine from doing wrong, had subsequently retained the mark of its origins. Being with her was not important, as long as I could prevent my 'runaway' from wandering here and there at will. In order to prevent her I had used as witnesses those who accompanied her, and, as long as their evening reports, however short, were safely reassuring, my worries would dissolve into a feeling of good humour.

Once I had convinced myself that, whatever I might need to do,

Albertine would be back home that very evening, this eased the suffering that Françoise had unleashed when she told me that Albertine had left (since at the time I was taken unawares and believed for the moment that her departure was irrevocable). But after a while, when the initial pain welled up again spontaneously inside me, throbbing with its own independent life, it was still as terrible as ever, because it preceded the soothing promise that I had made myself to bring Albertine back that very evening. My suffering heart was unaware of this declared intention, which ought to have assuaged it. In order to deploy the means necessary to ensure her return, I was condemned to act once more as if I were not in love with her and were not suffering from her departure, I was condemned to continue lying to her – not that I had ever been very successful with this course of action, but because I had always adopted it since I had been in love with Albertine. I could be all the more energetic in finding ways to get her to return, in so far as I was the one who appeared to have renounced her. I decided to write Albertine a farewell letter in which I would assume her departure to be final, while I would send Saint-Loup to exert the most brutal pressure on Mme Bontemps, as if I were unaware of it, in order to get Albertine back as soon as possible. Doubtless, I had learned with Gilberte the danger of writing letters whose indifference, at first feigned, finally becomes true. And this experience should have prevented me from sending Albertine letters of the same type that I had written to Gilberte. But what we call experience is only the revelation to our own eyes of one of our own character traits, which recurs naturally, and recurs all the more powerfully if we have already on some previous occasion brought it up into the clear light of consciousness, so that the spontaneous reaction which had guided us the first time becomes reinforced by all the suggestions of memory. The kind of plagiarism which it is most difficult for any human individual to avoid (and even for whole nations, who persist in reproducing their faults and aggravate them in so doing) is self-plagiarism.

I had commandeered Saint-Loup immediately, knowing him to be in Paris; he rushed to my side, as swiftly and effectively as previously at Doncières, and agreed to leave straight away for Touraine. I suggested the following stratagem. He would stop at Châtellerault, ask for directions to Mme Bontemps's house, and wait until Albertine had gone out, to avoid meeting her. 'But does this mean that the young lady you mention knows me?' he asked. I told him that I did not think so. The prospect of his action filled me with unbounded joy. And yet it was in total contradiction with what I had promised myself at the outset: which was to find a way to avoid appearing to send anyone to look for Albertine; now this would inevitably seem to be the case; but it had an inestimable advantage over 'what I should have done', in that it allowed me to say to myself that someone sent by me would see Albertine, and doubtless bring her back. And if I had been able to see clearly into my heart at the outset, it would have been this solution, which lay lurking in the shadows, but which I found deplorable, that I might have guessed would take precedence over the prudent course of action which I had decided to adopt, from lack of will power. Since Saint-Loup had already seemed slightly surprised that I had had a young lady living with me over the winter without telling him anything about it, and since in addition he had often asked after the young lady from Balbec and I had never replied, 'But she lives here', he could have been offended by my lack of confidence in him. It was true that Mme Bontemps might talk to him about Balbec. But I waited too impatiently on his departure and his arrival to be willing or able to consider the possible consequences of his journey. As for whether he would recognize Albertine (whom he had in any case systematically avoided looking at when he had met her at Doncières), everyone agreed that she had changed so much and put on so much weight that it was hardly likely. He asked me whether I might not have a portrait of Albertine. At first I said not, so that my photograph, taken at about the time we had met in Balbec, would not give him the opportunity to recognize Albertine, even though he had barely glimpsed her in the railway carriage. But I reflected that in her most recent photograph she would be as different from the Balbec Albertine as the living Albertine was now and that he would no more recognize her in the photograph than in real life. While I looked it out for him, he smoothed my brow gently with his hand, trying to console me. I was moved by the sorrow that he felt on imagining my suffering. In the first place, although he was separated from Rachel, what he had felt at the time

was not so far in the past that he did not feel a particular sympathy
and pity for this kind of suffering, as we feel closer to someone who
has the same kind of illness as us. And then again, he felt such affection
for me that he found the thought of my suffering unbearable. Thus for
the woman who caused it he felt a mixture of resentment and admiration. He saw me as such a superior being that for me to be so
subservient to another, she must be an absolutely extraordinary creature. I imagined that he would find Albertine's photograph pretty, but
even so I did not think that it would have the same impact on him as
Helen on the old men of Troy,[1] so while I kept searching for it, I said
modestly: 'Oh, you mustn't expect too much, you know, in the first
place it's not a good photo, and anyway she's not very striking, she's
no great beauty, but she is very sweet.' 'Oh, no, she must be marvellous,' he said with sincere and naïve enthusiasm, while trying to picture
the person who could throw me into such a state of agitation and
despair. 'I blame her for hurting you, but of course it was very likely
to happen to someone like you, artistic to your fingertips, loving
beauty in all things, and so passionately, you were bound to suffer
more than others when you found it in a woman.' At last I found the
photograph. 'She must be marvellous,' Robert continued, without
realizing that I was holding out the photograph. Suddenly he noticed
it and held it for a moment in his hands. His face registered a surprise
that bordered on stupefaction. 'Is this the girl that you love?' he said
finally, in a voice whose astonishment was muted by the fear of
offending me. He made no comment, but had taken on the judicious,
prudent and inevitably slightly condescending air that we adopt in the
face of an invalid – even if the patient has previously been a remarkable
man, or even your friend – who is no longer recognizable, for he is
stricken with raving madness and is talking to you of a celestial being
who has appeared to him and whom he continues to see exactly where
you, the normal man, see only his eiderdown. I immediately understood
Robert's astonishment, which was the same as that which had engulfed
me when I had caught sight of his mistress, with the only difference
that I had found her to be a woman whom I already knew, whereas
he believed that he had never seen Albertine. But doubtless in each
case the difference between what each of us saw in the same person

was just as great. It had been so long since I had tentatively started at Balbec to add the sensations of taste, smell and touch to the visual experience of watching Albertine. Since then, deeper, sweeter and less definable sensations had been added, and then painful feelings. In short Albertine, like a stone covered in snow, was no more than the core of an immense construction elaborated by my heart. All these layers of sensations were invisible to Robert, who grasped only the residue, which my system on the contrary prevented me from perceiving. What had disturbed Robert when he had seen Albertine's photograph was not the excitement of the old men of Troy saying, as they saw Helen pass:

Notre mal ne vaut pas un seul de ses regards,[2]

but exactly the opposite reaction, making him feel, 'But is this what has given you so much heartache, so much sorrow, led you into such folly?' We have to admit that this kind of reaction to the sight of the person who has wounded and disturbed the life, and sometimes caused the death, of someone we love is infinitely more common than that of the old men of Troy, and, we must admit, is the norm. This is not only because love is individual, nor because, when we do not feel it, we find it natural to judge it avoidable and comment upon the folly of others. No, it is also because when love has reached the stage when it causes such misery, the network of sensations interwoven between the face of the woman and the eyes of the lover, the fragile cocoon which protects and hides it, much as a layer of snow cloaks a fountain, has already grown so far that the point where the lover's eyes focus, the point where he confronts his pleasure and his pains, are as far from the point where others see them as is the real sun from the point where its condensed light makes us perceive it in the sky. And moreover during this time, beneath the chrysalis of pain and tenderness which renders the worst metamorphoses of the beloved invisible for the lover, her face has had time to age and change. With the result that, if the face which the lover saw for the first time is far removed from the one that he has seen since he has been in love and suffering, so, conversely, it is equally removed from the one that the indifferent spectator is able now to see. (What if, instead of the photograph of a young woman, Robert had seen that of an ageing mistress?) And we do not even have to see the woman who has caused so much distress for the first time in order to experience this astonishment. Often we knew her already, as my great-uncle knew Odette. In this case the difference of perspective affects not only someone's physical appearance but also their character and their individual impact. It is perfectly likely that the woman who makes her lover suffer has always been very friendly to someone who was not interested in her, as Odette, so cruel to Swann, had been the kind-hearted 'lady in pink' for my great-uncle; or likely perhaps that the person whose every move is anxiously anticipated by her lover, with all the awe that would be due to a deity, appears as an inconsequential person, only too pleased to do anything required, in the eyes of a man who does not love her, as did Saint-Loup's mistress for me, since I saw in her no more than 'Rachel, when of the Lord', who had so often been offered up to me. I remembered my stupefaction the first time that I had seen her with Saint-Loup, at the thought that one could feel tormented by not knowing what some woman had done one evening, what she might have said under her breath to someone, why she might have wanted to leave. Now I felt that this familiar story, although now that of Albertine, towards whom every cord of my heart and my life was straining in a frantic and chaotic process of suffering, must appear just as trivial to Saint-Loup, and that one day it must appear so to me; that gradually, in my feelings about the gravity or the insignificance of Albertine's past, I might pass from my state of mind at this moment to that of Saint-Loup, for I had no illusions as to what Saint-Loup must think, as to what anyone apart from the lover himself must think. And I was not too worried. Let us leave pretty women to men with no imagination. I remembered the tragic account of so many lives provided by a brilliant but an unrealistic portrait such as that of Odette by Elstir, which is, however, less the portrait of a woman in love than a portrait of love and how it disfigures. All that was missing was – an attribute present in so many portraits – that he should be not only a great painter but also her lover (and even then there were people who said that Elstir had been Odette's lover). This disparity is proved by the whole life of a lover, a lover like Swann, whose follies nobody understands. But if the lover is also a painter like Elstir, then the answer to the riddle is at hand, we at last have before our eyes the lips which common mortals have never perceived in this woman, the nose which nobody realized she had, that unsuspected allure. The portrait says: 'What I have loved, what has made me suffer, what I have always seen, is this.' By an inverse operation from the one where I had tried to invest Rachel in my mind with everything that Saint-Loup had added to her of himself, I tried to subtract my emotional and intellectual accretions from my composition of Albertine and to picture her just as she must appear to Saint-Loup, as Rachel had appeared to me. And even if we were to notice such differences ourselves, what importance would we ascribe to them? And when in former times at Balbec Albertine waited for me under the arcades of Incarville and leapt into my car, not only had she not yet 'filled out', but as a result of too much exercise she had rather melted away; she was so thin, and disfigured by an unattractive hat, which allowed only a glimpse of an unappealing part of her nose and a sidelong glance at cheeks as white as maggots, I recognized very little of her, yet enough for me to know as she leapt into my car that it was Albertine, that she had kept the appointment on time and had not gone elsewhere; and this was enough; what we love lives too deep in the past, consists too much in the time we wasted together for us to need the whole woman; we want to be sure only that she is the one, not to mistake her identity, which is far more important for the lover than her beauty; her cheeks may shrink, her body wither, even in the eyes of those who seemed to others at first most proud to possess a beauty, and yet her sharp little nose, that feature epitomizing her enduring personality, that algebraic remainder, that constant factor, is enough to prevent a man who frequents the highest social circles, if he is in love with her, from enjoying a single evening's peace, because he spends hour after hour, until bedtime, combing and uncombing the hair of the woman he loves, or simply staying at her side, to be with her, or to be sure that she is with him, or even simply to prevent her from being with anyone else.

'Are you sure', Robert asked, 'that I can just come right out and offer this woman thirty thousand francs for her husband's electoral committee? Is she so dishonest? If you are right, three thousand francs would be enough.' 'No, I beg of you, don't try to save money on something which I hold so dear. What you must say, and there is some truth to it, is this: "My friend had asked one of his relatives for these thirty thousand francs for a committee run by his fiancée's uncle. It's because of his engagement that they gave him the money. And he asked me to give it to you so that Albertine would know nothing about it. And now Albertine is leaving him. He does not know what to do. He is obliged to return the thirty thousand francs if he does not marry Albertine. And if he does marry her, she ought to return straight away, if only for the sake of appearances, because it would look really bad if she stayed on the run for too long." Does that sound as if I made it up?' 'No, not at all,' Saint-Loup replied, from kindness and from tact, and also because he knew that circumstances are often much more bizarre than we think. After all, there was no reason why there should not be, as I told him, a considerable element of truth in this thirty-thousand-franc story. It was possible, but it was not true, and it was precisely the most truthful element that was the lie. But Robert and I did lie to each other, as happens in any conversation when one friend sincerely wishes to help another who is suffering from despair in his love life. The friend who offers counsel, support and consolation can sympathize with the other's distress, but not feel it, and the more he tries to help, the more he lies. And his friend confesses all that he needs in order to be helped, but, precisely in order to be helped, may keep many things hidden. And it is the helper who is happy, whatever pains he takes, however long his journey, for he accomplishes his mission and feels no inner suffering. At this moment I was in the same position as Robert had been at Doncières when he thought that Rachel had left him. 'Very well, as you wish; if I encounter opposition I'll face it willingly, for your sake. And although I find it rather odd to set up such a blatant deal, I know well enough that even in our own circles there are duchesses, even the most strait-laced, who would do more embarrassing things for thirty thousand francs than tell their nieces not to stay in Touraine. But in any case, it doubles my pleasure to do you this favour, if that is what it takes for you to agree to see me. If I get married,' he added, 'might we not see more of each other, might you not come to feel as much at home in my house as yours?' He stopped suddenly, having thought, I presumed, that if I too were to marry, Albertine could not become a close friend of his wife. And I remembered what the Cambremers had told me about his likely marriage with the daughter of the Prince de Guermantes.

When he had consulted the time-table, he saw that he could not leave Paris before the evening. Françoise asked me: 'Should I remove Miss Albertine's bed from the study?' 'On the contrary,' I replied, 'please make it up.' I was hoping that she would return from one day to the next and I did not want Françoise even to guess that this might be in doubt. I needed Albertine's departure to seem to have been agreed with me, with no implication that she loved me any the less. But Françoise looked at me with an air, if not of incredulity, at least of doubt. She too had her own two hypotheses. Her nostrils flared as she scented trouble, and she must have been scenting it for some time. And if she was not perfectly sure, it was perhaps only because, like me, she was suspicious of believing absolutely in something that would give her too much pleasure. Now the burden of the affair weighed not on my exhausted mind but on Saint-Loup. I was buoyed up by the joyful feeling that I had reached a decision, saying to myself, 'I have returned her shot, on the volley.'

Saint-Loup could barely have caught the train when I bumped into Bloch in my lobby, not having heard him ring the door-bell, so that I had no alternative but to entertain him for a moment. Recently he had met me out walking with Albertine (whom he knew from Balbec) one day when she was in a bad mood. 'I have dined with M. Bontemps,' he told me, 'and as I have some influence on him, I told him that I was distressed to note that his niece was not more kindly disposed towards you, and that he ought to implore her to address this issue.' I seethed with rage: this imploring and complaining would undermine the whole impact of Saint-Loup's enterprise and would implicate me directly as far as Albertine was concerned by making me seem to beseech her. To add insult to injury Françoise had remained in the lobby and heard everything. I protested vigorously to Bloch, telling him that I had never asked him to undertake any such mission and that moreover the facts he mentioned were untrue. From then on Bloch started smiling more and more broadly, less, I believe, from amusement than from embarrassment at having annoyed me. He jokingly expressed his astonishment at having aroused such anger. Perhaps he said this to diminish in my eyes the importance of his indiscreet initiative, perhaps because he was of a cowardly nature and wallowed pleasurably and languidly in a life of lies, like a jelly-fish floating on the surface of the sea, or perhaps because, even had he been of another race of men, other people, since they can never share exactly our point of view, do not understand the extent of the harm that their randomly chosen words can cause. I had only just shown him the door, finding no remedy for what he had done, when the bell rang again and Françoise handed me a summons from a chief inspector of police. The parents of the little girl that I had taken home with me for an hour had decided to lodge a complaint against me for seducing a minor. There are moments in our lives when a kind of beauty is born of the multiplicity of the trials, interwoven like Wagnerian motifs, that assail us, as well as of the simultaneous realization that real events do not fit into the pattern of reflections pictured in the poor little mirror called the future that the intellect holds out before our eyes, but lurk on the threshold ready to pounce on us, like a detective waiting to catch someone *in flagrante delicto*. Already, left to their own devices, events evolve, whether because failure amplifies their importance in our eyes or whether because satisfaction reduces it. But they rarely come singly. The sentiments aroused by each of them contradict each other, and to a certain extent, as I felt while on my way to meet the chief inspector, fear is at least a temporary and fairly potent emetic for emotional troubles. At the police station I was greeted with insults from the parents, who told me that they would not 'swallow that kind of deal' and handed back the five hundred francs, which I refused to accept, and by the chief inspector, who, taking as his model the supreme talent of presiding magistrates for 'repartee', seized on a single word in each sentence I uttered and used it as part of a witty and crushing rejoinder. No one even discussed my innocence in the case, for it was the one hypothesis that no one would entertain for a minute. Nevertheless the difficulty of bringing a charge meant that I was let off with this ferocious grilling, which lasted as long as the parents were there. But as soon as they had left, the chief inspector, who had a weakness for little girls, changed his tone of voice and reprimanded me as a partner in crime: 'Another time you should take more care. Good Lord, don't pick them up so abruptly, it's bound to fail. Besides, you can find plenty of little girls better than her, and far cheaper. The price you paid was ridiculously steep.' I felt so sure that he would misunderstand me if I tried to explain myself that I took advantage of his invitation to leave, without saying another word. Each stranger I passed on the way home seemed to be a police inspector spying on my every act and gesture. But this leitmotif, like that of my anger against Bloch, faded, leaving room only for that of Albertine's departure. Now this motif started up again, but on an almost joyful note now that Saint-Loup had left. Since he had taken it upon himself to go to see Mme Bontemps, my suffering had become more diffuse. I believed that it was because I had acted, and I believed it in all good faith, for we never know what is hidden in the depths of our own souls. Deep down, what made me happy was not that I had passed the burden of my indecision on to Saint-Loup, as I believed. Actually I was not entirely mistaken; the specific remedy for the cure of an unfortunate event (and three-quarters of all events are unfortunate) is a decision; for deciding has the effect of suddenly reversing our thoughts and stemming the flow of those which derive from the past event and prolong its resonance, blocking it with a contrary flow of thoughts, brought in from outside, from the future. But these new thoughts are beneficial for us chiefly (as with those that invaded me at that moment) when what they bring us from the depths of the future is hope. Deep down what made me so happy was the secret certainty that, since Saint-Loup's mission could not fail, Albertine was bound to return. I understood this when as soon as I had not received a reply from Saint-Loup by the end of the first day, I started to suffer again. It was therefore not my deciding to surrender all powers to him that was the cause of my joy, which otherwise would have been boundless, but my thinking 'Success is certain' while saying 'What will be, will be.' And the thought, aroused by his delay, that in fact something other than success could arise was so hateful to me that I had lost my gaiety. It is in fact our prediction, our expectation of happy events that fills us with a joy which we attribute to other causes and which ceases only when it plunges us back into our sorrows, if we are no longer so sure that our wishes will be fulfilled. It is always this invisible belief that sustains the whole structure of our sensibility, which, when deprived of this, crumbles. We have seen how this determines for us the value or the nullity of people, our enthusiasm or boredom on meeting them. Similarly it decides whether a sorrow seems tolerable and unexceptional, simply because we are convinced that it will come to an end, or whether it suddenly expands until someone's presence becomes as important as our own lives, sometimes more. One extra thing finally made the pain I felt in my heart, which, I have to admit, had diminished, as acute as it had been at the start. This was rereading a phrase from Albertine's letter. However much we love a person, the suffering caused by losing her, when in our solitude we have nothing else on our mind, which can to a certain extent give the suffering whatever form it wants, is bearable and differs from the less human and personal suffering of those more unpredictable and eccentric accidents of our mental or emotional worlds – which are caused less directly by the person herself than by the manner in which we have learned that we will never see her again. As for Albertine, I could think of her and weep quietly, accepting that I would no more see her this evening than I had yesterday, but to reread 'my decision is irrevocable' was something else, it was like taking some drug so dangerous that it could cause a fatal heart attack. There are in the actions, details and letters of a separation, specific dangers which amplify and distort even the pain that people can cause us. But this suffering did not last long. Despite everything, I was so sure of Saint-Loup's skill and success, and Albertine's return seemed to me to be something so certain, that I started to wonder whether I had been right to want it. Unfortunately for me, who had thought the police affair was over and done with, Françoise came to announce that an inspector had called to enquire whether I might not be in the habit of inviting young girls home, and that the concierge, thinking that he meant Albertine, had replied that I was, and that, from then on, the house seemed to be under surveillance. From that moment on it would never again be possible for me to invite a little girl into my home to share my sorrows, without running the risk of being shamed in front of her by an inspector springing up and making her see me as a criminal. And at one and the same time I realized how we live more through certain dreams than we think, for the impossibility of ever cradling a little girl in my arms seemed to drain my life of all value for evermore, but in addition I realized how easy it is to understand that people may easily risk their fortunes and their lives, when we think that self-interest and the fear of death rule the world. For if I had thought that the arrival of the police could cause even a little girl who did not know me to form a shameful idea of me, how much I would rather have killed myself! There was not even any possible comparison between the two kinds of suffering. But in real life people never think that those to whom they offer money, or whom they threaten to kill, might have a mistress or even simply a companion whose esteem they value, even if they do not value their own. But, suddenly, in a moment of unwitting confusion (for in fact I had never imagined that if Albertine had not been over the age of consent, she would have lived with me, let alone been my mistress), I thought that 'the seduction of minors' could also refer to Albertine. Thus my life seemed walled in on all sides. And at the thought that I had not lived a chaste life with her, I found in the punishment inflicted on me for having cradled an unknown little girl in my arms the balance which always occurs in human punishment, suggesting that there is hardly ever either a just condemnation or a judicial error, but a kind of harmony between the false notion of an innocent act entertained by the judge and the culpable actions which he has ignored. But then, thinking that Albertine's return could bring upon me an ignominious charge which would degrade me in her eyes and would perhaps cause her some harm that she would not forgive me, I ceased to wish for her return, which terrified me. I wished I could telegraph her immediately not to return. Then immediately, drowning all else, a passionate desire for her return invaded me. It was because, having envisaged for a moment the possibility of telling her not to return and of living without her, I suddenly felt on the contrary ready to sacrifice all travel, all pleasure, all work, for Albertine to return! Oh, how my love for Albertine, whose outcome I had thought I could predict after what had happened to my love for Gilberte, had developed in exactly the

opposite way to the latter! How impossible it was for me to continue
not to see her! And with every action accomplished, even the most
trivial, as long as it had previously been bathed in the happy atmosphere
of Albertine's presence, I found it necessary each time, with further
effort and equal suffering, to renew my apprenticeship of separation.
Then competition with other forms of life cast this new pain into the
shadows, and during those days, which were the first days of spring, I
even experienced, while waiting for Saint-Loup to arrange to see Mme
Bontemps, a few moments of pleasant calm, imagining Venice and
meeting beautiful, unknown women. As soon as I realized this I felt
panic within me. The calm which I had just sampled was the first
appearance of the great but intermittent force which would struggle
within me against pain and against love, and would ultimately overcome them. What I had just had a foretaste and foreboding of, if only
for a moment, was that which would later become a permanent state
for me, a life where I would no longer suffer because of Albertine,
where I would no longer love her. And my love, which had just
recognized the only enemy able to vanquish it, the act of forgetting,
started to tremble, like a lion enclosed in a cage which has suddenly
seen the python that will devour it.

I thought constantly of Albertine, and when Françoise entered my
room she could never say, 'There are no letters' soon enough to cut
short my anxiety. But from time to time, by letting some current of
ideas or other flow through my sorrow, I managed to refresh and
ventilate a little the stuffy atmosphere of my heart. But then in the
evening, if I managed to get off to sleep, it was as if the memory of
Albertine had been the medicine which had induced my sleep, which
as its effects wore off, would waken me. I thought of Albertine all the
time that I was asleep. It was a very special sleep, which only she
could provide me with and, what is more, one where I would not have
been free, as I might during my waking hours, to think of anything
else. Sleep and her memory were like two substances mingled together
to form a sleeping-draught. Moreover during my waking hours my
suffering increased day by day instead of diminishing. Not that the
work of forgetting was not under way, but it was precisely this process
that enhanced my idealization of the missing image and thereby the

absorption of my initial suffering into the other analogous sufferings which reinforced it. Even then this image was bearable. But if I suddenly thought of her room, her room with its bed lying empty, of her piano, of her motor-car, I lost all my strength, I closed my eyes, and my head slumped on my shoulder as if I were about to faint. The sound of a door opening hurt me almost as much, because it was not being opened by her.

When there might be a telegram from Saint-Loup I did not dare ask, 'Is there a telegram?' One did finally come, but it only postponed everything by saying, 'The ladies have gone away for three days.' Doubtless, if I had tolerated the four days that had already elapsed since her departure, it was because I said to myself, 'It's only a matter of time, she will be back before the end of the week.' But this argument could not prevent the fact that for my heart and for my body, the actions which I had to perform were the same: to live without her, to go home and find her not there, to walk past the door to her room – the courage to open it still failed me – knowing that she was not there, to go to bed without saying good-night to her, those were actions which my heart had had to perform to the full, for all their terror, and in just the same way as if I were never to see Albertine again. Yet the fact that I had already performed them four times in my heart proved that I was now capable of continuing to do so. And soon perhaps I would no longer need to rely on this argument – the imminent return of Albertine – which was helping me to continue to live (I could say to myself, 'She will never return,' and carry on living regardless, as I had done for the last four days), just as a cripple who has learned how to walk again can throw away his crutches. No doubt in the evening when I came home I still found memories which left me breathless and suffocating with emptiness and loneliness, memories juxtaposed in an interminable series of all the evenings when Albertine was waiting for me; but already I found the memory of the day before, the day before that and the two preceding evenings, that is the memory of the four evenings which had passed since Albertine's departure, during which I had remained on my own without her, yet when I had none the less survived for four evenings already, composing a very thin layer of memories compared to the others, but which might perhaps thicken with every passing day. I need hardly describe the letter of proposal which I received at that period from a niece of Mme de Guermantes, reputedly the prettiest young lady in Paris, nor the advances made to me by the Duc de Guermantes on behalf of her parents, resigned in the interests of their daughter's happiness to such a misalliance and with such an unequal party. Such events, which might otherwise touch our self-esteem, are too painful when we are in love. We would like to reveal their import, were it not tactless to do so, to the other lady, who has formed a less favourable opinion of us, although this opinion would still not be modified if she learned that we might be the object of an entirely different opinion. What the Duc's niece wrote to me could only have irritated Albertine.

From the moment that I awoke and resumed my sorrows at the point where I had left off before falling asleep, like a book closed for an instant but which would haunt me all day until evening, it could only be with thoughts about Albertine that any feelings, whether arising from within or without, might be associated. The door-bell rang: it's a letter from her, perhaps herself in person! If I was feeling well, and neither too unhappy nor too jealous, and had nothing to reproach her with, then I wished I could see her soon, embrace her, and spend the rest of my life in happiness by her side. To telegraph her saying, 'Come quickly' seemed to me to have become an entirely simple thing to do, as if my new mood had changed not only my inner disposition but the external circumstances of our relationship and had made everything easier. If I was in sombre mood, and all my anger against her returned, then I no longer wanted to embrace her, I felt that it would be impossible ever to attain happiness through her, and I wanted nothing but to harm her and prevent her from belonging to anyone else. But the result of these two contradictory moods was identical, she must return as soon as possible. And yet, however much joy her return might give me when it happened, I felt that the same difficulties would soon arise again and that seeking happiness through satisfying my inner desires was as naïve as undertaking to reach the horizon by simply walking forward in a straight line. The more desire advances, the more true possession recedes. So that if it is possible to obtain happiness, or at least freedom from suffering, what we should

seek is not the satisfaction, but the gradual reduction and final elimin-
ation of desire. We try to see those we love, we should try not to see
them, for only the process of forgetting leads finally to the extinction
of desire. And I imagine that if an author wanted to express this kind
of truth, he would seek to approach the woman concerned by dedicating
his book to her, saying, 'This is your book.' And thus, in telling the
truth in the book he would be lying in the dedication, for he will want
the book to be hers only in the same way that he takes possession of
the gemstone that she gave him, which he will only consider precious
as long as he still loves the woman. The links between another person
and ourselves exist only in our minds. Memory weakens them as it
fades, and despite the illusions which we hope will deceive us and with
which, whether from love, friendship, politeness, human respect or
from duty, we hope to deceive others, we exist on our own. Man is a
being who cannot move beyond his own boundaries, who knows
others only within himself, and if he alleges the contrary, he is lying.
And I would have been so afraid that someone might take away my
need for her and my love for her, had they been able to do so, that I
convinced myself that these were essential for my life. To be able to
hear the names of the stations on the railway line to Touraine without
feeling pleasure or pain would have seemed to me a diminution of the
self (simply because deep down this would have proved that I was
becoming indifferent to Albertine). I told myself, while I could not
stop wondering what she might be doing, thinking and hoping at every
moment, wondering whether she intended to and was going to return,
that it was in my interest to keep open the communicating door that
love had unlocked within me and feel a different woman's life burst
through the floodgates and pour into the reservoir which would
otherwise have dried up. Soon, as Saint-Loup's silence continued, a
secondary anxiety – waiting for a telegram or a telephone call from
Saint-Loup – masked the first anxiety, worrying over the outcome,
wondering whether Albertine would return. Listening out for every
sound while expecting a telegram became so intolerable for me that
the arrival of this telegram, whatever it might say, was the only thing
that I could think of now that might put an end to my suffering. But
when I did finally receive a telegram from Robert, where he told me

that he had seen Mme Bontemps, but had been seen by Albertine despite all his precautions, which had ruined everything, I exploded with fury and despair, for this was what I had wanted to avoid above all. Now that Albertine had found out about it, Saint-Loup's journey would make me appear to hold her dear in a way that could only prevent her from returning, and what is more, my horror of this was the last shred of pride surviving from my love for Gilberte, and now it was lost. I cursed Robert, then told myself that if these means had failed, I would use others. Since man can have an impact on the external world, how could I not manage, by exploiting cunning, intelligence, money and affection, to suppress this atrocious thing: the absence of Albertine? We believe that we may change things around us to suit our desires, we believe this because otherwise we can see no acceptable solution. We do not think of the solution which occurs most frequently and which is also acceptable: when we do not manage to change things to suit our desires, but our desires gradually change. We become indifferent to a situation which we had hoped to change when we found it unbearable. We were not able to overcome the obstacle, although this was our only desire, yet life led us round or beyond it, and afterwards, if we turn back towards the past we can hardly catch sight of it in the distance, so imperceptible has it become. I heard some tunes from *Manon*³ played by one of our neighbours on the floor above ours. I applied their familiar words to Albertine and myself, and I was filled with such deep feelings that I began to weep. They were:

> Hélas, l'oiseau qui fuit ce qu'il croit l'esclavage,
> Le plus souvent, la nuit d'un vol désespéré revient battre au vitrage⁴

and the death of Manon:

> Manon réponds-moi donc! – Seul amour de mon âme,
> Je n'ai su qu'aujourd'hui la bonté de ton cœur.⁵

Since Manon did return to Des Grieux, it seemed to me that for Albertine I was the only love of her life. Alas, it is likely that if she had been able to listen to the same tune at that moment, it would not have been me that she would have cherished under the name of Des Grieux, and, if she had thought of it for even a moment, her memories of me would have prevented her from weakening as she listened to this music, which was however very much the kind of music that she liked, although better written and more subtle.

As for me, I was not brave enough to yield to the sweetness of thinking that Albertine used to call me her 'soul's only love' and had recognized that she had been mistaken over her 'seeming slavery'. I knew that one cannot read a novel without lending its heroine the features of the woman that one loves. Yet even if the book does have a happy ending, our love has not progressed an inch, and when we have finished it, the woman whom we love and who has finally surrendered to us in the novel, does not in real life love us any more than she did before. I sent Saint-Loup a furious telegram demanding his immediate return to Paris, to avoid at least the appearance of aggravating through added persistence the intervention which I had so wanted to keep secret. But even before he had returned in accordance with my instructions, I had received the following telegram from Albertine herself:

MY DEAR FRIEND, YOU HAVE SENT YOUR FRIEND SAINT-LOUP TO SEE MY AUNT, WHICH WAS RIDICULOUS. IF YOU NEEDED ME, MY DEAR, WHY DID YOU NOT WRITE DIRECTLY TO ME? I WOULD HAVE BEEN ONLY TOO PLEASED TO RETURN: DO NOT TRY ANY SUCH ABSURD APPROACH AGAIN. 'I would have been only too pleased to return!' If she said this, it must mean that she regretted having left, and that she was looking only for an excuse to return. So I only had to do what she said, write and tell her that I needed her, and she would return. So I was going to see her again, my Balbec Albertine (for, since her departure, this is what she had become for me. Like a sea-shell which we no longer notice because it is always placed on top of the same chest of drawers, but which, despite having entirely forgotten it, we call to mind as soon it has disappeared, whether because we lost it or because we gave it away, she recalled for me all the joyous beauty of the blue hills of the sea.) And it was not only because she had become an imaginary, that is, a desirable creature, but because my life with her had become an imaginary life, that is, a life liberated from all problems, that I said to myself, 'How happy we shall be!' But as soon as I was assured of her return, I should not appear to precipitate things, but on the contrary erase the bad impression created by Saint-Loup's intervention, which I might always disclaim later by saying that he had acted on his own initiative because he had always been in favour of our marriage.

However, as I reread her words I was none the less a little disappointed to realize how little of our person remains in our correspondence. Of course the characters we trace express our thoughts, as do our features; it is always a process of thinking that confronts us. But even so, in a person, thought appears to us only after being filtered through the bloom of the face, flowering like a water-lily only on the surface. And this, it has to be said, does modify it considerably. And perhaps one of the causes of our perpetual disappointment in love is this perpetual slippage, which causes every anticipation of the ideal being whom we love to be confronted at each meeting by a flesh-and-blood person who already has little in common with our dream. And then, when we expect something from this person, what we receive from her is a letter where very little of the person herself remains, as in those letters used in algebraic formulae, where there remains none of the qualities characterized by the arithmetical numbers, which themselves already no longer encapsulated the properties of the fruit or the flowers that were being assessed. And yet love itself, the experience of being loved, or reading love letters, are perhaps none the less translations – however unsatisfactory it is to pass from one to the other – of the same reality, since the letter seems insufficient only while we are reading it, and yet we sweat blood and tears as long as we await its arrival, and it does suffice to calm our anguish, even if its little black marks do not entirely assuage our desire, which feels in spite of everything that these are no more than an approximation to speech, smiles and kisses rather than those things themselves.

I wrote to Albertine:

'*My dear friend, I was in fact just about to write to you, and I am grateful to you for telling me that, had I needed you, you would have come with all speed; it is good of you to interpret in such noble fashion your duty to an old friend, and my esteem for you can only be enhanced. But, actually, no, I had not asked you to return and shall not ask you to; perhaps an unemotional young woman like you might not find it painful to meet again, at least in the distant future. But I, whom you have sometimes believed so indifferent, would find it much more so. Life has led us apart. You have taken a decision which seems to me very wise and is one which you have taken at the right moment, with remarkable foresight, for you left me the very day after I had just received my mother's consent to ask for your hand. I would have told you on waking, when I received her letter (at the same time as yours!). Perhaps you would have feared upsetting me if you had left in those circumstances. And perhaps we might have united our lives for what might, who knows, have been our misfortune? If that were to be our fate, bless you for your wise decision. We would lose all the benefit of this were we to meet again. I do not say that I would not find this very tempting. But I have no great merit in resisting. You know how inconstant and forgetful I am. So I am not much to be pitied. You have often said yourself what a creature of habit I am. The habits which I am starting to form in your absence are not yet very strong. Obviously for the moment those which we had acquired together and which your departure has disturbed are still stronger. They will not remain so for much longer. I even thought, for this reason, that I would make the most of these last few days where meeting you would not yet be for me what in a fortnight, or earlier perhaps (excusing my frankness), it will become, that is, a nuisance, — I had thought that I would make the most of it, before we finally forget each other, to settle one or two minor material matters with you, whereby the generous and charming friend that I know you to be might do a favour to the man who for a few moments believed himself to be engaged to you. As I had no reason to doubt my mother's approval, and as, on the other hand, I wished each of us to dispose of that freedom which you have too kindly and abundantly sacrificed on my behalf, which could be envisaged if we intended to spend even only a few weeks of our lives living together, but which would have become as odious to you as to me once we were due to spend the whole of our lives together (in writing this to you I feel almost hurt to think that we were only a few seconds away from bringing this to fruition), I had thought to organize our existence along the most independent lines possible and, to start with, I wanted you to have a yacht on which you might have sailed while I was too ill to do anything but wait for you in port; I had written to Elstir to ask for his advice, since you appreciate his taste. And back on dry land, I would have wished you to have a motor-car all to yourself, which you would use for your own visits and travel at your leisure. The yacht was already almost fitted out, it is called, in accordance with the wish that you expressed at Balbec, le Cygne.*[6] *And remembering that you preferred the Rolls to all other cars, I had ordered one for you. Now however that we shall never meet again, since I cannot hope to persuade you to accept either the boat or the car (which are of no use to me) I had thought – since I had asked an agent to order them on my behalf but giving them your name – that you might perhaps, by taking it upon yourself to cancel the order, spare me the embarrassment of owning a useless yacht and a useless car. Yet for this, as for many other things, we would have had to speak together. But I feel that for as long as I might be likely to fall in love with you again, which will not be for much longer, it would be crazy, merely for the sake of a sailing-boat and a Rolls-Royce, to meet again and prejudice your lifelong happiness, since you have decided that this consists in living far from me. So I prefer to keep the Rolls and even the yacht. And as I shall use neither of them, and as they are likely to remain unrigged in the harbour and parked in the stables, I shall have inscribed on the ——— of the yacht (heavens, I dare not use the wrong technical term and commit a solecism which would shock you) these lines from Mallarmé which you used to love:*

> Un cygne d'autrefois se souvient que c'est lui
> Magnifique mais qui sans espoir se délivre
> Pour n'avoir pas chanté la région où vivre
> Quand du stérile hiver a resplendi l'ennui.[7]

*Do you remember, it is from the poem whose first line is:* Le vierge, le vivace et le bel aujourd'hui.[8] *Alas, today is no longer either virgin or beautiful. But those who, like me, know that they will soon turn it into a better "tomorrow" for themselves, are themselves difficult to tolerate. As for the Rolls, it would have deserved rather the following lines from the same poet, which you claimed not to understand:*

> Dis si je ne suis pas joyeux
> Tonnerre et rubis aux moyeux
> De voir dans l'air que ce feu troue

Avec des royaumes épars
Comme mourir pourpre la roue
Du seul vespéral de mes chars.[9]

*Farewell for ever, my sweet Albertine, and thank you once again for the pleasant trip that we enjoyed together the day before we parted. I shall remember it fondly.*

*PS – I shall not reply to what you tell me of the proposals allegedly made to your aunt by Saint-Loup (whom I do not believe to be anywhere near Touraine). It's pure Sherlock Holmes. What can you think of me?*

No doubt, just as I had said to Albertine in the past 'I do not love you', in order to get her to love me, 'I forget people when I no longer see them', in order to get her to see me as often as possible, 'I have decided to leave you', in order to pre-empt any idea of separation, now it was because I desperately wanted her to return before a week had elapsed that I said 'Farewell' to her, 'for ever'; it was because I wanted to see her again that I told her: 'I would find it dangerous to see you again'; it was because living apart from her seemed worse than death that I wrote to her saying, 'You were right, we would be unhappy together'. Alas, this bogus letter, which I wrote so as to seem detached from her (the last shred of pride left over from my former love for Gilberte that survived in my love for Albertine) and also for the sweetness of saying certain things which could move only me, and not her, I ought to have guessed in advance that this might possibly provoke a negative response, that is, one confirming the truth of my words; that it was even quite probable that it would, for even had Albertine been less intelligent than she was, she would not have doubted for an instant that what I was saying was false. Even without lingering over my declared intentions in writing this letter, the simple fact that I was writing it, even if it had not followed Saint-Loup's intervention, was sufficient to prove to her that I wanted her to return and to imply that she should allow me to swallow the hook even deeper, then, having foreseen the possibility of a negative response, I should always have foreseen that this response would renew my love for Albertine more intensely than ever. And, even before sending my letter, I should have stopped to wonder whether, if Albertine were to answer in the same spirit and did not wish to return, I would be able to master my pain enough to force myself to stay silent, rather than telegraph her to say, 'Return' or send her yet another emissary, which, after writing to say that we would not see each other again, would be to give her detailed proof that I was unable to do without her and might lead her to refuse all the more strenuously to meet, which would then lead me, driven by my inability to contain my anguish, to go out to see her, without her even greeting me, as like as not. And no doubt, following three enormous blunders, this would have been the worst of all, after which my last resort would have been to kill myself on her doorstep. But the disastrous way in which the psychopathological universe is constructed implies that the clumsy act, the act which we should avoid at all costs, is precisely the act which soothes us, the act which, until we discover its outcome, opens up new prospects of hope for us and momentarily relieves us of the intolerable pain that rejection gave birth to within us, thus it is that when the pain is too strong, we fall into the clumsy error of writing to the person whom we love, or begging someone else to do so, or going to see her, and proving that we cannot do without her.

But I predicted none of this. The likely result of my letter seemed to me on the contrary to be to make Albertine return as soon as possible. So, since I was thinking of this outcome I felt greatly soothed as I wrote the letter. But at the same time I had not ceased to weep while I was writing it; at first rather in the same way as the day when I had faked a separation, because the words rendered present to me the idea that they expressed, although they aimed to produce the opposite effect (uttering their lies out of pride in order to avoid admitting that I loved her), they were charged with sadness, but I did also feel that there was some truth in the idea.

Since the effect of this letter seemed certain to me, I regretted having sent it. For in imagining Albertine's return as ultimately so simple, suddenly all the reasons that had made our marriage seem wrong for me returned in full strength. I hoped that she would refuse to return. I was starting to calculate how much my freedom and my whole future life hung on her refusal; how crazy I had been to write; how I should have retrieved my letter (alas, now sent), when Françoise brought it back to me, along with the newspaper which she was bringing upstairs. She was unsure how many stamps my letter required. But I immediately changed my mind; I did not want Albertine to return, however, in order to alleviate my anxiety, I wanted this to be her own decision, and so I decided to give the letter back to Françoise. I opened the newspaper. It announced the death of La Berma. Then I remembered the two different ways in which I had listened to *Phèdre*, but now there was a third way for me to think of the declaration scene. It seemed to me that what I had so often recited to myself and what I had listened to in the theatre, was the expression of laws that I would come to experience in my own life. There are in our soul things which are dearer to us than we realize. Or else, if we do yearn for them, it is because from day to day, for fear of failure or suffering, we delay taking full possession of them. That is what happened to me in the case of Gilberte, when I had thought that I could do without her. If, before the moment when we are entirely detached from these things, which occurs long after the moment when we first believe ourselves detached, if for instance the young lady gets engaged, we become insane and we find that we can no longer bear our life, which seemed so monotonous and calm. Or if the object of our desire is in our possession, we believe that she is a burden to us, that we would gladly be rid of her; which is what had happened to me in the case of Albertine. But just let the indifferent object be removed by her departure, and we can no longer live. Now did not the 'argument' of *Phèdre* combine the two cases? Hippolyte is about to leave. Phèdre, who until then has taken care to court his hostility, from moral duty, so she says, or rather, as the poet makes her say, because she does not believe that she could succeed, and because she does not feel loved, and can now hold out no longer. She comes to him to admit her love, and this is the scene that I had so often recited to myself:

On dit qu'un prompt départ vous éloigne de nous.[10]

Doubtless this reason for the departure of Hippolyte is incidental, we might think, compared with that of the death of Theseus. And even when, a few lines later, Phèdre pretends for a moment to have been misunderstood:

> . . . Aurais-je perdu tout le soin de ma gloire,[11]

we might suppose that it is because Hippolyte has rejected her declaration:

> Madame, oubliez-vous
> Que Thésée est mon père, et qu'il est votre époux?[12]

But even had he not had this indignant reaction, and had Phèdre seen happiness within her grasp, she might still have felt that it was of little worth. But as soon as she sees that it escapes her, that Hippolyte thinks that he has misunderstood her and makes his excuses, then, just as I did the moment after handing my letter to Françoise, she wants the rejection to come from him, she wants to try one last chance:

> Ah cruel, tu m'as trop entendue![13]

And even Swann's harshness towards Odette, of which I had heard tell, or mine towards Albertine, a harshness which substitutes for the former love a new one, composed of pity, tenderness and a need to find expression for emotion, and which is only a variant of the former love, even these can be also be found in this scene:

> Tu me haïssais plus, je ne t'aimais pas moins.
> Tes malheurs te prêtait encor de nouveaux charmes.[14]

The proof that 'care for her good name' is not what Phèdre holds most dear is that she would forgive Hippolyte and would turn her back on Oenone's good counsel, if she did not learn at this moment that Hippolyte was in love with Aricie. For jealousy, which in love is tantamount to the loss of all happiness, touches us so much more than the loss of reputation. Then it is that she lets Oenone (who is only a name for her baser self) slander Hippolyte without taking 'care to defend him' and thus sends the man who refuses to love her to a fate which, however calamitous, still offers her no consolation, since her own, self-inflicted death follows swiftly on from that of Hippolyte. This, minimizing the share of all the 'Jansenist' scruples,[15] as Bergotte would have called them, which Racine has allocated to Phèdre in order to make her seem less guilty, is at any rate how this scene appeared to me, almost as a prophecy of the kind of love-scenes that I would come to enact in my own lifetime. None the less, these reflections had not altered my determination in the slightest, and I held out the letter to Françoise for her to take it finally to the post, so as to have made this approach towards Albertine, which seemed indispensable to me the minute I heard that it had not been accomplished. And we are doubtless wrong to believe that fulfilling our desires is of little account, since as soon as we believe it possible for them not to be fulfilled, we need them once more, and it is only when we are quite certain that they cannot escape us that we feel that they are not worth pursuing. And, in a way, we are not wrong. For if this attainment of our desires and our happiness seem trivial only when they are secure, they none the less contain unstable elements from which nothing but sorrow can emerge. And the more completely our desires have been realized and the longer the happiness has been prolonged, against the laws of nature, and has been consecrated by habit, the stronger the sorrow, the more impossible to bear. In another sense too, the two tendencies, in this case the one which made me want my letter to be sent and, when I thought that it had been, to regret this, are both true in their way. As for the first tendency, it is only too easy to understand that we should pursue our happiness – or our unhappiness – while hoping at the same time, through the consequences of this new action as they start to unfold, to maintain expectations that will not leave us in total despair, in a word, which might manage to transform the misfortune which afflicts us into other forms that we imagine we must find less cruel. But the other tendency is no less important, for, born of our belief in the success of our enterprise, it is quite simply a beginning, the anticipated beginning of the disillusionment that we should soon experience if faced with the satisfaction of our desires, our regret at having settled on this form of happiness at the expense of excluding others. I handed the letter back to Françoise, telling her to take it quickly to the post-office. As soon as my letter had left, I again envisaged Albertine's return as imminent. This brought into my mind a constant stream of graceful images, whose sweetness could not help neutralize the dangers that I saw in this return. I was intoxicated by the prospect of recovering the long-lost sweetness of having her by my side.

Time passes, and gradually all the things which we have falsely alleged come true, an experience which had affected me only too strongly with Gilberte; the indifference that I had feigned while I sobbed day and night had come to exist; gradually, as I told Gilberte in a mendacious dictum which had retrospectively come true, life had driven us apart. I remembered this and thought: 'If Albertine waits for a few months, my lies will come true. And now that the worst is over, would it not be in her best interest to allow that moment to pass? If she returns, I shall have to renounce my true life, which I admit that I was not yet able to enjoy, but which could gradually start to become more attractive as the memory of Albertine becomes gradually weaker.' I cannot claim that the process of forgetting was not already at work. But one of the effects of forgetting was precisely to make many of the unpleasant sides to Albertine's character and the hours of boredom that I had endured at her side, no longer figure in my memory and thus cease to be reasons for me to wish that she were no longer there, as I had done while she was still with me, and to give me a summary image of her, embellished with all the love that I had felt for other women. In this particular guise, forgetting, although still working within me to accustom me to our separation, only made me see Albertine as sweeter and more beautiful than ever, and made me desire her return all the more.

On many occasions after Albertine's departure, whenever it seemed to me that I would not look as if I had been crying, I rang for Françoise and said: 'We ought to make sure that Mademoiselle Albertine has not left anything behind. Don't forget to clean her room so that everything is ready for her when she returns.' Or simply: 'Actually, it was only the other day, I suppose it must have been the day before she left, that Mademoiselle Albertine was talking to me about . . .' I wanted to

curtail the odious relish that Françoise took in Albertine's absence, by
making her realize that it would be short-lived; I also wanted to show
Françoise that I had no qualms about discussing her departure and to
present it – as do certain generals who refer to their forced retreats as
'strategic withdrawals executed according to contingency plans' – as
intended, as constituting an interlude whose true significance I was
momentarily dissimulating, but not at all as the end of my friendship
with Albertine. By constantly mentioning her, I hoped ultimately to
bring something of her back into the room, like a breath of fresh air,
since her departure had emptied the room and made it impossible to
breathe. And then again, we try to reduce the scale of our suffering by
bringing it into our everyday conversation between ordering a suit
and choosing the menu for dinner.

While she was tidying Albertine's room, Françoise's curiosity led
her to open the drawer of a little rosewood table where my friend used
to place the personal jewellery that she removed when she went to
bed. 'Oh, Monsieur! Mademoiselle Albertine has forgotten to take her
rings, she has left them in the drawer.' My first reaction was to say:
'We must send them on to her.' But that would look as if I were not
sure that she would return. 'Well,' I replied after a moment's silence,
'it's hardly worth the trouble for the short time that she will be away.
Give them to me and. I'll take care of it.' Françoise handed them to
me with some reluctance. She detested Albertine, but she judged me
by her own standards and imagined that no one could hand me a letter
written by my friend without fearing that I would open it. I took the
rings. 'I hope that Monsieur will be careful not to lose them,' said
Françoise, 'just look how beautiful they are! I don't know who gave
her them, whether it was Monsieur or somebody else, but I know it
must be somebody rich who has good taste!' – It wasn't me, I replied,
and besides the two did not come from the same person, one was given
her by her aunt and she bought the other herself. – Not from the same
person! Françoise cried, Monsieur must be joking, they are identical,
except for the ruby that they added to one of them, there is the same
eagle on both of them and the same initials inside.' I do not know
whether Françoise was aware of the pain that she was causing, but a
smile started to creep over her face and remained there. 'What do you

mean, the same eagle? You must be mad. On the one without the ruby you're right, there is an eagle, but on the other one there's an engraving of a sort of man's head. — A man's head? Where did Monsieur see that? Even with my reading-glasses I saw straight away that it was one of the eagle's wings; if Monsieur will take his magnifying glass, he will see the other wing on the other side and the head and the beak in the middle. You can see every feather. Oh, what a fine piece of work.' My anxious need to know whether Albertine had lied to me made me forget that I should have stood on my dignity in Françoise's company and denied her the cruel pleasure which she took, if not in tormenting me, at least in denigrating my friend. I gasped as Françoise went to fetch my magnifying glass, then I took it and asked her to show me the eagle on the ruby ring; she had no trouble in helping me to identify the wings, stylized in the same manner as on the other ring, with the head and every feather picked out in relief. She also pointed out similar insignia in the ruby ring, although in this case it is true that they were accompanied by others. And inside both were Albertine's initials. 'But I am amazed that Monsieur needed to take so much trouble to see that they were the same ring,' said Françoise. 'Even if you don't look close up, you can see the same craftsmanship, the same way of working the gold, the same shape. Just by looking at them I would have sworn that they came from the same place. It stands out like a dish by a good cook.' And indeed, the curiosity of the servant, accustomed to noting details with terrifying precision and spurred on by hatred, joined forces, in this expert scrutiny, with her good taste, the same taste in fact that she displayed in her cooking, and which was perhaps whetted, as I had noticed in the style of her dress when we set out for Balbec, by the coquetry of a woman who used to be pretty and who had taken note of the dresses and jewellery of other women. If I had opened the wrong medicine chest and if, instead of taking a few veronal tablets one day when I felt that I had drunk too many cups of tea, I had taken as many cups of coffee, my heart could not have beaten more violently. I asked Françoise to leave the room. I wished that I could have seen Albertine immediately. My revulsion at her falsehood and my jealousy of someone unknown were augmented by my pain at learning that she had accepted presents in this way. It is true that I had given her more, but a woman whom we are keeping does not seem to us to be a kept woman as long as we know that she is not being kept by anyone else. And yet since I had never ceased to spend so much money on her, I kept her despite this moral weakness; this weakness that I had allowed in her, perhaps encouraged, possibly even created. And then, just as we have the ability to tell ourselves stories in order to alleviate our pains, just as we manage when we are dying of hunger to persuade ourselves that some stranger is about to leave us a fortune of a hundred million francs, I imagined Albertine in my arms, explaining to me in a word that she had bought the second ring because of the similar design and that it was she who had had the initials engraved. But this exploration was still tender, it had not yet had time to put its salutary roots down into my mind, and my pain was not to be so easily appeased. And I wondered how many men who say that their mistresses are very kind suffer similar torments and thus lie to others as well as themselves. Yet they do not entirely lie; they do spend genuinely delicious hours with these women; but all the tenderness that these women show their lovers in the presence of their friends, to flatter their pride, and all the tenderness that they reserve for their lovers in private, to allow themselves to be worshipped, mask unknown hours where the lover has suffered, doubted and searched endlessly, but in vain, to discover the truth! Such suffering inevitably accompanies the sweetness of loving a woman and delighting in even her most trivial remarks, while knowing that they are trivial, as long as they are permeated with her scent. At this moment I could no longer delight in breathing Albertine's scent through my memory. I sat downcast, holding the two rings in my hand, looking at that pitiless eagle whose beak was tearing at my heart, whose wings with their chiselled feathers had flown off with the confidence that I still placed in my friend, and under whose claws my lacerated mind could no longer for a moment escape the questions ceaselessly raised about that stranger, whose name the eagle surely symbolized while none the less refusing to allow me to read it, the woman whom she had doubtless loved in the past and whom she had certainly seen again not so long ago, since it was on that unspeakably sweet and intimate day which we had spent walking in the Bois de Boulogne together that I had seen for the first time the second ring, the one where the eagle looked as if it was dipping its beak in the bright, bloody pool of the ruby.

Yet even if from morning to night I continually pined over Albertine's departure, this did not mean that I thought only of her. On the one hand her charm had gradually permeated objects which finally became very distant from her, but were none the less galvanized by the same emotions as those she inspired in me, if something made me think of Incarville, or the Verdurins, or Léa's latest role, a wave of suffering flooded over me. On the other hand, what I myself called 'thinking of Albertine' was in fact thinking of ways of getting her to return, of meeting up with her, of finding out what she was doing. So that if, during these hours of unremitting torture, my suffering could have been displayed in graphic form, it would have shown images of the Orsay railway station,[16] the banknotes offered to Mme Bontemps, Saint-Loup leaning over a post-office counter filling in a form to send me a telegram, but never a picture of Albertine. In the same way that during the course of our lives we, in our egoism, constantly see before our eyes the goals which our selves find valuable, but do not perceive the 'I' itself which never ceases to scrutinize them, so the desire that directs our actions swoops down upon them, but never looks back on itself, either because it is too utilitarian and, spurning knowledge, prefers to rush into action, or because we search out the future in order to compensate for the disappointments of the present, or even because the indolence of the mind tempts it to slide down the slippery slope of the imagination rather than to climb the steep slope of introspection. In fact in the moments of crisis when we are prepared to stake our very life, as the person on whom it depends reveals the increasingly vast place that she takes up for us, leaving nothing in our world undisturbed by her presence, proportionally the image of this person decreases until it is no longer perceptible. We feel the impact of her presence all around us through the emotions that we feel; but the cause, the person herself, is nowhere to be found. During those days I was so unable to call Albertine's image to mind that I might almost have thought that I did not love her, just as my mother, in those moments of despair when she found herself totally incapable of pictur- ing my grandmother (except on one occasion in a random encounter in a dream which made such an impression on her that, although she was asleep, she forced herself, with the little strength left to her in her sleep, to make it last), might have reproached herself and did in fact reproach herself with not missing her mother, whose dream had struck her a mortal blow, but whose features eluded her memory.

Why might I have believed that Albertine was not attracted to women? Because, especially in recent times, she had said that she was not attracted to them; but was not the life we lived together based on a perpetual lie? Never once had she said to me, 'Why am I not free to go out as I wish? Why do you ask other people what I do?' But our life was in fact too singular for her not to have asked if she had not understood the reason. And was it not understandable that my silence over the causes of her sequestration should be countered by an equally inflexible silence over her perpetual desires and countless memories, her countless desires and expectations? Françoise looked as if she knew that I was lying when I referred to Albertine's imminent return. And her belief seemed founded on rather more than the truth which usually guided our servant, that is, the fact that masters do not like to be humiliated in front of their servants and reveal to them only that part of reality which does not deviate too far from a flattering fiction, liable to maintain respect. On this occasion, Françoise's belief seemed to be founded on something else, as if she herself had awakened and fuelled the suspicions in Albertine's mind, and fanned her anger, in short as if she had driven her to an extremity where she could tell that her departure was inevitable. If this was true, my version of a temporary absence, known and approved by me, could have been met only with incredulity by Françoise. But her notion of Albertine's self-interested nature, which, inflamed by her hatred, caused her to magnify the 'profit' that Albertine was supposedly extracting from me, could to some extent cause her to doubt her convictions. Thus when in her presence I alluded to Albertine's imminent return as something wholly natural, Françoise looked into my eyes (in the same way as, when the butler teased her by reading out a piece of political news that she was reluctant to believe, altering the words so as to say, for example, they were going to close down the churches and banish the clergy,[17] Françoise, even from the depths of her kitchen, and despite not being able to read, instinctively and eagerly looked at the newspaper), as if she were able to see whether it was really written there or whether I had made it up.

But when Françoise saw me write a long letter and then check the right address for Mme Bontemps, her previously rather vague terror that Albertine might return welled up more strongly than ever within her. It reached a point of veritable consternation when she was obliged one morning to hand me among others a letter where she had recognized Albertine's handwriting on the envelope. She wondered whether Albertine's departure had not been purely theatrical, a supposition which she found doubly upsetting, in that it ensured Albertine's presence in the house permanently for the future and in that it constituted for me, that is, in so far as I was Françoise's master, for Françoise herself the humiliation of having been manipulated by Albertine. However impatient I was to read Albertine's letter, I could not help momentarily studying Françoise's eyes, drained of all hope as they read in this augury the imminent return of Albertine, just as a devotee of winter sports concludes joyfully that winter is nigh when he sees the swallows depart. At last Françoise left, and when I had made sure that she had closed the door, I opened her letter silently, so as not to seem anxious, reading as follows:

'*My dear friend, thank you for all your kind remarks, I am at your disposal and shall cancel the order for the Rolls if you think that I may be of assistance, and I do think this likely. You have only to tell me the name of your agent. You would be liable to let yourself be taken in by these people who have only one thing in mind, which is to make a sale; and what would you do with a car, since you never go out? I am very touched that you should have kept such a nice memory of our last outing. Please believe that for my part I shall never forget this excursion and its twofold twilight (since night was falling and we were destined to part) and that it will never be erased from my mind until blackest night finally invades it.*'

I felt confident that this last sentence was purely rhetorical and that Albertine could not have kept until her dying day such a sweet memory of an outing which had certainly given her no pleasure, since she had been impatient to leave me. But I also admired the talent of the cyclist and golfer from Balbec, who before making my acquaintance had read nothing by Racine apart from *Esther*,[18] and I realized how right I had been to feel that she had been enriched during her stay with me by new qualities, which had changed her and made her more complete. And thus, the words which I had uttered in Balbec, 'I think that my friendship would be valuable for you, that I am just the person who could provide you with what you lack' – I had written as a dedication to her on a photograph: *Certain to be providential*, – words which I spoke without believing them, only in order to persuade her that frequenting me would be profitable and to minimize the tedium that this might provoke, these words too turned out to be true; as, in fact, did my admission to her that I did not want to see her for fear of falling in love with her. I had said this because, on the contrary, I knew that with constant meeting my love tended to fade and that separation excited it; but in fact the constant meeting had given birth to a need for her infinitely stronger than that first love in Balbec.

But in the end Albertine's letter was unhelpful. She spoke only of writing to the agent. I must extricate myself from this situation and precipitate matters. I had the following idea. I immediately had a letter sent to Andrée telling her that Albertine was staying with her aunt, that I felt very lonely and that she would do me the greatest favour if she could come and take up residence with me for a few days but that, since I did not want to act behind Albertine's back, I begged her to let Albertine know. And at the same time I wrote to Albertine, as if I had not yet received her letter:

*'My dear friend, forgive me for something you will understand very well, which is that I so detest acting behind people's backs that I wanted you to be alerted by me as well as by her. Having had the experience of your sweet presence by my side, I have got into the bad habit of not living alone. Since we have decided that you would not return, I thought that the person who would best take your place, because she would change my life least, and would most remind me of you, was Andrée, and I have asked her to come. So that this should not seem too sudden, I have spoken to her of a period of just a few days, but between you and me I think that this time it is something permanent. Do you not think that I am right? You know*

*that your little group of girls at Balbec has always been the social group that has*
*exerted the most influence over me, the one with which I was most pleased to be*
*associated when allowed. There is no doubt that I still feel its prestige. Since our*
*fatal characters and life's misfortunes have determined that my little Albertine*
*could not be my wife, I believe that I should none the less take a wife – one less*
*charming, but one whose greater compatibility of character ought perhaps to allow*
*her to be happier with me – in Andrée.'*

But once I had sent this letter, I was suddenly assailed by the suspicion
that, Albertine having written, 'I would have been only too happy to
return if you had written to me direct,' she had said this only because
I had not written to her direct and that, if I had done so, she still would
not have returned, that she would have been pleased to know that
Andrée was living with me and was to become my wife, provided that
she, Albertine, remained free, because for a week now, foiling all the
precautions that I had taken hour by hour for more than six months,
she was able to give free rein to her vices and do every minute of the
day what I had been preventing her from doing. I thought that she
was probably applying her freedom out there to dubious ends, and no
doubt this idea as I formulated it made me sad, but it remained vague,
since it pictured nothing specific, and through the indefinite number
of women that she had led me to imagine might be her lovers, without
letting me dwell on any one in particular, it threw my mind into a sort
of perpetual motion which did cause me pain, but a pain which, for
lack of any concrete image, was bearable. But it ceased to be so and
became atrocious when Saint-Loup returned. Before saying why the
words that he uttered made me so unhappy, I must relate an incident
which occurred immediately before his visit and whose memory so
disturbed me that it diluted, if not the painful impression that I gained
from my conversation with Saint-Loup, at least the practical impact of
this conversation. This incident was the following. Burning with
impatience to see Saint-Loup, I was waiting for him on the staircase
(which I could not have done if my mother had been in the house, for
that, apart from 'talking out of the window', was what she hated most
of all), when I heard the following words: 'What do you mean! If
there is someone you don't like can't you get him dismissed? It's not

so difficult. All you have to do, for instance, is hide the things that they will ask him to fetch; then, just when his masters are in a hurry and call for him, he won't be able to find a thing, he'll lose his grip: my aunt will be furious with him and ask you: "Whatever can he be doing?" When he does arrive, he'll be late, everyone will be furious and he won't have brought what they'd asked for. By the fourth or fifth occasion you can be sure that he will be dismissed, especially if you take care on the sly to make the clean things that he was supposed to fetch dirty, and thousands of tricks like that.' I was struck dumb with stupefaction, for these cruel, Machiavellian words were uttered by the voice of Saint-Loup. Since until then I had always considered him to be someone so fundamentally kind, so sympathetic towards those who suffer, it had the same effect on me as if I had heard him reciting the part of Satan in a play; that is, he could not be speaking in his own name. 'But surely everyone should be allowed to earn his living,' replied the other man, whom I then saw and identified as one of the Duchesse de Guermantes's footmen. 'Why should you care a damn as long as you are all right?' Saint-Loup replied wickedly. 'You'll have the added pleasure of having a scapegoat. You can feel free to spill entire ink-wells over his livery just when he is preparing to serve at an important dinner, in short, never leave him in peace for a second, until he prefers to leave of his own accord. As for me, by the way, I'll put my shoulder to the wheel, I'll tell my aunt that I admire your patience in serving alongside such a clumsy, uncouth individual.' I announced my presence, and Saint-Loup welcomed me, but my confidence in him was shaken since I had heard him sound such a different man from the one I knew. And I wondered if someone who was capable of acting so cruelly towards a hapless wretch might not have acted treacherously towards me in his mission to Mme Bontemps. This reflection served above all, once he had left me, to help me avoid considering his failure as proof that I could not succeed. But while he was by my side, I had thoughts only for the Saint-Loup of old and above all for the friend who had just left Mme Bontemps, as I thought. He said to me straight away: 'You think that I should have telephoned you more often, but they kept telling me you were engaged.' Yet my suffering became unbearable when he said: 'To carry on from where my last despatch left off, I went through a kind of outhouse which led into the house, and they took me down a long corridor into the lounge.' On hearing these words – outhouse, corridor, lounge – and even before he had finished uttering them, my heart was wracked by spasms even more immediately than if it had been connected to an electric current, for the power that can circle the globe the most times per second is not so much electricity as pain. How I repeated these words, outhouse, corridor, lounge, renewing their shock at my leisure, when Saint-Loup had left. In an outhouse, you can hide with a girl-friend. And in that lounge, who knows what Albertine did when her aunt was not there? And yet, had I imagined the house where Albertine was living as able to include neither outhouse nor lounge? No, I had not imagined the house at all, or merely as a vague location. I had suffered first of all when the place where she was staying had become geographically specified for the first time, when I had learned that instead of being in one of two or three possible places she was in Touraine; the words spoken by her concierge had marked out in my heart as on a map the place where I would finally have to suffer. But even when I had got used to the idea that she was in a house in Touraine, I still had not seen the house; never could I have conceived the frightful idea of a lounge, an outhouse and a corridor, which I now saw staring out at me from Saint-Loup's retina, which had seen them, and appearing in the guise of the rooms which Albertine walked into, passed through and lived in; these specific rooms and not an infinity of other possible rooms which had neutralized one another. In the words outhouse, corridor and lounge, I perceived my folly in having left Albertine for a week in this accursed place, whose existence (rather than its simple possibility) had just been revealed to me. Alas! when Saint-Loup told me in addition that while in this lounge he had heard someone singing at the top of her voice in the next room, and that it was Albertine who was singing, I realized with despair that, once rid of me, she was happy! She had regained her freedom. And all the while I had been thinking that she would come back and take Andrée's place! My pain turned into anger with Saint-Loup. 'Letting her know that you were coming is precisely what I asked you to avoid. – How easy do you think that was! They promised me she wasn't there. Oh, I know you're annoyed with me, I could tell from your telegrams. But you are not being fair, I did what I could.' Set free once more, released once again from the cage where I had kept her for days on end without letting her come into my room, she had assumed in my eyes all her old value, she had become once again the object of everyone's pursuit, the wondrous bird of the earliest days. 'Look, to sum up. As for the money, I don't know what to say, the woman I spoke to seemed so discreet that I was afraid of offending her. But then she didn't even raise an eyebrow when I did mention money. And a little later she even told me that she was touched to see how well we understood each other. Yet everything she said subsequently was so discreet, so refined, that I found it impossible to believe that she could be talking about the money I was offering when she said: "We understand each other so well," for basically I was acting like a cad. – But perhaps she didn't understand; perhaps she didn't hear what you said; you should have repeated it, for it's surely the money that would have made everything work out. – But how can you imagine that she couldn't have heard me? I was talking to her as I'm talking to you now, and she is neither deaf nor mad. – And didn't she pass any remark at all? – Not one. – You could have repeated it, at least once. – How could I have repeated it? As soon as I went in I saw what she looked like, and I thought that you had been mistaken, that you were making me put my foot in it and that it was terribly difficult to just offer her money like that. Yet I still went ahead, in order to follow your orders, but convinced that she would have me thrown out. – But she didn't. Therefore either she hadn't heard what you'd said and you needed to repeat it, or you could have pursued the matter. – It's all very well for you to say: "she hadn't heard what you said" because you are here with me, but, let me say it again, if you had been there and listening to our conversation, there was no interruption, I said it quite bluntly, it was impossible for her not to understand. – But was she at least convinced that I have always wanted to marry her niece? – No, if you want my opinion on that, she didn't believe for one moment that you had the slightest intention of marrying her. She told me that you had told her niece yourself that you wanted to leave her. I don't know if she is convinced even now that you do intend to get married.' This reassured me somewhat, by making me feel that I appeared less humiliated, therefore more liable still to be loved, and freer to take some decisive steps. And yet I felt tormented. 'I'm so sorry, I can see that you are not pleased,' said Saint-Loup. 'Oh no, I am touched by your kindness and I am grateful, but it seems to me that you might have . . . – I did my best. Nobody else could have done more, or even as much. Try someone else. – But, how can I? If I had known, I wouldn't have sent you, but now that your approach has failed, it prevents me from trying again.' I reproached him again with trying to help me and failing. As he was leaving, Saint-Loup had met some young ladies on their way into the house. I had often previously suspected that she knew other girls in the region, but this was the first time that it tormented me so. We really have to suppose that nature has enabled our minds to secrete a natural antidote which cancels out the suppositions which we ceaselessly formulate and makes them harmless; but nothing could immunize me against the girls whom Saint-Loup had encountered. And yet were not all these details precisely what I had sought to glean from everyone about Albertine? Was it not I myself who, in order to know them more fully, had asked Saint-Loup, when he had been summoned to his Colonel's side, to come to see me at whatever cost? Was it not I who had sought out these details, or rather my ravenous pain, greedy to feed on them to give itself substance? Finally Saint-Loup told me that he had been pleasantly surprised to meet the only person in the vicinity whom he knew, a pretty actress who was on holiday nearby, a former friend of Rachel's, who had revived memories for him. And this actress's name was enough for me to think, 'Perhaps she was the one'; enough to make me see Albertine flushed and smiling with pleasure, held in the arms of a woman whom I did not know. And in fact why should that not have been the case? Had I ever deprived myself of thinking about other women since I knew Albertine? The evening when I had been to the Princesse de Guermantes for the first time, when I had returned home, was I not thinking much less about the latter than about the young lady who, according to Saint-Loup, frequented houses of ill-fame, and about Mme Putbus's chambermaid? Was it not for the latter that I had returned to Balbec? More recently, I had been very tempted to go to Venice, so why should Albertine not have been tempted to go to Touraine? Except that, deep down, as I now realized, I would not have left her, I would not have gone to Venice. And even, just as I was thinking, 'I shall leave her soon,' I knew in the depths of my heart that I would never leave her, just as I knew that I would never get down to work again, nor lead a healthy life, nor any of the things that I promised myself each day I would do the next. Only, whatever I might believe deep down, I had thought that I was behaving more cleverly by letting her live under the threat of perpetual separation. And doubtless my wretched cleverness had been all too convincing. In any case things could not continue in this way, I could not leave her in Touraine with those girls, with that actress; I could not bear the thought of the life that was slipping away from me. I would await her reply to my letter: if she was doing wrong, alas! one day more or less would make no difference (and perhaps I thought this because, having lost the habit of requiring an account of every minute of her life, a single one of which leaving her free would have driven me mad, my jealousy no longer observed the same time-scale). But as soon as I had received her reply, if it said she did not intend to return, I would go to fetch her back; I would tear her away from her girl-friends by consent or by force. Besides, would it not be better for me to go there myself, now that I had discovered Saint-Loup's previously unsuspected malice? Who could tell whether he might not have devised a whole conspiracy to keep me away from Albertine? Was it because I had changed, was it because until then I had not been able to suppose that natural causes would one day lead me into such an extraordinary situation, how I would have lied if I had written to her now what I had said to her in Paris, that I hoped no accident would befall her? Oh, if one might have occurred, my life, instead of being for ever poisoned by this ceaseless jealousy, would immediately have recovered, if not happiness, at least the peace bestowed by the suppression of suffering.

'Suppression of suffering'? Could I really have believed it, believed that death erases only what exists and leaves everything else in the state it was before, that it removes the pain from the heart of the man for whom the existence of his partner is no longer anything but a cause of pain, that it removes the pain and leaves nothing in its place? Suppression of pain! As I browsed through the news items in the papers, I regretted not having been brave enough to formulate the same wish as Swann. If Albertine could have fallen victim to an accident and had lived, I would have had an excuse to rush to her bedside; if she had died, I would have recovered what Swann called the freedom to live. Did I believe this? Swann, who was so refined and thought he knew himself so well, had believed it. How little we know of what lies in our hearts! How well I could have taught him a little later, had be still been alive, that his wish was as absurd as it was criminal and that the death of the woman he loved would have liberated him from nothing!

I abandoned all pride concerning Albertine, I sent her a desperate telegram asking her to return on any terms, saying that she would be able to do whatever she liked, that I would ask only to kiss her for a minute before bedtime three times a week. And had she said 'Only once a week', I would have accepted that 'once'. She never returned. My telegram had barely been sent when another arrived for me. It was from Mme Bontemps. The world is not given to each individual in advance. During the course of a lifetime things that we could never have guessed are added in. Ah! It was not suppression of suffering that the first two lines of the telegram produced in me: 'My poor friend, our little Albertine is no more, forgive me for having to tell you this terrible thing, knowing that you loved her so much. She was thrown against a tree by her horse while out riding. We did everything we could, but could not revive her. Would that I had died in her place!' No, not the suppression of suffering, but a previously unknown kind of suffering, that of learning that she would not return. But had I not told myself several times that she might not return? I had indeed said this to myself, but I now realized that I had never believed it for a moment. As I needed her presence and her kisses to help to bear the pain caused by my suspicions, I had acquired the habit, ever since Balbec, of being always with her. Even when she was out of the house and I was on my own, I would still be kissing her. I had continued to do so since she had left for Touraine. I needed her fidelity less than her return. And if my intellect could sometimes with impunity doubt this return, my imagination did not cease for one minute to picture it. Instinctively I stroked my neck and my lips, which had imagined themselves being kissed by her since she had left, yet which would never be kissed by her again; I stroked them as Mama had caressed me on my grandmother's death, saying to me, 'My poor child, your grandmother who loved you so much will never kiss you again.' My whole future life had been torn out of my heart. My future life? Had I then never on any occasion thought of living it without Albertine? No, never. Had I not for so long dedicated to her every minute of my life until my dying day? Of course I had! This future inseparable from her was not something that I had been able to perceive, but now that it had been cut loose I felt a gaping hole in the place where it had been in my heart. Françoise, who as yet knew nothing, came into my room; I shouted at her furiously, 'What is it?', then she said to me (and there are sometimes words that place an alternative reality in the same place as the one which we see before our eyes, making us reel with dizziness), 'There's no need for Monsieur to look angry. On the contrary, he is going to be very pleased. It's two letters from Mademoiselle Albertine.' I realized afterwards that I must have had the look of a man taking leave of his senses. I did not feel happy, nor even incredulous. I was like a man who sees the same place in his room taken up by a sofa and a grotto. Since nothing seems real any more, he collapses to the floor. Albertine's two letters must have been written shortly before the ride where she had met her death. The first one said: '*My dear friend, many thanks for showing your confidence in me by telling me of your intention to invite Andrée into your home. I am sure that she will accept with great pleasure and I think that she is very lucky. Gifted as she is, she will make the most of the company of a man like you and of the admirable influence that you are able to exert over a fellow creature. I think that your proposal will bring as much benefit to her as to you. So, should she show the slightest reticence (although I do not think this likely), send me a telegram, and I shall take her in hand.*' The second letter was dated a day later. In fact she must have written them both within a few moments of each other and then pre-dated the first. For all the while I had been absurdly misinterpreting her intentions, which had been merely to return to my side, whereas someone with no stake in the affair, say a man of no imagination, the negotiator of a peace treaty, or a businessman auditing a transaction, would have judged better than I. The letter contained only these words: '*Would it be too late for me to return to you? If you have not yet written to Andrée, would you agree to take me back? I shall be bound by your decision, which I beg you to let me know without delay, since you can imagine how impatiently I await it. If it were favourable, I would take the next train. Yours with all my heart, Albertine.*'

For Albertine's death to have suppressed my suffering, the mortal blow would have had to kill her not only in Touraine, but within me. There, she had never been more alive. To enter inside us, people have been obliged to take on the form and to fit into the framework of time; appearing to us only in successive instants, they have never managed to reveal to us more than one aspect, print more than a single photograph of themselves at a time. This is no doubt a great weakness in human beings, to consist in a simple collection of moments; yet a great strength too; they depend on memory, and our memory of a moment is not informed of everything that has happened since, the moment which it registered still lives on and, with it, the person whose form was sketched within it. And then this fragmentation not only makes the dead person live on, it multiplies her forms. In order to console myself, I would have had to forget not one but innumerable Albertines. When I had succeeded in accepting the grief of having lost one of them, I would have to begin again with another, with a hundred others.

So then my life was entirely changed. What had constituted its sweetness was not Albertine in person, but, in parallel with her, when I was alone, the perpetual rebirth of moments from the past called forth by identical moments. The sound of the rain brought back to me the scent of lilac in Combray; the sun's rays moving over the balcony brought the pigeons from the Champs-Elysées; the sounds muffled by the morning heat brought the coolness of cherries; the yearning for Brittany or Venice was borne by the sound of the wind and the return of Easter. Summer was on its way, the days grew longer. It was the season when pupils and teachers leave before mid-morning to go to the public gardens to prepare for their final examinations under the trees, to catch the last drop of coolness falling from a sky less burning than in the heat of the day, but already arid and bare. From my darkened room, with a force of evocation which equalled that of former times but now brought only suffering, I sensed that the sun hung heavy in the air outside as it set, garishly daubing the verticals of houses and churches. And if Françoise on her return were accidentally to ruffle the folds of the lined curtains, I would smother a cry escaping from the inner wound that had just been reopened by the sliver of antique sunlight which had made the modern façade of Bricqueville l'Orgueilleuse seem beautiful, when Albertine had said, 'It has been restored.' Not knowing how to explain my sighs to Françoise, I said, 'Oh, I am so thirsty.' She went out and then returned, but I had to turn away abruptly, assailed by the painful charge of one of those thousands of invisible memories which erupted in the shadows around me at every moment: I had just noticed that she had brought me cider and cherries, the cider and cherries which a farm lad had brought out to us in the car at Balbec, those substances which in former days would have enabled me to commune in perfect harmony with the rainbow filtering through shady dining-rooms on torrid days. Then for the first time I thought back to the farm at Les Écorres, and I thought that on certain days at Balbec when Albertine told me that she was not free because she had to go out with her aunt, she was perhaps with one or other of her girl-friends on a farm with which she knew that I was not familiar and where, while I was waiting around at the Marie-Antoinette farm[19] on the off-chance of a meeting only to be told, 'We have not seen her today,' she treated her friend to the same words that she had spoken to me when we had been for a drive together: 'He will never think of looking for us here, so we will not be disturbed.' I asked Françoise to draw the curtains to save me from seeing the ray of sunlight. But it continued to infiltrate my memory just as corrosively. 'I don't like it, it has been restored, but tomorrow we will go to Saint-Martin-le-Vêtu, and the day after to . . .' Tomorrow, the day after, it was a future life that we would share together, perhaps for ever, that was starting to take shape; my heart leapt out towards it, but it was no longer there, Albertine was dead.

I asked Françoise what time it was. Six o'clock. At last, thank God, the oppressive heat that Albertine and I used to so complain about, and so enjoy, was going to disappear. The day was drawing to a close. But what benefit did this bring me? The coolness of evening set in, the sun went down; in my memory, at the end of the road along which we were driving home together, I noticed, beyond the last village, something that looked like another resort in the distance, but too far to reach the same evening, so that we would stop in Balbec and stay there together. Together then. But now, alone, I had to pull up short before this same abyss, she was dead. It was no longer enough to draw the curtains, I tried to plug the eyes and ears of my memory, so as not to see this orange-tinted strip of sunset, so as not to hear those invisible birds who called to each other from tree to tree. All around me while I was being so tenderly kissed by the girl who now lay dead, I tried to avoid the sensations invoked by the dampness of leaves at evening, the switchback rise and fall of roads. But already these sensations had taken hold of me again, borne me quite far from the present moment, allowing the idea that Albertine was dead to fall back far enough to gather all the more momentum before it returned to strike me again. Oh, I would never again enter a forest and walk beneath the trees. But would the open plains be any less cruel to me? How often in order to fetch Albertine, or returning with her, had I crossed the open plain of Criqueville, sometimes in misty weather when the waves of fog gave us the impression of being surrounded by a vast lake, sometimes on limpid nights when the moonlight, draining the earth of matter and making it seem celestial just two feet away whereas in daylight it does so only at a distance, subsumed the fields and the woods into the heavens and sealed the whole in a single block of blue chalcedony! Françoise must have been pleased that Albertine was dead, and to be fair I must acknowledge that from a kind of decorum and tact she did not pretend to be sad. But the unwritten rules of her ancient code of law and the tradition of the medieval peasant weeping over tales of chivalry were deeper rooted than her hatred of Albertine or even Eulalie. Thus on one of those late afternoons, when I was too slow to hide my suffering, she noticed my tears, aided by her experience on a farm as a little girl who had been used to capturing animals and making them suffer, experiencing pure joy in strangling chickens and boiling lobsters alive, and when I was ill, in observing my sick complexion, as if I were an owl she had injured, and then commenting on it in lugubrious tones, as if it were a harbinger of doom. But her practice of the 'common law' of Combray would not allow her to take tears and grief lightly; she judged them as sinister as removing one's flannel vest or picking at one's food. 'Oh, no, Monsieur, you mustn't cry like that, you'll make yourself ill!' And in wanting to stop my tears she looked as worried as if they had been streams of blood. Unfortunately for her I adopted a cold expression which cut short her intended, but perhaps none the less sincere, effusions. She probably felt the same about Albertine as she had about Eulalie, and now that my friend could no longer derive any profit from me, Françoise no longer hated her. She was determined to show me, however, that she was well aware that I was crying and that, simply following my family's morbid habit, I did not want to 'let people see'. 'You mustn't cry, Monsieur,' she said, in calmer tones this time, rather to show me her insight than to display any pity. And she added: 'It was bound to happen, she was too happy, poor thing, she didn't know how happy she was.'

How long it takes the day to die on these never-ending summer evenings! The pale ghost of the house opposite continued for ever painting the sky with its persistent white water-colour. At last night fell inside the apartment, I stumbled into the furniture in the lobby, but, amid what I had taken for total darkness, the glazed panel in the door to the staircase shone translucent and blue, with the blue of a flower or an insect's wing, a blue that would have seemed beautiful to me if I had not felt that with this parting reflection the relentlessly cruel daylight dealt me a final thrust, as sharp as steel.

Complete darkness would, however, finally fall, but then I had only to see a star beside the tree in the courtyard to remember leaving by car after dinner for the woods of Chantepie, carpeted by moonlight. And even in the streets, I might happen to focus and reflect upon the natural purity of a beam of moonlight striking the back of a bench amid the artificial lights of Paris, as it brought the city into the countryside for a moment in my imagination, evoking the eternal silence of quiet pastures and permeating Paris with the painful memory of the rides that I had shared with Albertine. Would the night never end? But at the first cool draught of dawn I shivered, for it had brought back to me the softness of that summer when from Balbec to Incarville, from Incarville to Balbec, we had so often accompanied one another home and back again until the first light dawned. I had one single hope for the future, a hope much more poignant than a fear – which was to forget Albertine. I knew that I would forget her one day, I had after all forgotten Gilberte, Mme de Guermantes, and even my grandmother. And our most just and cruel punishment for the forgetting, as absolute and silent as that of the grave, which detaches us from those whom we no longer love, is that we should sense this same act of forgetting to be inevitable even in respect of those whom we do still love. To tell the truth, we know that it is a painless state, a state of indifference. But not being able to link simultaneously what I was then and what I would become, I thought in despair of this whole integument of kisses, caresses and friendly slumber, which I would soon have to shed for ever. The wave of such tender memories, coming to break over the idea that Albertine was dead, overwhelmed me with the clash of such contrary tides that I could not stay still; I got up, but suddenly I stopped dead in my tracks; the same early light of dawn that I used to see at the time when I had just left Albertine, feeling still warm and radiant from her kisses, had just drawn over my curtains its now funereal blade, whose cold, dense and implacable whiteness entered and struck me like a knife blow.

Soon the sounds of the street would start up, allowing me to read from the qualitative scale of their sonorities the constantly rising degree of heat amid which they resounded. But in this heat, which a few hours later would be saturated with the scent of cherries, what I found (as when replacing just one ingredient of a medicine by another is enough to change it from a tonic and a stimulant into a depressant) was no longer desire for women but anguish at Albertine's departure. Moreover the memory of all my other desires was impregnated as much with her and with suffering as with the memory of pleasure. Even Venice, where I had thought that I would find her presence intrusive (no doubt because I felt confusedly that I would find myself needing it there), no longer tempted me, now that Albertine was no longer alive. Albertine had seemed to me an obstacle placed between me and

449

all other things, because for me she had been their container, and it was from her as from a jar that I was able to take them. Now that this jar was broken, I was no longer able to face grasping them, there was not a single one of them from which I did not turn away, despondent, preferring not to taste of it. So that my separation from her was far from opening up for me the field of all possible pleasures that I had believed to be obstructed by her presence. Moreover the obstacle to travelling and to enjoying life that her presence may well have really been had only, as always, hidden other obstacles, which resurfaced intact, now that this one had disappeared. In similar fashion, previously, when some friendly visit prevented me from working, even if I remained alone the following day, I did not work any harder. If an illness, a duel or a runaway horse bring us face to face with death, we realize how richly we would have enjoyed the life, the sexual pleasure and the unknown lands that we are about to be deprived of. And once the danger is past, what we fall back on is the same monotonous existence where we knew none of all this.

Of course these very short nights cannot last long. In the end winter must return, when I would no longer fear the memory of driving with her all through the night until the all-too-hasty dawn. But would the first frosts not bring back to me, preserved in their ice, the germ of my first desires, when I sent the car for her at midnight, when it seemed to take so long before I heard her ring the door-bell, which I could now wait in vain for all eternity to hear? Would I not gather from them the germ of my earlier anxiety, when twice I believed that she would never return? At that time I saw her but rarely; but even the intervals that there were between Albertine's visits then, making her suddenly emerge from several weeks plunged in the depths of an unknown life which I could not attempt to possess, reassured me and pacified me by constantly interrupting the first inklings of my jealousy and preventing them from fusing into a solid mass in my heart. Just as they had been able to soothe me in those days, so retrospectively those intervals bore the imprint of suffering, now that I was no longer indifferent to the unknown things that she might have done during those periods, and above all, now that no visit from her would ever come again; so that those January evenings when she used to come, and which I had for this reason come to find so sweet, would now fill me not only with their bitter north wind but also with gusts of anxiety which I had not felt at the time, and which would return to me the first seeds of my love, but now grown toxic. And when I thought that I would once again see the start of the cold weather, which had always seemed so sad to me since the days of Gilberte and our games on the Champs-Elysées; and when I thought that evenings would return like that snowy evening when I had waited for Albertine in vain long into the night, then, like an invalid with a weak chest anxious for his body, what concerned me in my soul and what I still feared most at those moments, trying to spare my grief and my heart, was the return of this freezing weather, and I told myself that the hardest period for me to get through would probably be the winter. Since her memory was linked to every season, the only way of forgetting it would have been to forget all of them, even if it meant that I would have to learn to recognize them all over again, like an old man who has suffered from hemiplegia, learning to read again; I would have had to renounce the whole universe. Only a real death of my self, I told myself (were it not impossible), would be capable of consoling me for her death. I did not realize that the death of the self is neither impossible nor extraordinary; it is accomplished without our knowledge and, if necessary, without our consent every day, and I would suffer from the repetition of every sort of day that not only nature but accidental circumstances or more conventional arrangements could introduce into a season. Soon the date when I had gone to Balbec that last summer would return, when my love, which was not yet inseparable from jealousy and which was not concerned with what Albertine might be doing all day long, had so far to go before becoming a love so different and so special in its latter stages, so unique that this last year, when Albertine's destiny had started to change and had come to an end, appeared to me as full, diverse and vast as a century. Then there would be the memory of later days, but from earlier years; Sundays when the weather was bad and yet everyone had gone out, into the bleak emptiness of the afternoon, when the noise of the wind and the rain would in former times have incited me to act as a 'philosopher in the garret',[20] how anxious I would become as I saw the hour approach when Albertine had so unexpectedly come to see me and had caressed me for the first time, breaking off when Françoise had brought the lamp in, at that time, now dead twice over, when it was Albertine who was curious to learn all about me, when my affection for her could legitimately entertain such high hopes! And even, later in the season, those glorious evenings when the sculleries and the girls' boarding schools, like chapels with their doors ajar and bathed in a golden dust, allow their demi-goddesses to garland the streets and bring their private conversations so close to us that we feverishly desire to penetrate their mythical existence, now recalled nothing more than Albertine's affections, whose presence by my side prevented me from approaching them.

Moreover, to the memory of these purely natural hours I would have to add the mental landscape which makes of them something unique. When, later, I was to hear the goatherd's horn in the first days of fine, almost Italian weather, the same sunshine would now mingle with its light the anxiety of knowing that Albertine was at the Trocadéro, perhaps with Léa and the two girls, now the familiar, domestic and almost conjugal sweetness of a spouse, however cloying, whom Françoise was going to bring back home. I had felt that my pride was bolstered by this telephone message from Françoise, transmitting the homage paid by Albertine in returning with her. I had been mistaken. If it had intoxicated me, it was because it had made me feel that the woman whom I loved really belonged to me, lived only for me, and, even at a distance, without my needing to worry about her, looked on me as her lord and master, returning at a snap of my fingers. And thus this telephone message had been a package of sweetmeats sent to me from the farthest reaches of the Trocadéro region, which happened to contain sources of happiness irradiating me with their pain-killing molecules and healing balm, finally restoring me to such sweet and carefree spirits that all I had to do – yielding unrestricted by the slightest care to Wagner's music – was await Albertine's undoubted return, feeling a coolness and a total lack of impatience in which I ought to have recognized happiness, but failed to do so. And the cause of my happiness in her returning, obeying me, and belonging to me, was to be found, not in pride, but in my love. I would have found it pointless now to be able to snap my fingers and order fifty women to return, even from the Indies, let alone the Trocadéro. But that day, sensing Albertine approaching me submissively, while I was alone in my room playing music, I had breathed in, scattered like dust on a sunbeam, one of those substances which are good for the soul, as others are healthy for the body. Then, half an hour later, there had been Albertine's arrival, then, afterwards, the drive with Albertine, an arrival and a drive which I had considered boring because for me they were guaranteed in advance, but which because of this very guarantee, as soon as Françoise had telephoned me to say that she was bringing her back, had filled the following hours with a golden peace, had turned them as it were into a second day entirely different from the first, because its emotional foundations were entirely different, making the day quite unique, adding its original touch to the variety of those that I had previously known, a day which I could never have imagined – as we are unable to imagine a restful summer's day if such days have not existed in the calendar of days that we have experienced – a day which I could not be absolutely certain to recall, for its tranquillity was now overlaid with the suffering that I had not felt at the time. But much later, when I gradually moved backwards through the times that I had spent on the way towards loving Albertine, when my cauterized heart was able to detach itself from Albertine, long after her death, then, when I was at last able to recall without suffering the day when Albertine had gone shopping with Françoise instead of staying at the Trocadéro, I remembered that day pleasurably as one belonging to a mental season which I had not previously known; I at last remembered it while no longer adding suffering to it, but on the contrary, rather as we remember certain summer days which we found too hot at the time, and where it is only after the event that we extract from their alloys the pure, hallmarked gold and the indelible lapis lazuli.

In this way these few years not only imposed upon the memory of Albertine, which made them so unhappy, the changing colours, varying modalities and dying embers of their seasons and their hours, from their late June afternoons to their winter evenings, from moonlight over the sea to dawn on returning home, from snow in Paris to autumn leaves at Saint-Cloud,[21] but also transformed the particular ideas that

I had successively formed of Albertine, of the physical appearance with which I pictured her at each of these moments, and of the greater or lesser frequency with which I saw her in any particular season, making the season itself seem more or less diffuse or concentrated, of the hours of anxious waiting that she had provoked, of the desire that I felt for her at certain moments, of hopes nourished and then lost; all this modified the nature of my retrospective sadness just as much as the impressions of light and scent which were associated with it, and complemented each of the solar years that I had lived through and which even with just their springs, autumns and winters were already so sad because of their memory being inseparable from her, augmenting it with a sort of sentimental year where the hours were not defined by the position of the sun but by time spent waiting for a rendezvous; where the length of the days or the changes in temperature were measured by the rise in my hopes, the progress of our intimacy, the gradual transformation of her face, the places she had visited, the frequency and style of the letters that she had sent me during her absence, her greater or lesser eagerness to meet me when she had returned. And finally if each of these changes of weather and season yielded a different Albertine, it was not only through the evocation of similar moments. But we should not forget that, even before I fell in love, each season had made a different man of me, with different desires because he had different perceptions, a man who, having dreamed of nothing but storms and cliffs the night before, awoke ready to leave for Italy, once the indiscreet light of springtime had let the scent of roses seep through the cracks in the shutters of his uneven slumbers. And even when I was in love, had not my changing mental atmosphere and the varying pressure of my beliefs from one day to the next diminished the visibility of my own love, was it not one day high and rising, another day steady and fair, and another, falling to storm point? For we exist only through what we possess, and we possess only what is actually present, since so many of our memories, moods and ideas leave us and travel to faraway places, where we lose sight of them! Then we can no longer enter them into the accounting system whose sum is our whole being. But they find secret ways of returning within us. And some evenings, having fallen asleep hardly missing

Albertine any longer – we can miss only what we remember – I awoke to find that a whole fleet of memories had sailed into my clearest consciousness and had become marvellously distinct. Then I wept for the things which I saw so well and which for me the day before had been utterly absent. Albertine's name and her death had changed their meaning; her betrayals had suddenly resumed their old significance.

How could she have appeared dead to me, when now in order to think of her I had at my disposal only the same images that I saw alternately when she was alive: bent over the swiftly turning mythological wheel of her bicycle, harnessed on rainy days into the vulcanized warrior's tunic that made her bosom bulge, her turban-helmeted head swarming with serpents, as she spread terror throughout the streets of Balbec; on the evenings when we took our champagne out into the woods of Chantepie, her changed, provocative voice, her face lit by a pale fire reddening only at the cheekbones, which, since I found it difficult to see in the car in the darkness, I drew towards the moonlight and which I tried now in vain to recall or to visualize in the endless darkness. A small statuette in our crossing to the island, or a peaceful figure with her coarse-grained skin as she sat at the pianola, she was by turns swift and stormy, provocative and diaphanous, or an unmoved and smiling angel of music. Each Albertine was attached to a moment, to a date where I was transported when I visualized her again. Then again, past moments do not stay still; they maintain in our memory the momentum which was driving them towards the future – towards a future which itself has already become the past – dragging us in their wake. I had never caressed Albertine in her wet-weather rubber-wear, I wanted to ask her to remove her armour, in order to explore with her the love of life under canvas, the fraternity of travel. But it was no longer possible, she was dead. And then again, for fear of corrupting her, I had pretended never to understand her on those evenings when she seemed to offer me certain pleasures; pleasures however which, had I not adopted this attitude, she might not have sought elsewhere, and which now excited the most frenzied desire in me. I would not have felt them in the same way if they had been provided by someone else, but I could travel the whole world over in search of the girl who might do so without ever meeting her, for

Albertine was dead. It seemed that I had to choose between two facts and decide which was true, so blatantly did the death of Albertine – which arose for me out of a reality which I had not known, her life in Touraine – contradict all the thoughts that linked me to her, my desires, my regrets, my tenderness, my rage and my jealousy. Such a wealth of memories borrowed from her life's inventory, such a profusion of emotions evoking or involving her life, seemed to make it unbelievable that Albertine could be dead. Such a profusion of feelings, for while my memory preserved my affection it also preserved its whole variety. It was not Albertine alone who was only a succession of moments, it was also myself. My love for her had not been simple: to curiosity about the unknown had been added a sensual desire, and to my feelings of almost domestic sweetness, feelings sometimes of indifference, sometimes of jealous rage. I was not one single man, but the march-past of a composite army manned, depending on the time of day, by passionate, indifferent or jealous men – jealous men who were never jealous of the same woman. And doubtless this would be the source of an eventual cure, which I did not desire. The individuals in a crowd may without our noticing be replaced one by one, and others again may come to suppress or supplement them, so that at the end of the day a change has been accomplished which it would be impossible to imagine in a single, unitary being. The complexity of my love and my identity multiplied and diversified my suffering. And yet they could still be classified under the two heads whose alternation had ruled the whole life of my love for Albertine, ruled in turns by confidence and jealous suspicion.

If (bearing as I did the double yoke of the present and the past) I found it so difficult to accept that Albertine, who was so alive within me, was dead, perhaps it was just as paradoxical that my suspicion of misdeeds committed by Albertine, who today was stripped of the flesh that had enjoyed them and who was no longer capable of them or responsible for them, should excite in me such suffering, which I would happily have blessed if I could have seen in it the proof of the spiritual presence of a materially non-existent person, instead of the inevitably fading reflection of impressions which she had caused me in the past. A woman no longer capable of experiencing pleasure with other women should no longer have excited my jealousy, if only I could have brought my affections up to date. But this was impossible, because they could locate their object, Albertine, only in memories where she still lived on. Since at any moment when I thought of her, I resuscitated her, her infidelities could never be those of a dead woman, for the moment when she had committed them became the present moment, not only for Albertine but also for whichever of my selves was suddenly enlisted to contemplate her. So that no anachronism could ever separate the indissoluble couple where each new guilty woman was immediately matched with a woeful, jealous, but always contemporaneous, lover. During her last few months I had kept her locked up in my house. But now in my imagination Albertine was free; she used this freedom ill, she prostituted herself to all and sundry. Previously I had never stopped thinking about the uncertain future that unfolded before us, and I tried to read it. And now what was cast before me like the shadow of the future – as worrying as the future, because it was as uncertain, as difficult to decipher and as mysterious but even more cruel, because unlike the future, it did not allow me the possibility or the illusion of intervening to change it, and also because it would unfold as far as my life itself, without my companion being there to alleviate the suffering that it caused me – was no longer Albertine's future, but her past. Her past? This is not the right term, since in jealousy there is neither past nor future, for what it imagines is always present.

These changes in atmosphere cause other changes in the inner man, awakening forgotten selves, counteracting the lethargy of habit, reviving the force of memories here, of suffering there. How much more so for me if this new climate recalled days in Balbec when Albertine, despite the threat of rain, for instance, had set out, God knows why, for a long ride, strapped tightly into her rubbers! If she had still been alive today, she would doubtless be setting off, in similar weather, on a similar expedition in Touraine. But since she was no longer able to do so, I should not have suffered from this thought; but the slightest change in the weather renewed my aches and pains, as it would in the missing limb of an amputee.

Suddenly there came a memory which I had not seen for a long time, for it had remained dissolved in the transparent, fluid expanses of my memory, until it formed into crystals. Thus it had happened that several years before, when we were talking about her bath-robe, Albertine had blushed. In those days I was not jealous of her. But afterwards I wished I could ask her if she could remember this conversation and tell me why she had blushed. It had concerned me all the more since I had been told that Léa's two young girl-friends frequented her hotel's bathing establishment and, so people said, not only to take a shower. But for fear of annoying Albertine, or in the hope of better days to come, I had constantly postponed discussing it with her, and then I forgot about it. However, shortly after Albertine's death, I caught a glimpse of this memory, imprinted with the irritating but solemn character of an enigma left eternally insoluble by the death of the only person who could have shed light on it. Could I not at least try to learn whether Albertine might not perhaps have committed some real or even apparent misdemeanour in this bathing establishment? By sending someone to Balbec, I might possibly succeed. As long as she was alive, I am sure that I would not have learned anything. But tongues are strangely loosened and are swift to denounce people's faults when the revenge of the person accused is no longer to be feared. As the constitution of the imagination, which remains rudimentary and simplistic (not having passed through the various transformations which palliate the primitive models of human invention, which we now hardly recognize, whether we think of the barometer, the balloon or the telephone, etc., compared to their later improvements), allows us to see so few things at once, this memory of the bath-house took over the whole field of my inner vision.

Sometimes, in the dark alleyways of sleep, I stumbled over one of those bad dreams which we do not take very seriously, for the main reason that the sadness which they instil in us, like the sickness following an anaesthetic, rarely lasts more than an hour after our awakening, but for another reason too, which is that they occur very rarely, hardly more than once every two or three years. And even then we are not sure whether we have already encountered them – or whether our impression of *déjà vu* might not be either projected on to them by an illusion, or a reduplication (for it is more than a repetition) of our experience.

Of course, since I had my doubts about Albertine's life, and her death, I ought to have started my enquiries much sooner. But the same lethargy and cowardice that had kept me submissive to Albertine while she was there, prevented me from undertaking anything from the time that I no longer saw her. And yet sometimes a flash of energy may emerge from the weakness which has dogged us for years. I decided to make at least one enquiry, however partial. You might have thought that there had been nothing else in Albertine's life. I wondered whom I might send to try to make enquiries on the spot, in Balbec. Aimé seemed to be the right choice. Apart from the fact that he had an excellent knowledge of the location, he belonged to that category of working people who look after their own interests, are faithful to those they serve, are indifferent to all varieties of morality, and who – because if we pay them well they ignore anything that would hinder their devotion to our will, for they reveal themselves to be as incapable of indiscretion, lethargy or impropriety as they are of scruples – pass for 'good men'. These are men in whom we may place complete confidence. When Aimé had left, I thought how much more effective it would have been for me if I could have asked Albertine herself about what he was going to try to discover there. And straight away the thought of this question that I wished I could have put to Albertine, that I was going to put to her, brought her back to my side, not thanks to an effort of resurrection but through one of those chance encounters which – as happens in the kind of photograph which is a snapshot, rather than a 'posed' portrait – always breathe life into the person; at the same time as I imagined our conversation, I felt how impossible it was; approaching it from a different angle, I had again come up against the idea that Albertine was dead, Albertine, who inspired in me the kind of affection that we have for absent women whose embellished image is uncorrected by any real sighting of them, but also inspired sadness, from the thought that the poor young thing was deprived for ever of the pleasures of life. And immediately I shifted suddenly from being tortured by jealousy to feeling despair at our separation.

What now filled my heart, instead of suspicion and hatred, was the tender memory of hours of affectionate intimacy passed with the sister whom death had really made me lose, since my sorrow was directed not at what Albertine had been for me but at what my heart, desiring to participate in the more general emotions of love, had come to persuade me that she was; then I realized that this life which had so bored me – or at least so I thought – had, on the contrary, been delicious; I felt now that the briefest moments spent talking with her about even the most trivial things had been augmented and suffused with a voluptuousness which, it is true, I had not noticed at the time, but which had already caused me to seek them out so persistently and so exclusively; the slightest details which I recalled, such as the movements that she made when sitting beside me in the car, or sitting opposite me at the table in her room, sent through my soul ripples of sweetness and sadness which gradually spread out to overflow it entirely.

I had never found this room where we dined attractive: I had only told Albertine that I did, so that my friend would be happy to live in it. Now the curtains, the chairs and the books no longer left me unmoved. It is not only art which is able to imbue the most insignificant things with charm and mystery; this same power to bring them into an intimate relationship with ourselves is also granted to suffering. At the time I had paid no attention to the dinner which we had eaten together on our return from the Bois de Boulogne, before I went to the Verdurins', a dinner whose grave sweetness now filled my eyes with tears. The impressions created by love are disproportionate to our other impressions of life, but we do not realize this when they are mingled together. It is not from below, in the tumultuous streets and the close-packed neighbouring houses, it is only as we move away to the slopes of a nearby hill, to a distance where the whole town has disappeared or forms only a confused mass at ground level, that we are able, in the contemplative and welcoming solitude of the evening, to appreciate the unique, pure, and eternal height of a cathedral. I attempted to embrace the image of Albertine through my tears while thinking of all the serious and perceptive remarks that she had made that evening. One morning I thought that I glimpsed the oblong shape of a hill surrounded by mist, and felt the warmth of a cup of chocolate, while my heart was horribly wrung by the memory of the afternoon when Albertine had come to see me and when I had kissed her for the first time: it was because I had just heard the boiler gurgle as it was relit. And in my anger I threw away an invitation to Mme Verdurin's that Françoise had just brought me. How much more strongly the impression, which I had had when I went to dine for the first time at La Raspelière, that death does not strike all its creatures at the same age impressed me now that Albertine was dead so young, while Brichot continued to dine with Mme Verdurin, who was still entertaining guests and would perhaps continue to do so for years to come! Immediately Brichot's name reminded me how he had accompanied me home at the end of that same evening, and I had seen the light at Albertine's window from down below. I had already thought back to this on a number of occasions, but I had never approached this memory from the same angle. For, although our memories are entirely personal, they resemble those estates which have hidden side-gates, which often we ourselves have not discovered and have to have opened by a neighbour, so that we find ourselves arriving home from at least one direction which we had never taken before. Then, thinking of the void which would greet me on my return home and the fact that I would never again see Albertine's room from down below, since its light was for ever extinguished, I understood how mistaken I had been, on leaving Brichot that evening, to believe that I felt disappointment and regret at not being able to walk away and seek love elsewhere; I understood how mistaken I had been, and that it was only because I believed myself to be in absolutely safe possession of the treasure whose reflections poured down on me from above that I had neglected to assess its worth, which inevitably led me to see it as less valuable than other pleasures, however slight, to which I did attribute value because I was reduced to imagining them. I understood what a plenitude of sweetness and life this light, which seemed to emanate from a prison, contained for me, and how it was none other than the materialization of something that had intoxicated me for a moment but had then appeared for ever unattainable the evening when Albertine had slept under the same roof as me at Balbec; I understood that the life which I had led with her in my home in Paris, which was her home, was precisely the attainment of that profound peace of which I had dreamed.

I would never have been able to console myself if the conversation which I had had with Albertine when returning from the Bois de Boulogne before that last soirée at the Verdurins' had never taken place, that conversation which had tended to fuse Albertine with my intellectual life and had in certain areas made us one and the same being. For there is no doubt that if I lingered affectionately over her intelligence and her kindness for me, it was not because they were greater than those of other people whom I had known; had Mme de Cambremer not said to me at Balbec, 'How could you possibly spend whole days with your cousin when you could spend them with Elstir, who is a genius!'? I appreciated Albertine's intelligence because she evoked in me by association what I referred to as her sweetness, as we attribute to the sweetness of a fruit a certain sensation which exists only in our palate. And in fact, when I thought of Albertine's intelligence, my lips moved instinctively forwards to taste a memory whose reality I liked to think of as external and consisting in the objective superiority of a person. I have to say that I had known people whose intelligence was superior. But the infinite extent, or the egoism, of love causes us to love people whose intellectual and moral features are the least objectively defined for us, we readjust them endlessly according to our desires and our fears, we cannot separate them from ourselves, they are no more than a vast and vague terrain where we externalize our affection. Even our own bodies, where we are assailed by so many pains and pleasures, do not display a silhouette as clear as that of a tree or a house or a passing stranger. And perhaps I had been wrong not to try harder to get to know Albertine in her own right. Just as where her charm was concerned I had for some time considered only the different positions in the calendar of the years that she adopted in my memories, and just as I had been surprised to see her spontaneously enriched with transformations which seemed to go beyond any simple difference of perspective, so I ought to have tried to understand her character in the same way as that of any other person, and perhaps this might have explained to me why she hid her secret so persistently from me and might have enabled me to cut short this strangely savage conflict between us, which had led to the death of Albertine. And with my great pity for her at that time I felt great shame in surviving her. Indeed it seemed to me, in the moments when I suffered the least, that

I almost benefited from her death, for a woman is all the more useful in our lives if she is an agent of sorrow rather than an element of happiness, and there is not a single woman whose possession is as precious as the truths which she enables us to discover by making us suffer. In such moments, connecting my grandmother's death with that of Albertine, it seemed to me that my life was besmirched by a double murder for which only the cowardice of society could forgive me. I had dreamed of being appreciated by Albertine, of not being misunderstood by her, believing that it was for the greater satisfaction of being appreciated and not misunderstood, whereas so many others could have done it better. We wish to be understood because we wish to be loved, and we wish to be loved because it is we who are in love. Whether others understand us is unimportant, and their love importunate. My joy at having possessed a little of Albertine's intellect and of her heart did not derive from their intrinsic value, but from the fact that this possession was one more step on the way towards the total possession of Albertine, which had been my aim and my fantasy from the first day that I had seen her. When we speak of a woman's 'kindness', we are probably only projecting outside ourselves the pleasure that we feel on seeing her, like children when they say, 'My dear little bed, my dear little pillow, my dear little hawthorn blossom.' Which may also by the way explain why men never say of a woman who is faithful to them, 'She is so kind,' but do so often say it of a woman who is unfaithful. Mme de Cambremer judged, quite rightly, that Elstir had great spiritual charm. But we cannot judge in the same way the charm of someone who, like everyone else external to us, is depicted on the fringes of our consciousness and the charm of someone who, as a result of a series of unintentional but persistent errors of navigation, has become lodged within our own bodies, to such an extent that we ask ourselves retrospectively if having looked at some woman on a certain day in the corridor of a little coastal railway train has not made us experience as much suffering as would be caused by a surgeon trying to remove a bullet from our heart. A simple croissant, as we start to eat it, can make us experience more pleasure than all the bunting, rock partridge and leveret dined on by Louis XV, and the blade of grass quivering a few inches away from our eyes when we are lying down on the mountainside may mask the towering peak of the mountain top if this is several miles away. In fact our mistake is not that we over-appreciate the intelligence and the kindness of the woman we love, however small they may really be. Our mistake is to remain indifferent to the kindness and the intelligence of others. Falsehood or goodness only start to generate the indignation or gratitude that they should normally always stimulate in us when they come from a woman whom we love, and physical desire has the marvellous power of setting a true value for the intellect as well as providing solid foundations for our moral life. I would never again encounter that divine thing: a person with whom I could discuss everything, in whom I could confide all. Confide? But did not other people show me more confidence than Albertine? Did I not have more wide-ranging conversations with others? Is the point that confiding and conversing are in themselves paltry things, whose imperfections are neither here nor there, until they are blended with love, which alone is divine? I had a vision of Albertine's pink face beneath her black hair as she sat at the pianola; I felt her tongue against my lips as she tried to part them, her maternal, nourishing, holy, inedible tongue, whose hidden fire and secret dew prevented her caresses from being superficial, even when she did no more than slide her tongue along the surface of my neck or my stomach, as if they somehow issued from her inner flesh, turned inside out like a piece of material exposing its lining, endowing even the most external contact with the mysterious sweetness of a penetration.

I cannot even say that what made me feel the loss of all these moments of utter sweetness, which nothing could ever bring back to me, was actually despair. In order to despair of this life, when we see that it will be irremediably unhappy for evermore, we must still desire to cling to it. I had been desperate in Balbec when I saw day dawn and understood that no day would ever again bring me happiness. I had remained just as self-centred since then, but the self to which I had latterly become attached, the self that constituted my inner reserves, those which bring into play the instinct of preservation, this self was no longer alive; when I thought of my vital strengths, of my life force, of what was best in me, I thought of this one treasure which I had possessed (which I alone had possessed since others could not know precisely the hidden feelings that it had inspired in me) and which no one could now take away from me since I no longer possessed it. And to tell the truth, I had only ever possessed it in so far as I had always tried to imagine myself possessing it. I had not only been imprudent enough, while watching Albertine with my lips and lodging her in my heart, to make her live within me, as well as committing that other folly of mingling domestic love with the pleasure of the senses. I had also tried to convince myself that our relationship was one of love, that what we engaged in together was what people call love, because she obediently returned the kisses that I gave her. And from having acquired the habit of believing this, I had lost not only a woman whom I loved, but a woman who loved me, my sister, my child, my tender mistress. And finally I had experienced a happiness and an unhappiness which Swann had not known, precisely because, during all the time that he had loved Odette and had been so jealous of her, there were days when he had hardly seen her at all, since it was virtually impossible for him to go and call on her whenever she called off their appointment at the last moment. But afterwards he had had her to himself, as his wife, until he died. Whereas I, on the other hand, even while I was so jealous of Albertine, was happier than Swann, for I had her at home with me. I had in fact attained what Swann had so often dreamed of and what he had achieved in reality only when he had become indifferent to it. But ultimately I had not kept Albertine as he had kept Odette. She had fled, she had died. For nothing is ever repeated exactly, and the most analogous lives, even those which due to likeness of character and similarity of circumstance one may choose to present as symmetrical, remain in many aspects opposed. In losing my life I would not have lost much; I would have lost only an empty form, the frame for a missing masterpiece. Indifferent to what I might henceforth fill it in with, but happy and proud of what it had contained, I fell back on the memory of such sweet moments, and this moral support gave me a feeling of well-being that even the approach of death would not have disturbed.

How she would hurry to visit me in Balbec whenever I asked to see her, tarrying only a few last moments in order to lace her hair with perfume for my pleasure! These images of Balbec and Paris which I recalled with such pleasure, were the all-too-recent pages of her short life, which had been turned so quickly. Everything that for me was no more than memory had for her been action, the precipitate action of a tragedy, hurtling swiftly towards death. People evolve in one way within us, but also in another way outside us (I had felt this plainly on those evenings when I had noted how Albertine's character had become enriched with new qualities, and not only due to my memory), and each continually interacts with the other. Although, as I struggled first to understand Albertine, then to possess her entirely, I had done no more than obey our need to reduce the mystery of any person through experience to elements pettily similar to those composing our own selves, I had not been able to do so without in my turn influencing Albertine's life. Perhaps my wealth and the prospect of a dazzling marriage had attracted her; my jealousy had retained her; her kindness, her intelligence, her feelings of guilt or her sheer skill and cunning had led her to accept, and led me to render increasingly harsh, a captivity forged simply by the progress of the inner workings of my mind, but which had none the less had repercussions on Albertine's life, destined through their backlash to pose my psyche new and increasingly painful problems, since it was from my prison that she had escaped in order to kill herself riding a horse which without me she would never have owned, leaving me, even after her death, with suspicions whose truth, if confirmed, would perhaps be crueller for me than the discovery at Balbec that Albertine had known Mlle Vinteuil, since Albertine would no longer be there to soothe me. So much so that this long complaint of the soul which believes that it lives enclosed within itself is only superficially a monologue, since the echoes of reality cause it to change tack and since any single life resembles an improvised experiment in subjective psychology, yet one which at a distance provides the 'plot' of a purely realist novel belonging to a different reality, a different existence, whose reversals of fortune intervene one after the other to inflect the curve and change the direction of the psychological experiment. How taut had been the mechanism of our love, how swift its evolution and, despite some initial delays, interruptions and hesitations, as in some of Balzac's short stories or Schumann's ballads, how swift its resolution! It was within the course of this last year, which had seemed to me to last a century, so much had Albertine's position changed in my thoughts between Balbec and her departure for Paris, sometimes independently of me and often unbeknown to me, that I had to insert this whole life of affection, which had lasted such a short time and which however appeared to me as a plenitude or even an infinity impossible ever to grasp, and yet which I found indispensable. Indispensable without perhaps having ever been in itself or primarily anything necessary, since I would not have met Albertine if I had not read the description of the church at Balbec in an archaeological treatise; if Swann, telling me that this church was almost Persian, had not orientated my desires towards the Norman Byzantine style; if a company, in building a comfortable and hygienic grand hotel in Balbec, had not persuaded my parents to grant my wish and send me to Balbec. Doubtless once in the Balbec which I had so long desired, I had not found the Persian church of which I dreamed, nor the eternal mists. The charming ten-to-two[22] train itself had not matched up to my imaginings. But in exchange for what the imagination leads us to expect and what we take so much trouble to try to discover, life gives us something that we were far from being able to imagine. Who could have thought in Combray, when I awaited my mother's good-night kiss with such sadness, that these anxieties would be cured and would then one day be revived not in connection with my mother, but with a young lady who at first would be no more than a flower seen against the horizon of the sea that my eyes would every day be drawn to watch, albeit a thinking flower, and one in whose thoughts I desired to take an important place in so puerile a fashion that I suffered from the fact that she did not know that I knew Mme de Villeparisis? Yet it was on account of that good-night kiss from such a stranger that, some years later, I was to suffer just as much as I did as a child when my mother did not come to see me. But I would never have known this now so necessary Albertine, of whose love my soul had become almost entirely composed, if Swann had not spoken to me of Balbec. Her life would perhaps have lasted longer, and mine would have been void of what now constituted my martyrdom. And thus it seemed to me that through my totally selfish affection I had let Albertine die, just as previously I had murdered my grandmother. Even later, even after I had already got to know her at Balbec, I could not have loved her as I did after that. For when I renounced Gilberte and knew that I could one day pursue another woman, I hardly dared doubt that, at least in the past, I could not have loved anyone other than Gilberte. And yet in the case of Albertine I no longer even had any doubt, I was sure that she did not have to be the one that I must love, that it could have been someone else. All it would have needed was for Mlle de Stermaria, the evening when I was to dine with her on the island of the Bois de Boulogne, not to have called it off. There was still time then for this feat of the imagination, which enables us to extract from a woman a notion of the individual so special that she appears to us to be unique in herself as well as predestined and necessary for us, to have been focussed on Mlle de Stermaria. At best, viewing things from an almost biological viewpoint, I could say that I might have experienced the same exclusive love for another woman, but not absolutely any other. For although Albertine, who was plump and dark, did not resemble Gilberte, who was slender and red-haired, both none the less shared the same robust health, the same sensual cheeks and the same enigmatic look. They were the kind of woman who would not have caught the attention of some men who, on the other hand, would have done anything, however crazy, for another kind, who 'left me cold'.[23] A man nearly always has the same manner of catching cold, of falling ill, which is to say that he needs a particular combination of circumstances: it is natural that, when he falls in love, it will be with a certain type of woman, although the type may be loosely defined. The first time that Albertine looked at me and fired my imagination her eyes were not so different from those of Gilberte the first time. I could almost believe that the sombre and sensual personality and the cunning, wilful character of Gilberte had returned to tempt me, incarnate this time in the body of Albertine, which was quite different and yet was in some ways analogous. In Albertine's case, thanks to our totally different kind of life together, where within a block of thoughts into which no fissure of distraction or forgetfulness could insinuate itself, my painful preoccupations maintained a permanently cohesive whole, her living body, unlike Gilberte's, had never for a single day ceased to be the one where I located what I subsequently recognized as what for me was feminine attractiveness (although it would not have been for others). But she was dead. I would forget her. Who knows then whether the same hot-blooded, restless, fantastical qualities might not return again one day to upset me, but incarnate this time in a feminine form which I could not yet foresee. Starting out from Gilberte, I could have as little imagined Albertine, or the fact that I would love her, as the memory of Vinteuil's sonata could have enabled me to imagine his septet. Worse still, even on the first occasions that I had seen Albertine, I had managed to believe that it would be the other girls whom I would love. Moreover, if I had met her a year earlier, she might even have appeared to me as dull as a grey sky before daybreak. But if I had changed my attitude towards her, she herself had also changed, and the girl who had approached my bedside the day when I had written to Mlle de Stermaria was no longer the same as the one whom I had known at Balbec, whether simply because she had burst out into womanhood after appearing to me at the moment of puberty, or whether because there was some other set of circumstances that I had never been able to fathom. At all events, even if the woman I were one day to love should in some respects resemble her, that is, if my choice of a woman were not entirely free, even perhaps necessarily in some way directed, this meant none the less that it was directed towards something vaster than an individual, towards a type of woman, and this removed all necessity from my love for Albertine. We know full well that this unique woman, whose face we see before our eyes more constantly than the daylight itself – since even with our eyes closed, we never for a moment cease to cherish her lovely eyes and her beautiful nose, and will do anything we can to see them again – could have been a different woman, if we had visited a town other than the one where we met her, if we had walked down different streets, if we had been invited to a different salon. Do we believe her to be unique? She is everywhere. And yet she is consistent and indestructible before our loving eyes, irreplaceable for long after by anyone else. The reason is that this woman has done nothing but use all sorts of magic spells to invoke the thousands of elements of affection which exist within us in a fragmentary state, to assemble and unite them, bridging all the gaps between them; it is we ourselves who, in creating her features, have furnished all the solid substance of the beloved. From this it follows that, even if we are only one among thousands for her, and perhaps last in the line, for us she is the only one, and the one at whom our whole life is aimed. Of course I had even felt quite clearly that this love was not necessary, not only because it could have happened with Mlle de Stermaria, but even without that, as I came to know it better, and started to find that it seemed too similar to what it had been for other women, and also to feel that it was vaster than Albertine, enveloping her without taking any heed of her, like a tide engulfing a fragile reef. But gradually, by dint of living with Albertine, I could no longer disentangle myself from the chains that I myself had forged; the habit of associating the person of Albertine with emotions that I had not derived from her directly led me none the less to feel that they were special to her, just as habit, according to a certain school of philosophers, gives to the simple association of ideas between two phenomena the force and the necessity of a causal law. I had believed that my connections and my wealth would enable me to dispense with suffering, but perhaps too expeditiously, because this seemed to enable me to dispense with feeling, loving and imagining; I felt envious of some poor country girl, who, in the absence of connections or even the telegraph, might spend many months musing over a sorrow that she cannot artificially put to sleep. Yet I now realized that, whereas in the case of Mme de Guermantes, who enjoyed so many advantages that helped maintain an infinite distance between her and me, I had seen the gulf abruptly bridged by public opinion and my analysis, which found social privilege to be no more than an inert and changeable matter, by a converse but reciprocal process my connections, my wealth and all the material means from which both my position and the civilization of the day allowed me to benefit had done no more than postpone the moment of the hand-to-hand struggle with the contradictory, inflexible will of Albertine, which had resisted all pressure. Of course I had been able to exchange telegrams and telephone calls with Saint-Loup and remain in constant touch with the telegraph office in Tours, but had these expectations not been vain, their result null? And did a country girl with no social advantages and no connections, or people who lived before these advances of civilization, not suffer less? Because one desires less and misses less what one has always believed inaccessible and which has, for this reason, remained as it were unreal. We desire a person more when she is about to yield, expectation anticipates possession; but regret, too, amplifies desire. Mlle de Stermaria's refusal to come to dinner on the island of the Bois de Boulogne is what prevented her from being the person that I loved. This too could have been enough to enable me to love her, if I had seen her soon enough afterwards. As soon as I had found out that she would not come, entertaining the implausible hypothesis – which did however turn out to be correct – that if someone were jealous of her and kept her away from company, I might possibly never see her again, I had suffered so much that I would have given anything to see her again, and it was one of the greatest anxieties which I had ever known that Saint-Loup's arrival had assuaged. Yet after a certain age our loves and our mistresses are daughters of our anguish: our past, and the physical lesions within whose lines it lies inscribed, determine our future. For Albertine in particular, the fact that it was not necessary for her to be the one whom I loved was, even without these neighbouring loves, inscribed in the history of my love for her, that is for her and her girl-friends. For it was not even a love like that for Gilberte, but one created by its dispersal among several girls. It is possible that it was because of her, and because they appeared to me to be something analogous to her, that I had enjoyed the company of her girl-friends. And yet I must admit that for quite a time a hesitation among all of them was possible, as my choice wandered from one to the other, and when I thought that I preferred one, it was enough for her to keep me waiting or refuse to see me for me to start feeling love for her. On several occasions it could easily have happened, when Andrée was due to come to see me in Balbec, that if Albertine had let me down just before Andrée's visit, my heart would have started pounding, I would have thought that I would never see Albertine again and that she was the one whom I loved. And when Andrée did come, I was being perfectly truthful when I told her (as had I told her in Paris when I had learned that Albertine had known Mlle Vinteuil), although she might have thought that I was speaking disingenuously and for her benefit, whereas I would in fact have used the same terms if I had been happy the day before with Albertine: 'Alas, if only you had come earlier, now I am in love with someone else.' But even in this case of Andrée replaced by Albertine when I had learned that the latter had known Mlle Vinteuil, my love had alternated between the two of them, and consequently there had in fact been only one love at a time. But there had been cases previously when I had more or less fallen out with two of the girls. Whichever one of them took the first steps to make amends was the one who would soothe my spirits, and it would be the other one whom I would love if she was still sulking, which did not mean that it might not be the first that I would take up with permanently, for she would console me, however imperfectly, for the harshness of the second, whom I would ultimately forget if she never returned. And it did happen that, although I was convinced that one or the other would return to me in the end, neither of them did for quite a time. My anguish was therefore double, like my love, ensuring that I should cease loving whichever one did return, but, until she did, that I should suffer at the hands of both of them. This is a fate which befalls us at a certain age, which may be relatively young, where we may be less attracted by a person than by someone's rejection, where we ultimately know nothing more of the person we have chosen, whose face has grown dim and whose soul has evaporated, than our all too recent but none the less inexplicable choice itself: the fact is that the only thing that could put an end to our suffering would be if we could hear the words, 'Could I come to see you?' My separation from Albertine the day when Françoise had said to me, 'Mademoiselle Albertine has left' was like an allegory for so many other separations. For often in order to discover that we are in love, even perhaps in order to fall in love, the day of separation needs to arrive.

In these cases where it is waiting in vain or hearing a word of rejection that determines our choice, our imagination, spurred on by suffering, which sets to work so swiftly, creates with such speed a love which was until then so inchoate and formless, and destined for months past to remain only sketchy, that our intellect, which has lagged behind our heart, is astonished and cries out: 'You must be mad, what painful new thoughts are you plunging us into? None of this is real life.' And indeed at that moment, if the faithless lady were not to relaunch her pursuit, any distractions pleasant enough to bring physical peace to our heart would be enough to abort this love. At all events, although this life with Albertine was not in its essence necessary, it had become indispensable for me. I had trembled when I was in love with Mme de Guermantes because I thought that, with all the means of seduction at her disposal, drawing not only on beauty but on situation and wealth, she would be far too free to belong to far too many people and that I would have far too little hold over her. Albertine was poor and obscure, and ought to want to marry me. And yet I had not been able to possess her exclusively. Whatever social conditions prevail, however wise the precautions we take, we can never truly control another person's life. Why had she not said to me, 'I am that way inclined'? I would have yielded, I would have allowed her to indulge her inclinations. In a novel which I had read, there was a woman whom no exhortation by the man who loved her could persuade to speak. On reading it I had found this situation absurd; I myself, I thought, would have first forced the woman to speak, and then we would have come to an agreement. For what was the point of such futile misery? But now I saw that we are not free not to create this for ourselves and that, however well we know our own will, other people do not obey it. And yet how many times, without knowing it and without wishing it, have we uttered these painful and unavoidable truths, which dominated us although we were blind to them – the truth of our feelings, the truth of our destiny – in words which we no doubt believed mendacious but which gained prophetic value retrospectively after the event. I remembered many words which one or other of us had uttered without at the time realizing the truth that they conveyed, even words which we had exchanged believing that we were play-acting, but whose falsehood was very flimsy, insubstantial and born of our pathetic insincerity, compared to the implications which we failed to see in them. Lies and misunderstandings which fell short of the profound reality which we failed to see; beyond lay the truth, the truth of our characters, whose essential laws had escaped us, since they need Time to help them reveal themselves, as with the truth of our fate. I had thought that I was lying when at Balbec I said, 'The more I see you, the more I shall love you' (and yet it was this intimacy of every moment, which, through jealousy, had attached me to her), 'I feel that I could help improve your mind'; or in Paris, 'Try to be careful. Just imagine if you had an accident, I would be heartbroken' (and she said, 'But an accident could happen to me'); or in Paris, the evening when I had pretended to want to leave her, saying, 'Let me look at you once more, because soon I shall not see you again, and it will be for ever'; and she had said, when that same evening she had looked around her, 'To think that I shall never again see this room, these books, this pianola, this whole house, I cannot believe it and yet it is true'; in her last letters, finally, when, as she wrote, she probably thought to herself, 'I am faking it': *I leave you the best of myself* (and was it not in fact now to the faithfulness and the power of my memory, however fragile, that her intelligence, her kindness and her beauty were confided?) and: *That moment, with its twofold twilight (since night was falling and since we were destined to part), will never be erased from my mind until utter darkness finally invades it*, that phrase, written the day before the day when indeed her mind had been invaded by utter darkness and when, in those last fleeting glimmerings which anxiety multiplies into infinity, she had perhaps had a vision of our last drive together, and in that moment when everything abandons us and where we construct a faith for ourselves, as atheists become Christians on the battle-field, she had perhaps called for help from the friend whom she had so often cursed but whom she had so respected, who himself – for all religions are similar – had been cruel enough to wish that she herself should also have the time to recognize herself, to give him her last thoughts, to make her confession to him at last, to die within him. But to what avail, since even if then she had had the time to recognize her true self, both of us would have understood where our happiness lay and what we should have done, only when, and only because, this happiness was no longer possible and no longer attainable. As long as things are possible, we defer them, and they can assume their power of attraction and their apparent ease of accomplishment only when, projected into the ideal void of the imagination, they are withdrawn from immersion in the cloying, degrading morass of real life. The idea that we shall die is more cruel than dying itself, but less cruel than the idea that someone else is dead, than the idea that, when the waters of reality close after having engulfed a person's being, they smoothly, without so much as a ripple, cover the spot from which that being is excluded, where neither will nor knowledge exist any longer, and from which it is as difficult to return to the idea of what that person's being had experienced as it is difficult, even while memories of their life are still fresh, to think that this person is assimilable to the insubstantial images and memories left by the characters of a novel that we have read.

At least I was happy that before her death she had written me this letter and, above all, had sent that last telegram, which proved that she would have returned to me if she had lived. It seemed to me that this made things not only sweeter but also more beautiful, for the event would have been incomplete without this telegram and would have been less of a work of art and destiny. Yet, in fact, it would have been these just as much if it had been different; for any event is a kind of mould of a particular shape, and, whatever this may be, it imposes on the series of incidents which it has come to interrupt a design which seems conclusive and which we believe to be the only one possible, because we do not know the alternative which might have taken its place.

Why had she not told me, 'I do have those inclinations'? I would have yielded, I would have let her indulge them, and even then I would still have embraced her. How sad I felt to have to remember the way she had lied to me, three days before she left me, swearing that she had never had such a relationship with Mlle Vinteuil and her girl-friend, while her own blushes confessed the opposite! Poor girl, at least she had been honest enough not to wish to swear that the pleasure of seeing Mlle Vinteuil and her girl-friend again had nothing to do with her desire to go to the Verdurins' that day. Why did she not follow through with a complete confession rather than make up such an extravagant story? Perhaps, incidentally, it might have been partly my fault if, despite all my entreaties, which were repulsed by her firm denials, she had never been prepared to tell me, 'I do have those inclinations.' Perhaps it was partly my fault because at Balbec, the day when, after Mme de Cambremer's visit, I had had my first argument on this subject with Albertine and when I was so far from believing that she could have had anything but an over-passionate friendship with Andrée, that I had expressed my disgust for this kind of behaviour too violently and condemned it too categorically. I could not remember whether Albertine had blushed when I had naïvely uttered my abhorrence of all that, I could not remember, for often it is only long after the event that we wish we could know what the attitude of some person had been, at a moment when we were paying no attention to it at all, and which later, when we think back over our conversation, would clear up a sensitive problem. But there is a blank in our memory, no trace of it exists. And how often have we not paid sufficient attention at the time to things which could already have seemed important to us, have we not heard a phrase or noticed a gesture correctly, or else have simply forgotten them. And when later, eager to discover the truth, we proceed from deduction to deduction, leafing through our memory like a dossier of eye-witness accounts, we do reach this phrase or that gesture, there is no way we can remember, we keep starting the same journey all over again, but to no avail, for the path leads no further. Did she blush? I don't know if she did, but she could not have failed to have heard my words, and the memory of them had brought her to a halt when she may have been on the point of confessing to me. And now that she was nowhere to be found, I could have roamed the earth from pole to pole without meeting Albertine; reality had swallowed her up, formed a smooth surface and erased every trace of the person who had drowned in its depths. She was no more than a name, like a Mme de Charlus of whom those who had known her said with an indifferent air, 'She was delightful.' But I could not consider for more than a moment the existence of this reality which Albertine no longer knew, for within me, where all my feelings and my thoughts related to her life, my friend was only too alive. Perhaps if she had known this, she might have been touched to see that her friend had not forgotten her, now that her own life was finished, and she would have appreciated things which previously had left her indifferent. But as we would prefer to abstain from infidelity, however secret, as long as we fear that the woman whom we love does not abstain, I was afraid that if the dead live on somewhere, my grandmother would know my forgetfulness as surely as Albertine my memories of her. And when all is said and done, even in the case of this same dead woman, are we sure that the joy we would have of learning that she knew certain things would compensate for the terror of thinking that she knew them *all*? And, however savage the sacrifice, would we not sometimes renounce keeping them on after their death as friends, for fear of having them also as judges?

My jealous curiosity about what Albertine might have done was infinite. I paid who knows how many women, who taught me nothing. If my curiosity was so lively, it is because people do not die immediately for us, they remain bathed in a kind of aura of life which bears no relation to real immortality but which continues to occupy our thoughts in the same way as it did when they were alive. It is as if they had left on a voyage. Theirs is a very pagan survival. Conversely, when we have ceased to be in love, the curiosity aroused by the person we love dies even before the person herself does. Thus I would no longer have taken a single step to discover with whom Gilberte had gone for a walk on the Champs-Elysées on such and such an evening. And yet, even if I felt that such moments of curiosity were exactly similar, valueless in themselves and incapable of lasting, I continued to sacrifice everything to the cruel satisfaction of their passing pangs, despite knowing in advance that my separation from Albertine, enforced by her death, would lead me to the same state of indifference as had my intentional separation from Gilberte. If Albertine had been able to tell what was going to happen, she would have stayed by my side. But that was tantamount to saying that, once she had seen herself dead, she would have preferred to stay alive by my side. Through the very contradiction which it implied, such a supposition was absurd. But that did not make it harmless, for as I imagined how pleased Albertine, if she could know and retrospectively understand, would be to return to me, I saw her by my side, I wanted to embrace her, but alas it was impossible, she would never return, she was dead. My imagination sought her in the skies, on evenings like those when we were still able to gaze up at it together; I tried to wing my affections towards her, beyond the moonlight that she loved, to console her for no longer being alive, and this love for a person who had become so remote was like a religion, my thoughts rose towards her like prayers. Desire is so strong that it engenders belief; I had believed that Albertine would not leave, because it was my desire; because this was my desire, I believed that she was not dead; I started to read books about turning tables, I started to believe in the possible immortality of the soul. But that was not sufficient for me. I needed after her death to be reunited with her body, as if eternity could resemble life. Do I mean 'life'? I was even more demanding. I would have liked not to be deprived by death for ever more of those pleasures which death is not alone in taking from us. For even without death they would finally have withered, they had already started to do so through the action of long-standing habit and new attractions. Then, in real life, Albertine, even physically, would have gradually changed, and day by day I would have adapted to this change. But my memory, evoking only moments from her life, wanted to see her again in a certain guise that would no longer have been hers even if she had still been alive; what it wanted was a miracle to satisfy the natural, arbitrary limits of memory, trapped in the past. And yet I imagined this living creature with all the naïvety of the theologians of antiquity, granting me, not the explanations which she could have offered, but, through a supreme contradiction, those which she had always refused to give me while she was alive. And thus her death was a kind of dream, my love would seem to her an unexpected happiness; of death I retained only the usefulness and optimism of an outcome which simplifies and settles everything.

Sometimes I did not imagine our reunion as far away as in another world. Just as in former times when I knew Gilberte only as a playmate on the Champs-Elysées, in the evenings at home I imagined that I would receive a letter from her where she would admit that she loved me and that she was about to come home, so a similar force of desire, taking no more notice of the laws of physics which might prevent it than in the previous case of Gilberte, when, actually, my desire had not been mistaken because it did have the last word, led me now to believe that I was about to receive a message from Albertine, telling me that she had indeed had a riding accident, but that, like a character in some novel (and as does sometimes happen after all in the case of people long believed dead), she had not wanted me to learn that she had recovered and was asking me contritely, now that she was better, to take her back permanently. And, understanding perfectly well how people who otherwise seem quite rational entertain certain harmless follies, I felt coexist within me the certainty that she was dead, and the ceaseless hope of seeing her walk through the door.

I had not yet received any news from Aimé, although he had surely arrived in Balbec by now. No doubt my enquiry was directed at a peripheral and arbitrarily chosen point. If Albertine's life had really been laden with guilt, it must have been full of far graver events which chance had not let me encounter, as it had when Albertine had blushed over the question of the bath-robe. But these were precisely the things that did not exist in my eyes because I had not seen them. Yet it was quite arbitrarily that I had marked out that particular day as significant and, some years afterwards, was attempting to reconstruct it. If Albertine had loved women, there were thousands of other days in her life whose time-table had escaped me and yet which could be just as interesting for me to know; I could have sent Aimé to many other places in Balbec, to many other towns rather than Balbec. But precisely because I had no knowledge of her time-table on those days, I could not picture them in my imagination, they had no existence within it. People and things started to exist for me only when they took on an individual existence in my imagination. If there were thousands of others of the same sort, they became for me merely typical of the rest. If, concerning my suspicions about Albertine, I had for so long desired to know what had happened in the showers, it was in the same way that, although I knew that there were numerous young ladies or chambermaids who were equally likely candidates and who could equally well have come to my attention, those women whom I desired to meet – since it was those that Saint-Loup had told me about, those who existed individually for me – were the young ladies who frequented houses of ill fame, and Mme Putbus's chambermaid. The obstacles that my health, my indecision, my 'procrastination' as Saint-Loup called it, placed in my way when I tried to accomplish anything had led me to delay from day to day, from month to month, from year to year, the clarification of certain suspicions, just as it had the accomplishment of certain desires. But I kept them in my memory, promising not to forget to get to know the reality that lay behind them, because they alone obsessed me (since the others could not take shape before my eyes, and so had no existence) and also because the very chance that had selected them from the real world was a guarantee that it was indeed through them that I would be able to make contact with a little of reality, a little of the real life that I coveted but which eluded me. And again, would not one single little fact, if carefully chosen, enable the experimenter to decide on the general law which will make known the truth about thousands of analogous cases? Although Albertine existed in my memory only in the states in which she had appeared successively during her life, that is, subdivided into a series of temporal fractions, my thoughts, restoring her unity, reconstituted her as a person, and it is on this person that I wanted to form an overall judgement, to know whether she had lied, whether she had loved women, and whether it was in order to be free to frequent them that she had left me. What the bath-house girl had to say might resolve once and for all my doubts over Albertine's morals.

My doubts! Alas, I had thought that I would be indifferent, even pleased, at the prospect of never seeing Albertine again, until her departure revealed my mistake. Similarly, her death had taught me how mistaken I was occasionally to believe that I would welcome her death and to suppose that it would liberate me. It happened the same way when, on receiving Aimé's letter, I understood that, if I had not so far suffered too cruelly from my doubts over Albertine's virtue, it was because in fact they were not really doubts. My happiness and my life needed Albertine to be virtuous, thus they had posited once for all that she was. Armed with this salutary faith, I could safely allow my mind to play sadly with the suppositions which it formulated without believing in them. I thought, 'Perhaps she does love women,' as one thinks, 'I might die during the night'; we say the words to ourselves, but we do not believe them, we make plans for the morrow. This explains how, in mistakenly believing myself to be uncertain as to whether Albertine loved women or not and consequently believing that a guilty act proven against Albertine would add nothing to what I had often envisaged, I came, once faced with the images elicited by Aimé's letter, which others would have found insignificant, to experience an unexpected suffering, the most cruel that I had yet experienced and which, alas, formed with these images, with the image of Albertine herself, into a sort of precipitate, as one says in chemistry, where everything was indivisible and of which the text of Aimé's letter, which I have laid out in a purely conventional fashion, can give no idea, since each of the words that composed it was immediately transformed and coloured for ever by the suffering that it had just induced.

'*Dear Monsieur,*

'*Would Monsieur please forgive me for not having written to Monsieur sooner. The person that Monsieur had requested me to see had taken her leave for two days, and, wishing to respond to the confidence that Monsieur had placed in me, I did not want to return empty-handed. I have just had a chat at last with that person who remembers all quite clearly (Mlle A.)*'

Aimé, who had a certain smattering of education, wanted to place Mlle A. in italics or between inverted commas. But when he wanted to use inverted commas he drew brackets, and when he wanted to put something in brackets he used inverted commas. Similarly, Françoise would say that someone was waiting in the same street as me when she meant that he was resident there, but that someone could reside, rather than wait, for a minute or two, since the mistakes made by simple people consist most often in exchanging terms – as the French language itself has done – which over the centuries have changed places with each other.

'*According to her, what Monsieur had suspected is absolutely certain. Firstly, it was she who looked after (Mlle A.) whenever the latter came to the bath-house. (Mlle A.) very often came to take a shower accompanied by a tall woman older than herself, dressed always in grey, and whom the bath-house girl without knowing her name knew of as a result of often having seen her on the look-out for girls. But she paid no more attention to the others after she had got to know (Mlle A.). She and (Mlle A.) always locked themselves in the cabin, stayed inside a long time, and the lady in grey gave the lady with whom I had this chat a tip of at least ten francs. As the latter person said to me, you can guess that if they had spent their time making daisy chains they wouldn't have given me a ten-franc tip. (Mlle A.) also used to go there sometimes with a very dark-skinned woman, who wore a lorgnette. But most often (Mlle A.) came with girls younger than her, especially a very red-haired one. Except for the lady in grey, the persons that (Mlle A.) habitually brought along with her were not from Balbec and often must have come from quite far away. They never went in together, but (Mlle A.) went in, telling me to leave the cabin door unlocked, that she was expecting a friend, and the person with whom I have spoken knew what that meant. That person was unable to give me further details owing to her not remembering very well, "which is easy to understand after so long". Besides, this person did not attempt to find out, because she is very discreet and because it was in her interest, for (Mlle A.) brought her in lots of money. She was very sincerely moved by the news of her death. It is true that in one so young it is a great mishap both for her and her family. I await Monsieur's orders to know if I may leave Balbec where I am unlikely to learn no more. I wish to thank Monsieur again for the little outing that he has thus procured me and which I have found very pleasant all the more because the weather is more than favourable. The signs are good for this year's season. We hope that Monsieur will put in a brief apparition.*

*'I can't think of anything else of interest to tell Monsieur, etc.'*

To understand how deeply the words struck home, one should remember that the questions I had to put to myself about Albertine were not peripheral, unimportant questions, those questions of detail which are the only kind that we really ask ourselves concerning any person other than ourselves, thereby allowing ourselves, clad in waterproof thought, to wade through suffering, lies, vice and death. No, as regards Albertine, it was a question of essence: who was she deep down, what were her thoughts, whom did she love, had she lied to me, had my life with her been as lamentable as that of Swann with Odette? Thus the target struck by Aimé's reply, although it responded not in general but in specific terms – and precisely for that reason – was indeed the inner self, both Albertine's and my own.

At last, in Albertine walking with the lady in grey down the little street that led to the bath-house, I saw before my eyes a fragment of that past which seemed to me no less mysterious and terrifying than I had feared when I imagined it enclosed within Albertine's eyes and within her memories. Of course anyone other than I might have found those details, which, since Albertine's death, made it impossible for me to have her refute them, thus endowing them with what amounted to a likelihood of probability, quite insignificant. It is even probable that in Albertine's eyes, her own misdeeds, even if they were true, and if she had admitted them – whether in her conscience she found them innocent or blameworthy, whether in her sensual being she found them delightful or bland – would have been divested of that ineffable impression of horror of which I was unable to rid them.

Helped by my own love of women, and notwithstanding the fact that they were unlikely to have meant the same to Albertine, I was able to imagine something of what she had felt. And it was certainly already enough to trigger my suffering to imagine her desiring as I had so often desired, lying to me as I had so often lied to her, preoccupied with this girl or that, and incurring expenses on her behalf, as I had for Mlle de Stermaria and so many other young ladies, or for the village girls whom I met in the country. Of course, all my desires helped me to some extent to understand hers; it already caused me great suffering to have all my desires turned into torments, and the more intense the former, the more cruel the latter, as if in the algebra of the senses they reappeared with the same coefficient, but governed by a minus instead of a plus sign. But in Albertine's eyes, as far as I could judge for myself, however hard she had tried to hide her own misdeeds from me – which led me to believe that she felt that she was guilty or was afraid of hurting me – because she had nurtured them to suit her taste in the spotlight of the imagination where desire takes shape, they seemed to her none the less to be things of the same nature as the rest of life, pleasures for her, which she had felt unable to deny herself, pains for me, but which she had tried to prevent from hurting me by hiding them, yet pains and pleasures which could take their place among life's other pains and pleasures. But in my case it was from outside, without warning, without being able to elaborate the images myself, it was from Aimé's letter that I had received these images of Albertine going into the showers and preparing her tip.

It was obviously because I interpreted Albertine's calculated and silent encounter with the lady in grey as a meeting which they had planned, a convention of going to make love in a shower cabin, which indicated an experience of corruption and the carefully dissimulated organization of a whole double life, it was because these images brought me the terrible news of Albertine's guilt that they had immediately caused me a physical pain which would accompany them for evermore. But these images had immediately been affected by my pain; an objective fact or an image is different according to the state of mind in which one approaches it. And pain is as powerful a modifier of reality as is intoxication. Combining with these images, my suffering had immediately turned them into something absolutely different from what for any other person would be a lady in grey, a tip, a shower, or the street which Albertine and the lady in grey used for their calculated encounter – a glimpse of a life of lies and misdeeds of a kind that I had never envisaged –; my suffering had immediately eaten into their very substance, I no longer saw them in the light which illuminates earthly visions, it was a fragment of another world, an unknown planet of the damned, a vision of Hell. This Hell comprised the whole of Balbec and all its neighbouring villages where, according to Aimé's letter, she often found younger girls to take into the showers. How everything connected with Balbec now became fearfully permeated with that mystery which I had formerly imagined in and around Balbec, but which had dissolved while I was living there, which I had tried to grasp on a later occasion when I got to know Albertine because, as I saw her pass by on the beach, being mad enough to hope that she was not virtuous, I thought that she must be the embodiment of this mystery! The names of those stations, Toutainville, Épreville, Incarville . . . , which had become so familiar, so reassuring, when I heard them in the evening on my return from the Verdurins', but, now that I thought that Albertine had lived in one, walked to another and ridden her bicycle to a third, aroused an anxiety in me more cruel than the first time, when I had felt so disturbed on seeing them from the small local railway with my grandmother, before we arrived in Balbec, which I had yet to get to know.

One of the effects of jealousy is to make us discover how far the reality of external events and the sentiments of the soul are levied in unknown quantities which lend themselves to thousands of different interpretations. We think that we have an accurate knowledge of what things are in the world outside and what people think within themselves, for the simple reason that we are not directly concerned. But as soon as we acquire the urge to know, as the jealous person does, then they become a vertiginous kaleidoscope where we cannot recognize a thing. Had Albertine deceived me? With whom? In whose house? On which day? The day when she had made such and such a remark, and when I remembered having made some reply or other during the day? I had no idea. I had no better idea of what her feelings were for me, whether they were inspired by self-interest or affection. And suddenly I recalled a trivial incident, for instance that Albertine had wanted to go to Saint-Martin-le-Vêtu, saying that she found the name interesting, but perhaps quite simply because she had met up with some girl from the village. But what Aimé had learned from the bath-house girl was of little importance, since Albertine would for evermore be unaware that he had told me about it and since, during the period of my love for Albertine, my need to know was always surpassed by the need to show her that I knew; for this broke down between us the barrier raised by our separate illusions, without ever resulting in making her love me more, on the contrary. Yet now that she was dead, the second of these requirements had in fact become fused with the effects of the first: to imagine the conversation in which I would have tried to let her know what I had learned, as vividly as the conversation in which I would have asked her to tell me what I did not know; that is, I needed to see her by my side and to hear her answering kindly, to see her cheeks fill out, her eyes lose their mischief and fill with sadness, that is, to love her still and forget my jealous rage in the despair of my solitude. The painful mystery of the impossibility of ever letting her know what I had learned and of establishing a new relationship based on the truth which I had only just discovered (and which I might perhaps have been able to discover only because she was dead) substituted its sadness for the more painful mystery of her conduct. How ever could I have wished so much that Albertine should know what I had heard about the shower room, when Albertine no longer existed! This was yet another of the consequences of our finding it impossible, when we have to analyse death, to imagine it in terms other than those of life. Albertine no longer existed; but for me she was the person who had hidden the fact that she had made assignations with women at Balbec, who thought she had managed to prevent me from finding out. When we try to figure out what will happen after our death, are we not mistakenly still projecting the image of our living selves which we have at that moment? And in the end is it much more ridiculous to regret that a woman who no longer exists is unaware that we have found out what she was doing six years earlier, than to wish that the public should still speak well of us in a century's time, when we ourselves are dead? If there is more real foundation to the latter case than the former, the regrets of my retrospective jealousy proceeded none the less from the very same perspectival error as in other men the desire for posthumous fame. And yet, if this impression of the solemn and definitive side of my separation from Albertine had been substituted momentarily for the notion of her misdeeds, it only aggravated these by conferring an irremediable character on them. I saw myself lost in life as if I were alone, on a boundless shore where, whichever direction I took, I would never meet her. Luckily I came across something extremely apposite in my memory – as there are always all kinds of things, some dangerous, others salutary, in this dark cupboard where memories can only be brought to light one by one – I discovered, like a workman finding the right tool for his job, one of my grandmother's sayings. Commenting on an incredible story that the bath-house girl had told to Mme de Villeparisis, she had said to me, 'That woman must have caught lying sickness.' This memory was a great comfort to me. How much credit could I give to what the bath-house girl had told Aimé? Especially since in fact she had never seen anything. A girl can go to take a shower with her friends without having bad intentions. Perhaps the bath-house girl was exaggerating the amount of her tip in order to show off. After all I had once heard Françoise argue that Aunt Léonie said in her presence that she had 'a million a month to burn', which was quite absurd; another time she had seen my aunt Léonie give Eulalie four thousand-franc notes, when a fifty-franc note folded in four seemed to me already implausible enough. And thus I sought to discard, and gradually succeeded in discarding, the hurtful knowledge that I had taken so much trouble to acquire, buffeted as I was between the desire to know and the fear of suffering. Then my affections were able to revive, but so too, instantly accompanying these affections, was a sadness at being separated from Albertine, which perhaps made me even more unhappy than I had been during those recent hours when it had been jealousy that was torturing me. But this latter feeling itself did suddenly revive when I thought of Balbec, because of an image (which until then had never made me suffer and even seemed to be one of the most innocuous in my memory) which I suddenly revisualized, that of the dining-room in the evening, where, on the other side of the glass, Balbec crowded its whole population into the twilight, as if they were watching strange, glowing creatures moving past the illuminated glass of an aquarium, and (although I had never thought of it in these terms before) brought a whole medley of fisher-girls, working-girls and middle-class girls into close contact with each other, through their envy for this new luxury, a luxury which at least thrift and conservatism, if not wealth, prohibited their parents from enjoying, and among these middle-class girls almost every evening one could surely find Albertine, whom I had not yet met and who would no doubt pick up some little girl there and go to join her a few minutes later in the dark, on the sand or in an empty bathing cabin at the foot of the cliffs. Then my sadness revived, as I had just heard the lift, sounding like a sentence of exile as it continued to rise instead of stopping at my floor. Yet the only person whose visit I could have wished for would never again return, since she was dead. And despite that, when the lift did stop at my floor my heart fluttered, for a moment I thought, 'What if all this were only a dream! Perhaps she is here, she's going to ring, she has come home, Françoise will come in to say, more in fear than in anger, for she is even more superstitious than she is vindictive, and would be less afraid of the living woman than a woman she might perhaps believe to be a ghost, "Monsieur will never guess who is here."' I tried to think of nothing, to pick up the newspaper. But I found it insufferable to read all those articles written by people who felt no real pain. One said of a trivial song: 'It brings *tears to the eyes*' whereas I myself would have listened to it so joyfully if Albertine had been alive. Another, for all that he was a well-known writer, said that he had received *unforgettable* tokens of esteem, because he had been applauded as he got off a train, whereas I myself, if I had been so applauded, would not have given it a moment's thought. And a third argued that, without its tedious politics, life in Paris would be 'absolutely delicious', whereas I knew that even without politics life could only be odious for me, but would have seemed delicious, even with the politics, if I had Albertine back. The field sports correspondent (it was the month of May) said, 'This season is truly miserable, not to say calamitous, for the real hunter, since there is nothing, absolutely nothing, worth potting' and the Salon critic: 'Faced with this manner of arranging an exhibition one feels seized by deep discouragement, by infinite sadness.' If the strength of my own feelings made the expressions of those who felt neither real happiness nor real misfortunes seem mendacious and bland, on the other hand, the most insignificant lines which could be related however tenuously to Normandy, or Touraine,[24] or hydrotherapy, or la Berma, or the Princesse de Guermantes, or love, or absence, or infidelity, abruptly placed the image of Albertine before my eyes without leaving me time to turn away, and would start me weeping again. Besides, more often than not, I could not even read the newspapers, for the simple act of turning the pages reminded me both that I had performed the same action while Albertine was alive and that she was no longer alive; I dropped them back down again without having the strength to unfold all the pages. Each impression evoked an identical, but damaged, impression, in that Albertine's existence had been torn away from it, so that I never felt brave enough to live to the full these mutilated moments which lay bleeding in my heart. Even when she gradually ceased to be present in my thoughts and all-powerful in my heart, I felt a sudden pang if I had to go into her room, light a lamp and sit down beside the pianola as I used to do when she had been there. Divided into diverse divinities of hearth and home, she long inhabited a candle flame, a doorknob, or the back of a chair, and other less material domains, such as a sleepless night, or the emotions evoked by the first visit of some woman who had attracted me. In spite of this, the few sentences that my eyes read during a day, or that my thoughts remembered having read, often excited cruel jealousy within me. In order to do this, they needed less to provide me with evidence proving the immorality of women than to bring back impressions formerly linked to Albertine's life. As they were then transported into a forgotten moment whose force had not been blunted by the habit of thinking about it, a moment where Albertine still lived on, her misdeeds assumed a more intimate, agonizing and tragic character. Then I started once again to wonder whether I could be sure that the bath-house girl's allegations were false. A good way to find out would be to send Aimé to Touraine, to spend a few days in the neighbourhood of Mme Bontemps's villa. If Albertine liked the kind of pleasures that women enjoy together, the reason that she had left me would have been in order to be deprived of them no longer, and the minute that she was free she must have sought to indulge in them, and succeeded, in a neighbourhood that she knew and where she would not have decided to return if she had not thought that she would find more opportunities there than she would have if she had continued to live here with me. I do not claim that there was anything extraordinary in the fact that Albertine's death had changed so few of my preoccupations. While our mistresses are alive, a large number of the thoughts which go to make up what we call our love come to us at times when they are not by our sides. Thus we get into the habit of focussing our day-dreams on an absent object, and even if she is absent only for a few hours, she is during those hours no more than a memory. Thus death changes very little. When Aimé had returned, I asked him to leave for Châtel-lerault, and thus it was not only through my thoughts, my sadness and the emotion that I felt on encountering any name linked however tenuously with a certain person, but again through all my actions, through all the enquiries I undertook, through the use that I made of my money, devoting it entirely to learning of Albertine's activities, I can say that during that whole year my life continued to be filled with love, with a real relationship. But the object of this relationship was dead. People sometimes say that something of a person may live on after their death, if that person was an artist and placed something of himself in his work. It is perhaps in this way that a kind of cutting taken from a person and grafted on to another person's heart continues to live on when the person from whom it has been detached has perished.

Aimé went to take lodgings near to Mme Bontemps's villa; he became acquainted with a chambermaid and a man from whom Albertine often hired a car for the day. These two people had noticed nothing. In a second letter, Aimé told me that a young laundry-maid from the town had told him that Albertine had a special way of squeezing her arm when she brought her linen back. 'But', he said, 'this young lady had never done anything more than that with her.' I sent Aimé the money which paid for his trip and which also purchased the ill that his letter had just caused me, although I was struggling to cure this by telling myself that she had merely shown a sign of affection which proved no immoral intent, when I received a telegram from Aimé, saying: 'HAVE LEARNED MOST INTERESTING THINGS. HAVE LOTS OF NEWS FOR MONSIEUR. LETTER FOLLOWS.' The next day I received a letter whose envelope was enough to make me tremble; I knew that it was from Aimé, for everyone, however humble, is a master of those familiar little household creatures whose life lies as it were suspended on the paper, that is, the unique characters of his handwriting which he alone possesses.

'*At first the young laundry-maid didn't want to tell me a thing, she assured me that Mlle Albertine had never done more than pinch her arm. But to get her to talk I took her out to dinner and plied her with drink. Then she told me that Mlle Albertine often met her on the banks of the Loire when she went bathing; that Mlle Albertine, who rose early in the morning to bathe, used to meet her on the riverside at a place where the woods are so thick that no one can see you, and besides there's no one about to see you so early in the morning. Then the laundry-maid brought her girl-friends and they went for a dip, and afterwards, as it was already very hot out there and you could feel the heat beating down even under the trees, they stayed in the grass to dry one another, to tickle and caress one another and play games together. The young laundry-maid confessed that she enjoyed playing games with her girl-friends, and that when she saw that Mlle Albertine kept rubbing up against her in her bath-robe, she got her to take it off and caressed her by running her tongue down her neck and her arms, and even down the soles of her feet when Mlle Albertine stretched them out towards her. The laundry-maid also*

*got undressed, and they played around, pushing one another into the water. That*
*evening she told me nothing more. But dedicated as always to your service and*
*ready to do anything to please you, I took the young laundry-maid home to bed*
*with me. She asked me if I wanted her to do to me what she did to Mlle Albertine*
*when the latter removed her bathing-dress. And she said: (If you could have seen*
*how she quivered, that young lady, she said: (Oh! I'm in heaven) and she got so*
*excited that she could not help biting me.) I could still see the mark on the young*
*laundry-maid's arm. And I understood Mlle Albertine's enjoyment, for the young*
*wench is really very talented.'*

I had suffered badly enough in Balbec when Albertine had told me
of her friendship with Mlle Vinteuil. But Albertine had been there to
console me. Yet later, after I had managed to drive Albertine away
from me by trying to find out too much about her activities, and
Françoise had announced that she was no longer at home, and I found
myself all alone, I had suffered more. But at least the Albertine whom
I had loved remained in my heart. Now what I found in her place —
punishing me for having pushed my curiosity too far and contradicting
my supposition that death should have put an end to this curiosity —
was a different young lady, multiplying lies and deceit in just those
cases where she had so gently reassured me by swearing that she had
never tasted those pleasures which, intoxicated with regaining the
freedom that she had left me in order to savour, she had in fact
indulged to the point of swooning, to the extent of biting the young
laundry-maid whom she met at sunrise on the banks of the Loire and
to whom she declared, 'I'm in heaven.' A different Albertine, and not
only in the sense in which we employ the term when referring to other
people. When other people turn out to be different from what we had
imagined, this difference usually does not affect us deeply, and since
the diviner's wand of our intuition is unable to produce surface
movements greater than the inner swings which it detects, it is only
on the skin of other people's lives that we are able to situate these
differences. In former times when I learned that one woman loved
other women, this did not seem to me to make her a different woman,
a woman of a different essence. But when it comes to concern a woman
whom we love ourselves, we need, in order to rid ourselves of the

pain caused by the idea that it may be true, to find out not only what she has done, but also what she felt when she did it and what she was thinking about while she was doing it; then wading further out we enter deeper into our pain until we reach that mysterious essence. I suffered in the very depths of my being, in my body as well as my heart, much more than I would have done from the fear of losing my own life, from this curiosity which drew on all the united forces of my intellect and my unconscious mind; and in this way I projected into the very depths of Albertine's own being everything that I now learned about her. And the pain which had thus so deeply driven home the truth about Albertine's vice did much later render me one last service. Like the harm that I had caused my grandmother, the harm that Albertine had caused me was a last link between her and me and one link which survived even her memory, for, following the law of conservation of energy that is the law of all physics, suffering need not even be instructed by memory in order to function: thus a man who has forgotten the enchanted nights he had spent in the woods beneath the moonlight still suffers from the rheumatism which he contracted there.

These tastes which, despite her denials, she had, these tastes which were at last revealed to me, not through cold reasoning but through the searing anguish that I felt on reading the words, 'I'm in heaven,' a suffering which gave them a special quality, these tastes did not merely accrue to my image of Albertine as the hermit crab acquires a new shell that it drags along behind it, but rather as one salt which comes into contact with another changes not only that salt's colour, but even its nature. Whereas the young laundry-maid must have said to her girl-friends, 'Just imagine, who'd have thought it, d'you know that she's one too?', for me it was not merely a vice which they initially failed to suspect, which they then added into Albertine's character, but the discovery that she was a different person, a person like them, speaking the same language, making her the compatriot of strangers, making her even more foreign to me, proving that what I had known of her, what I harboured in my heart, was no more than a tiny fragment of her, and that the remainder, which took on such dimensions not only for already being that so mysterious and important thing, individual desire, but also for her sharing it with others, which she had always hidden from me, keeping me away from it, as a woman might have hidden from me the fact that she was an enemy spy, yet more treacherously than such a spy, who deceives only regarding her nationality, whereas Albertine deceived me regarding the nature of her deepest being, in that she did not belong to the common race of humanity, but to an alien breed that intermingles with it and hides within it, but never entirely fuses with it. As it happened I had seen two paintings by Elstir with naked women in a thickly wooded landscape. In one of them one of the girls raises her foot as Albertine must have done when she stretched it out towards the laundry-maid. With her other foot, she is pushing the other girl, who is raising one leg in the air and playfully protesting, and just skimming the surface of the blue water with her other foot as she falls. Now I remembered that the line of her raised thigh made the same sinuous swan's-neck of a curve against the angle of her knee that Albertine's thigh did when she lay beside me on the bed, and I had often wished that I could tell her that she reminded me of these paintings. But I had not done so, in order to avoid awakening within her visions of naked female figures. Now I saw her, along with the laundry-maid and her friends, re-composing the group that I had so admired when I took my place amid Albertine's girl-friends at Balbec. And if I had been a connoisseur responding to beauty alone, I would have acknowledged that Albertine recomposed this group a thousand times more beautifully now that its elements were statues of nude goddesses like those which great sculptors scattered around Versailles, whether planting them among the groves or leaving them to be washed and polished by the watery caress of the fountains. As I saw her now beside the laundry-maid, I saw her in terms of those girls at the water's edge, whose nude forms were reduplicated in feminine marble amid the bushes and undergrowth and steeped in water like some marine bas-relief. Remembering what she had been like on my bed, I thought that I recognized the line of her thigh. As I visualized it, it became the neck of a swan, seeking the other girl's mouth. Then I no longer saw even a thigh, but the bold neck of a swan, like the one in a sketch I knew where it tremulously seeks out Leda's mouth as she openly yields to the spasms of female desire, and where, because it is only a swan, she seems more alone, just as we discover over the telephone the inflexions of a voice that we do not notice until we are able to detach it from the face which for us gives its expressions their concrete form. In this study, pleasure, instead of being directed at the woman who inspires it but who is absent and replaced by a motionless swan, is focussed within the woman who feels it. There were moments when communications between my heart and my memory were cut. What Albertine had done with the laundry-maid was no longer signified by anything more than an almost algebraic shorthand which meant nothing to me: yet a hundred times an hour the current was restored and my heart was scorched by a hellish and pitiless fire as I saw Albertine brought truly back to life by my jealousy, stretching out beneath the caresses of the young laundry-maid, telling her, 'I'm in heaven.' As she was alive at the moment when she committed her misdeed, that is to say at the moment where I now found myself, I was not content merely to learn of this misdeed, I would have liked her to know that I knew. In this way, although in such moments I felt regret at the thought that I would never see her again, this regret was informed by my jealousy and quite different from the heart-rending regret which I felt in the moments when I loved her; it was the regret that I was not able to say to her: 'You thought that I would never know what you did after you left me, and yet I know everything, the laundry-maid on the banks of the Loire, you told her, "I'm in heaven," I saw the love bite.' Of course I also thought: 'Why torture myself? The girl who took her pleasure with the laundry-maid exists no more and therefore is not a person whose actions have retained any import. She cannot tell herself that I know. But nor can she tell herself that I do not know, since she cannot tell herself anything at all.' But I was less convinced by this argument than by my visions of her pleasure, which brought me back to the moment when she had experienced it. Nothing exists for us but what we feel, and we project this into the past, as into the future, without allowing ourselves to be restrained by the fictitious barrier of death. If at such moments my regret that she was dead was subject to the influence of my jealousy and took this particular form, this influence extended naturally to my dreams of the occult and the immortal, which were no more than an attempt to put my desires into practice. Thus at such moments, if I had been able to invoke her by turning a table, as Bergotte believed was possible, or to meet her in another life, as the Abbé X*** would have it, I would have wished to do so only in order to be able to repeat to her, 'I know about the laundry maid. You said: "I'm in heaven"; I saw the bite.' What I fell back on to help me fight against this image of the laundry-maid, was, admittedly after it had been there for some time, this image itself, because we only really take cognizance of something which is new, something which abruptly introduces a change of tone that strikes our sensibility, something that habit has not yet replaced with its pale replicas. But it was above all this fracturing of Albertine into many parts, into many Albertines, which constituted her sole mode of existence within me. Moments recurred when she had been nothing but kind, or intelligent, or serious, or even a lover of sport above all. And was it not right that this fragmentation should soothe me? For although in itself it was quite unreal, although it depended on the successive forms of the hours when it appeared to me, forms which remained those of my memory, as the curves in the images projected by the magic lantern depended on the curves of its coloured slides, did it not in its way represent a perfectly objective truth, which is the fact that none of us is a single being, for we are constituted of many people who do not all have the same moral qualities, and the fact that if the immoral Albertine had indeed existed, this did not preclude the existence of others, like the one who liked to chat about Saint-Simon in her room; the one who, on the evening when I had told her that we should part, had said with such sadness, 'To think that I shall never see this pianola and this room, again' and who, when she had seen what an emotional shock my own deceit had finally given me, had cried out in such sincere pity, 'Oh, no, anything rather than upset you, I agree, I shall not try to see you again!'? Then I was no longer alone. Once this kindly Albertine had returned, I had won back the only person whom I could ask for the antidote to the suffering caused by Albertine. Of course I did still want to discuss the affair of the laundry-maid with her, but no longer in the mode of a cruel triumph making a vicious display of the fact that I was in the know. As I would have done while Albertine was alive, I asked her tenderly whether the laundry-maid affair was true. She swore that it was not, that Aimé was not very truthful and that because he wanted to appear worthy of the wages that I paid him, he had not wanted to return empty-handed and had got the laundry-maid to say whatever he wanted. Of course Albertine had told me a string of lies. And yet in the ebb and flow of her contradictory statements, I felt that there had been a certain progress, thanks to my efforts. I could not have sworn that she did not confide in me even at the start (involuntarily, perhaps, in a phrase that slipped out): I could no longer remember. And then, she had such odd ways of referring to certain things that they might be significant, or they might not be. But her sense of my jealousy had led her afterwards to retract in horror what she had at first complaisantly admitted. Actually, Albertine had not even needed to say this to me. For me to be persuaded of her innocence it was enough for me to be able to kiss her, and now I could, now that the wall which had separated us, that invisible but intractable wall which rises between two lovers who have quarrelled and which kisses cannot breach, had fallen. No, she had no need to tell me anything. She might have done whatever she wished, poor girl, there were feelings which could unite us, beyond whatever divided us. If the affair were true, if Albertine had hidden her inclinations from me, it was in order to spare my grief. I had had the sweet pleasure of hearing this Albertine say so herself. Besides, had I ever known a different Albertine? The two main causes of misunderstanding in a relationship with another person are either that we ourselves are kind-hearted, or else that we are in love with the other person. We fall in love with a smile, the look in someone's eyes, a shoulder. That is enough; then during the long hours of hope or sadness, we create a person, we compose a character. And later, when we come to know better the person we love, we can no more, whatever cruel realities confront us, detach this kind disposition, this amorous feminine nature, from the person who has that look, or that shoulder, than we can remove her youth from a woman who has grown older but whom we have known since she was young. I called to mind the beautiful, kind, compassionate eyes of this Albertine, her plump cheeks and her neck with its grainy texture. It was the image of a dead woman, but since this dead woman was still alive, it was easy for me to do immediately what I would not have failed to do during her lifetime if she had still been by my side (and what I would do if I were ever to meet her again in another life), I forgave her.

The moments which I had spent in the company of this Albertine were so precious to me that I wished I had never forgotten a single one of them. Yet sometimes, as one comes across the remnants of a squandered fortune, I retrieved some which I thought I had lost: tying a scarf behind my neck instead of in front, I remembered a drive which I had never since recalled, when Albertine had kissed me and then arranged my scarf in this fashion to prevent the cold air from chilling my throat. So simple a drive, restored to my memory by so humble a gesture, gave me the pleasure afforded by those personal possessions which have belonged to someone we have dearly loved and which are priceless when they are brought to us by her old maidservant; my sorrow was enriched by this, all the more since I had never thought of this scarf again.

Now Albertine, once more set free, resumed her flight; men and women followed in her wake. She was alive within me. I realized that my vast, protracted love for her was as it were the ghost of the feelings that I had felt for her, reproducing their diverse phases and obeying the same laws as the emotional reality which it reflected beyond her death. For I understood plainly that if I had been able to insert some intervals between my thoughts of Albertine, and had these lasted too long, I would have ceased to love her; this interruption would have made me indifferent to her, as I had now become towards my grandmother. Too long a time spent not thinking of her would have broken in my memory the continuity which is the very principle of life, although it may sometimes be reconstituted even after it has lapsed for some time. Had this not been the case with my love for Albertine while she was alive, which had been able to pick up the threads where they had left off after long periods of not thinking of her? At all events my memory must have been subject to the same laws and equally unable to withstand extended intervals, for after Albertine's death it did no more than reflect, like the aurora borealis, the emotions that I had felt for her, as if it were merely the shadow of my love.

On other occasions my sorrow took on so many forms that

sometimes I did not recognize it; I wished I could have a great love, or I wanted to find someone to live with me, which seemed to me to be a sign that I was no longer in love with Albertine when it was a sign that I was still in love with her; for this need to experience a great love, just like my desire to kiss Albertine's plump cheeks, was only a part of my regret. Only when I had forgotten her would I be able to realize that I would be wiser and happier living without love. Thus missing Albertine, because that was what gave rise within me to the need for a sister, made that need impossible to assuage. And as I came gradually to feel the lack of Albertine less acutely, this need for a sister, which was only an unconscious expression of my need for her, would make it less imperious. And yet these two remainders of my love did not diminish with equal speed. There were hours when the former suffered such a total eclipse, while the latter on the other hand so maintained its full strength, that I decided to get married. And on the other hand, later on, when my jealous memories had died down, from time to time a surge of affection for Albertine welled up suddenly in my heart, and then, thinking of my loves for other women, I told myself that she would have understood and shared them, and her vice became almost a source of love. Sometimes my jealousy revived in the moments when I no longer remembered Albertine, although she was then the cause of my jealousy. I thought that I was jealous of Andrée because I had just learned of an affair she had had. But Andrée for me was only a accommodation address, a relay, a socket wiring me directly into Albertine. Thus it is in our dreams that we lend a different face or name to someone whose identity we have none the less perfectly well grasped. In short, despite the ebb and flow contradicting this general law in these individual cases, the sentiments left in me by Albertine found it more difficult to die than did the sentiment of their original cause. Not only the sentiments, but the sensations. Differing in this from Swann, who, when he had started falling out of love with Odette, had not even been able to revive within himself the sensation of his love, I felt myself still reliving a past that was no more than another man's story; as if my self were divided into two, while its upper half was already hard and cold, its lower half rekindled every time that a spark passed the old current back through it, even when my mind had long since ceased to think of Albertine. Since no image of her ever came to supplement the cruel palpitations that accompanied this phenomenon, or the tears brought to my eyes by a cold wind like the one which had blown through the prematurely pink apple trees at Balbec, I was led to wonder whether the rebirth of my pain was not due to entirely pathological causes and whether what I took to be the revival of a memory and the last phase of a love affair might not be rather the onset of a cardiac disease.

In certain ailments there are secondary infections which the patient is only too tempted to confuse with the illness itself. When they cease he is astonished to find himself less far from being cured than he had thought. Such was the suffering caused – the 'complication' induced – by Aimé's letters about the bath-house girl and the laundry-maid. But if a spiritual doctor could have visited me, he would have found that in other respects my sorrow itself was on the mend. No doubt, as I was a man, one of those amphibious creatures plunged simultaneously in the past and in present reality, there was still a contradiction inside me between the living memory of Albertine and my knowledge of her death. But this contradiction was in a way the reverse of what it had been before. The thought that Albertine was dead – which at first struggled so furiously against the thought that she was still alive that I was forced to run away from it as children do from an oncoming wave – had finally, precisely because of these incessant assaults, won over the place inside me still occupied until recently by the thought that she was alive. Without my realizing it, it was now this thought of the death of Albertine – and no longer the present memory of her life – that made up the greater part of my unconscious day-dreams, so that if I suddenly interrupted them to reflect on myself, what provoked my astonishment was not, as it had been during the first few days, that the Albertine so alive within me could no longer exist on this earth and could be dead, but that the Albertine who no longer existed on earth, who was dead, could have stayed so alive within me. The black tunnel shored up by my series of interlocking memories, where my thoughts had been dreaming for so long that they did not even notice it, was abruptly flooded by a sunny spell, bathing it in the light of a distant, smiling blue universe where Albertine was nothing more than a charming memory that left me indifferent. Is that her, I wondered, is she the real one, or is it that person who seemed during my long trek through darkness to be the only reality? A sort of self-multiplication made the character that I had been until so recently, and who lived for nothing but the permanent expectation of the moment when Albertine would come to kiss him good-night, appear to me now as only a small part of myself which I had already almost shed, and I felt the youthful freshness of a bud starting to open and burst through its leaves into flower. It is also possible that these brief flashes of illumination made me become more aware of my love for Albertine, as happens with all ideas which are too fixed and which need to feel resistance in order to affirm themselves. Those who lived through the 1870 war,[25] for instance, say that the idea of the war had gradually come to seem natural to them, not because they did not think enough about the war, but because they thought about it all the time. And to understand what a strange and momentous event a war is, something different was needed to shake them out of their constant obsession, to forget for a moment that war ruled their lives, and to find themselves as they had been when they had been at peace, until suddenly on to this temporarily blank screen the monstrous reality that they had so long ceased to see, since they saw nothing else, would at last be distinctly projected.

If for the time being this retreat within me of different memories of Albertine had at least been executed not in staggered ranks but in this instantaneous rout, along the whole front line of my memory, with the memories of her betrayals moving away at the same time as those of her favours, forgetting would have brought me peace. It was not to be. As on a beach where the tide runs out unevenly, I was already gnawed by the pangs of one or other of my suspicions when the image of her sweet presence had already receded too far away from me to be able to act as a remedy. As for the acts of betrayal, they made me suffer because, however many years previously they had been committed, they were new for me; but I suffered less as they grew old, that is, as I imagined them less vividly, for the remoteness of an object is proportionate rather to the visual power of the memory observing it than to the real distance of the number of days which have passed, as the memory of a dream from the night before may appear to us so faded and imprecise that it seems more remote than an event dating from several years earlier. But although the thought of the death of Albertine was making progress inside me, the ebb tide of the feeling that she was alive, even if it did not arrest that progress, did none the less oppose it and hinder its regular advance. And now I realize that during this period (no doubt because I had forgotten the hours that she had been sequestered by me, which, since they dispelled within me the suffering caused by her misdeeds and left me almost indifferent because I knew that she was no longer committing them, had become so much evidence of her innocence), I suffered the martyrdom of living habitually with an idea just as new as the one that Albertine was dead (until then I had always started out from the idea that she was alive), an idea that I would have thought just as impossible to bear and which, without my realizing it, was gradually forming the basis of my conscious mind and substituting itself for the idea that Albertine was innocent: it was the idea that she was guilty. At times when I thought I doubted her, I did in fact on the contrary believe in her: likewise I took as the starting-point for my other ideas the certainty – often contradicted, as had been the opposite idea – of her guilt, while still imagining that I was still in doubt. I must have suffered greatly during that period, but I realize now that it had to be thus. We may be cured of suffering only on condition that we experience that suffering to the full. By protecting Albertine from all contact, by forging the illusion that she was innocent, just as when later I took as the basis of my reasoning the thought that she was alive, all I was doing was postponing the moment of my cure, because I was postponing the long hours of preparation and the inevitable suffering that it would take. But when habit got to work on this idea of the guilt of Albertine, it would do so according to the same laws as those I had already experienced during the course of my life. Just as the name of Guermantes had lost the charm and significance of a road bordered with water lilies and of Gilbert le Mauvais's stained-glass window, so Albertine's presence had lost those of the blue valleys of the sea, the names of Swann, the liftboy, the Princesse de Guermantes and so many others, a charm and a significance each entrusted to a single word which they judged mature enough to live on its own, as someone who wants to train a servant will show him the ropes for a couple of weeks and then withdraw, so the painful power of Albertine's guilt would be expelled outside me by habit. Besides, by that time, as when an army attacks simultaneously on two flanks, in this action mounted by habit, two allies would take up arms on each other's behalf. It is because my idea of Albertine's guilt would become a more plausible and familiar idea for me as it would become less painful. But at the same time, as it became less painful, the objections raised to the certainty of this guilt and which were suggested to my intellect only by my desire not to suffer too much, would fall away one by one; and each process would facilitate the other, I would move fairly swiftly from the certainty that Albertine was innocent to the certainty that she was guilty. I needed to live with the idea of the death of Albertine, with the idea of her misdeeds, for these ideas to become habitual, that is for me to be able to forget these ideas and finally forget Albertine herself.

I had not yet reached this stage. Sometimes it was my memory, sharpened for instance by the intellectual excitement of reading, which renewed my sorrow; at other times it was, on the contrary, my sorrow, brought on for instance by the anguish induced by stormy weather, which dredged up some memory of our love and raised it nearer to the light. Moreover these revivals of my love for Albertine once she was dead might occur after an interval of indifference interspersed with other attractions, as when, after the long interval which had started with the kiss which had been denied me in Balbec, during which time I had been much more concerned with Mme de Guermantes, Andrée and Mlle de Stermaria, my love had revived once more when I had begun to see her frequently again. Yet even now different preoccupations could lead to a separation – from a dead woman this time – where I would become more indifferent to her. And all for the same reason, that she was still alive for me. And even later, when I loved her less, it nevertheless remained for me one of those desires which rapidly pall, but which rekindle when they have been left to rest for a while. I pursued one live woman, then another, then I returned to my dead one. Often it was in the darkest corners of my self, when I could no longer form a clear idea of Albertine, that a name would come by chance to excite painful reactions that I no longer believed possible, as in certain dying people whose brains have ceased to think but whose limbs may be made to contract when pierced by a needle. And for long periods, these stimuli were activated so rarely that I was led to seek out for myself a moment of sorrow or a fit of jealousy, to try to reconnect with the past and remember her better. For since missing a woman is no more than reviving a love that remains subject to the same laws as all love, the force of my regret was increased by the same causes which, while Albertine was alive, would have augmented my love for her and which had always given pride of place to jealousy and pain. But these occasions – for an illness, or a war, can last far longer than the most careful calculations had predicted – arose most often without my knowledge and caused me such violent shocks that I was much more concerned to protect myself from the suffering which they had caused than to appeal to them to yield me a memory.

Moreover it did not always even need a word like Chaumont[26] (even a syllable common to two different names could enable my memory – as an electrician can use the slightest conducting substance – to re-establish contact between Albertine and my heart) to refer directly to one of my suspicions in order to arouse it and to work as the password, the magic 'open sesame' creating access to a past which we had ceased to notice because, in having tired of looking at it, we literally no longer possessed it; we had been diminished by its loss, thinking that through this subtraction our own personality had changed shape, like a geometrical figure which loses a side if it loses an angle; just as certain phrases, for instance, which included the name of a street or a road where Albertine might have walked, were sufficient to incarnate a non-existent but virtual jealousy in search of a body, a dwelling, any material anchorage or specific concrete form. Often it was quite simply during my sleep that these reprises, these da capos of a dream turning several pages of my memory and of the calendar, returned me, or rather made me regress to, a painful but distant impression, which had long ago given way to others, but which now became present again. Usually it arrived accompanied by a whole theatrical staging, clumsy but striking, which created the illusion of a visible and an audible reality, which I thereafter dated back to that night. Moreover in the story of a love and its struggles against the process of forgetting, does not dreaming hold an even greater place than waking, since dreams take no notice of infinitesimal divisions of time, suppress transitions, reject blatant contradictions, undo in an instant the web of consolation so slowly woven during the day and during the night arrange for us to meet the woman whom we would ultimately have forgotten as long as we never saw her again? For, whatever people may say, it is perfectly possible during a dream to have the impression that what is happening is real. And this could be judged impossible only by using arguments drawn from our waking experience, but these are hidden from us at the time. As a result, this implausible life seems true to us. Sometimes through a flaw in the internal lighting which treacherously made the room disappear, as my carefully staged memories gave me the illusion of real life, I thought that I had really arranged to meet Albertine and had really met her; but then I found myself unable to walk towards her, to utter the words which I wanted to speak, to relight my extinguished lamp in order to see her: impossibilities in my dream which were simply the immobility, the speechlessness and the blindness of the sleeper, just as we may suddenly see in a magic-lantern show a great shadow, which is that of the lantern itself, or its operator, which were meant to be hidden, blotting out the images of the characters which were meant to be projected. On other occasions Albertine was in my dream and wanted to leave me again, without her decision managing to move me. It was because a warning ray of light from my memory had managed to infiltrate the darkness of my sleep; and what lay hidden within Albertine, and what removed all import from her future actions and her intended departure, was the notion that she was dead. I chatted with her and, while I was talking, my grandmother was walking about at the other end of the room. Part of her chin had crumbled to pieces like fractured marble, but I found nothing extraordinary in that. I told Albertine that I would have questions to put to her concerning the bath-house at Balbec and a certain laundry-maid from Touraine, but that I was leaving it until later because we had plenty of time and there was no longer any hurry. She promised me that she had been doing nothing wrong and that all she had done was kiss Mlle Vinteuil on the lips the day before. 'What? Is she here? – Yes, and what is more, it is time for me to leave, for I have to see her in a moment.' And because since her death I no longer held her prisoner at home as I had during the last phases of her life, her visit to Mlle Vinteuil perturbed me. But I did not want it to show. Albertine told me that she had done no more than kiss her, but she must be starting to lie again as in the days when she used to deny everything. In a moment she would probably no longer be content merely to kiss Mlle Vinteuil. Obviously from one point of view I was wrong to feel so worried, since, so we are led to believe, the dead can neither act nor feel. This is what people say, but it did not prevent my grandmother, who was dead, from living on for quite a few years and from walking around my room at that very moment. And doubtless, once I was awake, this notion of a dead woman living on would have become as impossible for me to comprehend as I find it to explain. But I had formulated it so many times, during these periods of temporary madness that we call dreams, that I had finally become used to it; our memories of dreams can become permanent if they are repeated often enough. And I imagine that even when cured and having recovered his reason, the man who must understand rather better than others what he wanted to say during an earlier period of his mental life, would be the man who had undertaken to explain to visitors to a mental hospital that he was not himself insane despite the doctor's claims, lucidly analysing the monstrous imaginings of each of the patients and concluding, 'Take that man who looks quite normal, you wouldn't think he was mad, and yet he thinks he is Jesus Christ, and that is impossible, because it is I who am Jesus Christ!' And a long time after the end of my dream, I remained tormented by the kiss which Albertine told me she had given, in words which I thought I could still hear. And they must in fact have passed very close to my ears since it was I myself who had uttered them. All day long I continued to converse with Albertine, I asked her questions, I forgave her, I made up for the things that I had always wanted to tell her but had forgotten to do during her lifetime. And suddenly I took fright as I realized that this person evoked by my memory, the person to whom all these remarks were addressed, no longer corresponded to anything in the real world, that her various facial features, given the unity of a person driven only by the continuous will to live, which was now annihilated, were destroyed. On other occasions, without having dreamed, I felt as soon as I awoke that my inner climate had changed, a cold wind was blowing relentlessly from another direction, from the depths of my past, bringing with it the chiming of far-off hours and the whistles of departures which I usually failed to hear. I tried to pick up a book. I opened a novel by Bergotte which I had particularly liked. I was very fond of its charming characters, and as I soon fell under the spell of the book once more, I started to take a personal interest in wanting to have the wicked woman punished; my eyes brimmed with tears when the happiness of the betrothed couple was safe at last. 'But then,' I cried in despair, 'I cannot conclude from the fact that I attach so much importance to what Albertine might have done, that her personality is something real which cannot be abolished, that I shall find her one day unchanged in heaven, if I desire so fervently, await so impatiently and welcome so tearfully the success of someone who has only ever existed in Bergotte's imagination, someone whom I have never seen, whose face I am free to imagine however I wish!' There were moreover in this book attractive girls, amorous correspondence and deserted paths on which to meet, which reminded me that clandestine love affairs could exist, which reawakened my jealousy, as if Albertine had still been capable of going for a walk along a deserted path. It also included the story of a man who meets a woman whom he had loved in her youth, fifty years earlier, but fails to recognize her and is bored by her company. And this reminded me that love does not last for ever, and I felt overwhelmed, as if I were destined to be separated from Albertine and meet her with indifference in my old age. And if I came across a map of France my fearful eyes conspired to avoid encountering Touraine, to save me from being jealous, and, to save me from being unhappy, Normandy, where at least Balbec and Doncières would be marked, between which I could trace all the routes which we had so often travelled together. Amid other names of French towns or villages, even if only read or heard, the name of Tours, for instance, seemed differently composed, not now of immaterial images but of toxic substances which acted instantaneously on my heart, making it beat more rapidly and painfully. And if this power extended to certain names, which she had rendered so different from others, then why, if I moved closer to home and concentrated only on Albertine herself, should I be surprised to find that this irresistible force, which might well have been exerted on me by any other woman, should be the outcome of a tangled confrontation and interplay of dreams, desires, habits and affections, duly disturbed by the intrusion of alternating pains and pleasures? And this process continued after her death, since memory suffices to sustain real life, which is mental. I recalled Albertine alighting from the railway carriage, telling me that she would like to go to Saint-Martin-le-Vêtu, and I also saw her before, with her polo cap pulled down over her cheeks; I discovered fresh possibilities of happiness and reached out for them, thinking, 'We could have gone to Infreville, or even Doncières.' There was not one resort near Balbec where I did not recognize her, so that this region, like some still-preserved mythological land, rendered the most ancient and charming legends of my love, however buried beneath later experience, alive and hurtful. Oh, how I would suffer if ever I had to sleep again in Balbec in that bed, around whose copper frame, as around a motionless pivot or fixed bars, my life had moved and evolved, winding around it in succession my cheerful conversations with my grandmother, the shock of her death, Albertine's sweet caresses, the discovery of her vice and now a new life where I knew, as I glimpsed the glass-fronted book-cases which reflected the sea, that Albertine would never again appear! Did not this Balbec hotel resemble the unchanging domestic interior on the stage of some provincial theatre, where year after year the most diverse plays are set, now for a comedy, now for one tragedy and then for a different one, and then again for a purely poetical drama, this hotel which already belonged to quite a remote period of my life? The fact that this single element, with its four walls, its book-case and its mirror, always remained the same during each new period of my life made me feel even more certain that overall it was everything else, that is, I myself, which had changed, thus giving me the impression that the mysteries of life, love and death (from which children optimistically believe themselves excluded) are not privileges reserved for others, but, as we realize later, proudly but painfully, have been part and parcel of our own lives and bodies throughout the passing years.

I tried from time to time to look at the newspapers, but I found reading them not only unpleasant but far from innocuous. In fact so many paths branch out from each idea within us, as from a crossing in a forest, that at the moment when I least expected it I found myself faced with a fresh memory. The title of Fauré's song, 'Le Secret',[27] had led me to *Le Secret du roi* by the Duc de Broglie,[28] the name of de Broglie to that of Chaumont. Or again, the words Good Friday had made me think of Golgotha, and Golgotha of the etymology of the word, which, apparently, is equivalent to *Calvus mons*, Chaumont. But no matter which path I had climbed on my way to Chaumont, when it emerged I was struck with a shock so cruel that from that moment on I thought far more of preventing it from hurting me than searching it for memories. A few moments after the shock, my intellect, lagging behind like thunder after lightning, brought me the explanation. Chaumont had made me think of the Buttes-Chaumont where Mme Bontemps had told me that Andrée often used to go with Albertine, while Albertine had told me that she had never seen the Buttes-Chaumont. After a certain age our memories are so interwoven with each other that the object of our thoughts or the book which we are reading has practically no importance. We have left traces of ourselves everywhere, everything is fertile, everything is dangerous, and we can make discoveries every bit as precious in an advertisement for soap as in Pascal's *Pensées*.

No doubt an incident like that of the Buttes-Chaumont, which had seemed trivial to me at the time, was in itself a much less serious and decisive charge against Albertine than the affair of the bath-house girl or the laundry-maid. But in the first place a memory which we experience fortuitously finds us with our powers of imagination, that is, in this case, with our powers of suffering intact, whereas on the other hand we have already partly blunted these when we have deliberately applied our minds to recreating a memory. And then, I had become accustomed to these memories (of the bath-house girl or the laundry-maid), always present in my memory, however dimly, like furniture placed in a dark corridor, which we somehow avoid bumping into without distinguishing them clearly. But, on the other hand, I had not thought of the Buttes-Chaumont for ages, nor for instance of Albertine looking into the mirror at the casino at Balbec, nor her unexplained expression the evening when I had waited so long for her after the reception at the Guermantes, all those parts of her life which remained outside my heart and which I would have liked to know in order to assimilate them and annex them to it, to add them to gentler memories formed in my heart by an inner Albertine that I really possessed. Raising a corner of the heavy veil of habit (habit which stultifies us and which during the whole course of our existence hides more or less the whole universe from us, and under cover of utter darkness, without changing their labels, substitutes for the most dangerous or intoxicating poisons of life something anodyne which procures no delight), these memories returned to me as on their first appearance, with the same sharp, fresh novelty that each new season brings as it returns, changing our routine time-table and providing us, even in the realm of our pleasures – if we climb into a carriage on the first fine day of spring or leave the house at sunrise – with an exultant awareness of our most insignificant actions, which invests this one intense moment with more value than the totality of the days preceding it. As they recede, passing days gradually cover over those which went before and are themselves buried by those that come after. But each past day remains deposited within us as in some vast library where there are copies even of the oldest books, which probably no one will ever ask to consult. And yet if this past day should pass through the translucent layers of the following eras, rise to the surface and spread out from within us until it covers our whole surface, then for a moment names will resume their former meanings, people their former faces and we our former souls, and we shall feel with a diffuse but newly tolerable and transient sense of suffering, the problems which remained intractable for so long and which caused us so much anguish at the time. Our selves are composed of our successive states, superimposed. But this superimposition is not immutable like the stratification of a mountain. A tremor is liable at any moment to throw older layers back up to the surface. I found myself back at the moment when I left the reception at the Princesse de Guermantes, waiting for Albertine to arrive. What had she been doing that night? Deceiving me? With whom? Aimé's revelations, even if I accepted them, did not in any way diminish my anxious and desperate interest in this unexpected question, as though each different Albertine, each new memory, asked a specific question of jealousy, which the answers to the others could not resolve.

But I would have liked to know not only with which woman she had spent the night, but what particular pleasure it had brought her, what was happenng inside her at that moment. Sometimes at Balbec Françoise had gone to fetch her and had told me that she had found her leaning out of the window, looking anxious and expectant as though she were waiting for someone. Now let us suppose that I learned that the girl she was waiting for was Andrée, what was Albertine's state of mind while she was waiting for her, what state of mind lay hidden behind her anxious, expectant expression? How important for Albertine were these inclinations, how large a place did they hold in her concerns? Alas, remembering my own agitation every time that I came across a girl who attracted me, and sometimes when I had only heard her mentioned and had not even seen her, my breaking into a cold sweat in my concern to appear handsome and interesting, I needed only to imagine the same voluptuous excitement in Albertine in order to torment myself, as if I had discovered the device which my aunt Léonie, after the visit of a certain physician who had seemed unconvinced by the reality of her malady, had hoped someone might invent in order to enable the doctor to feel all the sufferings of his patient, so that he would better understand them. And this was already enough to torment me, to tell me that compared to this she must have found our discussions of Stendhal and Victor Hugo truly insignificant, for her heart to be drawn to others, to fly away from mine and take root elsewhere. But even the importance that she attached to this desire and the reticence with which she protected it could not inform me of its qualities, let alone how she experienced those qualities when she talked to herself about it. When our bodies suffer, at least we cannot choose our pain. Our illness determines and imposes it. But with jealousy we are forced as it were to try out all types and scales of suffering before we settle for the one that seems to suit us. And what greater problem could we face than one which concerns the kind of suffering where our beloved takes her pleasure with people other than ourselves, who give her sensations that we are unable to give her, or at least with people who through their characteristics, their behaviour and the image they project, create an impression on her totally different from ours! Oh! If only Albertine had been in love with Saint-Loup! How much less I would have suffered, or so it seemed to me!

There is no doubt that we are unaware of the nature of each individual's personal sensibility, but generally we do not even know that we are unaware of it, for we are indifferent to other people's sensibilities. As far as Albertine was concerned, my happiness or unhappiness might have hung on what kind of sensibility she had; I was well aware that it was a mystery to me, and the fact that it was a mystery was already a source of pain. I did once have the illusion of seeing, and on another occasion of hearing, the unknown desires and pleasures felt by Albertine. Of seeing them, when Andrée came to see me, some time after Albertine's death. For the first time she seemed beautiful to me, I found that her curly, almost frizzy hair, and her moody eyes with their dark rings, must have been what Albertine had fallen in love with, and I saw materialize before my eyes what had nourished her amorous fantasies, what had fired her eyes with anticipated desire the day when she wanted to return from Balbec so precipitously. As if a dark, unknown flower belonging to someone beyond the grave from whom I had been unable to gather it were now recovered and presented to me, this miraculously exhumed and priceless relic seemed to present me with Albertine's desire incarnate in the form of Andrée as she appeared to me, just as Venus figured Jupiter's desire. Andrée mourned for Albertine, but I felt straight away that she did not really miss her friend. Forcibly deprived of her friend by death, Andrée seemed to have come to terms very easily with a final separation that I would not have dared request while Albertine was alive, for fear that Andrée would withhold her consent. On the contrary she seemed to accept this renunciation with no difficulty, albeit only at the very moment when this was of no further use to me; Andrée handed me Albertine, but only now that she was dead and had lost for me not only her life but, in retrospect, something of her reality, as I saw that she was not unique and indispensable for Andrée, who had been able to replace her with other friends.

While Albertine was alive, I would never have dared ask Andrée to confide in me the nature of the friendship between themselves and with Mlle Vinteuil's girl-friend, not being at all sure in latter days that Andrée would not tell Albertine everything that I had told her. Now this investigation, even if it delivered no results, would at least hold no danger. I spoke to Andrée, not as if I were questioning her but as if I had always been kept informed, perhaps by Albertine, of Andrée's own inclinations for women and her own relationship with Mlle Vinteuil. She admitted everything with no inhibition, and with a smile. From this admission I could draw the most hurtful conclusions; first and foremost, since Andrée, who had behaved so affectionately and seductively towards so many young men at Balbec, would never have given anyone to suppose that she indulged in those practices which she now made no attempt to deny, so that by analogy, on discovering this new Andrée, I was led to think that Albertine might just as easily have made a similar confession to anyone other than me, whom she guessed to be jealous. But furthermore, now that Andrée, who had been Albertine's best friend and the one for whom she had probably returned to Balbec on purpose, had admitted her inclinations, the conclusion which I was bound to draw was that Albertine and Andrée had always had a relationship together. Of course, just as we do not always dare take a look at gifts offered by strangers in their presence, preferring to wait until the donor has left before we undo the wrapping, so, as long as Andrée was there, I could not withdraw within myself to examine the pain that she caused, which I already felt greatly upsetting my bodily dependants, my nerves and my heart, although from politeness I pretended not to notice; on the contrary, I deployed all my reserves of charm in conversing with my young guest, without diverting my gaze towards these inner events. I found it particularly painful to hear Andrée say of Albertine, 'Ah, yes, she did like driving out with me in the Chevreuse valley.' The vague, non-existent universe where Albertine and Andrée drove out together seemed to be joined retrospectively by this new and satanic creation, adding to the work of God a valley of the damned. I sensed that Andrée was going to tell me everything that she used to do with Albertine, and, although I did everything I could, from politeness, cunning, self-esteem and perhaps even from gratitude, to appear more and more affectionate, while the space that I was still able to concede to Albertine's innocence shrank smaller and smaller, I had the impression that despite my efforts I appeared frozen, like an animal trapped but transfixed by the progressively narrowing circles described by a bird of prey taking its own sweet time, knowing that it can choose the moment to strike, since its prey can no longer escape. I looked at her however and summoning the last reserves of good humour, naturalness and self-confidence that remain in a person not wishing to seem to fear being hypnotized by someone's gaze, I dropped the following casual remark: 'I had never spoken to you about it before for fear of upsetting you, but now that it is a comfort to speak of her, I can tell you that for some time I had been aware of the kind of relationship that you enjoyed with Albertine; besides, you will be pleased to know, although you knew it already, that Albertine adored you.' I told Andrée that I would very much like her to let me watch her indulge in this kind of practice (even if she restricted her caresses to those which she would not be too embarrassed to perform in my presence) with those of Albertine's girl-friends who shared the same tastes, and I mentioned Rosemonde, Berthe and all of Albertine's friends, to see her reaction. 'Apart from the fact that in your presence I would not do what you mention for anything in the world,' replied Andrée, 'I do not believe that any of the girls you mention were that way inclined.' Moving closer, despite myself, to the monster that fascinated me, I replied, 'Come, now, you cannot expect me to believe that Albertine was the only person in your group that you did these things with! – But I never did do things like that with Albertine. – Listen, my dear Andrée, why deny something that I've known about for at least three years? I see nothing wrong in it, quite the opposite. I was just thinking of the evening when she was so keen to go with you to Mme Verdurin's the next day, perhaps you remember . . .' Before I had come to the end of my sentence, I saw an anxious look, like the face of someone allowed backstage before a play commences who peeps through the curtain then withdraws immediately to avoid being noticed, flash across Andrée's eyes, making them as narrow and piercing as certain gemstones which are so sharp that jewellers find them almost impossible to use. The anxious look disappeared, everything returned to normal, but I sensed that everything I saw from then on would be artificially arranged for my benefit. At that moment I caught sight of myself in the mirror; I was struck by a certain resemblance between myself and Andrée. If I had not long ceased to shave my upper lip, and if I had still had only the faintest shadow of a moustache, the resemblance would have been complete. Perhaps it was at Balbec, when she had observed my moustache as it was just starting to grow again, that Albertine had suddenly had that impatient, furious urge to return to Paris. 'But I can't tell you something that is not true just because you don't disapprove of it. I swear that I never did anything with Albertine and I am convinced that she detested that sort of thing. The people who told you that were lying, perhaps from self-interest,' she said, with a suspicious, questioning air. 'Well, so be it, since you don't want to tell me,' I replied, preferring to seem as if I did not want to reveal my evidence, rather than failing to have any. Yet I did refer in an offhand manner to the Buttes-Chaumont, just in case. 'I might have gone to the Buttes-Chaumont with Albertine, but is there anything particularly wrong with the place?' I asked her if she might not ask Gisèle about it, since she had at one time been very close to Albertine. But Andrée declared that Gisèle had recently stabbed her in the back, and asking her a favour was the one and only thing that she could never agree to do for me. 'If you see her,' she added, 'don't tell her what I've told you about her, there's no need to make an enemy of her. She knows what I think of her, but I have always preferred to avoid getting involved in violent rows with her and then having to patch things up. And then again, she is dangerous, but anyone who had read the letter she sent me last week, where she told such treacherous lies, would understand that nothing, not even the noblest actions in the world, could efface its memory.' In short, if, despite the fact that Andrée followed her inclinations to the point of not trying to hide them and despite the great affection which Albertine had certainly felt for her, Andrée had never had carnal relations with Albertine and had always been ignorant of the fact that Albertine shared her inclinations, then surely it must be because Albertine had not had such inclinations and had never had such relationships, which she would have sought to enjoy with Andrée in preference to anyone else. Thus as soon as Andrée had left, I realized that her trenchant affirmation had calmed me down. But perhaps Andrée had felt obliged by the sense of duty that she felt towards her dead friend, whose memory still lived on within her, not to let anyone believe what Albertine had most likely asked her during her lifetime to deny.

After that one moment when, looking at Andrée, I thought I caught a glimpse of the pleasures in which I had so often tried to imagine Albertine indulging, there was another occasion when I thought that I surprised their presence, but this time through my ears, not my eyes. I had asked for two laundry-maids from a neighbourhood which Albertine often used to frequent to be invited to a house of ill-fame. As one caressed the other, her partner started suddenly to make a noise which at first I was unable to interpret, for we never perfectly understand the significance of a strange sound which expresses a sensation that we do not ourselves feel. If we are listening in an adjoining room, without being able to see, we may take for a fit of giggles the screams of a patient operated on without anaesthetic; and as for the sounds made by a mother who has just learned of the death of her child, it could seem to us, if we did not know the cause, as difficult to ascribe to the human tongue as the sounds emitted by an animal or a harp. It takes us a while to understand that both kinds of sound express by analogy something we call suffering, however different from our own experience, and similarly it took me a while to understand that this particular sound expressed by analogy something, however different, which I had experienced, what I called pleasure; and this pleasure must have been very powerful to shake the person who felt it to such an extent that it drew from her this unknown language, which seemed to designate and comment on all the stages of dramatic delight experienced by the young woman hidden from my eyes by the curtain permanently drawn against anyone but themselves over what happens in the mysterious private depths of every human creature. At all events these two young things were unable to tell me anything, they had never even heard of Albertine.

Novelists often claim in their introductions that somewhere on their travels abroad they have met someone who has told them of another person's life. They then let this travelling companion tell the tale, and their novel is precisely the story they hear. Thus Stendhal heard about Fabrice del Dongo's life[29] from a canon in Padua. When we are in love, that is, when some other person's life seems to be a great mystery to us, how we would like to come across such a well-informed narrator! For he surely exists. Do we ourselves not quite dispassionately tell the life story of some woman or other to one of our friends or to a stranger who knew nothing of her love affairs but who listens to us out of sheer curiosity? The man I was at the time when I told Bloch about the Princesse de Guermantes or Mme Swann, the man who could have spoken to me of Albertine, there always is such a person . . . but we will never meet him. It seemed to me that if I could have met women who had known her, I would have found out everything that I needed to know. And yet to a stranger it must have seemed as if nobody could know her life better than me. Did I not even know her best friend, Andrée? Thus it is that we believe that a minister's friend must know the truth about certain affairs or he would not be caught up in his trial. But the friend knows from personal experience that each time he has discussed politics with the minister, the latter spoke in general terms and told him no more than he might read in the newspapers, or if he had a request, his repeated appeals for the minister's help were met each time by the phrase 'I can do nothing about it', which the friend himself can do nothing about. I thought 'If only I had been able to meet such and such a witness!' from whom, if I had met them, I would have been able to obtain no more than I had from Andrée, who was herself the guardian of a secret which she refused to deliver. I was different again in this from Swann, who, when he was no longer jealous, ceased to be curious about what Odette might have done with Forcheville; even when my jealousy had subsided, the only thing that held any charm for me to get to know Albertine's laundry-maid and other girls from her neighbourhood, in order to reconstruct her life and relationships there. And since desire always arises from something we have already found impressive, as I had found happened with Gilberte, or with the Duchesse de Guermantes, it was in the neighbourhoods where Albertine had formerly lived that I sought out women of her milieu, who were the only women whose presence I desired. Even if they could tell me nothing, the only women to whom

I felt attracted were those that Albertine had known or whom she might have known, women of her milieu or of the circles which she frequented, in short women who for me possessed the attraction of resembling her or of being those who would have attracted her. Recalling in this way either Albertine herself or the kind of woman that appealed to her, these women awakened in me painful feelings, whether of jealousy or regret, which later, as my grief subsided, changed into a curiosity which was not without charm. And these women were mostly working-class girls, since their lives were so different from my experience. Of course, it is only in our minds that we ever possess anything, and we do not possess a painting because we have it in our dining-room, if we do not understand it, nor a country because we merely reside in it without ever looking at it. But I have to say that in former times I did have the illusion that I possessed Balbec once more, when Albertine came to see me in Paris and I held her in my arms; just as I made a rather glancing not to say furtive contact with Albertine's life when I tasted the atmosphere of a workshop, shop-counter gossip, or life in the slums, in the arms of a working-girl. Always related to Albertine – as Albertine herself had been related to Balbec – Andrée and these other women were those kinds of substitutes for pleasure which replace each other in diminishing order and allow us to relinquish the pleasures that we are unable to attain, like staying in Balbec or loving Albertine, those kinds of pleasure which (just as going to the Louvre to see a Titian that used to be in Venice consoles us for being unable to go to Venice), as they fan out into a series of infinite nuances, arrange our lives into a set of concentric, continuous, harmonious but gradually fading circles, around an initial desire that has set the tone, eliminated everything that does not blend with it and has imposed its dominant tone (as happened to me for instance with the Duchesse de Guermantes and with Gilberte). Andrée and these other women acted the same part in my desire to have Albertine close at hand, which I knew I could no longer gratify, as had one evening, in the days when I knew Albertine only by sight, the fresh, sinuous, sunlit form of a bunch of grapes.

Now that they were associated with the memory of my love, the physical and social attributes of Albertine, whom I had loved in spite of them, had the opposite effect, that of orientating my desire towards what previously it would have least naturally chosen, dark-haired girls from the lower-middle classes. Of course what was starting partially to revive within me was the immense desire that my love for Albertine had been unable to assuage, that immense desire to know life which I used to feel on the roads near Balbec or the streets of Paris, the desire which had so made me suffer when, supposing that it also existed in Albertine's heart, I had attempted to deprive her of the means of satisfying that desire with anyone other than myself. Now that I was able to bear the thought of her desires, and since this thought was immediately aroused by the upsurge of my own desires, bringing our two boundless appetites into union, I would have liked us to have been able to indulge them together, and I thought, 'She would have liked that girl,' but as this oblique reference suddenly made me think of her and her death, I felt too sad to follow my desires any further. Just as in former times the Méséglise and the Guermantes ways had established the foundations of my taste for the countryside and would have prevented me from finding deep charm in a neighbourhood with no old church or cornflowers or buttercups, so in the same way it was by linking them within me to the charms of the past that my love for Albertine made me seek certain types of women to the exclusion of others; as in the days before I had fallen in love, I started to feel the need for harmonics emanating from her which could become interchangeable with my memory as it became gradually less exclusive. I could not now have found pleasure in the company of a proud, blonde duchess, because she would not have evoked in me any of the emotions which derived from Albertine, from my desire for her, from the jealousy I had felt for her loves, or from my suffering over her death. For in order to gain strength, our sensations need to trigger within us something other than themselves, a sentiment which cannot find its satisfaction in pleasure but which becomes added to desire, swells it and makes it cling desperately to pleasure. The more the love that Albertine might have felt for certain women gradually ceased to make me suffer, the more it attached these women to my past, making them into something real; just as the memory of Combray gave greater reality to its old buttercups and hawthorn than to the new flowers of spring. Even when I thought of Andrée, I no longer said furiously, 'Albertine loved her,' but, on the contrary, in order to explain my own desire to myself, I said tenderly, 'Albertine was fond of her.' I now understood those widowers whom one believes to be consoled and who prove on the contrary that they are inconsolable because they have married again, this time with their wife's sister.

Thus my dying love seemed to make new loves possible for me, and Albertine, like those women long loved for their own sake who later, feeling their lover's ardour waning, preserve their power by settling for the role of go-between, as La Pompadour did for Louis XV,[30] served up a whole series of new young girls for me. Previously my time had been divided into periods when I desired first one woman, then another. When the violent pleasures offered by the one had been appeased, I fancied the other, who offered an almost pure tenderness, until the need for more artful caresses brought back the desire for the first. Now this oscillation had come to an end, or rather, one of its phases had become indefinitely protracted. What I would have preferred was that the new arrival should come and live with me, and before leaving me in the evening, give me a friendly, sisterly kiss. So that I might have come to believe – had I not had the experience of the intolerable presence of the other person – that I missed the kiss more than any particular lips, the pleasure more than love, the habit more than the person. I would have also liked the newcomer to play Vinteuil for me as Albertine had, to discuss Elstir with me as she had. All of this was impossible. Their love was not worthy of hers, I thought; whether because a love which could include all those episodes, the visits to museums, the evenings at concerts, the whole complicated life which generates correspondence, conversation, the flirtation preceding the relationship itself and the solemn friendship that follows, draws on deeper resources than love for a woman who knows only how to yield, as an orchestra has more resources than a piano; or whether because at a deeper level my need for the same sort of affection that Albertine used to give me, the affection of a reasonably well-educated girl who acted at the same time as a sister, was only – like my need for girls from the same milieu as Albertine – a revival of my memory of Albertine, of my memory of my love for her. And once more I felt above all that memory is not creative, that it is incapable of desiring anything different or even anything better than what we have already possessed; and then that it is mental, so that reality cannot provide it with the state to which it aspires; and finally that the rebirth which it incarnates, since it emanates from a dead person, is less the rebirth of the need for love, as it would have us believe, than that of the need for the missing person. So that even the resemblance to Albertine of the woman whom I had chosen, and the resemblance of her affections, if I managed to obtain them, to those of Albertine, only made me feel all the more the absence of what I had been looking for without realizing it, of what was indispensable for the rebirth of my love, that is Albertine herself, the period that we had lived together, the past which I was seeking without realizing it. Of course on sunny days Paris appeared to me endlessly blooming with young girls whom I did not desire but who sprang from the dark roots of my desire for Albertine and the unknown nights that she had spent far from home. These were the sort of girl of whom when we first met, when she was not wary of me, she had said, 'What a ravishing little girl, look at her lovely hair!' All my former curiosity about her life when I knew her only by sight, and on the other hand all my desires to live life to the full, became fused in that one curious urge, to know the manner in which Albertine felt pleasure, to see her with other women, perhaps because thus, once they had left, I would remain alone with her, her last and only master. And if I could have seen her hesitate as to whether it was worth spending the evening with one girl or another, and noted her satiety or perhaps her disappointment when the girl had gone, I could have clarified and reduced to more sensible proportions the jealousy inspired in me by Albertine, because in seeing how she experienced her pleasures I would have taken the measure of them and discovered their limits.

How much pleasure and sweetness had been lost to us both, I thought, because of her fierce determination to deny her inclinations! And as I once again tried to find what had been the reason for this obstinacy, suddenly there came to me the memory of a remark that I had made one day in Balbec when she had offered me a pencil. In reproaching her with not letting me embrace her, I had told her that I found the thought of our kissing as natural as I found the thought of a woman having relations with another woman repellent. Alas, perhaps Albertine had remembered.

I took home with me the girls who should have appealed to me least. I stroked their sleek, prim tresses, I admired their finely chiselled little noses or their pale Spanish complexions. Of course even in former times, even with women whom I happened to glimpse on the roads around Balbec or on the streets of Paris, I had felt how singular was my desire and how false it would be to try to assuage it with a different object. But life, gradually revealing to me the permanence of our needs, had taught me that if a person is unobtainable we have to settle for someone else, and I felt that what I had asked of Albertine could have been supplied by another, like Mlle de Stermaria. But it had been Albertine; and between the satisfaction of my need for affection and the specific features of her body the cross-stitch of memories had become so intertwined that I could no longer tear my urge for affection away from the body of Albertine, which had become embroidered into my memory. Only she could bring me happiness. The idea of her uniqueness was no longer a metaphysical *a priori* deriving from Albertine's individual qualities, as formerly for various passing women, but an *a posteriori* constituted by my contingent but inseparably entangled memories. I could no longer yearn for any affection without needing her and suffering from her absence. In this way the very similarity of the woman I chose, and of the affection I sought, to the happiness that I had known, only made me all the more aware of everything they lacked in order to revive it. I felt the same emptiness in them that I had felt in my room since Albertine had left, the emptiness which I had hoped to fill by holding these women in my arms. For they had never spoken to me of Vinteuil's music or Saint-Simon's *Memoirs*,[31] had never put on too much perfume before coming to see me, never playfully brushed their eyelashes against mine, the kind of things which take on importance because they seem to allow us to cradle the sexual act itself within our dreams and create an illusion of love, but in fact because they were part and parcel of my memory of Albertine and because she was the person whom I was hoping to find. The qualities that these women shared with Albertine made me feel more keenly what they lacked, which was everything, but an everything which could never exist again, since Albertine was dead. And thus my love for Albertine, which had drawn me towards these women, made me feel indifferent towards them, and my regret for Albertine and the persistence of my jealousy, which had already outlasted my most pessimistic forecasts, would doubtless not have changed very much if their existence, isolated from the rest of my life, had been subject only to the play of my memories, to the actions and reactions of a psychology applicable to motionless states, and had not been sucked into a vaster system where souls move through time as bodies through space. As there is a spatial geometry, so there is a temporal psychology, where the calculations of a two-dimensional psychology would no longer be accurate because they would not account for Time and one of the forms that it assumes, that is, forgetting; the process of forgetting, whose force I was starting to feel and which is such a powerful tool of adaptation to reality because it gradually destroys in us the remnants of the past which constantly contradict it. And of course I might have guessed much sooner that one day I would no longer love Albertine. When I had understood the difference that there was between the importance of her person and her actions for me as opposed to for others, implying that my love was less a love for her than a love within me, I could have drawn diverse conclusions from this subjective character of my love, including the fact that, since it was a state of mind, it could clearly survive longer than the person concerned, but also that having no real link with this person, having no material support outside her, it must, like all states of mind, even the most long-lasting, one day find itself worn out and have to be 'replaced', and that on that day everything that seemed to me to be so sweetly and indissolubly linked to Albertine would no longer exist for me. The problem with people is that for us they are no more than prints in our mental museum, which fade on exposure. And it is precisely because of this that they form the basis of projects illuminated by our thoughts, but thoughts tire and memories collapse: the day would come when I would happily give Albertine's room to the first girl who wanted it, as I had given Albertine the agate marble or other gifts of Gilberte's.

CHAPTER 2

*Mademoiselle de Forcheville*

This is not to say that I did not still love Albertine, but it was already not the same kind of love as I had felt in recent times; rather, it was more like that love of former times when everything connected with her, both places and people, inspired in me a curiosity containing more charm than suffering. And in fact I now realized that before I could forget her completely, and regain my initial indifference, I would need, like some traveller returning down the same route to his point of departure, to experience in reverse order all the emotions which I had felt on the way out towards my great love. But these stages, these moments of the past are not inert, they have retained the terrible force and blissful ignorance of a hope which reached out then towards a time that has now become the past, but which, in moments of hallucination, we retrospectively take for the future. As I was reading one of Albertine's letters announcing her arrival for that very evening, I felt for a second the joy of expectation. In these journeys which return along the same track to a place where in reality we will never return, journeys where we recognize the names and the features of all the stations we stopped at on the outward journey, it sometimes happens that while we have halted at one or other of these stations, we experience for a moment the illusion that we have moved off, but in the direction of the place we have just left, as we did on the way out. The illusion swiftly dies, but for a second we felt ourselves driven forward once more: such is the cruelty of memory.

And yet if, in order to regain the point of indifference from which we started out, we cannot dispense with the need to cover in reverse order the same stages that we had covered on our way to attaining love, the itinerary or tracks which we follow are not necessarily the same itinerary or tracks as the first time. They are equally indirect, since forgetting proceeds no more regularly than love, but they do not necessarily follow the same routes. And on my return journey, there were, when I had nearly arrived, four stages which I particularly remember, doubtless because I now saw in them things that had no part in my love for Albertine, or at least which were connected with it only in so far as everything which our souls contained before our great love affair becomes associated with it, whether by nourishing it, by resisting it, or by setting up contrasts and images for our intellect as it analyses that love.

The first of these stages set in at the beginning of winter, one fine All Saints' Day when I had gone out. As I approached the Bois de Boulogne, I recalled with sadness Albertine's return, when she had come to meet me at the Trocadéro, for it was the same day of the year, but without Albertine. With sadness, yet not without pleasure, for the repetition in the minor key, in a melancholy tone, of the same motif that had punctuated my day the first time, and the very absence of Françoise's telephone call and of Albertine's arrival, were not something negative but, as my memories failed to materialize in reality, their suppression gave the day a poignant note and made of it something more beautiful than a single, uniform day, for what was lost, what had been torn from it, remained imprinted there as if etched between the lines. As I walked through the Bois I hummed phrases from Vinteuil's sonata. The thought that Albertine had played it for me so often no longer hurt me too much, for nearly all my memories of her had entered that second phase of their chemical reaction, where instead of oppressing the heart with anxiety, they soothe it. From time to time, as I reached the passages which she most frequently played and during which she would tend to reminisce, or pass some familiar remark that I found charming at the time, I thought, 'Poor little girl,' yet I thereby infused the musical passage not with sadness but with more value, the value of history and curiosity, just as Van Dyck's portrait of Charles I, already beautiful enough in its own right, gains even more in value from the fact that it entered the national collections through Mme du Barry's desire to impress the king.[1] When the little phrase, before entirely disappearing, disintegrates, and floats around for a moment as it dissolves into its various elements, it was not, as it had been for Swann, a messenger informing me of the disappearance of Albertine. The little phrase did not awaken quite the same association of ideas in me as it had in Swann. I had been particularly moved by the variations, experiments, repetitions and 'promise' of the phrase, which played in the sonata a role like that played in the course of my life by my love. And now, as I came to realize how far, day by day, another element of my love was drifting away, my jealousy or other aspects of my love gradually returning in a vague memory as the piece quietly started, I thought I saw my love dispersed or even dissolved in the little phrase.

As I followed the paths which ran through the shrubbery, veiled in a hazy foliage which became flimsier every day, I felt the memory of a drive beside Albertine in the car, when she was coming home with me and I had felt my whole life wrapped up in hers, swim up again around me amid the vague mist of darkening branches within which the setting sun lit up irregular horizontal layers of golden foliage, as if they were suspended in mid-air. Meanwhile I trembled at every moment, as does any man whose obsession turns any woman standing at the corner of a path into the possible likeness or identity of the woman he is thinking of. 'It might be her!' We look round, but the carriage moves on, and we do not turn back. I was not content to contemplate this foliage merely with the eyes of memory. It interested and moved me as do those purely descriptive pages in whose midst an artist, in order to make them more complete, introduces something fictional or a whole novel; and thus this natural scene took on the only melancholy charm which could touch my heart. The reason for this charm seemed to me to be the fact that I was still just as much in love with Albertine, while the true reason was on the contrary that inside me the work of forgetting was continuing to evolve and that the memory of Albertine was becoming less painful, that is, that it had changed; but however clearly we identify our own impressions, as I then believed I saw clearly into my melancholia, we are unable to plumb their deeper meaning: as with those attacks of sickness that a doctor hears his patient describing, but which lead him to detect a deeper cause, unknown to the patient, so our impressions and ideas count only as symptoms. While my jealousy was held back by the impressions of charm and sweet sadness that I felt, my senses were reawakened. Once more, as when I had stopped seeing Gilberte, a love for women surged up within me, freed of any exclusive association with a particular woman once loved, and wafted like those essences liberated by death and decay and which float suspended in the spring breeze, asking only to be united with some new entity. Nowhere do flowers, even those called 'forget-me-nots', bloom more readily than in a cemetery. I watched the girls who so profusely decorated this fine new day, as I would have in former times from Mme de Villeparisis's carriage or a carriage I had taken with Albertine on such a Sunday. As soon as I cast my eyes on one or other of them, they were given their focus by the curious, furtive, inviting looks, reflecting her elusive thoughts, which Albertine would have surreptitiously cast, and which, lending their mysteriously swift and blue-tinged wings to my own gaze, breathed into these hitherto entirely natural paths a shiver of the unknown, which my own desire, if left to its own devices, would not have been able to elicit, for my own desire held no secrets for me. And sometimes reading a rather sad novel carried me suddenly backwards, for some novels are like a period of great mourning which abolishes habit and puts us once more in touch with the reality of life, but for a few hours only, as does a nightmare, for the force of habit, the oblivion that it procures and the gaiety that it restores as the brain is unable to resist them and re-establish the truth, are infinitely stronger than even the most hypnotic suggestions of a beautiful book, which, like all suggestions, have a very fleeting effect. Moreover in Balbec, when I had wanted to meet Albertine for the first time, was it not because she had seemed to me to stand for all the girls whose sight had so often rooted me to the spot in the street or on the road, and because she could provide me with the quintessence of their lives? And was it not natural now that the waning star of my love in which they were condensed should be once again dispersed into this scattered stardust of the galaxies? They all looked to me like Albertine, the image which I bore within me made me see her everywhere, and even as I turned a corner in the road, the one I saw climbing back into a motor-car reminded me so much of her, and her figure was so similarly shaped, that I wondered for a moment if it wasn't Albertine herself that I had seen and if I hadn't been misled by the story of her death. I recalled her at just such a bend in the road, perhaps in Balbec, climbing back into the car in the same way, at a time when she had so much confidence in life. And as she climbed back into the car, the girl's movements not only struck my eyes as do those superficial visions that we glimpse so fleetingly during a drive: it became a more durable kind of action and seemed to me also to reach backwards into the past, through this newly acquired perspective which pressed so voluptuously and sadly upon my heart.

But the girl had already vanished. A little further on I saw a group of three slightly older girls, whose smart and athletic demeanour so perfectly echoed what had seduced me on the first day that I had seen Albertine and her friends that I followed in the footsteps of these three new girls, and when they took a carriage, I looked desperately around me to find one myself, but when I did find one, it was too late. I was unable to catch up with them. Yet a few days later, as I was going home, I saw emerging from under the archway of our house the three girls whom I had followed in the Bois de Boulogne. Although they were just a little older, they corresponded exactly, especially as far as the two brunettes were concerned, to those young society ladies whom I had so often seen from my window or walked past in the street, causing me to make a thousand plans and fall in love with life, but whom I had never managed to meet. The blonde one looked more fragile, perhaps sickly even, and attracted me less. Yet she was the one who made me dissatisfied with a momentary glance, as I stopped in my tracks and my eyes took on a fixed stare, as impossible to distract as if they were concentrating on one of those problems where we knowingly strain to reach far beyond surface appearances. I would no doubt have let them disappear like so many others, but just as they passed by, the blonde girl – was it because I was studying her so attentively? – cast me a first, furtive look, then, when she had gone past, turned her head back towards me and cast a second that finally set me alight. However, since she then lost interest in me and started chatting with her friends again, my ardour would have finally dampened, had it not been multiplied a hundredfold by the following fact. When I asked the concierge who they were, he replied: 'They asked for Mme la Duchesse. I think only one of them knows her and that the others only accompanied her to the door. Here is her name, I don't know whether I have spelled it right.' And I read: Mlle Déporcheville, which I easily corrected to: d'Éporcheville, that is, more or less, as far as I could recall, the name of the very well-connected young lady, loosely related to the Guermantes, whom Robert had mentioned after meeting her in a house of ill-fame and having been intimate with her. I now understood the significance of the look in her eyes, why she had turned round and hidden from her companions. How often I had thought of her, picturing her in terms of the name mentioned by Robert! And now I had just seen her, no different from her friends, except for that furtive glance which opened up for me a secret path to parts of her life which were evidently hidden from her friends, and which made her seem more accessible to me – already almost half mine – and more pliant than the usual run of aristocratic young ladies. In her mind, she already anticipated the hours that we might have shared together, if she had been free to make an assignation. Was that not what her eyes had tried to express with an eloquence that only I could read? My heart beat furiously, I would have been incapable of saying exactly what Mlle d'Éporcheville looked like, I vaguely recalled a blonde head seen from the side, but I was madly in love with her. Suddenly I realized that I was reasoning as if of the three girls Mlle d'Éporcheville was definitely the blonde one who had turned her head and looked at me twice. Yet this was not what the concierge had said. I returned to his lodge to question him again, but he said that he was unable to answer my question because today was the first time they had called and it had been while he was out. But he would ask his wife, who had seen them once before. She was cleaning the servants' staircase. Who has not had such delicious doubts during his life, more or less similar to these? A charitable friend to whom one describes a girl seen at a ball has deduced that she must be one of his friends and invites you to meet her. But among so many, and on the basis of a merely verbal portrait, will there not have been some mistake? Will the girl that you are about to see be different from the one whom you desire? Or will you on the contrary see the smiles and the outstretched hand of the girl that you wanted her to turn out to be? The latter good fortune is not infrequent and, without always being justified by arguments as decisive as mine concerning Mlle d'Éporcheville, results from a kind of intuition and also from the fair wind of fortune that may sometimes favour us, so that on seeing her we say, 'She is the one'. I recalled that I had correctly guessed which one of the little gang of girls walking along the sea front was called Albertine Simonet. This memory provoked a sharp but brief pain, and while the concierge went to fetch his wife, my main thought – thinking of Mlle d'Éporcheville and, as in one of those moments of waiting where a name or a fact, which you have for some reason fitted to a face, finds itself momentarily free to float between several, and ready, if it adheres to a new one, to render retrospectively the original face which it had brought to your attention alien, innocent and elusive – was that the concierge was likely to reveal that Mlle d'Éporcheville was one of the two brunettes. In which case the being in whose existence I believed would disappear, the being whom I already loved, who filled me with the desire to possess her, the blonde and sultry Mlle d'Éporcheville, whom the dread wrong answer would fatally dissociate into two separate entities, which I had arbitrarily united as does a novelist who merges diverse entities borrowed from real life in order to create an imaginary character, but which taken separately – if the name fails to confirm what the eyes had intended – would lose all significance, would be dissociated into two separate elements by the fatal reply. In this case my arguments would come to naught, but no, on the contrary, how much more strongly they were vindicated, as the concierge returned to tell me that Mlle d'Éporcheville was indeed the blonde!

From that moment on I could no longer believe that she was merely her namesake. The odds were too long against one of these three girls being called Mlle d'Éporcheville, and, in a first, limited corroboration of my supposition, being precisely the one who had looked at me in that almost smiling way and yet not being the one who frequented houses of ill-fame.

Then started a day of wild excitement. Even before going out to buy every garment that would help me dress up to create the best impression the day after next, when I would be visiting Mme de Guermantes, in whose company I would find a young lady of easy virtue and would make an assignation with her (for I would certainly find a moment to speak with her in a corner of the drawing-room), in order to make doubly sure I went out to send a telegram to Robert asking him for the name and the exact description of the young lady, hoping to have his reply before the day after next when, according to the concierge, she would return to see Mme de Guermantes; and when (without thinking for a moment of anything else, even of Albertine), whatever might happen to me in the meantime, even if I was ill and had to be taken there in a wheelchair, I would visit the Duchesse at the same time. If I went to send a telegram to Saint-Loup, it was not that I had any remaining doubts as to the identity of the person or that I made any distinction between the girl I had seen and the one he had described. I had no doubt that they were one and the same. But in my impatience at waiting for two days, it was a pleasure for me, it was almost already for me a secret hold over her, to receive a telegram full of details concerning her. At the telegraph office, while drafting my telegram with all the excitement of a man burning with hope, I noted how much less helpless I was now than in my childhood and in relation to Mlle d'Éporcheville than to Gilberte. I need do no more than take the simple trouble to write my telegram, and the clerk had only to accept it, for the swiftest of electric communications networks to transmit it across the length and breadth of France, right down to the Mediterranean coast. Robert would bring his whole libertine past to bear on identifying the person whom I had just encountered, would place it at the disposal of the fiction that I was starting to sketch and which I need not even worry about any more, for the reply would be bound to bring my romance to a conclusion in one way or another before twenty-four hours had elapsed. Whereas formerly, brought back from the Champs-Elysées by Françoise and left to foment my impotent desires alone at home, unable to exploit the technology of modern civilization, I loved like a savage, or even like a flower, since I had no right to come and go. From this moment on I spent all my time in a state of fever; a forty-eight-hour trip that my father asked me to take with him and which would have made me miss my visit to the Duchesse sent me into such a state of rage and despair that my mother intervened and persuaded my father to leave me in Paris. But it took several hours for my anger to abate, while my desire for Mlle d'Éporcheville had increased a hundredfold because of the obstacle placed between us, and my momentary fear that these hours at Mme de Guermantes', which I greeted as a well-deserved prize of which no one could deprive me, might not occur. Some philosophers argue that the external world does not exist and that it is only within ourselves that our lives evolve. Be that as it may, love, even in its humblest beginnings, is a striking example of how little reality means for us. If I had had to draw, describe or inventory the details of Mlle d'Éporcheville's features from memory, or even to recognize her in the street, I would have found it impossible. I had caught sight of her in profile as she passed, she had seemed pretty, unaffected, tall and blonde, and I could not have said more. But all my reactions of desire, anxiety, of mortal shock inspired by the fear of not seeing her if my father took me with him, all these, associated with an image which I had in fact invented but which I needed only to believe attractive, already constituted love. At last the next morning, after a night of blissful insomnia, I received Saint-Loup's telegram: 'De l'Orgeville, *de* noble particle, *orge* barleycorn, as in rye, *ville* as in town, short, dark and dumpy, is presently in Switzerland.' It was not her!

My mother had brought my mail to my room and placed it casually on the bed, as if thinking of something else. And as she withdrew immediately to leave me on my own, she smiled. And knowing my dear mother's stratagems and knowing that one could always decipher her expression with no fear of mistake if one took as its key her desire to please others, I too smiled, thinking: 'There is something interesting for me in the mail, and Mama has adopted her indifferent and absent-minded air to allow me to enjoy the surprise to the full, so as to avoid being like those people who ruin half of your pleasure by announcing it in advance. And she did not stay, because she feared that from pride I would hide the pleasure I felt, and thus feel it less keenly.' Meanwhile, as she was nearing the door, she had met Françoise, who was about to enter my room with my telegram in her hand. As soon as she had given it to me my mother forced her to beat a retreat and dragged her outside, flustered, offended and surprised. For Françoise considered that her duties included the privilege of entering my room at any time and staying there, if she wanted to. But already on her face astonishment and anger had disappeared beneath her sticky black smile of transcendental pity and philosophical irony, a viscous ointment secreted by her wounded pride to heal its scar. To avoid feeling despised, she despised us. For she knew full well that we were masters, that is, capricious creatures who are not noted for their intellectual brilliance and who enjoy using fear in order to show plainly that they are the masters, to impose on those more thinking creatures, their domestic servants, absurd obligations such as boiling water in times of epidemic, mopping my room with a wet cloth, and having to leave the room precisely when they had wanted to enter. Mama had placed my mail right by my side, so that I could not miss it. But I sensed that there was nothing but newspapers. No doubt there was some article by an author whom I liked but, because he wrote infrequently, it would be a surprise for me. I went over to the window and drew back the curtains. Above the pale misty daylight the sky, which was as pink as the stoves that are lit in the kitchens at this time of day, filled me with hope and the urge to spend the night and wake up in the morning at the little mountain resort where I had seen the pink-cheeked milkmaid. I opened the *Figaro*. How tedious! The leading article bore precisely the same title as the one which I had submitted but which had not been published.[2] But not only the same title, here and there were one or two identical words. That was too much. I would write in to complain. And I heard Françoise, who was indignant at having been expelled from my room where she considered that she was free to come and go as she pleased, grumbling: 'The very idea! A child that I saw born. Of course I didn't see him when his mother bore him, but let me tell you that when I first met him he hadn't been born for more than five years!' But there were not just those few words, there was everything, even my signature . . . It was my article, which had at last appeared! But my mind, which already in those days had started to age and to tire a little, continued for a moment to reason as if it had not understood that it was my own article, like those old men who are obliged to continue with a movement once they have started, even if it has become pointless, even if an unforeseen obstacle which they should immediately avoid has rendered it dangerous. Then I considered the spiritual bread that a newspaper constitutes, still warm and moist as it emerges from the press and the morning mist in which it has been delivered at crack of dawn to the housemaids who take it to their masters with a bowl of milk, this miraculous loaf, multiplied ten-thousandfold and yet unique, which stays unchanged for everyone while proliferating across every threshold.

What I was holding in my hand was not one particular copy of the newspaper, it was any one out of ten thousand; it was not only something written by me, it was something written by me and read by everyone. To appreciate the exact phenomenon as it occurs in each household, I must read this article not as an author but as one of the other readers of the newspaper; what I was holding in my hand was not just what I had written, it was the symbol of its incarnation in so many minds. Thus in order to read it I must for a moment stop being its author and become an ordinary reader of the newspaper. But now I feel a first pang of anxiety. Will the unsuspecting reader see this article? I open the newspaper absent-mindedly as would this unsuspecting reader, even wearing on my face my usual expression of not knowing what there is in the newspaper this morning and being impatient to look at the social or political news. But my article is so long that my eyes, which are trying to avoid it (to respect the truth and not load the dice in my favour, just as someone who is waiting deliberately counts too slowly), cannot help chancing on an extract in passing. Yet many of those who notice the leading article, and even of those who read it, do not look at the signature. Even I would have been unable to say who had written the leading article the day before. And now I promise myself always to read them and their author's name; but like a jealous lover, who avoids deceiving his mistress in order to make himself believe in her fidelity, I think sadly that my future attentions will not compel, as they have not compelled, the reciprocal attentions of others. And then there are the people who have gone out hunting and those who have left for work too early. And yet, some people will still read it. I follow their example. I make a start. As I read the article, even though I know that many of the people who read it will detest it, what I see behind each word seems to be printed there in black and white, I cannot believe that anyone who casts his eyes upon it will not see exactly the same images as those I see, for I assume, with all the naïvety of those who believe that it is the actual words we utter which travel down the telephone wires, that the author's thoughts are directly perceived by the reader, whereas it is other thoughts which are constructed in his mind; at the very moment when I am trying to be the ordinary reader, my mind, as I read, is rewriting the article. If M. de Guermantes did not understand such and such a phrase that Bloch would appreciate, he was able on the other hand to smile at some remark that Bloch would treat with disdain. Thus each passage that a previous reader seemed to cast aside would attract a new admirer, the whole of the article would be praised to the skies by the masses and would overcome my own self-doubt so that I would no longer need to defend it myself. For in truth the quality of an article, however remarkable, is similar to that of those sentences in Parliamentary reports where the words 'We shall have to see' uttered by the minister only take on their full import in the following context: 'THE PRIME MINISTER, MINISTER FOR HOME AND RELIGIOUS AFFAIRS: We shall have to see. (*Loud exclamations on the far left. "Hear, hear!" on some of the left and centre benches*)' (an ending which is finer than the middle of the passage, worthy of its beginning): for part of its beauty – and this is the original sin in this kind of literature, from which even the famous *Lundis*[3] are not exempt – lies in the impression which it produces on its readers. It is a collective Venus, of which we grasp only a severed limb if we merely take account of the author's thought, for this is completely realized only in the minds of its readers. That is where all is accomplished. And as a crowd, however select, is not an artist, its ultimate seal of approval always retains something of the common touch. Thus Sainte-Beuve, on Mondays, could imagine Mme de Boigne[4] in her four-poster bed reading his article in the *Constitutionnel*, appreciating some elegant phrase which he had lovingly crafted and which would perhaps never have materialized had he not seen fit to pack it into his weekly column in order to broaden its appeal. No doubt the chancellor, reading it himself, elsewhere, would mention it to his old companion when he visited her later. And taking him back that evening in his carriage, the Duc de Noailles in his grey suit would tell Sainte-Beuve what society had thought of it, if a comment by Mme d'Arbouville had not already informed him. And countering my own self-doubt with the ten thousand voices of approval that supported me, I drew as great a feeling of strength and of belief in my talent from the reading which I was undertaking at this moment as I had drawn self-doubt when what I had written was addressed only to me. I saw my thoughts or even, failing my thoughts, for those who were unable to understand them, the repetition of my name and a kind of glorified echo of my person radiate over so many people at that very moment, colouring their thoughts with a dawning light which filled me with more strength and triumphal joy than the rosy fingers of dawn which pressed simultaneously at countless window panes. I saw Bloch, the Guermantes, Legrandin and Andrée drawing from each sentence the images contained in the article; and now, at the very moment when I am trying to be an ordinary reader, I am reading as an author, albeit not only as an author. So as to help the impossible creature that I am trying to become to reconcile all the contradictions in the way most favourable to me, although I am reading as an author, I am judging as a reader, making none of the demands that a piece of writing faces from the person who expects it to match up to the ideal which he wanted it to express. When I wrote them, the sentences of my article were so weak compared to my thought, so complicated and opaque compared to my harmonious and transparent vision, so full of gaps which I had not managed to fill, that reading them caused me to suffer, they had only accentuated my feelings of impotence and an incurable lack of talent. But now in forcing myself to become a reader, if I delegated to others the painful duty of judging me, I was at least able to wipe the slate clean of what I had intended to do, by reading what I had done. I read the article, struggling to convince myself that it had been written by someone else. Then all my images, all my reflections and all my epithets, taken in themselves and with no memory of the failure of my aims that they represented, charmed me with their brilliance, their novelty and their profundity. And when I sensed too great a failure, I took refuge in the soul of your average admiring reader, and said: 'Well, how could a reader notice that? There may be something lacking there, I admit. But heavens above, they ought to count themselves lucky! It's full enough of good things as it is, far more than they usually get.'

Thus, hardly had I finished this reassuring reading than, despite not having dared reread my own manuscript, I wanted to start rereading it immediately, there being nothing better suited to the dictum 'if you can read it once you can read it twice' than an old article by oneself. I promised myself that I would ask Françoise to buy more copies, I would tell her they were to give to my friends, but in fact it would be to hold in my hands the miracle of my self-multiplying thought and read the same pages in a different copy, as if each time I were a different gentleman opening the *Figaro*. This turned out to be the same day when I intended to go to the Guermantes', whom I had not seen for ages, in order to meet Mlle d'Éporcheville, and during my visit I would find out from them what opinion people had formed of my article.

I imagined one such female reader in her bedroom, which I would have so liked to enter, to whom the newspaper would bring, if not my thoughts, which she would not be able to understand, at least my name as if in homage to me. But homage paid to something we do not care for is no more able to sway our hearts than the thoughts of a mind which we cannot understand are able to move our minds. As for other friends, I argued that, if the state of my health continued to deteriorate and if I could no longer see them, it would be pleasant to continue to write, to retain access to them in this way, to speak to them between the lines, to get them to follow my own trains of thought, to please them and be welcomed into their hearts. This is what I told myself, for social relations had until then figured as part of my daily life, so I was frightened by a future that might hold no place for them, and I found solace in this expedient which would enable me to retain my friends' interest, perhaps elicit their admiration, until the day when I would be well enough to start to visit them again; this is what I thought, but still I realized that it was not true, that although I liked to imagine their attention as the object of my pleasure, this pleasure was profoundly internal and spiritual, a supreme pleasure which they could not provide and which I could find not through conversing with them, but through writing at a distance; and I felt that, if I started to write, in order to meet them indirectly, to give them the best impression of me, to prepare a better social situation for me, perhaps writing might alleviate the desire to meet them and with it the social situation that literature might perhaps have procured me, and I would no longer want to enjoy it, for my pleasure would no longer be in society but in literature.

So after luncheon, when I went to visit Mme de Guermantes it was less on account of Mlle d'Éporcheville, who because of Saint-Loup's telegram had lost the better part of her character, than to see in the Duchesse herself one of those ladies who might have read my article and who might enable me to imagine what the public who subscribed to or bought the *Figaro* would have thought of it. Apart from which, it was not without pleasure that I went to visit her. It was all very well in my eyes to tell myself that what marked out her salon from the others for me was the long period it had spent waiting in my imagination, yet knowing the reason for this difference did not eliminate it. Moreover, there were for me several versions of the name of Guermantes. If the one which my memory had inscribed merely as in an address book was accompanied by no poetry, older versions, those which went back to the time when I did not know Mme de Guermantes, were liable to take shape again within me, especially when I had not seen her for some time and the crude light of the person with her human face did not extinguish the mysterious radiance of the name. Then once again I would start to think of Mme de Guermantes's dwelling as something beyond the real, in the same way as I used to start thinking of Balbec through the mist of my earliest day-dreams and as though I had not since then made the journey there, as though I had never taken the ten-to-two train. I would forget for a moment my knowledge that none of this existed, as we sometimes think of someone we love, forgetting for a moment that they are dead. Then notions of reality returned as I entered the Duchesse's hall. But I consoled myself with the thought that she was none the less for me the true point of intersection between dream and reality.

As I entered the drawing-room, I saw the young blonde lady whom I had believed for twenty-four hours to be the one referred to by Saint-Loup. She herself asked the Duchesse to 'reintroduce' me to her.

And in fact from the moment I arrived I had the feeling that I knew her rather well, but this feeling was dispelled by the Duchesse, who said to me, 'Oh, you have already met Mlle de Forcheville.' Whereas on the contrary I was quite sure that I had never been introduced to any young lady of that name, which would certainly have struck me, as it was so familiar to my memory since I had heard the retrospective account of Odette's love affairs and Swann's jealousy. In itself my twofold misunderstanding of the name, recalling 'de l'Orgeville' as being 'd'Éporcheville' and having reconstrued as 'Éporcheville' what was really 'Forcheville', was far from extraordinary. Our error stems from believing that things habitually appear to us as they are in reality, names as they are written, people as the static concepts presented by photography and psychology. But in fact reality is not at all what we usually perceive. We see, hear and conceive the world inside out and back to front. We repeat a name as we first heard it, until experience rectifies the error – but this does not always happen. Everyone in Combray spoke to Françoise of Mme Sazerat, and yet Françoise continued to call her Mme Sazerin, not through that wilful and proud persistance in error that was her habit, a habit which was only confirmed by our disagreement and which was the only concession to the egalitarian principles of 1789 which she allowed to modify the traditional French values of Saint-André-des-Champs (she claimed only one of her citizen's rights, that of pronouncing differently from us and maintaining that 'hôtel', 'été' and 'air' were of feminine gender), but because in fact she still continued to hear it as 'Sazerin'. This perpetual error, which is nothing but 'life' itself, does not invest with its thousand forms the visible and audible universes alone but also the social, sentimental, historical and other universes, too. As far as the wife of the High Court judge is concerned, the Princess of Luxembourg is little more than a tart and is, moreover, of little interest; what does take on more interest, where Swann is concerned, is the fact that Odette is a morally fastidious lady, and he constructs a whole fiction on the subject, which becomes all the more painful when he understands his error; what is even more significant is that in the eyes of the Germans the French dream only of revenge. We have only formless, fragmented visions of the world, which we fill out with arbitrary associations of ideas, creating dangerous suggestions. I should not therefore have been very surprised to hear the name Forcheville (and already I was wondering whether she was related to the Forcheville whom I had heard so much about) if the blonde girl, doubtless hoping tactfully to forestall questions which she might have found unpleasant, had not straight away said to me: 'Don't you remember that you used to know me very well, you used to visit my house, I am your friend Gilberte. I realized that you did not recognize me. But I recognized you straight away.' (She said this as if she had recognized me the moment I entered the drawing-room but the truth is that she had recognized me in the street and had greeted me, for later Mme de Guermantes told me that she had told her, as if it were most amusing and quite extraordinary, that I had followed her and brushed up against her as if I had mistaken her for a tart.) It was only after she had left that I learned why she was called Mlle de Forcheville. After Swann's death, Odette, who surprised everyone with her profound, prolonged and sincere suffering, found that she had become a very rich widow. Forcheville married her, after undertaking a long round of châteaux and reassuring himself that his family would accept his wife. (The family protested mildly but yielded to the overwhelming argument of no longer having to subsidize the expenses of a needy relative once he proposed to move from imminent poverty to sudden opulence.) Soon afterwards one of Swann's uncles, into whose hands an enormous fortune had fallen after the successive demise of a number of relatives, died, leaving this whole fortune to Gilberte, who thus became one of the richest heiresses in France. But this was the time when the aftermath of the Dreyfus case gave rise to an anti-Semitic movement, in conjunction with a movement towards a greater infiltration of society by the children of Israel. The politicians were not wrong to think that the discovery of the judicial error would strike a blow against anti-Semitism. But, at least in the short term, anti-Semitism in high society was on the contrary augmented and exacerbated. Forcheville, who like any self-respecting nobleman had drawn from family discussions the certainty that his name was more ancient than that of La Rochefoucauld, considered that in marrying the widow of a Jew he had acted with the same charitable spirit as a millionaire who picks up a prostitute in the street and saves her from poverty and the gutter. He was ready to extend his generous principles to include the very person of Gilberte, whose countless millions could hardly fail to help, but whose absurd name, Swann, made the marriage embarrassing. He declared that he would adopt her. As we know, Mme de Guermantes, to the astonishment of her social circle – which she was accustomed and delighted to provoke – had refused to talk to Swann's wife or his daughter after his marriage. This refusal had appeared all the more cruel in as much as what had for so long made his marriage with Odette appear viable was the likely introduction of his daughter to Mme de Guermantes. And no doubt, with all his experience of life, he should have known that these scenes which we picture never come true, for various reasons but among them one which made him think of this lost introduction with little regret. This reason is that – whatever the picture, from eating a trout at sunset, which inspires a stay-at-home man to take the train, to the desire to dazzle a high-minded cashier one evening by drawing up at her front door in a splendid carriage, which decides an unscrupulous man either to commit a murder or to yearn for the death and legacy of his family and, according to whether he is brave or lazy, either to rush to put his ideals into practice or to stay musing over the first step to take – the action which is destined to enable us to complete the picture, whether this action be a journey, a marriage, a crime, or whatever, changes us so profoundly that we attach no further importance to the reason which drove us to perform it in the first place. It may even happen that we never again see in our mind's eye the picture formulated by us when we were not yet the man who was to become the traveller, the husband, the criminal, or the recluse (the man who set to work in search of fame but has, through this very effort, become detached from the desire for fame), etc. Moreover, even if we did try obstinately to avoid acting in vain, it is probable that the effect of the sunset would not be repeated, that when the moment arrived we would feel cold and prefer hot soup by the fireside rather than trout alfresco, that our carriage would fail to impress the cashier, who might have had considerable esteem for us for entirely different reasons but who might feel suspicious of this sudden display of wealth. In short, we saw Swann, once married, attach importance above all to the relations of his wife and his daughter with Mme Bontemps and the like.

To all the reasons, arising from the Guermantes' manner of interpreting social affairs, which had decided the Duchesse never to have Mme and Mlle Swann introduced to her, we may also add the untroubled confidence with which people who are not in love keep their distance from anything they blame in lovers, explain it away by the fact that they are in love. 'Oh I don't have anything to do with all that; if it amuses poor Swann to play the fool and ruin his life that's his business, but you never know with that kind of thing, it could all turn out for the worst, I let them get on with it.' This was the *suave mari magno*[5] that Swann himself advised me to adopt towards the Verdurins when he had long since ceased to be Odette's lover and was no longer interested in the little set. It is what allows third parties to render such wise verdicts on passions which they do not themselves feel and on the complicated behaviour which these passions involve. Mme de Guermantes had in fact applied herself to ostracizing Mme and Mlle Swann with a tenacity that astonished people. When Mme Molé and Mme de Marsantes had started to frequent Mme Swann and to bring a great number of society ladies round to visit her, not only did Mme de Guermantes remain intractable but she managed to cut all their ties and to persuade her cousin the Princesse de Guermantes to follow suit. On one of the most serious days of crisis under Rouvier's[6] government, when it looked as if there would be war between France and Germany, I happened to be dining alone with M. de Bréauté at Mme de Guermantes's, and found the Duchesse looking worried. I had imagined, since she tended to be preoccupied with politics, that she wished thereby to show her fear of a war, as one day when she had sat down to dinner with such a careworn expression and had responded in such terse monosyllables to someone who enquired timidly as to the source of her concern, she had answered with gravity, 'I fret for China.' But now a little later Mme de Guermantes herself explained the preoccupied air which I had attributed to the fear of a declaration of war, saying to M. de Bréauté: 'I hear that Marie-Aynard wants to offer the Swanns a place in society. I absolutely must go to see Marie-Gilberte tomorrow to ask her to help put a stop to that.

Otherwise there will be no society left. The Dreyfus case is all very well. But then the grocer's wife down the road only has to say she's a nationalist and ask to be invited by us.' And hearing such a frivolous remark instead of the one that I expected, I felt the astonishment of a reader who looks in the usual place in the *Figaro* for the latest news of the Russo-Japanese war and finds himself faced instead with the list of people who contributed gifts to Mlle de Mortemart's wedding list,[7] the importance of an aristocratic marriage having pushed battles both on land and on sea to the back of the newspaper. Moreover, from her pride in this extravagantly protracted persistence, the Duchesse ultimately acquired feelings of satisfaction which she lost no opportunity to express. 'Babal', she said, 'claims that we are the two most elegant people in Paris because only he and I refuse to be greeted by Mme and Mlle Swann. You see he is convinced that elegance consists in not knowing Mme Swann.' And the Duchesse laughed heartily.

However, after Swann's death, it happened that her insistence on not inviting his daughter had provided Mme de Guermantes with all the satisfactions of pride, independence, 'self-government' and persecution that she was able to enjoy, and that these satisfactions were terminated by the disappearance of the person who gave her the delicious sensation that she was resisting him and that he was unable to get her to annul her decrees. So the Duchesse had passed on to the promulgation of other decrees, which, applied to living persons, were able to make her feel that she was sole mistress of all her actions. She had not given a thought to the Swann girl, but when people mentioned her the Duchesse felt a curiosity, as for a place never visited, which was no longer obscured by her desire to resist Swann's claims for attention. Besides, so many different feelings can come together to form one single feeling that it would be impossible to say whether one might not detect some affection for Swann in this concern. Doubtless – for at every level of society a frivolous social life paralyses sensitivities and incapacitates our power to resuscitate the dead – the Duchesse was one of those people who need someone's presence – that presence which as a true Guermantes she excelled at cultivating – if she were truly to love them, but also, more unusually, if she were to feel a little genuine hatred. So that often her kind feelings for people, interrupted during their lifetime by the irritation that one or other of their acts had occasioned, were revived by their death. She then experienced something approaching a desire for reparation, because she imagined them, however vaguely, with only their good qualities and free from the petty smugness and pretensions that had annoyed her during their lifetime. Despite Mme de Guermantes's frivolity, this sometimes lent a rather noble quality – however mingled with baseness – to her behaviour. For whereas three-quarters of the human race flatter the living and take no notice of the dead, she often put on a performance for those she had mistreated during their lifetime once they were dead.

As for Gilberte, no one who loved her and valued her self-respect could have failed to rejoice in the change in the Duchesse's dispositions towards her, in so far as they hoped that Gilberte, by contemptuously repulsing advances coming after twenty-five years of offence, could be finally avenged. But unfortunately our moral reflexes are not always identical with the promptings of common sense. A person who thinks that some ill-judged insult has spoiled his chances with a person he holds dear, may find on the contrary that it has salvaged them. Gilberte, who was fairly indifferent towards people who were pleasant to her, could not stop thinking with admiration of the insolent Mme de Guermantes and, pondering the reasons for this insolence, even wanted to write to the Duchesse on one occasion, although this would have caused those who felt the least friendship for her to die of shame, to ask her what she had against a girl who had done her no wrong. The Guermantes had taken on in her eyes proportions that their nobility alone could not have given them. She placed them not only above all the nobility but even above all royalty.

A few ladies who had previously been friends of Swann looked after Gilberte very carefully. Her most recent inheritance became known in aristocratic circles, people noted her exquisite manners and her potential as a charming wife. People said that a cousin of Mme de Guermantes, the Princesse de Nièvre, was thinking of Gilberte for her son. Mme de Guermantes loathed Mme de Nièvre. She announced to all and sundry that such a marriage would be a scandal. Mme de Nièvre took fright and protested that she had never even thought of it. One day after luncheon, since it was fine and M. de Guermantes was due to go out with his wife, Mme de Guermantes was adjusting her hat in the mirror, gazing at her own blue eyes and her still blonde hair, while the chambermaid held out various parasols for her mistress to choose from. The window was bathed in sunlight and they had decided to make the most of the fine day by paying a visit to Saint-Cloud. M. de Guermantes, who was ready to leave, having donned his topper and his pearl-grey gloves, said to himself, 'Oriane is still truly astonishing. I find her delicious.' And seeing that his wife seemed in good humour, he said: 'By the way, I had a message for you from Mme de Virelef. She wanted to ask you to come to the opera on Monday. But, as she is taking the Swann girl, she dared not ask and begged me to test the water. I have no opinion, I am simply transmitting the message. Good heavens, I wonder if we might not . . .' he added evasively, for since their attitude towards any person was a collective attitude and arose identically in each of them, he knew within himself that his wife's hostility towards Mlle Swann had abated and that she was curious to meet her. Mme de Guermantes finished adjusting her veil and chose a parasol. 'But as you wish, what should it matter to me? I see no objection to our meeting the girl. You know perfectly well that I have never had anything *against* her. It was simply that I did not want us to appear to be making advances to my friends' irregular connections. That's all.' 'And you were perfectly right,' replied the Duc. 'You are the soul of wisdom, Madam, and what is more, you look ravishing in that hat.' 'How very kind of you,' said Mme de Guermantes, smiling at her husband and moving towards the door. But before entering the carriage, she felt obliged to offer supplementary information: 'There are so many people now who invite her mother, besides which she has the good sense to be ill for three-quarters of the year. They say the little girl is quite charming. Everyone knows that we were great friends of Swann. Everyone will find it perfectly natural.' And they left together for Saint-Cloud.

A month later Swann's young daughter, who was not yet called Forcheville, was at luncheon with the Guermantes. They talked about all sorts of things; at the end of the luncheon, Gilberte said shyly, 'I believe that you knew my father very well.' 'But of course we did,' said Mme de Guermantes, with a melancholy air which proved that she understood the grief of a daughter and with an intentional over-emphasis which made her appear to dissimulate the fact that she was not sure she could recall the father very precisely. 'We knew him very well, I remember him very well indeed.' (And well she might have remembered him, indeed, since he had called on her every day for twenty-five years.) 'I know perfectly well who he was, let me tell you,' she added, as if she were seeking to explain to the daughter who her father had been and to offer the girl new information about him, 'he was a great friend of my mother-in-law and also well known to my brother-in-law Palamède.' 'He used to visit us, too, and even came to luncheon,' added M de Guermantes, displaying both his modesty and his concern for detail. 'I'm sure you remember, Oriane. What a good man your father was! How clear it was that he must spring from a worthy family! In fact I did once catch sight of his father and mother. What fine people they all were!' One felt that if the parents and their son had still been alive the Duc de Guermantes would have felt no hesitation in recommending them for employment as gardeners. But this is how the Faubourg Saint-Germain speaks to the bourgeoisie about anyone from the bourgeoisie, whether to flatter their listeners with the exception made in their favour for as long as the conversation lasts, or whether, preferably, to humiliate them at one and the same time. So it is when an anti-Semite tells a Jew of the faults of Jews in general while smothering him with affable remarks, thus enjoying being hurtful without seeming to be rude.

But since, when she saw you, she knew to perfection how to make you feel wanted and found it difficult to decide to allow you to leave, Mme de Guermantes was also a slave to this need for people's presence. On occasion, in the heat of an animated conversation, Swann might have deluded the Duchesse into feeling that she felt friendship for him, but now he was no longer able. 'He was charming,' said the Duchesse with a sad smile, casting an extremely tender gaze in Gilberte's direction just in case the girl should happen to be a sensitive soul, to show her that she was understood and that if she had been alone with her and if circumstances had permitted, Mme de Guermantes would have loved to reveal to her the full extent of her sensitivity. But M. de Guermantes, whether because he felt that these were precisely the circumstances which failed to warrant such effusion or because he considered that any exaggerated expression of sentiment was a woman's affair and that men had no more to do with this than with any other feminine concern except for menus and wine lists, which he had appropriated since he was better informed in these matters than the Duchesse, judged it wise not to encourage with any personal contribution a conversation that he listened to with visible impatience. Moreover, once her outburst of sensitivity had abated, Mme de Guermantes added a note of social frivolity by telling Gilberte: 'Just fancy, let me tell you that he was a *g-g-great* friend of my brother-in-law Charlus and also very much at home at Voisenon (the Prince de Guermantes's château),' not only as though Swann had happened to come to know M. de Charlus and the Prince quite by chance, as if the Duchesse's brother-in-law and her cousin had been two men whom Swann had encountered on some random occasion, whereas Swann was on familiar terms with everyone in that same social circle, but also as though Mme de Guermantes had wanted Gilberte to understand what sort of a man her father was, to 'place' him for her, through one of those typical reactions whereby, when we want to explain how we have met someone we are not supposed to know or want to make the account more striking, we invoke the patronage of someone else. As for Gilberte, she was all the happier to see the conversation falter since she wanted nothing better than to change tack, having inherited from Swann an exquisite tact and a charming intelligence which the Duc and the Duchesse recognized and appreciated, asking Gilberte to call again soon. Moreover, with that attention to detail typical of people whose lives have no aim, they sometimes descried in the people whom they frequented the most simple qualities, crying out in admiration with the naïve wonder of the town-dweller who discovers a blade of grass in the countryside or, on the contrary, magnifying their tiniest faults, as if under a microscope, with hair-splitting analyses and visceral objections, and often alternately in the same person. In Gilberte's case it was at first her attractions which excited the idle perspicacity of M. and Mme de Guermantes: 'Have you noticed the way she pronounces certain words,' the Duchesse asked her husband when she had left, 'a typical Swann, it sounded like the man himself. – I was about to make the same remark as you, Oriane. – She has wit, she has exactly her father's turn of phrase. – I find even that she is far superior. Just remember how well she told that story about the seaside, she has a brio that Swann did not have. – Oh but he was very witty, after all. – But I don't mean that he wasn't witty, I only said that he did not have such brio,' said M de Guermantes with a plaintive air, for his gout made him over-sensitive and, when there was nobody else to bear witness to his irritation, he displayed it to the Duchesse. But since he was unable to understand the deeper reasons, he preferred to affect a misunderstood air.

The favourable stance adopted by the Duc and the Duchesse meant that people might henceforth have dropped the words 'your poor father' to Gilberte when the occasion arose, had they not become pointless, since this was precisely the period when Forcheville adopted the young lady. She called Forcheville 'father', she charmed dowagers with her politeness and elegant manners, and people admitted that, while Forcheville had behaved admirably towards her, the little girl was very kind-hearted and had shown due gratitude. Doubtless because she sometimes wanted and felt able to show how much she felt at her ease in society, she had sought my approbation and had spoken of her real father in my hearing. But this was an exception, for no one dared pronounce Swann's name in her presence. It so happened that on entering the salon, I had just recognized two drawings by Elstir which had previously been relegated to an upstairs display cabinet where I had only come across them by chance. Elstir was now in fashion. Mme de Guermantes could not console herself for having given so many of his pictures to her cousin, not because they had become fashionable but because now she appreciated them. In fact fashion is composed of the enthusiasm of a group of people of whom the Guermantes are typical. But she would not dream of buying more pictures by him, since in recent times they had been attaining ridiculously high prices. She wanted to have something at least by Elstir in her drawing-room and had had the two drawings brought down, declaring that she 'preferred them to his paintings'. Gilberte recognized his style. 'They look like Elstirs,' she said. 'But they are,' replied the Duchesse, 'it was precisely your . . . some friends of ours who advised us to buy them.

They are admirable. In my opinion they are better than his paintings.'
I had not heard this dialogue when I went to look at the drawings, and
said, 'Oh look, it's the Elstir that . . .' I saw Mme de Guermantes's
frantic signals. 'Oh yes, it's the Elstir that I admired upstairs. It looks
much better here than on the landing. On the subject of Elstir, I
mentioned him in an article in the *Figaro* yesterday. Did you read it?
– You wrote an article in the *Figaro*?' exclaimed M. de Guermantes as
violently as he would have exclaimed, 'But she's my cousin. – Yes,
yesterday. – In the *Figaro*, are you sure? That would be surprising,
for we each have our own copy, and if one of us missed it the other
would have noticed it. Don't you agree, Oriane, there was no article.'
The Duc sent someone to fetch the *Figaro* and only accepted the truth
when faced with the evidence, as if until that moment it was most
likely that I had mistaken the newspaper for which I had written.
'What? I don't understand, do you mean you have written an article
for the *Figaro*?' the Duchesse asked me, making an effort to speak of
something of no interest to her. 'Well, Basin, look here, you must read
it later on.' 'Oh no, the Duc is fine as he is with his great beard all
over the newspaper,' said Gilberte, and I shall read it myself as soon
as I get home. – Yes, he's taken to wearing a beard now that everyone
is clean shaven, said the Duchesse, he never does what other people
do. When we married he shaved off not just his beard but his moustache. The country folk who saw him thought that he was not French.
At that time he was called the Prince des Laumes. – Is there still a
Prince des Laumes?' asked Gilberte, who was interested in anything
that concerned the people who had for so long refused to give her the
time of day. 'Oh no,' replied the Duchesse, with a melancholy, amorous
air. 'Such a lovely title! One of the finest titles in France!' said Gilberte,
in one of those lapses into banality which inevitably escape the mouths
of certain intelligent young women, as surely as the sun rises. 'But it's
true, and I regret it as much as you. Basin would like his sister's son
to take it on, but it's not the same thing; actually it would be possible,
because it doesn't have to be the elder son, it can pass from the elder
to the younger. As I was saying, Basin was absolutely clean shaven;
one day on a pilgrimage, do you remember, my dear,' she said to her
husband, 'that pilgrimage to Paray-le-Monial? My brother-in-law

Charlus, who rather likes to talk to the country folk, said to someone or other: "Where are you from, my friend?", and as he is very generous, he gave them a tip or offered to stand them a drink. For there's nobody more grand but simple with it than Mémé. You could find him snubbing a duchess if she's not enough of a duchess for him, and turn all his attention to a master of hounds. So I said to Basin: "Look, Basin, why don't you talk to them a bit too." My husband, who rather lacks imagination . . . – Thank you, Oriane,' said the Duc without interrupting his reading of my article, in which he was immersed – 'got hold of a local and repeated verbatim the words of his brother: "And you, where are you from? – I'm from les Laumes. – You are from les Laumes? Well then, I am your Prince." Then the countryman looked at Basin's whiskerless features and replied: "Not true, you are an English."' Thus in the Duchesse's anecdotes one saw these great titles, like that of the Prince des Laumes, emerge in their true place, in their former state and their local colour, as in certain books of hours one recognizes, amidst the medieval crowd, the steeple of Bourges. Some visiting cards left by a footman were brought in to her. 'I don't know what has possessed her, I do not know the woman. This is your doing, Basin. And yet you have scarcely made a success of this kind of relationship, my poor dear,' and then turning to Gilberte, she said: 'I couldn't begin to explain who she is, you certainly don't know her, she's called Lady Rufus Israel.' Gilberte blushed furiously: 'I don't know her,' she said (which was all the more false since Lady Israel, two years before Swann's death, had made her peace with him and since then called Gilberte by her first name), 'but I do know who she is from what people say, I know who you mean.' The fact is that Gilberte had become quite snobbish. Thus it happened one day, when a young lady who, whether from malice or from tactlessness, had asked her the name of her true rather than of her adoptive father, that Gilberte, in her confusion and in an attempt to disguise what she was forced to say, had pronounced the name as 'Svann' instead of 'Souann', a change which some time later she realized was pejorative, since it turned an originally English name into a German name. And she had even added, abasing herself morally in order to enhance her social status: 'I have heard so many different things about my birth that I prefer to know nothing.'

However ashamed of herself Gilberte must have been at certain moments when she thought of her parents (for even Mme Swann had seemed a good mother to her and had been one) at having adopted such an attitude to life, we must unfortunately suppose that its elements had doubtless been borrowed from her parents, for we do not create ourselves single-handed. But to the quantity of egoism given in the mother, a different portion of egoism, inherent in the father's family, comes to accrue, which does not always imply an addition or even a simple multiplication, but which creates a new breed of egoism, infinitely more powerful and fearsome. And ever since the beginning of the world, since families where such a flaw exists in one form have become allied with families where the same flaw exists in another form, creating a particularly complete and detestable form in the child, the accumulated egoisms (to talk here only of egoism) would take on such force that the whole of humanity would be destroyed, if from the same ill there did not arise, capable of reducing it to its just proportions, natural restrictions analogous to those which prevent an infinite pro-liferation of protozoa from annihilating our planet or the monosexual fertilization of plants from leading to the asphyxiation of the rest of the vegetable kingdom, and so on. From time to time a virtue emerges to compose with this egoism a new and disinterested force. The com-binations by means of which moral chemistry thus fixes and renders inoffensive down the generations elements which were becoming too dangerous are infinite and would be capable of giving an exciting variety to our family histories. What is more, the different kinds of egoism of the sort which Gilberte must have accumulated coexist with the most charming virtues, also inherited from the parents, which come for a moment to play their own individual, touching and entirely sincere part during the intervals. Doubtless Gilberte did not always go so far as she did on this occasion when she insinuated that she was perhaps the natural daughter of some great personage; but she did most often dissimulate her origins. Perhaps it was simply too unpleasant to confess them, and she preferred them to be related by others. Perhaps she really believed that she was hiding them, with that faltering belief which is still not doubt, as it reserves a possibility for what one desires and of which Musset gives an example when he speaks of 'hoping in God'.[8]

'I do not know her personally,' continued Gilberte. Had she, however, in calling herself Mlle de Forcheville hoped that no one would know that she was Swann's daughter? Perhaps hoping, where certain people were concerned, that this might in due course come to include almost everyone? She could not have harboured many illusions as to their present number and she must have known that many people would be whispering, 'She's Swann's daughter.' But she knew it only with the kind of knowledge that tells us of people yielding to despair and letting themselves die of starvation while we go off to a ball, that is with a vague and distant knowledge, for which we have no desire to substitute a more precise knowledge based on first-hand experience. As distance makes things appear smaller, less precise and less dangerous, Gilberte thought it pointless that the discovery that she had been born a Swann should be made in her presence. Gilberte belonged, or at least had belonged during those years, to the most frequently encountered species of human ostrich, those who bury their heads in the hope, not of not being seen, which they believe to be implausible, but of not seeing themselves being seen, which seems important enough to them and allows them to leave the rest to chance. Gilberte preferred not to be present when people discovered that she had been born a Swann. And as we are present to people whom we can picture, and since we can picture people reading their newspapers, Gilberte preferred the newspapers to call her Mlle de Forcheville. It is true that for those writings over which she did have some control, that is, her letters, she negotiated the transition for a while by signing G. S. Forcheville. The veritable hypocrisy of this signature was revealed far less by the suppression of the other letters of Swann's name than by those of Gilberte's name. Indeed, by reducing her innocent first name to a simple G., Mlle de Forcheville seemed to insinuate to her friends that the same amputation applied to the name of Swann was itself due only to the same desire for brevity. She even bestowed a particular importance on the S, giving it a kind of long tail that cut across the G, but one felt this to be as provisional and doomed to disappear as the one which, despite its length in the monkey, is absent in man.

Despite this, her snobbery retained an element of Swann's intellectual curiosity. I remember that on the same afternoon she asked Mme de Guermantes if she might not have known M. du Lau, and when the Duchesse replied that he was unwell and unable to go out, Gilberte asked what he was like, for, she added, blushing slightly, she had heard so much about him. (The Marquis du Lau had in fact been one of Swann's closest friends before the latter's marriage and perhaps even Gilberte herself might have caught a glimpse of him, but at a time when she was not interested in those social circles.) 'Might M. de Bréauté or the Prince d'Agrigente give me an idea?' she asked. 'Oh not at all!' cried Mme de Guermantes, who had a fine sense of these provincial distinctions and was able to offer a sober portrait, albeit coloured with the hoarse, gilded timbre of her voice and bathed in the warm light of her violet eyes. 'No, not at all. Du Lau was a charming nobleman from the Périgord, with all the refinements but casual manners of the provinces. At Guermantes, when the King of England, who was a good friend of du Lau, was there, they had tea after the hunt; this was the time of day when du Lau used to take off his boots. Well, the presence of King Edward[9] and all the grand dukes failed to impress him at all, he came back downstairs into the great salon of the Guermantes, wearing his thick woollen slippers. He felt that he was the Marquis du Lau d'Allemans who had no reason to feel inhibited by the King of England. It was he and the charming Quasimodo de Breteuil that I liked most of all. Besides, they were great friends of . . .' (she was about to say 'your father' and stopped short). 'No, that has no connection with Gri-Gri or Bréauté. He is an authentic Périgord nobleman. By the way, Mémé quotes a page from Saint-Simon about a Marquis d'Allemans, that's absolutely him.' I quoted the first words of the portrait: 'M. d'Allemans, who was one of the most distinguished members of the Périgord nobility, through his noble descent and through his own merit, was treated by everyone who lived there as judge and jury to whom everyone tended to appeal because of his honesty, his competence and his politeness, as well as being the cock of the walk in his province. – Yes, that sounds just like him,' said Mme de Guermantes, 'especially as he was always as red as a coxcomb. – Yes, I remember having heard that description,' said Gilberte, without adding that she had heard it from her father, who was in fact a great admirer of Saint-Simon.

She also liked talking about the Prince d'Agrigente and M de Bréauté for another reason. The Prince d'Agrigente was of the house of Aragon by descent but their estate is held in the Poitou. As for his château, at least the one where he resided, it was not one of his family's châteaux but came from the family of his mother's former husband and was situated at roughly equal distance from Martinville and Guermantes. So Gilberte spoke of him and M. de Bréauté as country neighbours who reminded her of her former province. Objectively speaking, there was an element of deceit in these words, since it was only in Paris that she had come to know M. de Bréauté, through the Comtesse Molé, who was, it should be said, an old friend of her father. As for the pleasure of speaking of the countryside near Tansonville, it may have been sincere. Snobbery for some people is analogous to those sweet-tasting cordials which we lace with more active ingredients. Gilberte took an interest in some elegant lady because she owned some superb books and some Nattiers,[10] which my former friend would certainly not have gone to see at the Bibliothèque Nationale or the Louvre, and I imagine that the attractions of Tansonville for Gilberte would have exerted their influence less through Mme Sazerat or Mme Goupil, despite their even greater proximity, than through M. d'Agrigente. 'Oh poor Babal and Gri-Gri,' said Mme de Guermantes, 'they are far more ill than du Lau, I'm afraid they won't last long, either of them.'

When M. de Guermantes had finished reading my article he addressed me some rather muted compliments. He regretted the somewhat hackneyed form of my style, which was 'as inflated and metaphorical as Chateaubriand's outmoded prose'; on the other hand he congratulated me wholeheartedly for having found an 'occupation': 'I like people to do something with their fingers and thumbs. I don't like layabouts who always take themselves too seriously or get overexcited. Foolish breed!' Gilberte, who had lost no time in adopting society manners, declared how proud she was to be able to say that she was the friend of an author. 'Just imagine how I shall tell everyone that I have the pleasure and the *honour* of knowing you.' 'Wouldn't you like to accompany us tomorrow to the Opéra Comique?' the Duchesse asked me, and I thought that this must be an invitation to the very bar where I had seen her for the first time and which had then seemed as inaccessible to me as the underwater realm of the Nereids.[11] But I replied sadly: 'No, I cannot go to the theatre, I have lost a friend. She was very dear to me.' The tears nearly came to my eyes as I said it and yet for the first time I felt something akin to pleasure in talking about it. It was from that moment that I started to write to everyone to tell them of my great sorrow and to cease to feel it.

When Gilberte had left, Mme de Guermantes said to me: 'You didn't understand my signals, it was to stop you talking about Swann.' And as I excused myself, she said to her husband: 'But I understand very well; I nearly mentioned him myself, I only just had time to cover up, it was awful, luckily I stopped in time. You know how embarrassing it is,' in order to diminish my fault a little by pretending to believe that I had complied with a propensity which was common to all and which was difficult to resist. 'What am I supposed to do about it?' replied the Duc. 'All you have to do is have the drawings taken back upstairs again, since they make you think of Swann. If you don't think about Swann, you won't talk about him.'

The following day I received two letters of congratulation which astonished me considerably, one from Mme Goupil, a lady from Combray whom I had not seen for many years and to whom even in Combray I had hardly spoken more than two or three times. She had had a copy of the *Figaro* sent by a lending library. Thus when something of any note happens to us in life, we hear the news from people situated so far from our present acquaintances and so far back in our memory that they seem to be situated at a great distance, especially in terms of depth. A forgotten school-friend, who might have remembered himself to you on a dozen occasions, shows up but this does turn out to have its compensations. Thus it was that Bloch, whose opinion on my article I would have so liked to know, did not write to me. It is true that he had read the article and was to admit this to me later but only in a delayed reaction. The fact is that a few years later he himself wrote an article for the *Figaro* and wanted to inform me of the event immediately. As he too had benefited from what seemed to him to be a privilege, his need to pretend to be ignorant of my article having suddenly ceased, as if a compress had been released, he mentioned it to me, very differently from the way in which he wanted me to talk about his own: 'I heard that you too had an article published,' he said. 'But I didn't think I should mention it to you, for fear of displeasing you, for one should not speak to one's friends of the humiliating things that happen to them. And obviously it is humiliating to write for the newspaper of the sword and the cross, of "five o'clock" tea parties, and other kinds of holy water.' His character had not changed, but his language had become less precious, as happens to certain writers who drop their mannerist style when they stop writing symbolist poems and start producing serialized novels.

In order to console myself for Bloch's silence, I reread Mme Goupil's letter; but it lacked warmth, for if the aristocracy has certain formulae which erect fences, between the opening 'Dear Sir' and the closing 'Yours faithfully' exclamations of joy and admiration can spring up like flowers and let their sweet-scented sprays spill over the boundary fence. But bourgeois conventions enclose even the heart of the letter itself within a network of 'your legitimate success' or at best 'your fine success'. Sisters-in-law, mindful of their upbringing and restrained by the stays of decency, believe that they have overstepped the bounds of pathos or enthusiasm, if they have written 'with kind regards'. 'Mother joins me in sending her best wishes' is a superlative which is rarely lavished. I received another letter apart from Mme Goupil's, but I did not recognize the name, Sautton. The writing was simple, the tone charming. I was very disappointed not be be able to discover who had written it.

Two days later I was delighted to think that Bergotte must have greatly admired my article, which he could not have read without jealousy. Yet after a while my joy subsided. In fact Bergotte had not written me a word. I had simply wondered whether he would have liked the article, fearing that he had not. The question that I had asked myself was answered by Mme de Forcheville, who had replied that he admired it greatly, finding it worthy of a great writer. But she told me this while I was asleep: it was a dream. Almost all our dreams answer the questions that we have asked ourselves with complex affirmations and scenarios involving several characters, but they fade with the dawn.

As for Mlle de Forcheville, I could not help feeling sorrowful when I thought of her. For all that she was Swann's daughter, whom he would have so loved to see at the Guermantes', they had refused to invite her, despite their great friendship for him, but then they had spontaneously sought her company after the passing of time, which, depending on what others have told you about them, renews the personality of those people whom we have not seen for a long time or invests them with another, since we too have shed our skins and acquired new tastes. But when on occasion Swann, holding his daughter in his arms and embracing her, said, 'It's nice, my love, to have a daughter like you; one day when I'm no longer here, if people still speak of your poor Papa, it will be to you alone and only because of you,' Swann, thus placing his timid and anxious hopes of survival after his death in his daughter, was as mistaken as some ageing banker who, having made his will in favour of a very respectful little dancer who is kept by him, thinks that, although he is no more than an old friend to her, she will remain faithful to his memory. She was very respectful but under the table she played footsy with those of the old banker's male friends whom she fancied, albeit with total discretion, preserving excellent appearances. She will wear mourning for the distinguished gentleman, will be greatly relieved, will benefit not only from the ready cash but from the properties and motor-cars that he has left her, but will everywhere erase the hallmarks of their previous owner, which cause her mild embarrassment, and she will never add to her enjoyment of the gift any regret for its donor. The illusions of paternal love are perhaps no less than those of the other kind; many daughters consider their father no more than the old man who will leave them his fortune. Gilberte's presence in a drawing-room, instead of being an occasion for people still to speak sometimes of her father, was an obstacle preventing them from seizing those increasingly rare occasions when they might still have been able to do so. Even on the subject of the words he had spoken and the gifts he had offered, people acquired the habit of no longer mentioning his name, and she who should have renewed, if not perpetuated, his memory turned out to be precisely the one who hastened and consummated the process of dying and forgetting.

And it was not only where Swann was concerned that Gilberte gradually consummated the process of forgetting: she had hastened this process within me in relation to Albertine. Under the impact of the desire, and consequently the desire for happiness, which Gilberte had aroused within me during those few hours when I had believed her to be somebody else, a certain number of painful sufferings and preoccupations, which until so recently had continued to obsess my thoughts, fell away from me, dragging away with them a whole block of memories, probably long since crumbling and precarious, connected with Albertine. For if many of the memories which were linked to her had at first helped to maintain within me a regret for her death, the regret itself had, in its turn, fixed the memories. So that the change in my emotional state, doubtless prepared obscurely day by day through the continual erosion caused by forgetting, but suddenly realized as a whole, gave me that impression of the void which I remember having experienced that day for the first time, that suppression within me of a whole section of the association of my ideas, as in a man whose worn-out cerebral artery ruptures and who finds a whole part of his memory erased or paralysed. I no longer loved Albertine. At most there were occasional days which brought the kind of weather that, modifying and stimulating our sensitivity, restores our contact with reality, making me feel bitterly sad when I thought of her. I suffered from a love that no longer existed. Thus when the weather changes do amputees feel pain in the leg they have lost.

The disappearance of my suffering and of everything that accompanied it left me diminished, as often does the cure of an illness which took up a great place in our lives. No doubt it is because memories do not remain true for ever, and because life is made up of the endless renewal of cells, that love is not eternal. But this renewal of memories is none the less delayed by our attention, which stops and fixes for a moment what is bound to change. And since sorrow, like desire for a woman, is magnified when we think of it, if we had more things to keep us busy, this would render forgetting, as it does chastity, all the easier.

While it remains the case that it is time which progressively causes forgetting, it is forgetting in its turn which, through a different reaction (although for me it was a distraction – the desire for Mlle d'Éporcheville – which suddenly rendered forgetting effective and palpable), contributes to profoundly disturbing our notion of time. There are optical illusions in time as well as space. The persistence within me of traces of my old urge to work, to make up for lost time, to change my way of life, or rather to start to live, gave me the illusion that I was still as young as ever; yet the memory of all the events which had succeeded one another during my life – and also those which had succeeded in my heart, for, when we have changed a great deal, we are led to suppose that we have lived for longer – during those last months of Albertine's existence, had made them seem to last much longer than a year, and this forgetting of so many things, separating me by empty spaces from quite recent events, which they made seem long gone because I had had what we call the 'time' to forget them, with its fragmented and irregular interpolation in the midst of my memory – like a thick ocean mist which blots out all the objects that aid navigation – was what had upset and dislocated my sense of temporal distances, shrinking them here, stretching them there, and making me believe that I was sometimes much further from, sometimes much nearer to things than I really was. And since in the new, as yet undiscovered, spaces which lay before me, there would no more be traces of my love for Albertine than there had been in my recent experience of traversing periods of loss of love for my grandmother, offering a succession of periods during which, after a certain interval, nothing that had sustained the preceding period remained in the following one, my life appeared to me to be something as much lacking the support of an individual, identical and permanent self, something as useless in the future as protracted in the past, something as easy for death to terminate here or there without any kind of conclusion, as those school courses in French History which stop arbitrarily, depending on the whim of the syllabus or the teacher, at the 1830 or the 1848 Revolution or the end of the Second Empire.[12]

Perhaps then the fatigue and sadness that I felt came less from having loved in vain than from the fact that I was already forgetting, that I was starting to take pleasure in the company of new, living people, simple society acquaintances, mere friends of the Guermantes, almost entirely uninteresting in their own right. I consoled myself perhaps more easily for the fact that the girl I had loved was after a certain lapse of time no more than a faded memory than for the fact that I found myself once more pervaded by that vain activity which makes us waste time in brightening our lives with a lively but parasitical human flora, which will also return to the void when it dies, which is already alien to everything that we have experienced, but towards which in our melancholia we none the less direct all our reserves of verbiage and flattery, in a senile attempt at seduction. The new person who would be quite able to live without Albertine had appeared within me, since I had managed to mention her to Mme de Guermantes as if I were afflicted, but without actually suffering much. The possible arrival of these new selves, which should bear a name different from that of their predecessor because of their indifference to what I loved, had always terrified me: on a former occasion in the case of Gilberte, when her father told me that if I went to live in the South Seas I would never want to return, and on a more recent occasion when I had read with such a heavy heart the memoirs of a mediocre writer who, separated by life from a woman whom he had adored when he was young, met her again as an old man, but felt neither pleasure nor any desire to see her again. Yet, on the other hand, this much-feared but beneficial person brought me, at the same time as forgetfulness, an almost complete suppression of suffering and the prospect of recovery, for he was none other than one of those alternative selves which fate holds in reserve for us, and which in spite of ourselves – paying no more attention to our prayers than a clear-sighted and all the more authoritarian doctor – it substitutes for our sorely wounded self, in a carefully timed operation. Moreover, it effects this renewal as the need arises, as happens with the wear and repair of bodily cells, but we take no notice unless our old self was nursing some great wound, some painful foreign body, which we are astonished no longer to find, in our marvelling at having become someone else, someone else for whom his predecessor's suffering is no more than the suffering of a third party, a suffering which we can discuss compassionately because we do not feel it. And we are even quite unmoved at having passed through so much suffering, for we remember only vaguely having suffered. In the same way it may happen that we are terrified by a nightmare. But when we awake we are another person, who little cares that the person he replaces had to flee from murderers in his sleep.

Doubtless this self still kept in touch with the old one, as someone unmoved by the bereavement of a friend nevertheless speaks to his guests with suitable sadness and returns from time to time to the room where his friend, the widower, who has asked him to greet the mourners on his behalf, continues to sob out loud. I was still sobbing when I became once more, if only for a moment, the person who used to be Albertine's friend. But I was tending to move into an entirely new character. It is not because others have died that our affection for them weakens, it is because we ourselves are dying. Albertine had no reason to reproach her friend. He who usurped that name had merely inherited it. We can be faithful only to what we remember, we can remember only what we have known. My new self, while growing in the shadow of the old one, had often heard him speak; through him, through the stories he told of Albertine; he thought he knew her, he sympathized with her, he liked her: but his affection was only second-hand.

Another person in whom the process of forgetting where Albertine was concerned probably evolved more rapidly at this time, and whose reaction allowed me to realize a little later how far this process had advanced within me (I now remember this as a second stage, before my final forgetting), was Andrée. Indeed I can hardly deny that forgetting Albertine was, if not the single or even the principal cause, at least the sufficient and necessary cause, of a conversation which Andrée held with me about six months after the one I have already recorded and where her words were so different from what she had told me that first time. I remember that it took place in my room because this was the period when I enjoyed a semi-carnal relationship with her, on account of the collective aspect that my love for the girls of the little gang had at first assumed, and had now resumed, long undifferentiated amongst them, and only briefly associated exclusively with the person of Albertine during the last months that had preceded and followed her death.

We were in my room for another reason again which allows me to place this conversation quite precisely. This is because I was banned from the rest of the apartment since it was Mama's at-home day. It was a day when Mama had gone to take luncheon with Mme Sazerat. As it was my mother's open day, she had hesitated before accepting Mme Sazerat's invitation. But since, as they do in Combray, Mme Sazerat always managed to invite you in company with boring people, Mama was sure not to enjoy herself and guessed that she would not miss out on any pleasures by leaving early. And in fact she had returned on time and with no regrets, since Mme Sazerat had invited nobody who was not deadly dull even before being frozen numb by her special society voice, which Mama called her Wednesday voice. Otherwise my mother liked her well enough and felt sorry for her lack of wealth – as a result of her father's ruinous cavortings with the Duchesse de \*\*\* – a lack of wealth which compelled her to live almost the whole year round in Combray, apart from a few weeks with a female relative in Paris and a long 'leisure excursion' once every ten years. I remember that my mother, after I had entreated her repeatedly for months, and because the Princess kept on requesting her to call, had gone the day before to call on the Princess of Parma, who never made visits herself and at whose house one usually simply left one's card but who had insisted that my mother should pay her a visit, since protocol forbade her to visit us. My mother returned very discontented: 'You made me put my foot in it,' she said, 'the Princess of Parma hardly said good morning to me, she turned away to continue talking to the ladies with whom she had been conversing, taking no notice of me, and ten minutes later, since she hadn't spoken a word to me, I left, and she didn't even shake my hand. I was very embarrassed; and yet when I left her house I met the Duchesse de Guermantes, who was very pleasant and who talked of you a lot. What a strange idea you had in telling her about Albertine! She told me that you said that her death had caused you such sorrow.' (I had indeed said so to the Duchesse, but had not given it much emphasis and had forgotten it myself. Yet the most absent-minded people often pay singular attention to words that we let slip, which seem quite natural to us but which excite their curiosity.) 'I shall never return to see the Princess of Parma. You made me put my foot in it.'

Now the following day, my mother's at-home day, Andrée came to see me. She did not have much time, for she had to go and fetch Gisèle, with whom she wanted to go out to dinner. 'I know her faults, but she's still my best friend and the person for whom I feel the most affection,' she said. And she even seemed rather terrified that I might ask to come out to dinner with them. She had a thirst for people, so that a third party who knew her too well, as I did, by preventing her from letting herself go, would prevent her from fully enjoying their company.

It is true that when she arrived I had not appeared; she waited for me to come, and I was on my way through my little sitting-room to go to meet her when I realized, from hearing a voice, that I had another visitor. I was in a hurry to see Andrée, who was waiting in my room, and since I did not know who the other person was, and he obviously did not know Andrée, since he had been asked to wait in a different room, I listened for a moment at the sitting-room door; for my visitor was speaking, he was not alone; he was talking to a woman: '*Oh! ma chérie, c'est dans mon cœur!*',[13] he crooned, quoting the lines written by Armand Sylvestre. 'Yes, you will always be my darling, whatever you have done to me':

> 'Les morts dorment en paix dans le sein de la terre.
> Ainsi doivent dormir nos sentiments éteints.
> Ces reliques du cœur ont aussi leur poussière;
> Sur leurs restes sacrés ne portons pas les mains.[14]

'It's rather old-fashioned, but isn't it lovely! And also what I could have said to you on the very first day:

> 'Tu les feras pleurer, enfant belle et chérie . . .

'Goodness, don't you know that?

> '. . . Tous ces bambins, hommes futurs,
> Qui suspendent déjà leur jeune rêverie
>    Aux cils câlins de tes yeux purs.[15]

'Oh, I almost thought for a moment that I could say:

> 'Le premier soir qu'il vint ici
> De fierté je n'eus plus souci.
> Je lui disais: "Tu m'aimeras
> Aussi longtemps que tu pourras."
> Je ne dormais bien qu'en ses bras.'[16]

Even if it meant delaying my urgent visit to Andrée for a moment, I was curious to know to which woman this deluge of poems was addressed. I opened the door. They were being recited by M. de Charlus to a soldier whom I soon recognized as Morel and who was about to leave for his thirteen days' training in the reserves. He was no longer on intimate terms with M. de Charlus but saw him from time to time to ask him a favour. M. de Charlus, who usually expressed his love in more virile terms, also had his sentimental moods. Moreover in his youth, in order to understand and feel poetic language, he had been obliged to imagine it addressed not to a beautiful and wayward lady but to a young man. I left them as swiftly as I could, although I felt that to call on friends with Morel gave M. de Charlus great satisfaction, giving him the momentary illusion of being married again. And what is more he combined within himself the snobbery of royalty with that of a domestic servant.

The memory of Albertine had become so fragmented within me that it no longer caused me sadness and was no more than a transition towards new desires, like a chord that announces a change of key. And even while discounting any idea of indulging fleeting sexual fancies, since I still remained faithful to the memory of Albertine, I was happier to have Andrée by my side than I would have been to have Albertine miraculously restored. For Andrée would be able to tell me more about Albertine than Albertine herself had ever told me. Now my problems concerning Albertine were still present in my mind, although my affections for her, whether physical or emotional, had already vanished. But my desire to know her life, which had diminished less, was now comparatively greater than my need for her presence. Besides, the idea that a woman might have had a relationship with her only provoked in me the desire to have this woman too. I told Andrée this while I caressed her. Then without making the slightest effort to reconcile her words with those which she had uttered a few months previously, Andrée told me with a half-smile: 'Oh, yes, but you are a man. So we can't do quite the same things together that I used to do with Albertine.' And whether she thought she would increase my desire (hoping to tempt her into confidential revelations, I had told her previously that I would like to have relations with a woman who had had them with Albertine) or my sorrow, or perhaps destroy a feeling of superiority over her that she might think I felt from having been the only person to have had a relationship with Albertine, she added: 'Oh we both had some good times together, she was so tender, so passionate. Besides, I wasn't the only one that she liked to take her pleasure with. She had met a handsome lad at Mme Verdurin's called Morel. They understood each other immediately. He took it upon himself – with her permission to take his own pleasure too, for he liked inexperienced young things and, as soon as he had set them off down the slippery slope, would cast them loose – he took it upon himself to lure young laundry-maids and young fisher-girls from farther along the coast, who could fall in love with a boy but would not have responded to the advances of a girl. As soon as the girl was well and truly under his thumb, he took her to a secluded spot and gave her over to Albertine. Fearing that they might lose Morel, who of course joined in the act, the girls always did what they were told but they lost him all the same, for, from fear of the consequences and also because once or twice was enough for him, he would disappear leaving a false address. He was once bold enough to take one of these girls along with Albertine to a house of ill-fame in Couliville, where four or five women took her together or in succession. But afterwards Albertine felt terrible remorse. I think that with you she had overcome her passions and kept postponing the day when she would yield again. And then her friendship with you was so great that her conscience was pricked. But it was inevitable that if ever she left you she would start again. She hoped that you would save her, that you would marry her. Deep down, she felt that it was a kind of criminal folly, and I often wondered if it wasn't after some such affair, causing some family suicide, that she killed herself. I have to admit that right at the beginning of her stay with you, she had not entirely renounced her games with me. There were days when she seemed to need them, so much so that once, when it would have been so easy elsewhere, she could not bring herself to say good-bye to me before she had taken me to lie down beside her, in your home. Our luck was running out, we nearly got caught. She made the most of the fact that Françoise had gone out on an errand and that you had not yet come home. Then she put out all the lights so that after you had turned the key in the lock you would waste some time searching for the switch, but she had not locked the door to her bedroom. We heard you coming up the stairs, I only just had time to adjust my dress and go downstairs. It was a waste of time, because by an incredible coincidence you had forgotten your key and had to ring. But we had none the less lost our heads so much that, without having time to confer, we both suddenly thought of the same way to hide our embarrassment, by pretending to detest the scent of syringa whereas on the contrary we both adored it. You had brought back with you a long branch of that shrub, which allowed me to turn my head away and hide my confusion. That did not prevent me from making the absurdly clumsy suggestion that Françoise had probably returned and could perhaps open the door for you, although only a second earlier I had lied to you, saying that we had just returned from an excursion and that on our arrival Françoise had not yet left (which was true). But our misfortune – thinking that you had your key – was to have put out the lights, for we were afraid that on your way up you would see them come back on; or at least we hesitated too long. And for three nights Albertine did not sleep a wink because she was constantly afraid that you would be suspicious and would ask Françoise why she had not lit the lamps before she left. For Albertine was very afraid of you, and sometimes was sure that you were deceitful and wicked and basically hated her. After three days she gathered, given your calmness, that you hadn't even thought of asking Françoise at all and she managed to sleep quietly once more, but she never took up her relationship with me again, whether from fear or remorse, for she claimed that she was very much in love with you, or perhaps she was in love with someone else. At all events, after that it was impossible to mention syringa in her presence without her turning bright red and hiding her face in her hands to try to cover her blushes.'

Like certain moments of good fortune, there are moments of misfortune which come too late, they fail to take on within us the significance that they would have assumed earlier. Andrée's terrible revelation was that kind of misfortune for me. Doubtless, even when a piece of bad news should make us sad, it may happen that some distraction or the intricate interplay of conversation makes it pass by unheeded, so that, having a thousand things to try to respond to, transformed into another person by the desire to please the present company and protected for a few moments, as we enter this new cycle, from the emotions and the suffering which we discarded on entry and which we will regain when the short period of enchantment is over, we have no time to take it in. Yet if these emotions and suffering are too predominant, we enter only half-heartedly into the ambit of a new and ephemeral world in which, too tied to our suffering, we are unable to become another; then the words strike home to our heart, which we have been unable to disengage. But for some time now, words relating to Albertine, like a poison which has evaporated, no longer retained their toxic powers. The distance was already too great; as a man out walking during the afternoon who sees a faint crescent in the sky and thinks 'Is that all there is to the great globe of the moon?', I thought: 'Goodness! That truth which I have sought and feared so much, is it only a few words spoken during a conversation and which one cannot fully take in because one is not alone!' Then again, the truth caught me totally unprepared, for Andrée had really exhausted me. Truly I would have preferred to have had more strength to devote to such a revelation; it remained external, for I had not yet found a place for it in my heart. We expect the truth to be revealed to us through new signs, not through a mere sentence, especially one so similar to those phrases that we have so often rehearsed in our minds. The habit of thinking sometimes prevents us from experiencing reality, inoculates us against it and makes it seem no more than yet another thought. There is no idea that does not carry within it its own possible refutation, no word that does not negate the word that negates it.

At all events, this was the sort of useless truth about the life of a dead mistress, if indeed it was true, which suddenly surfaces from the depths just when we no longer have any use for it. Then (doubtless thinking of another woman whom we love now and with whom the same process might occur, for we are no longer interested in the person we have forgotten) we are upset. We think, 'If only she were still alive,' we think, 'If only the woman who is alive understood all this and could realize that when she dies I shall discover everything she is hiding from me!' But it is a vicious circle. If I had been able to bring Albertine back to life, by the same token I would not have been able to make Andrée reveal anything. It is somewhat akin to the eternal 'You'll see, when I no longer love you', which is so true and yet so absurd, since we might find out much more if we were no longer in love, but then we would no longer be interested in learning it. In fact, the case is exactly the same. For the woman whom one sees when one no longer loves her, if she tells you everything, it is in fact because she is no longer the same person or because you are no longer the same self: the person who was in love no longer exists. There too death has intervened, has made everything easy and pointless. Such were my reflections, as I adopted the hypothesis that Andrée was telling the truth – which was possible – and inclined to be sincere with me precisely because she now had a relationship with me, showing the same Saint-André-des-Champs qualities as Albertine originally had done with me. She was helped in this matter by the fact that she no longer feared Albertine, for our grasp of people's reality does not long survive their death and after a few years they are like those gods of discredited religions that one may happily offend because one no longer believes in their existence. But the fact that Andrée no longer believed in the existence of Albertine might result in her feeling fewer moral scruples, not merely over betraying a truth which she had promised not to reveal, but even over devising a lie which retrospectively slandered her alleged accomplice. Was it this lack of fear which enabled her to reveal at last what I took to be the truth or, alternatively, to fabricate a lie, if, for whatever reason, she found me too full of happiness and pride and wanted to deflate them? Perhaps she was annoyed with me (with an annoyance that had been held in abeyance

as long as she had seen me miserable and disconsolate) because I had
had a relationship with Albertine and because perhaps she envied me
– thinking that for this reason I felt myself more favoured than she –
an advantage that she had perhaps neither obtained nor even sought.
Thus it was that I had often heard her tell people that they looked
very ill, when it was their healthy complexion and above all their
awareness of their healthy complexion that exasperated her, so that,
hoping to annoy them, she would tell them that she herself was very
well and continued to declare this even when she was quite ill, until
the day when the approach of death finally loosened her interest in
whether the happy were well or whether they knew that she was dying.
But, at the time, this day was still a long way off. Perhaps I had
irritated her for some reason unknown to me, as once she had been
furious with the young man who was so well-informed about sport
but so ignorant about everything else, the man whom we had met at
Balbec and who since then had been living with Rachel, and about
whom Andrée still spread libellous rumours, hoping to be sued for
libel in order to be able to publish dishonourable facts about his father,
the falsehood of which he would have been unable to prove. Now
perhaps this fury against me, which had abated as soon as she saw how
sad I was, was only a relapse. Indeed, even those people whom, her
eyes sparkling with rage, she had threatened with disgrace, death and
imprisonment, using false witness if need be, as soon as she thought
they were unhappy and humiliated, she wished them no ill and was
ready to shower them with favours. For she was not basically wicked
and if, below the surface, her slightly deeper, rather surprising nature
did not confirm the kindness that her first delicate attentions had led
people to suppose but rather envy and pride, yet, at an even deeper
level, her third-degree, that is, her true nature, even if never quite
fully realized, tended towards goodness and love of her neighbour.
Only, like all people who live in a state which they wish were better,
but know no more of this than their desire for it and do not understand
that the first condition is to break with their present state – like
neurasthenics or morphine addicts who would like to be cured but
only as long as no one deprives them of their tics or their morphine,
like certain rather worldly religious souls or artistic minds, aspiring to

solitude yet prepared to imagine it only in so far as it does not imply absolutely renouncing their former life – Andrée was ready to love all God's creatures but only as long as she had first managed to see them failing to triumph and, in order to do so, had humiliated them in advance. She did not understand that one should love even the proud and conquer their pride through love rather than more overweening pride. But the fact is that she was like those invalids who want to be cured by the same much-loved means as sustain their illness and which they would immediately cease to love if they abandoned these means. But one may learn to swim and still prefer to keep one's feet dry.

As regards the athletic young man, who was a nephew of the Verdurins and whom I had met during my two stays in Balbec, I have to say in passing, and by way of anticipation, that a short while after Andrée's visit, the account of which I shall resume in a moment, there occurred certain events which created a great impression on me. First of all, this young man (perhaps in memory of Albertine, although I did not know at the time that he had been in love with her) became engaged to Andrée and married her, despite Rachel's despair, which left him totally unmoved. At that time (that is to say a few months after the visit which I have mentioned) Andrée no longer said that he was a ne'er-do-well, and it was only later that I realized that she had said so purely because she was crazy about him but thought that he was not interested in her. But another fact was even more striking. This young man produced a series of short sketches, using stage-sets and costumes that he had designed himself and which introduced into contemporary art a revolution at least equal to that accomplished by the Ballets Russes.[17] In short, those in the know considered his works to be of crucial importance, almost works of genius, and I must say that I share their opinion, thus ratifying to my astonishment Rachel's earlier views. People who had seen him at Balbec attending only to whether the clothes of the people he had to frequent were well cut or not and spending all his time at baccarat or the races or playing golf or polo, who knew that he had always been the dunce of the class and had even got himself expelled from school (to annoy his parents, he had spent two months living in the notorious house of ill-fame where M. de Charlus believed he had seen Morel), thought that his works had perhaps been composed by Andrée, who, from love for him, wished him to take the credit, or that more probably he used his great personal fortune, only slightly reduced by his follies, to pay some brilliant but needy professional to write them (this kind of wealthy society – not having the gloss which is acquired by frequenting the aristocracy and having no idea of what an artist is like, since for them he is only either an actor whom they invite to recite monologues at their daughters' engagement parties, where, as soon as he has finished, his fee is discreetly handed him in an another room, or perhaps a painter for whom they will have the daughter pose once she is married, before she has had children and while she still has her looks – tending to believe that everyone in society who writes, composes or paints,[18] has his works created for him by someone else and pays to establish his reputation as an author as others do to have a seat in parliament). But none of this was true; for this young man was indeed the author of those admirable works. When I found out, I could not help wavering between different explanations. Either he had indeed spent long years as the 'thick-headed brute' that he had seemed and some physiological cataclysm had awoken the Genie slumbering within him, like a Sleeping Beauty; or else during his last turbulent years at school, failing his baccalaureate, running up large gambling debts at Balbec, avoiding riding in the 'tram' with his aunt Verdurin's acquaintances because of their dreadful clothes, there was already a man of genius, perhaps unaware of his genius, having lost the key to the door in the turmoil of his juvenile passions; or even, a man of genius and already aware of it, yet bottom of the class, because while his teacher was mouthing clichés about Cicero, he himself was reading Rimbaud or Goethe. Certainly nothing would have justified this hypothesis when I met him in Balbec, where his preoccupations seemed to me to resolve entirely around the form of horses and the preparation of cocktails. But this is not an irrefutable objection. Perhaps he was very vain, which may be allied to genius, and tried to shine in the way he knew would dazzle the society he lived in and which he could not achieve by showing a profound knowledge of *Elective Affinities*,[19] but rather by knowing how to drive a four-in-hand. Besides I am not sure even that when he had become the author of these fine and original works, he would have much wanted, in the theatres where he was known, to greet anyone who was not wearing a dinner-jacket, since people stay true to their former tastes, yet this would prove in him not stupidity but vanity and even a certain practical sense, a certain insight in adapting his vanity to the mentality of fools whose esteem he needed and for whom the dinner-jacket may well shine more brightly than the eyes of a thinker. Who knows, if seen from an external viewpoint, how many a man of talent or even without talent but with a fondness for things intellectual, like myself for instance, might not have struck someone meeting him at Rivebelle, at the Hôtel de Balbec, or on the promenade at Balbec, of the most utter and pretentious imbecile? Not to mention that for Octave the realm of art must have been something so intimate, lodged so deeply in his most hidden depths, that he would doubtless never have thought of talking about it, as would, for example, Saint-Loup, for whom the arts had the same prestige as teams of horses for Octave. Then he might have had a passion for gambling, and people would say that he never lost it. Even so if the piety which brought to light the unknown works of Vinteuil could emerge from the very dubious world of Montjouvain, I was no less struck to think that perhaps the most striking masterpieces of our times have been nurtured not by taking the *Concours Général*,[20] and following the classic academic route, like the Broglie family,[21] but by frequenting the paddock and fashionable cocktail bars. At all events during this period at Balbec the reasons which made me want to meet him and those which made Albertine and her friends anxious to prevent me from meeting him, fell equally wide of the mark, and their only value might have been to highlight the eternal misunderstanding by the 'intellectual' (represented in this case by myself) and society (represented by the little gang) of the character of a social figure (the young golfer). I detected no signs of his talent, and his prestige in my eyes – of the same type as that of Mme Blatin formerly – was to be, whatever they claimed, a friend of my young female friends, and more closely linked to their gang than I was. What is more, Albertine and Andrée, symbolizing thereby the inability of society people to exercise a valid judgment on things of the mind and their tendency in such matters to believe in deceptive appearances, were not only not far from finding me stupid because I was curious to find out about such a fool, but were astonished above all that, if I had to choose a golfer, I should go for the most insignificant. If at worst I had wanted to take up with the young Gilbert de Bellœuvre, he was at least a lad who had conversational as well as golfing talents, who had been runner-up in the *Concours Général* and wrote pleasant verses (and yet who was in fact as thick as they come). Or else, if my aim was to 'make a study', 'for a book', Guy Saumoy, who was completely mad and who had twice abducted a minor, was at least a curious figure who could 'interest' me. I would have been 'allowed' these two but whatever did I see in the other one? He was clearly a major specimen of the species known as the 'thick-headed brute'.

To return to Andrée's visit, after what she had just revealed to me about her relationship with Albertine, she added that Albertine's main reason for leaving me was what the girls of the little gang, and others, might have thought if they saw her living with a young man to whom she was not married: 'I know it was at your mother's house. But that makes no difference. You can't imagine what it's like, this society of young women, what they hide from each other, how afraid they are of other people's opinions. I have seen some who were terribly strict with their young men, simply because they knew their girl-friends and they were afraid that certain things might be repeated, and yet I have by chance seen the very same girls, much to their annoyance, on occasions when they were behaving very diferently.' A few months earlier Andrée's apparent knowledge of the motives that drove the girls of the little gang would have seemed priceless to me. Perhaps what she said was sufficient to explain the fact that Albertine, who was to yield to me later in Paris, had rejected me in Balbec, where I was constantly in touch with her friends, something which I had absurdly seen as a great advantage allowing me to be on better terms with her. Perhaps it was even the sight of some sign of my confiding in Andrée or the fact that I had rashly told Andrée that Albertine was coming round to sleep at the Grand Hotel which caused the latter, who an hour earlier might have been ready to grant me certain pleasures as the most natural thing in the world, to change her mind and threaten to ring for help. But in this case, she must have been more complaisant with many others. This idea revived my jealousy and I told Andrée that there was one thing I wanted to ask her. 'Did you do that in your grandmother's empty apartment? – Oh, no, never, someone might have disturbed us – And yet, I thought, it seemed to me . . . – Besides, Albertine used to prefer to do it when we were in the country – Whereabouts? – At first, when we did not have time to go very far, we used to go to the Buttes-Chaumont, there was a house she knew there, or even under the trees, there is never anyone there; or in the grotto at the Petit Trianon, too. – There you are, how do you expect me to believe you? You swore to me, less than a year ago, that you had never done anything at the Buttes-Chaumont. – I was afraid of hurting you.' As I have already mentioned, it was only much later that I thought that it was on the contrary with the second version of her confession that Andrée had tried to hurt me. And I would have guessed this immediately, while she was speaking, because I would have felt the need to do so, if I had still been as much in love with Albertine. But Andrée's words did not hurt me enough for me to feel it indispensable to judge them immediately to be false. In short, if what Andrée said was true, and at first I did not doubt it, the real Albertine that I now discovered, after knowing so many and various apparent Albertines, was not very different from the orgiastic girl that I had sensed when she had loomed up, walking along the promenade at Balbec, and who had afterwards offered me so many changing aspects, as when in approaching a town we see its buildings progressively modify their disposition until they smother and erase its principal monument, which was the only thing visible from a distance, but where finally, as we get to know it better and judge it more accurately, its true proportions turn out to be those indicated by the perspective of our first appraisal, the remainder of the buildings which we had passed being no more than the successive series of lines of defence that any person raises to block our vision and which must be crossed one after the other, whatever suffering it might cost, before reaching their heart. Moreover, just as I had not needed to believe absolutely in Albertine's innocence because my suffering had diminished, I should admit that the converse was true, that if I did not suffer overmuch from this revelation it was because, for some time past, the belief in Albertine's innocence that I

had forged had been gradually and unwittingly replaced by a belief
that had always been present within me, the belief in Albertine's guilt.
Now if I no longer believed in the innocence of Albertine, it was
because I no longer felt the need or the passionate desire to do so. It
is desire that engenders belief, and if we are not usually aware of this,
it is because most of the desires which engender belief – unlike the
one which had made me believe that Albertine was innocent – die only
when we do. Rather than accept all the evidence which corroborated
my original version, I had stupidly preferred to believe Albertine's
bald affirmations. Why had I believed her? Lying is essential to
humanity. It plays perhaps as great a part as the search for pleasure
and is in fact driven by this search. We lie to protect our pleasure or
our honour, if to divulge this pleasure would be contrary to our
honour. We lie all our lives, above all, or perhaps even only, to those
who love us. For in fact they alone make us fear for our pleasure and
desire their esteem. At first I had thought Albertine guilty and only
my desire, enlisting all the forces of my intelligence in its enterprise
of doubt, had led me astray. Perhaps we live surrounded by electric
or seismic signals, which we have to interpret in good faith in order
to know the truth about people's characters. But I have to admit that,
however sad Andrée's words had made me, in spite of everything I
found it more satisfying that reality should at last conform to what my
instincts had first intuitively felt, rather than confirm the wretched and
cowardly optimism to which I had later yielded. I preferred life to live
up to my intuitions; intuitions, moreover, which I had had the first
day on the beach, when I had thought that these girls were the incarnation of vice and frenzied pleasure, and also on the evening when
I had seen Albertine's governess take this passionate girl back into the
little villa, as one pushes back into its cage a wild beast that nothing
later, despite appearances, will be able to tame; did they not match
what Bloch had told me when he made the world seem so beautiful,
by showing me something which sent shivers down my spine every
time I went out for a ride, every time I met a woman, that is, the
universal nature of desire? Perhaps in spite of everything it had been
for the best that I should only now encounter these first intuitions a
second time, with the corroborating evidence. As long as my love for

Albertine was still entirely intact, they would have hurt me too much, and it was better that only a trace of them should remain, my perpetual suspicion of things which I could not see and which, however, were continually occurring so close to me, and perhaps yet another, earlier, vaster trace, which was *my love itself*. For indeed, did not my choosing and falling in love with Albertine, despite all the denials of my reason, entail knowing Albertine in all her vileness? And even in the moments when our mistrust recedes, is love not its prolongation and its transformation? Is love not a proof of clear-sightedness (a proof unintelligible to the lover himself) since desire, always seeking what is most opposite to us, forces us to love what makes us suffer? The charm of a person, of her eyes, her mouth and her figure, certainly also contains just those elements which, unbeknown to ourselves, are most likely to make us unhappy, so that to feel ourselves drawn towards this person, to start to love her, is, however innocent we claim her to be, already to start reading between the lines all her misdeeds, all her betrayals.

And did those charms which, in order to attract me, were thus embodied in the noxious,[22] dangerous, fatal parts of the person, have a causal relationship with these secret poisons more direct than that which the luxuriant attractions of some venomous flowers have with their poisonous secretions? Perhaps, I thought, it was Albertine's vice itself, the cause of my later suffering, which had produced in Albertine her frank and generous manner, creating the illusion that one enjoyed with her the same loyal and unrestrained camaraderie as with a man, just as a parallel vice had produced in M. de Charlus a feminine subtlety of wit and sensibility. In the midst of the most utter blindness, our perspicacity subsists in the very guise of predilection and tenderness, so that it is wrong in love to talk of a bad choice, since, as soon as there is a choice, it can be only a bad one. 'Did these walks in the Buttes-Chaumont take place when you came here to call for her?' I asked Andrée. 'Oh, no, from the day when Albertine went home with you from Balbec, except for what I've told you about, she never did anything with me again. She would not even allow me to mention such things to her any more. — But my dear Andrée, why keep on lying? Quite by chance, for I try never to pry, I learned in the minutest detail that Albertine did that kind of thing, and to be more precise, at

the seaside, with a laundry-maid, only a few days before her death. –
Ah, perhaps, after she had left you, I don't know. She sensed that she
had not been able to win back your confidence and never would be
able to again.' These last words overwhelmed me. Then I thought
again about the evening with the syringa and remembered that a
fortnight or so later, as my jealousy kept switching from one object to
another, I had asked Albertine if she had ever had a relationship with
Andrée and that she had replied: 'Oh, never! Of course I adore Andrée;
I feel great affection for her, but as for a sister, and even if I had the
inclinations that you seem to imagine, she's the last person that I would
think of for that. I can swear on anything you like, on my aunt, on
my poor mother's grave.' I had believed her. And yet even if I had
not been put on my guard by the contradiction between her former
partial confessions to things which she had later denied as soon as she
realized that I was not indifferent to them, I ought to have remembered
Swann, convinced that M. de Charlus's friendships were platonic and
affirming this to me on the evening of the very day that I had seen the
tailor and the Baron in the courtyard; I ought to have realized that
there are two worlds, one overlapping the other, one constituted by
the things that the best and sincerest people say, and behind it the
world composed by the series of these same people's actions; so that
when a married woman says of a young man, 'Oh, it's perfectly true
that I am terribly fond of him, but it's something very innocent, very
pure, I can swear to you on my parents' memory,' we ought, instead
of harbouring any doubts, to swear to ourselves that she has probably
just emerged from the bathroom where she hurriedly retires after each
tryst with the young man, in order to avoid having children. The
spray of syringa made me feel mortally sad and also the fact that
Albertine could have thought, could have told people, that I was
deceitful and hated her; and, more than anything perhaps, her lies,
which were so unexpected that I found it difficult to reconcile them
with my way of thinking. One day she had told me that she had been
to an airfield, where the pilot was a friend of hers (doubtless to divert
my suspicions away from women, thinking that I would be less jealous
of men), that she had been amused to see how entranced Andrée had
been by the pilot and how he had flattered Albertine, so much so that

Andrée had wanted to take a flight in the aeroplane with him. But this had been entirely invented, Andrée had never been to this airfield, etc.

By the time Andrée had left it was time for dinner. 'You'll never guess who came to visit me for at least three hours,' said my mother. I say three hours, it could have been longer, she arrived almost at the same time as my first guest, who was Mme Cottard, and sat there motionless while all my callers – more than thirty of them – were coming and going, and left me only a quarter of an hour ago. If you hadn't been with your friend Andrée I would have had someone fetch you. – Well, then, who was it? – Someone who never pays calls. – The Princess of Parma? – I do declare that my son is more intelligent than I would have thought. You spoil the pleasure of making you guess a name, you get it first time. – Did she apologize for being so cold yesterday? – No, that would have been stupid. The visit itself was her apology; your poor grandmother would have really appreciated it. It appears that she asked her footman at about two o'clock to find out if I had an at-home day. They told her that today was the day and up she came.' My first reaction, which I did not dare reveal to my mother, was that the Princess of Parma, who the day before had been immersed in the company of some of her closest and most illustrious lady-friends, those with whom she best loved to converse, had felt no need to hide the irritation she had felt on seeing my mother walk in. And this coldness, which moreover all the Guermantes had generally adopted, was absolutely in the tradition of great German ladies and they thought to make amends for it with scrupulous politeness. But my mother thought, and later I came to share her opinion, that the Princess of Parma had quite simply failed to recognize her and thought she need take no notice of her, but that after my mother had left she had learned who she was, whether from the Duchesse de Guermantes, whom my mother had met downstairs, or from the list of names which the footmen had requested of the lady visitors at the door before inscribing them in their register and allowing them to enter. She had thought it would be impolite to say to my mother or ask someone else to, 'I did not recognize you,' but, in a fashion no less suited to the rules of etiquette of the German principalities and the manners of the Guermantes than my first version, she had thought that a visit, an exceptional gesture by her Highness, and especially a visit lasting several hours, would transmit a similar message to my mother in indirect but equally expressive terms, which was in fact the result. But I did not want to waste time asking my mother for an account of the Princess's visit, since I had just remembered several queries concerning Albertine which I had wanted to put to Andrée but had forgotten. How little I knew, would ever know, may I say, on the subject of Albertine, the only subject whose details could really have interested me or were at least starting to interest me again from time to time! For man is a creature of no fixed age, a creature who has the ability to become years younger in only a few seconds and who, surrounded by walls formed by the periods of time that he has lived through, floats around in their midst but as in a pool whose level keeps constantly changing, thus putting him within reach now of one time period, now of another. I wrote to Andrée asking her to come back. She was not free until a week later. Almost as soon as she had arrived I asked her: 'Look, since you claim that Albertine no longer did that kind of thing when she was living here, you must think that she left me so as to be freer to indulge, but who was the girl-friend? – No, absolutely not, that was not the reason at all. – So was it because I was too unpleasant? – No, I don't think so. I think she was forced to leave you by her aunt, who had ideas for her with a "rascal" you know about, that man you called "the Also-ran", the young man who loved Albertine and had asked for her hand. Seeing that you were not going to marry her, they were afraid that her scandalously protracted stay with you might prevent that young man from marrying her. Mme Bontemps, who was constantly harried by the young man's friends and relations, called Albertine back to her side. Deep down Albertine needed her uncle and aunt and, when she realized that they were presenting her with a *fait accompli*, she left you.' In my jealousy I had never thought of this explanation but only of Albertine's desires for women and of ways of keeping her under surveillance; I had forgotten that Mme Bontemps also existed and that she might have eventually found strange something that my mother had found shocking from the outset. At least Mme Bontemps feared that it might shock the potential fiancé that she was holding in reserve for her like a pear to slake her thirst, in case I did not marry her. For Albertine, despite what Andrée's mother had previously thought, had in fact found a fine bourgeois match. And on those occasions when Albertine had wanted to visit Mme Verdurin, had spoken to her in secret, or had been so annoyed that I had been to one of Mme Verdurin's receptions without telling her, the intrigue between her and Mme Verdurin had been devised in order to allow her to meet, not Mme Vinteuil, but the nephew who was in love with Albertine and on whose behalf Mme Verdurin did not aspire to a rich marriage, taking her satisfaction in working to arrange one of those marriages which are surprising on the part of certain families if one does not entirely understand their mentality. Now, I had never given a second thought to this nephew, who had perhaps been the pioneer thanks to whom I had been kissed by her on the first occasion. And in place of all the layers of anxiety about Albertine that I had constructed I had to substitute a different one or overlay it, since it did not necessarily exclude them, just as a taste for women does not prevent women from marrying. Was this marriage the real reason for Albertine's departure and had she from self-respect so as not to seem to depend on her aunt or seem to be forcing me to marry her, preferred not to say so? I started to realize that the systematic explanation of a single action by multiple causes, which Albertine skilfully deployed in her relationships with her girl-friends when she led each of them to believe that it was for her alone that she had called, was no more than a rather artificial and self-conscious symbol of the different aspects that any act takes on according to the point of view from which we consider it. This was neither the first nor the last time that I felt astonishment and a kind of shame at never once having thought that Albertine was living with me in a false situation which could embarrass her aunt. How often has it happened to me, after trying to understand a relationship between two people and the problems that it entails, that I have suddenly heard a third party reveal his own attitude, since he had had even closer links than I with one of the couple, an attitude which might even have been at the heart of their problems! And if their actions are always so indeterminate, how could people themselves not be so? Listening to those who claimed that Albertine was a schemer who had tried to get herself married off first to one man then to another, it is not difficult to suppose how they would have qualified her life with me. And yet in my opinion she had been a victim, perhaps not an entirely innocent victim, but in that case guilty for different reasons, in respect of vices which nobody mentioned.

But the most important thing to admit is this: although, on the one hand, lying is often a trait of character, it is, on the other hand, in women who would not otherwise be liars, a natural defence, at first spontaneous and then gradually more organized, against that sudden danger which is capable of destroying anyone's life: love. Then again, it is not entirely due to chance if intellectual and sensitive men always offer themselves to insensitive and inferior women and yet still hold them dear, nor if the proof that they are unloved does not cure them of being prepared to sacrifice all in order to keep such a creature by their side. In saying that such men need to suffer, I am telling the truth, while passing over the preliminary truths which would explain this – in a sense involuntary – need to suffer as their perfectly comprehensible consequence. Not to mention the fact that, since entirely consistent characters are rare, a highly intellectual and sensitive man will generally have little will-power, will be the plaything of habit and of that fear of suffering in the immediate future which dooms him to perpetual suffering and that in these conditions he will never wish to repudiate the woman who does not love him. We may be astonished that he is satisfied with so little love, but we should rather imagine the pain that is caused by the love which he himself feels. A pain which we must not pity too much, for the terrible turmoil caused by an unhappy love affair or the departure or death of a lover is like an attack of paralysis which at first lays us low, but after which the muscles tend gradually to recover their vital energy and elasticity. And yet this pain is not without its compensations. These intellectual and sensitive people are generally little inclined towards lying. Lies catch them all the more unawares in that, for all their great intelligence, they have to live in the real world, but rather than reacting vigorously, they continue to live in thrall to the pain that a woman has just inflicted on them rather than in the clear awareness of what she wanted, of what she did, of whom she loved, an awareness mostly the preserve of strong-willed characters, who require it so that they may face the future rather than lament the past. So these intellectual and sensitive people feel betrayed, without quite knowing why. Thus it is that the mediocre woman, whom we were astonished to see them love, enriches their universe far more than an intelligent woman would have done. Behind each of her words they suspect a lie; behind each house she says she has visited, another house, behind each action and person, another action, another person. Doubtless they do not know exactly which ones and have neither the energy nor perhaps even the opportunity to find out. A deceitful woman can use a very simple trick, without bothering to vary it, to delude a great number of people and even use it to delude the same person more than once, when he ought to have been able to see through it. All of which confronts the sensitive intellectual with a universe whose complex depths his jealousy would like to plumb and which are not without their fascination for his intellect.

Without quite counting myself among their number, I might perhaps, now that Albertine was dead, learn the secret of her life. But do these revelations, which occur only after a person's terrestrial life is over, not prove that nobody, deep down, believes in an after-life? If these revelations are true, we should fear the resentment of the person whose actions are uncovered as much on the day we will meet her in heaven as we feared it during her lifetime, when we felt bound to honour her secret. And if these revelations are false, made up because she is no longer here to give the lie to them, we should fear the wrath of the dead woman even more if we believed in heaven. But nobody does believe in it. Thus it was possible that a long debate between staying and leaving was staged in Albertine's heart, but that her decision turned on her aunt or on that young man, rather than on women, whom she may not even have taken into account. The most weighty consideration which I faced was that Andrée, who however no longer had anything to hide from me about Albertine's morals, swore to me that there was nothing of this kind between Albertine on the one hand and Mlle de Vinteuil and her girl-friend on the other (Albertine was unaware of her own inclinations when she first met them and they, for fear of mistaking the object of their desire – a fear that leads us into as many errors as does desire itself – considered her to be very hostile to that sort of thing. Perhaps much later they might have learned the conformity of her inclinations with theirs, but by then they knew Albertine too well and Albertine knew them too well even to think about indulging in such things together.) In short, I was still no closer to understanding why Albertine had left me. If a woman's face is difficult to capture with the eyes, which cannot take in the whole of its mobile surface, or with the lips and even less with the memory, if her social position in relation to our own social level clouds our appreciation, how much thicker a curtain is drawn between those of her actions which we do perceive and her motives! People's motives lie at a deeper level, which we cannot perceive, and moreover engender other actions, which we fail to recognize and which are often in absolute contradiction with those that we do recognize. Was there any period in history when there was some public figure, believed saintly by his friends, who has not been exposed for committing forgery, robbing the state or betraying his country? How often every year is some great nobleman robbed by the steward whom he has raised on his estate, whom he would have sworn was an honest man and who perhaps was one! And yet how much more impenetrable does this curtain which veils others' motives become if we feel love for that person! For it confuses our judgment and also the actions of the woman, who, feeling herself loved, ceases suddenly to attach any value to things that otherwise she would have treasured, such as wealth, for instance. It may also tempt her partly to feign this disdain for wealth in the hope of obtaining more by causing us to suffer. Striking a bargain may be another factor, along with others, as may even material events in her life, an intrigue that she has confided to no one for fear that someone might reveal it to us, an intrigue which, despite this precaution, many people might well have discovered if they had had the same passionate desire to find out as we did, while exercising greater independence of mind and arousing less suspicion in the person concerned, an intrigue that was perhaps not unknown to certain persons – but persons whom we neither know nor know how to identify. And among all the reasons for her attitude towards us being inexplicable, one must include those individual traits of character, whether deriving from self-neglect, from hatred, from love of freedom, from sudden attacks of anger, or from fear of what certain people might think, which may drive a person to do the opposite of what we would have expected. And then there are the differences in background and education, which we prefer not to credit because, when we talk to each other, our language effaces them, but which, when each one of us is alone again, return to guide our several actions from such opposed viewpoints that no real encounter is possible.

'But my dear Andrée, you are lying again. Just remember – you admitted it to me yourself, I telephoned you the day before, don't you remember? – how badly Albertine had wanted to go to Mme Verdurin's reception on the day that Mlle Vinteuil was due to appear but hid it from me as something that I was not supposed to know. – Yes, but Albertine had no way of knowing that Mlle Vinteuil would be there.' 'Really? You told me yourself that she had met Mme Verdurin a few days earlier. Besides, Andrée, there is no point in our deceiving each other. I found a note this morning in Albertine's room, a message from Mme Verdurin urging her to come to her reception.' And I showed her this note, which Françoise had managed to bring to my attention a few days before Albertine's departure by placing it right on top of her affairs so that I would see it, and leaving it there, I fear, in order to make Albertine think that I had been rifling through her possessions or at least to let her know that I had seen this note. And I often wondered if this stratagem, devised by Françoise, had not strongly contributed to Albertine's departure, making her see that she could keep nothing private from me and feel discouraged and beaten. I showed her the note: *I am unrepentant, my perfectly normal family feelings are ample excuse*. 'You know, Andrée, don't you, that Albertine always used to say that Mlle Vinteuil's girl-friend was in fact a mother or a sister for her. – But you have misunderstood this note. The person that Mme Verdurin wanted Albertine to meet was not her girl-friend at all but the fiancé, "the also-ran", and the family feelings were those felt by Mme Verdurin for this scoundrel, who is in fact her nephew. And yet I think that Albertine did find out later that Mlle Vinteuil was due to attend, Mme Verdurin might have told her in passing. Of course she was pleased by the idea that she would see her friend, and it recalled past happiness but only in the way that you would be pleased, if you were going somewhere, to know that Elstir would be there at the same time, but no more, not even as much. No, if Albertine did not want to tell you why she wanted to go to see Mme Verdurin, it was because there was a rehearsal to which Mme Verdurin had invited just a very few people, including this nephew whom you had met at Balbec, whom Mme Bontemps wanted Albertine to marry and whom Albertine wanted to talk to. He was quite a rascal. And then there is no need to look for so many explanations,' added Andrée, 'God knows how I loved Albertine and how good-natured she was but, especially since she had had typhoid fever (a year before you met us all), she was a real tearaway. She suddenly became disgusted with what she had been doing, she wanted to change, and at a moment's notice, although doubtless she didn't even know why herself. Do you remember the first year you came to Balbec, the year when you met us all? One fine day she got someone to send her a telegram calling her back to Paris, with hardly any time for us to help her pack. But she had no reason to leave. All the excuses that she gave out were false. Paris would be desperately dull for her at that time of year. We were all still in Balbec. The golfing season was not over and even the trials for the championship cup which she had so set her heart on had not finished. She would surely have won it. There was only a week to go. But there you are, off she went, at a gallop. I've often asked her about it since. She said herself that she didn't know why she left, that she missed her little home (Paris as her "little home", can you believe it?), that she did not like Balbec, that she thought there were people there who were making fun of her.' And I thought that the element of truth in what Andrée was saying was that, if differences between minds explain the different impressions produced on one person and another by the same work of art and differences in feeling explain the impossibility of persuading someone to love you if they don't, there are also differences of character and even differing character traits within a single individual which may motivate an action. Then I stopped musing over this analysis and I reminded myself how difficult it is in life to know the truth. I had of course noticed Albertine's desire to go to Mme Verdurin's, and her dissimulation of it, and I had not been mistaken. But just as we grasp one fact, other facts – the underside of a tapestry, the secret behind an act or an intrigue or indeed the intelligence of the heart – of which we never see more than appearances, escape us, and we see only flat shadows pass, of which we say: this is it, that is what it is; it is because of her or some other person. The revelation that Mlle Vinteuil was due to come had seemed to me to be the explanation, especially since Albertine had made the first move in mentioning it to me. And later had she not refused to swear to me that she took no pleasure in Mlle Vinteuil's presence? And here on the subject of the young man in question I recalled what I had forgotten. A short time previously, while Albertine was living with me, I had met him and, in contrast with his attitude in Balbec, he had been extremely friendly, even affectionate, with me and had begged me to allow him to call on me, although I had refused for a number of reasons. Now, however, I realized that since he quite clearly knew that Albertine was living in my house, he wanted to be in my good books in order to have a free hand to come to see her and take her away from me and I concluded that he was a wretch. Yet when some time later I had this young man's first works performed for me, I am sure that I continued to think that, if he had been so keen to call on me, it was on account of Albertine and although I blamed him for that, I remembered that if formerly I had set out for Doncières to see Saint-Loup, it was in fact because I was enamoured of Mme de Guermantes. It is true that the two cases were not the same: since Saint-Loup was not in love with Mme de Guermantes, there may well have been an element of duplicity in my affections but no treachery. But afterwards I thought that we also feel affection for the person who owns the object of our desire, even if he himself also loves that same object. In this case of course we should struggle to resist a friendship that must lead directly to betrayal. And I believe that this is what I have always done. But in the case of those who are not strong enough to do so, we cannot say that the friendship which they display for the owner of the object of their desire is purely tactical, for they sincerely feel it and because of this they show it with such ardour that, once the treacherous deed has been perpetrated, it causes the deceived husband or lover to declare with indignation and stupor: 'If only you could have heard the protestations of affection that the wretch lavished on me! That someone should rob a man of his wealth, I can understand. But that he should feel the diabolical need first to assure him of his friendship shows a degree of ignominy and perversity that beggars the imagination.' And yet, there is no perverse pleasure involved nor even any entirely lucid untruth. The affection of this sort that Albertine's pseudo-fiancé had shown me that day had yet another excuse, for it was more complex than a simple offshoot of his love for Albertine. It was only very recently that he realized, and admitted to himself, that he wanted to be acknowledged as an intellectual. For the first time pleasures other than those of sport or debauchery existed for him. The fact that I was held in esteem by Elstir and Bergotte, that Albertine had perhaps spoken to him of my opinions of writers, which led her to believe that I could have been a writer myself, made me suddenly seem to him (to the new man that he at last perceived himself to be) someone interesting whom it would be pleasant to get to know better, someone in whom he would have liked to confide his plans and perhaps whom he might ask to introduce him to Elstir. As a result, he was sincere when he asked if he might call on me, expressing a personal sympathy, to which intellectual interest mingled with reflections of Albertine gave added sincerity. Of course it was not for that reason alone that he was so keen to call on me and would have dropped everything in order to be able to do so. But this last reason, which did hardly more than raise the first two to a level of paroxysmal passion, was perhaps unknown to him and the two others did really exist, as Albertine, when she wanted to go to see Mme Verdurin on the afternoon of the rehearsal, may well have really felt a perfectly honourable pleasure in seeing her childhood friends again, who were no more immoral in her eyes than she was in theirs, chatting with them, showing them by her very presence at the Verdurins' that the poor little girl whom they had known was now invited to a noted salon, as well as the pleasure that she may well have felt in listening to Vinteuil's music. If all that was true, the blush that had come to Albertine's cheeks when I had mentioned Mlle Vinteuil came from the fact that I had done so on the subject of the very reception which she had hoped to conceal from me because of the marriage proposal, of which I was supposed to know nothing. Albertine's refusal to swear to me that she had felt no pleasure at seeing Mlle Vinteuil that afternoon had at the time increased my torment and strengthened my suspicions, but proved to me retrospectively that she had wanted to be sincere and even in an innocent matter, perhaps precisely because it was innocent. There remained, however, what Andrée had told me about her relationship with Albertine. Perhaps, however, even without going so far as to believe that Andrée was making it all up solely in order to prevent me from feeling happy and from believing myself superior to her, yet I could still suppose that she had somewhat exaggerated what she used to do with Albertine and that Albertine, narrowing her analytic criteria and making casuistic use of certain definitions that I had foolishly formulated on the subject, also rather understated what she had done with Andrée, finding that her relationship with Andrée did not fall into the category of what she needed to confess and that she could deny it without telling a lie. But why should I believe that it was she rather than Andrée who had been lying? Truth and life are indeed an uphill path, and, without ever really getting to know them, I felt that the final impression which they left me was one where sadness was perhaps still overshadowed by fatigue.[24]

### CHAPTER 3

*Staying in Venice*

My mother had taken me with her to spend a few weeks in Venice, and – since we can find beauty not only in the humblest but also in the most precious things – I sampled there impressions analogous to those that I had so often felt previously in Combray, but transposed into an entirely different, richer mode. When someone came to open my shutters at ten o'clock in the morning, I saw the glow, not of the slates of St Hilaire splendidly transfigured into black marble, but of the gold of the angel on the bell-tower of St Mark's. With outstretched arms, and so gleaming with sunlight that it was almost impossible to behold him directly, he promised me joy half an hour later on the Piazzetta, a promise more reliable than his previous mission to bring tidings of Great Joy to men of good will. He was all that I could glimpse, as long as I lay in bed, but since the world is little more than a vast sundial where a single sunlit segment allows us to tell the time, from the very first morning I thought of the shops in the church square in Combray which were always about to close when I arrived for Mass on Sundays, while the smell of the straw in the market rankled under the burgeoning heat of the sun. But by the second day, what I saw when I awoke, and my reason for rising (because it had come to take the place of memories of Combray in my memory and my desires), were the impressions of my first day in Venice, Venice whose everyday life was no less real than that of Combray and where it was a pleasure, as in Combray, to go down into the festive street on Sunday mornings, but a street which was a whole stretch of liquid sapphire, cooled by soft breezes and so deep-dyed that my tired eyes could relax and look steadily at it with no fear that it might fade. Just as in Combray's rue de l'Oiseau the good citizens emerged from houses aligned side by

side in a row along the main street, so too did the inhabitants of this
new city; but the Combray houses' habit of casting a little shadow at
their foot was entrusted to palaces of porphyry and jasper, over whose
arched doorways heads of bearded gods jutted out of alignment, like
the door knockers in Combray, and their reflections darkened the
tones, not of brown earth, but of splendid blue waters. The shadow
that would have flowed from the awning of the dress shop or the
hairdresser's sign in Combray became, on the Piazza, the little blue
flowers that the relief of a Renaissance façade cast at its foot over the
desert of the sunlit paving stones, although it is true that, in Venice as
in Combray, when the sun beat down more strongly, they were forced
to lower their shutters on the banks of their canal. But these shutters
were deployed between the quatrefoils and the tendrils of Gothic
windows. You could say the same of our own hotel window, at whose
balustrade my mother waited for me, gazing at the canal with a patience
that she would never have shown before, in Combray, in the days
when she invested in me hopes that had never been rewarded and
wanted to hide from me the extent of her love for me. Now she clearly
felt that a show of coldness would change nothing, and the affection
which she lavished on me resembled the food that is no longer
forbidden to a sick person when we realize that they have no chance
of recovery. To be sure, the modest features that gave my aunt Léonie's
window overlooking the rue de l'Oiseau its individual character – its
asymmetry caused by the unequal distance between the two neighbouring windows, the excessive height of the wooden window-ledge, the
bent handle that opened the shutters and the two swathes of shiny blue
satin that were separated and held apart by tiebacks – could all find
their echo in our hotel in Venice. There too I heard that special,
eloquent language which helps us recognize from afar the dwelling
where we come home to dine and which later remains in our memory
like a testimony declaring that for a period of time this dwelling was
ours; but in Venice the task of saying so devolved, not as in Combray
and almost everywhere else, upon the simplest or even the ugliest
things, but upon an ogive still half recalling its Arabic origins, on a
façade that is reproduced in every illustrated book on art and cast in
plaster in every museum, as one of the masterpieces of medieval

domestic architecture; I glimpsed this ogive from far away, when I had only just passed by San Giorgio Maggiore, and as it caught sight of me, its soaring lancet arches supplemented its welcoming smile with a distinguished, superior, almost impenetrable gaze. And, because, behind its multicoloured marble balustrade, Mama waited for me, her face, while she read, surrounded by a light veil of tulle (as heart-rendingly white for me as her hair) which I sensed that my mother, on drying her eyes, had pinned to her straw hat partly in order to seem 'properly dressed' in the eyes of the hotel residents, but above all to seem to me to be less in mourning, less sad, almost consoled for the death of my grandmother; because, having not recognized me straight away, as soon as I called out to her from my gondola, she sent her love winging its way towards me, from the depths of her heart, a love that would cease only when it had no object left to sustain it, on the surface of the passionate gaze which she cast intensely in my direction, which she sought to enhance by forming her lips into a smile which seemed, within the frame and beneath the canopy of the more discreet smile of the ogive illuminated by the midday sun, to lean forward to embrace me, – because of that, this window has taken on in my memory the sweetness of things that played their part beside us just as a particular hour chimed, the same for us and them; and, however replete with admirable form its mullions may be, this illustrious window bears for me the familiar features of a man of genius frequented by chance for a month at a holiday resort and led to strike up a friendship with us, and if thereafter, each time I see a cast of this window in a museum, I have to fight back my tears, it is because it tells me quite simply the thing that I find most moving of all, 'I remember your mother very well.'

Then as I went to meet Mama, who had left the window, I felt the same sense of coolness on leaving the midday heat that I had experienced at Combray when I went up to my bedroom; but in Venice it was wafted by a sea breeze, and not up a small, narrow wooden staircase but up the noble surfaces of marble steps, constantly splashed with flashes of glaucous sunlight, adding the lesson of Veronese to the useful lesson of Chardin, which I had learned on a previous occasion. And since in Venice it is works of art and magnificent monuments that are entrusted with conveying the impressions of everyday life, it would distort the nature of the city, if, on the pretext that the most famous examples of the Venice of certain painters are coldly aesthetic (except for some superb studies by Maxime Dethomas[1]), we were to represent only its impoverished aspects, at the points where its habitual splendour fades, and if, in trying to make Venice more familiar and true, we were to make it look like Aubervilliers. Reacting quite naturally to the artificial Venice produced by bad painters, we could reproach the greatest artists with studying only the Venice that they found more realistic, with its humble campi and deserted side canals. This was the Venice that I explored in the afternoons, if I did not go out with my mother. For this was where I found it easier to meet women of the people, match-sellers and bead-stringers, glass- or lace-workers, young working-girls whose long black, fringed shawls were no barrier to my love, since I had nearly forgotten Albertine, yet some were more attractive than others, for I did still remember her a little. I wonder if anyone could have told me exactly how far, in this passionate perusal of Venetian women, what was due to them, and what to Albertine, or my former desire to travel to Venice. Our slightest desire, although striking its own, unique chord, contains within it the fundamental notes on which our whole lives are based. And if perchance we suppressed one or other of these notes, even unheard, even unconscious, a note bearing absolutely no relation to the object of our pursuit, we would none the less feel our whole desire for this object fade away. There was much that I did not attempt to elucidate in the midst of my excited pursuit of Venetian girls. My gondola followed the side canals, as if the mysterious hand of a genie were guiding me through the byways of this oriental city, the more I advanced along the canals the more they seemed to show me the way, slicing through a neighbourhood that they divided, as their narrow and arbitrarily traced furrows barely perturbed the tall houses and their small Moorish windows; and like a magical guide holding a candle between his fingers to light my passage, they cast ahead of them a ray of sunlight and opened a pathway for it. You could sense that between the humble dwellings that the little canal had just divided, and which otherwise would have formed a compact whole, there was so little space available that a church bell-tower or a garden trellis would directly overhang the *rio*, as in a flooded city. But for the churches, as for the gardens which underwent the same process of transposition as occurred in the Grand Canal, the sea was so willing to act as a means of communication, like a side or main street, that on either side of the Canaletto, churches rose out of the water in this old, crowded and poor neighbourhood. They had become busy, humble parishes, openly displaying the evidence of their run-down state and their frequentation by numerous people of the lower classes; thus the gardens traversed by the trough of the canal trailed their startled leaves and fruit down to the water's edge, and thus on the corner of a house whose rough-hewn sandstone was still as raw as if freshly cut, little boys, caught off-guard but maintaining their balance, dangled their seaworthy legs like those of sailors sitting on a swinging bridge whose two halves had just parted, letting the sea flow between them. Sometimes a more beautiful monument appeared, popping up like a present in a lucky dip, a small ivory temple with its Corinthian columns and its pediment adorned with an allegorical statue, somewhat out of place in the midst of the everyday things with which it was entangled, for although we made way for it to pass, the peristyle that the canal had allotted to it still looked more like a quay for unloading fruit and vegetables. I had the impression, further enhanced by my desire, that I was not out of doors, but rather that I was entering some increasingly secret place, for on every occasion I found something new moving into place to one side of me or the other, a small monument or an unsuspected *campo* still endowed with that air of surprise affected by beautiful things which we see for the first time but whose aims and functions we do not yet understand. I returned on foot by the narrow calli, stopping to talk to working-girls, as Albertine might have done before me, and I wished that she were with me. Yet they could not be the same girls; at the time when Albertine was in Venice they would still have been children. But whereas previously I had been unfaithful through cowardice in one way or another to each of the desires that I had at first believed unique, since I had sought an analogous object rather than the original which I no longer hoped to find, now I quite deliberately sought out women that Albertine had not known in person, and even avoided those women that I had previously desired. It is true that I often recalled, with the violence of unassuaged desire, some girl from Méséglise or Paris, like the milkmaid seen at the foot of a hill one morning on my first trip to Balbec. Alas, however, I remembered them as they were then, that is, such as they certainly were no longer. In this way, where formerly I would have been led to inflect my impression of the constancy of desire by seeking to replace a convent schoolgirl that I had lost sight of by a similar schoolgirl, now when I sought out the adolescent girls that had disturbed me or Albertine, I had to allow yet another exception to the rule of the uniqueness of desire; those I now must chase were not the girls who were sixteen at the time, but those who were sixteen now, for what I now loved, despite the specific qualities of the person, and what escaped me, was youth itself. I realized that the youth of the girls whom I had known existed only in the fires of my memory, and that it was not the girls themselves, however desirous of obtaining them I was when my memory presented them to me, that I should pluck, if I truly wanted to harvest the season's youth in full flower.

The sun was still high in the sky when I went to meet my mother on the Piazzetta. We hailed a gondola. 'How your poor grandmother would have loved such simple elegance!' Mama said to me, pointing out the Doges' Palace as it contemplated the sea, imbued with the ideas that the architect had entrusted it with and which it faithfully conserved, as it mounted a silent watch for its absent Doges. 'She would even have liked the delicacy of those shades of pink, because there is nothing mawkish about them. How your grandmother would have loved Venice, and how familiar, how close to nature, she would have found all this beauty, so full of things that it needs no arrangement, offering itself in its own guise, the Doges' Palace with its cubic forms, the columns that you say come from Herod's Palace, in the middle of the Piazzetta and, even less calculated, placed as if space were lacking elsewhere, the pillars of St John of Acre and the horses on the balcony of St Mark's! Your grandmother would have been as delighted to see the sun set on the Doges' Palace as over a mountain-top.' And there was indeed some truth in what my mother said, for, while the gondola brought us back up the Grand Canal, we watched the line of palaces as we passed between them reflecting the changing light and the passing day on their pink flanks, changing with them, less after the fashion of private dwellings and famous monuments than that of a chain of marble cliffs beneath which we travel by boat in the evening to watch the sun set. Thus the dwellings disposed on either side of the canal reminded us of natural sites, but inspired by a nature using the human imagination to create its works. Yet at the same time (because of the constantly urban nature of the impressions offered by Venice, despite being set almost out at sea, on its waves where the ebb and flow of the tide are perceptible twice a day and which first at high tide flood over, and then at low tide uncover the magnificent external staircases of the palaces), as we would have done in Paris on the boulevards, on the Champs-Élysées or in the Bois or any wide, fashionable avenue, we passed in the misty evening light the most beautiful women, nearly all foreign, leaning languidly on the cushions of their floating equipage, waiting in line, stopping at a palace, asking if the friend that they wanted to call on was at home and, while awaiting the reply, they prepared their card just in case, in order to leave it as they would have done at the door of the Hôtel de Guermantes, consulting their guide-book to check the period and the style of the palace, even as they were rocked all the while by the eddies of these sparkling, spirited waters, as if on the crest of a blue wave which reared in panic to feel itself caught between the dancing gondola and the resounding marble. And thus even an outing to call on a friend or to do some shopping was not only three things in one but still unique, in this Venice where the slightest social call takes on at once both the form and the charm of a visit to a museum and that of a naval manoeuvre.

Several of the palaces on the Grand Canal had been converted into hotels, and, whether because we fancied a change or from politeness towards Mme Sazerat, whom we had chanced to encounter – as one always meets some unforeseen, inopportune acquaintance on any journey – and whom Mama had invited out, we wished to try dinner in a different hotel from our own, one where they claimed that the cuisine was better. While my mother was paying the gondolier and escorting Mme Sazerat into the private room that she had booked, I preferred to take a look at the main dining-hall of the restaurant, with its fine marble pillars, once entirely covered with frescoes, which had since been badly restored. Two waiters were conversing in Italian, which I translate as follows:

'Are the old couple going to eat in their room? They never give notice. What a nuisance, I don't know whether to reserve their table (*non so se bisogna conservar loro la tavola*). Oh well, who cares if they do come down and find that it's taken! I can't understand why we invite *forestieri* like them to stay in such a chic hotel. They are not our kind of people.'

Despite his disdain, the waiter would have preferred to know what decision to take about the table, and he was on the point of sending the liftboy up to their floor to find out, when, before he had time to ask, the answer was given: he had just spotted the old lady entering the room. Despite the sad and tired air that the weight of passing years bestows, and despite a sort of red, leprous eczema covering her face, I had no difficulty in recognizing beneath her bonnet, in her black tunic, created by W***,[2] but looking to the uninitiated as if it belonged to an old concierge, the Marquise de Villeparisis. As chance would have it, the place where I stood studying the remains of a fresco on the fine marble wall was behind the very table where Mme de Villeparisis had just sat down.

'So M. de Villeparisis will soon be down. During the month that they've spent here they have only once eaten separately,' said the waiter.

I was wondering with which of her relatives it was she was travelling and whom they were calling M. de Villeparisis, when, a few moments later, I saw him approach her table and sit down beside her. It was her former lover, M. de Norpois.

His advanced age had affected the timbre of his voice, but on the other hand had made his language, formerly so reserved, truly intemperate. Perhaps the cause should be sought in the ambitions that he felt he no longer had time to achieve and which filled him with all the more vehemence and excitement; perhaps in the fact that, abandoned by the political life which he had longed to engage in, he believed, with the naïvety born of desire, that his withering criticism of those he aspired to replace would drive them into retirement. Thus we see politicians convinced that the cabinet to which they have not been appointed cannot last out the week. It would in any case be excessive to claim that M. de Norpois had entirely forgotten the traditional usage of diplomatic language. As soon as conversation turned to 'affairs of state', he became once more, as we shall see, the man whom we previously knew, but for the rest of the time he held forth about one rival or another with the senile violence that drives some octogenarians to run after women, despite being in no position to cause them harm.

For a few moments Mme de Villeparisis remained silent as if an old woman's fatigue made it difficult for her to return to the present from reminiscence of the past. Then, with the sort of quite practical question that bears the hallmark of the aftermath of reciprocal love, she asked:

'Did you go to Salviati's?'[3]

'Yes.'

'Will they send it tomorrow?'

'I brought the bowl home myself. I'll show you it after dinner. Let's look at the menu.'

'Have you instructed the brokers to deal with my Suez shares?'

'No, the stock market has no time for the moment to invest in anything but oil. But there is no cause for concern, given the excellent state of the economy. Here's the menu. There's mullet for the first course. Shall we have some?'

'I'll have it myself, but you know that you mustn't. Ask for a risotto instead. Except that they don't know how to cook it.'

'That doesn't matter. Waiter, bring some mullet for Madam to start with and a risotto for me.'

They fell silent again for a while.

'By the way, I've brought you some newspapers, the *Corriere della Sera*, the *Gazzetta del Popolo*,[4] etcetera. Did you know that a diplomatic reshuffle is confidently predicted and that the prime scapegoat is rumoured to be Paléologue,[5] who is notoriously inadequate in Serbia? They say he'll be replaced by Lozé,[6] which would leave a vacancy in Constantinople. But', M. de Norpois hastened to add bitterly, 'for an embassy of this scope, where it is quite evident that come what may Great Britain will always have to be seated at the head of the negotiating table, it would be advisable to seek out men of experience better equipped to detect the snares laid by the enemies of our British ally than the diplomats of the new school, who are bound to fall headlong into the traps.' The irritable loquacity with which M. de Norpois uttered these last words was inspired above all by the fact that the newspapers, instead of mentioning his name as he had advised them, gave as 'leading candidate' a youthful minister of foreign affairs. 'God knows what kind of tortuous manœuvres they use to prevent men of maturity from placing themselves *in loco* and *situ* of more or less incapable new recruits! I have known quite enough of all these so-called diplomats of the empirical school, who placed all their hopes in a trial run that soon ran out of steam. There is no doubt at all, if the government so lacks wisdom as to place the reins of state in unsteady hands, that there will always be a conscript ready to answer the call of duty with the cry of "present!". But, who knows' (and M. de Norpois appeared to know all too well of whom he was talking) 'whether the same reaction might not be obtained if peradventure one were to seek out some veteran replete with knowledge and skill. As I see it, and everyone will have his own interpretation, the Constantinople posting should be accepted only on settlement of our outstanding problems with Germany. We owe nothing to anyone, and it is unacceptable that every six months we should be inveigled over our dead bodies into fraudulent procedures in order to pronounce some spurious acquittal, advocated as usual by a venal press. This must cease, and it is natural that a man of great value, who has proved his worth, a man who, dare I say, has the ear of the Emperor, should enjoy more authority than any to bring the conflict to its ultimate conclusion.'

A gentleman who had finished dining greeted M. de Norpois.

'Why, if it isn't Prince Foggi!' said the Marquis.

'I'm afraid that I'm not sure who you mean,' sighed Mme de Villeparisis.

'But of course you do, it's Prince Odon. He's the actual brother-in-law of your cousin Mme Doudeauville. Surely you remember that I hunted with him at Bonnétable?'

'Oh, Odon! Is he the one that went in for painting?'

'Not in the least, he's the one who married the sister of the Grand Duke of N***.'

M. de Norpois held Mme de Villeparisis steadily in his gaze while he said all this, with the rather disagreeable tone of a teacher displeased with his pupil.

When the Prince had finished his coffee and left his table, M. de Norpois rose and walked meaningfully towards him, then, moving to one side with a lordly gesture, introduced him to Mme de Villeparisis. And during the few minutes that the Prince stood talking to them, M. de Norpois's blue eyes subjected Mme de Villeparisis to the relentless surveillance borne of the indulgence or sanctions of a former lover, and above all of fear that she might indulge in one of the lapses in linguistic propriety which he appreciated but dreaded. Whenever she said something inaccurate to the Prince, he corrected her remarks and looked straight into the obedient eyes of the subjugated Marquise with the sustained intensity of a hypnotist.

A waiter came to tell me that my mother was waiting for me. I went over to her and apologized to Mme Sazerat, explaining that I had been amused to see Mme de Villeparisis. On hearing this name, Mme Sazerat turned pale and seemed about to faint. She struggled to keep her composure:

'Mme de Villeparisis, Mlle de Bouillon?' she enquired.

'Yes.'

'Couldn't I look at her for a moment? I have dreamed of this all my life.'

'Yes, but don't take too long, Madam, for she will soon have finished dining. But why should she interest you so?'

'Because it was Mme de Villeparisis, the Duchesse d'Havré by her first marriage, as beautiful as an angel but as wicked as a witch, who drove my father mad, ruined him, then left him forthwith. And yet! Although she acted like a common whore and caused me and my family to live in straitened circumstances in Combray, now that my father is dead, I console myself with the thought that he loved the most beautiful woman of his day, and since I have never seen her, despite everything it will be a relief . . .'

I led Mme Sazerat, who was trembling with emotion, to the restaurant and pointed out Mme de Villeparisis.

But, like the blind, who direct their eyes everywhere but where they should, Mme Sazerat failed to focus her gaze on Mme de Villeparisis's dinner-table, and sought out another corner of the room.

'Well, she must have left, I can't see her where you say.'

And she continued to hunt for the detestable, adorable vision that had haunted her imagination for so long.

'No she hasn't, she's at the second table.'

'We must be starting our count from different ends. At what I call the second table there's only an old gentleman sitting beside a horrid little old lady with a red face and a hunchback.'

'That's her!'

Meanwhile, Mme de Villeparisis had asked M. de Norpois to invite Prince Foggi to be seated, and the three of them had struck up an amiable conversation. Politics were mentioned. The Prince declared that he was unconcerned by the fate of the cabinet and that he intended to stay in Venice for at least a week. He hoped that by then any ministerial crisis would have been averted.

At first Prince Foggi thought that these political issues were of no interest to M. de Norpois, for the latter, who had until then expressed himself so vehemently, had suddenly adopted an almost angelic silence, which seemed only likely to flower, if his voice were restored, into some melodious, innocent song by Mendelssohn or César Franck. The Prince also thought that this silence was due to the inhibitions of a Frenchman unwilling to discuss Italian affairs in the presence of an Italian. Here the Prince was entirely mistaken. In M. de Norpois's case, silence and an air of indifference had always been the sign not of inhibition but the customary prelude to his involvement in an important affair. As we have seen, the Marquis's goal was no less than Constantinople, and a prior settlement of the German question, in which matter he hoped to put pressure on the cabinet in Rome. Indeed the Marquis judged that his accomplishing an act bearing international repercussions might form a noble climax to his career, and perhaps even open the way to new honours, or tasks of a difficulty that he had not yet eschewed. For old age removes the ability to act, but not to desire. It is only in a third phase that those who live to a great age renounce desire, after being obliged to abandon action. They no longer stand for such petty elections as that of President of the Republic, where they so often formerly strove to succeed. They are content merely to go out, to eat, and to read the newspapers. They have outlived themselves.

In order to put the Marquis at ease and show him that he considered him a compatriot, the Prince started to speak of possible successors to the present Prime Minister, who would have a difficult task ahead of them. Only when Prince Foggi had cited more than twenty names of politicians whom he considered of ministerial capacity, which the former ambassador listened to without moving, half-closing the lids of his blue eyes, did M. de Norpois finally break his silence to utter the words which were to fuel conversation in ambassadorial circles for twenty years to come and which later, when they had been forgotten, would be exhumed by some personality signing themselves 'an insider', or 'Testis'[7] or 'Machiavelli' in a newspaper where the very oblivion into which they had sunk provided the impetus to generate a new sensation. So, Prince Foggi having cited these twenty-odd names for the benefit of a diplomat who remained as silent and motionless as a deaf man, M de Norpois raised his head slightly and, using the formula that had inspired his most influential diplomatic interventions, albeit this time with exceptional boldness and less brevity, finally asked, 'And has nobody mentioned the name of M. Giolitti?'[8] On hearing these words, the scales fell away from Prince Foggi's eyes; he heard the murmuring of celestial voices. Then suddenly M. de Norpois started to talk of this and that, with no concern for the noise he was making, as when, after the last note of a sublime Beethoven aria has sounded, nobody minds speaking out loud or going to collect his coat from the cloakroom. He made the transition even more brutal by begging the Prince to transmit his respects to their Majesties the King and the Queen when next he might see them, a parting shot matching the effect of someone shouting at the end of a concert, 'Coachman Auguste, from the rue de Belloy!' We cannot say what were Prince Foggi's precise impressions. He was certainly delighted to have heard this masterpiece: 'And has nobody mentioned the name of M. Giolitti?' For M. de Norpois, whose finest qualities had been extinguished or disrupted by age, had none the less perfected as he grew older his 'air of bravado', as certain musicians, with most of their faculties in decline, acquire towards the end of their days a perfect virtuosity in chamber music which they had not previously possessed.

At all events, Prince Foggi, who had intended to spend two weeks in Venice, returned to Rome that very same day and was received a few days later in audience by the King to discuss some properties, which I believe we have mentioned, that the Prince possessed in Sicily. The cabinet hung on for longer than anyone had predicted. When it fell, the King took advice from various statesmen as to who should lead the new cabinet. Then he sent for M. Giolitti, who accepted. Three months later a newspaper related Prince Foggi's interview with M. de Norpois. The conversation was reported in the terms that we have given, with the difference that instead of saying, 'M. de Norpois asked subtly', the article read: 'said with his notoriously subtle and charming smile'. M. de Norpois judged that 'subtly' already had explosive force enough for a diplomat and that this addendum was intemperate, to say the least. He had in fact asked the Quai d'Orsay to issue an official denial, but the Quai d'Orsay was out of its depth. For indeed, as soon as the interview had been revealed, M. Barrère[9] telephoned Paris several times a day to complain that there was an unofficial ambassador at the Quirinal and to report the displeasure that this fact had caused all over Europe. This displeasure was non-existent, but the various ambassadors were too polite to contradict M. Barrère when he assured them that everyone was outraged. M. Barrère, who brooked no counsel but his own, took their courteous silence for consent. He telegraphed Paris immediately to say: 'HAVE HAD AN HOUR-LONG CONVERSATION WITH THE MARQUIS VISCONTI-VENOSTA',[10] etc. His secretaries were at their wits' end.

Yet M. de Norpois benefited from the devoted services of a most ancient French newspaper,[11] which had even, in 1870 when he was French ambassador in a German country, done him a great favour. This newspaper, and especially its anonymous leading article, was admirably written. But, paradoxically, it aroused infinitely more interest when this leader (dubbed the 'Paris première' in those far-off days, and called now, we know not why, an 'editorial') was badly phrased, with endless repetitions of words. Then everyone felt moved, realizing that the article had been 'inspired', perhaps by M. de Norpois, perhaps by some other fashionable grand master. Anticipating later events in Italy, we might show how M. de Norpois used this newspaper in 1870, to no avail, one might feel, since the war none the less took place; but very effectively, in the opinion of M. de Norpois, whose axiom was that above all one should prepare public opinion. His articles, where every word was carefully weighed, resembled those optimistic medical bulletins published immediately after the death of the patient. For instance, in 1870, when mobilization was almost complete, M. de Norpois, still in the wings, of course, had judged it necessary to send this famous newspaper the following editorial:

'The prevailing opinion in official circles would appear to be that, since yesterday, towards the middle of the afternoon, the situation, without of course assuming an alarming aspect, might well be considered serious and even, from certain angles, susceptible of being judged critical. M. de Norpois is believed to have held several discussions with the King of Prussia, in order to examine in a spirit of firmness and reconciliation, and in the most concrete terms, the various causes of tension, if one may call them such. As we go to press we have unfortunately received no news as to whether their Excellencies have been able to come to an agreement which might serve as the basis of a diplomatic settlement.

'Latest news: it has been learned with satisfaction in well-informed circles that Franco-Prussian relations have apparently experienced a slight improvement. The most important factor would seem to be a meeting of twenty minutes' duration *unter den Linden* between M. de Norpois and the English ambassador. This news is considered by those with access to inside information to be satisfactory.' (The German word *befriedigend* had been added in brackets after its equivalent, 'satisfactory'). And the following day the editorial read: 'Despite all the subtlety of M. de Norpois, who is praised by all for the skilful efforts which he has managed to deploy in the defence of the imprescriptible interests of France, a breakdown in relations appears to be virtually impossible to avoid, if one may say so.'

The newspaper could not forgo the opportunity of following such an editorial with several commentaries, sent of course by M. de Norpois. The reader may perhaps have noticed how in the passages quoted the 'passive' mood was one of the ambassador's favourite grammatical forms for diplomatic writing. ('Considerable importance appears to be attached', rather than 'it seems that people attach considerable importance'). But the present indicative, taken not in its habitual sense but in that of the old 'optative', was no less close to M. de Norpois's heart. The commentaries that followed the editorial were these:

'Never has the public demonstrated a more admirable calm.' (M. de Norpois would have preferred this to be true, but feared that the opposite was the case). 'The people are tired of sterile agitation and have been satisfied to learn that His Majesty's government would accept its responsibilities in the case of whatever eventuality should materialize. The people ask (optative mood) for no more. To their admirably steady nerve, which already bodes well for success, we would yet add a piece of news sure to reassure public opinion, if need there were. We have been assured that M. de Norpois, who for reasons of health has long been expected to travel to Paris to undertake a brief cure, has left Berlin, where he felt that his presence was no longer necessary. Latest news: His Majesty the Emperor left Compiègne for Paris this morning in order to confer with the Marquis de Norpois, the Minister for War and Field-Marshal Bazaine, in whom the public places especial confidence. H M the Emperor has called off the dinner that he was to host in honour of his sister-in-law the Duchess of Alba. This measure has produced on everyone who has been informed of it a particularly favourable impression. The Emperor has reviewed his troops, whose enthusiasm beggars description. Several armed units, which were mobilized the moment that the royal family reached Paris, are standing ready to depart for the Rhine in case the eventuality should arise.'

Sometimes at dusk on my return to the hotel I felt that the Albertine of former times, although invisible, was none the less locked deep inside me, as if in the lead-lined cells of some inner Venice,[12] where from time to time an incident would shake the heavy lid enough to give me a glimpse into the past.

Thus for instance one evening a letter from my broker reopened for an instant the gates of the prison where Albertine lay living within me, but so far and so deep that she remained inaccessible to me. Since her death I was no longer engaged in the speculations that I had undertaken in order to have more money to spend on her. But time had passed; the received wisdom of the previous era was nullified by the present one, as had happened in former times to M. Thiers,[13] who declared that the railway could never succeed, thus the shares of which M. de Norpois had said, 'Doubtless their yield is hardly substantial, but at least the capital will never depreciate,' were often those that had lost the most value. If only for the English Consols and the Say Refineries, I had to pay the brokers such considerable differentials, not to mention the interest and the sums carried forward, that I suddenly took it into my head to sell everything, and found myself forthwith the owner of barely one-fifth of the wealth that I had inherited from my grandmother and had still possessed while Albertine was alive. This was known to those of our family and acquaintances who still lived in Combray, and because they knew that I frequented the Marquis de Saint-Loup and the Guermantes, people said, 'That's where delusions of grandeur lead you.' They would have been quite astonished to learn that it was for a young woman of such modest extraction as Albertine, more or less a protégée of my grandmother's old piano teacher, Vinteuil, that I had been speculating. Moreover in this world of Combray, where everyone is classified once and for all time, as in the Hindu caste system, according to his known income, they were unable to conceive of the great liberty that reigned in the world of the Guermantes, where wealth was considered of no importance, where poverty could be regarded as unpleasant but as in no way more undignified, and having no more impact on one's social status, than an upset stomach. No doubt, on the other hand, people in Combray imagined that Saint-Loup and M. de Guermantes were ruined noblemen with mortgaged châteaux to whom I lent money, whereas, if I had been ruined, they would have been the first to offer me assistance, albeit to no avail. As for my present, relative ruin, I was all the more embarrassed since my Venetian pursuits had just recently focused on a girl selling glassware, whose blooming complexion offered my ravished eyes a whole scale of amber tones, inspiring in me such a desire to see her every day that, realizing that my mother and I would soon be leaving Venice, I had resolved to try to find her some situation in Paris which would enable me not to be separated from her. The beauty of her seventeen years was so noble and radiant that she became a virtual Titian painting to be acquired before leaving. Yet would the reduced income available to me be sufficient to tempt her to leave her country and come to live in Paris at my entire disposal? But as I finished reading my broker's letter, a phrase where he said: '*I will take care of any sums to be carried forward*' brought to mind an almost equally hypocritical and professional expression, that the bath-house girl at Balbec had used when speaking of Albertine: '*I took care of her personally*,' she had said. And these words, which I had never before recalled, had the effect of crying 'Open, Sesame', making the hinges of the dungeon spring open. But a moment later they swung back again to reincarcerate the prisoner – whom I was not guilty of not wanting to visit, since I could no longer see her or remember her, and since people exist for us only in the idea that we have of them – who for an instant had been rendered more touching by my neglect, although she could not know of this: for one brief flash I had felt nostalgia for that already distant time when I suffered night and day from the company of her memory. On another occasion, at San Giorgio dei Schiavoni,[14] an eagle beside one of the apostles, and worked in the same style, revived the memory, and a great deal of the suffering caused by the two rings whose similarity Françoise had discovered, although I had never discovered who had given them to Albertine. One evening however it appeared that events were going to rekindle my love. Just as our gondola stopped at the steps of the hotel, the porter handed me a despatch that the telegraph boy had tried three times to bring round to me, for, because of the inexactitude of the name of the addressee (which I understood, however, despite the distortions wrought by the Italian operators, to be my own), I was required to sign a receipt certifying that the telegram was indeed intended for me. I opened it as soon as I was in my room, and running my eye down a text full of mistranscribed words, I managed to read the following: 'DEAR FRIEND YOU BELIEVE ME DEAD, MY APOLO- GIES, NEVER MORE ALIVE, WOULD LIKE TO SEE YOU TO DISCUSS

MARRIAGE, WHEN DO YOU RETURN? AFFECTIONATELY, ALBERTINE.'
Then occurred, but in inverse order, what had happened with my
grandmother; when I learned *the fact* that my grandmother was dead,
I at first felt no sorrow. And I had really suffered from her death only
when involuntary memories had rendered her living again for me.
Now that Albertine was no longer alive in my thoughts, the news that
she was alive did not bring me the joy that I would have expected.
Albertine had been for me but a bundle of thoughts, she had survived
her material death as long as these thoughts remained alive within me;
on the contrary now that these thoughts were dead, Albertine did not
come back to life for me along with the resuscitation of her body. And
on realizing that I felt no joy at finding her still alive, that I no longer
loved her, I should have been more overwhelmed than someone who,
looking at himself in a mirror, after months of travel or illness, realizes
that he has white hair or an expression altered by age. This upsets him
because it means: the man that I was, that fair-haired young man, no
longer exists, I am someone else. And is it not just as profound a
change, just as total a death of the self that one was, with its complete
substitution of this new self for the old, to see a wrinkled face coiffed
with a white wig? But we no more lament having become someone
else with the passing of the years and the fullness of time than we
lament being during the same period a sequence of contradictory
beings, the wicked, the sensitive, the fragile, the crass, the disinterested
or the ambitious that we are in turn day after day. And the reason for
which we do not lament is the same, it is because the self who is in
eclipse – momentarily in the latter examples, which affect our character,
permanently in the case I have mentioned and whenever the passions
are concerned – is no longer there to deplore the other self, the one
who at that moment, or henceforth, is entirely you; the crass man
laughs at his crassness because we are now that crass man, and the
absent-minded man feels no sorrow at losing his memory, precisely
because he has forgotten all about it.

I would have been incapable of reviving Albertine because I was
incapable of reviving myself, of reviving my former self. Life, with its
habit of changing the face of the world through incessant but infinitely
small adjustments, had not told me the day after the death of Albertine

to 'Become someone else', but, through changes too imperceptible to allow me even to notice the fact that I was changing, had renewed almost everything about me, in such a way that my thoughts were already accustomed to their new master – my new self – by the time they noticed that he had changed; and that it was he who mattered. My affection for Albertine and my jealousy depended, as we have seen, on the irradiation by association of ideas of certain kernels of sweet or painful impressions, on the memory of Mlle Vinteuil at Montjouvain, on the gentle good-night kisses that Albertine bestowed on my neck. But as these impressions grew weaker, the vast field of impressions that they dyed with their anxious or soothing tints had recovered their neutral tones. Once oblivion had captured one or two high peaks of suffering and pleasure, the resistance of my love was vanquished, I no longer loved Albertine. I tried to call her to mind. When two days after Albertine's departure I was horrified to find that I had survived forty-eight hours without her, that was an accurate foreboding. The same thing had happened when on a previous occasion I had written to Gilberte, thinking: if this goes on for another two years, I shall love her no longer. And if when Swann had asked me to see Gilberte again, I had felt as uncomfortable as if I were asked to welcome her back from the dead, in Albertine's case death – or what I had believed to be death – had functioned to the same effect as the prolonged separation in the case of Gilberte. Death functions only as absence. The monster whose appearance had made my love tremble, oblivion, had indeed finally, or so I believed, devoured it. Not only did the news that she was alive not reawaken my love, not only did it allow me to note how far I had travelled down the road to indifference, but it instantaneously accelerated the process so abruptly that I wondered retrospectively if formerly, the opposite news, that of Albertine's death, had not acted inversely, by completing the process of her departure, exciting my love and delaying its decline. And indeed, as soon as knowing that she was alive and that I could reach her had made her suddenly worthless to me, I wondered whether Françoise's insinuations, the separation itself, and even her death (imagined but believed to be real) had not prolonged my love, in so far as the efforts of third parties or even fate to separate us from a woman do no more than attach us more closely to her. Now it was the opposite that happened. Actually I did try to recall her, and perhaps because I had only to say the word to have her all to myself, the memory that recurred was that of a girl already quite stout and mannish, in whose faded features there sprouted like a seed the profile of Mme Bontemps. What she might have done with Andrée or other girls was no longer of interest to me. I no longer suffered from the malady that I had so long believed to be incurable, and in fact I might have guessed as much. Of course missing a mistress, and the jealousy that lingers on afterwards, are physical illnesses just as much as tuberculosis or leukaemia. Yet we need to distinguish among the physical maladies between those that are caused by a purely physical agency and those that act on the body only through the medium of the intellect. Above all, if the part of our intellect that serves as the means of transmission is memory – that is if the cause is annulled or removed – however cruel our suffering is, however deep seems the disturbance wrought on our organism, it is extremely rare, given the power of thought to renew itself or rather its inability to remain unchanged, unlike bodily tissues, for the prognosis to be unfavourable. After a period of time within which a patient suffering from cancer would have died, it is very rare for a widow or an unconsolable father not to have recovered. I recovered. Should I for the sake of that girl, who now appeared to me so bloated and who certainly must have aged as all the girls that she had loved had aged, should I for her sake renounce the dazzling girl who was my memory of yesterday, my hope for tomorrow (and to whom I would be unable to offer anything if married to Albertine), should renounce this 'new Albertine', '*non point telle que l'ont vue les Enfers*' '*mais fidèle, mais fière et même un peu farouche*'?[15] It was she who now was what Albertine had formerly been: my love for Albertine had been only a passing form of my devotion to youth. We think we love a girl, and in her we love no more, alas, than that dawn which their face momentarily reflects. The night passed. In the morning I returned the despatch to the hotel porter saying that it had been handed to me by mistake and that it wasn't addressed to me. He told me that the fact that it had been opened would cause him problems, that I would do better to keep it; I put it back in my pocket but promised myself that I would act as if I had never received it.

I had definitively stopped loving Albertine. In such fashion this love, after diverging so much from what I had foreseen, in the light of my love for Gilberte; after causing me to make such a long and painful detour, finally in its turn, after claiming exemption, surrendered, as had my love for Gilberte, to the universal rule of oblivion.

But then I wondered: I used to value Albertine more than myself; I no longer value her now because for a period of time I have ceased to see her. But my desire not to be separated from myself by death, to revive after death, was a desire unlike the desire never to be separated from Albertine, it continued to last. Was that because I believed I was more precious than she, because when I loved her, I loved myself more? No, it was because in ceasing to see her, I had ceased to love her, and because I had not ceased to love myself since my daily relationship with myself had not been interrupted as had that with Albertine. But what if the relationship with my body, and with myself, had also been interrupted? Surely the result would be the same. Our love of life is no more than an old affair that we do not know how to discontinue. Its strength lies in its permanence. But death, which interrupts it, will cure us of our desire for immortality.

After lunch, whenever I did not set out to wander around Venice alone, I got ready to go out with my mother, and I went up to my bedroom to fetch the exercise books in which I would take notes for the study of Ruskin that I was engaged in.[16] From the abrupt angles of the wall whose pressure distorted the corners of the room, I could sense the restrictions imposed by the sea and the scant provision of land. And as I went down to meet my mother, who was waiting for me, at this time of day when in Combray it was such a pleasure to sample the imminent sun in the darkness preserved by the closed shutters, here from top to bottom of the marble staircase, where one had no more idea than one would in a Renaissance painting whether it was built inside a palace or raised on a galley, the same coolness and the same feeling of external radiance were achieved thanks to the canvas blinds wafting before the ever-open windows, through which in a constant draught the warm air and the greenish sunlight slid as if on a floating surface, evoking the movements, the brightness and the instability of the neighbouring waves. Most often it was St Mark's that

I set out for, and with all the more pleasure because the church, which required a gondola to reach it, did not represent for me a mere monument, but as it were the terminus of a marine journey over springtime waters, with which St Mark's formed an indivisible, living whole. My mother and I entered the baptistery, both of us treading underfoot the marble and glass mosaics which paved it, and seeing before us the wide arches, whose waisted, pink surfaces have been slightly inflected by the passage of time, which, where time has respected the freshness of its colouring, lends the church an air of having been constructed from a soft and malleable material like the wax of giant honeycomb cells; but where, on the contrary, time has hardened the material and where artists have enhanced it with open-work and gold, it takes on the guise of some precious binding in Cordoban leather of the colossal gospel formed by Venice. My mother, seeing that I needed to spend a long time studying the mosaics representing the baptism of Christ and feeling the ice-cold air that fell around us in the baptistery, threw a shawl over my shoulders. When I was in Balbec with Albertine, I thought that she illustrated one of those misguided illusions that cloud the minds of so many people unable to think clearly, when she told me of the pleasure – which I judged entirely unfounded – that she would derive from seeing a picture in my company. Today I am sure that this pleasure, if not of seeing, then at least of having seen something beautiful in the company of certain persons, does exist. The time has now come for me when, on remembering the baptistery, facing the waters of the Jordan where St John immersed Christ while the gondola awaited us by the Piazzetta, I cannot remain indifferent to the fact that there was by my side in this cool twilight a woman clothed in mourning, whose respectful but enthusiastic fervour matched that of the elderly woman who can be seen in Venice in Carpaccio's *St Ursula*,[17] and that nothing can ever again remove this red-cheeked, sad-eyed woman, in her black veils, from the softly lit sanctuary of St Mark's where I am certain to find her, because I have reserved a place there in perpetuity, alongside the mosaics, for her, for my mother. Carpaccio, whom I have just cited, and who was the painter that we preferred to visit when I was not working at St Mark's, on one occasion almost revived my love for

Albertine. It was the first time that I had seen *The Patriarch of Grado exorcizing one possessed*.[18] I was looking at the admirable carmine and violet sky against which stand those tall, inlaid chimneys, whose waisted forms and red, tulip-like blooms call to mind so many paintings of Venice by Whistler. Then my eyes travelled from the old wooden Rialto bridge to the fifteenth-century Ponte Vecchio and its marble palaces decorated with gilded capitals, and returned to the Canal where the boats are steered by youths wearing pink doublets and caps topped with osprey feathers, almost identical to those which faithfully recalled Carpaccio in the dazzling ballet *The Legend of St Joseph*[19] by Sert, Strauss and Kessler. And finally, before leaving the painting, my eyes returned to the quay, which was teeming with scenes from the Venetian life of the time. I saw the barber wiping his razor, the negro carrying his barrel, the Muslims in conversation, Venetian noblemen dressed in ample brocade or damask robes and cherry-coloured velvet caps, when suddenly I felt a slight tug at my heart. On the back of one of the Companions of la Calza,[20] recognizable from the gold and pearl embroidery which inscribed on their collar or their sleeve the proud guild of which they were members, I had just recognized the coat that Albertine had worn to accompany me to Versailles in an open carriage, that evening when I was far from suspecting that hardly fifteen hours were to separate me from the moment of her departure. As she was always ready for anything, when I had asked her to leave, on the sad day that in her last letter she was to name: *twice twilit, since night was soon to fall and we would part*, she had slung over her shoulders a Fortuny coat that she was to take away with her the following morning and that I had never since recalled to mind. Now it was in this painting by Carpaccio that this brilliant scion of Venice had found it, it was from the shoulders of this Companion of la Calza that he had unclasped it, in order to drape it over the shoulders of so many Parisian ladies, who were doubtless as ignorant as I had been of the fact that the original could be found among a group of aristocrats in the foreground of the *Patriarch of Grado* in one of the rooms of the Accademia in Venice. I had recognized it all, and the forgotten coat having restored to me, as I looked at it, the eyes and the heart of the man who that night was to leave for Versailles with Albertine, for a few seconds

I was invaded with indistinct, impermanent feelings of desire and melancholy.

And finally there were days when my mother and I were not content to stay in the museums and the churches of Venice, and so one day when the weather was particularly fine, wanting to see those Vices and Virtues whose reproductions M. Swann had given me, and which were probably still pinned upon the wall of the study in our house at Combray, we travelled out to Padua; after crossing the gardens of the Arena Chapel under the midday sun, I entered the chapel with its Giottos[21] where the whole ceiling vault and the background of the frescoes are so blue that it seems as if the radiant daylight had crossed the threshold at the same time as the visitor and had come for a moment to seek out shade and fresh air for its limpid sky; whose purity, once cleansed of the gilding applied by the sunlight, took on only a very slightly darker tone, as happens during those brief moments of respite which interrupt the finest days, when, without a cloud in sight, the sun averts its gaze for a moment and the azure sky, growing still softer, darkens. In the sky thus transposed onto a blue-toned stone heaven, I caught my first glimpse of angels in flight, for M. Swann had given me reproductions only of the Virtues and Vices and not of the frescoes that retrace the story of Christ and the Virgin Mary. And now I detected in the flight of these angels the same effect of concrete and literally real action as I had in the postures of Charity or Envy. With all the celestial fervour, or at least, the well-behaved, childish concentration, that joins their little hands in prayer, the angels in the Arena Chapel are represented rather as if they were a distinct species of flighted fowl that had actually existed and had been portrayed in Old and New Testament times. These small creatures can always be relied on to flutter in escort ahead of any passing saint; there are always one or two in the air in readiness, and, since they are real creatures, actually able to fly, you can see them taking off, climbing and banking, looping the loop with the greatest of ease, diving head-first towards the ground with a great flurry of wings designed to keep them in the air against the laws of gravity, and they call to mind much more some extinct variety of bird, or the young pupils of Roland Garros[22] learning to glide, than angels of the art of the Renaissance or later periods, whose wings are purely emblematic and whose deportment is usually no different from that of flightless celestial beings.

On returning to the hotel, I met some young women, mostly from Austria, who had come to Venice to enjoy the first fine days of its flowerless spring. One of them had features that, without reminding me of Albertine, appealed to me through the same freshness of complexion and the same cheerful, humorous eyes. Soon I felt that I was starting to say the same things to her as I had said to Albertine at first, and that I was hiding the same pain when she told me that she would not see me the next day, for she was going to Verona, and immediately I too felt the desire to go to Verona. It was not to last, she was due to return to Austria and I would never see her again, but I was already vaguely jealous, as one is on starting to fall in love, and, while watching her charming, enigmatic face, I wondered if she too loved women, if what she shared with Albertine, the luminous complexion and bright eyes, the friendly, open airs that seduced everyone around her, and which arose as much from her total lack of interest in the actions of others as from the exaggeratedly childish lies with which she attempted to disguise her own actions, was not part of the morphological constitution of women who love other women. Was this the part of her that escaped my rational analysis, attracted me and caused me anxiety (perhaps the deeper cause of my attraction through its drive towards potential suffering), that gave me when I saw her so much pleasure and sadness, like those invisible magnetic elements in the air of certain countries that cause us to feel so ill at ease? Alas, I was never to know. When I tried to read her expression I would have liked to say, 'You should tell me, I would be interested to learn one of the laws of human natural history,' but she would never tell me; she professed a particular repulsion for this vice and maintained a studied coldness with her female friends. This might even have been evidence that she had something to hide, perhaps she had been teased or ashamed because of it, and the airs she adopted in order to prevent people believing it were like the eloquent distance kept by animals from men who have beaten them. As for finding out about her life, this was impossible; even in Albertine's case I had taken so long to discover the slightest thing! It had taken her death to loosen people's tongues, so prudent and circumspect had Albertine been in her behaviour, just like this young woman! And was I sure of knowing anything even about Albertine? And then just as the conditions of life that we desire the most become of no interest to us if we cease to love the person who unknown to us made us desire them because she allowed us to live by her side and, as far as we were able, to give her pleasure, so it is with certain kinds of intellectual curiosity. The scientific importance that I placed in knowing what kind of desire was hidden beneath the pale pink petals of her cheek, in the sunless light of her pale eyes glowing like early dawn, in the days that she never discussed, would doubtless disappear when I no longer felt the slightest love for Albertine or when I no longer felt the slightest love for this young woman. In the evenings I went out alone, surrounded by this enchanted city where I found myself in the middle of unknown neighbourhoods like a character from the *Arabian Nights*. It was most unusual for me not to chance upon some spacious, unknown square of which no guide or traveller had informed me. I had plunged into a network of alleyways, the *calli*. In the evening, with their tall, waisted chimneys turning the brightest of pinks as they were caught in the sunlight, there was a whole garden in flower on the roof-tops, with such a variety of shades that it looked as if a connoisseur of tulips from Haarlem or Delft had planted a garden on top of the city. And moreover the sheer proximity of the houses made each window the frame which a kitchen-girl looked dreamily through, a girl sitting having her hair combed by an old woman, whose face, half-hidden in shadow, seemed that of a witch – creating from the poor, silent individual houses, huddled together because of the extreme narrowness of the *calli*, a virtual exhibition bringing a hundred Dutch paintings together. Squeezed up against each other, these *calli* divided each part of Venice, sectioning it between a canal and the lagoon into a branching lattice of cracks, as if it had crystallized into this myriad of fragile, intricate forms. Suddenly, at the end of one of these little streets, the crystalline matter seemed to have produced a swelling. A vast, sumptuous *campo* of a size that I certainly could not have guessed, let alone found room for in this network of little streets, stretched out before my eyes, surrounded by enchanting palaces, in the pale light of the moon. It was one of those architectural ensembles towards which in other towns you are guided by streets that lead there, pointing the way. Here it seemed deliberately hidden in a criss-cross of alleyways, like those palaces in Oriental tales where a character who was led there by night and taken back home before morning is unable to find the magical dwelling and finally believes that he saw it only in his dreams. The next day I set off in search of my beautiful nocturnal palace, I followed *calli* which all looked the same and refused to give me the slightest indication, except to lead me further astray. Occasionally a vague allusion that I thought I recognized led me to believe that I would then see appear, in all the solitude of its silent and solitary confinement, the beautiful, exiled square. At which moment the evil genie, having taken on the appearance of a new *calle*, caused me to retrace my steps against my better intentions, and I suddenly found myself led back to the Grand Canal. And since between the memory of a dream and the memory of something real there is no great difference, I finally started wondering whether the strange drift into this sombre fragment of Venetian crystallization, revealing to my moonlit meditations a great square surrounded by Romantic palaces, had not occurred while I was asleep.

But it was the desire not to lose for ever certain women, rather than certain squares, that kept me, for as long as I was in Venice, in a state of agitation which turned feverish the day my mother had fixed for our departure, when at the end of the day, our trunks having already left for the station by gondola, I read in the hotel register of guests due to arrive at the hotel the name of the *Baroness Putbus and her entourage*. Immediately the impression of all the hours of carnal pleasure that our departure would cause me to miss raised this desire, lying endemic within me, to the status of an emotion, in a flood of vagueness and melancholia; I asked my mother to postpone our departure for a few days; but the expression on her face, showing that she did not for a moment entertain my plea, or even take it seriously, aroused in my nerves, already exacerbated by the Venetian springtime, my old desire to resist a fictitious plot hatched against me by my parents, who imagined that I would be forced to obey, awakened that urge to struggle which formerly drove me brutally to impose my will on those whom I most loved, even if it meant that I would hasten to obey their

wishes as soon as I had obtained their submission. I told my mother
that I would not leave, but she, believing it more subtle to look as if
she thought that I was not speaking in earnest, did not even deign to
reply. I insisted that she would soon see whether I was in earnest or
not. The porter came to deliver three letters, two for her, and one for
me, which I put in my wallet with all the others without even looking
at the envelope, and when the time came for her to leave for the
station, followed by all my effects, I asked for a drink to be served me
on the balcony overlooking the Canal and settled down to watch the
sunset, while a musician, on a boat moored opposite the hotel, sang
'*O sole mio*'.[23] The sun sank lower in the sky. My mother would have
nearly arrived at the station. Soon she would be gone, and I would be
alone in Venice, alone with the sad knowledge that I had upset her
and without her presence to console me. It was nearly time for the
train to leave. My irrevocable solitude loomed so large that it seemed
to me to have already started, and to be absolute. For I felt alone in
the world, alienated from all things, and I was not calm enough to
detach myself from my palpitating heart and impose some stability on
the world around me. The city I saw before me was still Venice. Its
personality and its name appeared to me as mendacious fictions that I
no longer had the heart to relate to its stones. The palaces appeared
reduced to their congruent parts and their portions of indifferent
marble, and the waters to a combination of nitrogen and hydrogen,
eternal and blind, anterior and exterior to Venice, ignorant of Turner
and the Doges. And yet this unexceptional place was as alien as a place
where you have just arrived, which does not yet know you, or a place
that you have left and that has already forgotten you. There was
nothing now that I could tell it about me, nothing of mine that I could
invest it with, it forced me to withdraw within myself, I was no more
than a beating heart and a mind anxiously following the words of '*O
sole mio*'. However much I tried to anchor my thoughts to the familiar
and beautiful curve of the Rialto, it appeared to me both proven and
banal that the bridge was not only inferior, but as alien to the idea that
I had gained of it as would be an actor whose blond wig and black
doublet failed to persuade me that essentially he was Hamlet. Like the
palaces, the Canal and the Rialto were bereft of the ideas that made

them original and were dissolved into their crudely material elements. But at the same time this mediocre place seemed far distant from me. In the dock of the Arsenal, for a perfectly scientific reason, its latitude, things took on a peculiar aspect, as they do, even when they seem similar to those of our own country, once they are exiled to foreign climes, revealing their otherness; I felt that this horizon, however close, barely an hour away, was a far-flung curve of the Earth's surface which the vagaries of travel had moored close beside me; so that the Arsenal dock, however trivial and distant, filled me with the same mixture of fear and disgust that I had experienced when as a child I accompanied my mother to the Deligny baths;[24] for in that fantastic site composed of dark waters, delimited neither by the sun nor by the heavens and yet whose cabin-bound surrounds made us feel in communion with invisible depths lurking beneath human bodies clad in bathing-costumes, I had wondered whether these depths, hidden from ordinary mortals by a series of sheds that prevented them from being seen from the street, did not provide a direct entrance to the neighbouring ice floes of the polar seas which already flowed through them, and if this narrow space were not precisely the open seas of the poles; this unsympathetic Venice, where I was to stay alone, seemed to me no less isolated and unreal, and it was my distress that the song '*O sole mio*', rising like a lament for the Venice I had known, seemed to call to witness. Doubtless, if I had wanted to catch up with my mother and take the train with her, I should have stopped listening to it, I would have had to make up my mind to leave without an instant's hesitation, but that was precisely what I could not do; I stayed motionless, incapable not only of rising to my feet but even of deciding that I wanted to stand up. My thoughts, most likely to avoid taking any decision, were entirely taken up in following the progress of the successive verses of '*O sole mio*', mentally singing along with the singer, anticipating the moments when his voice would soar in flight, and letting myself rise and then fall back with him. Doubtless I was not in the slightest bit interested in this trivial song, which I had heard a hundred times before. Listening to it religiously all the way through brought pleasure neither to myself nor to anyone else. And, finally, none of the motifs of this vulgar romance, all of which I knew in advance, could help me with the decision that I needed to take; although each of the verses which went by in turn became an obstacle to effectively taking that decision or rather obliged me to take the contrary decision not to leave, for it kept me waiting. In this way the intrinsically pleasureless business of listening to '*O sole mio*' became imbued with a profound, almost desperate sadness. I knew well enough that, in sitting there without moving, I was really taking the decision not to leave; but admitting to myself, 'I am not leaving', which I was unable to do in such direct terms, became possible for me in these other terms: 'I want to listen to one more verse of "*O sole mio*"'; but the practical significance of this figurative language did not escape me, and while I was telling myself 'All I am doing, actually, is listening to one more verse', I knew that this meant: 'I am going to stay in Venice on my own.' And it was perhaps this sadness, resembling a kind of cold numbness, which constituted the desperate but fascinating charm of the song. Each note that the singer launched, with a voice almost muscular in its strength and ostentation, struck me to the very heart; when the phrase with its low notes was consummated and the piece seemed to be over, the singer was not satisfied, and repeated it on a high note as if he felt bound to proclaim once again my solitude and despair. My mother must have arrived at the station. Soon she would be gone. I was choking with the anguish caused by this banal Rialto that was no longer the Rialto, with its view over the Canal that had shrunk now that the soul of Venice had drained away from it, by this song of despair that '*O sole mio*' had become, and which, thus declaimed before the inconstant palaces, finally made them crumble and reduced Venice to ruin; I was watching over the gradual realization of my misfortune, constructed artistically, unhurriedly, note by note by the singer, watched by the astonished sun, which had stopped still behind San Giorgio Maggiore, so that this crepuscular light was for ever to forge my trembling emotions and the singer's voice of bronze into an equivocal, unchangeable and poignant alloy in my memory.

In this way I remained motionless with my will-power dissolved, taking no apparent decision; doubtless at such moments the decision has already been taken: even our friends can often predict it. But we ourselves cannot, otherwise we would be saved much suffering.

But at last, from caverns darker than those from which more predictable comets are launched – thanks to the unsuspected defensive powers of inveterate habit, and the hidden reserves that it can suddenly mobilize and throw into the ring at the very last moment – my action suddenly materialized: I ran for dear life and reached the train after the doors had closed, but still in time to get on board and find my mother, flushed with emotion, holding back her tears, believing that I was not going to come. Then the train left and we saw Padua then Verona move up to the window, coming nearly into the station to wave us good-bye, and, since they were not leaving, they let us move away and went back to their usual occupations, one in her fields, the other on her hillside.

The hours passed. My mother was in no hurry to read the two letters which she had merely opened, and she tried to prevent me from getting out my wallet straight away to take out the letter that the hotel concierge had given me. She was always worried that I would find a journey too long and too tiring, and she put off until as late as possible, so as to give me something to do during the last hours, the moment when she would unpack the hard-boiled eggs, pass me the newspapers and unwrap the packet of books that she had bought to surprise me. First I watched my mother reading her letter with astonishment, then she raised her head, and her eyes seemed to struggle with a whole series of separate, incompatible memories that she could not manage to reconcile. Meanwhile I had recognized Gilberte's handwriting on my envelope. I opened it. Gilberte announced her marriage to Robert de Saint-Loup. She said that she had sent a telegram to me in Venice on this subject but had received no reply. I remembered how unreliable the Venetian telegraph service was reputed to be. I had never received her despatch. Suddenly my brain felt a fact that had lodged there in the guise of a memory leave its place to make room for another. The despatch that I had recently received and that I had thought came from Albertine was from Gilberte. Since the rather factitious originality of Gilberte's handwriting consisted principally in placing, in the line above the line she was writing, the crosses on her *t*'s, making them look as if they were underlining the words higher up, or making the dots on her *i*'s look as if they were breaks in the sentences of the line above, and on the other hand to insert in the lines below the tails and the curlicues of the words that were written above, it was natural enough that a telegraph clerk should have read the scrolls of the *s*'s or the *y*'s of the upper line as a final *'ine'* closing the name of Gilberte. The dot on the *i* of Gilberte had ridden up to make a dash. As for her *G*, it had the appearance of an *A* in Gothic script. The fact that in addition to this, two or three words had been misread, entangled as they were (besides, I myself had found some incomprehensible), was enough to explain the details of my error, and it was not even necessary. How many characters in each word does a person read when his mind is on other things and when he is already sure that he knows who the letter is from? How many words in each sentence? We guess as we read, we invent; everything stems from one initial error; those that follow (and this not only in reading letters and telegrams, not even only in all acts of reading), however extraordinary they may seem to someone who does not share the same starting-point, are natural enough. Thus it is that a great deal of what we believe to be true, not to mention the ultimate conclusions that, with equal perseverance and good faith, we draw from it, results from an initial misconception of the premiss.

CHAPTER 4

*A New Side to Robert de Saint-Loup*

'Oh, how incredible! said my mother. Listen, I know that at my age
one should no longer be surprised by anything, but I assure you that
nothing could surprise me more than the news in this letter. – Yes,
but listen to me, I replied, I don't know what it says, but whatever the
news, it cannot be more amazing than what I have just learned from
my letter. It's a marriage. Robert de Saint-Loup is going to marry
Gilberte Swann. – Ah!' my mother replied, then that must be what I
shall find in the other letter, the one that I haven't opened yet, for I
recognized your friend's writing.' And my mother smiled at me with
the tenderly concerned air that every event, however trivial, evoked
in her if it affected human beings capable of suffering, remembering,
and sharing others' mourning. Thus my mother smiled and spoke to
me with a gentle voice as if she feared that, if she treated the marriage
lightly, this might disparage the melancholy feelings it was likely to
evoke in Swann's widow and his daughter, as well as Robert's mother,
preparing to be separated from her son, on to whom my mother, out
of kindness and out of sympathy inspired by their kindness to me,
projected her own sensitivity, at once filial, conjugal and maternal.
'Wasn't I right to tell you that you would find nothing more amazing?
I asked her. – Well, actually, no, she replied gently, it is I who have
the most extraordinary news, if not 'la plus grande, la plus petite', for
that quotation from Mme de Sévigné made by people who knew
nothing else of her work exasperated your grandmother as much as
'La jolie chose que c'est de faner'.[1] We do not stoop to glean such
common-or-garden Sévigné. This letter announces the marriage of the
young Cambremer. – Oh, yes, I said, with no interest, to whom? But
in any case the nature of the bridegroom has already removed from

this marriage any element of excitement. – Unless the nature of the bride were to restore it? – And who is this bride? – Ah, if I tell you straight away you won't have deserved it, come on, try a little harder,' said my mother, seeing that we had not yet reached Turin and wanting to leave me something substantial to get my teeth into, and something to wash it down with. 'But how am I supposed to know? Is it someone brilliant? If Legrandin and his sister are pleased, we can be sure that it is a brilliant marriage. – I don't know about Legrandin, but the person who has told me of the marriage says that Mme de Cambremer is delighted. I don't know whether you will call it a brilliant marriage. For me it calls to mind those marriages from the days when a king could marry a shepherdess, except that the shepherdess is even less than a shepherdess, although very charming. Your grandmother would have been stupefied, if not displeased. – But whoever is this bride? – It is Mlle d'Oloron. – She sounds imposing, and most un-shepherdess-like, but I just don't see who you mean. It's a title that used to run in the Guermantes family. – Precisely, and it was granted by M. de Charlus to Jupien's niece when he adopted her. She it is who is due to marry the young Cambremer. – Jupien's niece! That's impossible! – It is virtue rewarded. It's a marriage from the end of a novel by George Sand,' said my mother. 'It's the wages of sin, it's a marriage from the end of a novel by Balzac,' I thought. 'After all, I said to my mother, when you come to think about it it is natural enough. It allows the Cambremers to drop anchor at the Guermantes', where they never dared hope pitch their tent; what is more, the child, since she was adopted by M. de Charlus, will have plenty of money, which was indispensable for the Cambremers since they had lost their own; and finally she is the adopted and, according to the Cambremers, probably the real – that is, the natural – daughter of someone whom they consider to be a prince of the blood. A bastard of an almost royal house has always been considered a flattering match by nobility, French or foreign. There is no need even to go back so far as the Lucinges,[2] for only six months ago you will recall the marriage of one of Robert's friends with that young lady whose sole claim to a place in society was that she was supposed, rightly or wrongly, to be the natural daughter of a sovereign prince.' My mother, while maintaining the caste distinctions of Combray according to which my grandmother would have been bound to be scandalized by this marriage, wanted above all to prove her mother's good judgment, and added: 'In fact the girl is perfection itself and your dear grandmother would not even have needed her enormous kindness and infinite indulgence to avoid severity in judging young Cambremer's choice. Do you remember how distinguished she found the girl one day long ago when she called in to have her skirt mended. She was only a child then. And although now so to speak an old maid left ripening on the shelf, she is quite another woman, a thousand times more perfect. But your grandmother had taken that all in at a glance. She had found the great-niece of a waistcoat-maker more "noble" than the Duc de Guermantes.' But even more than praise my grandmother, my mother needed to find that it was 'better' for her not to be able to witness these events. This was the supreme aim of her affection, as if she were sparing her one last sorrow. 'And yet,' my mother asked me, 'would you believe that old father Swann, although it is true that you never knew him, could have thought that one day he would have a great-grandson or a great-granddaughter in whose veins would mingle the blood of old mother Moser, who used to say "Goot mornink, Chentlemen", and the blood of the Duc de Guise!³ – Actually, Mama, it is even more extraordinary than you say. For the Swanns were very fine people, and given their son's position, if only he had made a good marriage, then his daughter could have made an even finer one. But everything had to start from scratch again because he married a tart. – Oh, a tart, now really. We must have been cruel. I never believed everything people said about her. – Oh yes, she was a tart, and I'll let you into some of the 'family' secrets one of these days.' Plunged in her day-dreams, my mother said: 'The daughter of a man your father would never have allowed me to greet, and she's marrying the nephew of Mme de Villeparisis, whom your father refused to allow me to call on at first, because he found her socially too grand for us!' She continued: 'Mme de Cambremer's son, to whom Legrandin so feared to recommend us because he didn't find us classy enough, marrying the niece of a man who would never have dared come to see us without using the servants' staircase! . . . After all, your poor grandmother was right, you remember, when she said that great aristocrats did things which would shock the petty bourgeoisie, and that Queen Marie-Amélie was spoiled for her by the advances which she had made to the Prince de Condé's mistress to get her to persuade him to make a will in favour of the Duc d'Aumale.[4] Do you remember how shocked she was to learn that for centuries the maidservants of the house of Gramont, who were veritable saints, bore the name of Corisande in memory of the liaison of a progenetrix of theirs with Henri IV?[5] These things may also happen in the bourgeoisie, but they are more carefully hidden. Imagine how it would have amused your grandmother!' my mother said sadly – for the pleasures we were sad for my grandmother to miss were the simplest of life's pleasures, a piece of news, a play, or even a mere 'skit' that would have amused her. 'Don't you think that she would have been amazed? Yet I'm sure that these marriages would have shocked your grandmother, that she would have suffered, I think it's better for her to have known nothing about them,' my mother continued, as she liked to think that, given my grandmother's marvellously singular nature, she would have been most peculiarly struck by them and that her impressions would have been extraordinarily important. Formerly, faced with any sad and unpredictable event, the disgrace or ruin of one of our old friends, some public calamity like an epidemic, a war, or a revolution, my mother believed that it was probably better that my grandmother should never have known about it, for she would have been too upset and might not have been able to survive it. And when the subject was an event as shocking as these, my mother, from an emotional reaction opposite to that of the ill-willed, who prefer to hope that those whom they dislike have suffered more than people think, did not, in her affection for my grandmother, want to admit that anything sad or belittling might have happened to her. She continued to imagine my grandmother beyond the reach of all ills, even the most unpredictable, thinking that the death of my grandmother had perhaps on balance been a blessing in sparing this so noble nature the all too ugly sight of modern times, which she would not have been able to accept. For optimism is the philosophy of the past. Since the events which actually happened, among all those which might have, are the only ones that we know, the harm that they have done us seems inevitable, and we credit them with being responsible for the little good which they have been unable to avoid bringing with them, imagining that without them it would never have come to pass. At the same time she tried to guess what my grandmother would have felt on learning the news, and simultaneously wanted to believe that our minds, being of a lower order than hers, were unable to guess it. 'Just imagine', my mother started to say, 'how astonished your poor grandmother would have been!' And I felt that my mother suffered from not being able to pass on the news, sad that my grandmother would never know it, and found something unjust in the way life could bring to light facts which my grandmother would have found unbelievable, thus rendering false and incomplete after the event the knowledge of people and society that she had taken to her grave, the marriage of the young Jupien girl with Legrandin's nephew having been of a nature to modify my grandmother's general philosophy just as much as the news – if my mother had been able to convey it to her – that the problems of aerial navigation and wireless telegraphy, which my grandmother had believed insoluble, had been resolved. But we shall see that this desire to enable my grandmother to share in the benefits of our knowledge seemed to my mother yet too selfish. What I learned – for I had not been able to witness it all while in Venice – was that Mlle de Forcheville had been solicited by the Duc de Châtel-lerault and the Prince de Silistrie, while Saint-Loup had been trying to marry Mlle d'Entragues, daughter of the Duke of Luxembourg. This is what had happened. Mlle de Forcheville, with her hundred million francs, seemed to Mme de Marsantes an excellent match for her son. Her mistake was to say that she was a charming girl, that she had no idea whether she was rich or poor, and preferred not to know, but that even without a dowry it would be a boon for even the most discriminating young man to have such a wife. This was going rather far for a woman tempted only by the hundred million and indifferent to the rest. Everyone immediately realized that she had her own son in mind. The Princesse de Silestrie uttered shrieks of protest, expatiated on the grandeur of Saint-Loup, and proclaimed that if Saint-Loup married the daughter of Odette and a Jew, that would be the end of the Faubourg Saint-Germain. No matter how sure of herself she felt,

Mme de Marsantes did not dare pursue her claim further, and withdrew in the face of these protestations by the Princesse de Silestrie, who immediately forwarded a proposal from her own son. Mme de Marsantes had cried out in protest only in order to reserve Gilberte for herself. However, unwilling to settle for failure, Mme de Marsantes had immediately turned to Mlle d'Entragues, the daughter of the Duke of Luxembourg. The latter party, with a mere twenty million francs to her name, was less suitable, but Mme de Marsantes made it publicly known that a Saint-Loup could not marry a Mlle Swann (the name of Forcheville was not even mentioned). Some time afterwards, when someone tactlessly said that the Duc de Châtellerault was considering marriage with Mlle d'Entragues, Mme de Marsantes, who was unrivalled for her susceptibility, took umbrage, readjusted her fire, switched to Gilberte, had a proposal made on behalf of Saint-Loup and concluded the engagement forthwith.

The engagement elicited animated commentaries in the most diverse milieux. Several lady-friends of my mother's, who had seen Saint-Loup in our house, called on her during her 'visiting hours' to ascertain whether the fiancé was indeed the same person as my friend. Some people went so far as to claim that it was not the Cambremer-Legrandins who were involved in the other marriage. They had this on good authority, since the Marquise, née Legrandin, had denied it on the eve of the very day that the engagement was announced. I for my part wondered why M. de Charlus on the one hand and Saint-Loup on the other, who had both had occasion to write to me shortly beforehand and had spoken so amiably of their travel plans, whose execution would have prevented all possibility of such ceremonies, had made no mention of it. I concluded, without considering how people keep such matters secret until the last moment, that I was less their friend than I had thought, which, in the case of Saint-Loup, distressed me. And why indeed, having remarked that the friendliness and openness of the aristocracy, 'peers and fellows on an equal footing', was a charade, should I expect to be an exception? In the house of pleasure – in which men rather than women were increasingly procured for one's pleasure – where M. de Charlus had surprised Morel and where the 'vice-Madam', a fervent reader of the *Gaulois*, who commented on events in high society, declared, when speaking to a stout gentleman who came to drink endless bottles of champagne in her establishment in the company of young men, because he wanted to develop his already considerable girth into an obesity certain to ensure that he would never be 'caught up' in any war that might break out: 'It appears that young Saint-Loup is "that way inclined" and young Cambremer too! Pity their wives! In any case, if you know the betrothed pair, do please send them along, they will find their heart's desire here, and help us earn a lot of money.' Upon which, the stout gentleman, although himself being 'that way inclined', protested, replying, on slightly snobbish grounds, that he often met Cambremer and Saint-Loup at his cousins', the d'Ardonvilli-ers, and that they were great connoisseurs of women and very far from such 'inclinations'. 'Ah!' concluded the vice-Madam with a sceptical air, but possessing no proof, and remaining convinced that in our century the perversity of morals was second only to the libellous absurdities spread by gossip. Some people whom I hardly knew to speak to wrote to me and asked 'what I thought' of these two marriages, absolutely as if they were conducting an inquiry into the height of the hats which women wore to the theatre, or into the psychological novel. I was unable to face replying to these letters. Confronted with these two marriages, I did not think anything at all, but felt an immense sadness, as you do when two parts of your past existence, previously moored alongside you and in which perhaps from one day to the next you may have been harbouring some half-hearted, secret investment, leave for ever, with all flags proudly flying, like two ships sailing for foreign parts. As for the parties themselves, they considered their marriages perfectly natural, since they themselves and not others were concerned. They had always had endless scorn for these 'great marriages', founded on some hidden flaw. And even the Cambremers, of such ancient but unpretentious lineage, would have been the first to forget Jupien and remember only the forgotten splendours of the house of d'Oloron, if an exception had not occurred in the shape of the person who should be most charmed by the marriage, the Marquise de Cambremer-Legrandin. For her spiteful character led her to prefer to humiliate her relatives rather than seek to bask in her own glory. Thus, since she did not love her son and had taken a premature dislike to her intended daughter-in-law, she declared that it would be a misfortune for a Cambremer to marry a person whose origins were more or less unknown, and whose teeth were exceptionally irregular. As for the propensity of the young Cambremer to frequent men of letters like Bergotte for example or even Bloch, it is easy to imagine why such a brilliant alliance should not have aggravated his snobbery, since seeing himself as the successor of the Ducs d'Oléron, 'sovereign princes', in the words of the press, made him sure enough of his grandeur to feel able to frequent anyone. And, on days when he did not worship some Highness or another, he left the lower nobility to join the ranks of the lower bourgeoisie. These notes in the press, especially concerning Robert de Saint-Loup, gave my friend a new grandeur, as they enumerated his royal ancestors, but one whose only effect was to sadden me further, as if he had become somebody else, the descendant of Robert le Fort[6] rather than the friend who had so recently sat on the folding seat in the car so that I could have the more comfortable seat in the back; the fact that I had been taken by surprise by his marriage to Gilberte, which suddenly surfaced in the letter which I had received, as unsuspected as a chemical precipitate, making them seem so different from how I had imagined them the day before, made me suffer, whereas I should have realized that he had been very busy and that society marriages often come to pass in this sudden fashion, and often in order to replace a previous, unsuccessful arrangement. And the sadness which I felt, as depressing as moving house and as bitter as jealousy, resulting from the abrupt and accidental clash caused by these two marriages, cut so deep that people would remind me of it later, as if, absurdly, I should be proud of it, as if it were quite the opposite of what I had felt at the time, a double, triple or even quadruple foreboding.

Those in society who had never taken any notice of Gilberte told me with an air of profound concern, 'Ah! So she's the one who is to marry Saint-Loup,' and cast on her the attentive eyes of people who not only avidly follow the events of Parisian life, but also seek instruction and believe in the profundity of their insight. On the other hand, those who had met only Gilberte observed Saint-Loup with extreme attentiveness and, despite often being people who hardly knew me, asked me to introduce them and returned from their introduction to the bridegroom brimming with festive joy, saying, 'He is such a fine figure of a man.' Gilberte was convinced that the name of the Marquis de Saint-Loup was a thousand times greater than that of the Duc d'Orléans,[7] but, as she belonged above all to a generation of (rather egalitarian) wits, she did not want to appear any less witty and took pleasure in calling herself *mater semita*, to which she added, in order to consummate her wit, 'whereas for me he is my *pater*'.

'I hear that it was the Princess of Parma who arranged the marriage of the young Cambremer,' said my mother, and it was true. For some time the Princess of Parma had known, on the one hand Legrandin through his works, and on the other hand, Mme de Cambremer, who changed the subject whenever the Princess asked her if she was really Legrandin's sister. The Princess knew how disappointed Mme de Cambremer was at remaining on the fringes of high aristocratic society, without being invited inside. When the Princess of Parma, who had taken it upon herself to make a match for Mlle d'Oloron, asked M. de Charlus if he knew the identity of the pleasant, cultivated man who went under the name of Legrandin de Méséglise (for this was how Legrandin now styled himself), the Baron at first replied that he did not, then was suddenly struck by the memory of a man whom he had met one night in a train and who had left him his card. He smiled vaguely. 'Perhaps it's the same man,' he thought. When he learned that he was the son of Legrandin's sister, he said: 'Well, that would be quite extraordinary! If he took after his uncle, after all, that shouldn't put me off, I have always said that they make the best husbands. – They? Who do you mean? asked the Princess. – Oh, Madam, I would willingly explain if we were better acquainted. You are someone it's easy to talk to. Your Highness is so intelligent,' said Charlus, seized with a need to confide, but which he did not take further. He liked, if not the parents, at least the name of Cambremer, while knowing that it was one of the four baronies of Brittany and by far the best he could expect for his adoptive daughter; it was an ancient and honourable name, with good connections in the region. A prince would have been impossible, and actually not desirable. This was what was needed. Then the Princess summoned Legrandin. He had changed physically quite a bit in recent years, and rather to his advantage. Like those

women who resolutely sacrifice their faces for the sake of a slim
waistline and spend all their time at Marienbad, Legrandin had taken
on the casual swagger of a cavalry officer. While M. de Charlus
had become stouter and slower, Legrandin had become slimmer and
quicker, the contrary effect of the same cause. Besides, his swiftness
had its psychological reasons. He had become a regular client of certain
houses of ill-fame. Since he did not wish to be seen entering or leaving
them, he dashed in and out, and vanished. When the Princess of Parma
spoke to him of the Guermantes or Saint-Loup, he declared that he
had always known them, creating as it were an amalgam of the fact
that he had always known the *name* of the Lords of Guermantes and
the fact that he had made the acquaintance in *person*, at my aunt's, of
Swann, the father of the future Mme de Saint-Loup, that same Swann,
one might add, whose wife and daughter Legrandin refused to frequent
in Combray. 'I even travelled recently in the company of M. de
Charlus, the brother of the Duc de Guermantes. He spontaneously
struck up a conversation with me, which is always a good sign, for it
proves that he is neither a starched-shirt nor a pretentious fool. Oh! I
am well aware of what they say about him. But I never believe that
kind of thing. In any case other people's private lives are none of my
concern. He struck me as a sensitive man, with a truly cultivated soul.'
Then the Princess of Parma mentioned Mlle d'Oloron. In Guermantes
circles people were most affected by the noble heart of M. de Charlus,
who, with his proverbial generosity, had secured the happiness of a
poor but charming young lady. And the Duc de Guermantes, who
suffered from his brother's reputation, let it be understood that, however fine the action might seem, it was only natural. 'I am not sure if
you catch my meaning, but everything about this affair is natural,' he
said, with an awkwardness exaggerated by his attempt to be subtle.
But his aim was to suggest that the young lady was a daughter of his
brother, who wished thus to acknowledge her. At a stroke, this
accounted for Jupien too. The Princess of Parma favoured this version
in order to show Legrandin that Mlle de Cambremer, all things
considered, would be marrying someone of the ilk of Mlle de Nantes,
one of the bastard daughters of Louis XIV who were snubbed neither
by the Duc d'Orléans nor the Prince de Conti.[8]

These two marriages, which my mother and I discussed in the train back to Paris, had fairly remarkable effects on some of the people who have so far figured in this story. First, on Legrandin; needless to say he dashed headlong into M. de Charlus's mansion, for all the world as if he were entering a house of ill-fame where he did not wish to be recognized, but also simultaneously to display his bravado and dissimulate his age, for our habits persist even in situations where they are no longer of any use to us, and hardly anyone noticed that in greeting him M. de Charlus addressed him with a smile even more difficult to interpret than to detect; this smile was apparently the same – although actually exactly the opposite – as that exchanged by two men who habitually frequent high society if by chance they meet in dubious circumstances (for example at the Elysée Palace, where Général de Froberville, when in former times he used to meet Swann there, affected on noticing Swann that air of ironic and mysterious complicity appropriate to two familiars of the Princesse des Laumes compromised by meeting at M. Grévy's[9]). But what was rather remarkable was the real improvement in his character. Legrandin – ever since the days when as a child I went to spend my holidays in Combray – had long been cultivating aristocratic relations which at best yielded no more than the odd invitation to an unproductive stay in a resort. Suddenly, the marriage of his nephew having intervened to join these long-separated branches, Legrandin enjoyed a social situation to which in retrospect his former relations with people who had frequented him, however closely, only in private, gave a certain substance. Ladies to whom people wanted to introduce him made out that he had spent two weeks in the country with them every year for the last twenty years, and that it was he who had given them the charming antique barometer in the small drawing-room. He had by chance been involved in 'circles' which included dukes who now became related to him. Yet as soon as he acquired his social position, he ceased to take advantage of it. It was not merely because once he was an official guest he no longer experienced any pleasure at being invited, but also, because of the two vices which had competed so long within him, the least natural, snobbery, gave way to the other, more natural one, since it marked a return, however devious, to nature. No doubt these two vices are not incompatible, and the back-streets of the suburbs may well be explored on the way home from a duchess's shindig. But, cooling with age, Legrandin turned away from the accumulation of too many pleasures, from sallying forth without taking all due precaution, thus rendering his natural pleasures, consisting above all in friendship and time-consuming chatter, increasingly platonic, making him spend most of his time with the lower classes and leaving him little time for life in high society. Mme de Cambremer herself became relatively indifferent to the friendly advances of the Princesse de Guermantes. The latter, obliged to frequent the Marquise, had realized, as always happens when we spend more time with any fellow-beings, with their inevitable mixture of qualities which we finally discover and defects which we eventually accept, that Mme de Cambremer was a woman gifted with an intelligence and endowed with a culture which I for my part appreciated little, but which seemed remarkable to the Duchesse. Thus often towards nightfall she called on Mme Cambremer to pay her a lengthy visit. But the magical charm that Mme de Cambremer had imagined the Duchesse de Guermantes to possess evaporated as soon as she found herself solicited by the latter. And she invited her from politeness rather than pleasure. A more striking change, at once symmetrical with and different from that which had occurred in Swann after his marriage, became apparent in Gilberte. Certainly during the first few months Gilberte had taken pleasure in inviting the most select society. Doubtless it was only because of the inheritance that she invited the close friends who mattered to her mother, albeit on certain days only, when they came on their own, cloistered apart from people of fashion, as if the contact of people like Mme Bontemps or Mme Cottard with the Princesse de Guermantes or the Princess of Parma might, like that of two unstable compounds, have produced some irreparable catastrophe. None the less, the Bontemps, Cottards and company, however disappointed at having to dine alone, were proud to be able to say, 'We dined with the Marquise de Saint-Loup,' all the more so because Gilberte occasionally made so bold as to invite them at the same time as Mme de Marsantes, who, in the interests of the inheritance, cut a truly distinguished figure with her tortoiseshell and feather fan. She merely took care from time to time to sing the praises of those people discreet enough not to call unless invited, which announcement was intended as a gracious but haughty salutation for those who had ears to hear, such as Cottard, Bontemps and company. Perhaps because of my 'young friend from Balbec', whose aunt I would have liked to see me in these surroundings, I would have preferred to be invited to those evenings. But Gilberte, for whom I was now above all a friend of her husband and of the Guermantes (and who – perhaps way back in Combray, in the days when my parents would not speak to her mother – at an age when we not only attribute some particular quality to each and every thing but also classify them by species, had invested me with the sort of prestige which we never lose afterwards), considered those evenings unworthy of me and would say to me as I was leaving: 'I was very pleased to see you, but why don't you come back tomorrow, you will meet my aunt Guermantes and Mme de Poix, today it was Mama's friends, to keep Mama happy.' But this lasted only a few months, and soon everything was totally changed. Was this because Gilberte's social life was bound to display the same contrasts as that of Swann? Be that as it may, Gilberte had not long been Marquise de Saint-Loup (and soon after, as we shall see, Duchesse de Guermantes) before, having achieved what was most spectacular and most difficult, thinking that the name of Guermantes was now incorporated within her like a gilded enamel and that whomsoever she frequented, she would remain the Duchesse de Guermantes for all and sundry (which was a mistake, for the value of an aristocratic title, like that of a share quoted on the stock exchange, rises when in demand and falls when on offer. Everything we believe imperishable tends towards destruction; a social position, like everything else, is not given once and for all but, just like the power of an empire, is reconstituted from moment to moment through a sort of endless renewed process of creation, which explains the apparent anomalies of social or political history over half a century. The creation of the world did not happen 'in the beginning', it happens from day to day. The Marquise de Saint-Loup thought, 'I am the Marquise de Saint-Loup,' in the knowledge that the night before she had turned down three invitations to dine with duchesses. But if to a certain extent her name enhanced the distinctly un-aristocratic circles

633

which she entertained, by an inverse movement the circles which invited the Marquise devalued the name that she bore. Nothing resists such movements, the greatest names finally succumb. Had Swann not known a princess of the royal house of France whose salon, because anyone at all could be invited, had fallen to the lowest rung? One day when the Princesse des Laumes had felt duty-bound to spend a moment with her Highness, but had found nothing but the lowest sort of company, she had afterwards visited Mme Leroi and had said to Swann and the Marquis de Modène: 'At last I am out of enemy territory. I have just escaped from Mme la Comtesse de X., where there were no more than two or three friendly faces'.) Sharing in a word the opinion of the comic-opera character[10] who declares, 'My name excuses me, I think, from further explanation,' Gilberte started to show her contempt for what she had so desired, to declare that the inhabitants of the Faubourg Saint-Germain were fools unfit for company, and, matching words with deeds, did indeed cease to seek their company. People who first made her acquaintance only after this period, and, when they first met her, heard this Duchesse de Guermantes make fun of the society which she could so easily have frequented, or yawn openly in the face of any one of them, even the most brilliant, who ventured to call on her, blush retrospectively at having themselves found some prestige in high society, and would never dare confide the humiliating secret of their past weaknesses to a woman whom they believe, through the essential grandeur of her nature, to have always been incapable of understanding such weakness. They hear her mock dukes with such brio, and see her, even more significantly, acting in such close accord with her mockery! Doubtless they would not think of investigating the causes of the accident which turned Mlle Swann into Mlle de Forcheville, and Mlle de Forcheville into the Marquise de Saint-Loup and then the Duchesse de Guermantes. Nor perhaps would they guess that the effects of this accident would help no less than its causes to explain the later attitude of Gilberte, since she no longer regarded the frequentation of commoners in quite the same way as she would have when Mlle Swann, a lady addressed by everyone as 'Mme la Duchesse', but addressed by the duchesses whom she found tedious as 'my dear cousin'. We are easily tempted to disdain an ambition which we have failed to fulfil or which we have satisfied and outgrown. And we suppose such disdain inherent even in people whom we did not know at the time. Perhaps if we could go back down the years, we would find these people ravaged, more furiously than anyone, by those same faults which they have managed so completely to hide or overcome that we consider them incapable not only of ever having been affected themselves but even of ever excusing them in others, since we assume that they are unable to imagine them. Meanwhile the salon of the new Marquise de Saint-Loup soon took on its definitive aspect (at least from a social viewpoint, for, as we shall see, all sorts of disturbances of a different nature would erupt there later). Yet this aspect was surprising for the following reason: people still remembered that the most sumptuous and refined receptions in Paris, as brilliant as those of the Princesse de Guermantes, were those of Mme de Marsantes, Saint-Loup's mother. What is more, in recent times, Odette's salon, although held in infinitely less esteem, had none the less been resplendent with luxury and elegance. Whereas Saint-Loup, who thanks to his wife's fortune enjoyed all the comfort that he could wish, dreamed of nothing more than the tranquillity of finishing a fine dinner in the company of artists playing him good music. And this young man, who had once appeared so proud and ambitious, invited to share these luxuries friends to whom his mother would never have spoken. Gilberte for her part put into practice Swann's words, 'I care little for quality, but I fear quantity.' And Saint-Loup, who was completely at his wife's feet, both because he loved her and because it was precisely to her that he owed this supreme luxury, took care not to interfere with her tastes, which so closely resembled his own. In this way Mme de Marsantes's and Mme de Forcheville's great receptions, given for years in order above all to set up their children as brilliantly as possible, did not generate any great receptions by M. and Mme de Saint-Loup. They had the finest horses for riding together, the finest yacht for their cruises – but they never invited more than two guests at a time. When in Paris they never had more than two or three friends to dinner; with the result that, by a process of unforeseen and yet natural regression, their two mothers' great aviaries had been replaced by a silent nest.

The person who benefited least from these two unions was the young Mlle d'Oloron, who, already infected with typhoid fever on the day of her religious nuptials, dragged herself painfully to church and died a few weeks later. The obituary notice which followed shortly after her death mingled names like that of Jupien with almost all the great names of Europe, such as those of the Vicomte and the Vicomtesse de Montmorency, HRH the Comtesse de Bourbon-Soissons, the Prince of Modena-d'Este, the Vicomtesse d'Edumea, Lady Essex, and so on. Doubtless, even for those who knew that the departed was Jupien's niece, this quantity of grand alliances was no surprise. The main thing above all is to have such grand relations. Then the *casus foederis* comes into play and the death of a petty commoner throws all of the princely families of Europe into mourning. But many of the young people of the new generations, not knowing how things really stood, apart from being liable to take Marie-Antoinette d'Oloron, Marquise de Cambremer, for a lady of the noblest birth, might have been liable to commit many another error on reading the obituary notice. Thus if their excursions through France had led them into the countryside near Combray, they might not have been astonished to see that Mme L. de Méséglise and the Comte de Méséglise were among the first of the mourners, alongside the Duc de Guermantes: the Méséglise way and the Guermantes way lie side by side. 'Traditional aristocracy from the same region, perhaps intermarried for generations,' they might have thought. 'Who knows, perhaps it's a branch of the Guermantes which bears the name of the Comtes de Méséglise.' Yet the Comte de Méséglise bore no relation to the Guermantes at all and did not even belong to the world of the Guermantes, but rather to the world of the Cambremers, for the Comte de Méséglise, whose rapid social ascent had seen him spend only two years as Legrandin de Méséglise, was our old friend Legrandin. And no doubt of all false titles, no false title could have been more disagreeable to the Guermantes than this. They had been related in former times to the genuine Comtes de Méséglise, of whose line there remained only one woman, the daughter of obscure folk fallen on hard times, herself married to one of my aunt's tenant farmers, who had become prosperous and bought Mirougrain from her. He had transformed his original name of Ménager into the appellation Ménager de Mirougrain, so that when people said that his wife's maiden name was de Méséglise, they thought this meant that she had been born and bred at Méséglise just as her husband had been at Mirougrain.

Any other false title would have caused the Guermantes fewer problems. But the aristocracy knows how to accommodate such problems, and worse, as long as a marriage judged useful, from whatever point of view, is at stake. Legrandin, backed by the Duc de Guermantes, was the true Comte de Méséglise for some people of that generation and for everyone in the next.

Another error that any uninitiated young reader might have been tempted to commit would have been to believe that the Baron and Baronne de Forcheville signed the obituary notice in their capacity as parents and parents-in-law of the Marquis de Saint-Loup, that is, as the Guermantes connection. Yet they had no call to figure on their list since it was Robert rather than Gilberte who was related to the Guermantes. Yet if, despite such false inferences, the Baron and the Baronne de Forcheville did figure on the bride's list and not on that of the Cambremers, the truth is that it was not through the Guermantes but through Jupien, whom our more knowledgeable reader will recognize as a first cousin of Odette.

After the marriage of his adopted daughter, M. de Charlus brought all his favours to bear on the young Marquis de Cambremer; the latter's tastes resembled those of the Baron, who, since he had found them no obstacle to the marriage with Mlle d'Oloron, could only find him all the more estimable once he became a widower. This is not to say that the Marquis did not have other qualities, which made him a charming companion for M. de Charlus. But even in the case of a man of great value, it is a quality not to be despised by someone who seeks his personal friendship, and one which comes in very handy if he also plays whist. The young Marquis's intelligence was remarkable and, as people said even in Féterne when he was still only a child, he really 'took after his grandmother', being just as enthusiastic and musical as she. Certain other family characteristics recurred in him, but more through imitation, as happened with the whole family, than through atavism. Thus it was that, a little while after the death of his wife, having received a letter signed 'Léonor', which I did not recollect as one of his baptismal names, I understood who my correspondent was only when I read the final flourish: 'Please accept my true sympathy.' This *true*, when 'placed in context', added to the first name Léonor the surname Cambremer.

As the train entered the station in Paris, my mother and I were still discussing these two reports, which, in order to make the journey seem less protracted, she had tried to save for the second stage and had managed to keep from me until we had passed Milan. My mother had very quickly reverted to what was for her the only true opinion, that of my grandmother. My mother had at first thought that my grandmother would have been surprised, and then that she would have been saddened, which was simply a way of saying that my grandmother would have enjoyed such a surprising event and that my mother, unable to tolerate depriving my grandmother of a pleasure, preferred to think that all was for the best, since such news was of a kind that could not have failed to upset her. But hardly had we arrived home than my mother already felt that she had been too selfish in wishing that she could have made my grandmother share all the surprises that life reserves for us. She still preferred to suppose that these would not have surprised my grandmother, whose predictions they merely ratified. And in these surprising events she was determined to see confirmation of my grandmother's prophetic visions, and proof that she had had a mind that was even profounder and more far-sighted than we had thought. Thus my mother, in her quest to adopt a position of perfect admiration, lost no time in adding: 'And yet, who knows whether your poor grandmother might not have approved? She was so understanding. And you know, don't you, that she counted social connection as opposed to natural distinction for nothing. Well, don't you remember, surely you remember, however strange they were, both of these girls caught her fancy. Think back to the first time she went to meet Mme de Villeparisis, then when she returned to tell us how vulgar she had found M. de Guermantes, and yet how lyrically she praised Jupien. Poor mother, do you remember? She said of the father: "If I had another daughter, I would give her to him, and his daughter is even better than he." And Swann's little girl! She said: "I must say that she is charming, just wait and see what a fine marriage she will make." Poor mother, would that she could see how well she had judged! Right to the end, even after her departure, she will give us lessons in foresight, kindness and good judgment.' And since the pleasures that we saw my grandmother deprived of were all the simplest and humblest of life's pleasures: enjoying an actor's tone of voice, appreciating a favourite menu or the latest novel by a favourite author, Mama said: 'Wouldn't she have been surprised! Wouldn't she have been amused! What a lovely letter she would have written in reply!' And my mother continued: 'Just imagine how pleased our poor Swann would have been, since he was so anxious for his daughter to be invited to the Guermantes', if he could have seen his daughter become one of the Guermantes! – Under a name not his own, led to the altar as Mlle de Forcheville? Do you think that he would have been as happy as all that? – Ah, that is true, I hadn't thought of that. – That's what makes me unable to rejoice for the little "hussy"; it's the thought that she could find it in her heart to drop the name of her father, who was so good to her. – Yes, you are right, after all, perhaps it is better that he never knew of it.' It is as difficult to know whether something would be more likely to cause pleasure or pain to the dead as it is to the living! 'I hear that the Saint-Loups are going to live at Tansonville. I wonder if Swann's father, who so wanted to show off his pond to your poor father, could ever have imagined that the Duc de Guermantes would often see it, especially if he had come to know of his son's dishonourable marriage. But since you yourself have talked so often to Saint-Loup of the pink hawthorn, the lilac and the irises at Tansonville, he will understand you better. Now they will belong to him.' Thus under the dining-room lamp which encourages them, there unfolded one of those conversations where the wisdom, if not of nations at least of families, seizes on some event – a death, an engagement, an inheritance or a ruin – and places it under the magnifying glass of memory, throwing it into high relief, dissociating, distancing and placing in perspective at different points in time and space things which, for those who have not experienced them, seem to run together on a single plane – the roll of the deceased, changes of address, sources of and changes in wealth, transfers of property. Is this wisdom not inspired by the Muse, whom we should fail to recognize for as long as possible if we want to preserve the freshness of our impressions and some creative power, but whom precisely those of us who have avoided her shall meet in the evening of our lives in the nave of some old village church, at a moment when all of a sudden they feel less touched by the eternal beauty expressed in the carvings on the altar than by the diverse fates which they have suffered, as they moved into a distinguished private collection or a chapel, then into a museum, or by the feeling that we are treading on an almost sentient flagstone, composed of the last remains of Arnauld or Pascal, or quite simply by deciphering the names of the daughters of the nobleman or the commoner inscribed on the copper plate of a wooden prie-dieu, imagining perchance the fresh young faces of these village maidens, the Muse who has assumed everything rejected by the higher Muses of philosophy and art, everything unfounded in truth, everything which is merely contingent but which also reveals other laws: the Muse of history!

Some old friends of my mother's, from Combray or nearby, came to see her to talk about Gilberte's marriage, which did not overawe them at all. 'You know who Mlle de Forcheville is, she's quite simply Mlle Swann. And her best man, Charlus, who passes himself off as a "Baron", is the old man who used to keep her mother in full sight of Swann, who found it advantageous. – Why, whatever do you mean?' my mother protested. 'In the first place, Swann was extremely rich. – Not rich enough, it would seem, not to need other people's money. But how does the woman do it, how does she manage to hang on to her old lovers like that? She managed to persuade the first one to marry her, then the third, and then she hauls the second one back from the brink of the grave to get him to act as best man for the daughter she had with the first, or someone else, since the sheer number is confusing! Even she has lost count! I said the third, but the three-hundredth would be more like it. Besides, you know that she's no more a Forcheville than you or I, which makes her a good match for the husband, who obviously isn't noble either. You can be sure that only a fortune-hunter would marry such a creature. They say he's some M. Dupont or M. Durand or other. If we didn't have a radical mayor in Combray now, who won't even talk to the curé, I would have got to the bottom of it. Because you know, of course, that when they published the banns they must have had to give the real name. It's all very well for the newspapers and the stationers who print the invitations to call you the Marquis de Saint-Loup. It doesn't harm a soul, and if it suits these good people, I'm the last to want to spoil their fun, what's it got to do with me? Since I'll never visit the daughter of a woman with a reputation, she can be a marchioness for her servants till the cows come home. But for the registrar it's another matter. Ah, if my cousin Sazerat was still deputy mayor, I would have written to him, and he would have told me what name he had used for the banns!'

This was, moreover, a period when I saw quite a lot of Gilberte, with whom I had resumed my friendship: for in the long term the rhythm of our lives does not scan with the timescale of our friendships. Once a sufficient period of time has elapsed, we see ( just as we see the revival of former ministries in politics or of forgotten plays in the theatre) friendly relations resumed, after long years of interruption, between the same people as before, and revived with pleasure. After ten years of reasons for one person to be too much in love, and reasons for the other not to tolerate such despotic demands, the reasons cease to exist. Only affinities matter, and everything that Gilberte would have refused me previously, she easily granted me, no doubt because I no longer desired it. Doing something that had always seemed intolerable or impossible to her, she now, without our ever discussing the reason for the change, was always ready to come to me and never in a hurry to leave; this was because the obstacle had vanished, that is, my love.

A little later I was in fact due to spend a few days at Tansonville. I was rather embarrassed by the trip, for in Paris I kept a girl-friend who slept overnight in the *pied-à-terre* which I had rented for myself. As some need the scent of a forest or the sound of the lapping waters of a lake, I needed to feel her sleeping beside me at night and, during the day, to have her always beside me in the car. For even if we forget a love affair, it may determine the form of the love affair that follows. Already in the very heart of the earlier love affair daily habits existed whose origins we ourselves had forgotten; it was the anguish we first felt one day which made us desperately desire, then systematically repeat like rituals whose original meaning is forgotten, our beloved all the way back to her door, to move her into our home, to attend in person or through the presence of a trusted friend all her comings and goings – all these habits are smooth highways where every day our love follows paths which in former times were scored out by the molten lava of our ardent emotions. But these habits survive the disappearance of the woman concerned, even her memory. They shape, if not all our love affairs, at least certain of our loves, as they recur in turn. And thus in memory of the forgotten Albertine, my home had demanded the presence of my current mistress, who was hidden from visitors while filling my life in the same way as Albertine. And in order to go to Tansonville, I had to get her to agree to be looked after for a few days by one of my friends who was not attracted to women. I was going because I had learned that Gilberte was unhappy, since Robert was deceiving her, but not in the manner which everyone believed and which perhaps even she still believed, or at any rate declared. But self-respect, the urge to deceive others and deceive oneself, and the inevitably imperfect knowledge of one's betrayal which is the lot of all deceived people, were aided and abetted by the fact that Robert, a true nephew of M. de Charlus, showed himself off in public with women whom he compromised and whom everyone, no doubt even Gilberte, believed to be his mistresses . . . Society even felt that he did not take enough care, refusing to leave the side of the woman he had brought to a soirée and even escorting her home, leaving Mme de Saint-Loup to make her own way home. Anyone who thought to say that the other woman whom he compromised in this way was not his mistress would have seemed naïve, given the blinding obviousness of the evidence. But unfortunately I had been put on the track of the truth, a truth which caused me no end of suffering, by a few words that Jupien let slip. What was my stupefaction when, a few months before my visit to Tansonville, having gone to take news of M. de Charlus, who had been suffering from cardiac irregularities which gave rise to considerable concern, and finding Jupien on his own, I mentioned some love letters addressed to Robert and signed Bobette, which had been intercepted by Mme de Saint-Loup. I had then learned from the Baron's former factotum that the person signing himself as Bobette was none other than the violinist and critic whom we have mentioned and who had played a considerable part in the life of M. de Charlus! Jupien was unable to speak without indignation: 'The lad was free to do whatever he liked. But if there was one direction he should not have strayed in, it was that of the Baron's nephew. All the more because the Baron loved his nephew like a son; he tried to upset the marriage, it's a disgrace. And he had to employ the most fiendish stratagems, for nobody was more opposed by nature to such things than the Marquis de Saint-Loup. Just think of his extravagant behaviour with his mistresses! No, the fact that this wretched musician left the Baron in the underhand way that he did, you can say that that's his business. But to take up with the nephew! There are things that one just does not do.' Jupien's indignation was sincere; those people we call immoral have a moral indignation just as strong as others', except only that the object of their indignation is slightly different. Moreover, people whose own hearts are not directly concerned and who constantly judge which relationships are inadvisable and which marriages bad, as if one were free to choose whom one loves, take no account of the delicious mirage which love projects and which so entirely and uniquely enfolds the person whom one loves that the 'folly' committed by a man who marries a kitchenmaid or his best friend's mistress is in general the only poetical act that he will accomplish in the course of his whole existence. I understood that there had very nearly been a separation between Robert and his wife (without Gilberte being aware yet of what the problem was) and that it was Mme de Marsantes, a loving, ambitious and philosophical mother, who had arranged, or rather imposed, the reconciliation. She belonged to that milieu where the endless mingling and recycling of blood, and the dilapidation of inheritances, may at any moment reawaken hereditary vices and compromises, either in the realm of the passions or in that of financial interest. It was with just such energy that she had formerly sponsored Mme Swann or Jupien's daughter's marriage, and arranged the marriage of her own son with Gilberte, employing on her own account, with painful resignation, the same atavistic wisdom that she had lavished on the whole Faubourg. And perhaps the only reason why she had suddenly rather clumsily precipitated the marriage between Robert and Gilberte, which certainly gave

her less trouble and caused fewer tears to be shed than making him
break up with Rachel, was the fear that he might take up again with
another tart – or even with the same one, for Robert took a long time
to forget Rachel – and perhaps find salvation without her. Now I
understood what Robert had tried to tell me at the Princesse de
Guermantes': 'It's a shame that your girlfriend from Balbec does not
have the fortune required by my mother, I think that the two of us
would have got on well together.' He had meant to imply that she was
from Gomorrah as he was from Sodom, or perhaps, if he had not yet
arrived there, he enjoyed the company of only those women whom he
could love after a certain fashion and in the presence of other women.
If I had not thus, apart from some rare flashes of recollection, lost all
curiosity to find out anything about my young friend, I could have
questioned not only Gilberte but also her husband on her account. In
the end it was the same factor that had inspired both in Robert and in
me the desire to marry Albertine (that is, her love for women). But
the causes of our desire, like its ends, were opposite. I had been driven
to it by the despair I had felt at the discovery, Robert by his satisfaction;
I in order to prevent her though constant surveillance from yielding
to her inclination; Robert in order to cultivate it and to enjoy the
freedom that he would allow her to offer him her girl-friends. Whereas
Jupien situated so recently the new orientation that Robert's carnal
tastes had taken, so different from the original, a conversation which
I held with Aimé and which made me very unhappy, showed me that
the former *maître d'hôtel* from Balbec dated this divergence or inversion
much earlier. This conversation took place during a two- or three-day
stay that I made in Balbec, where Saint-Loup himself, during a long
period of leave, had come with his wife, whose side, in this first phase,
he never left. I had admired how Rachel's influence on Robert could
still be felt. Only a newly-wed who has lived for a long time with a
mistress knows how to remove his wife's coat on entering a restaurant
and show her proper respect. During his affair he has received the
education that a good husband should have. Not far away, at a table
near mine, Bloch, surrounded by pretentious young university dons,
exuded an air of bogus relaxation, shouting aloud to one of his friends,
'No, no, my dear friend, you give the order. I have never in my life

been able to choose a menu. I've never been able to give orders!' he repeated with suspect pride and, mingling literature with gourmandise gave his instant opinion on the bottle of champagne that he liked to see enhance a conversation 'in totally symbolic fashion'. Whereas Saint-Loup knew how to give orders. He was seated beside Gilberte, who was already pregnant (later he ceaselessly got her with child), just as he slept with her in their double bed at the hotel. He spoke only to his wife, the rest of the hotel seemed not to exist for him, but as soon as a waiter took an order or came near, he raised his limpid eyes and looked straight at him for no more than two seconds, while his clear-sighted gaze seemed to display a series of interests and requests entirely different from those which any other client might have inspired, however long they spent eyeing a page or a waiter in order to make remarks about him, witty or otherwise, that he could retail to his friends. This brief, discreet, indifferent glance, showing that he was interested in the waiter in his own right, would reveal to anyone who observed it that this excellent husband, the previously passionate lover of Rachel, had another dimension to his life, and one which seemed to him to be infinitely more interesting than the one to which his duty assigned him. But this was the only visible sign of it. His eyes had already returned to Gilberte, who had noticed nothing, he introduced her to a friend of his who was passing through, and he left to take her for a walk. Now on this occasion Aimé told me of a much earlier time, the time when I had made the acquaintance of Saint-Loup, also in Balbec, through Mme de Villeparisis.

'But, my dear Sir, yes, of course, it's common knowledge, I've known it for ages. The first year that your good self was in Balbec, M. le Marquis took my liftboy upstairs, on the pretext of developing some photos of your own lady grandmother. The lad tried to complain, we had to go to an awful lot of trouble to keep things quiet. And then, Sir, I'm sure Sir will remember the day when he came to dine with the Marquis de Saint-Loup and his mistress, who served as a screen for M. le Marquis. I am sure Sir will remember that M. le Marquis left on the pretext of a fit of temper. Of course you know that I am not saying that Madam was right. She really made him suffer. But you can't stop me believing that on that occasion M. le Marquis's anger was faked, and he needed to get away from Sir and Madam.' At least as far as that day was concerned, I am sure that, even if Aimé was not deliberately lying, he was entirely mistaken. I remembered only too well the state that Robert was in and the slap that he had administered to the journalist. And indeed it was the same for Balbec, either the liftboy had lied, or it was Aimé who was lying. At least that was what I believed; absolute certainty eluded me; we never see more than one side of things, and had it not made me suffer, I would have found a certain beauty in the fact that, while for me the errand of the 'lift' to Saint-Loup had been an easy way to deliver him a letter and receive a reply, for Saint-Loup it had served to get him acquainted with someone who had attracted him. There are at least two sides to every question. Starting from the most insignificant action that one man accomplishes, another would launch into an entirely different series of actions. There is no doubt that I was no more likely to guess the repercussions of the episode involving Saint-Loup and the liftboy, if it ever took place, that would follow the banal despatch of my letter than someone with no knowledge of Wagner other than the duet from *Lohengrin* could foresee the prelude to *Tristan*.[11] Doubtless, objects present man with no more than a limited number of their innumerable attributes, because of the poverty of our senses. Things are coloured because we have eyes; how many other epithets might they not deserve if we had hundreds of senses? But this different aspect that they could have had is made easier for us to understand by what in life is a minimal incident of which we know only a part, believing it to be the whole, and which someone else perceives as if through a window on the other side of the house giving a different view. Supposing that Aimé was not mistaken, Saint-Loup's blush when Bloch had mentioned the 'lift' to him did not perhaps spring only from the fact that he pronounced the word as 'lifed'. But I was convinced that Saint-Loup's physiological evolution had not started at this time and that then he still loved only women. I was able to deduce this retrospectively more from the friendship that Saint-Loup had shown me at Balbec than from any other evidence. It was only as long as he still loved women that he was really capable of friendship. Afterwards, at least for a period of time, the men who did not interest him directly were subject to a display of indifference, which was, I believe, partly sincere, since he had become very cold, but which was also partly an act, designed to make people believe that he was interested only in women. None the less I remember that one day at Doncières as I was setting out to dine with the Verdurins and as he had just been looking rather lingeringly at Charlie, he had said to me: 'It's strange how this lad reminds me of Rachel. Doesn't it strike you too? I find that they have some identical features. Not that it is of any interest to me.' And yet meanwhile his gaze remained afterwards trained for some time on the horizon, as when, before returning to a round of cards or leaving to dine on the town, we are thinking of one of those long journeys which we suspect we will never undertake but for which we have felt a sudden pang of yearning. But if Robert saw something of Rachel in Charlie, Gilberte, for her part, tried to take on something of Rachel in order to please her husband, tying her hair with yellow, pink or poppy-red silk ribbons and adopting the same hair-style, for she was jealous because she thought that her husband was still in love with Rachel. It may well be possible that Robert's love hovered on the boundary between that of a man in love with a woman and that of a man in love with another man. At all events the memory of Rachel played no more than an aesthetic role, and it is even improbable that it could have acted otherwise. One day Robert went so far as to ask her to dress as a man and to let her forelock hang loose, and yet he was content merely to look at her, feeling no satisfaction. He remained none the less attached to her and paid her scrupulously, if coldly, the enormous allowance which he had promised her and which did not prevent her later from dealing with him in the most despicable manner. Gilberte would not have suffered from this generosity towards Rachel if she had known that it was simply the dutiful discharge of a promise which no longer corresponded to any real love. But love was precisely what he feigned to feel for Rachel. Homosexuals would be the best husbands in the world if they did not pretend that they loved women. Actually, Gilberte did not complain. It was the fact that she had thought that Robert had been loved by Rachel, over such a long period of time, that had made her desire him, and had made her renounce on his behalf the most attractive matches; she felt in some way that he was making a concession by marrying her. And indeed at first he made comparisons between the two women (who were yet so different in charm and in beauty) which were unfavourable to the delicious Gilberte. But afterwards the latter grew in her husband's esteem while Rachel diminished visibly. Another person who had to eat her words was Mme Swann. If, in Gilberte's eyes, Robert was already surrounded before the marriage by the double halo generated, on the one hand by his life with Rachel, constantly impugned in Mme de Marsantes's lamentations and, on the other hand, by the prestige which the Guermantes had always had for her father and which she had inherited from him, Mme de Forcheville, however, would have preferred a more dazzling marriage, perhaps with a prince (there were impoverished royal families who would have been glad of the money – which it should be said turned out to be considerably less than the eighty million francs that had been mentioned – once rendered odourless by the attribution of the name of Forcheville) and a son-in-law less devalued by a life spent outside society. She had been unable to vanquish Gilberte's will, complained bitterly to everyone and poured scorn on her son-in-law. But one fine day everything had changed, the son-in-law had become an angel and he was mocked only in private asides. This was because age had not deprived Mme Swann (now Mme de Forcheville) of her habitual tastes as a kept woman, but, since her admirers had deserted her, it had deprived her of the means to gratify them. She desired a new necklace every day, a new dress sewn with diamonds, a more luxurious car, but she did not have a large fortune, since Forcheville had spent nearly everything, and – what Jewish ancestry had thus informed Gilberte? – she had an adorable but dreadfully mean daughter, who calculated every penny of her husband's budget and, naturally, that of her mother even more so. Now, suddenly she had caught scent of and found a protector in Robert. The fact that she was no longer in her prime was of little importance in the eyes of a son-in-law who did not love women. All that he asked of his mother-in-law was that she smooth over the occasional difficulty that might arise between him and Gilberte and consent to a trip which he planned to make with Morel. As soon as Odette had got to work, she was rewarded with a magnificent ruby. Which meant that Gilberte needed to be even more generous to her husband. Odette persuaded her all the more fervently since she herself would be the beneficiary. Thus, thanks to Robert, she was able, on the threshold of her fiftieth (some said her sixtieth) year to dazzle with extraordinary luxury at any dinner-table and every soirée to which she was invited, without needing as she had done before to have a 'friend', who now would no longer have forked out, or even acted his part. Thus she embarked upon a final period of chastity, which seemed definitive, and she had never been more elegant.

It was not only the ill-will and resentment of the former pauper for the master who has made him rich, while none the less making him feel the difference in their conditions (which was in Charlus's character, and showed even more in his vocabulary), that had driven Charlie towards Saint-Loup in order to inflict more suffering on the Baron. It was also perhaps self-interest. I gained the impression that Robert must be giving him considerable sums of money. At one reception where I had met Robert before leaving for Combray and where his manner of exhibiting himself with an elegant woman who passed for his mistress, clinging to her sides and publicly entangled in her skirts as if they were one and the same being, made me think of a sort of ancestral gesture, albeit in this case more nervous and excited, that I had noticed in M. de Charlus, as it were billowing in the drapery of Mme Molé or her like, bearing the standard of a *gynophile* cause which was not his own but which he liked, however undeservedly, to flaunt in this fashion, whether because he found it afforded protection, or whether aesthetic pleasure, I was struck on my return by how economical this young man, who was so generous when he was far less rich, had become. That people care only for their possessions, and that he who was profligate with his occasional windfalls should then start saving when he comes into his fortune, is no doubt a fairly common phenomenon, but one which none the less seems in this case to take on a different aspect. Saint-Loup refused to hire a cab, and I noticed that he had kept a tramway transfer-ticket. Doubtless in this way Saint-Loup exploited, to different ends, talents which he had acquired during his long liaison with Rachel. A young man who has spent a long time living with a woman is very different from the virgin whose bride is his first woman. It was sufficient, on the rare occasions when Robert took his wife out to a restaurant, to observe his skill and respect in removing her hat and coat, his art in ordering dinner and having it served, his care in smoothing Gilberte's sleeves before she put her jacket back on, to realize that he had spent a long time as another woman's lover before becoming this one's husband. Similarly, having been obliged to intervene in the minutest details of Rachel's housekeeping, partly because she herself had no idea how to manage it, then later because his jealousy drove him to supervise her servants with a firm hand, he managed in administrating his wife's property and her household to sustain this skilfully learned role which Gilberte might possibly not have been able to play and which she willingly left to him. But no doubt he did it above all to enable Charlie to benefit from the slightest cheese-paring savings, ultimately keeping him in style without Gilberte noticing or suffering. Perhaps even because he believed the violinist to be a spendthrift 'like all artists' (Charlie used the title in this way with no pride and little conviction in order to provide an excuse for not replying to letters, etc., and for a host of other faults that he thought were universally agreed to be part and parcel of an artist's psychology). Personally I found that it made no difference from a moral point of view whether one took one's pleasure with a man or a woman, and only too natural and human to take it wherever one could find it. So that if Robert had not been married, his liaison with Charlie ought not to have caused me the slightest pain. And yet I did feel that the pain I experienced would have been just as sharp if Robert had still been a bachelor. Coming from anyone else, what he was doing would have left me indifferent. But I wept to think that I had in times gone by felt so great an affection for a different Saint-Loup, and that I felt clearly from his newly cold and evasive manner that this was no longer reciprocated, for, since he had found that men could arouse his desire, they no longer inspired his friendship. How could that have occurred in a young man who had so loved women that I had seen him in despair when 'Rachel, when of the Lord' had tried to leave him? Had the resemblance between Charlie and Rachel – which was lost on me – been the springboard for Robert to pass from the tastes of his father to those of his uncle, thus accomplishing the evolution that even in the latter had happened rather late in life? And yet on occasion Aimé's words returned to disturb me; I remembered Robert that year in Balbec; he had a way of not looking at the liftboy when he was talking to him in a way that much recalled M. Charlus's manner of speaking to certain men. But Robert could very well have inherited this from M. de Charlus and a certain hauteur and physical deportment of the Guermantes, and not at all from the Baron's special tastes. Thus it was that the Duc de Guermantes, who had absolutely no such tastes, had the same nervous manner of twisting his wrist, as if he were fastening a lace cuff around it, and also some shrill and affected tones in his voice, all mannerisms which in M. de Charlus would have invited a different interpretation and to which he himself gave another, as the individual expresses his particularities through impersonal, atavistic traits which are perhaps merely personal characteristics from former times which have become crystallized in terms of voice and gesture. In the light of this latter hypothesis, which borders on natural history, one would not call M. de Charlus a Guermantes affected by a flaw and expressing it partly through the characteristics of the Guermantes race, rather, it would be the Duc de Guermantes who would be the odd one out in a perverted family, an individual whom the hereditary malady has so well spared that the external stigmata which it has marked him with have lost all their meaning. I remembered that the first day at Balbec when I had seen Saint-Loup, with his fair complexion and refined physique, seemingly wrought from some precious substance and looking so mannered as he waved his monocle in front of him, I had found that he had an effeminate air, which was certainly not the result of what I was now learning about him, but a grace specific to the Guermantes, that fineness of Dresden porcelain in which the Duchesse too was modelled. I also remembered his affection for me, and his tender and sentimental way of showing it, and thought that this too, which might have misled someone else, meant something entirely different at the time, even quite the opposite, from what I was now discovering. But when had it started? If it was the year when I had returned to Balbec, how was it that he had not returned even once to see the 'lift', and had never mentioned him to me? And as for the first year, how could he have noticed him, being as passionately enamoured of Rachel as he was at the time? That first year, I had found Saint-Loup eccentric, like a true Guermantes. But he was even more peculiar than I had thought. Yet when we have had no direct intuition of something but have learned it only from others, it is too late, we are unable to transmit it to our soul, for its lines of communication with reality are closed; so we cannot enjoy the discovery, it comes too late. Besides, in any case, this discovery hurt me too much for me to take any intellectual pleasure in it. Of course, after what M. de Charlus had told me at Mme Verdurin's in Paris, I no longer doubted that Robert's case was common to a host of honourable citizens, even the best and the most intelligent among them. Learning it of anyone but Robert would have left me indifferent. The doubts which Aimé inspired in me tarnished our whole friendship in Balbec and Doncières, and, although I believed neither in friendship nor that I had ever really felt it for Robert, when I thought back over these stories about the 'lift' and the restaurant where I had dined with Saint-Loup and Rachel, I had to make an effort not to weep.

However, I should not have to dwell on this visit to the country near Combray, and at the time in my life when perhaps I thought least of Combray, if it had not provided, precisely because of this, at least temporary confirmation of certain ideas which had first struck me on the way to Guermantes, and of other ideas that had struck me on the way to Méséglise. Every evening I retraced, albeit in the opposite direction, the steps of the walk which we used to take in the afternoon in Combray when we went out towards Méséglise. Now at Tansonville we dined long after the hour when in Combray in days gone by we would have been asleep. And because of the hot weather, and because Gilberte spent the afternoons painting in the château chapel, we did not set out for our walk until about two hours before dinner. Our former pleasure, of observing on our way home how the crimson sky framed the wayside calvary or dipped into the Vivonne, was replaced by that of leaving at nightfall and finding the village deserted except for the shifting blue tones and irregular triangular forms of the sheep coming home. Over one half of the fields the sun was setting; over the other the moon was already lit and preparing to bathe them entirely in its light. Sometimes Gilberte let me go on my own, and I walked onward leaving my shadow in my wake, like a boat sailing forth through enchanted waters; but usually she came with me. The walks we took then were most often the same as those we had taken in earlier days when we were children: now on my way to Guermantes, how could I have avoided experiencing even more strongly than ever the feeling that I would never be capable of writing, added to the realization that my imagination and my sensitivity had weakened, when I saw how little curiosity Combray inspired in me? I was sad to see how little I relived my past years. I found the Vivonne narrow and ugly beside the tow-path. Not that I discovered any major material discrepancy with what I recalled. But, since I had been separated by my totally divergent life from the places which I now happened to rediscover, there was not between them and me that contiguity which, even before one is aware of it, gives birth to the sudden, delicious, all-enveloping irruption of memory. Doubtless because I did not understand their nature, I felt sad to think that my faculties of feeling and imagining must have diminished if I was experiencing no pleasure on these walks with Gilberte. Gilberte herself, who understood me even less well than I did myself, increased my sadness by sharing my astonishment. 'However can you not be moved,' she asked, 'when you take the same steep little track that you used to climb in the past?' And she herself was so changed that I no longer found her beautiful, and in fact, she was no longer beautiful at all. While we walked, I saw the landscape change, as we first climbed steep slopes, but then walked downhill. I chatted with Gilberte, which I found very pleasant. And yet it was not all that easy. In so many individuals there are different, dissimilar layers, the character of the father, the character of the mother; we traverse first one, then the other. But the next day the order of the layering is reversed. And ultimately we no longer knows who could separate the parts and who could be trusted to sit in judgment. Gilberte was like one of those countries with which we dare not conclude an alliance because they change government too often. Yet basically we are wrong. However discontinuous the life of an individual, memory establishes within him a sort of identity, with the result that he does not want to break promises that he remembers, even if he did not sign them himself. As for intelligence, Gilberte's was very shrewd, give or take a few eccentricities inherited from her mother. But independently of her intrinsic qualities, I remember how greatly she astonished me on several occasions, during the conversations which we held while out walking. Once, the first time, by telling me that, 'If you weren't too hungry and it weren't so late, if we took the path on the left and then turned to the right it would take us less than a quarter of an hour to reach the Guermantes.' It was as if she had said, 'Turn left, then turn right, and you will grasp the intangible, you will reach the distant and unattainable goals of which on earth we know only the direction, and only' – something I had always previously thought of as all I could ever know of the Guermantes, and perhaps in a sense I was not entirely wrong – 'the "way" towards them'. One of my other moments of astonishment was to see the 'source of the Vivonne', which I had imagined to be something as extra-terrestrial as the entrance to Hell, and which was no more than a kind of square wash-tub full of bubbles. And the third time was when Gilberte said: 'If you like, we could still go out one afternoon to walk towards Guermantes, but we could walk past Méséglise, it's the prettiest route,' a sentence which overturned all the ideas of my childhood by revealing that the two ways were not as irreconcilable as I had thought. But what struck me the most was how little, during this stay, I relived my former years, how little I wanted to revisit Combray, and how narrow and ugly I found the Vivonne. Yet it was during one of those quasi-nocturnal albeit pre-prandial walks – since she dined so late! – that she did authenticate for me the fantasies which I had formed around the way to Méséglise. Just as we were about to enter a mysteriously smooth and deep valley bathed in moonlight, we stopped for a moment, like two insects about to dive into the depths of a blue-tinted calyx. Then Gilberte, perhaps merely acting the well-mannered hostess, reluctant to let you leave so early and wishing she could have given you a deeper appreciation of the countryside that you seemed to like, spoke to me with all the skill of a sophisticated woman adept at mingling silence, simplicity and sobriety with the expression of feeling, leading you to believe that you have a place in her life which no one else could replace. Gushing suddenly with an affection inspired by the sweetness and warmth of the evening breeze, I replied, 'You mentioned the steep little track the other day. How I loved you then!' She answered, 'Why didn't you tell me? I had no idea. I loved you too. And I even once threw myself at your feet. — Whenever was that? — The first time, at Tansonville, you were out walking with your family, I was on my way home, and had never seen such a handsome little boy. I used', she added with an absent and modest air, 'to go to play with my young friends in the ruins of the dungeon at Roussainville. And you can guess how naughty it was, for it was a group of boys and girls of all sorts, and we took full advantage of the darkness. The choir-boy from Combray, Théodore, who, I have to admit, was very nice (my God, he was handsome!) but who has become extremely ugly (now he's the chemist at Méséglise), had fun with all the little village girls for miles around. Since they let me out on my own, as soon as I could get away, I rushed off to join them. I can't tell you how much I would have loved to see you there; I remember only too well, since I had only a moment to tell you, given the danger of being seen by your parents and mine, how I showed you so crudely what I wanted that I'm ashamed of it now. But you looked at me so fiercely that I realized that you didn't want to.' And suddenly I thought that the real Gilberte and the real Albertine were perhaps those who offered themselves up in a single glance, one by a hedgerow of pink hawthorn, the other on the beach. And it was I, unable to understand something which I was to retrieve only later in my memory, after a delay during which the whole emotional undercurrent of my conversation had made them fear to be as frank as they had been in the first instance, who had spoiled everything with my clumsiness. I had 'bungled' things more completely with them than Saint-Loup had with Rachel, and for the same reasons, although I have to say that my relative failure with them was less absurd. 'And the second time', continued Gilberte, 'was years later when I saw you in your doorway, the day before I met you at my aunt Oriane's; I didn't recognize you straight away, or rather I recognized you without realizing it, since I felt the same urges that I had at Tansonville. — But in between, there was the Champs-Elysées. — Yes, but then you were too much in love with me, I felt that you were spying on my every move.' I did not think to ask her the identity of the young man with whom I saw her walking down the Champs-Elysées the day that I had set out to meet her again, when I might have been reconciled with her while there was still time, on a day which would perhaps have changed my life if I had not met two shadowy figures coming towards me side by side in the twilight. If I had asked her, she might have told me the truth, as might Albertine, if she had come back to life. And indeed, does death not come between us and women whom we no longer love but meet again years later, just as if they were no longer of this world, since the fact that our love no longer exists makes of the women that they used to be, or the men that we were, dead people? Perhaps also she might not have remembered, or she might have lied. In any case I no longer saw any interest in finding out, since my heart had already changed more than Gilberte's face. It no longer appealed to me, but the main thing was that I was no longer unhappy, and I could not have imagined, if I had thought of it again, that I could have been so unhappy to see Gilberte walking slowly side by side with another young man that I could have thought, 'It's all over, I refuse ever to see her again.' Of the state of mind which, for the whole of that far-off year, had been nothing but endless torture to me, nothing remained. For in this world where everything wears out, where everything perishes, there is one thing that collapses and is more completely destroyed than anything else, and leaves fewer traces than beauty itself: and that is grief.

If, however, I am not surprised not to have asked with whom she was walking down the Champs-Elysées, for I had already seen too many examples of how Time dulls our curiosity, I am a little surprised not to have told Gilberte that before meeting her that day I had sold an antique Chinese vase in order to buy her some flowers. My only consolation during those very sad times that followed was in fact that one day I might be able without embarrassment to tell her of this so tender intention. More than a year afterwards, if I saw that a car was in danger of striking mine, my only reason for not wanting to die was to be able to tell this to Gilberte. I consoled myself with the thought, 'Let's not rush things, I've all my life ahead of me for that.' And because of that I did not want to lose my life. Now it would have seemed to me unpleasant to recount, almost ridiculous and 'compromising'. 'Besides,' Gilberte went on, 'even on the day that I met you on your doorstep, you were still so like you were at Combray, if only you knew how little you had changed!' I pictured Gilberte again in my memory. I could have drawn the rectangle of light shed by the sun beneath the hawthorns, the spade that the little girl held in her hand, the lingering look that she cast in my direction. Except that, given the crude gesture which accompanied it, I had seen it as a look of contempt, because what I wanted seemed to me to be something of which little girls knew nothing and complied with only in my imagination, during my hours of solitary desire. Even less could I have imagined that, so easily and so swiftly, almost under my grandfather's nose, one of them might have been so bold as to spell it out.

Thus after so many years I had to touch up the image that I recalled so well, an operation which made me relatively happy by showing me that the uncrossable abyss which I had at that time believed to exist between me and a certain kind of little girl with golden hair was as imaginary as the abyss described by Pascal, and which I found poetical because of the long series of years I needed to cross in order to perform this operation. I felt a renewed pang of desire and regret on thinking of the dungeons of Roussainville. And yet I was pleased, as I realized that the happiness which I had striven with all my might to achieve in those days, and which nothing could ever now restore, had existed elsewhere than in my thoughts, and indeed so near to me in the Roussainville which I talked of so often and which I glimpsed from the toilet scented with iris. And I had had no idea! In short, she had subsumed everything that I had desired on my walks, when I reached the point where I could not bear to go home, as I felt that the trees were on the point of becoming human and parting their limbs. What I had then so feverishly desired, she had almost, if only I had been able to understand and accept it, made me taste while still an adolescent. Even more than I had thought, Gilberte was already at this time fully engaged in the Méséglise way.

And even on the day when I had met her in a doorway, although she was not the Mlle de l'Orgeville whom Robert had met in a house of ill-fame (and how extraordinary it was that the person whom I had asked to enlighten me on this subject was none other than her future husband!), I had not been entirely mistaken as to the significance of her glance, nor as to the kind of woman that she was and now admitted to me that she had been. 'All that is so long ago,' she said, 'I've never thought of anyone but Robert since the day we were engaged. And, you know, those childish pranks are still not what I regret the most.'

# *Notes to* The Prisoner

1. *Mme de Sévigné*: seventeenth-century aristocrat, famous for her letters, most of which are addressed to her daughter, Mme de Grignan.

2. *Et la mort ... qu'il me fasse appeler*: 'And death is the reward of any audacious person/Who without being called appears before his eyes ... // Nothing can protect one from that deadly order,/neither rank nor sex, and the crime is equal./Even I ... am subject to this law like anyone else,/And without forestalling him, if I am to speak with him/I must wait for him to come to me or at least have me called.' These lines come from Racine's play *Esther* (Act I, Scene iii), which Proust frequently quotes (from memory) in *The Prisoner* and in other volumes of *In Search of Lost Time*. Originally written for performance by a girls' school, *Esther* was often chosen as a text for young girls to study in Proust's day. It is supposed to be the only classical play Albertine knows, from having studied and acted in it at school.

3. *the Buttes-Chaumont*: a park on the north-eastern edge of central Paris.

4. *My landlady, Mme de Guermantes*: having originally lived in a different part of Paris, the narrator's family moves at the beginning of *The Guermantes Way* (pp. 7–8) to a flat in the Hôtel de Guermantes, in the Faubourg Saint-Germain. The side ranges of the front courtyard of the old aristocratic town house are now divided into flats and let to middle-class families, while on the ground floor are small workshops of various kinds. The furthest range is occupied as a single house by the owners, the Duc and Duchesse de Guermantes, whom by this point in the story the narrator has got to know. Many of the main characters in the story (the narrator, Albertine, the Guermantes, Jupien and his niece) are thus now living on the same site, and can plausibly meet and observe each other's comings and goings on the stairs and in the courtyard. The Baron de Charlus, brother of the Duc de Guermantes, erstwhile sexual partner of Jupien and protector of his niece, visits them all at this address. This is all extremely convenient to the novelist's purposes, but not in itself implausible: such multiple use of old aristocratic dwellings was

common in Paris throughout the nineteenth century, and its traces could still be seen in the Marais until the recent renovation of that quarter.

5. *an umbrella*: carrying an umbrella was, in the nineteenth and early twentieth centuries, the very symbol of bourgeois status. Aristocrats were supposed to ride in carriages, poor people to get wet. Louis-Philippe, the 'Citizen King', was often caricatured with an umbrella in his hand.

6. *Pampille*: pen-name of Mme Léon Daudet, wife of a friend of Proust and author of *Les bons plats de France: cuisine régionale* (1913).

7. *Xerxes . . . that had swallowed up his fleet*: after the battle of Salamis the Persian fleet was destroyed by a storm in the Hellespont. Xerxes, the King of Persia, is said to have vented his feelings by having his servants beat the sea with rods. See also p. 92.

8. *the terrifying jumping girl of Balbec*: see *In the Shadow of Young Girls in Flower*, II, p. 372.

9. *Rosita and Doodica*: Siamese twins exhibited by Barnum's Circus in 1901–2.

10. *at right angles, it rose*: sic.

11. *Boris Godunov . . . Pelléas*: Mussorgsky's opera *Boris Godunov* was first performed in Paris in 1908, Debussy's *Pelléas et Mélisande* in 1902, but Proust first heard them in 1911–13, at the time when he was first working on *The Prisoner*. The novelty of these music-dramas was that they did not observe the old operatic distinction between recitative and aria, but were through-composed, their essential dialogue delivered with only small variations of pitch.

12. *Rameau*: these words appear, not as Proust seems to have thought in an opera of Rameau, but in Quinault's libretto *Armide*, set to music first by Lully in 1686 and then by Gluck in 1777.

13. *Arkel . . . Golaud . . . the King of Allemonde*: characters in *Pelléas et Mélisande*.

14. *'Per omnia saecula saeculorum' . . . 'Requiescat in pace'*: 'World without end' (a very frequent concluding formula for prayers) . . . 'May he (or she) rest in peace' (concluding formula for prayers for the dead). Both usually intoned with the last syllable falling a minor third, and followed by *Amen*.

15. *Quel mortel insolent vient chercher le trépas . . . et jamais ne me lasse*: 'What insolent mortal comes here to seek death? //Was it for you that this stern order was made?//I find only in you a certain grace/Which always charms me and never tires me' (from *Esther*).

16. *Mnemotechne*: (Greek), the art of memory: here confused, perhaps deliberately, with Mnemosyne, Memory herself, the mother of the Muses.

17. *'Here's mackerel' . . . Shudder*: an untranslatable pun. *Maquereau* is French slang for a pimp.

18. *Praeceptis salutaribus . . . dicere*: 'As our Saviour Christ commanded and taught us, we are bold to say.' This formula introduces the Lord's Prayer in the Mass liturgy.

19. '*Rags, old iron to sell*': *sic*.

20. *Suave mari magno*: 'It is pleasant, when the wide sea . . .' The opening lines of Book II of Lucretius' poem *De rerum naturae* observe how pleasant it is, when we are on dry land, to watch another man battling to stay afloat in a stormy sea. Though the poet was commending not *schadenfreude* but philosophical detachment, the phrase is used proverbially to allude to someone who takes pleasure in the suffering of others. Proust, however, seems here to be using it literally and not figuratively.

21. *they don't sell ices in the street*: small ices, to be eaten immediately, were certainly sold in the street before 1900: there is a nineteenth-century photograph of an ice-cream man with his cart by Eugène Atget. But what the characters are discussing here are sizeable, elaborate iced desserts sold in expensive shops.

22. *Scheherazade*: the fictional narrator of the *Arabian Nights*, a book which Proust loved both as a child and as an adult.

23. *his crucifix*: the steering-wheel of some cars at this time was cruciform, with no outer ring.

24. *Gregory the Great . . . Palestrina*: Gregory the Great, Pope from 590 to 604, is supposed to have set the rules for Gregorian chant. A sixteenth-century Pope, Gregory XIII, had Palestrina adapt the old chants to the new liturgy of Pius V.

25. *Danaids . . . Ixion*: figures from Greek legend condemned to never-ending tasks. The Danaids (the fifty daughters of Danaos) murdered their husbands and were condemned to spend eternity pouring water into a bottomless vessel. Ixion was attached by Zeus to a burning wheel which turned eternally in the Underworld.

26. *The Longjumeau Postilion*: the critic Frédéric Masson had written in 1915 that he preferred the work of this name, a light opera by Adam, to Wagner's *Die Meistersinger*.

27. *Human Comedy . . . The Legend of the Centuries . . . The Bible of Humanity*: the first of these was the title given by Balzac to his collected novels; the second is a collection of narrative poems by Hugo and the third an imaginative attempt at a synthesis of human history by Michelet.

28. *those hundred-and-twenty-horsepower Mysteries*: the *Mystère* was a make of aircraft.

29. *L'Éducation sentimentale*: in Flaubert's novel of that name, the woman the hero loves sees in his house a portrait of a former mistress of his, whom she

661

had known. She says, 'I've seen that woman somewhere,' but he replies, 'Impossible, it's an old Italian painting.'

30. *great slut*: the original expression is *'grand pied-de-grue'*. This does not appear in any dictionary, including those of slang and low language, as an insult that might be addressed to a woman, though *'une grue'* is a prostitute. *'Faire le pied de grue'* is to wait, to be kept waiting or hanging about, but that is plainly not the meaning here. 'Slut' is an approximation.

31. *he*: Elstir. See *Sodom and Gomorrah*, p. 408.

32. *the Trocadéro whose giraffe-neck towers*: the building described stood on the small hill above the Place du Trocadéro from 1878 until 1937, when it was replaced by the present Palais de Chaillot.

33. *the Champs-Elysées Circus*: this auditorium was used for a variety of performances, including subscription concerts.

34. *a large Barbedienne bronze*: Ferdinand Barbedienne (1810–1892) specialized in drawing-room bronzes. By 1900 his sculptures were regarded as a sign of quintessentially bourgeois taste. A Barbedienne bronze is the only decoration of the anonymous hotel-room in Sartre's *Huis clos*.

35. *a 'Rambuteau shelter'*: the once familiar green metal Parisian *pissotières*, more elegantly known as *vespasiennes*, began to be erected during the Comte de Rambuteau's tenure as *préfet* of the *département* of the Seine, just as the dustbin (*poubelle*) was introduced under M. Poubelle. One can imagine that the Rambuteau family would not wish their name to be attached to such a utilitarian innovation.

36. *a more Cambronnesque word*: General Cambronne commanded Napoleon's Imperial Guard at Waterloo. Official history relates that when called upon to surrender with his men, he answered, 'The Guard dies but does not surrender.' All Frenchmen believe, however, that his real reply was *'Merde!'* Hence a euphemism for *merde* is 'le mot de Cambronne'. The word Proust uses in the text is *'se débrouiller'*: the 'Cambronnesque' alternative would be *'se démerder'*.

37. *the choice between breaking . . . and completely falling out with M. de Charlus*: sic.

38. *the Tissot painting*: this passage describes a real painting by Tissot, now in a private collection, in which the distinguished figures mentioned appear in company with Charles Haas, generally regarded as the real-life model for Swann. It was reproduced in *L'Illustration* of 10 June 1922.

39. *Otto . . . Lenthéric*: a fashionable photographer and hairdresser of the time.

40. *Landru*: a serial killer of women, convicted in 1921 and executed in 1922. This passage must therefore be one of Proust's last additions to *The Prisoner*.

41. *La Bruyère*: this observation occurs in La Bruyère's *Caractères* (1688), in the chapter 'On Fashion'.

42. *Mounet-Sully*: a celebrated tragic actor of the day.

43. *We must say . . . the postmarks*: this sentence is incomplete in the original.

44. *an Ingres pen*: the painter Ingres was also a talented amateur performer on the violin. Hence a gifted man's 'second string' is referred to as his 'violon d'Ingres'. As Morel is a violinist, M. de Charlus is able wittily to invert the set phrase.

45. *Il Sodoma*: the nickname given by his contemporaries to the sixteenth-century Italian painter Giovanni Antonio Bazzi.

46. *the abbé Le Batteux*: should be simply 'the abbé Batteux', eighteenth-century author of a guide to literature.

47. *Mrs Todgers, Sarah Gamp and Mrs Harris*: M. de Charlus's reference in the original is to Mme Pipelet, Mme Gibout and Mme Joseph Prudhomme, minor creations of the nineteenth-century writers Eugène Sue and Henri Monnier. They are chosen as examples of women utterly lacking in social distinction: Mme Pipelet, for example, is a concierge. Three comparable characters from Dickens have been substituted.

48. *Reichenberg . . . Bernhardt*: Suzanne Reichenberg was a light comedienne, while Sarah Bernhardt excelled in intensely dramatic roles.

49. *Reinach . . . Hervieu*: Joseph Reinach, politician and journalist, an early Dreyfus supporter, went on to write a 7-volume *Histoire de l'affaire Dreyfus* (1901–11). Paul Hervieu was a society novelist and also a Dreyfusard.

50. *Anatole France*: one of the most highly regarded novelists of the day (Nobel Prize for Literature 1921).

51. *Picquart . . . Labori . . . Zurlinden, Loubet, Colonel Jouaust*: all official figures involved in the Dreyfus case.

52. *Jaurès*: Jean Jaurès, socialist politician, newspaper editor and writer, assassinated in 1914.

53. *Gaeta*: King Theodosius and Queen Eudoxia are invented characters, but the Queen of Naples was a real person. At the siege of Gaeta in 1861 she had actually given the order to fire on the invading Piedmontese troops before being driven into exile.

54. *'the poet is speaking'*. . . *'the child is asleep'*: Proust gives French translations of the titles of piano pieces in Schumann's *Kinderszenen*. These pieces are not intended for children to play, but are, in the composer's own words, 'retrospective reflections of an adult, for adults'.

55. *as Buffon says of the camel*: Buffon, the eighteenth-century naturalist, wrote an account of the animal kingdom in supremely elegant prose. His descriptions of such animals as the lion or the horse often endow the beasts with almost human moral qualities, and were given to schoolchildren as models of style. He in fact says that the docility of camels is equal to their courage.

**56.** *Beckmesser's parody*: a character in *Die Meistersinger* who tries to compete in a singing contest and is laughed off stage.

**57.** *Moscow decree*: Napoleon I signed a decree in Moscow in 1812, establishing a new constitution for the Comédie Française and spelling out the rights and duties of members of the company. Mme Verdurin aspires to similar control over 'her' artists.

**58.** *Hoyos*: Count Hoyos, Austrian ambassador to Paris from 1883 to 1894.

**59.** *grande mortalis aevi spatium*: 'a long period in a man's life' (Tacitus, *Life of Agricola*).

**60.** *Doña Sol's time*: heroine of Victor Hugo's play *Hernani*. On the evening of her marriage to Hernani, all the guests have left when the sound of a horn reminds Hernani that he has promised to die before sundown.

**61.** *Couture's philosophers*: the reference is to Couture's large history painting, *Les Romains de la décadence* (1847), once held in the Louvre and now in the Musée d'Orsay. It shows a Cecil B. De Mille-style Roman orgy, but downstage right two philosophers are deep in discussion, unmoved by what is going on behind them.

**62.** *Hernani again*: this is perhaps a play on Charlie's name and that of Don Carlos, another character in Hugo's play.

**63.** *Enesco, Capet or Thibaud*: leading violinists of the day.

**64.** *Théodore Rousseau*: landscape painter of the School of Fontainebleau.

**65.** *Vacqueries and Meurices*: Auguste Vacquerie and Paul Meurice, literary disciples of Hugo.

**66.** *the bedel in all his chains*: these are chains of office, worn by (non-academic) university officials on ceremonial occasions. At the University of Oxford at the time of writing (2002), distinguished visiting lecturers (but not the native product) are still preceded to the rostrum by bedels carrying silver maces.

**67.** *sursum corda*: 'lift up your hearts': the priest's exhortation to the faithful which begins the Proper of the Mass. The phrase was used in French in Proust's day as a general expression of encouragement.

**68.** *the Citizen King*: Louis-Philippe, installed by the July Revolution of 1830. His reign, from 1830 to 1848, was known as the July Monarchy. Legitimists, like the Duchesse de***, regarded him as a usurper and had only contempt for his middle-class manners (see note 5 above).

**69.** *Barrès*: Maurice Barrès, right-wing novelist, politician and journalist.

**70.** *Leverrier's planet*: Neptune. The nineteenth-century French astronomer had shown, by mathematical calculation, that this planet must exist, well before its presence could be confirmed by observation.

**71.** *Lucien Daudet*: a close friend of Proust, right-wing journalist and author of seemingly far-fetched spy stories, notably *La Vermine du monde, roman de l'espionnage allemand* (1916).

72. *arbiter elegantarium*: (Latin) the chief authority on taste. The title was given to the writer Petronius (hence known as Petronius Arbiter) in the reign of the emperor Nero.

73. *Monsieur*: like 'Madame' (p. 280), this was a title given to a close relative of the King under the *ancien régime*. 'Monsieur' was the King's eldest brother, 'Madame' his wife. The 'Monsieur' referred to here, Louis XIV's only brother, was notoriously an effeminate homosexual. He had two wives (and several children): the second Madame was Charlotte-Elizabeth, a princess from the Palatinate (hence her further name of La Palatine). She was a stocky, down-to-earth German girl who was at first appalled and finally moved to shocked laughter by the atmosphere of Louis XIV's court, where she lived for fifty years, describing it in regular, vivid letters to her relations at home. These were edited and translated in 1863, giving nineteenth-century Frenchmen a new view of the court of the Sun King. Most of M. de Charlus's scandalous anecdotes come from La Palatine's letters: not, however, the suggestion that Molière was a homosexual, which is not found in seventeenth-century sources.

The verses in macaronic Latin might be translated as follows: 'My dear friend La Moussaye/Good God, what weather/Hey nonny nonny/We shall drown in this rain . . . Our lives are safe/For we are Sodomites/And destined to die in fire/Hey nonny no.'

74. *M. Bourget*: Paul Bourget, society novelist admired in Proust's day for his careful, theoretically based psychological analysis.

75. *la Rochefoucauld . . . Heliogabalus*: François, Duc de la Rochefoucauld (1613–80), makes this observation in the *Réflexions diverses* added to his more famous *Maximes*. Heliogabalus was a third-century Roman emperor famous for his excesses, particularly sexual.

76. *Tobias . . . Archangel Raphael . . . pool of Bethsaida*: in the Book of Tobias, the young Tobias brings to the house of his father, also Tobias, a stranger who turns out to be the Archangel Raphael and who cures his father's blindness. M. de Charlus distorts the story to fit his own preoccupations: Brichot is invited to bring the young man to the house, and promised the reward of the old Tobias. The pool of Bethsaida is the scene of one of the miracles of Jesus (John 5: 2–4).

77. *Mgr d'Hulst*: founder of the Catholic University in Paris and its first Rector (1880–96). The phrase attributed to him ('*je ne m'embête pas*') is surprisingly colloquial and in no sense requires the authority of such a figure.

78. *Monday Conversations*: the *Causeries du lundi* (1851–62, 15 vols.) and

*Nouveaux lundis* (1863–70, 13 vols.) of Charles-Augustin Sainte-Beuve were collections of the weekly essays which he published between 1849 and 1869 in *Le Constitutionnel*, *Le Moniteur* and *Le Temps*. The most famous French exponent of the biographical method of literary criticism, Sainte-Beuve was Proust's critical *bête noire*: his writings on literature, published posthumously, were given the title *Contre Sainte-Beuve*. No doubt it amused him to present, through Brichot, Sainte-Beuve's work as a collection of stale gossip.

**79**. *Plato in the house of Aspasia*: Aspasia was a *hetaira*, famed for her beauty and intelligence, the companion of philosophers and statesmen in Plato's day.

**80**. *Dii omen avertant*: literally, 'may the gods turn aside the omen': 'Heaven forbid'.

**81**. *Sylvestre Bonnard*: eponymous hero of Anatole France's *Le crime de Sylvestre Bonnard* (1881).

**82**. *Horrors! That is what she would have preferred*: '*Casser le pot à quelqu'un: le sodomiser*' (*Dictionnaire de l'argot*, Larousse, 1990). This is the first and only mention of a possible taste in Albertine for anal sex. The explanation which follows ('Only to another woman', etc.), however, suggests that the expression may have been in use among lesbians to denote penetrative sex in general.

**83**. *La Tour*: seventeenth-century painter famous for chiaroscuro effects.

**84**. *charlatante*: this is a coinage of Françoise's: there is no feminine of *charlatan*. It has been made by substituting for the final *-tan* the feminine noun *tante*, aunt (which also has the slang meaning of (male) homosexual).

**85**. *the Pont-aux-Choux drawings*: production drawings surviving from the former Pont-aux-Choux porcelain factory, destroyed in 1789.

**86**. *Roettiers . . . Mme du Barry*: Roettiers was court silversmith to Louis XV, Mme du Barry the King's mistress.

**87**. *Barbey d'Aurevilly*: nineteenth-century novelist. Like Hardy's, his novels are usually set in provincial towns far from the capital, and in the surrounding countryside. His works include *Une vieille maîtresse* (An Old Mistress) (1851), *L'Ensorcelée* (The Woman Bewitched) (1854), *Le Chevalier des Touches* (1864) and a collection of short stories, *Les Diaboliques* (1874), which includes 'Le Rideau cramoisi' (The Crimson Curtain). Aimée de Spens, La Clotte and La Vellini are characters in these various fictions.

**88**. *Nastasya Philippovna . . . Grushenka*: characters in Dostoevsky's novels: Nastasya Philippovna in *The Idiot*, Grushenka in *The Brothers Karamazov*.

**89**. *Paul de Kock*: a prolific, low-brow mid-nineteenth-century novelist whom no one would be likely to compare with Dostoevsky.

**90**. *here is a description*: no description follows. However, a passage of Mme de Sévigné is compared to Dostoevsky in *In the Shadow of Young Girls in Flower*, p. 232.

91. *Choderlos de Laclos . . . Mme de Genlis*: Laclos was the author of *Les Liaisons dangereuses* (1782), Mme de Genlis of a collection of *Contes moraux* (Moral Tales) (1802). She had been governess to Louis-Philippe in his childhood and at the same time the mistress of his father, the Duc d'Orléans.

92. *Si le viol . . . n'est pas assez hardie*: 'If rape, poison, daggers, arson . . . / It is because our soul, alas, is not bold enough.'

93. *the Princess of China shut up in a bottle*: the reference is to a letter by Merimée in which he tells the story of a madman who thought he had the Princess of China, the most beautiful of all princesses, shut up in a bottle. When he broke the bottle – and lost the Princess – he changed from madness to imbecility.

94. *Jugez combien . . . qui partent de vos yeux?*: 'Judge how much this face, angry with me,/Must have sown alarm in my disturbed soul . . . /Alas! What audacious heart could, without trembling,/Bear the lightning that flashes from your eyes?'

95. *'Booz endormi'*: an anthology piece by Victor Hugo. In the last stanza, the moon in the sky is compared to a golden sickle.

96. *Parisian, get up, get up*: the morning bugle-call in the French army is given the words *'Soldat, lève-toi'* (Soldier, get up). (Cf. e.g. 'Come to the cook-house door'.) Proust imagines a bugle sounding *'Parisien, lève-toi'*.

97. *. . . une majesté terrible/Affecte à mes sujets de me rendre invisible*: 'a fearsome majesty/Affects to keep me unseen by my subjects' (from *Esther*).

98. *the river Ocean*: in some medieval maps, the sea is represented as the river Ocean, winding around the land.

# *Notes to* The Fugitive

1. *Helen on the old men of Troy*: a reference to Ronsard's sonnet sequence, *Sonnets pour Hélène*. See note 2.

2. *Notre mal . . . de ses regards*: Pierre de Ronsard, *Sonnets pour Hélène*, Book II, LXVII, line 4: 'Our ills cannot match one look from her eyes.'

3. *Manon*: the opera of 1884, adapted from the Abbé Prévost's eighteenth-century novel *Manon Lescaut*. Music by Jules Massenet, libretto by Henri Meilhac and Philippe Gille.

4. *Hélas . . . au vitrage*: 'Alas, the bird who seems to flee her plight/Most oft returns at night/To beat against the pane in desperate flight,' sung by Manon in Act III, Scene II, imploring her lover Des Grieux, who is then reconciled with her.

5. *Manon . . . de ton cœur*: 'Manon do answer me! – My soul's only love,/It was only today that I found how kind was your heart.' Sung by Des Grieux in a duet at the end of Act V, where the dying Manon asks for forgiveness.

6. *le Cygne*: 'The Swan'.

7. *Un cygne . . . l'ennui*: a stanza from Mallarmé's sonnet 'Le vierge, le vivace et le bel aujourd'hui': 'A swan of past days recalls it is he/Magnificent but without hope who is freed/For not having sung the realm where to live/When sterile winter's ennui has shone forth.'

8. *Le vierge . . . aujourd'hui*: 'This virgin, beautiful and lively day.'

9. *Dis si . . . de mes chars*: 'Say if I am not joyous/Thunder and rubies at the axles/To see in this fire-pierced air/Amid scattered realms/As though dying purple the wheel/Of my sole chariot of evening.' (Two stanzas from another sonnet by Mallarmé, 'M'introduire dans ton histoire'; both extracts in Roger Fry's translation, Stéphane Mallarmé, *Poems*, Chatto and Windus, 1936.)

10. *On dit . . . de nous*: Jean Racine, *Phèdre*, Act II, Scene V, where Phèdre

admits her incestuous love for her stepson, Hippolyte: 'I hear that you must leave, and travel far from us.'

11. *Aurais-je . . . de ma gloire*: Phèdre: 'Could I have lost all care for my good name.'

12. *Madame . . . votre époux?*: Hippolyte: 'Madam, do you forget/That Theseus is my father, and that he is your husband?'

13. *Ah cruel . . . entendu!*: Phèdre: 'Oh, cruel friend, you understood too well!'

14. *Tu . . . de nouveaux charmes*: Phèdre: 'You hated me more, I loved you no less./Your misfortune revived all the charms that you held.'

15. *'Jansenist' scruples*: 'Jansenism' is so called after the Christian doctrine expounded by Jansenius (1585–1638) in his *Augustinus* of 1628. This doctrine favours grace and predestination rather than free will and good works. In this light, Phèdre would be less responsible for her actions, and less guilty.

16. *the Orsay railway station*: this Parisian railway station served the south and south-west of France, including Châtelleraut and Touraine.

17. *they were going to close down the churches and banish the clergy*: an allusion to the legislation passed in 1904 and 1905 in France leading to the separation of Church and State ('Loi sur les Congrégations').

18. *Esther*: See *The Prisoner*, n. 2.

19. *Les Écorres . . . the Marie-Antoinette farm*: it was fashionable at the time to drive out into the countryside in Normandy and take tea on a farm.

20. *'philosopher in the garret'*: reference to a novel by Émile Souvestre, *Un philosophe sous les toits, journal d'un homme heureux*, 1850.

21. *Saint-Cloud*: one of Marie-Antoinette's châteaux, where Napoleon and Napoleon III both declared themselves Emperor in their turn (in 1804 and 1852). It was sacked in 1870 during the Franco-Prussian war, and demolished in 1891. But its gardens, designed by Le Nôtre, still provided an attractive, and perhaps nostalgic, weekend excursion.

22. *ten-to-two*: I have homogenized the time of this train, which Proust noted variously as 1.35 (here), and elsewhere as 1.22 or 1.50.

23. *. . . 'left me cold'*: here I have omitted a sentence repeated inadvertently by Proust twice on the same page.

24. *Touraine*: here Proust actually wrote 'Nice', left over from an earlier draft where Mme Bontemps's villa was stuated on the Côte d'Azur.

25. *the 1870 war*: Franco-Prussian war. Napoleon III surrendered to the Prussians at Sedan in 1870. This was traumatic for civilians because of the resulting uprising of the Paris Commune in 1871.

26. *Chaumont*: cf. note 28, and *The Prisoner*, n. 3.

27. *'Le Secret'*: 'The Secret', by Gabriel Fauré, opus 23, no. 3, in D flat, set to a poem by Armand Sylvestre, 1882. The *Figaro* regularly published such songs.

**28.** *the Duc de Broglie*: Albert de Broglie was a historian who wrote *Le secret du roi* ('The King's Secret') in 1878. De Broglie, the grandson of Madame de Staël (whose daughter was called Albertine), was the owner of a château at Chaumont-sur-Loire, where glamorous society events were held at the end of the ninteteenth century.

**29.** *Fabrice del Dongo's life*: Fabrice is the hero of Stendhal's *La Chartreuse de Parme*, 1839.

**30.** *as La Pompadour did for Louis XV*: Mme de Pompadour (1721–64) retained influence with Louis XV through such means, after ceasing to be his mistress.

**31.** *Memoirs*: the Duc de Saint-Simon (1675–1755) wrote his *Memoirs* of life during the reign of Louis XIV.

### CHAPTER 2

**1.** *Mme du Barry's desire to impress the king*: the Goncourt brothers, in their *La Du Barry*, recount that Mme du Barry had displayed Van Dyck's portrait of Charles I in her bedroom.

**2.** . . . *which had not been published*: from 1903 onwards Proust himself had published a number of articles in the *Figaro*.

**3.** *Lundis*: Sainte-Beuve published his *Causeries du lundi* from 1851 to 1862. In his *Les Nouveaux Lundis*, published in 1886, he reproduces the Comtesse de Boigne's obituary from *Le Constitutionnel* of 18 May 1866 and recalls her thanks to him in 1863 for his obituary on chancellor Pasquier.

**4.** *Mme de Boigne*: in 1907 Mme de Boigne published *Les Récits d'une tante: Mémoires de la comtesse de Boigne née Osmond*, which spurred Proust into writing his anti-Beuvian article in the *Figaro*, 'Journées de lecture', published posthumously in his *Contre Sainte-Beuve*.

**5.** *suave mari magno*: from the Stoic philospher Lucretius' *De Rerum Natura*. The complete sentence is: 'Suave, mari magno turbantibus aequora ventis,/e terra magnum alterius spectare laborem;/non quia vexare quemquamst iucunda voluptas,/sed quibus ipse malis cares quia cernare suave est.' ('What joy it is, when out at sea the stormwinds are lashing the waters, to gaze from the shore at the heavy stress some other man is enduring! Not that anyone's afflictions are in themselves a source of delight; but to realize from what troubles you yourself are free is joy indeed.' Trans. R. E. Latham, Penguin, 1951.)

**6.** *Rouvier's*: Rouvier was Prime Minister in 1905. The reference is probably to a controversial speech made in Tangier by Kaiser Wilhelm II.

**7.** . . . *Mlle de Mortemart's wedding list*: the Russo-Japanese war ran from 1904 to 1905, whereas Mlle Antoinette de Rochechouart de Mortemart's wedding was recounted in the *Figaro* of 4 August 1916, while the battles of Verdun and the Somme were both raging.

8. *Musset . . . 'hoping in God'*: a reference to Alfred de Musset's poem 'L'Espoir en Dieu', *Poésies nouvelles*, 1838.

9. *King Edward*: Edward VII reigned from 1901 to 1910. He is remembered for sponsoring the Entente Cordiale between Britain and France in 1904. He had spent many years previously as Prince of Wales, living a life of social amusement under Victoria's long reign.

10. *Nattiers*: Jean-Marc Nattier, 1685–1766, court painter under Louis XV.

11. *Nereids*: water nymphs, daughters of Nereus.

12. *the Second Empire*: (1852–70) ended with the defeat of Napoleon III by the Prussians at Sedan. This would have been very recent history for a *fin de siècle* school syllabus.

13. *'Oh! ma chérie, c'est dans mon cœur!'*: 'Oh, darling, with all my heart!'

14. *'Les morts dorment . . . les mains'*: 'The dead sleep in peace in the womb of the earth./Thus must my deadened feelings sleep./These bones of my heart have also their dust:/Let us not lay hands on their sacred remains.' From Alfred de Musset, 'La nuit d'Octobre', *Poésies complètes*.

15. *'Tu les feras pleurer . . . tes yeux purs'*: 'You will make them weep, my beautiful, beloved child . . ./All those children, future men,/Already suspending their young daydreams/From the tender lashes of your pure eyes.' From Sully-Prudhomme, 'Aux Tuileries', *Les Varnes Tendresses*.

16. *'Le premier soir . . . dans ses bras'*: 'The first night that he came to me/I lost all care for self-esteem./I told him: "You may hold me fast/As long as still your love can last." I could not sleep outside his arms.' From Charles Cros, 'Nocturne'.

17. *Ballets Russes*: one of the most revolutionary – and fashionable – artistic phenomena in Paris from their inauguration in 1909. The character of Octave probably owes something to Proust's young acquaintance, Jean Cocteau, who collaborated with Picasso, Satie and Diaghilev on *Parade*, 1917, and whose artistic talents were underestimated because of his reputation as a socialite.

18. *who writes, composes or paints*: this phrase is difficult to construe in the French. In order to make sense of it, I have preferred the Folio edition's reading of *qui* instead of the Pléiade reading of *lui*.

19. *Elective Affinities*: novel by Goethe, 1808–9.

20. *Concours Général*: this was, and is, a nationwide competitive examination, for which lycées might enter their star baccalaureate pupils.

21. *the Broglie family*: this family had produced not only Albert, the historian quoted earlier, but a whole series of historians and physicists.

**22.** *noxious*: here I have preferred the Folio reading *nocives* to the Pléiade's *novices*.

**23.** . . . *overshadowed by fatigue*: the Folio edition adds the following sentence from one of Proust's typescripts, which helps make the transition to the next section: 'As for the third time that I remember realizing that I was nearing complete indifference where Albertine was concerned (and this last time, to the point of feeling that I had completely succeeded) it occurred one day in Venice, quite some time after Andrée's last visit.'

CHAPTER 3

**1.** *Maxime Dethomas*: this artist (1867–1929) had illustrated Henri de Régnier's *Esquisses venitiennes* in 1906 and Proust's 'À Venise', *Feuillets d'Art*, 1919.

**2.** *W\*\*\**: the couturier Worth, 1825–95, who created his Parisian fashion house in 1860.

**3.** *Salviati's*: the best-known Venetian glass merchant, situated on the Grand Canal.

**4.** *the Corriere della Sera, the Gazzetta del Popolo*: liberal, centre-left newspapers, founded respectively in Milan in 1876 and Turin in 1848.

**5.** *Paléologue*: Maurice Paléologue (1859–1954), a diplomat who gave evidence during the trial of Dreyfus.

**6.** *Lozé*: Henri Lozé (1859–1915), ambassador to Vienna between 1893 and 1897.

**7.** *'Testis'*: literally, a witness, the pen-name used by the painter Gabriel Hanotaux when he wrote articles in the press on foreign policy.

**8.** *M. Giolitti*: Giovanni Giolitti (1842–1928), a liberal, centre-left Italian Prime Minister in 1892–3, 1906–9, 1911–14, 1920–21.

**9.** *M. Barrère*: Camille Barrère (1851–1940), French ambassador to Rome 1897–1924.

**10.** *VISCONTI-VENOSTA*: Emilio Visconti-Venosta (1829–1914), Italian foreign minister working in collaboration with Barrère.

**11.** *a most ancient French newspaper*: probably an allusion to *Le Temps*, founded in 1861.

**12.** *the lead-lined cells of some inner Venice*: the Doges' Palace in Venice held its prisoners in the 'piombi' – lead-lined cells in the attics, or the 'pozzi' – basement dungeons, likened to wells. Proust seems to conflate the two.

**13.** *M. Thiers*: Adolphe Thiers (1797–1877), historian and politician.

**14.** *San Giorgio dei Schiavoni*: the Scuola contains paintings by Carpaccio, including depictions of St George, St Jerome and St Augustine, but not of St John, whose emblem is the eagle. But the evangelical eagle is a motif likely to found in almost any Venetian or indeed Christian church.

15. *'non point telle . . . un peu farouche'*: from Racine's *Phèdre*, Act II, Scene V: 'not as Hell hath seen her' 'but faithful, and loyal, if not entirely tamed'. Phèdre's speech alludes to her husband Thésée, presumed dead, alleging that her love for him is reincarnated in his son Hippolyte – Marcel has transposed the genders of the speaker and the reincarnated loved one.

16. *a study of Ruskin that I was engaged in*: Proust himself had translated Ruskin's *Bible of Amiens* (1904) and *Sesame and Lilies* (1906).

17. *Carpaccio's St Ursula*: Carpaccio's cycle of paintings of the life of St Ursula is in the Accademia. The painting referred to here is *The Martyrdom and Funeral of St Ursula*.

18. *The Patriarch of Grado exorcizing one possessed*: also in the Accademia.

19. *The Legend of St Joseph*: ballet, Paris 1914, for Diaghilev's Ballets Russes; music by Richard Strauss, décor and costumes by Misia Sert, scenario by Hugo von Hofmannsthal and Harry Kessler.

20. *Companions of La Calza*: members of the hosiers' guild. Each guild had its own distinctive livery.

21. *the chapel with its Giottos*: the Arena Chapel, or Capella degli Scrovegni, is entirely covered in frescoes painted by Giotto. Below the coloured frescoes depicting the life of Christ are the monochrome figures of the vices and virtues whose reproductions Swann had given the young Marcel.

22. *Roland Garros*: (1888–1918) French aviator.

23. *'O sole mio'*: lyrics by Giovanni Capurro, music by Eduardo di Capua, Naples 1898.

24. *the Deligny baths*: the Bains Deligny is a swimming-pool inside a barge moored to the banks of the Seine in Paris. The cold baths were recommended by Proust's father, who was professor of public hygiene at the University of Paris.

### CHAPTER 4

1. *'La plus grande . . . de faner'*: letters from Mme de Sévigné to her cousin Coulanges. Letter of 15 December 1670 announcing the marriage of La Grande Mademoiselle and de Lauzun as 'the greatest and the least' event; letter of 22 July 1671 on haymaking: 'haymaking is the most delightful thing in the world.'

2. *the Lucinges*: the Princesse de Lucinge was one of two natural daughters of the Duc de Berry (who on his deathbed when assassinated in 1820 recommended them to his wife for recognition and advancement).

3. *the Duc de Guise*: he plotted to kill Henri III (king of France 1574–89), who had him killed at Blois in 1588.

4. *Queen Marie-Amélie . . . Duc d'Aumale*: the Orléans family wanted to inherit the wealth of the Prince de Condé, which had fallen in 1830 into the hands of his son the Duc de Bourbon. Bourbon's godson, the Duc d'Aumale, was able to be named in the will only on condition that Bourbon's mistress, Mme de Feuchères, was received at court.

5. *the name of Corisande . . . Henri IV*: la Belle Corisande was Diane d'Andouins (1554–1620), who when a widow became mistress of Henri de Navarre (Henri IV, king of France 1589–1610) from 1573 to 1591.

6. *Robert le Fort*: (d. 866) Comte d'Anjou et de Blois, Marquis de Neustrie, and ancestor of the Capetian dynasty of Frankish kings.

7. *the Duc d'Orléans*: the Orléans line was one of the ancient French royal families, most recently on the throne under Louis-Philippe (king, 1830–48).

8. *Mlle de Nantes . . . Prince de Conti*: three of Louis XIV's natural daughters were legitimized, Mlles de Blois and Mlle de Nantes.

9. *M. Grévy's*: Jules Grévy, 1807–91, President of the Third Republic 1879–87, firm republican sympathizer and opponent of the aristocracy.

10. *the comic-opera character*: Agamemnon in *La Belle Hélène*, 1864, music by Jacques Offenbach, libretto by Henri Meilhac and Ludovic Halévy.

11. *Lohengrin . . . Tristan*: *Lohengrin*, one of Wagner's first operas, 1845. The duet between Elsa and Lohengrin is in Act III, Scene II. *Tristan und Isolde*, 1865 is a more complex and mature work.

# *Synopsis of* The Prisoner

*Life with Albertine: day one.* Street noises, a musical awakening (3). Albertine under my roof in Paris (4). Albertine's favourite songs (5). The little weather-house man (6). Mama's letter, her disapproval of my plan to marry Albertine (6); she herself cannot leave Combray (7). I set rules for Albertine regarding my sleeping hours (8). Françoise's respect for tradition (9). Albertine's intellectual development and changes in physique (11). Andrée now Albertine's companion on her outings: I advise them not to go to the Buttes-Chaumont (12). My trust in Andrée (13). I no longer love Albertine; but my jealousy has outlived my love (13). Impossible to cut her off from Gomorrah, which is present everywhere (14). My pleasure in being alone after Albertine has left (18). The smell of twigs in the fire recalls Combray and Doncières (19). Unknown women, glimpsed from the window, make me regret my life shut up with Albertine (20). Jealousy an intermittent fever (22).

My late afternoon visits to the Duchesse de Guermantes (24). She is no longer the mysterious Mme de Guermantes of my childhood (24). I visit her to ask her advice about dresses for Albertine (24). The Duchesse's Fortuny dresses (25). Her deliciously French conversation (26). She has forgotten Mme de Chaussepierre's appearance at the Princesse de Guermantes's party, a tiny consequence of the Dreyfus case (31). I hastily turn the conversation back from the Dreyfus case to the Duchesse's dresses (34). Leaving her house I meet M. de Charlus and Morel crossing the courtyard on their way to have tea at Jupien's (35). M. de Charlus quarrels with Morel over the expression 'treating to tea' (36). A note from the pageboy at a gambling club to M. de Charlus (37). M. de Charlus and M. de Vaugoubert; the author explains to the reader his reasons for dwelling on such strange scenes (38). The expression 'I'll treat you to tea': Jupien's niece had learnt it from Morel (39). The girl's natural good manners (39). The Baron happy to see them married (40). He imagines himself as guide and protector to the young couple (42). Morel's heartless plans (42); his excessive susceptibility (43), as shown in his dealings with Bloch and M. Nissim Bernard (45).

Returning home from Mme de Guermantes's, the syringa incident (46). I can usually rely on the works of Elstir, Bergotte or Vinteuil to calm my impatience as I wait for Albertine's return, and to intensify my love for her; I make sure my friends do not know she is living with me (47). Albertine's discretion now that she knows I am jealous (48). My pleasure in seeing her again (49). Andrée has become less likeable; her sourness (50). She spreads lies about the young golfer of Balbec (50). I question her about Albertine's outings, but learn nothing; how jealousy breeds mistrust and deceit (51). Once she has gone Albertine, in her indoor clothes, comes and sits with me (53). Her taste for the fine points of dress (53); her elegance and her growing intelligence (54). Our ever-changing view of the nature of young girls (55). Jupien's niece, too, has changed her opinion of Morel and M. de Charlus (55). Evenings when Albertine plays for me; the desire I formed for the free-spirited girl, desired by all, at Balbec survives even now, when she is shut up in my house (57). The different Albertines, over time (59). Albertine asleep: I watch her (59); sometimes, a less spiritual pleasure (62). How she wakes (64); 'Darling Marcel' (64). I am no longer seeking a mysterious Albertine, as I was the first year at Balbec, but an Albertine I know through and through (65). Her kisses can pacify me as my mother's used to do (66). Little by little I am coming to resemble all my relations (67); and especially Aunt Léonie (67). The sweetness of my erotic games with Albertine hides a permanent undercurrent of danger (69).

*Day two.* I awake to find the weather changed, as if to a different climate; this fosters my laziness (71). I remember Aimé telling me, at Balbec, that Albertine had arrived. Why had he said she looked 'not quite the thing' (73)? I suspect all of Albertine's friends (74). Jealousy after the event (75) and even after the death of the woman one loves (75).

That evening, Albertine says she means to visit Mme Verdurin the following day (76). I see through her words and expression (77). To stop her going, I suggest other places to visit (79). She is one of those people whose essence is flight (81). My anxiety is constantly intensified by the things she says to me (83). We sacrifice our lives not so much to a person as to the web of habits we have woven around him or her (85). Françoise's hatred of Albertine, her cryptic remarks about her (86). While Albertine goes to take her outdoor things off, I telephone Andrée; the telephone goddesses (87). I am the only one who can say 'Albertine' with that note of possession in my voice (87). I ask Andrée to stop Albertine going to the Verdurins', then announce that I will go there with them myself (88). When Albertine comes into my room, I tell her that I have been speaking to Andrée; Albertine tells me that the girls had met Mme Verdurin while they were out (90). The fluctuations of jealousy (91). Albertine wants to discourage me from going to the Verdurins' with her; she announces her intention of going to a department store instead; all she can offer me now is a series of insoluble problems (92). More of her time is mine now than when we were at Balbec; I go out with her to aerodromes near Paris (92). But I do not return from these outings in a more peaceful state of mind, as I did at Balbec (93). I suggest that she goes next day to a charity performance at the Trocadéro; I say the same things to her as my parents used to say to me when I was a child (94). The stern adult I have become in my manner to her is superimposed on the highly strung, sensitive creature I used to be (95). It is natural to be unfeeling and devious with the person one loves; my anguish when she refuses to kiss me (98), or gives me kisses that fail to satisfy me (98). Sometimes I trick her into going to sleep in my room (100). Once more I watch her as she sleeps (100) and wakes (101).

*Day three.* The following day, I wake to a spring morning, occurring unexpectedly in the midst of winter (102). Françoise brings me the *Figaro* and gives me the news, to which I am now quite indifferent, that Albertine is going to the Trocadéro and not to the Verdurins' (106). Albertine comes in, quoting *Esther*; we speak untruthfully to each other (106). A hint of her death in a riding accident (107). Digression on the different kinds of sleep and the paralysis and loss of memory which they involve (108). Renaissance *pietàs* (111). Cries of Paris again; Albertine's liking for food sold in the street (112). Her eloquent speech about ices and what it suggested (115).

As soon as Albertine leaves, I realize how tiresome her presence is to me (116). I am relieved that Andrée should be going with her, for I no longer trust the chauffeur as I did; on a visit to Versailles, Albertine had dispensed with his services for seven hours (117). Information from Gilberte's maid; at the time when I loved Gilberte, she was deceiving me (119). Alone at the window, I begin listening again to the noise and cries of the street (121); I watch the young shop-girls making their deliveries (123). I ask Françoise to call up one of these girls to run an errand for me: the girl from a dairy, whom I had noticed before (124). While I wait, I read a letter from mother at Combray: she is worried that Albertine should still be living in our flat (125). Francoise brings in the dairy-girl (126). The gap between the women we imagine and those we can actually approach (127); the girl is soon reduced to her unremarkable self (128). As I talk to her I see in the *Figaro* that Léa, whose reputation I know all too well, is appearing in *Naughty Nérine* at the Trocadéro matinée (129). Albertine had talked about her at Balbec, and then changed her story (129). I must stop Albertine meeting Léa at the Trocadéro

(130). I send the little dairy-girl away so as to concentrate on this (132). Jealousy recalls to my mind the image of a perverse, unfaithful Albertine (133). I send Françoise to find her at the Trocadéro (136). Decadence of Françoise's language, under the influence of her daughter (138). She rings me to tell me that Albertine is coming home (139), and Albertine confirms the message by sending me a note (140). Now I am no longer impatient to see her, and even feel irked by my slavery: to pass the time, I play Vinteuil's sonata on the piano (141). Vinteuil's music, like Wagner's, helps me to explore my own mind (142). Essential if retrospective unity of the great works of the nineteenth century, both literary (143) and musical (144). My musical reverie turns to Morel, and M. de Charlus's difficulty in understanding how he spends his day (145). Soon afterwards, I witness, in the courtyard, the violinist picking a quarrel with Jupien's niece, calling her 'great slut' (147). I feel calm as I wait for Albertine to return; she has a new ring (148). We go in the car to the Bois (149). All the young women I see from the car make me regret my present life more intensely (149). Apropos the Trocadéro, Albertine and I talk about architecture (150). I do not tell her that I have decided to go to the Verdurins' in the evening (151). Living with Albertine is depriving me of a journey to Venice, as well as of all the young working-girls I see; my friend seems to be looking at them as well (152). My disappointment with the women I have got to know, as with the cities I have visited (153). Albertine's captivity returns all other girls to their place in the beauty of the world, but, as a prisoner, she has lost her own beauty (155): only the memory of my original desire for her at Balbec can restore it (156). Our parallel shadows in the Bois; as we turn for home, the full moon over the Arc de Triomphe (157).

We dine in her room; 'no such thing as a fine prison' (158). Despite her docility, certain things make me wonder whether Albertine has not decided to break her chains (159). A chance meeting with Gisèle – despite, or perhaps because of, her cautious speech – confirms my suspicions (160). The girls of the little gang support each other in their lies (162) as, in another world, do publishers and editors of magazines and their staff (162). Albertine's confessions hide further lies; every person we love is Janus-faced (163). I say nothing for the moment about my plan to break off our relationship; to distract her from such thoughts I want to order her a dress from Fortuny (164).

I learn that Bergotte has just died; his illness was artificially prolonged by medical treatments (165). He had not been out of the house for years; he had little girls visit him, which revived his enthusiasm for writing (165). His nightmares in the last months of his life (167). Contradictory advice of his doctors (167). He tried every kind of sleeping draught (168). His death while visiting an exhibition of Dutch painting, in front of Vermeer's *View of Delft*;

dead for ever? The artist's moral commitment, so evident in his work, make a negative reply at least a possibility (169). Albertine's lie: she told me she had met Bergotte that day, when he was in fact already dead (170). The evidence of my senses would not have alerted me to her lying (171); examples show that such evidence is processed by the mind; the butler's *pistières*, for instance, or the restaurant doorman's 'old trout' (172). Albertine an inspired liar; outdone, however, by one of her friends (173).

*The Verdurins quarrel with M. de Charlus.* Albertine has decided not to go out; I suggest to her various other places I might be going, and then head for the Verdurins' (174). In the street I meet Morel, who is in tears of regret at having insulted his fiancée (175). His changeability and shamelessness (176); the resentment he feels towards those he has hurt (178). My day has led me to two conclusions: one, a decision to break with Albertine, and the other, a conviction that Art is as meaningless as the rest of life; but they will not last, and indeed will be overturned in the course of the evening (179). Arriving at the Quai Conti, I see Brichot getting down from a tram; even with his powerful spectacles he is almost blind (180). We talk about Swann, and I recall his death, which at the time had so upset me (180). His name will live on, because I have made him the hero of a novel (180). There were things I had still wanted to ask him (182). Brichot describes to me the Verdurins' old salon in the rue Montalivet, where Swann had first met Odette (183).

Nearing the Verdurins', we meet M. de Charlus, followed, as so often nowadays, by a street-boy determined not to lose sight of him; he has become monstrous (185). Brichot is distressed at his appearance (186). Homosexuality and the refining of moral qualities (187). M. de Charlus's moral decline is written on his face and informs his conversation (188). He talks to me about my 'cousin' Albertine's dresses; he excels in such descriptions, he might have become an accomplished writer (189). His familiarities (192); his conjugal and paternal manner with Morel (192). He now ignores social convention and has adopted mannerisms that he previously deplored (194). He tells us he met Morel by chance that morning, which convinces me that he was with him not an hour since (195). Shortly after the evening in question, he will open by mistake a letter from Léa to Morel in which she calls him 'dirty girl': sorrow and astonishment of the Baron (196). What does it mean to say 'you are one'? Being only an amateur and not a professional writer, M. de Charlus cannot put such incidents to use (197). He asks me for news of Bloch (198) and expresses admiration for Morel's success with women (199).

M. de Charlus explains to me that he has organized the evening at the Verdurins'; the Patronne is 'off the case', he has sent out the invitations (201) to a hand-picked audience that will get Morel talked about (201). He also wants to launch his protégé in literary journalism, and that is why he is keeping up his contacts with Bergotte (202). M. de Charlus tells me that Mlle Vinteuil and her friend are expected at the party (204). My pain on hearing this (204). My jealousy is redirected on to them (206). In the courtyard of the Verdurins' house we are approached by Saniette (206). In the entrance-hall, Charlus's familiar manner to the footman; M. Verdurin rudely corrects Saniette when he uses archaic expressions (208), and then snubs him for having mentioned Princess Sherbatoff's death (209). The Verdurins' fondness for matchmaking or fomenting quarrels among their guests (210). Mme Verdurin is furious with M. de Charlus for rejecting the names she put forward for her party (211). The Baron's unpredictable temper (213); his diatribes against Mme Molé (214). First fruits of the Dreyfus Affair for the Verdurins' salon (215). The Russian Ballet will also contribute to Mme Verdurin's standing (217). She does nothing to hide her indifference to Princess Sherbatoff's death (218). Her medical precautions before listening to Vinteuil's music (220). She tells me that Mlle Vinteuil and her friend will not be coming (221). Morel's manners have improved (222). *Sotto voce* conversations between M. de Charlus and several important figures who share his tastes (223). Mme Verdurin decides to make trouble between Charlus and Morel (223). The Baron's guests behave badly towards Mme Verdurin (224), all except the Queen of Naples (226).

M. de Charlus imposes silence on his guests; the concert is about to begin (227). An unpublished work of Vinteuil's is to be performed (228); it reminds me of the sonata, but with new elements (228). Postures of Mme Verdurin, the musicians and Morel (230). The music brings back my thoughts to my love for Albertine (231). And yet, the beginning of the work seemed to promise something more mysterious (232). Vinteuil's daring sonorities (233). Art is perhaps more real than life (234). Vinteuil's particular intonation (235). Each musician has his lost homeland (235). Music, sole example of the soul-sharing that might have been (237). Reprise of the septet (238), ending with the triumph of the joyful motif (239). Shall I ever know such joy (239)? The revelation of Vinteuil's music was the work of Mlle Vinteuil's friend, who transcribed his papers after his death (240). The strange appeal which she had thus conveyed to me (241). Profound ties between genius and perversion which ensured the survival of Vinteuil's work (242).

After the concert, M. Verdurin drives Saniette out of the house; he collapses in the courtyard (244). The guests file past the Baron; he does not suggest that they thank Mme Verdurin (244). Examples of M. de Charlus's wit (245). Mme de Mortemart prepares the ground for an evening at which she wants to have Morel play (247). Charlus begins to draw up the invitation list, not at all on the lines that the hostess intended (249). M. d'Argencourt and homosexuals (250). Mme Verdurin's fury, as she is ignored by the guests and irritated by M. de Charlus's remarks (251). The Queen of Naples has left behind her fan (252). The Baron's self-satisfaction (253); he congratulates himself on Mme Molé's absence and its beneficial effects (253). Mme Verdurin cannot tolerate the threat to her role as Patronne (255). Conversation between M. de Charlus and General Deltour (256). Mme Verdurin asks Brichot to keep M. de Charlus talking while her husband approaches Morel (257). Brichot reluctantly accepts (259); his pedantic self-justifications (259). He calls up the image of the old Verdurin salon, adding to each object its spiritual counterpart (261). Brichot and M. de Charlus drag me off with them (264). M. de Charlus goes over Morel's performance: the Lock (264)! He does not give me any information about Vinteuil's daughter, but he is friendly towards me (265). His reasons for enjoying Brichot's witticisms (266). The pity I feel for M. de Charlus; my own lack of self-regard (267). M. de Charlus at Brichot's lectures at the Sorbonne (268). I ask the Baron if he will warn me when Mlle Vinteuil is likely to return; he reminds me of the interest he formerly took in me; Mme de Villeparisis's death, her real standing in society (269). The certainty of finding Albertine waiting for me makes me reluctant to go home (271); I decide that on my return I will pretend to break with her (272). Brichot starts Charlus on the subject of homosexuality (272). M. de Charlus's statistics (274). He speaks of Swann, of Odette and her many lovers, of whom he was one (276). M. de Crécy (277). Homosexuality through the ages: the seventeenth century (279); M. de Charlus's observations (281). He is disconcerted to see the most enthusiastic ladies' men dabbling in homosexuality (282) and scandalized that women should now talk about such subjects (284).

Meanwhile, Morel is being lectured by M. Verdurin (285) and then Mme Verdurin (286). She has no difficulty in convincing him (286). Her accusations against the Baron become more extreme (287). We return to the drawing-room, Morel cuts M. de Charlus, who is left speechless (292). He cannot understand this public rejection (293). The Queen of Naples comes back for her fan, reacts indignantly to the scene (296). She proudly offers her arm to M. de Charlus and leads him away (297). The Baron de Charlus is profoundly shaken by the evening's events, he falls ill (298). His moral improvement, which lasts only as long as his illness (299). Kindness of the Verdurins to Saniette, now ill and penniless (299). Words peculiar to particular families (300). My discovery of the unsuspected good nature of M. Verdurin (301).

*

*Albertine disappears.* I return from the Verdurins' party with Brichot (302). He comments on M. de Charlus's remarks, adding erudite details (304). Arriving at my own door, I see the lighted window of Albertine's bedroom (305). It is the symbol of my enslavement (306). Albertine hides her feelings, but her anger explodes when she realizes I have been to the Verdurins' (307). I too am angry (307). She admits having pretended to go to Balbec (308). I wish to shame her by referring to Mlle Vinteuil (309), but Albertine had only pretended to know her well in order to make herself more interesting to me (310). I see a new and unsuspected Albertine when I reconstruct her expression *casser le pot* (311). In order to hold on to her, I pretend to desire a separation (315). A new revelation about the photograph of Bloch's cousin Esther (316). Memories of my former sadness when I told Gilberte we must part (317). Albertine has never openly showed any desire to leave me (319). Difficulty of being the narrator of one's own story (320). Albertine's deviousness, confirmed by her new-found disapproval of girls who looked 'fast' (322). Albertine now confesses that she once went away for three weeks with Léa. Ease with which lesbians home in on each other (323). Unsuspected role of heredity in these comedies of separation: Aunt Léonie's behaviour to Françoise (326). I am caught up in the game (328). I beg Albertine never to see me again (330). My detailed requests (330). Albertine's plan to go to her aunt's house in Touraine appals me; I quickly bring the scene to a close by 'signing a new lease' (331). Prophetic significance of this scene; Albertine asleep in her room is an allegorical figure of death (332).

*Fourth sequence of days.* The following morning I analyse the scene of the night before: it was a bluff, like those used in diplomacy (334). A letter from my mother: she is worried about my intentions towards Albertine (336). Albertine tries to calm my suspicions in the old way, but without success (337). Françoise's perceptiveness and disparaging remarks about my friend (337). She wants to break up our friendship, as no doubt do the Verdurins (338). Artistic tastes of the fair prisoner (340). The Fortuny dresses (341). She is nothing more than a demanding slave of whom I wish to be rid; she plays music for me on the pianola (343). An angel-musician (344). She plays pieces by Vinteuil (345). The truth of this music; I relate it in my mind to the pleasure I felt before the steeples of Martinville or the trees of Hudimesnil, or on drinking a certain cup of tea (346). The proof of genius is not in the content of a work but in the unknown quality of a unique world revealed by the artist, whether in literature or music (347). I show Albertine examples of this point in Barbey d'Aurevilly, Thomas Hardy and Dostoevsky (348). Going over my own impressions once more, I opt for the materialist hypothesis: that art means nothing (352). Is Albertine's role in my house that of a work of art, a St Cecilia at the pianola (353)? Not at all: if I love her, it is for reasons quite unrelated to art, for all the things that I do not know about her (354). My painful, indefatigable curiosity about her past life; love is space and time made perceptible to the heart (356). She is like a great goddess of Time; her peaceful sleep (357).

*Last sequence of days.* Spring has come; I resolve in vain to change my life (358). I learn from Mme Bontemps about Albertine's visits three years ago to the Buttes-Chaumont, and also why she was so ready to leave Balbec with me the previous year (359). I recall two traits of her character: her ability to put a single action to several uses – here, to please both Andrée and myself (361), and the avidity with which she seized on any temptation to pleasure (361). I know she is bound to leave me some day, but I want to choose the moment, when I can take it calmly (362). My anger, one evening when she had put on a Fortuny dress (364). I apologize to her (365), then I hark back to the Trocadéro matinée and the Verdurins' party; she makes further admissions and I continue to press her about her relations with Andrée and her reasons for leaving Balbec (366). I apologize again and she refuses to kiss me good-night in her usual way (369). Premonitions (369). She twice refuses to return my kiss (369). I hear her window open in the night, another forewarning of death (371).

The following morning, on awaking, I fear that Albertine has left; when Francoise tells me that she is in her room, my indifference to her returns. A further premonition of death (372). We go out to Versailles together (374). Buzzing sound of an aeroplane in the sky (375). While we are having tea she keeps staring at the tea-shop owner (376). We return as night falls (378); the moonlight over Paris reminds me of descriptive passages in the great poets of the nineteenth century, I quote them to Albertine (378). She wants to look in at the Verdurins', but agrees to go straight home when I suggest it (379).

I awake to a beautiful spring morning, familiar sounds and scents (379). The smell and sound of a motor-car remind me of Balbec and make me dream of going into the country with a strange woman (380). I long to leave for Venice without Albertine, and decide to leave her at once (381). I ring for Françoise to ask her to buy me a guide-book and a railway time-table, but she announces that Miss Albertine left that morning at nine o'clock (383).

# Synopsis of The Fugitive

CHAPTER I: *Grieving and Forgetting*

'Mademoiselle Albertine has left!' Acute suffering which I have to assuage immediately by imagining that she will return (387). Thinking that I no longer loved her was a mistake. The new face of Habit is that of a formidable deity (388). Farewell letter from Albertine (389). I look for ways of getting her to return that very evening: money, yacht, Rolls-Royce, independence, marriage (389). My other desires fall away (390). There is no easy way to part. I attempt to analyse my anguish and to detect forewarnings of her departure (392). Was her flight premeditated (394)? My pain is unaffected by the prospect of her early return, which I have promised myself, from an instinct of self-preservation (396). My previous loves were not driven by Habit (397). She must return without my seeming to care (397). All my 'selves' have to learn of this departure, since every familiar object recalls it (398). I hope that Albertine has left for Touraine. When this is confirmed, I feel tortured by the news (399). I invite an innocent poor girl home, then send her away (399). If Albertine left in order to weaken my resolve I ought to try to gain time, but I cannot (401). Saint-Loup agrees to help me (402). Forced to dissimulate, I pretend to approve of her departure, and I ask Saint-Loup to work on Mme Bontemps (403). I hand him a photograph of Albertine which causes him considerable surprise (405). A lover's eyes see things differently from others (407). I suggest a series of lies that Saint-Loup may use in order to explain the thirty thousand francs to be offered to the Bontemps and I tell other lies to Françoise in order to dissimulate the quarrel which she suspects, but hardly dares believe and rejoice in (410). Angry with Bloch, whose direct appeal to Mme Bontemps interferes with Saint-Loup's approach (410).

A chief inspector summons me: I am insulted by the little girl's parents and my innocence is not accepted (411). Convinced that Saint-Loup cannot fail, I am almost joyful; then, having no news from him, I start to suffer once more (412). Rereading a phrase in Albertine's letter revives my pain (413). Françoise informs me that the house is under surveillance; cradling little girls in my arms is henceforth forbidden: I wrongly interpret this ban as including Albertine, seeing in it a punishment for having lived with her unchastely (414). I am immediately swamped by a passionate yearning for her return (414). A few days of waiting, the first days of spring, bring me some moments of pleasant repose; as I become aware of this I feel a wave of panic; my love, facing forgetfulness, trembles like a lion faced with a python (415). I think of Albertine in my sleep; on waking, my suffering increases every day (415). Saint-Loup's first telegram: 'The ladies are away for three days' (416). While my mind awaits the return of Albertine, my body and my heart start to learn to live without her (416). I receive a letter of proposal from one of the Guermantes' nieces and the Duc approaches me in such a way that I feel neither flattered nor advantaged (417). I think ceaselessly of Albertine, sometimes tenderly, sometimes in a rage (417). I feel that her return would not restore my happiness; the more desire advances, the more true possession recedes (417). Relationships between people exist only in the mind; memory, as it grows weaker, dissolves them (418). I convince myself that my need for Albertine is vital for my life. Second telegram from Saint-Loup; Albertine saw him, and his manœuvre failed (419). Furious and desperate, I seek another solution, not realizing that the suppression of desire is the most ordinary solution (419). A melody from *Manon* reminds me of our love but I cannot confuse fictional characters with those of real life. I call Saint-Loup back to Paris (420). Albertine sends me a telegram telling me that if I had written to ask her to return she would have done so. Certain now of her return, I do not wish to appear to be in a hurry (421). My letter is only a translation of, or a substitute for, the reality which I desire (421). I reply to Albertine: I bless her wisdom in leaving, since to unite our two lives could have been disastrous for us; I am inconstant, and shall forget her (422). My first reaction would have been to ask her to cancel the order for the Rolls-Royce and the yacht which were destined for her, but now I intend to keep them; I embellish them with poetical quotations (423). Writing this deceptive letter was a clumsy action, I should have foreseen a negative response, but, convinced now of the contrary, I regret having sent it (425). Françoise brings it back to me (426). The papers announce the death of La Berma (426). I think of *Phèdre* and interpret the scene of her declaration as a prophecy of the love-scenes in my life (427). I send my letter to be posted (428). As time passes, lies become true; what I wrote to Albertine might well come to pass, as had been the case with Gilberte (429). But forgetfulness erases the memory of the periods of tedium, and Albertine's image becomes more beautiful (429). I endlessly speak her name (430). Françoise tortures me by discovering two rings Albertine had left behind, each bearing the same figure of an eagle (430). My suffering is dispersed among diverse objects, I envisage ruin and consider suicide but meanwhile the image of Albertine starts to fade (433). Françoise does not believe that she will return (434) but is filled with dismay by her letter (435). Albertine offers to cancel the order for the Rolls-Royce. I admire the way that our life together has enriched her with new qualities (436). I call Andrée to my side in order to precipitate matters and I tell Albertine of this, referring to the likelihood of my marriage with Andrée (437). I suddenly imagine that she does not wish to return and that she has been using her week of freedom in order to indulge in debauch (437). Saint-Loup returns (437). I overhear his conversation with a footman; my confidence in him is shaken and his failure seems inconclusive (438). The details which he reveals rekindle my jealousy and inflame my desire (439). I decide to wait for Albertine's reply and to go to seek her myself if she fails to return (442). I am suspicious of Saint-Loup (442). Like Swann with Odette, I imagine that the death of Albertine would put an end to my pain (443). I send her a telegram asking her to return and setting no conditions (443). Mme Bontemps sends me a telegram to tell me that Albertine is dead (443). Renewed suffering teaches me that I had always thought that she would return, that I needed her presence; my future life has been torn from my heart (444). Françoise brings me two letters from Albertine, one approving my proposal to Andrée, the other asking if she herself might return (444). My life is changed (445). Albertine is not dead within me, her innumerable selves are reborn, as moments from the past are called forth by identical present moments (445). Summer arrives, a ray of sunshine tears me apart, recalling thousands of memories of excursions around Balbec (446). Evening assaults me with sensations that I try to avoid (447). Françoise does not even pretend to be upset, but she is concerned by my tears (448). The slow death agony of summer evenings (448). The sight of a star is enough to revive my memories. I am afraid of the forgetfulness which is to come (449). Dawn, like a knife blade, reawakens the anguish of Albertine's departure (449).

I no longer wish to go to Venice: the obstacle placed between myself and the world by her presence was imaginary (450). I am afraid of the arrival of winter when I shall rediscover the germ of my first desires (450). I would have to ignore all the seasons and renounce the whole world (451). There would also be anniversary dates, with a mental climate corresponding to the memories inspired by the dates (451). Thus, when the fine weather returned, I would recall the sweetness and calm of the moments when I was waiting for

Albertine to return from the Trocadéro, then the moment when we left for an excursion together. That day, remembered subsequently without suffering, has retained its unchanging brightness (453). The sadness of my memory takes on different colourings according to the diversity of the days evoked and the successive notions of Albertine which I entertained (453). There is not just one Albertine but innumerable Albertines, and I too am the march-past of a composite army (456). The jealous self is a contemporary of the images evoked: pain of the amputee. Memory of Albertine blushing over the bath-robe incident at Balbec (458). I send Aimé to Balbec to make enquiries (459). Jealousy ceases to torture me, my heart is filled with despair and tenderness (459). My room takes on a painful charm which, like art, is able to embellish the most insignificant things (460). Memories of our first kiss, of the gurgling of the water heater and the evening with Brichot make me realize that, in this life which I had found tedious, I had found that profound peace of which I had dreamed (461). Remembering Albertine's intelligence and sweetness, I regret my selfish love and feel guilty for her death, as I do for that of my grandmother (462). What we value in a woman is a projection of our pleasure on seeing her (463). All other pleasures leave us unmoved. Love alone is divine (464). Albertine at the pianola, her kisses (464). Only the memories of such sweet moments prevent me from feeling despair for I no longer value life (464). I have known a happiness and an unhappiness that Swann never knew (465). Nothing is ever exactly repeated: the main difference (art) has not yet appeared (465). Recapitulation of our story (466). I might never have met Albertine, nor, having met her, have fallen in love, and yet she is necessary to me (467). Comparison with Gilberte (468). Woman unique and multiple (469). What it is that forges the chains of love: habit, hope, regret (471). After a certain age our loves are born of our anguish (472). Separation makes us discover love (472). We have no hold over the life of another human being (473). The prophetic value of phrases which we intend to be mendacious (473). Perhaps she did not admit her tastes to me because I had declared my disgust for that kind of thing (476). Had she blushed? The uncertainty of memory (476). Terror inspired by the thought of being judged by the dead (477). My curiosity survives the death of Albertine (477). Desire engenders belief: I start to believe in the immortality of the soul (478). I imagine her alive, but similar to the Albertine of my dreams (478). Arbitrary nature of my enquiry into the incident in the showers at Balbec: people and things exist only when they occur to my imagination (479). One single little fact may determine the truth (480). When I receive Aimé's letter, I realize that I was merely playing with suppositions, I did not believe that Albertine was guilty (480). Damning evidence given by the shower attendant (482). A new

Albertine surfaces, I try to imagine her desires, which torment me (483). Pain modifies reality decisively; Balbec and its familiar scenes become a kind of hell (484). Jealousy has the power to reveal the fragility of our notions of reality (485). I suffer from not being able to tell her what I have learned (485). Soothing memory of my grandmother accusing the shower attendant of mendacity (486). My affection revives and increases my sadness (487). I find reading the newspapers painful (487). Each impression evokes a former impression (488). My jealousy revives and I decide to send Aimé to Touraine (489). I am spending my life and my money on a relationship with a dead woman (489). Aimé discovers a young laundry-girl whose evidence – Albertine saying 'I'm in heaven' – is cruel (491). The reality of Albertine's vice turns her into a stranger and she is no longer there to console me (491). The deepest suffering resists the process of forgetting (492). In Albertine a different race lay hidden; Elstir's nude bathers help me to imagine erotic and mythological scenes at the water's edge (493). This renewed communication makes my heart ache (494). We project what we feel without allowing the fictitious barriers of death to interrupt us (494). But the instability of the images, the fragmentation of Albertine into innumerable Albertines saves me (495). The kind Albertine is the only antidote to the suffering caused by the other Albertine (495). If she lied to me, it was to spare my grief. I forgive her (496). The intermittence of memory (497). My feelings – the need to feel a great love – and my very sensations – tears on feeling the spring breeze – continue to make me live in a past which is no more than someone else's story (499). I attribute my pain to pathological causes (499). Man is an amphibious being plunged simultaneously in the past and in present reality (499). But unwittingly I am recovering, for I think so much of Albertine's death that I find the idea of it natural (499). Yet the memories do not recede uniformly and the idea that she was guilty tortures me without my being able to find consolation in the image of her sweet presence (500). This idea too will become habitual one day, and therefore less painful (502). I have not reached that point yet. Our regret for a woman is no more than the revival of love and obeys the same laws. Between intervals of indifference my regrets are revived above all by jealousy and pain (502). A name or a word opens a door on to the past, as do the da capo reprises of a dream (503). Dreams undo the consolatory work of wakefulness; their staging creates an illusion of life (504). I meet Albertine as well as my grandmother, they are dead but continue to live (504). Once repeated, dreams produce a lasting memory: during the day I continue to converse with Albertine (505). Does Albertine's continuing existence depend on my feelings? My attachment to the imaginary characters from a novel by Bergotte fills me with despair (506). The fragility of love terrifies me. On a map I avoid reading the names of places which make my heart pound (506). These places are the permanent stage on which my life has evolved, it is I myself who have changed. Nor are the newspapers inoffensive; here and there some name will evoke another by association: everything is dangerous and therefore precious (508). An ancient memory, like that of the Buttes-Chaumont, resurfaces with its power intact, whereas habit has dulled those memories to which we have applied our intellect (508). Each new memory renews my jealousy (509). I try to imagine what Albertine felt: on one occasion I experienced the illusion of seeing her hidden pleasures, on another, of hearing them (511). Andrée comes to see me (511): she seems to me to be Albertine's desire incarnate (511); I question her about her taste for women, pretending to know all about it (512); she confesses, but affirms that she did not have sexual relations with Albertine (513). The cries of the young laundry-maids (515). I would like to find, as one does in novels, a witness who would recount Albertine's life to me (516). I seek out women who resemble her, or who might have attracted her (517). Amid my latest desires, it is Albertine herself whom I seek (520). The idea of Albertine's uniqueness is no longer a metaphysical *a priori* but an *a posteriori*, an entanglement of memories (521). My love and my regrets might have lasted for ever if psychology were applicable to motionless states (522). But love is within me, and my soul is mobile within time (522). A day will come when I shall have forgotten Albertine (522).

CHAPTER 2: *Mlle de Forcheville*

To attain a state of indifference, we need to pass backwards through all the feelings through which love has first passed; but the process of forgetting is irregular (524). The first stage, an All Saints' Day in the Bois de Boulogne (524). I think tenderly of Albertine while humming phrases from Vinteuil's sonata (524). The charms of melancholia depend on the evolution of the process of forgetting (525). I look at girls (526). They all seem to be Albertines (526). I follow, then lose sight of, three girls. I see them again in front of my house and one of them, the blonde one, looks at me. Her sidelong glance, and her name, Mlle d'Éporcheville, set me on fire (528). Certain to have guessed right, I check with the concierge (529) then by telegram with Saint-Loup that the blonde girl who looked at me is none other than the aristocratic girl who frequented brothels (530). I would be sure to meet her at Mme de Guermantes's (530). Rage and despair when my father proposes to take me away from Paris with him for forty-eight hours (530). Saint-Loup's telegram reveals my mistake (531). My mother brings me my mail (531); she hurts Françoise's feelings by preventing her from entering my room (532). My article has appeared in the *Figaro* (532). It is being read by everyone; I try to put myself in the place of the reader, I am charmed by my article (533). I want to go and check whether others read it in the same way that I do; literary activity could replace my social life (536). I go to see the Duchesse de Guermantes; the attraction of this salon, which is a point of intersection between reality and the dream (537). I am introduced to the blonde girl again: I did not think that I knew Mlle de Forcheville (538). Mistakes in how we represent the world (538). The story of Gilberte Swann, who has become a rich heiress, adopted by Odette's second husband (539). Swann dreamed of introducing his daughter to the Duchesse, but the pictures we paint never turn out to be true (540). The Duchesse's refusal and the reasons for her persistence (542). M. de Guermantes obtains an introduction for her (544). Gilberte's rapid progress with the Guermantes, who appreciate in her the qualities inherited from her father (545). Patronizing comments on their old friend; the Duchesse's sudden attack of sensitivity; Gilberte's adoption accelerates her forgetfulness (547). Elstir's drawings, now fashionable and appreciated by the Duchesse (547). I mention my article; the Duc, greatly astonished, starts to read it (548). The anecdote about the Prince de Laumes and the peasant at Paray-le-Monial (549). Gilberte claims not to know Lady Rufus Israel (549). Ashamed of her parents, she has inherited her faults from them (550). The complex combinations of moral heredity (551). Gilberte behaves like an ostrich; her new signature (551). Her snobbery secretes an intellectual curiosity: her tactful questions about her father's former friends (552). The Duc's muted compliments on my article (553). I refuse an invitation because of my mourning (554). Once Gilberte has left, the Duchesse comments on how difficult it is not to mention Swann: the Duc declares that all one has to do is not to think of him (554). I receive two letters congratulating me on my article, one from Mme Goupil, the other from someone unknown to me, and nothing from Bloch (554). I dream of Bergotte admiring my article (555). I am dismayed at the thought of Gilberte hastening her father's death and oblivion (556). She has a similar effect on me concerning Albertine (557). The disappearance of my suffering leaves me diminished (557). My life seems to lack the support of a stable, individual self (558). The changes in the self are accompanied by fatigue and sadness (558). The second stage of the process of forgetting: a conversation with Andrée, six months after the previous one (560). Mme Sazerat's misfortune (561). My mother's visit to the Princess of Parma (561). In my little sitting-room, M. de Charlus quotes love poetry to a soldier who turns out to be Morel (563). Andrée is waiting for me in my room

(563). While I caress her I tell her of my curiosity over Albertine's pleasures (564). She shamelessly contradicts her previous denials (564). Morel used to pick up young working-girls for Albertine (564). Albertine's terrible remorse, feeling herself in the grip of a kind of criminal folly from which she hoped I would save her (564). I had almost caught her with Andrée on the day of the syringa incident (565). The awful truth emerges too late to touch me deeply (566). A sentence or an idea can always be refuted (566). Andrée might have been sincere because she no longer fears Albertine; on the other hand, for the same reason, she might have been lying in order to hurt me (567). Her kindness and her cunning (568). Anticipation of her marriage with Octave, the Verdurins' nephew (569); behind the pretentious fool encountered at Balbec, there was an artist of genius (570). His prestige for me; masterpieces do not spring from intellectual merit (571). The real Albertine glimpsed the very first day (573). I did not believe her guilty as long as I loved her (574). Lying is essential to the human race (574). The charms of a person lie in his or her secrets; love is linked to suspicion (575). After Andrée's departure, Mama tells me of the Princess of Parma's visit, an exception to her rule (577). I write asking Andrée to return in order to question her again (578). The cause of Albertine's departure: the Bontemps wanted to marry her to Octave, and it was in order to meet him that she wanted to go to the Verdurins' (579). Albertine both schemer and victim (580). Mediocre women are suitable for sensitive intellectuals since their lies create for these men a universe in depth (580). The elusive figure of Albertine (582). The innocence of her relations with Mlle Vinteuil and her girl-friend (583). Albertine a wild creature (584). Octave's friendliness towards me derived from his desire to meet Albertine (585). I pass judgment on him and realize that a similar duplicity filled me with affection for Saint-Loup when I was in love with his aunt (585). Perhaps this young man sincerely sought the friendship of an intellectual (586). My doubts over Andrée's declarations, over the significance of Albertine's blushes; my sadness and fatigue (587).

CHAPTER 3: *Staying in Venice*

My third moment of awareness of the process of forgetting: travelling to Venice. Venetian analogies and transpositions of my former impressions of Sunday mornings in Combray (588). Mama no longer hides her affection (589). Her sweet smile is now forever linked in my memory with a jewel of medieval architecture, an ogive in the Arabic style (590). Comparisons between the splendours of Venice and the poverty of Venice: the lesson learned from Veronese comes to complete the lesson learned from Chardin (590). In the afternoon, without Mama, I explore the back-streets of Venice looking for working-girls (591). At sunset I ride in a gondola with my mother; urban and social impressions in the city of art and the sea (594). Dinner with Mme Sazerat in a palazzo converted into a hotel (594). The waiters' disdainful comments on an old couple: who turn out to be Mme de Villeparisis and M. de Norpois (595). Their conjugal behaviour (596). M. de Norpois is interested in the international situation (596). He introduces Prince Foggi to the Marquise (597). Mme Sazerat discovers a little old woman instead of the *femme fatale* who had ruined her father (598). The Marquis's diplomatic arts and secret ambitions. The press mentions this conversation and provokes his ire (601). How he manipulated public opinion in 1870 (602). Albertine enclosed within me (603). My inheritance is severely depleted (604). Nobody in Combray would be able to understand how I had allowed myself to be ruined by Albertine (604). Might I be able to take home to Paris a girl I had found selling glassware in Venice (605)? Elusive reminders of Albertine (605). A telegram arrives: Albertine is alive and wants to discuss marriage (606). I can no more resuscitate Albertine than I can the past self who used to love her; oblivion has devoured my love (607). I say that the telegram was not addressed to me (608). Study trips with Mama, when I work on Ruskin at St Mark's (610). She remains in my memory, cloaked in her mourning, like the old woman in Carpaccio's painting (610). Albertine's coat, recognized in a different painting, momentarily revives my love (611). I visit the Arena Chapel in Padua, with its Giotto frescoes (612). Like the allegorical figures which Swann had given me in Combray, the angels perform real actions (612). An Austrian girl on holiday in Venice attracts me through what she has in common with Albertine (613). Solitary, nocturnal walks through enchanted streets (614). When I learn of the imminent arrival of Mme Putbus, I refuse to leave Venice with my mother (615). Under the influence of my anguish, Venice ceases to be Venice (616). I rush to the station (619). In the train I read my mail (619). Gilberte informs me of her marriage to Saint-Loup; the telegram was from her; her handwriting explains the confusion (620).

## CHAPTER 4: *A New Side to Robert de Saint-Loup*

My mother's emotion on hearing the news (621). She informs me of the marriage between the young Cambremer and Mlle d'Oloron, that is, between Legrandin's nephew and Jupien's niece (622). Transgressions of caste boundaries which shock the bourgeoisie (622). My mother tries to imagine what my grandmother would have thought (623). The intrigues which precede a marriage (625). My sadness as my past recedes; but it would be wrong to interpret this sadness as prescience (628). Gilberte becomes a salon celebrity. The awkwardness caused by social matches (630). The consequences of marriages. Snobbery (631). Legrandin yields to a less artificial taste, but one rendered platonic by age (632). Mme de Cambremer grows indifferent to the amiability of Mme de Guermantes (632). Gilberte, thinking that she has attained the summits of the Faubourg Saint-Germain, is filled with contempt for high society and her salon falls from favour (634). Mlle d'Oloron dies shortly after her marriage (636). The pitfalls awaiting the uninitiated reader of the obituary notice (636). Charlus appreciates the young Cambremer (637). Return to our family commentary in the train, then in Paris (638). The lore of families and the Muse of history (640). The people of Combray make fun of Saint-Loup's marriage (640). I go to see Gilberte since I no longer love her (641). In order to leave for Tansonville, I entrust my mistress to a friend who is not attracted to women (642). Gilberte, deceived by Robert, is unhappy (642). Jupien informs me that the letters signed by Bobette are from Morel, who has left the Baron for Saint-Loup (643). Jupien's indignation (643). Mme de Marsantes enforced a reconciliation between Gilberte and Robert (643). Robert could have married Albertine, for the same reasons as mine, but with the opposite intention (644). Conversation with Aimé in Balbec where I met Saint-Loup (645). My friend's tastes may be long-standing: the liftboy scandal (646). Who was lying (646)? A new interpretation of Saint-Loup's blushes (646). He finds something of Rachel in Charlie (647). Gilberte attempts to resemble Rachel, believing that Saint-Loup is still in love with her (647). Having found a protector in Robert, Odette, at first hostile to the marriage, works to support it (648). Saint-Loup's deplorable behaviour during his liaison with Morel (650). I shed tears for my lost friendship (650). I go to stay at Tansonville. Walking and talking with Gilberte at nightfall (652). I am devastated to realize how little emotion I feel on revisiting Combray and the neighbourhood: my childhood visions are overturned (653). Gilberte reveals her desires: I had misinterpreted the look in her eyes, the first time we met, at Tansonville (655). I had understood it well enough, on a second occasion, the day before we were introduced at Mme de Guermantes's (656). My grief having disappeared, I no longer try to linger over the circumstances of our parting (656). But I am obliged to modify my views of our first meeting and to convince myself that the happiness I dreamed of then was not inaccessible (657).